STRONG BONES

STRONG BONES

Robert J. Peterson

A California Coldblood Book
Los Angeles, Calif.

THIS IS A GENUINE CALIFORNIA COLDBLOOD BOOK
Los Angeles, Calif.
californiacoldblood.com

Set in Minion
Cover design by Dale Halvorsen

Printed in the United States

Publisher's Cataloging-in-Publication Data

Names: Peterson, Robert J., author.
Title: Strong bones : a novel / Robert J. Peterson.
Description: Los Angeles, CA: California Coldblood Books, 2021.
Identifiers: ISBN: 978-1-955085-16-8
Subjects: LCSH Friendship--Fiction. | Family--Fiction. | Magic--Fiction. | Video games--Fiction. | Dungeons and Dragons (Game)--Fiction. | Great Smoky Mountains (N.C. and Tenn.)--Fiction. | Horror. | BISAC FICTION / Horror
Classification: LCC PS3616.E84749 S77 2021 | DDC 813.6--dc23

Dedication

Sing, goddess!

This is for all the families of choice, including my own.

Author's Note

This novel includes depictions of emotional and physical abuse.

Disclaimer

This book is about many things, including the slippery nature of our senses and memory. Although it takes place from 1989 to 1990, it includes references to events and media that weren't exactly contemporary to those years. You won't see the Internet, but you might see a reference to a game or movie that hadn't come out yet, or maybe had come out many years earlier.

*PART ONE
ALL ABOARD!*

I was eleven the first time I dreamed about the magic traincar.

I had the dream shortly before my mom died, before she married the biggest asshole I ever knew, before an escaped serial killer snatched me and a bunch of my friends, and before all of us teamed up to battle an ancient horror that had been menacing the Smokies for years.

If I'd known that every detail of this dream would be crucial to my survival over the next year, maybe I'd have been paying more attention.

If I'd known that a pair of competing ancient powers would spend the next year communicating with me and my friends through dreams, visions, and all manner of visual media, maybe I'd have been taking notes.

If I'd known that this dream would be my first step toward discovering a constellation of magic realms, dark and light, good and evil, maybe I would've taken this dream more seriously.

But maybe my initial ignorance was for the best, because if I'd known that so many families around the Smokies would come to count on me and my friends discovering the secret location of one of these magic realms, and if I'd known the high price this quest would exact from us, I might've lost my nerve.

I did a lot of sleepwalking in those days. That's a common symptom for kids from screwed-up homes, I guess. Mine wasn't the most screwed-up, but we'd have made the podium, for sure.

This was one of those dreams that simulated reality. Boring, right? I stumbled down the stairs of our tiny two-bedroom house into the cozy chaos of a living room in the seminal year of 1989, baby: shag carpeting, cheap wood paneling, chintzy brass fixtures, hand-me-down mid-century furniture that emitted a faint puff of our late grand-dad's cigars when you sat on it.

My father, Deacon Gresham, had died when I was four and my sister, Mackenzie, was eight. Over the years, our mom, Corrie Blackledge Gresham, had swapped out his travel posters for ones that better reflected her tastes: The Grateful Dead, *Hair, Jesus Christ Superstar,* as well as posters from various Shakespeare festivals (*The Tempest, A Midsummer Night's Dream, Coriolanus, Twelfth Night, Othello*). A roll-top desk sat at the foot of the stairs, covered with Mom's third-grade worksheets that she'd covered with red ink.

My attire for the occasion was *somnambulant-kid-casual:* dark blue jammie pants with a sweet Masters of the Universe iron-on T-shirt.

A door stood next to the stairs. Next to that door hung a photo of me and Mac. (Everyone called my big sis Mac or Gresh.) About a month before he died, Dad had snapped a shot of us on the front porch, capturing us in all of our gingery, chunky glory. Mac draped an arm around my shoulder, her big-boned self wearing the one-piece swimsuit she lived in every summer, while I'd opted for a collared golf shirt Dad had given me, my burgeoning belly already poking out underneath. Summer sun slanted under the porch-front roof and lit our frizzy hair in orange halos.

I opened the door. Darkness awaited me. Unconsciously, I flicked on the light to reveal a walk-in closet. You know the room—it's the catch-all for every errant whatsamadoodle and thingamajig you're not quite ready to part with yet: Christmas decorations, old toys, diplomas that never got framed, stacks of *National Geographic,* and our Auntie Hanna's old Nancy Drews. Clipped magazine pages and album covers checkered the walls: Toni Basil, Bananarama (the one where they're supposed to be floating underwater), and my most recent addition: a movie magazine promoting the "upcoming release" of Tim Burton's *Batman.*

A pathway wide enough to admit a chunky eleven-year-old (or a side-stepping grown-up) led between these stacks to the closet's rear, where it took a U-shaped left turn into a crawlspace under the stairs. Dad had tacked a movie poster to the slanted ceiling before he died: *The Adventures of Buckaroo Banzai Across the Eighth Dimension.* The poster was a collage of screenshots from the movie. In one, a latticework of orange lines crawled across an old monochrome computer monitor like a robotic spiderweb.

I had turned this space into my hidey-hole. I moved a small work-desk from mine and Mac's room and lay a sleeping mat under it like a daybed. A footstool was my secret throne.

But the main event was wedged into the space at the far end: an old-time fifties radio, one of those standing units with dark, finished wood and a half-dozen black knobs. It hadn't worked in years.

I used to pretend I could talk to my dad through it.

The night I dreamed about the magic traincar, I *did* talk to him.

Or rather, he talked to me.

"Itza linda adda."

They say our dreams are messages from our subconscious. I say bullshit. Most of the time mine are just a screensaver; my mind clearing out old memories and ruminating on the day's detritus. But this dream? This dream was something else. And it came from some*where* else. I didn't know the voice's origin then, but I do now. It's what this story is about. Well, partially. It's also about how I didn't really get to know my mom until she was gone and about how sometimes our closest family members aren't related to us by blood.

Dad spoke again: "Itza linda adda."

I had only the most fleeting memories of my Dad, but for some reason, I remembered his voice perfectly. I could pick it out of a crowded room, and this was unmistakably him, speaking in Lovecraftian gibberish.

"What?" I said. I wonder if I said it out loud while I sleepwalked.

"Gedda brusha. Trap. Trap. Itza linda adda."

Itza linda adda? Eetza Leenda ad-uh.

Gedda Brusha. Gedduh Bruh-shah.

What was he saying?

Light flickered to my right. A line of blinding white slashed between two of the wood panels. Another slash of light appeared at a ninety-degree angle to the first.

It was a door, opening toward me.

I reached out . . .

. . . and found myself in the woods near my house.

Mackenzie

A voice pulled Mackenzie "Mac" Gresham from a deep slumber.

She jolted awake with a gasp, the horizon of her dreamscape rapidly receding. Her hair, like her baby brother's, was a bright orange disaster that would've made Albert Einstein proud.

What was that voice? she thought, sitting up and sliding into slippers. Her bedroom stood on the cusp between childhood and adolescence: posters for *She-Ra* and *My Little Pony* shared wall space with Widespread Panic, *Red Sonja,* Drivin' and Cryin', Phish, *Xanadu,* Peter Gabriel, Phil Collins, and others. An array of art supplies crowded her built-in desk: plasticine, clay, and oil paints. A hand-carved wooden pistol lay next to a few heavy-duty rubber-bands. Papers spilled out of the drawers, which never quite shut all the way.

The voice had come from downstairs; a woman's voice, but what had it said? Mac stood, accidentally knocking over a Barbie Dream House with one of her muscular calves. She stood almost five foot ten and had been ducking the field hockey coach's overtures for two seasons now. As for the Dream House, she'd recently evicted it from her desk in favor of a new sculpting project. She paused, lingering on the hot-pink toys.

"Dream House," Mac whispered.

As if in response, the voice spoke again. It was definitely coming from downstairs:

"Fall me."

Follow me? Mac thought as her gaze drifted to her sculpting project, a statue of the Terpsichore, muse of song and dance. She'd deviated from the assignment and made her to look like a combination of Wonder Woman, Artemis, and Olivia Newton John from *Xanadu:* Mac's riff on Terpsichore wore an armored halter and skirt, and instead of strumming on a harp, she wielded a combination bow-harp that could fire flaming arrows as well as play music. The final touch was Mac's favorite: a pair of leg-warmers.

Mrs. Robertson had given her a C-minus with the note, *What kind of outfits did you learn Greek goddesses wear?*

Mac shook her head. What did *she* know, the dummy? Pulling on a robe, she crept to her door, which was plastered with cut-out pages from *Teen Beat* and *Bop* that showcased her ever-changing celebrity crushes. Ralph Macchio and Jonathan Taylor Thomas were this week's, but there was a boy at school who topped them both. She slid aside a target bullseye she'd pinned to her door to reveal a cut-out yearbook photo of a boy with close-cropped black hair and a kind smile.

Out in the hallway, the voice spoke again, louder this time:

"Feels balmy."

Balmy? Why is she talking about the weather? And am I dreaming?

Cr-r-r-eeeak! Her baby brother's bedroom door swung open in a gentle breeze. Mac's mind suddenly delivered up the night's dream: it was her dream house, the kind of mansion kids draw for fun. It had a game room and a library, but it also had features she'd never think to include, like an observatory and a small chapel. Padding down to Hiram's bedroom, she found it empty—for the third time this month.

She was already running back to her bedroom to throw on some night clothes, her dream forgotten.

"Mom! MOMMMM! Hiram's got out again!"

Hiram's Journal

In classic dream fashion, the magic door had teleported me into a glen of birch, hickory, and maple, all staples of the Great Smoky Mountains and our hometown of West Chimney Top, Tennessee, about an hour east of Knoxville and nestled comfortably between Gatlinburg and Pigeon Forge. A full moon shone from an autumn-crisp and cloudless sky while trees bowed and moaned in the wind.

It's funny how dreams can create information inside your head. I remember the first time someone told me a joke in a dream. I wondered how I couldn't know the punchline when it literally existed inside my own mind. That night, my mind didn't conjure a punchline but a hunch; a hunch that I should follow a pathway that appeared before me and snaked into the woods ahead.

I rounded a cluster of trees and brought a wide depression into view, a bowl of green about fifty feet wide, all of it surrounded by thick, overhanging trees. That same harsh moonlight slanted through openings in the tree cover, dappling the main event:

The traincar.

Imagine an old-west-style train caboose, painted a deep burgundy-red and adorned with dozens of brass fixtures and wrought-iron railings and features. The windows were intricately crafted stained-glass affairs, depicting a coiling array of otherworldly shapes—snakes and tentacles—all of them coiling around a train locomotive and lined with hundreds of eyes that stared at me.

What was weird was I recognized the traincar.

I'd seen it before, but it was somewhere *outside* my dreams, in my waking life.

But where?

Remember when I said every detail of this dream would be crucial to me not winding up a lampshade in some serial killer's evil lair? Case in point: the words painted on the traincar:

Zo vaxap dis en zo flestulo

What the heck? I didn't know what "Zo vaxap dis en zo flestulo" meant, but if I was going to make it through the next year alive, I had to find out.

Snap.

I whirled around. Something was in the woods behind me. I could only see its silhouette. The figure slowly stepped out. It was a guy in a double-breasted navy blue suit with emerald highlights that caught the moonlight in surging sparkles. Every square inch of exposed flesh was the shiny, livid pink of a new burn victim, its texture an endless ocean of swirling, ragged ridges and pockmarks. Freddy Krueger would've thought this guy needed a makeover.

But his face.

He had no face; no face that I could *see*, that is, because it was covered by a patch of plaid fabric so threadbare it could've been clipped from a pair of thirty-year-old pajamas. It was staple-gunned to the man's face in a jagged picket fence of steel. Whoever had done it had been in a hurry, because the staples stood at weird angles, some of them driven deep into his flesh, others hanging by one tine. The rise of his nose cast a small shadow. His lips whispered against the fabric, which ballooned with his every breath.

This was the first time I saw the Plaid Man.

I wanted to scream, but all I could do was wheeze. It felt like my lungs had shrunk by half. If you'd held your ear next to my lips, you might've heard the faintest utterance:

"Help. Help."

I tried to run, but my feet felt bolted to the earth.

The Plaid Man took a couple steps forward, strangely tentative given his status as the most pants-shittingly scary thing I'd ever seen. He moved in fits and starts, like a flip-book cartoon missing a few pages. His limbs left ghostly trails like smears of blue watercolor.

I kept count. I had this dream one more time over these awful six months. This was the first. I wouldn't have it again until I had my first near-miss with the aforementioned serial killer:

Lenny Skelton, aka the East Tennessee Strangler, aka the Blue Ribbon Killer.

Who incidentally, had broken out of Tennessee State Pen a month before. No one had seen him since, although there were rumors he was hiding out in the woods near West Chimney Top.

Somehow I remembered that detail in my dream—that there was an actual, living, breathing serial killer on the loose—and in that instant of distraction, the Plaid Man launched at me like he'd been shot out of a cannon. My arms made an X in front of my face.

I was standing in that position when I woke up screaming in the middle of the woods.

Chest heaving, I surveyed the scene: no pants-shittingly scary monster, and more importantly, no traincar. My breath puffed in little clouds, the night air creeping past my thin layer of sleepy-time clothes. A shiver racked through me. A still silence surrounded me, the kind only found when you subtract the ambient racket of the city.

It was hell and gone past the witching hour. I'd somehow sleepwalked out of my house and into the bush.

Lucky for my poor single mom, I was a weirdo who always came prepared. From my pocket I pulled a well-worn piece of college-rule notebook paper and a No. 2 pencil I'd worn down to a nub.

It was my map of the area surrounding my house.

I loved maps. Love 'em, all kinds. Still do. At school, I used to get in trouble for sneaking into the back room of the library to page through the giant World Atlas. I also got obsessed with mapping out video game worlds, overlands and dungeons, secret passages, and hidden warp zones.

All this meant when I was suddenly transported by the dreamtime express out to the middle of the woods, I was ready. Luckily, our house sat in a region that included some useful landmarks.

"Hmmm," I muttered. "Uh where's the mill?"

In case you're wondering why I said "uh" to myself, it's because I was a stutterer. Still am, and as strange as it might sound, I stuttered even when I was alone. I stuttered when I talked to myself—which was often—and I even stuttered inside my own thoughts.

"There it is," I said, spotting the mill's silhouette whirling over the tree line. I rotated my map a few degrees, trying to situate myself. I didn't have a compass, but who needed one? Casting my gaze skyward, I looked for the Big Dipper, which pointed at . . .

"Polaris."

The North Star. Basic navigation stuff, but crucial for finding your way home before freezing to death. I rotated my map a few more degrees, lining up north with north.

"Good on you, little buckaroo," I said to myself.

Good on you, little buckaroo? Where had I heard that before?

It didn't matter. Now that I'd found north, I pivoted about ninety degrees to the left and headed west, toward my house.

If only I had a sextant, I thought. Or hell, maybe I said it aloud. I got those mixed up a lot. Still do.

"Oh, wait," I said, stopping to make a note on my map: "Traincar? Caboose?" I paused and chewed the end of my pencil. I wasn't much a dream-journaler, but this one felt important, even to my chuckleheaded, primordial, eleven-year-old brain.

I was writing, "Plaid Man?" when I heard the shouting.

"Hiram! Hiiii-rammmm!" I knew the voice: *Mom!*

I was already running due west, wincing as brambles and roots dug into my bare feet. Flashlights swept back and forth over the tree line like miniature spotlights. Another voice joined the shouting:

"Hiram Deacon Gresham! I demand you show yourself immediately!"

The voice belonged to Auntie Hanna, or should I say, *Sheriff* Hanna Blackledge. I had to have been gone awhile if Mom had already called the cops. I popped out of the trees onto a stretch of faded pavement lined with small one- and two-bedroom tract homes, a typical subdivision. I spotted Mom and Auntie Hanna about thirty yards away, shouting over the neighbors' houses into the surrounding woods. I guess they didn't care who got woken up.

I called out: "Uh Mom?!"

Flashlights whipped toward me, followed by rapid-fire footfalls. Mom and Auntie Hanna faded into view; Mom with her feathered strawberry-blonde hair just starting to take on streaks of gray; Auntie Hanna, the sheriff, almost a decade older than Mom's forty-three years, her hair slate-gray and pinned away from her square-jawed face, her eyes the same pale green as Mom's but somehow warm where her baby sister's were icy. Mom had thrown on a flannel and jeans, while Auntie Hanna was wearing her duty uniform over body armor; it gave her the V-shape of a middle linebacker.

Their contrasting physicality told the tale of apples that fell from the same tree but landed in different worlds. Mom, brittle and jagged, skittered to a stop and lurched to her knees before me, absentmindedly letting her flashlight clatter to the pavement. Hanna, who seemed to live in a state of perpetual mosey, glided over, her frame a beige block, and scooped up the flashlight.

Mom's tone was that classic motherly combo of *relieved yet furious.* She squeezed my shoulders. "Ohmigod, Hiram, Hiram! Where *were* you? I thought I was gonna be sick when I couldn't find you."

"Dropped something there," Hanna said, tucking the flashlight into her sister's hand. Hanna always sounded like she should be spinning a yarn on a front porch somewhere, strumming on a guitar while she kicked back in a rocking chair.

I was still a little dazed from being asleep. "I found something. And someone found me."

But Mom didn't hear me. She'd already jumped to her feet.

"Mac!" she screamed toward our house. *"We found him!"*

I checked my map. I'd written the word "Plaid" but stopped.

Plaid? Plaid what? What was it I saw?

Another woman's voice joined the scene, the lungs behind it huge and powerful:

"Hi, what the *fuck,* man?!"

Mac pounded up the pavement wearing a jumper and galoshes, another thrown-on outfit. Her hair was overly teased and about five years out of style. She came to a stop next to Mom, standing almost a full head taller. Mac had an easy athleticism that had skipped me genetically—where she taught herself how to swim and ride a bike, I hid in the shallow end till I was seven and still couldn't ride a two-wheeler. I guess you could've called her a tomboy, but she might knock your block off for it. I'd still yet to beat her at arm-wrestling.

In response to Mac's question, Auntie Hanna drawled, "You kiss my sister with that mouth, young lady?"

Mom stood up, her tone sharp. "I got this." Turning to Mac, she said, "Easy on the F-words, all right?"

Mac had already moved on, waving her arms at me and saying, "Where were you? Third time this month you're up and around, middle of the night!"

Hanna's eyebrows hopped. "Third time?"

Mom winced and whirled toward our house. "C'mon, gang. Back inside. Night's ruined anyway."

She left me standing there. Hanna smiled and held out her hand.

"Hey there, champ," she said. "Want to show this old fart your drawing?"

I was too old to hold hands, but I took it anyway—and that's when it came to me.

"Auntie, I saw a man with a plaid face."

She scuffed to a stop and looked down at me.

Hanna

Hanna Blackledge always had to keep one eye on her little sister, from when they were kids living in Sedalia, Missouri, to the last few years, when they all landed in the Smokies to take care of their ailing parents. After hanging on for a few years, both their mother and father passed within months of each other, leaving Hanna with their big, rambling house near Gatlinburg. Hanna asked if Corrie wanted to move her family in after Deacon died, but her sister, always so bullheaded, refused.

Now they were all wondering if something was seriously wrong with her youngest son.

"Where'd you see him?" she asked.

"Out in the woods. Near the traincar."

Corrie's voice rang out: *"Are you coming?"*

"We better go tell your mom," Hanna said, leading Hiram back to their house, one of a zillion split-level tract homes: white wood siding on a short brick foundation. They entered through the garage into a side door that led straight into a kitchen that bore all the hallmarks of a hectic household fraying at the edges: tired yellow linoleum floors, splintering faux-wood cabinets, and an electric range that was crusted with remnants of Chef Boyardee. Corrie was brewing some Sanka on the range while Mac lingered in the door to the living room.

"You've got maybe two hours' sleep before I've got to wake you for school," Corrie said. "Try and get some rest. Sorry, Hi, but I've got to lock your door again."

Hanna: "Hi? Something you want to share with us?"

"I saw a guy out there. He had a plaid face."

Corrie: "You saw someone?"

Hiram started to speak but instead merely nodded. Hanna recognized the behavior; he knew he was going to stutter, so he chose not to speak.

Hanna touched his knee. "Where'd you see him?"

"Uh I don't know," he said. "There was a traincar that had . . . monsters on it. Or squids. Or letters." He scrunched up his face, trying to summon the memory. "The sacks something? Flow uh sax? I can't remember. And it disappeared. He was near that."

Hanna held out her mug at almost the same time Corrie poured the coffee, a sisterly synchronization. After filling her own cup, Corrie sat, her face full of questions. Hanna knew that Hiram's sleepwalking frightened her sister, but she'd never ask her for help. Hanna pursed her lips and turned her attention back to the boy.

"Hiram, is it possible you simply dreamed this man? Or were you awake when you saw him? It might be important."

"Um," he said. Blood started to rush to his face. *He's stuttering again, the poor kid.*

A hand came to rest on his shoulder: Mac's.

"It's okay," she whispered.

"I don't know if I can remember," he said.

Hanna nodded and sipped her coffee. "Honey, why don't you and Mac get you some shut-eye before school? Your mom and I need to catch up on a few things."

"Come on, goofball," Mac said, ushering him out of the kitchen.

"Have you taken him back to that sleep specialist?" Hanna asked.

"Yeah, we had to stop," she said. "Couldn't afford it."

"You know you can just ask," Hanna said. Part of her wondered if Corrie had simply pissed away her share of the inheritance, while another figured it was because she had two kids.

Judge not, lest ye be, Hanna thought.

"I know. I just . . . don't want to. Not right now."

"You might *have* to, you know."

"You don't have anything better to do than hassle us?"

"Getting out three times in a month is one thing, but c'mon—if he's sleepwalking, he's upset about something. That's step two in the parenting handbook."

A ruckus came from above, followed by Mac's hushed—but perfectly audible—voice: *"Get in bed, Hiram!"*

Corrie and Hanna met eyes, rolled them.

"We can *hearrrr youuuuu!*" Corrie barked. "Get to bed!"

Scrambling footfalls sounded overhead. Corrie listened.

"Close the door!"

Slam.

Hiram's Journal

"We can *hearrrr youuuu!* Get to bed!"

Busted! Mac and I scrambled into our bedrooms. Mine was a glut of toys, books, and games, all of it arrayed around my messy-as-heck bed, which sported some totally badass and non-dorky Transformers sheets, while my dresser was covered in a platoon of my favorite Transformers, all in robot mode and all of 'em standing at attention.

I was about to climb into bed when I noticed shadows moving in the upstairs hallway.

Mac was lingering.

I snuck into the hallway to see her sitting in her bedroom doorway.

"Close your doors!" came Mom's voice from below.

Mac and I pulled an old trick: we both slammed our doors . . . and very lightly opened them back up in one smooth motion. Mom heard the slams but didn't know we could still listen in. I lumbered over and sat next to my sister. She gave me a look, and for a moment I thought she was going to shoo me back to bed, but instead she draped her arm around my shoulder and gave me a squeeze.

"Hey, goofball," she whispered.

"Hey," I said, leaning into her hug. "Is there another room behind the walk-in closet?"

Mac ignored my question. Mom and Auntie Hanna were still talking:

"You know about Skelton's been sighted 'round Asheville, right?"

"That's half a state away," Mom said.

"Not for me it isn't," Hanna said. "He's at large and on the move."

"You don't think Hiram saw him out there, do you?"

Mac and I looked at each other, our eyes widening.

"Did you see Skelton?" Mac asked me.

I shook my head. "No. I saw . . . someone else. The Plaid Man."

"You sure?" Mac asked. "Maybe Skelton was there, and that's just how you saw him in your dream."

"Uh maybe, but—"

Mac shushed me; Hanna was talking: "I don't mind getting woken up to help a neighbor, much less my sister. And I get it. My little Reggie used to sleepwalk. But if it looks like you can't hold down the fort here, some busybody might report you to Child Protective Services, and I won't be able to stop it."

Mom didn't answer. Mac prodded me. "You know we've got to start keeping this door locked."

I nodded, my face hot. "I'm sorry. I'm a big derk." I meant to say "jerk," but eleven-year-old me had a bit of a speech impediment. "I'm messed up."

"You're not a jerk," Mac said. "And you're not messed up. But we can't let them take us away from Mom."

After a silence, Mom finally said, "Is this payback for how I used to kick you in the shins when you pissed me off?"

"You read the news about Skelton? What he did to those kids? Got me back in church."

Mom snorted. "Yeah, for a week or two."

"Six of one," Hanna said. "I have nightmares about it all the time. Did you know we still can't find half his victims' remains?"

Mom didn't answer. Mac un-draped her arm from around me, her body growing tense.

"Are you sure you didn't see him out there?" Mac whispered.

I suddenly wasn't so sure, and on that note, I guess I should tell you about Leonard Shane "Lenny" Skelton, aka the East Tennessee Strangler, aka the Blue Ribbon Killer.

And if I'm going to tell you about Skelton, that means I have to tell you about the man who almost caught him: Justin Johnson.

First, let's make something clear: Lenny Skelton was way worse than a strangler. The guy had a thing—and a way—with kids. He was a specter straight out of a nineteen-eighties public service announcement, stalking neighborhoods, hiding in the woods. A master of disguise, he would pose as repairmen to trick latch-key kids into letting him in. He'd steal security uniforms and snatch kids away from distracted parents at banks or the mall. He once posed as the musical act at a state fair just to get backstage, where he saw a target.

The disguises always baffled me, because regardless of what he was wearing, Skelton had one incredibly distinctive feature: he'd lost an eye as a kid and replaced it with a glass one that always rolled out of sync with the other. Kids around the playground traded tall tales about how he lost the eye. Billy Gunderson told me Skelton's dad hit him in the face with a bicycle chain, while Maggie Benson insisted the cops shot it out. Billy's story seemed more plausible, given the ink-vine scar that ran from Skelton's hairline to the middle of his cheek, bisecting his eye like that guy from James Bond.

But only having one eye or scars doesn't make anyone look like a bad guy. No, Skelton's evil welled up from a bottomless store deep in his gut. His pupil was a pinprick, his gaze never meeting yours but always glancing at some unseen horizon where his demons beckoned. He moved in uneasy jerks and feints, like he was always about to lash out.

Skelton just *looked* like a bad guy.

He was a master of makeup, too. After they finally caught him, they found one of his secret lairs. He'd moved into the basement under a warehouse near Alcoa and converted it to a darkroom where he'd hung dozens of photos of his makeup tests. He'd photographed himself from every angle to make sure he looked perfect. A jar of glass eyes of every color sat next to his assortment of multi-colored contacts along with wigs, spirit gum, and makeup putty. When he played old men, he's swallow cordite to make his skin look tired and gray. The room was also dotted with Skelton's calling cards:

Prize ribbons. He left one on every victim.

Every victim they found, that is.

I hate to even mention Justin Johnson's name in the same breath as Skelton, but there's no getting around it. Their names are inextricably linked due to one fateful night in West Chimney Top.

Here's a primer on Justin Johnson, aka "JJ Flash," the hero of Polk High's still-legendary upset over mighty Brentwood Academy. He was a multi-talented skill player who could play runningback, quarterback, as well as single-wing-style halfback. (Justin was basically running the wildcat almost two decades before it got popular.) Justin was a marvel on the field, but even though the Polk coaches begged him to play other sports, he always acted in school plays in the offseason, foregoing basketball, wrestling, baseball, track—everything. He even directed his own productions, rounding up the other Black kids at Polk to put on August Wilson's *Fences*.

Justin took a scholarship at NC State, and although he ran all over the ACC and SEC, he skipped his senior year not to go pro . . . but to focus on his major, theater. He even gave up his scholarship. His mom and dad both took on extra work to help out with his tuition, all while fielding phone call after phone call from Justin, who often called them in tears. After he stopped playing football and started chasing his dream, he didn't have a friend in the world in North Carolina.

Well, I'm exaggerating. Justin had plenty of friends, but after he gave up football, the steady stream of bullshit and micro-aggressions every Black person has to put up with got ten times worse for him. Hate mail to him and his folks. Graffiti on his car and his home. Name-calling and slurs. I can't even imagine how hard it must be to be a Black man anywhere, much less the South, and much less as Justin Johnson, who didn't do anything but chase his dream.

He chased it all the way to New York City, where he tried his luck on Broadway. He landed some roles but didn't quite make it, so he came back in West Chimney Top and followed in his dad's footsteps at the sheriff's department. He was living a quiet life. After all, the Smokies aren't exactly a hotbed for crime.

But then Skelton came.

He'd confined his mayhem to northern Georgia for a while before making his way up through western North Carolina to the Smokies, leaving a wake of death and sorrow. Authorities had only identified Skelton as the perp behind all these killings about a month before Justin crossed paths with him.

When they finally nabbed him over in West Chimney Top, things almost got bloody. Skelton slipped up, letting himself be seen in a neighborhood park, and the town's parents turned out in force to hunt him down. It was shaping up to be a repeat of the Ken McElroy affair. McElroy, who menaced the small town of Skidmore, Missouri, was shot to death in 1981. Almost fifty people watched it. No one ever went to jail.

The people of Skidmore made McElroy disappear, and the people of West Chim were poised to do the same to Skelton. They had him corralled under the bleachers at Polk High, all of 'em spitting mad and armed with baseball bats, knives, and an assortment of firearms. Justin screeched onto the scene in his police cruiser, sprinted up behind the crowd, and shot his gun in the sky. He stopped the crowd—and gave Skelton the diversion he needed to escape.

The authorities caught up with Skelton over in Gatlinburg, but not before he added another victim to his tally.

They blamed Justin for Skelton's escape, even though it was bullshit. He was only doing his job, and he said so in court.

"I stand my decision," he told a packed courtroom. "I couldn't do it. I couldn't just allow those folks to sentence him outside the law." When asked how Skelton had slipped away, he said: "I have no idea. It never made sense to me. They had him surrounded, and the bleachers were too close together for him to slip through. He just . . . vanished."

It took the jury less than an hour to come back with a unanimous guilty verdict. The sentence was death, but Skelton spun it out in the appeals for years, slowly doling out the location of victim after heartbreaking victim. In all, he led the FBI to five poor souls, each one marked with one of his prize ribbons.

But he never revealed them all.

The FBI said he'd hidden away at least a dozen more victims. They practically begged him to give them up, but all he said was:

"They ain't anywhere someone could find 'em, not even if they found 'em. I done tore up the map. I cain't reveal what ain't real. I cain't reveal what ain't real. I cain't reveal what ain't real."

That was about three years ago.

Skelton vanished from Tennessee State Pen about six months before I first dreamed of the traincar.

He hadn't been seen since.

But I'd seen him in the flesh in less than seventy-two hours.

"I . . . uh I don't think it was Skelton," I whispered to Mac as we huddled in our bedroom doorway. "He had a plaid face."

"You were dreaming." It wasn't a question.

"No."

"No, you didn't see Skelton?"

"Uh no, I don't think I was dreaming."

Chairs scooted downstairs. Mac held up her hand to say *quiet*.

"How about I come by every week or so, check in, see how y'all are holding up?"

"You don't need to," Mom said.

I nudged my sister. "Hey."

"Shh."

Hanna: "I wanna do a favor for my sweet little sister who's done me so many. Easy enough to swing by after my shift on Fridays."

I pressed on: "Mac, I've got a question."

"*Shh*," Mac hissed.

Mom: "Okay. Just so long as it's no trouble."

"It's no trouble at all," Hanna said. "I gotta get back on the road. Change those locks for me, would ya? And make sure the office is locked up tight."

Office? I thought.

"Will do," Mom said. "Good night."

The side door shut. Hanna's police cruiser fired up with an errant *whoop* and rumbled away. A silent moment passed before we heard coffee mugs clank into the sink, followed by the click of Mom's bedroom door. Mac and I didn't move.

"Mac, I've still got a question."

"What is it? I'm really tired."

"Is there another room behind the walk-in closet?"

"Yeah, the Office."

"The Office? We have an office?"

"It's not an office. That's only what we call it. It's just an empty room."

"Is that what Auntie Hanna was talking about keeping locked up tight?"

"Yeah, it's dangerous. Don't go in there."

I frowned. "Are you making fun of me?"

Mac heaved a sigh and stood. "I'm not making fun. Go to sleep."

"There's a whole 'nother room back there?"

"Yes." She shut her door. I sat there.

I whispered at her door: "In our *house?*"

"*Yes.* Now go to bed."

"How long has it been there?"

"It's always been there."

It's always been there?

The next day at school was pure misery. I tried to sneak into the walk-in closet before we left, but Mom hauled me out of the house and plopped me in the Sentra.

Mac and I attended the same school, Polk Middle-Senior High. Someone at the Board of Education thought it'd be a good idea to squeeze middle and high schoolers together into the same building. Whoever it was, I hope they're in the lowest circle of hell getting pitchforks in the butt. Polk High had been built sometime in the twenties, and I'm ninety-nine percent certain it used to be a prison or an insane asylum. It was a solid block of red-brick brutalism crawling with rusty fire escapes that clung to its sides like barnacles, while the windows all wept black tears. Graffiti on the side screamed, *SUCK MY DICK TUCKER.*

Speaking of Mr. Tucker, I had him for homeroom, where I always sat in the back and fended off the overtures of someone who was—at the time—my least-favorite person, Lee Dockery.

"Greetings, Admiral," he said as I sat.

Rolling my eyes, I mumbled, "Hey, Lee."

He was a few inches taller and about thirty pounds lighter than my fat ass. (If I hadn't made it clear, I was Mama's well-fed boy.) He wore a light brown windbreaker with jeans and enormous glasses that made him look like a robot. He was the weirdest kind of dork, awkward and strange. I was always trying to shake his tail at Polk High, but he made it a point to take all the same classes as me, even if it meant he took ones that were beneath his learning level. (I heard the gifted teacher say he had a one-fifty IQ.)

If I sound like a mean kid when I describe Lee, it's because I was. Eleven-year-old Hiram was too much of a dipshit to recognize a great person.

But I would. Eventually.

Another kid sat down ahead of us, Danny Sizemore, who had been held back twice and towered over everyone in seventh grade. Looking back, I feel bad for him—he always came to school with a new bruise—but at the time, he was my biggest bully.

"Nice shorts, piggy," he said to me. I wore shorts almost every day, no matter how hot or cold, because they all had elastic bands; none of my pants were comfortable.

Lee stood. "Don't address the admiral in such a disrespectful manner."

Danny's eyes took on a delighted, evil gleam.

"Don't address the admiral in such a disrespectful manner," he said, widening his eyes and locking his arms in place to imitate a robot. "Shut your fuckin' mouth, computer-brain. I guess having a one-fifty IQ don't make you smart enough to mind your own business."

Lee

His mind wasn't a computer. It never felt like one. He couldn't solve math problems faster than anyone else. The rumor about his one-fifty IQ was bunk. (He had declined to take an IQ test because he thought they were silly.) No, Lee liked to imagine his mind was like a series of interwoven epicycle machines. He'd seen one at a museum in Chicago, an elegantly crafted piece of bizarro brass and bronze clockwork. The fact that it depicted an interstellar configuration that never existed only added to its mystique. Lee liked to imagine his thought processes as divinely crafted quantum clockwork with a quintillion moving positronic parts that spun, always spun along on parallel tracks.

And yes, he thought of them as *divinely* crafted, for though he was a strict student of the sciences, he felt the benevolent hand of a prime mover behind it all.

Lee's mom liked to say he had an "active internal life." He could divert himself for hours by simply thinking. He'd ponder comic-book storylines, dissect movies, or recall scenes he especially loved from pop-culture. Sometimes he'd recite entire scenes to himself, playing both parts in his head. Once in a while, his sister or mom would catch him playing these scenes, his lips moving slightly or his arms acting out a gesture.

When Danny Sizemore insulted the admiral, Lee's decision to stick up for him was an easy one. Lee recognized a kindred spirit in Hiram, even if he didn't reciprocate the feeling. Hiram's rudeness didn't bother Lee, who knew with a happy certainty that he'd come around eventually. Hiram was trapped in the limited mindset of someone who could only perceive a few months at a time.

He was a kid.

So was Lee, but he saw his life in larger and longer terms. He thought about his future a lot and could easily project himself into a far-flung time where there weren't any bullies and life was easier. It was an ability that helped him stave off the sadness that always lurked at the periphery of his mind. Thinking about a future when he had more friends made Lee happy, so he did it a lot.

He didn't know it, but he was about to make a lot of new friends, including Hiram.

Hiram's Journal

I stared at my desk and pulled out my map just as *she* walked in.

She, as in Christy Hodges.

My primordial brain had absolutely no idea what to do with the feelings Christy summoned. She had black hair and blue eyes and rang every bell I had. She wore a blue-jean jumper and was the girl of my idiotic eleven-year-old dreams. She sensed me looking and turned. I snapped my head back down.

Mr. Tucker rolled in wearing his usual purple flannel and matching Doc Martens.

"Today's worksheet is on the power of volunteering!" he said. "I expect your full attention."

As we distributed the worksheets, Mr. Tucker passed by my desk and gave my shoulder a little chuck.

"I think you'll like those new cartoons, Hiram."

I nodded, smiling. "Uh yes, sir." He smiled and pressed on with his lecture. The new cartoons were indeed awesome—a series of panels from a strip called *Ernie Pook's Comeek.* The art was bizarre and a little disturbing . . . and I *loved* it. I discreetly laid the worksheet on top of my map and worked on both. If I couldn't get back into the walk-in closet until tonight, I was going to keep working on my map. I sketched in details of the area surrounding the traincar: the wooded glen, the wide depression in the earth.

But when I woke up, the traincar was gone. Why?

Another voice in my head answered: *Because you were dreaming, dummy.*

"That's quite good work," Lee whispered.

"Gee, *thanks,*" I said, rude as hell.

"Would you mind if I added something?" he asked.

"Uh, I don't know. It's pretty specific, what I'm drawing." As if he were asking to touch up the Mona Lisa.

"I understand, Admiral," he said, sliding the map onto his desk.

Danny heard him say "Admiral" and glanced back with that same shit-eating smirk. Christy looked over, too, and smiled.

Is she smiling at me or laughing at Lee? Or is she laughing at us both?

"You don't have to call me 'Admiral,'" I said.

"Understood, sir," Lee said, returning the map. While Mr. Tucker admonished us to get out and volunteer, I marveled at Lee's craftsmanship. He hadn't added any new structures or landmarks, but he'd delicately shaded in every detail, from the trees to the traincar. The one detail he *had* added was a compass rose that looked like it had come from a pirate's treasure map.

"Whoa," I said. "That's really good."

"Thank you. My mother taught me."

"This looks like a real map," I muttered. The world faded away. Lee was saying something about his mom's secret club meetings, but I didn't hear him. Next to the traincar, I wrote, *How to get back here? What is hidden?*

"What is this intended for?"

It was Lee who'd asked. I honestly didn't have an answer. "It's hard to explain."

"Would you like to come over after school? I have a Masterminder Home Edutainment System with a game that is most fascinating."

"Oh. I've got a Nintendo. I don't know if I'd know how to play a Masterminder."

That's actually what I said. When I think back on this moment, I cringe so, so hard.

Lee was crestfallen. "Oh, I see. I understand."

But I didn't hear him, and I hadn't even noticed Christy trying to get my attention. All I could think about were my map and those strange words I'd heard:

Itza linda adda. Gedda Brusha. Zo vaxap dis en zo flestulo.

On a hunch, I drew our little house, taking care to highlight a space at the rear: *The Office,* I wrote in delicate script before adding arrows emanating from it in several directions. Something flashed across my mind. I scribbled next to the traincar: *Is this Itza Linda? Is the Office the key to Itza Linda?*

Mackenzie

"Settle down, everyone!"

Mac's homeroom teacher, Mr. Evanston, was in his usual state of high dudgeon. Balding, bearded, and wearing a short-sleeve button-down with a knit necktie, he waved around a worksheet about the evils of eating sugar. The room's decor was *eighties high school drudgery*: linoleum floors, fluorescent lights, and motivational posters like *THE ONLY WAY TO GUARANTEE FAILURE IS TO NEVER TRY*.

Mac was sitting at her desk, with her friends arrayed around her: Dawn Dockery, Becky Hubert, Sabrina Terrence, among others, but it was Dawn who commanded the bulk of her attention and affection. They'd bonded during Brownies when they got rained out of a camping trip and had to ride a jon boat back to safety, and they knew each other's every tic and mannerism. Everyone called them "Dawn-n-Gresh"; that's one word, mind you: *Dawn-n-Gresh.*

They'd coordinated outfits: Mac wore her favorite Dan Marino Dolphins 13 jersey, while Dawn wore her Joe Namath Alabama 12. A mangy fur coat hung on the back of Dawn's chair, while Mac had elected for her favorite denim jacket, which she'd draped across her shoulders. Both had pulled their hair into pigtails, although Dawn's straight blond hair fared better than Mac's frizzy red mop. (She looked like Pippi Longstocking had stuck a fork into a wall socket, but in the most adorable way possible.) Dawn was shorter and skinnier, Mac strapping and stocky. They were a reverse-image Helena and Hermia, an odd couple bound at the hip, their destinies intertwined—more intertwined than they knew.

"Here's today's human dev worksheet, everyone!" He passed a stack of papers to the kids in the front row, who passed them back.

"Psst, Gresh."

It was sweet, handsome Dave Shuler, with his close-cropped black hair and gorgeous eyes. She hadn't noticed him slide in next to her, otherwise she might've moved, for although she'd placed him in the same exalted company as Ralph Macchio and Jonathan Taylor Thomas, the thought of actually talking to him turned her insides to ice. She thought about moving seats, but she didn't want to hurt his feelings. He was in the ninth grade but had been held back for football, so he already sported a five-o'clock shadow.

"Gresh, hey, Gresh," he whispered as Mr. Evanston droned on. "You going to Randall's party this weekend?

Mac didn't stutter like her brother, but she did any time a good-looking boy spoke to her. She knew Dave had been carrying a torch for her since seventh grade. He'd even politely asked her out a few times—never one-on-one—but he'd asked her to parties and group outings. Nice, low-pressure overtures. But she'd found excuses to say no every time, her mom's voice echoing in her head:

You don't have time for boys. You're too busy, and they'll just break your heart anyway.

"No, I don't think so, Dave. I'm too busy."

Dave's look of disappointment was diverted by a tap on the shoulder from Dawn, who was twirling a pigtail and frowning at her worksheet.

"Dave, can you help me with this?"

Mac smiled at Dawn's "ditzy" act. She was fairly certain Dawn had the same high IQ as her brother, but she hid it deep inside. Most other girls would be upset by Dawn's diversion; not Mac.

She was relieved.

BRRRRRING! Everyone jumped from their seats and scrambled into the hallway. Mac hadn't even noticed how quickly the time had passed. She'd planned to stall and let Dave leave first, but he was already gone. Dawn was waiting for her by the door, waving her along.

"Randall's having a kegger this weekend! Wanna go?"

She thought of having to tell poor Dave Shuler she wasn't interested.

"I dunno," Mac said. "I'll have to think about it."

Dawn looked disappointed. "Oh, okay. That's all right. I figured your mom might've—" She stopped.

"Figured my mom might've what?" Mac asked.

But Dawn was already running to her next class.

"Nothing! Tell ya later!"

Hiram's Journal

When I got home, I decided find this "office" for myself, regardless of the danger. The way Mac described it, it sounded like it was *behind* the walk-in closet, but that wasn't possible. The walk-in closet was at the very back of the house.

The golden light of a setting sun cast my mom in silhouette as I slipped past her through the kitchen and outside. It was right on the borderline of being too late to play outside, so I eased the kitchen door shut and ran around to the side of the house. (Flat land is hard to come by in the Smokies, so architects had to build a lot of stuff *into* the sides of hills and mountains.)

Almost half of the house's rear end was buried under a gently sloping hill. One side window peeked in at the living room, where I could see the door to the walk-in closet. Past that was the kitchen, where I saw Mom hunched over the sink, smoking and scrubbing away at the dishes. (Our dishwasher was always on the fritz.)

Standing by the side of the house, I noticed something strange: behind the house, situated on the same parallel as the walk-in closet and right below Mac's bedroom, was a slight rise in the earth, a swelling, like something was buried there. There was something else:

When I looked in the side window, the walk-in closet was open.

I ran inside.

Mom didn't notice me running by her into the living room, where I found the closet door closed again.

Weird.

I opened it, flicked on the light—and had an idea. I thought of the actor Donald Pleasance counting off steps in *The Great Escape,* so I counted the steps from the closet door to the back of the room:

One, two, three, four, five, six . . . seven.

Seven steps.

I went back outside, ran around to the side of the house, and counted the number of steps from the closet door to the back of the house. It was about seven steps.

But what about that swell in the earth behind the house?

I counted the number of steps from the closet door to the end of the swelling.

Eleven steps.

There was something back there.

Back in the walk-in closet, I crawled into my hidey-hole and examined the walls. I felt along the grooves in the wood paneling, pressing in, looking for secret buttons or switches; basically, everything you'd do if you'd grown up watching stuff like *The Private Eyes* and *Clue* on repeat. I was ready to give up when it jumped out at me:

A small brass handle.

It was inlaid into the paneling, the kind used for pocket doors. I pulled it, and a panel slid into the wall, revealing a door leading into pitch darkness.

"Holy crap," I whispered.

In my dream, the door had opened outward. This was a sliding door. But it was the same shape and size, set in the same position as the door from my dream. I poked my head in the door. Darkness engulfed my face like a hood. Musty, rotting smells hit my nose and sent me scooting back out.

I almost went running to Mom. I don't know what stopped me, but I found some nerve and reached back through the door. (When you're a kid, there's a tense interplay between what terrifies you and what fascinates and attracts you.) Patting around the inside wall, I flicked on a light. It illuminated a room about ten feet deep and six feet wide. I crawled inside and paused on my hands and knees. Somewhere, a bird chirped. Roughly trapezoidal in shape, the room included a small school-desk, the kind with a bookshelf built into the seat. Books and papers spilled out of the shelf, while a box filled with clothes and other detritus sat in the seat. I stood and plunged my face straight into a spiderweb.

"Eeeee!" I staggered back before I realized it wasn't a spiderweb but a pull-cord for another light. Heat pressed against my chest; the earth overhead kept this space well insulated. The school-desk beckoned to me, but when I approached it, I froze.

A patch of fabric hung over the side of the cardboard box.

Plaid fabric, the exact same color and pattern as the man from my dreams.

I bolted from the room so fast I banged my forehead into the tiny doorjamb.

There's a phenomenon called "The Mandela Effect." Large groups of people share collective *false* memories. One of the most common examples is the death of Nelson Mandela. A bunch of people think he died in the eighties, when he actually lived until 2013. There's a related—and outlandish—hypothesis that the people with the false memory don't actually have a false memory but instead are simply from a nearby parallel reality that got collapsed into our own.

The Office was like that for me.

When I saw that little brass handle, it felt like a joke. I'd gone back there I don't know *how* many times and never noticed it when in reality it had been there, *right next to me,* the entire time. Maybe I was from a nearby parallel reality where the Office didn't exist. Looking back at the unreal magical mayhem that was in store for me over the next several months, such an explanation doesn't seem so outlandish anymore.

After seeing that patch of plaid fabric, I ran straight into the kitchen, where Mom was sitting at the kitchen table, smoking and writing in a small book with a green-and-purple cover, her diary. I coughed from the smoke. She made a half-hearted attempt to wave it away.

"Sorry, honey," she said.

"When did we add the room behind the walk-in?"

"Add the what? What room?"

"Mac called it the 'office'? The little room behind the walk-in closet?"

"Don't go in there. It's dangerous."

"Okay, but when did we add it?"

"Add it? It's always been there."

There's a saying about the youngest kid in a family: they think they're coming in at the beginning of a story, when they're really coming in at the end.

I frowned.

"It's always been there? The door and everything?"

"Yes, of course it's been there. It's part of the house."

It felt like Mom was telling me that the world had an extra continent or that the Earth had rings. The Office was magic to me, mundane to them, because it had always been a part of *their* story. They'd existed in the swirling darkness before my birth, learning untold wonders about the world.

"What's it for?" I asked.

"Hm? Oh, I don't know. The attic's hard to get to, so I think the architect added it for some extra storage. Your dad used to keep his Peace Corps stuff in there before I moved it."

"Where's it now?"

"Where's what, honey?"

"Uh Dad's Peace Corps stuff."

Mom scribbled something into her diary. I'd only seen her diary a handful of times over the years. Its cover had the color and texture of a lime, highlighted by a royal purple spine.

"It's, uh, in the attic."

I lingered, not sure why, though looking back, I think it was because I wanted to know more about her.

"What're you writing?" I asked.

"Nothing."

Mom had this way of actively ignoring you. She'd delete you from the room and somehow fill it with her impatience at your presence. She lit another cigarette and kept writing in her diary.

Without looking up, she said, "Was there something else?"

"Uhhh," I said before adding in a faint whisper, "uh can . . ."

Me and my awful stutter. I wanted to say the following sentence to my mom:

Can I use the Office?

But I couldn't say it. There are all kinds of stutters and stutterers. Naturally, plosive consonants—your b's and p's and t's and even some g's—are harder to say, especially if they're at the beginning of a sentence, so you find ways to work around them. A lot of times, I'd just tack an "uh" to the beginning of the sentence in question.

But you couldn't always get away with that. Then the anxiety would start up. You knew you were going to *have* to start a sentence with a B or a P—or in this case, a dreaded C—and you'd freeze up. You'd be forced to do what, in my head, I called a "skip," where you begin a sentence with an easy-to-say word or sound—like "uh"—and use that sound to get a running start so you could skip over the difficult-to-say word or sound.

But I still couldn't quite get it out. Mom's active impatience had filled me with anxiety.

"Uhhh . . . can . . . Uh, can—"

"Can you *what?*" she said, her head whipping toward me, her eye contact sudden and aggressive.

"Use it?" I skipped over that dastardly first word "can" entirely.

"Can you use what? Use your words, honey."

"The office. Uh can I use it?"

"For what?"

"I don't know. A clubhouse, maybe? Or a little theater?"

Like I said, when you're a kid, there's a tense interplay between what terrifies you and what attracts you, plus it's not like I knew my weirdo dream from the night before had been a missive from the beyond. At least not yet. Most of its deeper, more crucial details had already faded from memory.

Mom wrinkled her nose in amused affection at my suggestions just as her cigarette burned down to her fingers.

"Shit!" she yelled, dropping the butt.

"Sorry!" I yelled it on instinct.

"Oh, honey. It wasn't anything you did. Don't say sorry so much."

"Sorry."

I winced as soon as I said it. Mom gave me a semi-dirty look, but let it slide.

"I don't know if anyone should be back there, sweetie. There's only one way in or out of that room, and the ventilation's not great. If the door got stuck, you could suffocate."

"Maybe you could take the door off so the . . . uh so the air could get in?"

"It's too much work to take the door off," Mom said, her voice higher and a few decibels louder. "And I don't want to clean your dad's stuff out of the attic."

If anyone had been listening in on this exchange, they'd have probably thought she was yelling at me. But she wasn't. Her volume had increased because I'd inadvertently overstepped one of countless invisible boundaries she'd erected. One of them was Dad. How was I supposed to know that asking her about the Office would remind her of him?

I felt the very beginnings of tears behind my eyes. My lower lip wasn't trembling, but my lips had pursed together. Mom knew the expression and took mercy on me. She set aside her diary, taking care to lock it with a tiny gold key, and faced me.

"Maybe I can take the door off some other time," she said. "It's just that we're going to be busy this weekend."

"Uh we are?"

"Yeah. We're going to the Gold Rush."

My stutter vanished: *"We are?!"*

"Didn't Mac tell you?"

As if summoned by the utterance of her name, Mac appeared in the door next to me.

"Tell him what?"

"We're going to the Gold Rush this weekend!"

"We are?!" she yelled with a squeal. "Holy shit!"

We busted up laughing, not knowing that Mom had a surprise in store for us at the park:

A secret boyfriend she hadn't told us about.

Mackenzie

Mom can really be fun sometimes, but how can she afford this?

Mackenzie "Mac" Gresham wore her favorite bespangled T-shirt to honor the namesake of the theme park they all visited that weekend: country music legend Susie Schuppe, whose park—Susie Schuppe's Smoky Mountain Gold Rush—was the centerpiece of a newly-revitalized West Chimney Top metro area.

Mac's T-shirt depicted the curvy crooner in her classic ensemble: skintight, bright blue dungarees, a rhinestone-studded ten-gallon hat, and a button-down that shimmered with footlong fringe and hugged her legendary figure.

"It costs a lot to look this cheap," Susie Schuppe always said, part of her regular onstage patter.

Mac had glued an assortment of rhinestones and sequins onto the shirt, which an airbrush artist had made for her on their first trip to the park some six years ago, before Hiram was old enough to come. She'd nearly grown out of it, even though her dad, Deacon Gresham, had had the foresight to buy her a shirt three sizes too big.

That had been the last time they'd visited the park with Dad.

Years later, the day after Hiram said he dreamed of a man with a plaid face, Mac, Hiram, and their mom all ran across the parking lot on an autumn-golden Friday afternoon. Laughing and cheering, they raced each other toward the park's entrance, a pair of giant, cartoony wooden farm gates.

The date was Friday, October 13, and Halloween season was in full swing.

As she always did, Corrie won the footrace, while sweet, chubby Hiram came in last. Mac, with her powerful frame and natural gifts, came in a close second to her mom . . . but she was getting close to beating her. They all came scampering into the main entrance area, where a giant pumpkin smiled mischievously at them.

"I almost got you that time!" Mac said, laughing.

"Only counts in horseshoes, dear," Corrie said with a cough. She was already lighting a cigarette.

Red-faced and looking slightly hurt, Hiram pounded up. He was always a sore loser, but he was getting better at playing it off. Mac raised her hand for a high-five.

"Great job, goofball!" she said as they slapped hands. "Good form!"

"Really?' Hiram said, flattered. It had been the right thing for her to say. He actually checked his muscles in the reflection of a kiosk. As always, he wore shorts in spite of the chilly temperatures and his Masters of the Universe T-shirt, the same one he'd slept in, even though he was getting a little too old for that kind of thing.

Leafy gold-and-red garlands lined the gates, while various harvest-time crops lay strewn around the entranceway, the occasional cornucopia dotting the perimeter. A line of pumpkin-head scarecrows flanked the ticket booths, where Corrie paid cash, adding an extra fifty bucks for tickets to a live show later that evening, a band called Little Women.

"Oh, Mom," Mac said. "That's okay, we don't need to see an extra show."

Corrie shooed them away from the ticket booth and toward the main entrance turnstiles.

"Well, I want to see it. I've been dying to see Jerry Joseph live again," she said, slipping on a pair of sunglasses and sticking her tongue out at Mac, who giggled.

Sometimes she's like a big sister, other times she's like a wicked step-mother, Mac thought. *And where does she get all this money? The way Auntie Hanna was talking, she's already spent most of our inheritance from Grandma.*

Hasn't she?

Corrie jerked her chin toward the park. "C'mon, guys. I wanna squeeze in a few rides before the show."

Hiram had grabbed a park brochure-map from a nearby kiosk and lingered, poring over it. Mac prodded him.

"C'mon, goofball," she said. "Let's go have some fun."

An intricately carved wooden sign set into a stone foundation greeted them at the turnstiles: *SUSIE SCHUPPE'S SMOKY MOUNTAIN GOLD RUSH.* As they passed through the turnstiles, Hiram continued to examine the brochure, much to his big sister's chagrin.

"You're gonna walk into something," she said, guiding him around a stanchion as they passed through a tunnel that led into the park proper. The Gold Rush achieved a remarkably immersive atmosphere with its sunken nature; most of the park resided a few feet underground. Each area of the park was separated by a series of tunnels. Like Disneyland, a train ran around the park, although unlike that train, which only ran in a circle around the park's perimeter, the Gold Rush Express zigged and zagged and swooped through the park, passing over each themed area at least once every ten minutes.

They ran to keep up with Corrie, who strode ahead on her long legs. Mac, already five-nine, inherited her mom's height, while Hiram got stuck with the Gresham side's more hobbit-sized proportions; he'd been five-three for years. (Mac's mental images of her dad floated in the mists of distant memory, but she remembered Mom always seemed to tower over him.)

Hiram prattled on: "Susie Schuppe acquired the old Santa's Holiday Kingdom theme park and used it as the basis, as the *foundation,* for the Gold Rush, re-theming several lands to reflect the look of her hometown in the Smokies."

Mountains rose up around the park pathways and cradled it in green. The initial area, "Hootin' Hollow," was styled like a magical old country hamlet. Miniature villages, made smaller to their eyes by forced perspective, peppered the hillsides and swarmed with Lilliputian animatronic activity: tiny villagers scurrying to and fro, windows opening and closing. A tiny windmill spun in an imaginary distance. Cobblestone pathways lined with wrought-iron lamps led between quaint little shops and buildings: a fire station, a hair salon, a magic shop.

But the park wasn't all quaint—it had a wild streak, too. Buildings teetered and tilted, and roughly half the rooftops bore an occupant: some were costumed woodland creatures, while others were thematically costumed musicians laying out top-tier bluegrass, including a classic song familiar to any Tennessean, "Rocky Top."

Hiram kept chattering away: "But in other places, Susie Schuppe had her engineers build directly over existing attractions, in some cases retaining the ride technology but completely swapping out the animatronics and . . ."

Her brother's sudden silence drew her attention away from keeping up with Corrie. Hiram was frozen in place, the map spread between his hands, squinting into the distance, almost looking straight into the sun. Mac checked for Mom; they'd already lost her.

I'll find her later, Mac thought, slowly approaching her brother.

"Hi?" she said. "What's wrong?"

He spoke, but his lips moved out of sync with his words. He looked like a foreign movie with bad dubbing, and although she couldn't swear to it, he sounded to Mac like he was speaking in tongues.

"Zo vaxap dis en zo flestulo," he said.

Hiram's Journal

It's him, I thought. *Oh shit, it's him.*

Him.

The Plaid Man.

Dozens of performers were scattered across the rooftops, including a bunch who stood among the miniature villages like giants. One man—the one who was playing "Rocky Top"—was staring right at Hiram, belting out the chorus. The performer was wearing the same blue suit as the Plaid Man, his head situated directly between the setting sun, which blazed over his right shoulder, and the moon, which was just fading into view over his left. Shimmer-blazing sunbeams carved his face into a plaid pattern. For some reason, the previous night's dream heaved into view, the magic traincar plain as day in my mind's eye:

"Zo vaxap dis en zo flestulo," I muttered, remembering the strange writing on the side.

But what does that mean?

"Hi?"

It took me a moment to realize I was being spoken to. (It was a common mistake for me, as my nickname often sounded like someone saying, "hi!") Giving my head a shake, I looked into my sister's eyes. Her eyebrows were raised, her mouth hanging open in concern. She took a step closer.

"What's wrong?" she asked.

"Zo vaxap dis en zo flestulo," I said, which caused her eyes to pop even wider.

"*What?*"

"Help me remember it," I said. "Zo vaxap dis en zo flestulo. It's from my dream. It means something."

"Okay, okay," Mac said. "Zo zaxxo deslo fartoolo."

"No, *no*," I said, blushing. I always got red in the face when I couldn't explain myself. "Zo vaxap dis en zo flestulo!"

"Zo vaxap dis en zo flestulo," she repeated, rolling her eyes, all while the Plaid Man's voice kept singing from above, recounting the bad luck of a certain group of G-men. But when I looked, he was gone. Or rather, he wasn't *gone*, but the man in the blue suit had been replaced with a more theme-appropriate good ole boy in overalls who was plucking away on a banjo.

"Where'd he go?" I muttered, but Mac was already pulling my arm.

"C'mon, goofball. We lost Mom."

The song continued from above but stopped abruptly. I'd heard "Rocky Top" approximately a bajillion times growing up in East Tennessee. I knew every word, and the singer had stopped mid-chorus. As Mac tugged me along, I stared at the ground. For some reason, I knew when I looked back up, I'd see something fucking terrifying, though I didn't know what. I didn't want to look, *couldn't* look . . . but I had to. I tilted my head slowly upward.

He was staring straight into my eyes.

Gone was the good ole boy in overalls, once again replaced by the man in the blue suit—only his face wasn't plaid, thank God. It looked human . . . but strange. His face was frozen in a rictus, his mouth open in a wide grin, his eyes in a half-squint, looking directly into mine. The song that had just short-circuited suddenly fritzed back to life out of his mouth, which remained still.

Oh, it's a robot, I thought. *An animatronic.*

It sure looked like it. The animatronic performer in the blue suit moved in the herky-jerky rhythm of an animatronic, repeating the same poses over and over.

But why was it the only animatronic on that particular hill?

"Hiram!" Mac said, a little louder this time. "Come on! I see Mom!"

She pulled me down the main drag toward a tunnel leading deeper into the park. Other park workers roamed the crowd, performing bits: comedy sketches, musical interludes, and, in some cases, fully interactive stories. One guest got whisked away on an interactive story that would play out around the park. Other characters posed for photographs taken on plastic disposable cameras.

Finally, Mom came into view on the far side of the tunnel, which bore a sign reading, "THIS WAY TO CHRISTMASVILLE!"

"C'mon, guys!" Mom called. "I see Santa!"

I pelted ahead, my belly bouncing, instantly forgetting about the weird animatronic guy on the hillside. Such was the world of Kid-dom.

I caught up with Mom right on the border of Christmasville, a realm of perpetual holiday cheer and my second favorite place in the Gold Rush. Hidden machines borrowed from Ober Gatlinburg—the nearby ski resort— kept a steady stream of snowfall across the land, no matter the season, while employees dressed as Santa's elves goofed around with park guests. The architecture was a polyglot of German and Scandinavian styles, all

A-frame, chalet-style cottages and inns, all of them covered with faux snow and glittering with tinsel.

The running joke with Christmasville was that it was connected to the North Pole via a magic gate located in the middle of the land. The gate itself stood near one of the tunnels leading out of the land. It was a simple illusion—a few cleverly placed mirrors made the gate look like it was nothing more than a stone arch, the words *THIS WAY TO THE NORTH POLE* carved into its keystone. But all the same, it captured my imagination every time I saw it. Santa's elves streamed in and out of the gate, some bearing gifts from the big guy himself, who made regular appearances in the land. I ran up to Mom and tugged her sleeve like I was five years old and not eleven.

"Mom, Mom! Can we go see Santa?! I wanna tell him about that new Nintendo game I read about!"

My poor mom had to find a way to run interference between me and Santa, lest the fat old fuck promise me the moon for Christmas during a year when my mom was—unbeknownst to me and Mac—completely, flat-on-her-ass broke. To distract me from the charms of the Claus clan, she went to her old standby at the Gold Rush:

"We can see Santa later! It's time for the Mystery Mansion!"

Mackenzie

Hiram charged ahead, devil-may-care of who he might run into. Mac smiled, feeling a surge of warmth for her little brother. He was a sweet kid but quick to anger, empathetic to others but also an exposed nerve. And he held grudges. Hoo boy, did he hold grudges. Hiram grappled with angers beyond his understanding and emotions he didn't yet have the vocabulary to describe.

Their mom was waving them past a miniature version of Santa's Village toward another pedestrian tunnel. A placard over the tunnel read:

THIS WAY TO MAD SCIENCE MOUNTAIN!

On the far side of the tunnel rose a hill capped with the silhouette of a twisty, creepy old mansion right out of Tim Burton's dreams. Tilting parapets sprouted crazy towers that clawed at the evening-orange sky like the knobbly-gnarled fingers of a witch. Corrie was intent on going through the tunnel, but Hiram was tugging at her sleeve and pointing at a map—only it wasn't the brochure-map he'd grabbed earlier; it was a yellowing piece of notebook paper that bore a custom map of the park he'd drawn himself.

"Let's take Statuary Row!" he said, pointing toward another tunnel that led away from Mad Science Mountain.

Corrie sighed. "Okay, sweetie. Lead the way."

They left Christmasville. On the far side of the tunnel was a cozy little pathway that wound through a wooded glen. More Halloween-y decorations—garlands and tiny Jack-O-Lanterns—lined a foot-high wrought-iron fence that ran along the path, separating guests from a collection of four- to five-foot statues depicting characters from fairy tales and mythology.

Hiram stopped and pointed out two of the statues, a depiction of Narcissus and Echo.

"Susie Schuppe had the statues of Narcissus and Echo in the backyard of her house in Johnson City growing up. It's the only depiction on Statuary Row that *predates* the opening of the park."

Corrie smiled. "I know, honey. You tell us every time. I think it's time to go, sweetie."

Like someone had flipped a switch, Hiram shifted gears, stowed away his maps, and loped off toward the woods, almost tripping over his own feet. "This way!" he trumpeted, pointing the way. The rapid change in attention and intent was so awkward, so goofy, and just so totally *Hiram*. Mac felt a stab of sadness that Dad never got to know him.

"Here, I know a shortcut," he said. "It goes right through here!"

He indicated a "path" that was little more than a slightly worn strip of earth that led into the trees. Mac peered ahead.

"How'd you even know about this?" she asked.

"When they added Enchanted Whippoorwill Hollow to the back of the park, they covered up the old path between Statuary Row and Mad Science Mountain," Hiram said, walking down the path. "It's still here; they just tried to conceal it with some fake trees. See?"

As promised, a bunch of the trees had an unnatural crayon-green hue. Hiram pressed ahead, but his headlong progress was interrupted by the *whoop* of a train whistle. Corrie jogged ahead and stopped him from entering the forest just as the Gold Rush Express came charging past, spewing steam and sparkling with the intermittent flashes of the passengers' cameras.

"That way looks dangerous," Corrie said, calling over the racket from the train. "C'mon. Show us next time."

"*Mommmmm!*" Mac was waving her arms up and down. "Let's go!"

Corrie looked at Hiram. The train continued to pass by.

"Honey?" she said. "Come on."

"Okay," Hiram said, turning—but as he turned, something caught his eye. He seemed to freeze mid-turn, one sneaker-clad foot dangling in the air. He gawked at the train, which was completing its passage. His mouth hung open long enough for a drop of drool to form. Corrie frowned.

"Hiram, honey, what's wrong?"

Mac walked up, taking note of the strange scene. Hiram muttered something she could just barely make out:

"It's a Leenda," he said.

Hiram's Journal

"Itza Linda."

It popped into my head. I don't know why, but as that train charged past, I flashed on the strange words I'd heard my dad say through the old radio in my dream:

Itza linda adda.

Gedda brusha.

Zo vaxap dis en zo flestulo.

I felt dizzy. All those words cycled through my head, alternating with images of the man with the plaid face.

The Plaid Man.

Words warbled out of my mouth, a few words from "Rocky Top." The train had almost completely passed. Only the caboose was left. It rattled past—and my eyes popped wide. It was the same traincar from my dream, only instead of gibberish written on the side, it said: *SUSIE SCHUPPE'S GOLD RUSH EXPRESS! ALL ABOARD!* The writing, though, was in the same script and color—a gleaming gold—as what I saw in my dream.

Is there something inside that traincar?

I frowned, lost in thought. Somewhere in the distance, I could hear Mom and Mac talking to me, but they sounded like grown-ups from a Charlie Brown cartoon: *Wah wah wahhh wahhh wahhh.* I had more important matters to consider.

Was there something hidden in that traincar? If so, what?

Did it have something to do with Lenny Skelton?

But why? And *how*? *How* could my subconscious know something secret about the most notorious serial killer in the country? And even if I *did* somehow know something secret about Lenny Skelton, what I knew was all in gibberish. I needed to figure out how to decipher what my dreams were trying to tell me.

Suddenly another voice spoke up in my mind, my dad's: *There's another train.*

But what did that mean?

"Hiram? Sweetie?"

It was Mom, looking down at me, trying to smile but looking worried as hell. Mac stood just off her shoulder with the same expression, an expression that asked, *Are you all right?*

I felt dazed. "There's no train coming. Why don't we cross here? We'll get to the Mansion faster that way."

"I don't want to do that," Mom said with finality. "But I do want to get some elephant ears. How about that? Trade me?" She turned to Mac and said, "How about you, Mackenzie? Elephant ears?"

"Can I get cocaine on mine?"

Mom smiled and cocked an eyebrow. "It's called *confectioner's sugar*. Don't say that in front of people, or they'll call Sheriff Blackledge on me."

I was still freaked out, but in a few steps, all my worries were wiped away when we made the journey from a world of classical myth to the world of Mad Science Mountain. It was my favorite land in the park, by far, a world of perpetual Halloween that was somehow scary and silly all at once. It was a "Saturday morning cartoon" version of classic horror movies. The land retained the rest of the park's down-home aesthetic—picket fences, clapboard cottages, brick and wrought-iron details—but overlaid it with a patina of Hammer Horror-style gothic details: a canopy of bare trees, a sheet of mist that crawled along the black cobblestone pathways, and cobwebs aplenty. The Halloween decorations seen around the rest of the park in October were permanent fixtures here.

Up ahead, Mom was tucking the last of her elephant ear into her mouth and chatting with someone; someone really freakin' tall. Mac walked an elephant ear back to me and jerked her chin forward.

"C'mon, goofball! Last one there's a wacko!"

Mackenzie

Mac thought of her mom with such longing. Corrie was tall, about five-eleven, and slender, with feathered hair that never seemed to get messy. She moved with an elegance that always seemed to elude Mac. (Though when she got upset, Mom was about as elegant as a jack-knifing truck.) Deacon had been the same way, with a movie-star face and a ready smile that he used to charm his way into free stuff all the time.

But right now, her mom was being the spectral opposite of elegant.

"Were you really first through the door?" she cackled, her laughter shrill and peppered with snorts. It was at odds with her carefully crafted facade of color-coordinated outfits, fresh-from-the-salon hair, and just the right amount of jewelry. That night, she was wearing a burgundy turtleneck, white vest, and her favorite blue jeans. Her wrists jangled with a few gold bracelets—imperfect ones she got for a song at Miller Brothers—while her favorite gold herringbone necklace glittered around her neck. She was beaming at a hulking man who stood at least six foot six.

"Oh, yeah!" the hulking man said, dropping into a comical "soldier" pose, sweeping an invisible machine gun back and forth. *"Budda-budda-budda!"* he said, imitating gunfire. His blond hair was graying at the temples but still as thick as a teenager's. He wore a sport-coat over a plaid sweater-vest with beige chinos. Stonily handsome, he reminded Mac of an older version of the mean blonde guy from *The Karate Kid.* The hulking man went on: "They didn't stand a chance once we got the drop on 'em."

Corrie's eyebrows rose in concert with her voice. "I can't even imagine the nerve that must've taken. You're so *brave.* And those muscles!" She sounded ditzy, air-headed, and not at all like herself. Mac took a tentative step toward them, already intimidated—or was she put off?—by her mom's gigantic new friend.

"Mom?"

Corrie went on like she hadn't spoken: "Was it plaid? Was that what they called you?"

The gigantic man nodded. "Plaid. Took about fifteen minutes of my first day at BUD/S." When he laughed, his stomach pumped like a bellows, his heavy, heaving shoulders seeming to push the sun away.

Mac hated it when her mom ignored her.

"Mom? The line's getting long. Can we go?"

Hiram came blundering up, finishing the last of his elephant ear. The gigantic man's expression darkened for an instant at Hiram's arrival. Mac knew the look; it was how a certain kind of cruel thin person looked at a fat person, a detestable cocktail of disgust and pity. In spite of herself, Mac felt ashamed of her brother for one awful moment. She chased the feeling out of her head immediately, instinctively draping an arm around Hiram's shoulder.

Mac said again: "Mom? Can we go?"

But before Corrie could answer, the gigantic man was offering his hand. "Well! Are these the little ones I've been hearing about?" He added *sotto voce:* *"They're not so little.* The name's Trent Sutton. Pleased to make your acquaintance."

Mac took his hand, which was the size and texture of a baseball glove.

"Mackenzie," she said, then with a jerk of her chin added, "This is my brother, Hiram."

Hiram offered his hand, which was still covered with confectioner's sugar. Trent's brow creased; he hesitated. He actually *hesitated* to shake her brother's hand.

Trent cocked an eyebrow. "Looks like ya didn't quite get it all there, big guy."

Hiram's jaw went slack, his eyes vacant. It was an expression Mac knew well: the poor kid was confused. He'd breached some boundary of social etiquette that was unknown to him, and now he was scrambling in his poor head for a way to respond.

The only reason why Hiram's confused is because this big snob doesn't want to get sugar on his hands.

Mac didn't want to embarrass her brother any more than he already was, so she ran interference. She jabbed her finger at the Mystery Mansion and said, "Hey, is it okay if we get in line?"

Trent's face lit up. He swung his shoulders around, nearly knocking someone over, and clapped, the sound as loud as a gunshot. Mac and Hiram winced.

"Right! That's the ticket. Jase and Kaity already hopped in line. C'mon, Cor, let's join 'em."

Cor? Mac thought. *Only Auntie Hanna calls her that.*

Corrie hooked arms with Trent and strutted off. Mac and Hiram followed, the little boy's gaze stuck to the ground.

Mac sighed. "What is it, goofball?"

"Did I do something wrong? Why didn't he want to shake my hand?"

"Because he's an asshole," Mac said. "C'mon, last one there's a wacko."

Hiram smiled. Mac snagged a disposable wet napkin from a snack stand, unwrapped it, and slipped it to her brother.

"Missed some," she said casually. "Why don't you clean yourself off before we get in line?"

"Oh! Right," he said cheerfully, not making the connection between his sister's suggestion and Trent's reluctance to shake his hand. Mac felt relieved that she saved him the embarrassment, but she made a mental note to chat with him about it later.

After Dad died, there was so much she had to keep track of.

Hiram's Journal

Our memories aren't reliable.

They exaggerate and elide, highlight and hide. I've experienced my share of trauma. Part of me wishes my brain would block it all out. Yeah, sure, I've forgotten *some* of my trauma, but a lot of it I remember as vividly as if it happened moments ago. If anything, the passage of time has only made these memories more upsetting. To be clear: a lot of kids had it worse than me and Mac. A lot worse. Like I said, we didn't grow up in the most fucked-up home in the world, but we'd have made the podium, for sure.

But sometimes the capricious nature of memory works in our favor.

That's how it is with Professor Cletus J. Wizardo's Mystery Mansion.

Here's a confession: one of my first goals as a kid was to get turned into a Saturday morning cartoon. (Also acceptable would be getting teleported into a live-action/animated world like *Mary Poppins* or being the only human in a world of Muppets.) Visiting the Mystery Mansion was like *going into* a Saturday morning cartoon. Imagine an old Victorian mansion capped with hundreds of parapets, towers, ramparts, and little balconies, all of it enhanced with forced perspective. Like the rest of the park, Mad Science Mountain sat on a series of rolling hills. The Mystery Mansion was the main attraction, accompanied by a roller coaster called the WOW-ZO, so named because it ran on "Wow-Zo-brand Superfuel," one of Professor Wizardo's many inventions. Pipes bubbling with fluorescent-green Wow-Zo fuel lined each of the roller coaster's cars, while the ride itself coiled around—and partially *through*—the mansion itself.

The passage of time has only enhanced my memory of the Mystery Mansion, to say nothing of what happened there that night—or on another fateful night six months later.

Mac and I jogged to catch up with Mom, passing by a series of signs warning people away from the ride:

PROFESSOR CLETUS J. WIZARDO, PHD IN ALL EARTH SCIENCES, LIVES AT THIS RESIDENCE

NO WACKOS ALLOWED!!!

NON-WACKOS NEED NOT APPLY!!!

BEWARE: AHEAD LIES THE MOST INTENSE DIMENSION: THE SEVENTH HYPERCUBE!!!

IMMINENT DEATH AND DISMEMBERMENT RISK!!!

ACCIDENTAL BEHEADING RISK TODAY: HIGH

THRILLS! SURPRISES! THRILLING SURPRISES! SURPRISING THRILLS!!!

VISIT THE MANSION ANYTIME—DAY OR NIGHT RAINPROOF!

Mac and I caught up with Mom at the back of the line, which ran along a stone wall that led up a gentle incline to the mansion's front door. She was still arm in arm with that gigantic Trent guy, who was shouldering his way past a bunch of people to move farther ahead in line. Mac and I hesitated.

"Um, Mom?" Mac called. "The back of the line's here."

Clank! A stanchion fell over, bringing with it an entire length of chain. A few park guests jumped back in surprise.

"What the hell?" one annoyed-looking father muttered.

Up ahead, another gigantic person, this one a teenager about seventeen years old and almost a photocopy of Trent, stepped over the stanchion and beckoned to us.

"Get up here, losers!" he yelled, much louder than he needed to.

Trent bulldozed his way past a few more parties, all of who were glaring daggers at him.

"Jerks," one young mother fumed.

Trent affectionately elbow-prodded the gigantic teenager, who was only a few inches shorter than him.

"Hey there, Jase." Trent leaned out and waved. "Up here, guys! Come on!"

Mac and I were frozen. We'd never broken in line before. In the pause, another kid appeared from behind "Jase," this one a girl about fifteen or sixteen. She had the same stony good looks as Trent and Jase, but she was much smaller, about my height. She wore white slacks and a shimmering, sapphire-blue blouse along with a fur coat and round sunglasses. Her makeup was perfect, her eyebrows neatly plucked. She looked like she was walking a red carpet, not waiting in line for a theme park ride. She carried a paper cup by the rim, the straw stained with dark red lipstick, and walked over to us.

Lowering her sunglasses, she asked: "Max and Heidi?"

The smell of booze wafted over. A scar curled under her right eye, capped with a teardrop-sized clot of flesh connected to her lower eyelid. Every time she blinked, it stretched her cheek a tiny bit.

Mac and I stared at her, baffled. The girl rolled her eyes and heaved a sigh.

"Are you Max and Heidi?" she asked, finishing her drink with a *slur-r-r-p.* "C'mon, we don't wanna lose our spot."

Mac's brow creased. "I'm *Mac* and he's *Hiram.*"

The girl cocked an eyebrow. "Weird names, dudes. I'm Kaitlyn, the big shit-for-brains is Jason. C'mon."

She spun on a heel and left us standing there. On her way to join the others, she tossed her cup at a trash can. It bounced off the side and spilled ice in front of an oncoming family, who gave her dirty looks. Mac and I still didn't move.

"Are we doing this?" she asked.

"Uh you tell me. I'm not breaking in line."

"But they're already up there."

Before I could answer, Kaitlyn came marching back.

"*Dudes,*" she snapped. "We're about to go inside. Come on!"

She grabbed our hands and tried to pull us forward. I stumbled forward a step, but unsurprisingly, Mac didn't move, her bulk yanking Kaitlyn back like she was bound to a wall. Giving us an annoyed grimace, Kaitlyn released our hands and turned around, smirking.

"Lift weights much, Gibraltar?" she asked Mac.

"Huh?"

"*Huh?*" Kaitlyn aped my sister and cackled. "Come on, tons of fun. Let's go. I love this ride."

She skedaddled back to the group. I started walking, but when I didn't sense Mac next to me, I stopped and looked. She was standing in the same place, her face bright red. Her lower lip was trembling.

"Hey, you all right?" I asked.

She nodded, swallowed a lump in her throat, and started walking.

"Yeah, I'm fine," she said. "Let's break in this stupid line."

The Suttons were *big*.

And I don't only mean in terms of size, because Kaitlyn and I were about the same height. No, they were hulking and loud and boisterous, broad-shouldered and bold. They took up space. Trent and Jason kept bumping into people and jostling stanchions and signage, while Kaitlyn snuck pulls from a flask and cackled at the mansion's every detail—details that Mac and I held dear. The line spilled onto a small porch under an awning from which hung cobwebs and orange garlands. Laid into the porch itself was a multi-colored cobblestone mosaic depicting a labyrinth. The mansion's facade was faded, crumbling wood and Georgia red-clay brick. Animatronic effects gave the illusion that the mansion itself was *breathing*: the walls surged in and out, while goofy cartoon eyes peeked at us from between curtains.

A sign by the front door read:

PROFESSOR CLETUS J. WIZARDO'S MYSTERY MANSION
DANGER: MAD SCIENCE AHEAD

Jason and Kaitlyn hooked their thumbs at the signs and rolled their eyes. I wanted to tell 'em both to shut up but didn't dare. Fortunately, I didn't have to, because the mansion's foreboding double doors suddenly shook in their frame. Everyone jumped or whooped in delighted fear, including Jason and Kaitlyn, although they tried to play it off like they were faking. The doors opened, and one of the coolest people I'd ever know emerged. He was a Black man, about five-ten and dressed in a tuxedo overlaid with a white lab coat. He was powerfully built, with a broad chest and muscles that filled out his costume. Gray was just starting to dust his neatly trimmed hair and beard. A name-tag on his lapel read *JUSTIN*.

Hm. Justin. Where have I heard that name before?

He scowled at us like intruders and intoned in a British accent:
"None shall pass. *Mwah-ha-ha!*"

I was about to laugh at the *Monty Python* reference when I noticed Kaitlyn rolling her eyes. The Mystery Mansion was a hallowed place of fun and escape for me and Mac, but to the Suttons, it was just another townie dump.

Justin continued, his British accent flawless: "Welcome, victims! I mean, *guests,* to Professor Cletus J. Wizardo's Mystery Mansion! Please wait here while the professor's minions prepare the mansion for your entrance!" A little boy, about six, made a move to sneak in the door, but Justin gently held up a hand and once again intoned, "None shall pass."

The kid flinched a little, in spite of the care Justin had taken, and it was then I saw what a gentle soul he was. When he blocked the small boy's passage, his hand came down in a gentle arc, his shoulders lowering a few delicate inches to bring him closer to the child's level.

But despite the care he took, the kid still flinched.

And he noticed it. Even with all the hubbub—the park guests, the crowded space—Justin noticed that he'd frightened a little kid. From his pocket he produced a pair of 3D glasses, which he offered to him.

"Young man?" he said in a quiet voice. "The professor himself has asked me to present you with these." Turning his attention to the mother, he asked, "May I give him these? He'll need them inside in order to see all the mad science."

The mother smiled. "Of course," she said, nudging her child. "Go on, honey."

The boy took a tentative step forward and accepted the glasses, which he immediately put on.

"Thanks, Mister!" he said as he nestled back under his mom's arm.

Justin resumed his previous act and turned to the crowd. "None shall pass!"

The words leaped out of me: "He turned me into a newt."

I whispered it, but it was loud enough for Justin to hear. He looked at me.

"An outstanding movie, isn't it?"

I started babbling: "My fourth grade English literature teacher showed it to us as an example of satire and parody! She said it was at once a spoof of adventure movies and some of the high literature of the middle ages."

For whatever reason, I felt a surge of confidence that led me to start blathering about a movie at full volume to a stranger in a room full of strangers. Even stranger was how the sentence began with an *M,* one of my problem letters. A brief hush fell over the crowd while I spoke; not a long one, no . . . but long enough for me to notice, for Mac to blush, and for Mom to avert her gaze from me. I detected the awkward silence mid-sentence—around "an example of satire and parody"—but it was too late. I was already blushing bright red. (It'd be several years before I learned the virtue of an "inside" voice.)

Mac instinctively hooked her arm around me. The moment was about to (thankfully) pass when someone decided to make it worse:

A finger jabbed me in the shoulder. Blushing, I turned to see Jason's face gaping down at me in a cruel, open-mouthed smirk.

"Hey, what's your name?"

"Uh w-w-wuhh?" It was no use. My brain had frozen. Here's why: when we walked over, I assumed that the other family—Trent, Jason, and Kaitlyn—all knew our names. Why was Jason asking me my name if he already knew it? It didn't occur to me that *they did,* and Jason was simply being mean. One thing about bullies and abusers is they have a keen instinct for your weaknesses. For a stutterer, they know to ask unusual questions, change the subject, interrupt, or any of a hundred other verbal tricks used to derail you.

Jason saw me struggling and leaned down. He was so tall, it seemed like his head was descending from the clouds. He made a guttural sound in his throat, imitating my struggle to talk: *"Wuh-wuh-wuh."* He and Kaitlyn cackled.

"Jase, come on, man," Kaitlyn said, elbowing him.

He resumed his full, towering height and adjusted his jacket, a gleaming orange Tennessee Volunteers warm-up. (I hadn't gotten a new piece of clothing in at least a year. Mom had to clothe us in roughly unisex garments so I could get Mac's hand-me-downs.) Jason bared his teeth at me in a cruel simulacrum of a smile.

"He turned me into a newt!" he yelled, prodding Kaitlyn with his elbow.

Kaitlyn rolled her eyes but joined in, using her index finger to push a pair of invisible glasses back into place and aping my voice: "My fourth grade English literature teacher showed it to us as an example of satire and parody!" In case you think Kaitlyn *raised* her voice to make fun of me, she actually *lowered* it. My voice had cracked and dropped into my chest by fifth grade. I scanned the area for Mom, but she was behind Trent, whose back faced us. He'd propped an arm on a wall and appeared to be in deep conversation with Mom.

Can she hear them? Can she hear how mean they're being? I wondered.

"Assholes," Mac said under her breath.

BWOOOONK! From within the mansion, a siren sounded in tandem with a bank of red lights that flashed overhead. Justin held up his hands for our attention, raising his voice over the mayhem:

"Welcome, *victims*, to Professor Cletus J. Wizardo's Mystery Mansion! Before I allow you inside this palace of wonder and doom, there are matters we must discuss: First! Parents, keep an eye on your little one at all times, lest they wind up as the subject of an experiment in the professor's lab! Second, no flash photography! Third, be aware that your exploration of the mansion will unfold in two stages: the first will be a self-guided tour of some of the professor's failed experiments—ha ha, I mean most *successful*, Nobel Prize-*winning* experiments!"

Jason and Kaitlyn continued to roll their eyes at Justin's monologue, and God help me, I found myself wanting to join in. I'd visited this attraction a zillion times and loved it every time, but now that these two good-looking rich kids were making fun of it, I felt ashamed of my joy. Part of me wondered why I ever even liked it? Was it because it was a kiddie ride, and I was a kid?

Justin continued: "The *second* and most exciting, most dangerous, most *fantastimazing* part of your exploration will be a guided tour in one of our systemated-automated, semi-roboticized humanless carriages—ha ha, I mean horseless carriages! If you will make sure all your feets and toes are behind the yellow line." He indicated a yellow line that swept into a holding area. Guests backed up to get out of the way—except for Trent, whose arm was still propped on the wall. Justin gently tapped his shoulder.

"Sir?" he asked.

Trent whirled around, his eyes wide, and snapped, "What?"

Justin held up his hands in a calming gesture but didn't back down: "Sir, I need you to stand behind the yellow line."

Trent folded his arms. "Why?"

"So we can open the doors."

A park guest yelled: "Get out of the way, man!"

A band of red broke out across Trent's broad face, from one ear to the other. He looked like a volcano about to erupt, and he might have, if not for Mom.

"Plaid?" she said, coming around his side. "We're holding up the show. C'mon."

Plaid? I thought. *Why does she keep calling him that?*

Mom's admonition apparently did the trick, because Trent stepped behind the yellow line.

I leaned over to Mac and whispered, "Did you know Mom had a boyfriend?"

"No, did you?"

"No."

Trent and Mom joined us just as Justin stepped behind the yellow line and raised his hands in proclamation:

"The doors to Dr. Wizardo's mansion are about to open!"

The mansion's doors swung open to reveal a hallway lined with dark-finished wood, brass fixtures, and dozens of paintings of imaginary mad scientists from throughout the ages. Now that the attraction had actually started, my embarrassment of it faded a little. As we all headed inside, I leaned over to Justin and whispered:

"Thank you *so* much for the educational introduction."

"You got it, kid."

I smiled. The actor sounded different. He'd been putting on a British accent until that moment, when he suddenly spoke with his normal voice. I wasn't sure, but I thought I'd heard him before; maybe on TV?

"Hey, goofball."

It was Mac, standing inside the mansion and beckoning me to hurry up.

I turned to say goodbye to Justin, but he was gone.

Mackenzie

How long has Mom been dating this asshole? And how did we not know about it?

Everyone crowded down the Mansion's main entry hallway. A bank of speakers bleated out a goofy refrain of haunted-house music—"Toccata and Fugue in D Minor" by way of a jam band at the peak of an acid trip. Mac and her little brother hustled down the hallway and past portraits of mad scientists from the past and the future:

PROFESSOR LEXICON JONES, inventor of the rocket-powered shoes made famous by Magnum Louise Studebaker in the futuristic year nine hundred billion.

DR. DEBRA QUANTUMFLUX, discoverer of the spectral realms between our atoms and under your dreams.

DR. BLARPINGTON WHATSAMADOODLE, winner of the 1876 Nobel Prize for his invention of the Queef-O-Matic Fart Silencer.

DR. EUREKA J. BREAKTHROUGH, best known for shouting "EUREKA" loud enough to set off the Clapper.

ZYGOR, the professor's loyal assistant and future "Mad Scientist of the Year."

DR. CLEOPATRA VON WIZARDO-SORORA, the professor's wife and Revelation General of the East Tennessee—the rest of her plaque was scuffed over and illegible. A triangular glyph bore the letters *ETSOSD.*

Mac always smiled at Dr. Wizardo-Sorora. She looked like that frizzy-haired lady from *The Rocky Horror Picture Show,* which she'd watched giggling with Dawn Dockery on a sleepover last year. Mac liked that the mansion had some women who were as accomplished as the men when it came to mad science.

And finally, the main madman himself, *DR. CLETUS J. WIZARDO, PhD in all earth sciences and inventor of the Third Hypercube.* All of these scientists were members of the mansion's Board of Trustees and occasionally appeared as costumed characters like Frankenstein's monster or Santa's elves.

The mansion's initial hallway felt like the innards of a magician's manor: dark, gleaming wood, hardwood floors, brass light fixtures, but as they progressed farther inside, the hardwood was replaced by scattered stone floors and walls intercut with wood beams.

It felt like they were going underground, because they were. The hallway led guests from the mansion's outer facade underground into the actual ride area. The temperature dropped a few degrees as they walked. Mac scanned the crowd for the rest of their group but couldn't find them. Hiram came scampering up.

"Uh that Justin guy was really cool."

"Yeah, he sure was, goofball. You see Mom anywhere? I'm ready to run the barrel."

"Uh me too!

The hallway rounded a corner to bring a madcap chamber into view: large punching bags dangled from the ceiling and swung to and fro as laughing park-goers bumped and bonked into them. Circus and carnival-style theming adorned the room: funhouse mirrors and ornately decorated signs advertising various acts: *JIMBO THE STRONGMAN, THE FLYING FLAMBINO BROTHERS,* and someone called *THE MYSTERIOUS FACELESS FIRST.* Park-goers streamed around Mac and her little brother.

"Why wouldn't Mom tell us she had a boyfriend?" Hiram asked.

"I don't—"

A nightmarish howl jolted them into silence. After sharing a look of panic, Mac and Hiram looped around a hanging bag to bring a red-faced monster into view. The monster was hanging upside-down, its arms and legs fully extended in a quivering spread-eagle. Its tweedy tail-feathers hung and flapped behind its beet-red face.

It was Trent, and he was riding the barrel.

The giant rotating barrel welcomed guests to the Mystery Mansion. For those guests too unsure of their footing, a pair of alternate paths curved to either side of it, but most everyone—and always Mac and Hiram—braved the barrel. Its spinning, spiral-painted interior hypnotized guests as they approached, rendering them dizzy and happy before they ventured into the rest of the mansion's mysteries.

Trent had lodged himself in place and was rotating like a gigantic Vitruvian Man, his blazer's tail-flaps hanging behind his head. Mac was mildly impressed with the feat for a moment before she noticed two things: Jason and Kaitlyn grinning evilly at her, and an increasingly impatient crowd of people waiting their turn to run the barrel.

Kaitlyn sidled over and prodded her. "Hey there, tons of fun. Why the long face?"

"Don't call me that," Mac said, hooking an arm around Hiram. Kaitlyn shook her head and giggled.

"Don't be so touchy," she said before yelling at Trent: "Get a move on, old man! You're holding up the show!"

"Mom?" Mac repeated and pointed at Trent. "How long have you been dating?"

Corrie started to babble: "He's former Navy! He was a SEAL! Goodness, isn't that something? It's just something! I *told* you we were dating. When I met Willie Bates down in Panama City back in sixty-three, he said he was going to try out for the SEALs—" Babbling was another of her mom's defenses. The truth was slowly dawning on Mac that their mom had been dating this man for a while, had kept it from them, and now wanted to act like it was common knowledge. She was giggling and snorting, but Mac could tell she wasn't really *laughing.* Mac knew what her mom sounded like when she legitimately got the giggles—the times she got them were some of Mac's most cherished memories—but this wasn't it.

Her mom was trying to distract her.

Trent let his feet fall and performed a nimble cartwheel out of the barrel. He swept Corrie into his arms and escorted her out of the room. She called over her shoulder: "Honey? Why don't you let Jase and Kaity chaperone you through the rest of the ride? Trent and I want to catch up."

Mac's face fell. Jason and Kaitlyn were both giving them evil grins.

For once, Mac was the oner who was stuttering: "Uh M-Mom, I don't know. We don't need babysit—"

Hiram's voice cut her off: "When did you two meet, Mom?"

The question, innocent as it sounded, must've set off alarm bells inside Corrie's head, because her next words came in a shout: "Plaid! Why don't you tell me about the time you and your SEAL team had that mission in the Persian Gulf?!" She laughed for no reason—"Ha! Ha! Ha!"—and escorted Trent around the side of the barrel, still chattering away: "I don't know how you boys slept outside. Did I ever tell you about what a light sleeper Deacon—that's my ex-husband, my *old* husband—was?"

They vanished into the crowd. Mac and Hiram were left standing with Jason and Kaitlyn. Park-goers flowed around them, some giving them annoyed looks. Jason bent over, placing his hands on his knees, and looked Hiram in the face with a big, toothy grin.

"Hi, buddy! I wanna learn about parody and satire. Maybe you can teach me?"

Hiram's face turned bright red. Mac held her little brother closer. He said something inaudible.

"What'd you say?" Mac asked.

"High reason."

Hiram's Journal

"High reason."

It slipped out of my mouth for reasons I couldn't fathom. When Mom said, "Plaid! Why don't you tell me about the time you and your SEAL team had that mission in the Persian Gulf," my vision went . . . white. Pure nothingness. Images floated before me:

The Christmasville gate leading to the North Pole, only this one was capped with a strange symbol: a pair of snakes eating each other's tails, entwined around a dragon's skull. A wrought-iron lamp-post standing by a cliff. And a small cabin with an A-frame overhang like an old Howard Johnson's, only this one was powder blue instead of orange. The cabin appeared to be tucked away in the Smokies based on the soft, rolling silhouette of the surrounding mountains. A voice sounded in the distance:

"High reason."

The words leaked out of my mouth again: "High reason."

Jason checked over his shoulder, looked back, and shook his head. He prodded Kaitlyn, jerking his chin forward.

"Come on," he said. "I don't wanna lose 'em."

He led the way, Kaitlyn at his side, and skirted around the spinning barrel. We followed, the sound of a locomotive *chug-chug-chugging* away growing louder. Mac bumped me with her shoulder.

"You all right, goofball?"

I wasn't even remotely all right. "Sorry for asking that uh question. I was only wondering when they met."

We passed through a small tunnel that spilled into the next room, a "slanted" room straight out of a mystery-spot-style attraction. Mac gave me a quick squeeze.

"It's okay, goofball. She kept me in the dark too—*whoa!* Hang on!"

The walkway tilted to the left, forcing us all to grasp at a guardrail to our right. On the other side of the guardrail lay the source of the *chug-chug-chugging* sound. Roughly the size of a locomotive, it looked a little like a gigantic beer fermenter outfitted for space travel; every inch of it blinked and hissed and spun with lights and pipes and servos. Hundreds of multi-colored wires coiled around it. If Willy Wonka and Dr. Frankenstein had collaborated on a machine to create monster candy, it would've resembled this contraption:

Professor Cletus J. Wizardo's Flambonium Airscoop 3000.

"Watch out for the flambonium!" Mac hooted happily as we struggled along the slanted pathway.

Dozens of brightly colored signs covered it:

FLAMBONIUM AIRSCOOP 3000 GENERATING DEVICE, Copyright Dr. Cletus J. Wizardo.

DANGER! DANGEROUS LEVELS OF SCIENCE

WE'RE WATCHING YOU RIGHT NOW AND ALL THE TIME

FLAMBONIUM ORE BEING PRODUCED IN ALARMING QUANTITIES — EXERCISE EXTREME AND/OR MAXIMUM LEVELS OF CAUTION

THERE'S NO POINT IN EVEN TRYING

A pair of percentage sliders read:

INTENSITY: 100%

SCIENCE: 100%

An arrangement of readouts and gears across the flambonium device's front resembled a rudimentary face. The "mouth" emitted a conveyor-belt that circled up to the guardrail. Shivering piles of sand and rock rattled along the belt, passing within arm's reach of the park-goers.

Also behind the guardrail stood another park worker dressed like a "mad scientist" version of Keith Richards: topped with a mop of wild mop of black hair, the guy wore a red vest over a white lab coat. A fluorescent orange headband tried and failed to tame his Einstein-ian hairdo.

"Awww, yeahhhhhh! Check it *oooout*, everyone! Professor Wizardo's mastered the creation of flam-flam-flam*bonium! Whoooo!*" He plucked a green rock from the conveyor belt. Carved into the rock was the number seven. Keith Richards presented it to the crowd.

"It's prospectin' time, my fellow science maniacs, except we're not prospectin' for gold—we're panning for *flambonium!* Get the brochure!" He indicated a bank of brochures set into a series of slots on the guardrail. "I'm watching you!" He indicated another sign that read *GUESS WHAT?* Below it was a strip of siding held to the wall with hinges. Keith flipped it down to reveal another sign that read: *I WATCH FROM THE FOREST, I WATCH*

FROM THE TREES.

I prodded Mac and asked, "Was that sign always there?"

But when I looked back, it was gone. Mac was looking at me.

"Did you say something?"

"No," I muttered. Now Keith Richards was indicating a stack of steel pans on the wall behind us.

"Now grab a pan and get to panning some flambonium for the professor, and keep an eye out for those prime numbers!" Keith Richards indicated a stack of steel pans. "Find a rock with a *priiiiime* and get somethin' *fiiiiine* in the gift shop! *Awww, right!*"

Clank, clank, clank, clank went the pans as park-goers collected their own and started awkwardly panning the conveyor belt for fluorescent rocks bearing numbers. I'd just grabbed my own pan when someone jostled me—a *big* someone.

"What's your name again?" Jason asked, hulking over me. "C'mon, we're losing 'em."

His hand closed like a vise around my bicep. He yanked me ahead so hard I yelped. A sign up ahead read:

THIS WAY TO THE ENCHANTED FOREST!

Mackenzie

Kaitlyn was drunk.

Like, *really* drunk. She'd snuck in a second flask and was ducking into alcoves to pull from it. She and Mac had passed from the flambonium ore "mystery spot" room into a low-rent recreation of an enchanted medieval forest. The main pathway split into several paths that snaked and crisscrossed through the tiny forest of plastic trees.

Kaitlyn stumbled through the room, which was admittedly hard to navigate; the light throughout the mansion was kept at a dim, golden glow, and the pathway through the imaginary forest was uneven, making unexpected rises and falls. The pathway narrowed to two abreast and spilled onto a cheesy-looking rope bridge made out of what appeared to be plastic and twine. The bridge swung back and forth under the weight of passing guests. Kaitlyn paused at the start of the bridge, using both hands to hold herself upright.

"Come on, wide load," Kaitlyn said. "Let's hustle. I don't wanna lose track of shit-for-brains."

They crossed the bridge and emerged into a small clearing. The far wall was painted to look like a medieval stone fortress. Woodland sound effects—

chirping birds, the occasional lion's roar—could be heard underneath a plucky medieval lute. A drawbridge sat open, admitting guests into the mansion's next chamber, but in order to reach the drawbridge, guests had to traverse a spiderweb-like jungle gym. Two chain webs hung in an A-frame tent; guests were awkwardly climbing up and over it, laughing as they struggled and cheering on their friends. Mac was about to bark out a comeback to Kaitlyn's insult when another voice called out from above:

"My ghoulish prince!"

On the far side of the chain-web, a young woman dressed as a low-rent Disney princess looked down from one of the fortress's second-story windows. She waved at someone in the crowd below. It was obvious who it was: Jason's head rose above everyone else's. The princess leaned farther out and winked.

"I'll see you then."

Kaitlyn rolled her eyes and yelled, "Quit flirting with my brother, ya slut!"

The Bride frowned, and Jason's shoulders perceptibly jerked. He threw Kaitlyn a nasty look over his shoulder but turned his attention back to the princess. Kaitlyn stepped up to the chain-web.

"What is that slut doing trying to chat up shit-for-brains?" she asked herself, her legs already tangled in the chains.

Mac, still stinging from Kaitlyn's insult, had crossed her arms and was settling in for a good sulk when it occurred to her, *Where's Hiram?* The answer came in the form of a sharp cry from the far side of the chain-web. Mac uncrossed her arms and stepped around a few park-goers to bring her little brother into view.

He had fallen.

"Hiram!"

Mac's reflexes kicked into high gear. She shouldered her way past Kaitlyn, who emitted a drunken "whoa" as she passed, but wait, wait, wait:

Something grabbed Mac's attention.

It came from her right: a sharp flash, like the sun glinting off a mirror, followed by a general dimming of the lights, like a raincloud speeding overhead on a windy day.

Somewhere in the distance, a woman's voice spoke:

Feels balmy.

It came from her right, so that's where she looked, and when she did, the impossible looked back at her.

The Mystery Mansion had a new room.

A library.

A set of wooden double doors stood open, giving view to a sweeping, multi-story library complete with a rolling ladder to help reach the topmost shelves. Somehow, Mac knew that the room was spatially impossible; the mansion simply wasn't large enough to contain such a room.

She blinked, and it was gone. Well, not exactly *gone,* but transformed. Where the double doors had been now stood nothing more than a painting that depicted the same library but rendered in crude, carnival funhouse-quality muralship.

Mac wrote it off as a trick of the lights and started climbing up the chain-web.

Behind her, Kaitlyn slurred, "Hey, wait up!"

Hiram had fallen into one of the web's support pylons, a cement cylinder set into the floor. Somehow, he'd brought another guest down with him, a little boy who was a couple inches taller and about fifty pounds lighter than Hiram. The skinny little boy wore a light brown windbreaker that was streaked with old stains, torn jeans, and inch-thick horn-rimmed glasses that gave him an owlish look. His black, bowl-cut hair encircled his face.

His voice carried across the room: "Are you injured, Hiram?"

Mac was still scrambling over the chain-web, but despite her stress, the little boy's voice gave her some comfort. It was Lee Dockery, little brother of her best friend Dawn. Lee worshipped Hiram for some stupid reason, and to date, Hiram had treated him like garbage, turning down his every invitation to hang out at their place.

I don't understand why Hiram doesn't like him, Mac thought as she looped her leg over the top of the chain-web. *Hiram doesn't have any friends, and Lee is so nice.*

A sob broke her heart.

It came from below, from where Hiram had fallen. Mac's heart thudded; she turned and saw Hiram sitting cross-legged by the pylon, holding his arm. He bore an expression that was all too familiar to Mac: he was trying not to cry. The poor kid's mouth was downturned in a sorrowful grimace, his cheeks red, the underside of his nose already slick and gleaming in the darkness with snot.

And there was Jason standing under the princess's window like a dipshit, broad-shouldered Romeo.

From the top of the chain-web, Mac yelled, *"Hey!"*

Jason—along with everyone else in the room—turned at the sound and watched Mac skim down the web with the ease of a gymnast. She landed on the balls of her feet and ran to Hiram. Lee Dockery had vanished, and she felt irrationally annoyed that he'd ditched Hiram so quickly. Jason was ignoring them, still flirting with the princess. Mac shot Jason a dirty look and knelt down, taking Hiram's hands in hers. His head was hung, his shoulders shaking.

"Hey, goofball. Are you okay?"

"I fell. Hit my shoulder."

Mac nodded and gave him a kind smile. Hiram could be dramatic sometimes, but when she lifted his sleeve, a purple welt marked the beginnings of a bruise. It must've been a pretty bad fall.

"Aw, buddy," she said. "Did you trip?"

Hiram nodded. He still hadn't looked her in the eye.

"Did someone push you?"

No response.

Mac used her index finger to lift Hiram's chin. "Goofball, you can tell me. Did someone push you?"

"I want to go home," Hiram said.

Mac sat next to him and scanned the room. No sign of their mom. Hiram was swallowing sobs, his Adam's apple bobbing in tune with his shaking shoulders. The scene was almost too much for Mac to bear. The last time Hiram had melted down like this, they'd been in an empty park, and he was three. Now he was surrounded by dozens of strangers, a lot of who were stifling giggles and jabbing their fingers at him.

Not all of them, though.

"I procured some ice."

It was little Lee Dockery, who had somehow gotten a Ziploc bag of ice in the last minute and a half. He stood a few inches too close, offering the bag and staring at them, unblinking. Mac half expected him to give the Vulcan salute.

"Thanks, Lee," she said, taking the bag and holding it to Hiram's shoulder. "Where's the rest of your family?"

"You see, we were together a moment ago, but when we encountered Hiram with, um," he scanned the room, located Jason and pointed directly at him. "With him, that large lad, Dawn ventured ahead while I elected to stay behind and . . . um, *hang*." When he used slang, the little kid sounded like he was searching for a vocabulary word in an unfamiliar tongue. Lee turned his attention to Hiram: "That was quite the spill you took, at least two meters off the chains."

Mac looked aghast. "Hi, you fell?"

Hiram nodded. "I lost my grip."

Mac was on her feet before he finished saying "grip." She crossed the room in a few great strides, zig-zagging around guests, until she reached Jason. She wrenched his shoulder around, and despite his sheer mass, he almost lost his footing.

"Hey!" he yelled.

"You wanna explain what happened here?"

Jason checked the upper window, but the princess was gone. Fuming, he said: "I was talking to someone."

He tried to step past Mac, but she blocked him.

"I'd like an answer to my question."

Jason smirked, looked her up and down, sizing her up. Mac braced herself to get into a fistfight in the middle of the Mystery Mansion.

"What up, dipshits!" They turned. It was Kaitlyn, who'd slipped on her sunglasses despite the room's darkness. She offered up her flask. She started mugging and adopted a goofy British accent: "Do *not* go back that way, for I just left the raunchiest fart ever. Care for a nip of Buffalo Trace, my dears?"

Mac locked eyes with Jason again. Whatever moment that had been brewing had passed, although a dark twinkle in his eyes said, *I could take you.*

Someone was tugging Mac's sleeve. It was Hiram, Lee by his side, still holding the ice pack to his shoulder.

"I lost my grip is all," he said.

Mac gave Jason one more hard look and headed for the next room.

"Come on, guys," she said. "Let's go find our families."

Hiram's Journal

The flambonium ore room gave way to the world's cheesiest, most fake-looking enchanted forest ever. We were surrounded by plastic tree trunks and felt-cloth foliage. The pathway divided into a small labyrinth. Despite their cheesiness, the trees were grouped thickly enough to block our view. Jason stopped at a fork in the path, my arm still held in his enormous fist.

"Which way do you think they went?"

My brain produced the answer *to the left,* but I opted against saying it. (I knew the T would trip me up.) Mac and I always went to the left because it had the cool swinging bridge. The righthand path was more boring, but there was no stopping Jason; he yanked me along.

"Uh hey, let go of my arm," I whined. He released me, stopping so fast I staggered ahead a few steps, nearly crashing into a guest. I rubbed my bicep, which was already smarting. "Owwww." Even in the moment, I inwardly cringed at my tone. This new kid was so much bigger, so much older, so much better-looking than I could ever *dream* to be.

And I was trapped with him. The Mystery Mansion was one of my favorite places. Now it was a prison.

"What's your name, kid?"

I knew I'd already told him, but I answered anyway: "Uh Hiram. Or just Hi."

"That's not your name."

"Huh?"

He stepped closer, his head blocking one of the overhead lights. His face fell into a swimming silhouette.

"Your name isn't what you said. You need a new one. Don't you?"

"No."

"You need a new name, kid." He said it like he was annoyed he even had to deal with me. I stood dumbfounded, chewing on a response that didn't exist—my brain had gone blank. He strode past me. "C'mon, stupid. You're really *dumb,* God. Let's try to think of a better name for you before we get through this dumb-shit ride."

We looped around some trees and brought a spooky tableau into view: a banquet table straight out of the middle ages, packed with a murderer's row of *very* cheesy-looking movie monster mannequins: a wolfman, a Lugosi-style vampire, a creature from the Black Lagoon, all of them dressed in medieval attire for some reason. Stanchions dangling ropes surrounded the table.

One of the monsters, though, wasn't a dummy but a park performer outfitted as the Bride of Frankenstein. She vamped and gaped at the crowd as we passed.

"Come and be our dinner! Whoops! I mean—join us *for* dinner! I promise not to turn you into a newt!"

She cackled. Jason stopped by the table and fell weirdly silent as the crowd flowed by. I pulled up beside him, rubbing my bicep and—no kidding— trying to think of a way to win his approval. It's funny how these things seem like super-powers when you're a kid: the ability to fall silent and hold you in thrall to their approval. Even though Jason and his sister had been making fun of my voice only moments before, I still wanted his approval. He was tall and good-looking and probably very rich—richer than our wildest dreams— and all of those things made him cool. When you're in first grade, a second-grader seems like a worldly grown-up. And when you're eleven, an eighteen-year-old seems like an ancient, unattainable sage. When they fall silent, you start negotiating with yourself to get . . . anything.

Jason was always one step ahead of me.

And except for one moment in our lives, he always would be.

That moment was still months away, though. I still had many more magic rooms . . . and magic *maps* . . . to discover and *uncover*. We both still had a kidnapping in store at the hands of Lenny Skelton, a shared trauma that, for once, would leave *him* struck silent and *me* with all the answers. It would not only be my time to shine, but it would also be my chance to undo one of Jason's biggest fuck-ups, because in retrospect, our falling into Skelton's hands was his fault.

Kind of.

It's hard to explain, so I better tell the rest of the story.

The Bride continued to toss out bon mots and one-liners to the crowd—stuff like "Won't you step into my cauldron; I mean *my office?*" or "I'm giving away free hexes today, two for the price of one!"—and Jason kept staring at her with an intensity that made me squirm. That's when it occurred to me:

The Bride was pretty cute.

She was older than me but younger than Jason, I could tell. He fiddled with the dangling rope that surrounded the banquet table and stared at her. He opened his mouth, apparently to yawn, but instead, a stream of saliva jetted from under his tongue. It carved a perfect parabola from his gaping maw to the Bride's hair, where it dangled and glittered in the amber light. She didn't notice it—or us. Jason snapped his fingers like he'd just remembered something.

"Oh, it's Wimpy. Wimpy, what's your name?"

"Huh?"

"Wimpy, you ever gleeked?"

He might as well have been speaking in tongues. All I could muster was, "Um."

"Wimpy, you ever gleeked? Answer me, Wimpy. You ever gleeked?"

The Bride was finally taking note of us; Jason's voice carried.

"Uh evergleeked? Uh what does that mean, evergleeked?"

New input can be tough for me. Sometimes people use phrases that are familiar to them, but for whatever reason, my brain can't process. For the uninitiated, to "gleek" is a childish term for emitting a string of spit from your mouth, or at least it was in late-eighties east Tennessee.

But I'd never heard it. And now Jason sounded like he was speaking in gibberish.

Jason had already gone back to staring at the Bride, who was still wearing his spit in her hair.

"Hey," he said.

Her face lit up: "Hey."

Wow, I thought. I couldn't imagine a girl looking at me like that, and for many, many years to come, I wouldn't be able to. Jason continued to leer at her.

"Nice costume," he said, his spit still dangling in her hair.

"Thanks!" she said, practically bouncing in her chair. Looking back, it occurs to me that the kids who worked the Gold Rush park were middle-class or poorer. Not like Jason, who probably never had to work a day job in his life. He probably looked rich and glamorous to her. Little did she know.

"What's your name?"

"Jenny."

Jason leaned so far over the rope I thought he might fall over. He angled his face away from me and whispered something. Even in the dim, amber light, I could tell Jenny blushed.

"Half an hour," she said.

"Great, I'll come find ya," Jason said, then frowned and pointed at her. "You've got something in your hair."

My stomach dropped. *Why is he telling her he spit in her hair?* I asked myself, too naive to see what was coming. Jenny touched her temple, her hand coming away shiny with Jason's gleek. She made a grossed-out grimace.

"Ugh!"

Jason sprang his trap. Wheeling on me, he barked, "You little shit! Apologize to her! Fucking gross!"

Jenny glared at me and yelled, "Fuck you, kid!" She stood and pulled off her wig, checking it. Makeup and dye stained her fingers. She looked horrified. "This is gonna come outta my paycheck. Oh, no."

"Say you're sorry, you little shit," Jason said.

Looking back, I remember some deep-seated, Cro-Magnon part of my brain wanted to protest, wanted to say he was lying. Another part of my brain was already flash-fried with humiliation, incapacitated for the foreseeable future. Now when I look back, I can appreciate how diabolical Jason's gambit was: If I *did* respond, I'd look like a stupid little kid, especially next to him, who was so tall and beautiful; and if I *didn't* respond—if I stood there with that stupid fucking look on my face—then I'd be codifying his lie into truth.

All of that happened in an instant, but still, the words trickled out of me in a strangled whisper:

"I-I-I'm sorry."

And people ask me why I stutter.

Jenny was using the hem of her costume to try and dab Jason's spit out of her wig. She was on the verge of tears, her face clenched and flushed. In response to Jason, she gave a quick wave and nodded.

"Hey," he said, but she was already heading toward a staff exit. He raised his voice: "Hey!" She stopped. He added, "I can spot you for a new one."

Her expression cycled through an array of emotions, starting with an immediate surge of gratitude, followed by a frown that came down like the blast door on a submarine.

"Oh, you don't gotta do that," she said, though her frown wavered. She leaned forward, her eyebrows rising: "Could you really?"

Jason's smile looked like a knife coming out of its sheath. "Happy to."

Jenny was already chattering: "See, I'd pay for it myself, but I had to get an advance to get my mama's car out of the shop, and if my paycheck gets any more garnished, I might as well quit."

Jason leaned back an inch or two, the disclosure causing his smile to flicker.

"Oh, that's okay," he said. "I . . . uh, I get it."

She sighed, giving him a big smile. "Okay, I gotta work one more bit before I get off." She pointed up the path ahead. "Up by the chain-link jungle gym? I'll be the princess in the castle. You can come find me after that. I can let you inside the staff gate 'round back."

"See you in a few minutes, then," he said, and with one last fluttering smile, she vanished through the rear door. Without a word, Jason turned and pressed on. A few moments later, we reached the end of the enchanted forest, where a sort of chain-link web slid into view. You had to climb over it to reach the next part of the attraction, which was reached by passing through a goofy-looking drawbridge. A crude-looking castle-fortress was painted on the walls surrounding the drawbridge.

A voice rang out: "My prince!"

It was Jenny, formerly the Bride, now dressed in a gold-and-blue "Snow White"-style princess gown, waving down at Jason from a window in the "top" of the faux medieval fortress. Jason smiled and waved back. That's when Jason threw me a curveball:

He ditched me.

Jason made his way nimbly up the chain-link web. I guess flirting with a girl was more important than bullying me. Ahead, Jason had already spanned the chain-link web and landed lightly. He was chatting up Jenny, whose ruined wig was a distant memory. I stood in relieved silence, my skin tingling with gratitude to be rid of him, if only for a moment.

A shrill voice shattered my reverie: "Hiram!"

I jumped so hard I almost fell. Two dark figures emerged from behind me, two familiar ones: Dawn and Lee Dockery, Mac's best friend and my least favorite person. (Well, as of that evening, Lee had been downgraded to my *second* least favorite person.) Dawn was wearing her usual mangy fur coat over a black T-shirt with pigtails, while Lee was wearing his daily uniform of a light brown windbreaker with jeans, his eyes rendered owlish by his coke-bottle glasses.

They were both smiling at me. Dawn gave me a quick hug.

"Hey, Hiram! We didn't know y'all were coming tonight. Where's the rest of your family?"

"I dunno. I lost track of 'em."

Dawn frowned. "That's weird. Why didn't y'all stick together?"

I glanced over at Jason, shrugged. "Mom's on a date."

A knowing look crossed Dawn's face. "Oh."

"What?" I asked.

"It would seem they've not been told," Lee said, prompting an immediate rebuke.

"Shhh!" Dawn said.

My face fell. "Aw, jeez. How long have you guys known?"

Dawn shrugged. "Well, your mom and our mom are pretty tight. She's been talkin' about this new guy she met."

"We might've been eavesdropping," Lee said.

Dawn elbowed him with a smile. "Kinda hard *not* to be eavesdroppin' in a double-wide." She turned to me. "Well, I was gonna run on ahead, see if I can find Mac. You mind if Lee keeps you company?"

I *did* mind, but I gritted my teeth, smiled and said, "Sure. Fine."

"Awesome, thanks!" Dawn said and turned. She smiled at something across the room. "Well I'll be. Haven't seen her in years." She ducked around the side of the chain-link web.

Lee and I stood awkwardly for a moment, him smiling stupidly at me.

"Have you played the new *Masterminder Presents Theseus's Labyrinth of Terror* game?"

I sighed, already cranky. "I don't have a Masterminder. I already *told* you that. I only have an Atari and a Nintendo."

"Oh," Lee said. "Well, it's easy enough to connect one to any standard television set. I could bring mine over and . . ."

While Lee prattled on, I checked ahead for Jason. He was still flirting with the Bride/Princess, and now I was stuck with my second least favorite person in the world, who wouldn't shut up. I needed some time to think. Behind Lee was a bathroom.

"Excuse me," I said. "I've got to go."

Lee's owlish eyes bulged momentarily. "Of course, my good sir. I'm reminded in this moment of a line from *Star Trek II: The Wrath of Khan*—"

"*Tell me later.*" The words came out in a harsh rush. I stopped at the bathroom door and lowered the temperature. "Sorry. You can tell me later."

Lee was unfazed. "Yes, Admiral."

Dawn

How long had it been since she'd seen her? Five years? Six? She looked all grown up now, but it was definitely her.

Jenny Miles, her first bestie-bestie.

She'd moved five miles away in second grade, but it was like she'd moved to another planet. Jenny belonged to a curious corner of Dawn's memory—an amber-hued, magical *before* time when she would pull on her Rainbow Brite T-shirt and go charging through the woods around West Chim without any worry of a monster lurking in the shadows.

In the Mystery Mansion, Dawn stepped under the princess's window. Jenny was done up in a chintzy but adorable costume dress with about three layers too much makeup. She was leaning over the windowsill, arms crossed, making eyes at a tall boy below. He was the tallest boy Dawn had ever seen, easy, taller even than Max Stanford up in Knoxville, with blond hair and a stern face.

"I'll meet you around back?" he was asking her.

The moment derailed Dawn. She was simultaneously happy to see Jenny and jealous of her for attracting the attention of this good-looking guy. His clothes—from his Air Jordans to his Tennessee Volunteers warm-up—shone with new-ness. Dawn suddenly felt self-conscious in her fur coat. A final gift from her father, she treasured it, but even though she missed Jenny sorely, she couldn't bring herself to say hi.

She was looking at her.

It happened before she knew it. Jenny was looking straight at her with a nasty look that said, *Try your luck elsewhere.* Even worse was the lack of recognition in her eyes. Dawn broke eye contact and shouldered her way across the room to her brother.

"I'm gonna go on ahead. You okay to hang here, wait for Hi and Mac?"

"That will be fine," he said. "But if I could pose a question—"

"You can just ask me," Dawn said, a little harsher than she intended. "Sorry, buddy. What's on your mind?"

"Is there something the matter?"

Dawn watched Jenny flirt with that tall boy. She looked older and worldly . . . and a million miles away.

"Nothing's wrong," Dawn said. "The world's different, and I don't like all the ways it's changing." Hiram emerged from the bathroom. "There's Hiram. I'll catch up with you later, buddy."

She turned and rushed from the room as Lee said: "There's a line from *Star Trek II: The Wrath of Khan* I wanted to share with you."

Hiram's voice came back, sounding nasty: "You've told me before, Lee—"

Why is he so mean to my baby brother? she thought, lingering on how special it is to have even *one* bestie-bestie in your life. She'd never heard of Hiram having any friends, much less a best one. *Mac and I need to talk about that.*

Hiram's Journal

Park-goers rushed in and out of the bathroom. A couple of nattily-dressed teenagers checked their hair in the mirror, adjusting their pinstripe blazers and artfully untucking a single shirt-tail.

"Think she's into me?" one asked the other.

"You're *in*, dude."

They left, giving me access to the mirror just in time for my tears to bubble up again. My face clenched. I turned on the faucet and splashed ice-cold water on my face, rubbing it on my fat forearms and biceps, too.

It looked like a splash of blue and purple paint.

I stopped. Pulling my sleeve up, I saw it: a huge welt near my shoulder. Livid and purple, it appeared to be getting bigger.

I muttered: "Where did that . . ."

But I knew. It was from where Jason had grabbed me earlier. Jesus, the huge fucking asshole was strong as an ox. I hadn't even noticed how badly my arm was throbbing until I went into the bathroom. I'd been yelled at I don't know how many times by my mom, but no one had ever laid hands on me like that before.

I don't know what to do.

It was the truth. I could tell on Jason, but I'd had it drilled into me that you shouldn't be a tattletale. Still, part of me knew that what Jason had done was worse than, say, Jimmy Sheridan putting a booger in Lily Goff's hair. It wouldn't be tattling to tell everyone he'd physically hurt me.

But another voice in my head said: *Stay quiet.*

Why? I asked back.

Because if you do *tell on him, it'll only get worse.*

I was an extremely stupid kid, but even extremely stupid kids have some sense of intuition. Part of me knew that Jason, Kaitlyn, and Trent were shortly going to become part of our lives. Another part of me agreed that, yes, if I told on Jason, he'd only hurt me worse.

I had to keep it a secret, but how was I going to hide the bruise?

I wish I could go home and get into bed.

My head snapped up. That was it. I'd conjure a way to hide the truth while also forcing my mom to take me home: I'd pretend to get hurt. It wouldn't be a tough sell, given what a blundering fatass I was.

I was going to take a fall.

When I emerged from the bathroom, Dawn was gone, and Lee was already chattering away:

"There's a line from *Star Trek II: The Wrath of Khan* I wanted to share with you."

"You've told me before, Lee. Is it about the Kobayashi Maru?" The Kobayashi Maru was a scenario taught to students at Starfleet Academy. It was an impossible-to-solve rescue mission that was supposed to test the cadets' character. I felt like I was in my own little Kobayashi Maru scenario that day in the Mystery Mansion, and like Captain Kirk so infamously did, I was about to cheat my way out of it.

Lee was shaking his head. "No, no, it's another line."

"Here, let's climb this thing," I said, hauling myself up a few lengths of the chain-link web. A little kid went toppling down past me, while a couple of teenagers had turned around to sit and chat. Lee and I climbed around them, Lee blathering about Star Trek the whole time.

"I don't know if you remember the scene with Captain—excuse me, *Admiral*—Kirk and Mr. Spock, when Kirk comes upon Captain Spock in repose, but there's a moment that truly resonated with me—"

We reached the top. I looped a leg over the top and checked below. Jason was still flirting with the Bride/Princess. At the bottom of the web stood one of several concrete pylons.

Below, the Bride/Princess said, "My ghoulish prince!"

Lee was saying: "It's after Spock turns over command of the Enterprise to Kirk—"

Another voice, Kaitlyn's, rang out: "Quit flirting with my brother, ya slut!"

I flipped myself over the top of the web, pretended to lose my grip, slid down the web, rolling and aiming myself at the pylon, coming to rest on my stomach, whereupon I really *did* lose my grip.

"Oh, shit!" I yelled as I skimmed the rest of the way and really crashing into the pylon. Pain blossomed from my bicep and shoulder. I'd managed to hit myself right where Jason had left his welt, but in the process, I'd hurt myself a little worse than I intended. I cried out.

My sister's voice, bless her heart, came calling: "Hiram!"

Rolling over, I saw her scrambling over the chain-link web when something strange happened: She stopped. Cold. Like someone had deactivated her. She stared at the wall to her right, her jaw falling slack. Tracking her gaze, all I saw was a painted depiction of a set of double doors leading into a library.

But what was that?

It moved. The painting fucking *moved*, ladies and gentlemen.

There was someone *inside* the painted library, an animated man. He wore a dark blue suit, and although I couldn't see his face, I instantly recognized his gait.

The Plaid Man.

A scream welled up in my belly. At that same instant, Mac reactivated and continued her frantic scramble over the web.

A drunk Kaitlyn yelled, "Hey, wait up!"

I looked again. The Plaid Man was gone.

"Are you injured, Hiram?"

It was Lee, who'd somehow managed to descend the web without me noticing. I crossed my legs and girded myself against tears. Jason was only a few feet away, and I couldn't let him see me cry, not after everything he'd already done.

But I couldn't hold it in. A single sob racked out of me.

It was an awfully sublime paradox. I felt humiliated to have let out a sob in front of Jason, but at the same time, it felt so, so good to cry.

After her near confrontation with Jason, Mac and I rushed through the mansion's next section, a brief mirror maze. Neither of us wanted to look at the other or at ourselves. Her shoulders were shaking, she was so angry, while my lower lip was still quivering from my run-in with Jason (and that pylon.) Slices and segments of reflected park-goers slid all around us. Mac and I actually pulled ahead of Jason and Kaitlyn—we'd navigated this maze a million times. (We lost Lee somewhere behind us, too, thank goodness.)

I broke the silence: "You okay?"

She said nothing, and even though I was the one who got hurt, I suddenly found myself much more concerned for her well-being.

I spoke again: "Hey, what happened?"

We passed into the second half of the ride. Mac still said nothing. The first half was a walk-through funhouse, while the second half was a sit-down dark ride. The mirror maze shunted everyone into a stone-walled hallway lined with broad dark-wood beams and dotted with more portraits of the mansion's mad alumni: Dr. Prevington T. Schmippington III, nicknamed

"Grid-Runner," glared at us, his skin bright green, while Dr. Bellanna Valdemar, nicknamed "Havoc-Wrangler," cackled at a test tube filled with glowing green fluid. There were others, each wackier (and mad-science-ier) than the last, and all of them had backlit eyes that followed you down the passage.

The portrait hallway deposited everyone into a library packed with catawampus shelves and more paintings and statuary of the mansion's many denizens. A moving sidewalk emerged from a dark hallway to the right, carrying ride vehicles that resembled little spaceships, all retrofitted with gears, servos, and readouts that blinked with all kinds of crazy alphanumerics. Jason and Kaitlyn rolled in behind us, conspiratorially whisper-laughing about something.

Kait jabbed a finger at us, yelling, "There they are, the little shits!"

Two newcomers had joined the scene, the same pair of nattily dressed teenagers I'd seen in the bathroom adjusting their clothes. They flanked her, hanging on her every word and laughing at her every joke. Mac and I managed to slip into a ride-car together. Jason got into the one behind us, while Kaitlyn crammed into one with her two friends.

I had to ride my favorite ride in the world with Jason less than two feet away, dammit.

But then Jason threw me another curveball. He discreetly handed the ride operator one of the green chunks of flambonium ore that was labeled with the number forty-seven, a prime. The ride operator in turn handed him a special pair of 3D glasses, which he stowed in a pocket.

Wow. I've ridden this ride a million times and never found a rock with a prime on it. I wonder what those 3D glasses are for?

The ride-vehicles crept along the moving sidewalk toward a stone archway. An animatronic Professor Wizardo stood by the archway wildly and jerkily waving his hands.

"I've done it!" Wizardo said. "I've DONE IT! I've cracked the code of the most intense dimension! COME WITH ME AND BEAR WITNESS TO ITS WONDERS!"

I gently prodded Mac once more: "Is there something—"

"*Nothing,*" she snapped. "Sorry I was crying. You seen Mom? Or that guy? Trent?"

I hadn't noticed she'd been crying. The last time I saw her cry was when we were going through the old cedar chest. We came across a photo of Dad. It was from the two or three years when he wore a beard. He and Mom were backpacking the Appalachian Trail; he bore Mac in a sling across his back while he whittled a piece of wood into a small pistol. The sky was gray, the trees heavy with moisture. Rainwater beaded on his red parka. Mom was farther behind, blurry but visible, waving at the camera and smiling. Mac had the baffled look of a baby seeing everything for the first time. Mom said Auntie Hanna met them to walk the trail for a few miles and took the photo with a disposable camera.

The photo had sparked no memory in me, but it had made Mac cry.

We rode through stone archway; the ride was underway! It suddenly occurred to me to look around for Lee and Dawn, but all I'd been able to think about was avoiding Jason and Kaitlyn. As we entered the first room—a massive mad-science laboratory—Jason said *"psst"* at me. I looked over.

"Hey, Wimpy, I've got a question for you," he whispered.

Mac gave me a look. "Wimpy?"

I rolled my eyes. "He says it's my new name and I should like it."

"We've gotta get out of here," Mac grumbled.

The first room was the quintessence of mad science: test tubes, pipets, and various readouts and machinery packed the room, which also included animatronics of Professor Wizardo and his henchman, Zygor.

Our cars paused. We took in the tableau: the professor labored over a worktable, mixing various neon-glowing chemicals. His voice was an electronic howl: "When I combine these two elements, I shall have cracked the code of the most intense dimension! Science will have been achieved!"

Zygor protested: "Wait, Professor! You don't know what will happen! THE RAMIFICATIONS!"

Throughout the ride, the animatronic Zygor always gestured toward a curious detail: one of many large black panels that were spread throughout the sit-down portion of the ride. They looked like chalkboards waiting for the day's first lesson. I always wondered why they were there.

Meanwhile, Jason was still trying to get my attention.

"Psst, psst!"

Kaitlyn reached over and smacked him. "Shut up, shit-for-brains! I wanna listen." She addressed her two admirers: "You too, morons. Queen Kaity demands silence."

Mac fumed, muttering under her breath: "Bitch."

Jason persisted: "No, it's not that. I wanna show him something." He turned back toward me and reached out, offering me something. I ignored him.

"What'd she say to you?" I asked Mac.

"Nothing."

Before I could ask her again, she burst out in a gale of laughter. I immediately knew why: it was her favorite part of the ride. We rode out of the mad science laboratory into a smaller transitional chamber that depicted poor Zygor in a slapstick tableau:

He was rushing from one room (labeled the CHAMBER OF MAXIMUM SCIENCE) into another (THE MOST INTENSE DIMENSION), but along the way, he slipped on a puddle of glowing green glop. Unfortunately for Zygor, he'd been carrying a full tray of beakers, pipets, and an array extremely dangerous-looking chrome implements, all of which went flying, forever suspended in the air over his perpetually pratfalling form.

Even though I didn't find the image half as funny as Mac, her laughter lifted my spirits. Despite Jason and Kaitlyn's assholery, this ride was one of our favorite places on earth. We were going to enjoy it, no matter what.

Still . . . what the heck is going on with Mom?

"How long do you think they've been dating?"

"You mean Queen Bitch and the Dickhead Twins?" Mac said, jerking her chin at Kaitlyn. Mac knew damn well I was talking about Mom and Trent, but she sometimes deflected when she was upset.

"No, not her. Mom."

"Ugh. They're probably off making out somewhere."

"What if Mom starts dating that guy?"

As we rode into THE MOST INTENSE DIMENSION, Mac gave me a sad look; a look that said, *Oh, buddy, you don't get it, do you?*

"I think they've been dating for a while, goofball."

I gave my head a quick shake, a longtime tic that came out when I was confused. "Oh. Right. She—Kaitlyn—said they'd already met. I forgot."

But I didn't exactly *forget*. Even at that age, I'd trained my brain to block out things I didn't want to think about, and the prospect of Mom bringing these three assholes into our lives was too much for my addled little eleven-year-old brain to process.

And I still hadn't asked Mac about what she'd been looking at earlier.

"Psst!"

It was Jason, still trying to hand me something. Blood rushed to my face, both out of anger and lingering embarrassment. He was waving something in the air just beyond my peripheral vision. I concentrated on the ride, which progressed into THE MOST INTENSE DIMENSION:

It was the same scene as the first one, but a few moments later: Professor Wizardo had just combined the two fateful chemicals and unlocked the most intense dimension. The lab's walls melted away to reveal a view of interstellar space, which in this case were masses of fiber-optic lights hung against a black scrim. Professor Wizardo and Zygor floated in the void, their proportions bizarrely distorted into funhouse-mirror versions of themselves.

Wizardo: "GREAT SCOTT, IT'S FULL OF STARS!"

Zygor: "AAAA! TOO MANY RAMIFICATIONS!"

Floating in space all around them were a school of glowing alien creatures. They flowed and blooped around the lab. Some look like jellyfish, others like huge, tentacled blobs, others like "graymen," but with neon-yellow, glow-in-the-dark skin. (The discontinuity of the "Zygor slipping and falling" tableau never bothered me or Mac. It delighted us, even on an awful day like this one.)

Jason was still hissing: "Hey, kid. Kid. Sorry I called you Wimpy, all right?"

The apology got my attention. It turned out that Jason was offering me the 3D glasses.

"Are you serious?" I asked.

"Yeah," he whispered. "This room's really cool. Have a look."

My words sounded strangled: "Have a look?"

"Yeah," he said, suddenly chummy, his tone kind. "There's this weird paint all over the place. You can only see it with these."

It's strange how much a moment's kindness from a cool kid means to you, even if that cool kid has also been torturing you. I donned the 3D glasses, and fluorescent words leaped from the walls. Most were goofy dad jokes:

Q: WHAT DO YOU CALL A SICK CHEMIST?

A: IF YOU CAN'T HELIUM, AND YOU CAN'T CURIUM, YOU MIGHT AS WELL BARIUM.

And:

NEVER TRUST ATOMS! THEY MAKE UP EVERYTHING.

And:

WHAT DOES A SUBATOMIC DUCK SAY? QUARK.

But splattered across the far wall, seemingly thousands of imaginary light-years away, was this:

I WATCH FROM THE FOREST, I WATCH FROM THE TREES, I WATCH FROM ABOVE

And:

ALL ABOARD!

I snatched the glasses off my face, my skin tingling.

We rode into the next room, which depicted the continued deterioration of reality. Gone was the lab, replaced instead with endless space. In the distance, miniature animatronics of Professor Wizardo and Zygor floated, both of them still screaming about "DISCOVERIES" and "RAMIFICATIONS," their voices tiny and distant.

Jason was still prodding me: "Put 'em back on. This room's really rad."

My hands shaking, I donned the glasses once more, this time revealing massive interstellar creatures, like luminescent jellyfish.

But there were more words, too.

IT'S A PLEASURE TO WATCH YOU

SHE'S CRYING BECAUSE SHE'S UGLY

And this, which made my blood run cold:

HIGH REASON

The writing was so small you could've looked right past it. It looked like someone had snuck into the park after hours and scribbled the messages using a needle and a thimbleful of magic ink.

And I'd spoken those words earlier: *High reason.*

But what did they mean? What did *any* of these words mean, these riddle-words I'd been hearing in my dreams and speaking in waking dream-states?

Itza linda adda.

Gedda brusha.

High reason.

I felt certain that Itza Linda was a place. The magic traincar was there, and I had to find a way back to it.

But as for the others? I had no idea what they meant. Were they a message? A warning?

Was Mac seeing them too? Or *hearing* them? Earlier, when I saw the Plaid Man skulking in the walls of the mansion, did she see her own message?

Jason tapped my shoulder and whispered, "Give 'em back."

I returned the 3D glasses, relieved to see the strange messages disappear. Glancing back, I saw Kaitlyn clowning around with her two dates, while Jason slipped on the 3D glasses and appeared to sulk. We rode into the ride's final chamber, THE SPACE-WITHIN-SPACES, which depicted a return to an off-kilter reality. The professor's lab had reappeared, but its proportions were as wildly exaggerated as a Tim Burton fever dream: the stone archway doors had transformed from gentle arches into kooky trapezoids, while the floor had returned—but only in part. A lone pathway led through the room, seeming to float in interstellar space.

Mac couldn't stop giggling. She was smile-crying; they were the kind of tears you can only shed as you rise up from a pit of grief to see the sun again. We loved the entire Mystery Mansion, but this was hands-down our favorite room. The imagery was somewhat grisly but undeniably silly, as we learned that the alien creatures didn't really understand human physiology. One of them tries to pull off the professor's head.

Mac and I knew every line:

"Is this their hat?" she quoted in tandem with one of the well-meaning aliens.

Another alien produced a ray gun and zapped Zygor, causing his feet and hands to change places.

"I fixed him!" I quoted.

Professor Wizardo and Zygor made "zoinks" cries in response to the aliens' goof-ups. It was all kiddie stuff, but damn if it didn't cheer us up. Too bad the next thing we saw was a glittering cloud of spit. Two cars back, one of the teenagers was tickling Kaitlyn, causing her to spew a mouthful of booze all over the room, including Jason.

"Hey!" he yelled.

We left the final chamber and rolled into the load-out area, a dungeon hallway. Various animatronics—other mad scientists, by the looks of their white lab coats—all stood in a row of cells, their body parts all scrambled. One headless animatronic asked if we could help find her "noggin," while another animatronic (this one normal-looking) complained of a "missing spleen." Other "angelic" aliens held the professor and Zygor captive at the ride's exit. Zygor's hands and feet were still switched. He waved goodbye with a foot.

"Have a scientastic day and enjoy all the park's ramifications!" Zygor said.

"May God have mercy on my soul!" Professor Wizardo said. "Make sure to get a brochure on your way out!"

The animatronic Wizardo pointed at a bank of park maps. Mac and I jumped out of our cars and made for the exit while Jason and Kaitlyn argued their way out behind us.

"You got it *all over* me!" Jason yelled, hulking over Kaitlyn, whose two dates had made themselves scarce.

"Oh, you like it," she spat back, sipping from her flask. "Almost as much as you like your new little brother."

Little brother? I thought.

"Shut up," he said, pocketing his 3D glasses. They had both defaced our favorite ride in so many ways, and even though the glasses were cheap, plentiful, and disposable, it felt like the worst of their offenses.

"He's not my little brother," Jason said. "Now *apologize* for spitting all over me."

Kaitlyn's two teenage dates tried to slink past us, but she barked, "Bye, boys!" She mimed "call me" with her thumb and forefinger. Jason actually smacked away her gesture, prompting her to scream, "Hey! Don't touch me!"

They were blocking the exit with their fight. A family tried to sidle past.

"Look out, kids," the father said to his children, a pair of wide-eyed moppets wearing Gold Rush T-shirts.

Jason yelled, "Shut your fuckin' face, old man!"

Kaitlyn howled with laughter. *"Awwww! You tell him, big bro! Big tough bro, bein' all tough!"*

By this point, Mac and I were thunderstruck. We'd gotten into fights in public before, but never anything like this. They were both shouting at the tops of their lungs, drawing stares from all around.

"Shut the fuck up!" Jason screamed.

"Why don't you *make* me, ya big asshole?!"

We blushed; never in our lives had we heard this kind of language uttered in public, much less at this volume. I scanned the crowd and spotted Mom and Trent on a bench about twenty yards away. He was nursing a beer, while she sipped from a root beer float. They both giggled like teenagers. Mac's face darkened when she saw Mom.

She hooked her thumb. "Let's go."

We ran over. I dumped Lee's bag of ice in a trash can and covered up my bruise. (I knew my mom would freak out if she saw it.) Mom was in the middle of one of her interminable stories: "I always related the most to the professor. I loved his little apartment; looked so cozy. I thought, 'I could live there.'"

"Mom," Mac said, but she went on like we weren't there:

"But I'd want that bottomless bottle of wine, too! Y'know, I almost did before I met Deak. Did all that. Moved to that apartment. Got that bottle of wine. I was *this close* to getting my master's when I met him. If I got my master's, I could've stopped teaching elementary, maybe moved up to high school and worked on a PhD over the summers. I could've been teaching at Northwestern by now."

If you've ever had a withholding parent freeze you out for no reason, then you might find it hard to relate with the previous moments. Mac and I were both clearly upset, and Mom just pretended like we weren't there. Part of me has to respect the focus it would take to *completely* ignore someone you know—and supposedly love—and simply go on with a fairly involved story you were telling. Mom had the power to freeze us out entirely.

It didn't just feel like we weren't there. It felt like we'd never been there.

"Mom," Mac said, almost yelling. Mom fell silent and sipped her drink, not even bothering to look over. Mac pressed on: "Where *were* you?"

Jason and Kaitlyn had withdrawn to the edge of the walkway, where they continued their fight at a lower—but still embarrassingly loud—volume.

"You're drunk!"

"Well, at least I'm having some fun!"

"Oh, go fuck yourself."

Trent ignored his kids' fight and responded to the last thing Mom said.

"You still can, you know—teach college."

"I think that's sad. I can still remember the moment when I decided to go meet him instead of going to grad school. I was living over on Ridge, in this little dorm for singles. Remember those? Had a chalkboard on my door for messages. I felt so clever, hanging it. Adella—she was so cute, we used to do spring break in Myrtle Beach and Fort Lauderdale—Adella, she left me a message, 'Let's finish those applications!'"

Kaitlyn came traipsing over. "Sorry for the little kerfuffle, but Jason was being a royal douchebag."

Trent ignored her and asked Mom: "Why didn't you finish your application?"

Mom's brow clenched, and Trent got a taste of what Mac and I got all the time. Whenever we stumbled onto one of the million topics we weren't allowed to talk about—Dad's death, her aspirations to teach college—she would retreat into her mind and have a conversation with herself before coming back to the real world with a non sequitur.

"I did college part-time so I could work as a TA over at Oakton. That's where Deak went to grade school, funny coincidence. Took me six years to get through forty credits, so thank goodness for Adella. She took time off from Stiller Brothers—she was the office manager for a construction company—to spend all my extra spring breaks together."

Trent's confusion was manifest, but he tried to maintain the thread:

"You can still do it, even with kids. You can do it all."

Mom sipped her root beer float, leaving an ice cream mustache on her lip.

"I think that's sad," she said in response to nothing. Finally, she looked over, scowling. "What?"

"Where *were* you? We were scared!"

"I hadn't spoiled myself yet today, so I got a root beer float."

"It was scary," Mac said. "We couldn't find you. What if something happened?"

"Want a sip?" Mom asked. God, sometimes her deflecting pissed me off.

I pointed directly at Jason and Kaitlyn and blurted: "They were being mean to us."

Everyone got quiet. I instantly knew I'd fucked up.

A silence settled over the scene for three reasons: One, I'd implicated Trent's kids. He sat forward, suddenly engaged in the conversation. Two, because Trent was engaged in the conversation, now Mom had to come back from Cloud Nine and get involved.

And three, because I'd just committed one of the great childhood faux pas: I tattled.

Per the now-defunct rules of the eighties, tattling was somehow a greater crime than being a bully, at least in the Gresham household. Because neither Mac nor I was allowed to be anything but perfect, if either of us stepped out of line, it was automatically our fault. The fact that I'd tattled on Trent's kids and disrupted Mom's date with a rich guy was even worse. One thing you could always count on with Corrie Gresham: you could *never* count on her. If you embarrassed her or in any way made her have to step out of her comfort zone, she'd treat you like you were a fucking stranger.

Jason and Kaitlyn's faces filled with fire and cunning. They were mad, yes, but they were more interested in spinning the situation to their advantage.

"Who was being mean to you?" Mom asked.

She asked me this even though I was pointing straight at Jason and Kaitlyn. "*Them?*" Mom asked. "Put your hand down, honey. Don't point at people." "But—"

"They didn't do anything."

My brain froze up: "D—D—"

My mom continued like she didn't see me trying to talk:

"They weren't being mean to you." She addressed Mac: "Were they?"

It'a hard to describe the humiliation of being scolded by my own mother in front of these assholes.

Mac finally spoke up. Folding her arms, she cocked her head at Kaitlyn and said: "She was calling me fat. And Hiram fell."

Trent finally activated: "Is this true?"

Kaitlyn looked thunderstruck at being called out. Must not have happened often.

But Jason broke in: "We were just fooling around. Telling some jokes. It was fun."

Trent stood. It was like a redwood sprang from the earth. He put his hands in his pockets, and damn if Jason and Kaitlyn didn't shrink a few inches. He addressed me:

"You say you fell?"

I nodded. Mom rolled her eyes.

"Honey, you fall down on that ride all the time. How bad could it be?"

Nobody said anything for a moment. I thought about showing my bruise. Mac gave me a look that said, *Go ahead,* but at the time, I decided not to.

I shrugged.

"Not that bad," I said.

Trent's temperature was on the rise, though. He addressed his kids: "You *just* met these two. Not everyone has the same sense of what 'fun' means to you."

"We didn't mean anything by it," Jason said.

"Look at this one," Trent said, indicating Mac, whom he addressed: "Honey, have you been crying?"

The question disarmed her. She unfolded her arms and nodded.

Trent addressed his kids: "Do people having fun usually cry, in your estimation?"

"Folks sometimes cry when they're happy," Kaitlyn said under her breath.

Trent took his hands out of his pockets. To me and Mac, it was an innocuous gesture, but to Jason and Kaitlyn, it was like he'd pulled a gun. They both shrank a few more inches. When Trent spoke, his voice was a few decibels louder, his tone weirdly stilted, like he was working the PA system for a sports event.

"Jason, I want to honestly and sincerely apologize. We all know that I lost some hearing in this ear when I was a kid. Pneumonia. Malpractice. Sued and won. But I couldn't win back my hearing! And sometimes, *sometimes*, *sometimes* on *rare* occasions, my hearing aid goes on the fritz. Funny!" Trent made a sound like he was hawking something up. I guess it was what passed for laughter. "Jason, I'm really, honestly, and truly sorry about all this. My hearing aid was on the fritz when you answered me just now." His jaw flexed, his voice dropped a full octave: "Would you mind. If I asked you. To repeat yourself?"

Now Jason was the one stammering: "I—I—"

"And this time—really sorry about this—but can I trouble you to speak up, not only so *I* can hear but so we can *all* hear?"

Kaitlyn finally let loose a big, annoyed sigh.

"We're sorry."

Trent raised his eyebrows.

Kaitlyn repeated, louder: "We're *sorry. God.*"

Trent nodded. I guess her response was good enough.

"Anything you'd like to add, Jase?"

Jason's expressions in that moment sketched a whole journey: His lip trembled. His jaw clenched. His eyes went glassy (like he was going to cry), then steely (like he was going to scream). Was he about to pick a fight or beg for mercy? His next (and final) expression wasn't facial but physical: his shoulders slumped; his jaw went slack; and his eyes went blank. Looking back, I know now why his eyes went blank.

But at the time, I felt more pity than schadenfreude, even though he'd spent the last hour bullying the shit out of me.

Jason stormed off.

Mackenzie

Corrie leaped to her feet. "Oh! I'm sorry!"

"Don't apologize to that one," Trent said. "He's a hot-head sometimes. I know he's sorry. Sometimes, it just takes him some time to come around. He'll be back in a few."

Jason vanished around the back of the Mystery Mansion. Trent faced the group, curiously unconcerned about his now-absent son.

"Look, my kids acted like little brats. I wanna make it up to all of you." Trent stooped, hands on knees, and addressed Hiram and Mac, who half expected him to bellow, *Fee-fi-fo-fum!* Instead he said: "So let me ask you kids this: What's the fanciest place you've ever been for dinner?"

Uh oh, Mac thought. Somehow she knew they were in dangerous territory. Corrie smiled, but it didn't reach her wide eyes. She was a portrait of tension.

Stepping around Trent, she started prattling: "We've been to a lot of fancy—"

"Hang on, now. I asked the towheads here. I'd like to know. Name the fanciest place. The one with your favorite food and best service."

He might as well have asked them what their favorite Fabergé egg was. Mac sensed her mom's fear that they'd say something to embarrass her. After all, Trent was a hotshot who probably ate at all kinds of fancy places they'd never heard of, and if he found out that their mom had never taken them to anyplace *fancy,* well then—that'd be horrible! He might not want to keep dating her.

"Hardee's," Mac said with a smirk. Kaitlyn had gone silent, but Mac detected the hint of a smile from her.

Corrie's face fell. "Aw—now, honey, that's not a fancy place."

"*I* think it's fancy."

Kaitlyn snickered, and for an instant Mac thought she would, too, but she held it in.

Corrie: "Mackenzie, Mr. Sutton asked you a serious question."

"I like Ryan's!"

Everyone gawked at Hiram, who beamed like he'd just answered a tricky question in class. Corrie covered her face, while Trent gave him a pitying look that made Mac want to smack him. "Ryan's" of course referred to Ryan's Steakhouse, a family-style buffet joint comparable to a Sizzler or a

Ponderosa—in other words, not the kind of "fancy" restaurant Trent had in mind.

Who cares if we've never been to one of your stupid fancy restaurants? Mac thought.

"Can't you think of anyplace nicer?" Trent asked. "C'mon. Sky's the limit."

Something flashed across Hiram's face; Was it recognition? Did he finally understand the question? He started chewing on words again.

"Ohhhhh," he said. "Uh you mean like a place where you, um, where you uh call ahead?"

Both the Suttons, Trent and Kait, took on the same pitying look.

"Yeah, Howdy-Doody," Kaitlyn said, giggling. "A place where you call ahead. They're called *reservations.* Can you say 'reservations,' little guy?"

"Shut up," Mac said. Before either of the grown-ups could respond, she added: "We've never been to one. Have we, Mom? Maybe before Dad died?"

Everyone got quiet. Mac had somehow stumbled onto two anathema subjects at once.

Trent fidgeted. "Sorry . . . uh, I'm so sorry about your husband. For your loss."

Mac and Hiram shared a stunned glance. *Had she not told him she was a widow?*

"Oh, it's stupid," their mom said, and even Trent was a little thrown by that one.

"Oh," Trent said, even more baffled. "Well, hey . . . That's not stupid. I lost my Marie—" he broke off that thought and shifted gears: "Listen, there's this little place I like in Ober Gatlinburg. Ottokars. Take the kids there sometimes. It's small, it's quiet. And I already booked a table for three. Easy enough to add a few more. Whaddaya say?"

Hiram practically squealed: "Ooooh!"

Trent: "What's up, fella?"

"Um, uh," he stammered. Mac wanted to intervene but knew if she finished his sentence it'd only made him grouchy. Hiram managed to say: "Otto—?"

"Yeah, Ottokars!" Trent said with a smile. "That's the one! Up in Ober."

Mac lit up: "The place at the foot of the ski slopes? Ohmigod, I've always wanted to go there!"

"Uh are we really going to go?" Hiram asked. "I've always wanted to take the, um, the chairs!"

Corrie suddenly turned all her energies on Hiram: "The *chairs?*"

Mac sighed. She knew what was coming.

Hiram was about to get a stuttering lesson.

Hiram's Journal

When you're a stutterer, everyone around you learns what turns of phrase strike dread into your heart.

In this case, the turn of phrase was "ski lift."

Susie Schuppe's Smoky Mountain Gold Rush was located right on the edge of Gatlinburg, Tennessee, which during the winter months moonlighted as a ski resort. "Ober" Gatlinburg was the "ski" part of the ski resort. You got there one of two ways: by driving a scary switchback road or riding a ski lift.

When you're a stutterer, you're constantly thinking a few words ahead, and if you see a word that's going to trip you up, you try and talk around it. I didn't want to say "take the ski lift," so I said, "take the chairs."

I was looking at a map of Gatlinburg one day when I spotted Ober. A snaky filament of green—a small ridge of impassible mountains—separated it from the rest of the city. I was *dying* to see what it looked like up there, but this was before the Internet, so I couldn't just Google it. I asked my mom about it, and while she was out one day, she dropped by a motel near Gatlinburg and grabbed a bunch of brochures, including one for Ober. Do they still have those? Every little hotel or tourist trap around here used to have these banks of pamphlets inside the door. I used to grab as many as I could and just pore over them, look at all the cheesy and silly little places I dreamed of going to: The Ancient Sea. Enchanted Caverns. Rock City. Ruby Falls.

I didn't know it at the time, but I'd be visiting one of those places in the next year.

But more on that later. My mom was asking me something: "Are you sure they're called 'the chairs'? What would a cool person call them?"

"Uh . . ."

Great. She's giving me a stuttering lesson.

My mom *hated, hated, hated* my habit of talking around words. I'm pretty sure "cool" was her codeword for "normal." Sometimes she'd let it slide, but sometimes—like that day in the Gold Rush—she'd bring all conversation to a halt and try to get me to say the word I had trouble saying.

Everyone stared at me. Mac looked pained—she knew I hated this. She waved at someone leaving the mansion and ran off; I didn't see where. Trent and Kaitlyn, having stumbled onto a strange Gresham family ritual, looked confused. You'd think my mom might be looking at me with love or patience, but nope—she simply looked annoyed. Maybe even a little pissed.

"What would a cool person call it? It's easy, honey, just say it."

I felt like someone was holding a hot iron next to my cheek, I was blushing so hard. I'd shed a lot of tears that day, so they were close to the surface, but I swallowed a lump in my throat and soldiered on: "Uh the . . ." God, in times like this, I felt out of breath, I was so stressed out. I whispered: "Uh the ski li—"

Mom snapped: *"Don't say uh. Just say the words like a cool person."*

Mackenzie

Sandra Dockery was maximum Mom.

She and Corrie Gresham were best friends, but unlike their daughters, *Dawn-n-Gresh,* who dressed so much alike, Sandy Dockery wasn't the fashion plate Corrie was. Nope, Sandy had forgotten about fashion back in the late seventies. She wore whatever was clean and comfortable, and for her, that meant high-waisted "mom" jeans, a succession of long-sleeve T-shirts, and an emerald green fleece vest she practically lived in.

She was escorting her two kids out of the Mystery Mansion when Mac came running up.

"Hey! Wait up!"

Sandy was already smiling.

"Well, hello there, Mackenzie Lynn."

"Hi, Mrs.—sorry, I mean *Ms.* Dockery." Mac kept forgetting that their dad, Hank, had died when his eighteen-wheeler jack-knifed. It was weird: she always remembered that Dawn's *dad* was dead, but not necessarily that Sandra's *husband* was. They didn't seem like the same person to Mac. She'd met Dawn's dad once before the crash. He was kind-hearted and funny, but also macho in a way that didn't seem to mesh with Sandy's vibe.

"Hi, Ms. Sandy," Mac said. "Hi, Lee."

Lee gave a curt, formal nod.

"Greetings. How is the admiral's shoulder?"

"He's a little banged up, but he's okay. Thanks for getting that ice."

"Yes, my lady."

Lee is such a strange one. But he's not who I need to talk to.

"Dawn, got a second?"

Dawn had been weirdly hovering behind her mom. She came forward, looking grumpy.

"Be right back, Mama."

"We'll be right here."

Mac and Dawn stepped to the side of the walkway. Mac started to talk, but Dawn cut her off:

"Can I ask you something about Hiram?"

Mac dodged the question with: "Did you know my mom had a boyfriend?"

She figured Dawn was angry about how Hiram had treated Lee. Truth be told, so was Mac, but she was way more pissed off about Dawn keeping such a big secret from her.

Dawn nodded. "She let it slip the other night when she came over."

"Why didn't you tell me?"

Dawn's tone changed: "Can I ask you something?"

"Sure."

"Why are you askin' *me* this and not your mama?"

Hiram's Journal

Mom snapped: *"Don't* say *uh.* Just say the words like a cool person."

I had almost said it. I had almost spat out all three words—"the ski lift"—when she snapped at me and made me start over without my crutch, the little "uh" I'd put at the start of a sentence so I could getting a running start; so I could skip across that problem sound.

It wasn't good enough for her, though. At least in that moment. Maybe she was still embarrassed because I'd called Ryan's Steakhouse a fancy restaurant. Maybe it was because Mac had blown her secret about Dad being dead.

But there's a part of me that fears the worst: that she thought my stutter made me stupid, and she didn't like having a stupid kid. It meant she didn't raise me right. Even though my mom didn't even seem to particularly *like* being a parent, it made her furious to think that people might see her as a bad one.

I think. Her inner life was hidden from me by a wall a million miles high.

Regardless, I gave up.

I let out a long rush of air and let my arms go limp by my side. New tears started to stream down my cheeks. Not much elicited my mom's sympathy, but tears sometimes did.

"It's okay, honey," she said. "Say *uh* if you want. But can you say it for me? Say what a cool person would say?"

I hated my mom in that moment. Everyone was staring at me. And I can tell you this: no force on earth could've made me talk again. I'd have jumped off a fucking cliff before I'd say another word.

"Um, it's Hiram, right?"

It was Kaitlyn. I barely even recognized her voice. She'd stepped over closer to me. Her tone had changed. Heretofore, she'd been adopting some goofy English accent or shouting dirty words. But now, her voice had softened. She sounded somehow younger but *wiser*—more like Mac, honestly.

I was a crimson statue, but I managed to nod.

"Hi? That's your nickname?" she asked.

I nodded. Mac came back over, shooting Mom a dirty look before noticing that Kaitlyn was talking to me. Kaitlyn didn't notice Mac; no, she smiled in a way she hadn't that day. Her face glowed with a kindness I didn't know was in there.

"That's a really cool name. Hi, Hi. Can I tell you a secret?"

I nodded again.

"I love the ski lifts. Maybe we can take one together, just the two of us?"

Incredibly, my tears vanished. I assume I smiled because Kaitlyn's smile grew in response. For some reason, my arm chose that moment to get itchy, so I pushed up my sleeve; pushed it up high enough to reveal my bruise.

Mom's jaw dropped. "Oh, my God, Hiram—"

"Wait a minute."

Trent had spoken, his voice a low, urgent whisper. I hid my bruise again. Mom was still staring at me, confused. I could see the wheels in her head turning as she tried to calculate why I'd kept such an injury hidden from her. Trent stalked around the immediate area, looking in every direction. He turned to us.

"Where's Jason?"

The next half hour was one of burgeoning panic. As night fell, we checked behind the Mystery Mansion and even went through the ride again with a park employee. We checked all the restaurants, snack bars, and the one place in the park that served booze.

No sign of Jason.

Trent hauled us all down to the security center, a general-store-looking outpost near the back of the park. The building's conceit included a huge set of double doors that stood open, letting the cool autumn breeze into the reception area. In front of the station, a set of benches encircled a friendly old oak tree with a massive trunk whose hovering branches hugged the area. Moonlight shone through the tree's remaining leaves and dappled the area with fall-time burnt oranges, golden yellows, and deep reds.

Mom, Mac, Kaitlyn, and I all sat on the benches while Trent paced. An employee had told us that the Head of Security would be right with us. That had been ten minutes ago.

"Where the hell is he?"

On cue, a Black man emerged from the building wearing a beige park security uniform, the same guy who'd been performing in front of the Mystery Mansion. An embroidered name-tag on his chest read JUSTIN.

"Help you folks?" he said.

Trent propped his hands on his hips and cleared his throat upon seeing him; my guess is the huge asshole wasn't expecting to see a Black man running security.

"Trent Sutton," he said, offering his hand. "What should I call you, son?"

"Mr. Johnson's fine."

Johnson. Ohmigod, it's Justin Johnson!

Indeed it was Justin Johnson, "JJ Flash," hero of Polk High, former Broadway actor . . . and the man who almost caught Lenny Skelton.

Justin continued: "What seems to be the problem?"

"Mr. Johnson, is there a police officer on duty we could speak with?" Trent had adopted the same "announcer" voice he did with his kids. It didn't occur to me at the time—again, I was a very, very stupid kid—but I know now that Justin had to put up with assholes like Trent all the time every day.

"That'd be me," Justin said.

"You're an officer?"

"Private security."

"But that's not an officer."

"If it's important enough for the police, maybe you can tell me what it is?"

"My son is missing."

Justin nodded; this was familiar territory. "I understand. Mr. Sutton, families get separated here all the time. They usually turn up close to where you left them, or a park employee brings them down to Guest Relations. I can make an announcement—"

"May I use your phone?"

"There's a bank of pay phones right there," Justin said, indicating a bank of pay phones a few yards away. Trent headed for them, but Justin added: "If you're calling the police, you should know they'll just call me. They don't respond to calls about kids gone missing here 'cause we get at least three, four a day."

"Even with Skelton out there?" Trent said with some asperity.

Seeing someone like Justin Johnson in person for the first time is hard to describe. Stories of his exploits on the football field had taken on the aura of myth, as had his encounter with Skelton. My mental projection of him was that of a superhero, but somehow seeing the real person was even cooler. He wasn't as tall as I imagined, but he was brawnier than I'd pictured. Cords of muscle had jumped out of his forearms when he'd shaken Trent's hand. More than anything, though, he projected calmness, gentleness, kindness. He only seemed to move when absolutely necessary. By contrast, someone like Trent was always sawing the air and carrying on.

Trent had about six inches and fifty pounds on Justin, but he seemed pint-sized in comparison.

When Trent mentioned Skelton, Justin's brow creased for an instant, but his manner didn't change. If he was upset, he didn't show it. "We've got his photos up at every park entrance. I know the guy." His voice rarely rose above a hushed tone; you found yourself leaning in to better hear him.

Trent was fuming. "This is bullshit."

Mac and I met eyes. I could tell she wanted to crawl under a rock as much as I did. We looked to Mom for support, but she was deeply focused on picking her cuticles.

"Sir, there's no need for that kind of language," Justin said. He reminded me a little bit of Auntie Hanna, which is one of the best compliments I could pay anyone. "Mr. Sutton, can I at least make an announcement? Kids get lost all the time."

Kaitlyn spoke: "He's not a kid. He's eighteen." She was leaning back and making little Xs with her feet.

"Beg pardon?" Justin asked.

"Graduates next June. Got held back a year for football. Too bad he can't play because of his knee."

She kept her eyes downcast, but her words drew a dirty look from Trent. If Justin detected the interaction, he didn't let on.

"You sure he's lost?" Justin asked. "You didn't see him sneak off? Maybe go meet a friend? I'm not trying to be indelicate, but maybe he went off to have a drink or do . . . some of the things that teenagers do? Happens all the time, believe me."

"Him and Dad were fighting," Kaitlyn said.

"There was no fighting," Trent said. "And he doesn't do that kind of thing."

"Mr. Sutton, I'm not trying to suggest—"

Trent: "He's not some pot-head."

Kaitlyn snorted.

Justin: "Folks, I don't care if he is. Busting up kids with joints is half the job. I'm not gonna call the cops on some kid for that." He addressed Trent: "Or if the two of you are on the outs."

"You said they turn up where you saw them," Trent said, flaring. "We looked all around that stupid—whatzitcalled? That stupid mansion ride. Nothing. How do you *know* it's not Skelton? He could be in disguise."

"He's right. You were in disguise."

For a moment, I didn't know who had spoken. When I noticed everyone staring at me, I realized it was me. Justin looked a little embarrassed but still smiled.

"Good eye, kid," he said with a small nod of approval.

Trent looked like he was trying to figure out the square root of something. "Disguise?"

Justin waited for me to solve the puzzle.

"You were back at the Mystery Mansion," I said, indicating Justin. "The greeter at the front door. With the monocle?"

Trent stared at Justin and shook his head. *"No, you weren't."*

Corrie covered her mouth. My jaw hung open. Kaitlyn snickered. "Um, Dad, are you kidding? You didn't realize that?"

Justin nodded. "I do some acting at the park. It's fun. Lots of folks do it."

Trent blustered, his brow furrowed, his eyes darkening. Kaitlyn let loose an outright guffaw, which sent the huge dickhead stomping out the door.

"We need a *real* cop!"

He crossed to the pay phones and snatched one up. I got the feeling Trent was the kind of person who was used to making other people the butt of the joke but not being it himself. Kaitlyn sprang up and padded over to Justin, twining her fingers in a posture of contrition.

"I'd like to personally apologize for my dad being not only a huge asshole, but also a gigantic asshole. Can you go ahead and make that announcement?"

Half an hour later, we were still waiting.

The announcement sparked some activity around the park. Justin dispatched a few more security guards to search some of the park's remote corners, to no avail, while we waited back at the security center, getting hungrier and hungrier. Meanwhile, Trent's anger was doubling every few minutes. At some point, Mom finally came and sat next to me.

"Show me your arm, sweetie."

I did. She checked out my bruise, made a *tsk-tsk* sound, and kissed my forehead.

"Did you fall?" she asked. "Is that how you got this?"

For a moment, I considered telling the truth, but instead, I nodded.

"Why didn't you tell me?

An interesting question. Looking back, I can say that I was rarely incentivized to tell the truth about my hurts and inner turmoil, but at the time, all I could say was, "I thought I'd get in trouble."

Her tone was almost angry: *"Why* would you get in trouble?"

Again, there's a divide between what I know now versus what I thought then. *Then,* I knew that if I ratted on Jason for hurting me, I'd ruin Mom's date, she'd be upset, and . . . well, I wasn't sure what after that. Telling on Jason would've given my mom a moral test: *Dump this new guy because his son hurt yours,* or *Take your new boyfriend's side against your own son.* I hate to put it in such stark terms, but at the time, I honestly didn't know how my mom would've reacted.

Now, I know I should've told the truth. *How* I know that is basically what this journal is about.

But I didn't, and the events that led to me being held captive by Lenny Skelton continued their inexorable progression.

Footsteps heralded the arrival of Justin with a police officer in tow. I recognized her drawl immediately.

"What're *y'all* doing here?"

Mac and I jumped up, simultaneously shouting: "Auntie Hanna!"

Broad-shouldered, gray-haired, and beautiful, Hanna Blackledge accepted our hugs. She wore her usual duty uniform and campaign hat. "They said it was a teenage boy went missing?"

"Hanna?" Mom asked, standing. "What're you doing here?"

Mac and I returned to our seats while Mom folded her arms and shot us an annoyed glance; she always thought we favored Auntie Hanna. (*Psst.* Can you keep a secret? We kind of *did* favor her.)

"Park security put out a call for police help. I was in the neighborhood. But who went missing?"

"Oh, it's not one of mine," Mom said.

Trent thudded over. "*He* is my son, the one who's missing." He shook Hanna's hand. "Trent Sutton. Hope you can be more help than this one." He jerked his chin at Justin, who didn't react.

Hanna: "Of course we will. Now, where was the last place where—"

"Excuse me," Trent broke in. "Where's everyone else?"

"Everyone else?"

"The rest of the police."

"There's a crash over in Pigeon Forge got most of 'em busy," Hanna said before addressing Justin: "You always send up a flare when a kid goes missing?"

"No, ma'am," Justin said. "But it's been a few hours. They usually turn up by then."

"You made all the usual moves? Extra eyes on the exits, check all the bathrooms?"

"And we looked in all the 'fall' areas. Yes, ma'am. All the usual steps."

Hanna paced a bit, took off her hat. "And still no sign. That's strange." She addressed Trent: "Johnson said on the radio you two had a tiff?"

"Nothing I can remember," Trent said.

Hanna pursed her lips, replaced her hat. "If you had a fight, that's helpful for us to know, me and Johnson. Out of curiosity, you got your keys on you?"

Wind kicked through the trees. Clouds slipped across the moon. There were whispers on the wind, I could've sworn: *itza linda adda gedda brusha high reason zo vaxap dis en zo flestulo.*

"Itza linda," I whispered. "Zo vaxap." Mom's ears pricked up. She sat next to me.

"What was that you said?"

"Um, it's some of those weird words I saw in my dreams," I said.

Hanna asked Trent if Jason might've pickpocketed the keys to Trent's car. Turned out he had.

"Damn," Trent said, checking his pockets.

Mom asked, "What were those last words you said?"

"Zo vaxap."

"The . . . map?" she asked, her eyes wandering.

"Huh?"

Hanna was questioning Trent: "He's eighteen, your boy? Got his license?"

"Yeah," Trent said. "He drives."

The wind caught the brochure in my hand. Instinctively, I snatched it out of the air, holding it open—with my thumb on the Mystery Mansion. I prodded my mom.

"You said something about a map?"

She wrinkled her nose at me. "But you weren't even alive then. Were you?"

"What're you talking about?"

"Deak—your father—and I had a secret language. 'Zo vaxap' means 'the map.'"

"It *does?*"

Hanna flipped open a notebook. "Make and model of your car?"

"It's an eighty-seven Mercedes-Benz G-Wagon. But he wouldn't steal my—"

"The hell's a G-Wagon?" Hanna asked.

"A four-wheel-drive Mercedes. Slate gray. Cost me forty Gs. We parked in the FairyTown lot. It'll be the only one there."

While Trent kept bragging about his stupid car, I stared at the brochure. The map was hand-drawn, like a Saturday-morning-cartoon version of the park. Mom was still lost in her memories.

"But we never used our code around you," she said. "Unless you were a baby at the time."

"Do you know what *itza linda adda* means?" I asked, eyes wide.

She shook her head. "No, that doesn't sound like our language."

While Mom and I talked about secret languages, Trent was arguing with

Hanna about whether he needed to give her his license plate numbers.

"You don't need my plate numbers," he said condescendingly. "It's the only G-Wagon in the Southland region."

"Well, isn't that special," Hanna said.

I asked Mom: "What about *gedda brusha?*"

"Nope."

"And what about *dis en lo flestulo?*"

"Flestulo means 'book,'" Mom said instantly. "Or maybe *guide.* We had a lot of homonyms."

"Homonyms?"

"Words with the same spelling that mean different things," she said.

Hanna was losing patience. "Sir, I'm gonna need those plates. What if I need to put out an APB?"

Mom stood and addressed Trent: "Baby, just give her your plate number."

Mac and I met eyes. Our expression said, *Gross. She called him "baby."*

Trent finally relented: "NDT four thirty-one."

Flestulo, I thought. *Book. Guide.*

"Or maybe brochure?" I said to myself.

Zo vaxap dis en lo flestulo.

The map is in the brochure.

I still held the brochure-map of the Gold Rush park, its corners flicking in the wind. In the middle of the park sat the Mystery Mansion. It looked like a kooky version version of the Bates Motel, its proportions all swollen and out of whack, like it had been filtered through a funhouse mirror.

Kind of like Professor Wizardo and Zygor when they enter the Most Intense Dimension.

Which reminded me of something. I pulled out my personal map of the park in all of its graphite and yellowing notebook paper glory. I superimposed it on the official brochure-map, lining up the two depictions of the Mystery Mansion.

I jumped to my feet and triumphantly stuttered:

"Uh! *Uhhh!* Um! Uh, yes, I was uh thinking!"

Hanna

"Uh! *Uhhh!* Um! Uh, yes, I was uh thinking!"

The poor kid was basically making noises to draw attention. Hanna, who knew of Hiram's stutter, gave him a kindly look.

"Something on your mind?"

"And so uh there's someplace else we can look."

Justin shook his head, crossed his arms. "We searched the whole park."

"Uh the new park, yeah," Hiram said. "Uh but you didn't search the old one."

"Old one?" Justin asked.

"Here, check it out!" Hiram said, running as fast as his little legs could carry him to the benches, where he spread out a park brochure-map and an ancient-looking piece of notebook paper. Hanna scanned everyone's faces: Trent, her sister's shithead of a new boyfriend, looked at Hiram like he was deficient.

Don't you dare judge my blood because he's a little overweight, Hanna thought. She'd done everything she could to talk Corrie out of dating him, but when Corrie Blackledge Gresham got it in her, she'd dig in her heels worse than an ornery stallion. Hanna didn't like what she'd heard about Trent's son, either, though she'd yet to meet the young man, but as for Kaitlyn . . . well, there might be something to work with there.

Hanna stepped closer, peering over Hiram's shoulder. The ancient paper was a makeshift map the boy had sketched; good work, too. He had talent, if only he'd try to cultivate it. Everyone else gathered around, too. Mac and Kaitlyn were both smiling at Hiram's exuberance.

Corrie asked: "Sweetie, what's going on?"

Hiram went on like she hadn't spoken: "Look: Susie Schuppe's Smoky Mountain Gold Rush used to be another park."

Hanna: "I remember. Santa's Holiday King—"

"Kingdom, yeah," he said. Hanna noticed he managed to say "kingdom" without stuttering. *He must really be excited.* Hiram continued: "You can still see the remnants of the old park in Christmasville. When Ms. Schuppe bought the park, she built everything else around it—or *on top of it.*"

"If you're talking about the old gondola stations, we searched 'em both," Justin said.

"Did you search the third one?" Hiram asked.

"Hell if there's a third one," Justin said. "Where?"

"There were two gondola lines back in the seventies. There was the line that went from one end of the park to another—"

Justin indicated two points on the brochure-map. "With stations here and here. We searched 'em both."

"And there was also a *second* gondola line with a *third* station," Hiram said, waving a hand in a theatrical flourish. "Guess where it is?"

Mac smiled and Kaitlyn stifled a giggle. Corrie's expression was inscrutable, while Trent gritted his teeth. Hanna sensed he was about to explode.

"Don't keep us in suspense, buddy," Hanna prompted.

"Right here." He pointed at the Mystery Mansion.

Justin looked incredulous.

"There's a gondola station *there?* In the Mystery Mansion?"

"Look," Hiram said, indicating his old map, which depicted a gondola station in the center of the park. He overlaid his hand-drawn map onto the official brochure-map. His drawing of the old gondola station exactly matched the kooky silhouette of the current Mystery Mansion. "They closed it down in seventy-nine."

"Where'd it go?" Justin asked. "The gondola?"

"Up to Ober Gatlinburg," Hiram said. "When Susie Schuppe—"

"Hold that thought, little guy," Hanna said, making for the door. "You can tell us on the way."

Hiram's Journal

The back hallways of the Mystery Mansion were hallowed ground for me. I'd only ever gotten the occasional peek at them when performers slipped backstage, and now here I was being escorted into the most secret-secret parts of my favorite ride. Plywood walls and cement floors abounded, interrupted occasionally by unusual machinery and apparatuses: hulking driveshafts chugging away and rubber belts spinning. Overhead, catwalks led to various doorways, all marked PRIVATE or EMPLOYEES ONLY. Posters hung here and there; mostly movie posters along with some Cindy Crawfords and Kathy Irelands clipped from *Sports Illustrated.*

The park was still open, so voices of guests filtered through the walls. Laughter and squeals mixed with delighted shrieks, the latter of which seemed to rattle Trent. I already didn't like the guy, but I couldn't blame him for feeling anxiety when his son was missing and the most notorious serial killer in the country was at large.

Justin came up beside me. "Where to, kid?"

"We need to get into the ride itself," I said. "Can we do that?"

"Can you pause the ride for a minute?" Hanna asked.

"Sure, give me a sec," Justin said, disappearing through an access door. A moment later, he poked his head back in the door and waved us through. "Come on!"

A muffled voice announced throughout the ride: *"Ladies and gentlemen, we are experiencing a brief technical difficulty. Remain seated. The ride will continue shortly."*

Justin led us down a narrow passage that ran alongside the ride vehicles. Our way was lit by red emergency lights set into the floor. A slash of light flashed, and Justin opened another door, leading us into the ride's first scene, where Professor Wizardo first combined the two fateful chemicals to unleash the Most Intense Dimension. Ride vehicles stood idle. Employees were escorting guests out emergency exits. Halogen lights cast everything in a strange cold haze. Dust motes danced. Trent stood with his arms crossed, grimacing, breathing shallowly.

Everyone turned to me.

"Okay, kid, what now?" Justin asked.

"Sheriff?" It was Trent. He looked green. "Can we please call in more help? Please."

"I done did, but they're tied up, same as before," Hanna said, crossing to him. She looked him dead in the eyes. "Let's follow this lead till it ends. Unless you got something better to do?"

"No."

Hanna turned to me. "Hiram? What's our next move?"

I frowned, looked at the walls. "It's not in here. Maybe a couple rooms down? The outer-space room?"

Kaitlyn: "How do you *know?*"

My stutter returned: "Uh um the wall. It's the wrong shape."

She cocked an eyebrow comically and adopted a fussy British accent: "The wrong *shape*, you say?"

"Johnson, can you clear a path for us?" Hanna asked. "Don't want folks flippin' their lid when a law officer comes traipsing through."

Justin nodded and ran ahead.

Mac walked over and elbowed me. "You sure about all this?"

I shrugged. "Nope. But I know there's a secret room in here."

Justin leaned back in and waved us ahead. We walked through the "Zygor pratfalling" room and into the Most Intense Dimension. Black curtains and fiber optics hung in the bright lights, which revealed that the miniature animatronics of Professor Wizardo and Zygor were held aloft by thin lengths of wire. The emergency lights further revealed that the animatronics were incomplete; they were only the front shells of Wizardo and Zygor; tucked into the open cavity were more fiber-optics lights.

Auntie Hanna was saying something behind me, but I didn't hear it. I was too focused on the black scrim. It was showing its age—sections were threadbare and thin, showing ghostly glimpses of the walls beyond.

Spaces create shapes.

That weird secret room in my house, the Office, created a little convexity that poked out into the walk-in closet. When I saw that shape, I knew there had to be a room back there. I knew there had to be a secret.

Shapes hold secrets.

But it wasn't a secret. Mom knew about the Office. Mac knew about the Office. It was just that they knew about it before I was born and forgot to tell me. In their minds, I *did* know, and its existence was mundane, a fact of everyday life.

I couldn't believe that something happened in the past that I didn't know about. There must be a bespoke-beautiful German word for that feeling, that silly sense of amazement at how people who were alive before you were born knew stuff you didn't.

That night in the park, I didn't know if we'd find Jason, but I knew that room held a secret.

I muttered to myself: "Spaces hold shapes. Shapes hold secrets. Spaces hold shapes. Shapes hold secrets."

I took hold of the scrim and looked up. It hung from a rod like a giant shower curtain.

"Can I pull this back?" I asked Justin.

"Sure," he said with a shrug.

I pulled the scrim aside to reveal the facade of a German chalet-style building protruding from the wall. It was like the ride had swallowed the building. Everyone gaped at it.

"The old gondola house," I said.

"Has this always been here?" Justin asked.

I grinned at him. I knew the feeling. We all stepped closer. It looked like something out of a storybook, the facade, with a gilded front door and stained-glass windows criss-crossed with lattices of wood.

Shoonk. Metal slid against leather.

"Quiet, everyone." It was Hanna. She'd pulled her service revolver. That's when I saw it: one of the windows had been smashed. She stepped closer to the gilded door and addressed Justin over her shoulder: "They let you pack here?"

"Just this, ma'am." He drew a can of pepper spray.

"That'll do," she said. "Get it ready. Better stand back, folks." She called inside: *"Police! I'm entering with my weapon drawn! Throw down your weapons and get on the floor with your hands on your head! Acknowledge you heard me!"*

Silence. More silence.

And then a groan. Trent lurched forward.

"Jason?"

Another groan. It was unmistakably Jason's voice.

Trent burst into tears. "I'm so sorry I yelled at you! Wanna get some

TCBY?"

Mac, Kaitlyn, and I all looked at each other. When you're a chuckleheaded little kid, you don't really understand how grief and distress work. Trent's question sounded ridiculous and childish. I wanted to laugh, but I knew I shouldn't. All the same, a distant and cruel part of me enjoyed seeing him so vulnerable.

It'd be a long time before I'd see him that way again.

Hanna came and gripped his shoulder. "Sir, I'm gonna need you to gather yourself. The boy's name is Jason, right?"

"Jason Lewis Sutton."

"Thank you," Hanna said and turned back toward the facade. "Jason! It's the police. Are you alone?"

The next moment remains seared in my memory. Jason's voice was slurred. I didn't know it then, but it was the kind of slurring that comes from head trauma: "Ee ed ay ud lie."

A fell wind blew through the room. Trent turned stark white. Justin's jaw clenched. Jason voice was slurred, but we all heard the words:

Ee ed ay ud lie.

He said I could fly.

Hanna swallowed and made a battlefield decision:

"Johnson, we gotta move. I think he's alone. You agree?"

"The hell do I know?"

"I know you were a cop. You agree? Got a gut feeling?"

Justin gave a curt nod. "Yeah, I think he's alone."

"Okay. We're going in."

Moments later, the coast was clear. Justin came and escorted us into the old gondola house. A dark and dusty foyer greeted us. Cartoony portraits of Christmas characters dotted the walls—Santa's uncle, Wilbur Claus; the nine Muses of the Holidays—all ghostly with vignettes of cobwebs. Dim light slanted into a room ahead where a pair of prone legs could be seen through a doorway. Trent shouldered his way past us.

"Jase!"

We all filed into a the gondola house's main room. A boarded-over set of glass doors stood on the far side while another set of double doors stood closed to the right. A wooden sign hung over the glass doors, burn-engraved with the words *THIS WAY TO OBER GATLINBURG SKY-GONDOLA, LOWER STATION.* The decor was that of an old-world German chalet done in a cheesy, American caricature. The hardwood floors bowed and splintered under our feet.

Trent kneeled next to Jason, who sat with his back against a wall. A cone of dusty-orange light cut through the gloom. When I entered, a strange instinct made me raise my hand. I swiped at the sky before I realized nothing was there. Lowering my hand, I wondered what the heck I was doing when it hit me:

The room was the same trapezoidal shape as the Office. I'd been reaching for the light switch, but it wasn't there.

Even weirder, Jason was sitting in the same place where a school-desk was in the Office, while a bank of brochures mirrored the location of a box of old junk. A shiver ran through me.

Trent took Jason's hands in his while Kaitlyn hovered over his shoulder.

"Ohmigod, ohmigod, ohmigod," Trent said.

Mom, Mac, and I hung back with Hanna, while Justin ducked back out the front door. Another set of double doors stood behind us. A nasty gash split Jason's forehead, the wound scored with pitch and wood splinters. A few rivulets ran down his cheek, but the injury was already scabbing over.

This had happened a while ago.

Hanna got on her shoulder radio: "Radio, this is Blackledge over at the Gold Rush park. I need an ambulance and EMTs out front of the park ASAP. I've got a white male, approximately seventeen, head trauma."

"Copy that, Blackledge," a female voice responded.

Kaitlyn was crying. "Is he gonna be okay?"

The question passed by Hanna, who said: "Mr. Sutton, I'm gonna have to ask you to step back so I can have a word with your boy."

Justin returned with a first-aid kit. He kneeled and opened it, dabbing alcohol on gauze to clean Jason's wound. Kaitlyn and Trent both stepped back next to us. Hanna took a knee and doffed her hat.

"Son, do you know where you are?"

Jason blinked, squinted, shook his head. "No."

His voice sounded normal again. Trent exhaled. Hanna took Jason's hand.

"You're in the Gold Rush park," she said. "You know what day of the week it is?"

"Friday?"

"Right you are. What year?"

"Nineteen eighty-nine."

"You have any idea how you got back here—"

Everyone's hands clamped over their ears. Justin was so startled he fell on his rear. Hanna almost pulled her gun before she realized what was happening. Mom stared at me like I'd lost my mind.

I was screaming.

Something had exploded inside me; some deep-seated instinct had taken over so all I could do was scream . . . and point. My finger wagged at something over Jason's head, but no one noticed. Justin stood and slowly approached me.

"Kid, kid . . ."

My voice lost meaning. It became white noise, a shrill beacon sounding from someplace else. I was pointing; Why wouldn't they look?

"Hiram? Honey?" It was Mom. Her words meant nothing.

Arms engulfed me. I shut up. Rough polyester crinkled across Kevlar as I was swaddled in the scent of Emeraude and liniment. Auntie Hanna was hugging me, hard.

"Shhh, shhh," she whispered. "It's okay. It's okay." She glanced at Justin and said, "Keep an eye out."

Justin nodded, pulled his mace, and scanned the scene. Everyone relaxed a little once I got quiet. Mom was giving Auntie Hanna a hard look, which she didn't notice. Holstering her weapon, she took my shoulders.

"What's the matter, big guy? I know it's scary in here, but—"

"Over his head," I said, pointing. Jason was sitting under a bank of framed posters hawking the wares of Ober Gatlinburg. One poster was for the very same restaurant Trent had been talking up earlier: Ottokars, only this poster included an unusual detail: a medieval coat of arms for the Ottokars family, divided into quadrants . . . one of which was the same plaid pattern as the man from my dreams.

But of course no one knew that.

Trent squinted at me. "The . . . restaurant? What? What're you talking . . ."

"Uh no," I whispered. "Uh pattern fabric. Uh the plaid."

The moment passed; Trent turned his attention back to his son: "Jase? Answer the sheriff's question. We need to know what happened. If there's anything you can remember, you need to tell us."

Jason finally started talking, but we couldn't hear him. While he and his father exchanged whispers, Justin quietly stepped over to the Ottokars poster, frowning. Hanna seemed to sense Justin's unease. She stood and crossed over next to him. Justin bent over for a closer look. Swooping underneath the coat of arms was a motto: *Scio ubi sit locus.*

"What in the—" Justin whispered.

He tapped the Latin words with a fingertip, and white fluid oozed out from underneath them. He used his fingertip to press harder. More white oozed out. Dabbing some onto his fingertip, he smelled it.

"Glue," he said, and that's when he noticed the same white ooze outlining the quadrant of plaid. He pressed the plaid quadrant, and it slid aside, revealing a medieval lion underneath, smeared with glue. He did the same with the motto, revealing another underneath: *Venite ad me avolare.*

"Oh, my God," Hanna said. "Do . . . do you think they had to fix the poster at some point? Change mottos?"

"I don't know," Justin said. "That glue seems pretty fresh."

"If we're gonna lock down this park and cause a panic, I wanna be completely sure."

"Right."

Trent noticed the exchange. "What's wrong?"

"Nothing, we don't think," Hanna said, then addressed Justin: "Are we closing this park down or not?"

"He says he hit his head," Trent said.

"Well, that much is obvious," Hanna said.

Trent: "You don't need to shut down the park."

"That'll be our call to make, Mr. Sutton."

Jason sat up a bit. "I came in here to look around and hit my head."

"Got it," Hanna said. "What we need to know is if you had help. How'd you even know *how* to get in here? Justin works the ride and didn't even know this was here."

"Someone let me in."

"Who?"

A moment passed before Trent spoke: "He came up here with a girl."

"He tell you that?" Hanna asked.

"He did."

"Think he can tell a law officer the same thing, or do we need to make this official?"

Trent looked at Jason. "Son?"

"I met a girl on the ride earlier. She was in costume working one of the scenes."

The Bride, I thought. *What was her name?*

Justin asked: "She brought you up here?"

"Yeah, there's another way in through there." Jason indicated the double doors behind us. My skin tingled; I suddenly felt creeped out that I'd been standing with my back to them that whole time. Justin gave a wry smile.

"Damn. Folks had been saying they smelled something funny on the ride."

Trent: "He didn't come up here to get high."

"I already said I don't care, sir."

"*We* don't care," Hanna said. "I just want to know if there's a chance Skelton is working the park; if we need to do something." She addressed Jason:

"What's this young lady's name?"

"Jenny something."

"Any idea where Jenny is now?"

Jason shook his head, his eyes going a little glassy.

"You don't know?" Hanna asked, cocking an eyebrow.

"It was . . . We came up here. To look around."

Hanna scoffed quietly. "And after you had a 'look around,' what happened?"

"Jenny wanted to get something to eat. We were on our way out . . . I lost her . . . and I hit my head."

"You fell?"

Jason grimaced. "No, I was . . . running. After her. I ran into something. Through there."

He pointed at the double doors. Hanna and Justin shared a look.

"Might coulda happened," Hanna said. "Wanna have a look?"

Justin nodded. "Sure."

Hanna shouldered her radio up to her mouth: "Radio, what's the ETA on that ambulance?"

A squawk, and: "Sorry, still en route, Blackledge. ETA twenty or thirty. That wreck's still got most of 'em tied up."

"Copy that, thanks, radio." She addressed us: "All of you, stay here. Mr. Sutton, keep cleaning that wound. Johnson and I are gonna check out this next room."

Justin

Justin Johnson's police training was coming back online like an old program left dormant in a forgotten memory bank. He slid against the wall, wishing his mace were a gun and praying to holy God there weren't any prize ribbons waiting for them in this dank hallway.

Prize ribbons. Skelton's calling card.

Click. Blackledge lit her flashlight, nodding at him to do the same. He clicked his on and crossed his wrists so both his light and the mace aimed forward. They crept down the hallway, which featured more faux German cheese and faded hardwood floors turning to dust. Blackledge's lungs had a slight rasp at the bottom of every breath; he wondered if she was (or had been) a smoker. His momma sounded like that.

Before she passed.

He dismissed the memory. *No time for that.*

The sheriff's voice rumbled: "Wary eyes, Officer."

"Not what I am anymore," he said. "Officer."

"You got a raw deal. We all know it. Who'd you draw from Knoxville IA?"

"Colquitt," he said, thinking of his cruel eyes. Bo Colquitt attended every day of Skelton's monthlong trial, sitting in the front row and smirking at Justin all while the district attorney blamed him for the killer's escape.

In response to Colquitt's name, Blackledge audibly shuddered.

"Colquitt. That guy is a serious asshole."

"Tell me about it."

"You were only doing your job."

As they crept forward, their lights brought various details flashing into view: more posters for Ober Gatlinburg, graffiti, some Polaroid photos stuck to the wall.

"I dunno," Justin said. "Sometimes I think I should've let those folks do theirs."

"Think you could live with yourself if you did?"

"Not for a solitary moment," Justin said, stopping to study something on the wall. "Look at this."

Hundreds of Polaroid photos covered the wall. Another wood-engraved sign over them read, *TAKE A PHOTO WEARING OBER SKY-GONDOLA TEE, AND RIDE FOR FREE.* The pics showed people in various worldwide locales, all wearing Ober Gatlinburg Sky-Gondola merchandise. Hanna stepped closer.

"What am I looking at here, Johnson?"

Most of the photos looked normal, except one: It was nothing but a gleaming bar of white against a black background. Justin plucked it off the wall and showed it to the sheriff.

"See anything?"

Blackledge took the photo and shined her light on it. "Looks like someone left their thumb over the lens. Probably got put up there as a joke."

"But look."

Justin flipped the photo over. Its back was smeared with white paste, same as the Ottokars poster. Hanna inhaled slightly.

"Okay, that's weird," she said. "But doesn't Skel—y'know, doesn't he leave prize ribbons?"

"You can say his name. It's okay." He took the photo and looked at the front. "Skelton left ribbons at his murder scenes, all right. Except for one."

"Which one was that?"

Justin's breath caught in his chest. He steadied himself. "Jamie Scott Glenn. Victim number seven. Skelton forgot to bring any ribbons with him that night. But Jamie had one of those disposable cameras in his room. Skelton left a picture of himself on it. God Almighty, but I still get nightmares about it." He tapped the Polaroid. "The frame's white. Looks brand new." He held it up against the rest of the photos, which were yellowing.

Hanna shook her head. "You sure about that?" She shined her flashlight across more photos, some of which had white frames and depicted various Mystery Mansion employees clowning around in costume. "Looks like lots of kids knew about this place. Probably became a hangout for 'em."

Justin kept staring at the Polaroid.

Hanna lowered her flashlight. "Johnson, I get it. They did you dirty back in the day and you wanna make it right. I would, too. But we gotta do our jobs, and unless there's conclusive proof Skelton was here—"

"Wait," Justin said, shining his light over her shoulder. "You're right. Look."

He crossed to a low-hanging wooden cross-beam. His light revealed a bloody divot notched into it. Blackledge came and ran her fingers through it; they came away stained with blood and pitch.

"Didn't the Sutton boy have some pitch on his head?"

"Yeah. I bet he and that girl came up here, fooled around, then went runnin' out this way."

"He hits his head. Tall kid like that, be easy to do. Rings his bell, staggers back in there . . ."

"Hits the floor, out cold. Probably got a concussion."

Blackledge stowed her firearm.

"We need to quit playing Sherlock Holmes and get ready for that ambulance."

"Yeah, for sure," Justin said, heading back.

"Johnson?" He stopped. She went on: "You sure you feel right about lettin' this go?"

Justin fidgeted, frowned. "What if Skelton—"

A voice rang out: *"Sheriff!"*

Hanna

Johnson took off like he was shot out of a cannon, the double doors back into the gondola house already swinging wildly from his momentum. Hanna tried to keep pace, but she nearly pulled a hamstring.

Mental note, Blackledge: Next time, stretch out before you go on duty.

Hanna stumbled back into the main room to find Johnson facing down Trent, who was brandishing a piece of paper.

"Have a look," he said, handing it to Johnson, who read it and passed it to Hanna.

The note was scrawled in wriggly cursive: *Talk to you later, sexy. 615 555-*

6958. Jenny.

"Where'd this come from?" Hanna asked.

"It was in your pocket, wasn't it, big guy?"

Jason nodded, but he looked like he was going to be sick. He burst into tears. Hanna's radio squelched.

"Blackledge, we've got an updated ETA on that ambulance. Should be there inside of ten minutes."

"Thank you, radio," Hanna said, stepping toward Jason. "Son, what's wrong?"

Suddenly Kaitlyn was screaming: "Shut up! Don't fuckin' laugh at him! Don'cha got any feelings?!"

Hiram and Mac were the targets of her rage, but they didn't appear to be laughing.

Mac started: "But we weren't—"

"Shut up!" Kaitlyn yelled.

"We weren't laughing!" Mac screamed.

Corrie, who seemed to have gone into hibernation, sprang to life with a shout:

"Mackenzie Lynn Gresham! Don't raise your voice like that!"

Hanna opened her mouth to defend her niece and nephew, but a nasty look from Corrie shut her up. It was an old story: Corrie yelling at her kids for the wrong reasons, while Hanna tried to take up their cause. Hanna knew it wasn't her place—after all, they were Corrie's kids, not hers—but she couldn't stand how unfairly Corrie treated her own flesh and blood.

But instead of picking a fight with her sister, Hanna shifted gears, offering a hand to Jason:

"Let's get you to that ambulance, kiddo." She hefted the kid to his feet, almost getting pulled off balance by his bulk. She addressed Trent: "Mind if I take down that phone number, Mr. Sutton? I'd like to make sure Ms. Jenny made it home okay."

Hiram's Journal

The diagnosis was: a mild concussion and a few stitches. Mac and I were hoping it'd be enough to scuttle our dinner plans, but as soon as the doctors at urgent care gave Jason a clean bill of health, Trent hopped in his fancypants G-Wagon and led us (in Mom's non-fancypants Sentra) up the switchback road. As much as spending more time with these jerks made me want to hurl, I was still bouncing in my seat all the way up the mountain, watching the city lights shrink below us.

I was finally going to see Ober Gatlinburg!

It was like someone grabbed a fistful of Buellton and dropped it in the Smokies. Little restaurants, wineries, and attractions were spread across the mountainside. The sky was foreboding, the land festive. The change in elevation was somehow modest yet dramatic—West Chim was autumn cool, but Ober Gatlinburg was locked in the dead of a fertile winter. Wind howled and snow flew, all while the moon glinted and peeked through heavy steely-black storm clouds. Meanwhile, golden lights pushed back the winter darkness, shining the way for hundreds of chattering tourists who all flowed between and among Ober Gatlinburg's cozy chalets, cabins, and cottages. Gatlinburg PD even had a small outpost tucked up here that, for some reason, resembled a medieval pub, complete with a wooden shingle hung out front.

"Right this way," Trent crowed, leading us to an unmarked wooden door with a stained-glass inlay. I learned that night that some of the most chi-chi places didn't have signs at all.

White tablecloths, dark-finished wood, and exposed, hanging light bulbs were the order of the day at Ottokars, which looked like a cross between a classic mountain lodge and a gentrified Brooklyn eatery. The atmosphere immediately put me ill at ease; I was wearing my usual dorky combo of jeans and a T-shirt, while Mac's outfit wasn't much better. Jason and Kaitlyn had emerged from Trent's G-Wagon looking like they were ready for a cocktail party: Jason had thrown on a navy blue sport coat, while Kaitlyn had put on a black dress.

"Do they keep a change of clothes in their car?" Mac whispered to me.

Inside, the maître d' discreetly slipped me my own sport coat. Because I was too fat for all the kids' blazers, I had to wear an adult-sized one that swam on my frame—as if I didn't already feel self-conscious enough. Mac, though, had me beat in that department. When she saw the caliber of guests at Ottokars, her face turned bright red. She and Mom had put on a little extra makeup, but she still looked underdressed. She picked at the rhinestones she'd glued to her Susie Schuppe T-shirt and looked miserable.

"You look like you're going to a county fair, sweetheart," Kaitlyn said the moment we sat down. Mac looked like she wanted to crawl under the table, but before she could, Kaitlyn took her hand and whispered, "You're a size seven, right?"

Mac's head snapped up. "Shhh."

"Oh, boo hoo. Am I right or not?"

I couldn't hear Mac's next words.

"Close enough," Kaitlyn said, standing. "Come with me." She addressed

Trent: "Dad, we gotta go do girl stuff."

Trent looked horrified. "She's not . . . is she?"

Kaitlyn looked like she'd just sniffed a fart. *"Ugh, Dad!* You're re-*volt*-ing."

"Well, I'm only asking."

Corrie volunteered: "She's had it, but she's not on it." She hesitated. "Are you?"

By this point, Mac had buried her face in her hands. "No."

"Oh-*kay!*" Kaitlyn said. "Soooooo all you creepers stay here while I go help her look a little less like a hobo. We'll be right back."

"Wait, wait, wait," Trent said, eyeing Jason's stitches. "You're just going out to the car, right?"

"*Daaaaaaa*d. There's nothing to worry about. Those cops were *tres merde-*heads."

Mom's eyelids fluttered. "Deak—Hiram—Mac—*Mackenzie Lynn*, just be careful, okay?"

That happened a lot with Mom. She could never remember anyone's name, so she rattled off the name of every person in the family until she got to the right one. At the time, I found it mortifying the way a kid always feels about their dorky parents. Looking back, I wish I'd been more perceptive.

With the keys to Trent's mighty G-Wagon in hand, the girls left. Trent twined his fingers and regarded my mom.

"Hey, can I ask why you didn't tell me about your husband?"

My skin went cold on instinct. This wasn't the kind of question that got asked around our house, but because it came from an outside party, Mom had to answer.

"It's none of your business," she said brattily, eyes downcast.

Trent leaned back. It was like a tectonic plate shifting. His eyes went steely. I thought he was about to lay into her, but the moment passed. He shrugged.

"Next time you'll tell me," he said flatly. "So, Ms. Elementary School Teacher, are your students as tough as mine?"

"Oh, they're fine," she said, chuffing my shoulder. "Do you always bring your 'students' with you on a second date?"

So it's only their second date, I thought, frantically trying to conjure a way to break them up.

Jason swayed in his seat.

"Um, is your head okay?" I whispered.

"My knee hurts," he whined. "Was anyone else there?"

Trent: "Not usually. But it's been a while since my last second date."

"How long?" Mom asked.

Trent's eyes rose as he did the math. "Twenty years?" He corrected himself, astonished: "Twenty-seven. God, it's been that long. *Marie* and I had our first date in eighth grade, if you can call sneaking into *The Music Man* a first date."

Mom smiled at the way he pronounced his late wife's name; he said it trippingly, with a slight lilt.

"Was she French?"

"No, German. I could never keep the accents straight, though."

Jason's question confused me. "Uh was anyone else where?"

"When you found me in that ride. Was anyone else there?"

Mackenzie

The snowfall had become a blizzard.

Lights and happily chattering voices pushed through the swirling snow while Mackenzie followed Kaitlyn, who seemed to glide over the mess like she was on snowshoes. She yelled something over her shoulder.

"What?" Mac said.

"What're you, about five-eight?"

"Five-nine," Mac said, bracing herself. She'd learned to brace herself for insults any time her size was the subject of conversation, and with this bitch, she knew she had to be extra careful.

Trent's idiotically gigantic Mercedes-Benz G-Wagon came hulking into view like a megalith emerging from a stormy sea. Kaitlyn unlocked the back and opened a trunk full of clothes. Kaitlyn pulled out another black dress, this one quite a bit longer than the one she was wearing.

"Well, bully for you, tons of fun."

There it is, the insult, Mac thought ruefully. Kaitlyn held the dress up to her torso.

"Here, I think you can cram your ass into this."

"Hey, I'm only a couple sizes bigger than you," Mac said.

Kaitlyn snorted. "Yeah, a couple *dozen*."

Mac wanted to scream and run, but instead she snatched the dress.

"Fine, I'll *cram my ass* into it."

"Wait. When's the last time you got a haircut?"

"Two weeks ago."

Another voice floated through the snow: "Feels balmy."

It was a woman's voice. Mac had heard it before and felt an impulse to investigate, but she was too busy bracing herself for whatever insult Kaitlyn had in store about her hair.

"That's what they gave you at the stylist?" Kaitlyn said. "Like, you *asked* for that cut? On purpose?"

"Yeah," Mac said, advancing on her. "What's wrong with it?"

That same woman's voice again, but quieter, farther away: "Balmy. Balmy." *Where is it that coming from?*

"What's *wrong* with it is one hundred percent of absolutely everything. You look like a reject from *Desperately Seeking Susan*."

"I *like* that movie."

Kaitlyn opened one of the G-Wagon's rear doors. "Me too, but I don't wanna *look* like it."

"Hey, bite me."

"You're the one who wanted a new outfit."

"I didn't ask to come out here."

"The look on your face inside communicated maximum mortification, sister. Listen, no offense intended."

"Like when you called me a fat pig?"

She cackled and patted Mac on the head. Kaitlyn was so effortlessly gorgeous and thin and rich, without a worry in the world, and now here she was laughing at her like she was some stupid hayseed.

"That. Was. A. Joke. Ain't you gotta sensa humor?"

Kaitlyn didn't know it, but she came very close to getting punched that night. Instead, Mac turned on her heel.

"I'm going back inside."

"Wait, wait, wait! At least put on the dress!" She cocked her head at the Benz. "Tinted windows. I'll keep a watch out for pervs."

Mac hesitated, but the prospect of going back inside wearing her current outfit was too much to bear. She climbed in the G-Wagon and slammed the door, cutting off the howling wind. A few stray snowflakes snuck inside and melted across the dress. Mac checked the label—*Valentino*—and realized it probably cost thousands of dollars. A sudden urge to tear it to pieces seized her but was halted by a strange realization:

It was quiet inside the car.

Between her and Hiram having to share a room and the near-constant racket (from music to shouting to video games), she rarely got to sit alone in silence. God, it was nice to be alone for once. Leaning over, she breath-fogged the glass and fingertip-wrote a single word:

Dad.

Kaitlyn's silhouette hovered outside.

"C'mon, you fall in? It's a cocktail dress. Just pull it on over your head."

"I know how to put on a stupid dress!" she yelled, wiping away the word with her forearm. "Sheez."

It took her a couple of minutes to change. A dark shape blocked the light outside.

"Slimy."

"What?" Mac asked.

It was that strange woman's voice, only she hadn't been saying *balmy*.

"They felt slimy," she said.

Kaitlyn, outside: "Lady, are you all right?"

"Her teeth. Her teeth."

Hiram's Journal

"Evening, Trent."

A middle-aged man with leathery-tanned skin was standing before us, hands clasped. His attire almost matched Trent's: sport coat, slacks, button-down with no tie. He'd slicked his silverback-gray hair to his skull. I don't know if you've ever seen the movie *Love at First Bite,* but he reminded me of the guy who played Count Dracula, George Hamilton. It occurred to me that this was our waiter.

"Georgie!" Trent said, and I had to stifle a giggle at the coincidence. "How are ya, buddy?"

Bafflingly, they shook hands. I leaned over and whispered: "Mom? I thought he was the waiter."

"Shhh, honey. He is."

Until Ottokars, the fanciest restaurant I'd ever been to was indeed a Ryan's Steakhouse or maybe an Applebee's, and and the oldest waitstaff I ever saw was a booger-brained teenager. Now there was a grown-up man waiting on us, and he seemed to be friends with one of the customers? Suddenly George Hamilton was smiling at me.

"First time here?" He was speaking to Trent but indicating me.

Trent patted my shoulder cheerfully. It almost knocked me to the ground.

"It's his first time anywhere, I'd wager!"

The men both laughed. Mom blushed, but the source of embarrassment eluded me. As Trent and George kept joking around, Jason touched my knee.

"What about Jenny?"

"Who?" I asked. "Oh, your girlfriend."

That's how little I knew about anything. Jason and Jenny hung out for one afternoon, so I thought they were boyfriend-girlfriend.

"Not my—" He broke off, massaging his brow. Even then, I knew we all should've gone home. He was really hurt.

I whispered: "Uh maybe you can go home?"

"Was Jenny there? Did her mom come get her?"

"Uh no. She wasn't there. Don't you remember? She was gone when we found you."

Jason said nothing. His eyes looked glassy, vacant. I thought about telling Trent, but he was too busy fucking around with George.

"How's the tasting menu this week?"

"Kitsy just changed it," George said. "Added two new courses, one an aperitif, the other a new dessert that he picked up from a sabbatical in Osaka."

"Perfecto," Trent said. "Let's do that and wine pairings."

Does this guy ever look at his own son? He looks really bad.

Corrie touched Trent's hand. "Baby, I don't want any wine—"

"You know this is my treat, right?"

Jason's eyes were suddenly burning into me: "Are you sure I was alone? He said he was going to be watching from the attic."

Mackenzie

Mac climbed out of the car to find an older woman, maybe mid-fifties, wearing only a black T-shirt (for the band Heart) and pajama pants. No shoes. The temperature must've been in the twenties, and she had no shoes. The weird part was she didn't look like she was homeless; no, she looked more like she'd been rousted from bed.

Something wet glistened on her shirt; What was it?

"Mom, my teeth feel slimy! I can't stop licking them," she said. Her attention was elsewhere, her gaze locked on the horizon. She dry-washed her hands, pausing to tap her teeth with a fingernail: *click, click.* "Braces. I thought that was funny because you lick your teeth every day, don't you? Gone."

The woman wandered past them, kicking up snow-eddies in her wake.

"Lady, are you all right?" Kaitlyn called.

"I should probably call her school to let them know she won't be in this week."

Mac shivered. "What's wrong with her?"

"Micah said he wanted to stay at a friend's house. That makes sense. Braces. Her braces. I think I maxed out the Discover. I'll have to call her—" The woman broke off her thought and spun back toward them, responding to something they hadn't said: "Oh, you're right. I should call Vickie, see if she can take him for a week or two, shouldn't I? Goodness, that's two calls I need to make: her school and Vickie."

Hiram's Journal

Before I could respond to Jason's weird question, I realized George was asking me something.

"Uh what?"

Mom patted the table, a mild admonition: "Be polite, dear. Don't say 'what.'"

"Oh, uh excuse me, sorry. I didn't hear you, sir."

"Nothing to be sorry about," George said. "I was wondering if you were a spring baby or a winter baby?"

"April."

"No kidding!" George said, his eyes aflare with happy crow's feet. "Me too. How old are you going to be?"

"Twelve."

"Got it. Y'know, Kitsy has something special cooking for all our April birthday guests. I'll bring it out a little bit at a time with everyone else's food. That okay with you?"

"Okay," I said. I didn't know it at the time, but George was doing me a kindness. A gourmet tasting menu might've been too much for me to handle, so he had a kiddie menu on tap, just in case. He concocted the "spring baby or winter baby" schtick to save me the trouble of asking for it. Not for nothing, but I liked the way George spoke to me. He spoke to me like I was a grown-up.

I never got to see the meal, though.

"Kitsy's also got a signature cocktail on tap tonight," George said. "You two all right with a surprise?"

Trent looked to my mom for her okay.

"Water's fine for me," she said to Trent's disappointment.

"Count me in," Trent said. "None for this clown, though." He elbowed Jason.

"Of course not," George said. "How about an Arnold Palmer, big guy?"

Jason stared at the table. Silence settled and unsettled.

"Water's fine," Trent said, wincing. He was rubbing his knee.

"Be right back, folks."

George bustled off. My mom looked dazzled.

"Kitsy?"

"Oh, that's short for Kittredge, Teddy Kittredge. Sorry, *Theo* Kittredge now. Old Duke buddy, Kitsy. He runs this place."

"You *know* the owner?"

"You kidding? He and I used to do keg stands together before the old homo became *Chef Theo*," he said with a snort. A look of disgust crossed Mom's face, but she said nothing. The big asshole twined his fingers behind his head. "Tempus really does fugit, doesn't it?"

Jason whispered: "When did she leave?"

"Wait a minute," I whispered back. "Who was in the attic? And *where* was the attic?"

"He didn't say?"

"*Who* didn't say?"

The grown-ups kept talking like we weren't there.

Trent: "You don't see it when it's happening. It's funny, the way people look back on the sixties with so much nostalgia. Feels like last week to me."

Mom: "Yeah, the decades don't feel like decades. When we flipped from seventy-nine to eighty, I didn't think, 'We're in the eighties now.' It was just another year."

"There was an attic. Some secret room. He said he was going to be watching from the attic."

The words reared up before me:

I WATCH FROM THE FOREST, I WATCH FROM THE TREES, I WATCH FROM ABOVE

They'd been written on the black scrim back in the Mystery Mansion.

But who'd written them? I was trying to think, but Trent wouldn't shut the fuck up: "Twenty years with Marie went by so fast. Sometimes I think, what if a few years ago, someone had come up to me and said, 'Your wife has a month to live'? How would I have reacted? What would I have done? Would I have taken her on a vacation to her favorite places? She was kind of a homebody. Maybe she would've been happier just spending time with Jase and Kait."

"Mind if I ask how it happened?"

"Leukemia. Some rare form they didn't know about. The doctors fucked up. Bad. One night, she has a headache. They give her something for it, and when it slams into this leukemia, that's it. Her brain's bleeding, she's gone in minutes. They said they'd never think to look for it in someone her age. I say *fuck you.* Cover all your bases, no matter who it is."

Trent paused a moment to slow his breathing. Boy, that guy could get his blood up in a hurry.

I whispered to Jason: "He was in the attic?"

"Yeah. The ride. There's an attic. He was watching you."

My blood turned to ice, my heart to stone.

"Hey, folks!"

No kidding: I almost peed myself. It was George, holding a tray of drinks.

"Who's ready for the best Old Fashioned east of the Mississippi?"

Mackenzie

The woman's feet were turning blue. Kaitlyn hung back, arms crossed, chewing on a fingernail and looking freaked out.

"Ma'am?" Mac asked. "Do you need some help?"

"Oh, no. Thank you, dear. They're helping . . ."

She trailed off, arms limp at her sides, her eyes vacant. Kaitlyn took a tentative step forward.

"Lady?"

It was like an air-raid siren suddenly blasted to life all around them. Its source was no mystery—the woman was screaming—but it was somehow different and worse. Her screams had transformed her into something other than human; she had quantum-leaped to a universe of horror and sorrow, a hellscape where all she could do was howl and howl. The sound froze the girls. They were fixed in place and fixated on this poor woman whose world was disintegrating. Whatever course of action they were contemplating—bringing her inside, calling her a cab—vanished in the face of her grief, which transposed onto Mackenzie, whom she hugged.

Yes, the woman hugged Mac.

She hugged her hard and close, like a dear friend, but not because she knew her and not because she was a friend, but because she was *there,* real and present, and in that moment, that terrible evening in 1989 when her life was shattered forever, the strange woman hugged Mackenzie Lynn Gresham and howled to a Heaven that ignored her plight, her sorrow, her grief.

"No no no god no god god no no god god no no god god god god god god!"

In a flash, it exploded before Mackenzie, and in her mind's eye, she saw the library, the impossible room she'd seen in the Mystery Mansion, and she remembered, she *remembered* what she heard not only in that uncanny moment, but also just this week when she woke to find her brother sleepwalking:

Fall me.

Feels balmy.

Feels slimy.

"It was her," Mac whispered with a voice she barely recognized.

Men, shouting in the distance: "There she is!"

The strange woman must have heard them because she went instantly silent, releasing Mac and staggering past her. Headlights swung over their heads; it was a car just pulling into the lot. Kaitlyn lunged toward the woman.

"Lady, look out!"

Bwooonk! The car's horn blared, its wheels hurling a sheet of slush that hit the woman. Rubies glittered and sparkled all around the woman in a nimbus of crimson light.

Crimson light.

The driver yelled: "Look out! Jesus, lady!"

Crimson light. Mac saw it at last: the woman was covered with blood; the sheet of icy water splashed some off in a gory cloud. *Ohmigod ohmigod she's covered in blood she's covered in blood.*

Footsteps approached, followed by bursting breath-clouds from a pair of harried men. One was in a shirt and tie, a badge lanyard dangling around his neck, while the other wore a full police uniform. The plainclothes cop chased after the woman.

"Ma'am! Ma'am! Please, get out of the road!" He grabbed her around the shoulders, his shirt slicked with red.

Oh, God, he's bloody, too, Mac thought.

"Her shoes, her shoes," the plainclothes cop said. "She lost her shoes!"

The uniformed cop addressed the girls, bent at the waist, arms extended, palms up; he looked like he was playing basketball defense. It occurred to Mac he was trying to keep them away from the strange woman.

"You girls okay?" he said, breathing hard.

"Look around for her shoes!" the other yelled, hefting the woman into his arms. "Jesus, her feet, her feet."

The uniformed cop didn't hear the other cop; he merely yelled: *"Are you girls okay?!"*

"Yes!" Kaitlyn cried. "What the hell happened?"

The plainclothes cop carried the woman toward the police outpost.

"Call the doc! Might be frostbite, *damn* it!"

The uniformed cop spun and followed, the girls forgotten, yelling into his shoulder radio: "I need Doc Lyman up here ASAP! We might have a case of—"

Slam. Both cops vanished into the outpost. Mac looked down at the dress.

"Oh, no. I got blood on your dress."

Hiram's Journal

"Why didn't you tell the sheriff?"

Mom was occupied with Trent while I was trying to coax the truth out of Jason. If someone else was in the gondola house with us, we needed to tell the cops right away.

"Care for some quid pro quo?" Trent asked.

"About *my* dearly departed?"

"If you're up for it."

"Sure. Widowmaker. Thirty-eight. Went out for a run. The garbageman found him. The end."

Sheesh, Mom can be really mean sometimes.

Mac and Kaitlyn finally came back in, both of them shivering and pale. I did a double take, not only at how haggard they looked, but also because I don't think I'd ever seen my sister in a dress. She looked like her skin was crawling. They sat and looked at their laps. The restaurant's front door swung open again, admitting a burst of snow and a blond woman wearing a winter coat. She ran across the room, right past me, and hunched over next to one of the guests, an older man in a tweed coat.

"Welcome back, ladies!" Trent said. "Thought you'd boosted the Benz!"

I prodded Jason: "We should tell the sheriff."

"Who?" he asked.

"The. Sheriff."

Crash! Dishes shattered in the back. We all jumped. A busboy came running out of the kitchen, hurrying out the front door. Mac mumbled something. Trent comically cupped a hand around his ear.

"Couldn't hear you, little lady."

"We saw something," Mac said.

Kaitlyn added: "Outside."

"Was it in the attic?" Jason asked Kaitlyn, who wrinkled her nose in confusion. The man in the tweed coat hurried past us, the blond woman in tow. Another person, this one a waiter, practically sprinted out of the kitchen, pulling on a peat coat and calling over his shoulder:

"Cover me!" I think he said.

Kaitlyn answered Jason: "No. There were cops. And some lady, talking about teeth."

"*Teeth?*" Trent asked.

"Is everything okay?" Mom asked.

A shriek sounded from across the restaurant. The front door was swinging back and forth now as people rushed in and out. The kitchen was a mass of activity with people throwing on coats, exchanging whispers, shouting orders and calling in favors.

What's going on?

Mom, to both girls: "What did you see?"

Swing, swing went the front door. This time, more people were leaving. One middle-aged man almost forgot his coat and ran into someone as he rushed back in to retrieve it. Beige, a familiar color, emerged. Big and broad-shouldered, she appeared as if magically summoned, her hat's brim bearing a drift of new-fallen snow. She stepped around the mass of increasingly panicked guests and made eye contact with me.

It was Auntie Hanna.

Her eyes were kind, but her face was drawn. Her look told the story we were about to hear, and it wasn't a happy one.

Mom spotted her next. She shot out of her chair. Sirens sounded outside, a distant wail.

"Hanna?"

"Was she in the attic, too?" Jason was tugging my coat sleeve, but there was too much going on for me to track. Auntie Hanna was crossing the restaurant toward us, doffing her hat and knocking snow off it. She stopped before our table.

"Son, I've got some bad news," she said. "I need to ask you to come over to the station."

Exactly who Hanna was addressing was a moment's mystery for everyone else, but not for me, and not for Jason, whose eyes were welling up. Now Trent was on his feet. Everyone was on their feet, either coming, going, running, or screaming. Everyone except Jason.

Trent: "What happened? What's this about?"

"We can talk about it there," Hanna said, turning. "Come on."

"He was in the attic, wasn't he?"

Jason had uttered the riddle as he finally stood, lurching to his feet, his lips quivering now, the tears starting, a trickle of blood leaking from his stitches. He kept talking about an attic, but *what* attic?

Why oh why did we come out to dinner after what happened? He's hurt so bad.

Hanna pivoted back toward us, toward him. "You knew?"

"No," Jason said. "I couldn't remember if I knew or not."

Trent: "Knew what? Sheriff, what's going on?"

"*Oh, fuck.*" Now Kaitlyn was telling riddles, profane ones that drew her father's ire.

"Watch your mouth, young lady," he said before addressing Hanna, my dear, sweet aunt, who I then saw was spattered with blood herself. Trent was talking, but I didn't hear. Without knowing it, I'd pulled out my two maps, dropping the new one, the world's clamor fading to silence as my aperture narrowed around my sketch of the old gondola house, where I saw—in my own hand—the words *Secret Attic,* with a line indicating an A-framed space at the building's top. At some point in the past, I'd written those very words and completely forgotten about them, even when I looked at the map that day while trying to find Jason.

Wish that I was on old Rocky Top . . .

It exploded in my mind's eye, the memory of the strange singer from earlier, the man in the same blue suit as the Plaid Man, the guy singing "Rocky Top" with a frozen face.

Frozen.

Because he'd been wearing a mask.

An image of the park's train charged past: *SUSIE SCHUPPE'S ROCKY MOUNTAIN GOLD RUSH EXPRESS!*

"All aboard," I whispered. Or thought. Like I said, I get those mixed up sometimes. I'm pretty sure I said this last part out loud: "He was watching us."

In response, my aunt gave a sorrowful nod.

"He was gone," she said. "But that's where we found her. Jenny."

Mom covered her mouth, the tumblers falling into place. Trent's eyes widened. Mac burst into tears. So did Jason. Kaitlyn was dead silent, her gaze locked on her brother's grief.

"I couldn't remember," Jason sobbed. "I swear to God I couldn't remember."

Hanna: "We need to ask you a few more questions, son."

Trent was already striding away from the table. "Not without a lawyer. I'm calling Uncle Billy. Don't say a word till he gets here!" He almost shouldered someone to the ground on his way out the door.

"Sheriff? Auntie Hanna?"

It was Mac, grimacing with grief. Hanna smiled.

"What is it, sweetie?"

"Did her mom get to make those two phone calls?"

Outside was awash in lights and sound: police cruisers had crowded into the parking lot while a TV truck sat at the far end of the lot, its antennae extended skyward. A familiar face was intoning important words into a microphone; my mind dimly registered him as a local TV reporter.

"—here in Ober Gatlinburg, where word of the killing has just broken. We've learned that a young man may have been witness to the murder . . ."

Hanna hooked an arm around Jason.

"Didn't know the media had already gotten wind," she said, hustling us along.

Trent's voice rang out: "My God! *Goddammit!*" He was a few doors down from Ottokars, screaming into a pay phone, his form cast in a silhouette that surged with the flash of the police lights. As he screamed at Uncle Billy, Hanna escorted us across the lot toward the police outpost.

With a gush of wind and breath, Trent was upon us, his bulk everywhere, his arms a hundred feet long, his hands grasping at nothing. "Goddammit, god-*damn*-it, Sheriff! You can't question him without a lawyer!"

The reporter heard him and spotted us. Lights swiveled our way. Hanna threw a coat over Jason's head.

"We'll get you in the back way, son," she yelled. "Follow—"

Splashing footfalls approached. It was a producer who'd leaped out of the TV truck, clad in a windbreaker and soaking wet jeans. He waved at the reporter.

"Bill, they're bringing him in now!"

The reporter, Bill, lowered his mic and waved to his cameraman.

"Andy, set up! Perp walk! Perp walk!"

"Perp walk?" Hanna said, but now the lights were swiveling *away* from us. The cameraman had his lens trained on the entrance to the parking lot, on the road leading *up from* Gatlinburg.

Bill was breathless: "The perpetrator was Leonard Shane 'Lenny' Skelton, aka the East Tennessee Strangler, aka the Blue Ribbon Killer, known to have been at large for the last—"

Red and blue lights slanted up from below: they were coming. Shouts erupted from the police outpost. More police cruisers rolled into the lot, lights flashing. A half-dozen cops flowed out of the outpost, holding out hands to block the camera.

"Get back! Get *back!*"

"Holt, move those reporters back!"

"Turn those fucking lights off!"

The TV crew ignored the order and kept their cameras trained on the newly-arrived cruisers. One cruiser in the lead parked near the outpost. A uniformed cop jumped out and opened the cruiser's rear door, which was shrouded in a shadow cast by a nearby ancient oak.

Snow fell. Lights flashed. No one breathed.

A leg emerged, clad in blue, followed by a body, also clad in blue.

A blue suit.

He stood, the man in blue, revealing a black bag over his head, hands bound behind him. At a glance, his suit looked like blue-and-black camouflage, but it wasn't. The patches of black were blood, and he was covered in it. More cops clustered around him, grabbing him roughly by the arms and his lapels. Stepping from the tree's shadow, the flashing lights brought the man into better view, revealing that the bag over his head wasn't black.

It was plaid.

My aperture snapped shut. I'd been dropped into a sensory deprivation chamber, my only view a pinprick peek at the world. I sensed I was backpedaling, my breath wheezing, my lungs empty.

"Kid? You okay?"

I think it was Kaitlyn who asked. Mom and Mac turned my way.

"Hi?"

"Hiram?"

"Kid?"

A distant part of me felt guilty. This had happened to Jason; Why was *I* so upset?

Snap. My aperture flew open, admitting an onrush of input—too much, too much—and even though he was twenty yards away, Skelton was right in front of me, facing me. A concavity sank into the bag: he was taking a deep breath and sucking the fabric to his wide-open mouth in preparation for an ear-splitting scream:

"ALLLLLL ABOAAAAAARD!"

Darkness, welcome darkness, swallowed me.

PART TWO
THE TWO MAPS

Hiram's Journal

I didn't dream about the magic traincar again until Christmastime. The voices were drawing me downstairs, to the walk-in closet.

To the Office.

Some voices were family, like my parents.

"C'mon, it's interesting stuff!" My dad's voice, Deak.

"Oh, all right." Mom.

Others weren't family. A newscaster repeated words I couldn't get out of my head:

"Bob, I'm standing outside what used to be Susie Schuppe's Smoky Mountain Gold Rush amusement park. Three months ago, the body of a teenage girl, Jenny Miles, was discovered inside one of the park's abandoned buildings accompanied by one of Skelton's grim, all-too-familiar calling cards: a prize ribbon."

Another voice, the district attorney, thundered: "Employees and guests were able to access this space regularly to drink, do drugs; it didn't matter how clearly dangerous it was, and steps were never taken to properly seal it off. *And it is the fault of one man and one man alone: Justin Joseph Johnson, head of security for the Gold Rush park!*"

Stairs creaked under my feet. Trent had paid to take out our shag carpeting in favor of hardwood floors, and they made it hell to sneak around our home. (Which wasn't going to be our home much longer, but more on that later.)

As I crept closer to the walk-in closet, the newscaster spoke again: "Authorities are still in the dark as to how Skelton infiltrated the park that fateful day, though blame has fallen squarely on one man, former Gatlinburg Police Sergeant Justin Johnson, whose previous run-in with Skelton ended in tragedy."

I opened the door. A baby cried. I froze. Dad spoke again:

"Aw, how's our little Buckaroo Banzai doing?"

"We're not naming him that. We're naming him after my father."

"Hiram?" Deak laughed. "That's such a grandad name."

Mom, arctic cold: "It's a beautiful name."

Wow. So that's where I heard "Buckaroo Banzai" for the first time. I was in the room with them. God, I must've been in my crib, back in the old projects we lived in before the house. Looking back, I wish this meant more to me. I keep thinking about stories where the kid hears his dead father's voice coming from a magic radio in his dreams, and the camera slowly pans in on his face . . . slowly, slowly . . . as a single tear streams down his cheek. But not me.

I wish this meant more to me.

You'd think it would. My subconscious was delivering up one of my only true-blue memories of Dad. Somewhere in my brain, this memory had been lurking around, this pillow talk between my mom and dad.

And it didn't mean anything. Until it meant everything.

Mom said: "Pum dreto dit din vupp danavreece."

What the hell?

"Holo?" Deak asked.

"Where?" Mom said, and I realized: this was their secret language. *Holo* must have meant *where*.

"You know *where* I wrote it," she said as I entered the walk-in closet.

Pum dreto dit din vupp danavreece

I wrote it in the danavreece.

But what the hell was a "danavreece"?

The hardwood floors continued into the closet. A new voice entered my dream, Auntie Hanna's:

"I'm responsible for that girl's death," she said in court. "I was the officer on duty. It was my call, not his."

The newscaster: "Johnson was fired but all charges against him were dismissed, mostly because of the testimony of Hanna Blackledge, the former sheriff of West Chimney Top, who resigned from her job in protest of Johnson's firing. She was replaced by former head of Knoxville PD's internal affairs, Bo Colquitt. Justin later sued Schuppe's company, Salty Grits LLC, for wrongful termination. They settled out of court for an undisclosed amount. He has since gone into seclusion."

I'd made it underneath the stairs. The door to the Office was inches away. To my left was Mom's old radio.

But it was silent.

"I *know* you wrote it in your diary, sweets." Dad's voice, only it wasn't coming from the radio.

It was coming from the Office.

"It's much more than a diary," Mom said.

Diary. Danavreece. Maybe the danavreece is that green-and-purple book she's always writing in.

Light shone around the door's edges.

"Yeah, but Frederick Buckaroo Banzai Gresham would be such a cool name!"

"We're not naming him after the inventor of quantum funneling."

"*Tunneling*, my dear," Dad said. "And why not? You love *A Wrinkle in Time*, and that's all about quantum tunneling and tesseracts. Me, I think Buckaroo Banzai used the same kinds of tesseracts Meg Murry did."

The light grew brighter.

"You and that movie. We were the only ones in the theater."

"Yeah, yeah, yeah. Next time we'll go see that one with your boyfriend again."

"Michael Douglas is not my boyfriend. Yet. And you said Kathleen Turner was sexy, so we're even."

"I said her *voice* was sexy. Different beans."

"Different *beans?*"

"It's an old Gresham family saying," Dad said.

I reached out to open the door.

"You wanna know a saying we had in the Blackledge family?"

"What?"

"*Pillows!*"

The *thwack* of Mom's pillow hitting Dad's face sounded from the Office. I hesitated, listening.

"*That's not a saying!*"

They burst into merry gales of laugher. Something inside me sank, while tears rose to my eyes. I'd heard Mom laugh, but I'd never heard her laugh *like that* in my life. Why didn't she laugh like that anymore? Maybe the answer was inside the danavreece.

Or the Office.

This time, the door matched reality: it was a pocket door with a small brass handle. With a shaking hand, I gripped the handle—just as a voice boomed from behind:

"*ALLLL ABOOOOARD!*"

It came from the radio, the voice, *his* voice, Skelton's, and suddenly the radio was breaking and shattering and shivering to pieces as he smashed his way out, his glass eye glinting, his scar purple and livid, his hands clawing at me with cracked, yellowing fingernails. *Slam* went the pocket door as I threw it open, my stupid fat legs propelling me into the Office in a headlong dive.

But I didn't land in the Office.

I landed in an execution chamber.

The newscaster's voice boomed: "The jury took thirty minutes to find him guilty of the murder of Jenny Miles. Per Tennessee state law, he has foregone the option for lethal injection, choosing instead to die in the electric chair. Since his conviction, the park has been thoroughly searched for the remains of his other victims. None have been found."

It was the same size and shape as the Office, the Tennessee State Pen electric chamber. Sitting on a dais was the chair, a grim throne. Lightning licked around the room, converging on a television screen the size of a galaxy that reared up before me and filled with Skelton's face. He was being interviewed on a tabloid show.

"You've refused to reveal the location of your victims," the reporter asked off camera. "Even though it might have meant a commuted sentence."

Skelton's inkvine scar coiled around his eye socket. "I cain't reveal what ain't real. I cain't reveal what ain't real. I cain't reveal what ain't real. Lookit, I took the fall for that girl outta the goodness of my heart 'cause she had them strong bones. Had I *had* the wherewithal to undergo and enact the murder and slaughter any other young'uns with the kinda strong bones of Ms. Jenny's caliber, I'da done tore up the map by now."

They'd searched every inch of the park, including every traincar, every attic, every crawlspace. So why was I still dreaming about a Gold Rush traincar?

Skelton's words echoed:

I'da done tore up the map.

I'da done tore up the map.

My dad's voice echoed:

There's another train.

There's another train.

He had found me.

Skelton's eye suddenly shined on me like a demented moon. His cackles were thunder strikes, his laughter a wail from hell. I ran, *ran* pell-mell straight at the wall ahead, not knowing or caring what would happen when I hit it, only to have it fall before me and open out onto the forest near my house. In moments I found myself in the same wooded glen where I'd first discovered the traincar—*and there it is!* I'd found it! It had reappeared—reappeared just in time for an earthquake that threw me off my feet with a *thud.*

Brains rattled, I looked up to see that the traincar was rattling and rumbling in tune with the earth, transforming and expanding. Its roof swelled and burst like a wooden bubble, engorging and upthrusting slats and beams that assembled into an A-frame attic overtop the structure.

It looked just like the hidden attic on top of the old gondola house.

Where Skelton killed Jenny.

Light shone from within the A-frame addition, casting slanting-dancing shafts of gold in every direction. The light flickered, drawing my eye.

What's in there? Is that . . . a bird?

Slam! The traincar's front door flew open and revealed the *thing,* the *him,* the *it*, the Plaid Man himself, his skin a boiling and bubbling-bloody horror, his plaid mask billowing with his brimstone breaths. He pointed at me.

"Itza linda adda!"

He sounded like Skelton. He sounded like Trent. He even sounded a little like Dad.

He sounded like Skeltontrentdad, his voice a layer-distorted overhowl of memories and harbingers, oracles and omens.

He also simply sounded scary as holy fucking shit, because I spun on a heel and sprinted into the endless woods with every ounce of energy my fat ass could muster. As I ran, I realized I'd already forgotten the previous few moments.

What had I been looking at? I was looking at something, and then the Plaid Man appeared.

But where had he come from?

Spectral lights shone through the trees, landing on curious new landmarks: a chair here, a couch there, a smattering of lamps and a clustering of cabinets. Entire freestanding rooms sprang from the earth around me as I ran, ran, and ran, all while Skelton's voice—this time only his, from his tabloid interview—bellowed from an unseen everywhere:

"Jenny was strong, *is* strong, and had it inside her, that strength. Iron! She deserves to rest easy now that she's gone. But I ain't done her or nobody else; it's the *Hightower* what's responsible. Look for 'em in—"

"The 'Hightower'?" the reporter asked.

I had the same question: *What is the Hightower?*

Now I was running past Susie Schuppe's Smoky Mountain Gold Rush, its cartoony front gates shuttered and covered with a sign that read *CLOSED FOR RENOVATIONS.* They hadn't even taken down the Halloween decorations.

And he was gaining. For a fatass, I could *scoot* when an ancient specter of evil was chasing me, but despite my best and most fatasstic efforts, the Plaid Man was roaring up behind me, leaping over the strange furniture sets that had no business being in a forest. I nearly crashed into a dining room set— *ON SALE SPECIAL $399.99!*—when an idea occurred to me.

Actually, Skelton was the one who gave me the idea.

I'da done tore up the map.

I pulled out my hand-drawn map of the forest, dodging around shelves packed with groceries and leaping over a fallen tree, where I stopped, spun . . . and faced off against the Plaid Man, who stopped a few yards away, crouched like a predatory beast. My map bore all the same landmarks I'd run past, including the weird grocery aisles and furniture sets and the shuttered Gold Rush park. In a burst of intuition, I gauged the locations of myself and the Plaid Man on the map—

—and I tore it in half.

It was like Zeus punched the earth. The ground heaved, trees fell, and sporting goods and groceries went flying. A massive chasm opened between me and Mr. Tall, maps Dark 'n' Ugly, swallowing up dinettes and hundreds of pounds of produce. I fell on my ass, graceful as hell. The Plaid Man peered at the chasm like something feral. He hissed at me—*yes, he freaking hissed*—and ran off.

Standing, I inched toward the chasm's edge, expecting to look down and see, y'know, a *chasm,* an opening in the earth, but instead I found myself standing on the edge of existence and staring into the nothingness beyond Euclidean space . . . only it wasn't nothing; something in the deep was calling to me:

"Itza lindaaaaaaa. Iiiiiitzaaaaa lindaaaaaaa."

I knew the voice, but who was it?

It was . . .

"Gotcha!"

Arms encircled my massive midsection. He had me. The Plaid Man had me.

"What are you *doing* out here?!"

It wasn't the Plaid Man, and I wasn't in a magical dream-forest.

She set me on the ground before her. Stars twinkled overhead, while the slopes of the Smokies rose up before me. She sat on a parking lot curb, still wearing her dark blue apron. A name-tag on her chest read WAL-MART SECURITY: CORRIE GRESHAM. About a hundred yards to my left stood a gigantic Wal-Mart, its facade covered with wreaths, garlands, and other Christmastime decorations.

She'd found me at the far rear edge of the parking lot, where I was two steps away from plunging into a ravine.

I'm not too proud to say I bazooka-barfed.

My poor fucking mom. She led me back to her security booth at Wal-Mart, where she'd set up a cot for me. I'd gotten out a few more times in the last few months, and it was too much to ask of Mac to keep track of me every night; she needed sleep, too.

She sat at her desk, unhooked her belt, which hung with a flashlight and mace, and stretched. Trent had been been moving in on her fast over the past few months, but she hadn't accepted any of his monetary offers—yet. She'd taken the second job at Wal-Mart to cover the mortgage, all while teaching third and fourth grade full-time. I still wonder what happened to the inheritance. Auntie Hanna turned her share into a big house that overlooked the Smokies.

But then, Auntie Hanna didn't have two kids.

Mom yawned. "What were you dreaming about? You were screaming when I found you."

"I was?"

She nodded.

"Uh I can't remember." I remembered a lot of my dream—the radio, the Office, the electric chair—but there was something I *couldn't* remember. Something to do with the traincar. But what was it?

I sat up on my cot. "Is there a place called Itza Linda?"

"Itza Linda?" She thought for a moment. "Hm. Not that I know of. There's a place in Mexico called Chichen Itza. Your dad and I went there for our honeymoon. Well, we went to *Cancun*, but Chichen Itza's near there, so we took a day trip. I remember Deak, your father, actually made fun of me because I kept trying to speak Spanish with the vendors, and—"

"Mom?"

"—I said, 'I've forgotten half of what we learned in the Peace Corps, and there's nothing better than immersion,' oh? What was that, honey?"

I smiled. "I got it. I'm pretty tired."

"Oh! I'm so sorry. Look at me, prattling on. Get some sleep and try not to scream this time. Oh, I'm taking you to Dr. Eldridge tomorrow. Okay?"

Ugh. Dr. Eldridge. "Okay."

"I know it's tough, but it's good for you to talk to him. Maybe you can talk with him about changing schools."

I can't believe Mom's transferring me and Mac to Montmarnass.

"Okay," I said. "Have you heard from Mr. Johnson?"

"Mr.—oh, the security guard who helped us? No. Why?"

"Auntie Hanna talked about him in the court case. Are they friends now?"

"Honey, if they are, your aunt hasn't told me." She paused. "Hasn't told me anything. I'm sure he's fine, though. He got a big settlement after the court case, so he has a lot of money now."

I lay silent, pretending to sleep. After a time passed, Mom pulled out her purple-and-green diary.

The danavreece. There it is.

But for the time being, I forgot about my mom's mysterious diary, instead fixating on Justin Johnson. No one had heard from him since the court case. What happened to him made me feel rotten inside. It was such bullshit. And on top of that, Skelton still hadn't revealed where he'd hidden the rest of his victims. I couldn't stop thinking of all the families he'd shattered; the lives, the peace, and the closure they'd been denied. Even worse was how he gloated about it, the evil glint in his eye, the smug way he joked about the lives he'd taken.

There had to be something I could do.

Maybe there is, a voice inside me said. *When you tore up your map, you opened a hole in the earth.*

I don't know where these voices came from. Maybe they emanated from the same place as my dreams about the traincar. But there's no doubt in my mind now that these voices were real and that they were trying to help me.

But that was in my dream, I responded.

Another voice asked: *Who says that wouldn't work in the real world?*

Mackenzie

She was Queen Shit of Fuck Mountain.

Homeroom was Mac's royal court now. Gone was her previously teased-up orange disaster of a hairdo in favor of delicately straightened locks she'd pinned back in a pair of ponytails. Her attire was a few years ahead of the curve: skirt and blazer, both in primary colors—a look Alicia Silverstone would make famous in *Clueless*. Mac had her usual retinue gathered around her—Dawn, Jarra, Becky, and Sabrina—but now she wasn't sitting in her chair but on her desk.

"I love this outfit, Gresh," Jarra said.

"It's so chic," Sabrina said.

"It's a few years out of date, but it's still cute," Becky said.

"Yeah, who's your stylist?" Dawn asked with some asperity. She was wearing jeans and a sweater; an outfit that would've been standard for Mac only a few months before.

Mac shrugged. "Oh, no one special. I've been keeping an eye on trends."

It burned Mac to admit it, but it had been Kaitlyn who'd helped with her look. They'd been regulars at Blue Ridge Supermall over the last three months, where Kaitlyn maxed out her MasterCard and taught her how to smoke a bong.

"Focus up, everyone!" yelled poor Mr. Evanston. "Here's today's human dev worksheet!"

"Human development" was code for "sex ed," which meant poor Mr. Evanston had to contend with oodles of sophomoric jokes, chortling, and derailing every day, to say nothing of Mac's newfound attitude.

"And Ms. Gresham?"

Mac fluttered her fake eyelashes and spoke in a falsetto. "Yes, Mr. Evanston?"

He took a deep breath. "I think you can take your seat now."

She sat with a theatrical flip of her hair that made Dawn roll her eyes. As always, sweet Dave Shuler had grabbed the seat next to her, only now he had to fend off three other boys for it.

"Psst, Gresh," he whispered.

"What is it?" Mac said, more impatiently than she intended.

"How much longer you here?"

Mac's heart simultaneously boomed and fell. No one knew she and Hiram were transferring schools next semester. Or so she thought.

"How'd you know?"

Dave shrugged. "I think Looney Balls heard it from Randall."

Mac rolled her eyes. *Fucking Randall and his big mouth.*

"I hadn't really told anyone," she whispered. By "anyone" she mostly meant Dawn. "I'm transferring next semester."

"To Montmarnass?"

"Shh," she said but nodded. "Yeah."

The corner of Dave's mouth rose in a sweet half-smile. His eyes were sad.

"We're gonna miss ya, Gresh."

Mac almost asked him out on the spot. The words rose up in her, but she squelched the impulse as soon as it was born. After all, how could she go out with anyone when she was changing schools in a matter of weeks anyway?

A new school. Where she didn't know anybody.

And where she *wasn't* anybody.

She'd have to start all over.

BRRRRRING! Everyone jumped from their seats and scrambled into the hallway. Mac hadn't even noticed how quickly the time passed. She'd planned to stall and let Dave leave first, but he was already gone. Dawn was waiting for her at the door. Her expression was a mixture of disappointment and anger, which was strange; Dawn was slow to anger.

"What's up?"

"Why don't your brother wanna hang out with mine?"

Dawn

Dawn Dockery missed her best friend already. Mac had let it slip last Friday in Randall's wood-paneled basement that her mom's rich new boyfriend was moving her and Hiram over to that snooty-posh prep school on the ridge.

"We'll still hang out!" Mac promised amidst the mayhem of a high school kegger. Randall was arguing with someone about who was better, Bon Scott or Brian Johnson, while Looney Balls was in the corner, trying and repeatedly failing to do a keg stand. Becky, Jarra, and Sabrina were flirting with boys someplace, but Dawn was right next to Mac on Randall's swaybacked felt couch. Someone had puked on it last week, so they threw an afghan over the stain. Dawn sipped her Bud Ice and nodded, thinking back to when Jenny moved away.

I miss Jenny, Dawn thought. *I should really reach out to her—*

No. She couldn't reach out to her. Because she was gone.

Dawn kept forgetting Jenny was dead. She didn't know which was worse—that she kept forgetting she was dead, or that Jenny hadn't recognized her in the Mystery Mansion.

She almost didn't go to her funeral.

"You should go," Dawn's mom had said. "It would mean so much to her mama."

And she was right.

At the observance, which was held at West Chim Funeral Home, Dawn spotted Jenny's mom easily; she had the same auburn hair as her daughter. (She was also walking on a cane because she'd lost three toes to frostbite.) To Dawn's surprise, she remembered her immediately and hugged her for a full minute, thanking her for coming. Dawn scanned the crowd for that tall boy, Jason. The word was he was with Jenny when . . . Dawn didn't like to think about it. Jason skipped the funeral. Dawn wondered why, but given that she nearly skipped it herself, she could somewhat understand. When everyone lined up to view the body, Dawn demurred and slipped out the back door to go cry.

When Sandra picked her up, Dawn was almost in shock from grief. She walked like a ghost across the parking lot and sat in the car, silent.

"Are you glad you went?" her mom asked.

She thought. "I dunno if 'glad' is the right word, but . . . yeah. I'd have felt bad if I didn't go." She leaned over and hugged her mom's arm. "I love you, Mama."

That morning as she and her brother came walking up to Polk High, Lee spotted the Greshams getting out of that stupid Mercedes truck they drove now. Mac was wearing one of her fancy new outfits, while Hiram was wearing shorts in the dead of winter like always. Lee brightened immediately upon seeing Hiram and scampered over. Dawn watched him go, wincing a little in anticipatory dread. They had a brief exchange, and Lee came running back, silent. His expressions were inscrutable, but Dawn had learned to read him over the years.

He let loose a sigh that flapped his lips: *b-b-b-b-bbbbb.*

"What'sa matter, buddy?"

He shrugged. "Nothing whatsoever. I asked the admiral how his shoulder was faring and if he might like to come over Friday night."

"His shoulder? Oh, you mean the one he hurt a few months back?"

They passed under a fire escape covered in rust. Mr. Johannsen, the custodian, was cleaning off some graffiti that screamed, *BURN IN HELL TUCKER!* The school's only inviting quality this time of year were the Christmas lights and garlands glowing inside.

Lee nodded. "That's correct. The admiral took quite a spill, and I was worried about permanent damage."

That was Lee for you, always weirdly out of sync with the world. His mind was constantly jumping around from subject to subject. He remembered *everything,* from the cast and crew of every movie he saw to the details of every conversation he'd ever had with you. He would sometimes pick up a thread from a conversation you'd been having a month earlier, only to be surprised when the other person didn't have the same total recall he did.

He was also incredibly smart. The only reason why he wasn't at the top of his class was because he threw the occasional test. ("I don't want to make the other kids feel bad," he'd said with a shrug.)

The fact that Hiram was constantly blowing him off—and worse, sometimes making fun of Lee behind his back—kept Dawn up at night. Lee didn't have any other friends, and he *worshipped* Hiram for reasons she couldn't fathom. And Hiram treated him like garbage.

Dawn paused by the door. Kids hurried past, racing to beat the bell. Lee hesitated.

"Would you like for me to wait with you?"

"Nah, go on in," she said, then called: "And you don't gotta call him 'Admiral'!"

"I'll take it under consideration," he said and vanished inside.

Dawn turned and looked out. The school sat at the top of a series of gentle slopes. A yellowing football field flanked by sagging bleachers sat in a basin one slope below, while misty mountains rose to every side.

Even though she hated Polk High, she loved this view . . . and it wasn't lost on her that Mac had stopped going in the side door with her. After she met that rich Kaitlyn girl, Mac had suddenly become scarce. Dawn and Mac used to sit on these steps every morning before class and watch the last few minutes of the sunrise. Now she didn't have time because she spent half her morning getting dolled up for school.

She and I are going to have words after homeroom.

Mackenzie

"What're you talking about?"

Dawn had been acting weird ever since Randall's kegger last weekend. Mac strode up the hallway toward Algebra II, making eyes with a couple of boys—football players!—who hadn't noticed her before. Kids ran to and fro, snatching books out of lockers, shouting, waving to each other, and generally acting like a bunch of hormone-addled goofballs. The styles included big hair, sports jerseys—lots of swag from around the SEC and ACC: Tennessee, Alabama, Auburn, a few Kentuckys, a few stray North Carolina Tar Heels—as well as ripped jeans with high waists.

The usual.

And Mac was so far above them.

Dawn tagged along behind her. "Lee invited your baby brother over this Friday to play video games."

"So?"

"He invites him over *every* Friday, and he says no every time."

Mac almost shrugged and said something snide and tossed-off, but something flashed to her right. It was Mr. Gilbert's AP Euro class, filling up with the Junior-year supernerds, but for an instant, she caught the sunrise blazing over the mountaintops and filtering through the Smoky Mountain mists. The effect blinded her, revealing a moment's glance back into a sight that was at once uncanny and familiar:

The library. But it wasn't just *any* library.

It was *her* library.

She'd first seen it in the Mystery Mansion, and now she was once again peering into its endless stacks. Through a window stood craggy, snow-capped mountains—nothing like her native Smokies—as well as a strange new sight: hovering over the mountains was what appeared to be a geodesic grid of luminescent hexagons.

Why is there a grid in the sky? she thought with a distant voice. Her mind made unusual connections; she suddenly remembered she'd dreamed about this very sight, the memory timestamped a few years' distant by the brains' arcane inner filing system.

She'd dreamed about the magic library—and the Grid—years before she saw it in the Mystery Mansion. But when?

This was a dream, the library, *her* dream, and it struck her silent and filled her with awe.

The vision—and the feelings—faded, but she was left with an afterimage of magic and contrition. She turned to her friend, whom she'd met down by the lakeside cottages one summer morning a million years ago. Her face must've been a sight, because Dawn quantum-leaped from cranky to concerned.

"Aw, honey, what is it?"

Mac: "I miss you. Sorry I haven't been around."

Dawn's face fell. "You've been around."

"You know what I mean."

"It's okay, sis. You've got some new friends now."

"Hey, Kaitlyn's no Dawn Dockery, you hear me? You're my bestie-bestie, got it? Let's *do* something that's not gettin' drunk in stupid Randall's stupid basement, and I promise to spend less time with her and more time with you. Dealio?"

"Dealio."

Hiram suddenly went charging by wearing his dumb-ass shorts. "Himacbyemac!"

Mac shook her head. "And I'll have a talk with him, too."

Hiram's Journal

School was *out!* I'd managed to stay awake through the rest of my classes, all while fending off Lee Dockery's overtures and steering clear of Danny Sizemore. As I ran through the halls, I drew a few passing insults from the bigger kids—"Nice shorts, blobbo"—but I ignored 'em.

I was a man with a plan—a plan to help Justin Johnson.

"Hold it, Hiram!"

It was Mr. Tucker, looking cool as *heck* in his purple flannel. He was only twenty-three, but he seemed so worldly to me, a real grown-up. He'd gone to some school I'd never heard of in Maine and was the only faculty member who didn't have a Southern accent. He was holding a small book, which he held out to me. It was by a cartoonist named Lynda Barry.

"You're always laughing at her cartoons, so I thought you might enjoy this."

He may as well have handed me a bar of gold. I cradled the book in my palms, marveling at the cover.

"Uh can I open it?"

He smiled. "It's yours. Yes, you can open it."

The pages parted to reveal untold bizarre wonders. Barry's cartooning was squiggly and cantankerous and flat-out gorgeous. Laugh-out-loud funny, too. It was like Mr. Tucker had peered straight into my deepest hopes and needs and presented me with this gift. I hugged the book to my chest.

"Thank you so much, Mr. Tucker."

He got the warmest, kindest look on his face and shook his head. "The gratitude's all mine. Happy holidays, and, hey—how's the sleepwalking?"

"Um, better. I think."

"Okay," he said. "It's none of my business. I've just become—"

"What?"

He shrugged. "Nothing. Happy holidays."

He walked away, and as much as I wanted to know what he was going to say, my curiosity vanished into my swirling eleven-year-old mind. *Slam* went the double doors leading out to the side steps, where Mac was sitting on a wall. We sat out here every day, waiting for our ride. Over the last three months, Trent had been showing up more and more often, much to our chagrin.

As hundreds of other kids poured out of the school's every exit, I plopped down next to her and pulled out my map, the same one Lee had improved a few months earlier. I had an idea for how I could get back to the traincar, but I wasn't sure if it was possible. But before I even *tried* to get back to the traincar, I had to remember that detail from my dream I'd forgotten.

It was something about the traincar.

"Hi, sis!" I chirped.

"Hey," she said, her tone strangely dark, although I barely noticed it at the time; I was too fixated on my map.

Something was different about the traincar. What was it?

I tried to imagine the traincar. I saw it in my mind's eye, its every detail, the weird writing along the side, the stained-glass windows.

But there was something else . . .

Another voice: "Hey, Gresh!"

It was Mac's friends, Dawn, Becky, and Sabrina, along with Lee, who was tagging along. My concentration was broken. They came chattering over just as the Dockerys' mom, Sandra, pulled up in her station wagon.

Becky scooted in next to Mac.

"You comin' to Billy Bones' farm this Friday night? Or do you gotta go to church?"

"We're not religious, Becky," Mac said. "And Billy Bones has a farm?" Mac asked as Sabrina hopped up on the wall opposite us and started ripping off cheerleader kicks.

"Naw, silly!" Sabrina said. "Billy Bones don't have a farm, but he's got a line on the old Soddy Farm."

"Dave Shuler might be there!" Becky cooed. "You could break his heart again!"

"Shhhh!" Mac said, waving her hands. "I'll be there. I just gotta work it out with my mom."

Dawn pointed at her. "And this time, *you know who* ain't gonna come?"

"Just us, Dawn-n-Gresh," Mac said, offering her pinky. "Pinky swear."

They pinky swore as Lee sat next to me.

"Greetings, Admiral."

I ignored him. Mac gave me a hard look out of the corner of her eye.

Lee indicated my map. "I see you've added some of the surrounding landmarks. It's well done, if I may say so."

"Yeah, thanks."

Dawn and Mac made eye contact.

Lee: "Would you like to come over this Friday? I was hoping to show you that Masterminder game I'd previously mentioned."

"Uh—" I said, but Dawn cut me off:

"We'd love to have ya over, Hiram. Mama can make dinner and everything."

I shrugged. "Sure, maybe!"

A new voice: "Hi, kids!"

Sandra Dockery walked up wearing her usual dark green vest. She'd affixed a purple pin to it; some kind of triangular symbol that rang a bell, but I couldn't remember where.

"Well, hey there, kids. How was school?"

Dawn scrunched her mouth up, looking disappointed. "School was fine, Mama. Hiram said he might come over this weekend."

My head snapped up in panic. "Uh—"

Sandra propped her hands on her hips. "That'd be great, Hiram. We'd love to have ya."

"I'm gonna be busy."

"Oh," Sandra said with a frown. "Fair enough. Lee, you ready?"

He hopped up. "Yes, my lady."

"You don't gotta call me that, buddy," Sandra said, chuckling. They climbed in their station wagon and pulled off. Becky and Sabrina's rides showed up, and they went running off.

"See ya, Gresh!"

"Bye, Mac!"

Mac silently waved goodbye. We sat for a moment, staring at the parking lot, before she sighed.

"Trent's late again."

I grunted in response and kept working on my map.

"So are you going to spend the night at Lee's this Friday?"

"Yeah. I don't think so. He doesn't have a Nintendo, and we do, and I don't know if he even lives in a house."

Snap! The map was gone. My face fell as I clawed at the air before me.

"W-w-what?!"

Mac had snatched it from me and crumpled it in her fist.

"What the hell is wrong with you?"

I swiped at the map. "Give it back!"

"Are we even fucking related? *'He doesn't have a Nintendo'? 'He doesn't live in a house'?* You have any idea how *lucky* we are to be in that house? That Mom was able to *save* the house when Dad died? But you don't remember any of that, do you?"

Mac and I fought about stupid shit all the time, but this was my first memory of her really *angry* at me about something important, something that mattered.

In response, I shook my head.

"Yeah, no, because the whole world didn't exist until Hiram Deacon Gresham was born. Well, you know the townhouse we used to live in? Those were housing projects, set up by the county. Mom and Dad had to go down to the county every month and beg for the assistance check. When Dad died, his asshole family tried to take the house, and we'd have had to move right back into the townhouse. And ya know what? *That'd have been fine. We'd have figured it out.* But Mom busted her ass working three jobs to make ends meet so we could have our own rooms and you could have your stupid Nintendo."

A dark cloud-circle of shame closed around my mind. Even then, as a chuckleheaded eleven-year-old, the cruel snobbery of my words stunned me now that Mac had thrown them in my face.

He doesn't have a Nintendo. They don't live in a house.

What *was* wrong with me?

The tears were coming fast, and Mac was already cooling off. She wrapped an arm around me and pulled me close.

"Hey, I'm sorry, goofball. That was pretty harsh. But Lee's a cool kid. You should hang out with him, ya dumbo."

Now I was really crying. "I'm a stupid jerk. I'm a stupid jerk."

She hugged me closer. "You're not a jerk."

"I'm a stupid *fucking* jerk." You read that right. Sometimes I swore to get attention or to deflect blame from myself. In this case, I absolutely hated myself in that moment.

"Hey," Mac said, looking me in the eyes. "You're not a jerk. But we all *act* like jerks sometimes. What's important is we learn from it and maybe act like a little less of a jerk the next time. How's that sound?"

I wonder if someone reading this might think Mac was being too hard on me. After all, I started crying, didn't I? But if anything, she took it *easy* on me. I often think about how I treated Lee Dockery, how quickly and easily I slipped into the role of a bully, how I looked down on him, how I couldn't tolerate his presence even though he was so kind to me.

It's impossible for me to overstate my shame. It's boundless.

I know I was only a stupid kid. Stupid kids fuck up and do stupid shit that makes them cringe years later. I get it. But at the same time, I think there comes a point in our lives when we can't blame our shortcomings or our mistakes on what age we were. There comes a time when we're given a choice, and if we make the wrong one, it's only because of a failure of our moral imagination.

And moral courage.

I was only eleven, and it's asking a lot of an eleven-year-old to develop a moral imagination, but luckily, my big sister was there to show me what one looked like. And in addition to that, I was about to become friends with a group of brave souls who all had beautiful moral imaginations. That group would include Mac, Lee, Dawn, and a few other surprising faces.

Including mine.

Even though I'd treated Lee like garbage, there was at least the beginning of a moral imagination in me. If there hadn't been, I don't think I would've made it through the next year alive. My moral imagination had been awakened by people like Justin Johnson and it would be cultivated and honed by my friends.

Before I started hanging out with Lee Dockery, I didn't have any friends.

But I was about to make some.

Sitting next to my sister, I yawned.

"I'm sorry I cried."

"Goofball, you can always cry around me."

Vrooom! Trent's idiotic Mercedes tank came charging into the lot, swerving and *honk*-ing around other cars. Someone actually had to scoot out of the way or get hit.

"What an asshole," Mac said.

With a chirp of tires, he pulled up, the truck radiating heat like a grease fire.

"Hey guys! Get on in!"

Mac and I looked at each other and rolled our eyes.

The truck was a prison. We rumbled along, Mac in front, me in back, while Trent chattered away and tried to connect with us. He was wearing his usual sport coat over a button-down with slacks. Neither of us could believe Mom had started dating this guy, much less that they might actually get married.

But if we were transferring to Jason and Kaitlyn's school, marriage was probably the next step.

"So how was everyone's day at school?" he asked.

We sat silent. I was trying to remember a detail from my dream the night before. The traincar had some kind of new feature. Was it a new door? Something new written on the side?

All I could remember was *Itza Linda.*

"That's where it is," I said, unaware I was speaking out loud.

"What'cha working on there, buddy?"

"Homework," I said absentmindedly.

"Homework, huh? What subject?"

What was different about the traincar last night?

Trent was pulling into the parking lot of the medical center where I saw my therapist, Dr. Eldridge. He parked the G-Wagon across two spots like an asshole and proceeded to turn around and shake my knee.

"What subject, buddy?"

"Math—geometry," I said shortly. In the rearview mirror, Mac's eyes widened. Trent's jaw clenched, and I held my breath. This kind of thing happened all the time. If you didn't act *in just precisely the perfect, proper, and right manner,* Trent might fucking *explode.* We teetered on a knife's edge for a moment before his jaw unclenched.

"You don't sound so happy about it. Anything I can help with?"

I put on a happy face. "No. Thank you. I'll figure it out."

Bwoooooonk! We all jumped. A car was pulling into the lot behind us. Trent had somehow managed to park across two spots and left the truck's backside blocking the way in. Looking back, I saw a pissed-off guy in a filthy Toyota. Suddenly a bomb exploded:

"SHUT THE FUCK AHHHHHP! WE'RE GOING, WE'RE GOING!"

Mac yelled: *"Can we just go?!"*

Trent's entire body clenched; every muscle flexed while veins burst from his forehead and neck. His rage filled the car like a dense, dank stench you couldn't escape; it made your eyes squint and water. My lower lip was already trembling, my face a beacon of fright. Trent wrenched around, revving the engine and pounding the wheel. He tried to move the car but couldn't. *Bwoooooonk!* The motorist was inching up behind us now. Trent's biceps bulged through his coat. He looked like he was trying to rip the wheel off its column. Mac's eyes were dinner-plate-big in the rearview. Trent swung around, his face a sudden red sun that filled my world:

"MOVE!"

Imagine trying to yell loud enough to be heard, for example, on the other side of the Grand Canyon. You'd really put your back into it, wouldn't you? That's how loud Trent yelled at me. And he was three times my size, his face as red as a stop sign. Fucking enormous. Terrifying. This kind of shit had been happening all the time since Mom started dating him.

This is one example. I could list a hundred. A *thousand.*

Other people had it worse than me growing up. I know that. All I can say is these incidents, a thousand wounds both superficial and severe, added up. I was sobbing in the back seat.

Somewhere in the haze of my terror, Trent had downshifted into damage control. He was shaking my shoulder.

"Hey, hey, hey. It's okay. You shouldn't cry." He grabbed my arm. "Hey. Don't cry for me, okay?" His smile was a wheedling grimace, evil and pathetic. "Okay? It's okay. It's okay. Heck, you don't even *need* to cry. Can you stop crying for me? It's a big boy thing. You need to stop. When I need to stop crying, I make my Adam's apple jump. Here, watch!"

He tilted his head back and swallowed several times, making his Adam's apple jump.

"Now you give it a shot!" he said. "Gulp, gulp, gulp!"

Bwoooooooonk! My stomach clenched in anticipation of another Trent explosion, but he was fixated on stopping up my tears. I tilted my head back and swallowed over and over. It actually helped, that and the sheer mortal terror I felt. My tears subsided, and I was fumbling for the handle. The door fell open, heavy as a barn door—I swear, the car had been built for giants—and I hurried out of the truck.

"The door!" Trent yelled.

I slammed it shut. It felt like closing a safe. Trent fired up the truck and managed to inch it out of the Toyota's way. A shadowy figure shot him the finger as he passed and circled around the side of the building. Trent's expression in the side mirror was one of mania: his brow was misted with sweat, his eyes goggling. I was on autopilot by this point, heading in to my appointment.

But Trent wasn't done with me yet.

"Buddy! Hey, buddy!" He'd taken a knee before me. I hadn't even heard him get out of the car. "What's on the docket today, champ?"

"Huh?"

"I dunno what you're planning to talk about, but if you needed some prompts, I had some ideas for ya!"

"I—"

"See, Tripod's a smart guy, but he probably doesn't remember what y'all've been talking about this whole time. Probably the dreams you keep having, right, and the bed wetting?"

"Uh it's sleepwalking."

"Sleepwalking! Right! Kid takes some constitutionals now and then, everyone gets their panties in a bunch!" His volume and tone lowered: "Listen, we're off limits, okay? You and me, we're off limits."

I opened my mouth but decided my best option for survival was to keep quiet.

"Just . . . don't talk about me with Tripod. Guy's such a joker, I'll never hear the end of it. Focus on what matters: your dreams and the sleepwalking." He was yelling again: "You've got your mother worried sick, kid, and that's not good. It's really not good, because she works her *ass* off for you. You understand?"

I wanted to ask why he kept calling Dr. Eldridge "Tripod," but I merely nodded.

"Lemme hear you say it."

"Uh I understand."

His tone shifted from pissed-off back to sweaty-eyed terror.

"There ya go!" He chucked my shoulder. It felt like a punch. He finally stood and climbed back in the G-Wagon. Mac looked like she was on her way to be executed. They pulled away.

I went inside.

Mackenzie

She was terrified to move.

Trent climbed back in the car, growling to himself, sweating and swearing, his every move violent. He didn't turn the key, he *wrenched* it. He didn't press the accelerator, he *stomped* on it. Mac sat like a statue, hoping against hope that if she didn't move a muscle on the drive home that she'd be spared Trent's wrath that afternoon.

They rumbled down the road in silence. He didn't even turn on the radio.

There were so many things Mac wished she had said to Trent in that moment, but all she could think of was survival. She was hyper-aware of the present, because that's all there was, and all she could think of was trying to escape that awful moment in one piece.

His face clenched. "*Mother-fucker.*" But it sounded more like "*mother-fehhhker!*" He barely sounded human. He spun the G-Wagon in a vicious U-turn and floored it. Mac's feet pressed into the floor, her hand gripping the door handle, her teeth clenching. He roared back into the medical center's lot and around the side of the building where the offending Toyota was. He stopped the truck, ripped out the keys, and jumped out, forgetting to put it in park. Mac lunged to pull the emergency brake, watching as Trent stormed over to the Toyota.

He spent a full minute keying it, sawing back and forth, metal screeching against metal like an awful orchestra, his face a rictus of off-the-charts rage, his spittle flying in glittering arcs.

He paused and observed his handiwork.

"Fuck you," he whispered with a curt nod. He climbed back in the truck, pinched the Toyota's paint off the key, and started up the truck, all in silence. That end of the lot was a dead end, so Trent pulled a three-point turnaround, giving Mac a view of the Toyota.

Damn if the pattern he'd left didn't look like plaid.

Hiram's Journal

"Want to know what I'm getting for Christmas?"

It was Dr. Eldridge who'd asked the question. I'd been sitting in silence for the first ten minutes of our session, partially because I was still rattled from my encounter with Trent, but mostly because I hated being here.

"Come on," he said. "Take a guess."

It had nothing to do with him. He was nice enough. But coming here made me feel like I was stupid or broken. The other kids didn't have to do this. Why did I?

I shifted on the squishy couch, which threatened to swallow me up. Bold colors dominated the room: the couch was a deep, apple-y red adorned with banana-yellow pillows. Paraphernalia from around Central and South America peppered the room: travel posters from Belize and Nicaragua, an icon marked *CHILE,* an another etching of two goddesses sitting in repose.

The doc himself was wearing a complementary outfit: a royal blue button-down with a bright green tie. A few strands of beads hung around his neck, while his face was clean-shaven except for a soul patch. He was about as tall as Trent but much thinner; he had the build of a long-distance runner.

"How about if I give you a hint?"

I relented: "I don't know. Maybe plane tickets somewhere?"

"Nothing," he said. "I'm Jewish!"

This might've been funny to a lot of other people but not me in my current state. I'd been mean to Lee, and now I was being mean to Dr. Eldridge. My tears welled up.

"I'm sorry," I squeaked. "I forgot."

He held up his palms. "Oh, my gosh, Hiram, I was only kidding! Well, I wasn't kidding about being Jewish, but I didn't mean to embarrass you. I'm so sorry about that."

I nodded. "I'm sorry I was mean."

"You weren't being mean. It's hard to remember everything all the time, isn't it?"

"Yeah."

"Wanna tell me what you're doing for Christmas?"

I *wanted* to talk about the way I'd treated Lee Dockey, but I didn't really understand therapy yet. I didn't know *I* could ask questions and guide the discussion.

"We're doing Christmas Eve at our house, then Christmas morning at his. The Suttons."

"That sounds nice. Like you get two Christmases. You've mentioned that you have a hard time with them. Maybe we can talk about that now?"

"Um," I thought about what Trent had said. "I can't."

"You can't?"

I shook my head.

"Why can't you? Do you not want to?"

"Trent said that we were off limits."

"He said you and I were off limits?"

"Uh no. That him and me were off limits."

"Oh. Did he say why?"

Is there any way for him to find out? I didn't know. All I *did* know was that I was straying into tricky territory, so I clammed up. Dr. Eldridge leaned forward and twined his fingers.

"Maybe it'd be easier if you told me more about this conversation?"

"He was showing me a trick. Uh but not a magic trick. Something he does to stop crying."

Dr. Eldridge's brow furrowed. "Why was he showing you how to stop crying?"

"Uh I didn't want to cry, so he showed me how to stop."

"You . . . didn't want to cry, so he showed you how to . . . stop crying?"

"Yeah, like this."

I tilted my head back and swallowed repeatedly. When I was done, Dr. Eldridge was looking at me the way Mac did when I was feeling sad. He had his "empathy" face on.

"I want you to know that everything we talk about in here is confidential. You know that, right?"

I shrugged.

He nodded. "There's no way he could ever find out. You understand that, right?"

Really? "Are you sure? What if he asks you?"

"I won't tell him anything. It's against the law."

"Okay."

"Do you want to tell me what was happening when he showed you this trick?"

Something inside me cowered and ran for cover. I spat: "He calls you Tripod."

Dr. Eldridge sat back and gave a small chuckle. But he wasn't amused.

"Did he? Funny guy."

"You two know each other?" I asked.

"Yeah, we went to Duke together."

"He said you two were really good friends."

"Huh. Well, we weren't friends. But things change when you grow up. I guess you could say we're contemporaries." He paused. "Tripod. Hadn't heard that one in a while."

"What's it mean?

"Long story. And I don't know if it'd be appropriate for this room." He shifted gears: "Hiram, I want to say again: you can tell me anything."

I nodded. Shame was creeping up on me again. Some part of me knew that Trent had infected this room, that he'd transported a little bit of himself in here with me, that no matter what Dr. Eldridge said about laws or secrets, he would always know everything that happened. That he would be everywhere in my life.

Just like . . .

"I dreamed about him again," I said.

"The Plaid Man?"

Nod.

"Was he at the traincar again? The one you keep dreaming about?"

"Yeah, and I think . . ." I trailed off.

"What?"

"I think my dreams are trying to tell me something."

Dr. Eldridge pursed his lips. "What are they trying to tell you?"

They're trying to tell me where Skelton's hidden his victims, I wanted to say but couldn't.

"I think they're trying to tell me how to get back to the traincar."

I knew this was a weird thing to say, but it was all I had. I was too scared to talk about Trent, too ashamed to talk about Lee, and too weirded out to talk about Skelton. I felt like I was trying to communicate with Dr. Eldridge in code, same as my subconscious—or whatever higher power was at work— was trying to do with me. But even saying *this* much felt dangerous; I was sure he was about to call my mom or Trent and rat me out.

But all he said was: "I want to hear about the dream you had last night, but do this for me: instead of telling me about the *events* of the dream, tell me how you *felt.*"

Frowning, I nodded. "All right." I replayed the dream in my head:

First I was in walk-in closet, listening to my parents talk.

"I don't know how to describe this feeling. When I found that new room in my house—"

"The Office?" Dr. Eldridge asked.

"Yeah, the Office. When I found it, I felt . . . wonder? Like the world had gotten bigger. But also sad."

"Sometimes we don't have words for all the things we feel. Go on."

Next I was in the Office (which was also the electric chair chamber) watching the newscast of Skelton.

"I'm angry."

Next I was being chased by the Plaid Man through the forest. (Which was also the aisles of the Wal-Mart.)

"I'm scared."

Next I got the idea to escape the Plaid Man by tearing my map in half.

"I'm . . . excited? I got a cool idea, but . . . wait. I forgot something. Something that happened."

Where had the Plaid Man come from? He came out of the traincar, yeah I remember that, but there was something different about it.

"What was different about it?" I mumbled.

"What was different about what?" Dr. Eldridge asked.

I snapped my fingers. *"That's it!"*

"What? What?"

"The traincar had a new room," I said, then thought: *It grew that new room on top, the little A-frame attic. That's what I dreamed. That's where they're hidden. Skelton's victims.*

In the attic of the traincar in Itza Linda.

Now all I have to do is get back there.

"Dr. Eldridge, thank you. This was a really big help!"

I was (and remain) a seriously stupid person. A true dips hit, I didn't even start to find my sea legs as a person until I was almost thirty, and even then, I was only getting started. It took years of therapy and tiny, incremental improvements to get myself to anyplace even approximating a functioning adult. Looking back at my formative years, I see nothing but a wasteland of unhealthy thinking and bad decisions.

But every so often, I got something right.

Like Lee Dockery.

It took my sister kicking me squarely and rightfully in the ass to *get* it right, but starting that December night, I finally made a good friend.

"Who are you calling?" Mom yelled from the kitchen.

I was in the living room, standing by our Christmas tree, which we always put up in front of the walk-in closet. Our rotary-dial phone sat on a side table by the roll-top. Keeping a nervous eye on the walk-in closet, I dialed Lee's number and yelled in response:

"Lee Dockery! Can I sleep over this Fridayyy?"

"Is it okay with his mommm?"

Our entire exchange unfolded in this state of half-shout.

Lee's mom picked up:

"Dockery residence, this is Sandra speaking, how can I help you?"

My stuttering levels ratcheted up to maximum: "Uh hi Ms. . . . uh-ockery, uh this is Hi is it okay if I sleep over uh this Friday."

"Why, Hiram Gresham! What a delight to hear your voice. Goodness, you sound like quite the young man these days! Here, let me get Lee for you." Her phone clunked around and: *"Leeee phoooone it's your friiiiiend Hiiiiiram!"*

"Uh wait is it okay if I sleep—"

Lee was on: "Hiram?! Why, good e'en to you, Admiral. I've never received a phone call before!"

"Are you serious?" I thought for a moment. "I guess I haven't, either! My dad used to write me letters sometimes."

Mom: *"Did Sandy say it's okayyyy?"*

"Oh!" I said. "Lee, can I sleep over Friday? My mom needs your mom to say it's okay."

Silence. "You'd like to come over?"

"Yeah! I mean, if you still want me to. I figured we could play that video game you told me about, the one about the maze?"

"Masterminder Home Edutainment Presents Theseus's Labyrinth of Terror."

"That's it. Sounds really cool! So can I—"

His voice was a siren: *"Mommm can Hiram—"*

Sandra's voice: "I'm right here, honey."

"Would y'all shut up!" Dawn was yelling, too, her voice more distant. *"I'm tryin' to study in here, sheez!"*

I smiled. Lee had some *pipes,* and I knew they had a small place. I could relate.

Lee: "Oh, I beg your pardon. May Hiram sleep over this Friday?"

"As long as it's okay with his mom, of course."

"Hiram, do you have your mother's permission?"

The next couple exchanges happened at roughly the same time:

Me: *"Mommmm, Lee's mom says it's okay!"*
Lee: *"His mom says it's okay!"*
Sandra: *"Then it's okay!"*
My mom: *"Then it's okay!"*
"Splendid!" Lee said.
"Great! Do I need to bring anything?"
"If you have any graph paper, that would be a boon."
"I think Mac has some. I'll bring it. Well, I'll see you at exams—"
"Wait, Hiram—if I may. I wanted to explain why I call you 'Admiral.'"
My face got hot. I didn't know why, at least not at the time.
"It's okay, Lee. I figured it had something to do with *Star Trek II,* the Kobayashi Maru?"
"It wasn't that. Of course, that sequence is a master class in misdirection, but I wanted to bring your attention to the scene where Captain Kirk tells Mr. Spock, his first officer, of the trouble at Regula One."
"Right. I remember that scene. Spock was praying?"
"Correct, though I believe he's meditating." He hesitated, taking a long breath. "Spock tells Kirk that he will always be his friend, even though he is his superior officer. That's why I call you Admiral. I have been and always shall be your friend."
Every detail about this moment is enshrined in a proud place in my mind. The wintertime sun cast an orange glow through the side window. Our old rotary phone had the numbers 4, 1, and 2 rubbed out because we used them so much. Mom was making spaghetti. Christmas was right around the corner.
Lee was my first good friend.
Let me clarify: he was my first close friend who was also a truly good person. I'd had neighborhood friends or playground buddies, but they were little assholes, for the most part, constantly calling each other names or looking for ways to tear you down. Not Lee. He was the first friend who was kind to me and who was secure enough in his sense of self to express his affection in such unvarnished terms—no small feat for a boy in the late eighties.
A moment ago, I said my face got hot, and I didn't know why. Now I know I was blushing out of the simple joy that comes from being paid an open kindness. What I said next came easily:
"Lee, we're both admirals. Nobody outranks anyone here, deal?"
"Very well."
"Lee . . ." I trailed off.
"Yessir?"
"Nothing. See you tomorrow."

We hung up. I'd almost asked him for his help finding Itza Linda, but I decided against it. I thought it might be too frightening a quest for him.

Like I said, I'm a dipshit.

But in the meantime, I had a plan to get back to Itza Linda, and it was happening tonight.

Mackenzie

Her baby brother ran in with a complicated expression. Corrie was stirring the spaghetti sauce, which steamed up the kitchen.

"Is Lee excited to have you over?" Corrie asked.

"Huh?" Hiram said. "Yeah, how'd you know?"

"Your sister was telling me about what a sweet kid he is."

Mac and Hiram shared a look. His expression was still inscrutable, but it registered happiness and a deep contentment combined with something darker; some unspoken disappointment, maybe?

"Yeah, he's excited, and we're gonna play a cool game he's got. *Labyrinth of something-or-other.*"

"Well, I'm glad you're spending some time with him. I've met his mother, and she's a really sweet lady. Reminds me of my old friend Pepper who introduced me to Willie Bates down in Panama City over spring break my freshman year at—"

Now that she was babbling, Mac enacted her plan: "Oh, Mom, I'm spending the night at Sabrina's this Friday, too. Her mom says it's okay."

Hiram frowned at her. Mac loved her brother, but he had the tendency to blab at the wrong moment. She shot him a *keep your mouth shut* look and winked. The gears in the goofball's head turned for a moment before his eyes lit up. He nodded and theatrically winked in return.

Thank God Mom's so clueless, Mac thought.

"Well, I'll have the place to myself this Friday! How nice. Maybe I'll drop by Video Village and pick up a movie."

"Maybe you could go out on a date? I know Mr. Tucker at school, and he's really—"

Clank! Corrie dropped her stirring spoon on the range and leaned forward, resting her hands on the counter. The temperature seemed to drop a few dozen degrees.

Hiram had fucked up. Mac winced and tried to shush him, but he was already talking:

"Uh I'm sorry—"

"Did I ever tell you that Willie went on to coach the Demon Deacons?

He was the head coach, can you believe it? But I remember meeting him at Rustler's Reef and I thought . . . what a great smile!" Her speech was endless and breakless. She spoke without periods or purpose, just filling the void with her stories of times and triumphs past.

Even though she'd known her mom much longer than her dad, Mac felt a stronger connection with her father. He didn't protect his inner life as jealously as her mom did. You could ask him tough questions, and he'd usually give a straight answer.

"Mom, are you working Wal-Mart tonight?"

"We only dated the one summer, but we walked the boardwalk every—Oh? What was that, sweetie? No, I've got the night off. I was planning to turn in early." She turned and leaned against the stove. "Think you can keep an eye on this little guy so your mom can get a good night's sleep?"

"You got it, Mom." She addressed Hiram: "Think we can keep you from getting lost tonight, goofball?"

"Of course you can," Hiram said with that same inscrutable expression. *What's he up to?*

Justin

He loved being able to see satellites.

The cottage was a cross between a craftsman and something out of a fairy tale, with a kooky slate-tile roof and walls built from alternating red brick and stucco of varying shades of mustard and deep blue. Wavy glass windows looked in on comfy, distorted interiors. One of the stained-glass windows had been liberated from an old brewery and depicted a beer-fermenting tank. Getting there was an ordeal of switchback roads and dirt grooveways. The nearest supermarket was a general store twenty minutes away in town.

The real estate agent jokingly called it "Snow White's wintertime getaway."

Justin Johnson took it on the spot.

He sat outside his front door—thick red wood inlaid with a steel speakeasy spy door—and watched the sunset. His cottage sat next to a cliff that overlooked a sweeping green valley. Rolling mountains surrounded him. Twin lakes sat below. A lawn of grass and gravel pathways encircled the cottage, enclosed by a stucco retaining wall capped with the same red tile as the roof. Various quaint ornaments dotted the lawn, most of which had been there when he moved in: a birdbath, various steel sculptures, a miniature medieval village complete with a working windmill.

Justin sat in a fold-up camping chair and sipped a cocktail as the Milky Way emerged. He wore a fluffy robe, pajama bottoms, and a T-shirt that read

Florida A&M Marching 100. A black cat with gold eyes slinked out of the house and bounded into his lap, immediately head-bonking his chin.

"Hey, Rusty," he whispered, scanning the sky for his nightly visitor. After a few moments, he spotted it: a twinkling speedster that zipped across the sky like it did every night. "There you are," he said. Rusty nudged his hand, purring away, and Justin obliged with some extra pets. He was about to stand when something caught his eye:

The satellite illuminated something.

"What the . . ."

He squinted, trying to get a bead on it. It was big, whatever it was, and it seemed to enclose the entire planet.

"A . . . grid?"

That's what it looked like. A massive, hexagonal, geodesic grid flashed into view for the slightest of seconds.

Then it was gone.

"Huh." Justin shrugged and went inside. He left his door open so Rusty could come and go as he pleased. (He'd found him goofing around his front yard when he moved in; they bonded immediately.) The cottage was comfy and cluttered, with hardwood walls and floors, the floors covered with the occasional shag throw rug. Christmas decorations glowed: candoliers in the windows, garlands on the mantle, a tree in the corner. A fireplace flickered happily, its mantle overhung with photos and artwork. His movie collection lay strewn next to a TV/VCR combo, including *Coming to America, Eddie Murphy: Raw,* anything with Richard Pryor, *The Great Escape,* all the *Star Wars* and *Indiana Jones* movies, the *Shaft* series, all of Spike Lee's joints, *Purple Rain,* and a hundred others. He'd framed a copy of Langston Hughes's poem "Harlem." Photos of Justin's glory days on the football field alternated with shots of him acting on Broadway, including as the understudy for Dan Kaffee in *A Few Good Men.*

That was one of the happiest nights of his life. The lead actor (a truly sweet guy) took a spill in the subway, so Justin had to go on, and it just so happened to be on the night his mother came to see him. He had a nice enough part (Corporal Barnes), but he was so proud his momma got to see him during one of his finest hours as an actor.

Justin always chuckled when he thought back to that night. The play's dramaturge assigned the understudy roles. Right before Justin was about to go onstage, he bumped into the director, a gray-haired old white guy. He was nice enough, but his expression definitely said, *My lead understudy's a Black guy?* After Justin brought the house down, the director caught him outside the theater and whispered in his ear:

"I should've cast you as Kaffee in the first place," he said.

But he never reached out to Justin about any other roles.

Oh, well, Justin thought as he lingered on the photo of him as Kaffee. His momma had snapped it from the audience and made him sign it for her. She'd signed it, too.

It read: *JJ's big night! Love, Sue. AYF.*

"Aw, Momma," he whispered, smiling and shaking his head at the inscription. He'd always wondered why she'd signed it with her first name. He sat in his favorite easy chair, opposite his fireplace and overlooked by his Christmas tree. A table-lamp combo sat next to him, bearing a rotary-dial phone and some papers. Justin picked up the phone, dialed, and waited.

"Momma? Hey, it's JJ. No, no, everything's fine, sorry to call so late. Couldn't sleep."

He laughed.

"You either, huh? Birds of a feather. Yeah, yeah—I wanted to hear my momma's voice. You got me. Hey, I wanted to ask you a couple things, if that's all right. Y'know that old photo of me in *A Few Good Men?* Why'd you sign it 'Sue' instead of 'Momma' or something?"

He sat silent.

"Oh, it's your little secret, huh? All right, I get it. Huh? Oh, what else was I gonna ask? Well . . . do you think what I did all those years ago was right? Yeah, with him, with Skelton."

He sat silent.

"Yeah. Thanks. I guess I needed to hear that." His eyes were glistening, his voice hoarse. "Thanks, Momma. Well, Sandman's calling. I'm gonna hit it. Love you, too."

He hung up and sat for a moment, gathering himself. Once he was sure he wasn't going to cry, he picked up a paper from his side table and took up the evening's primary project:

A map.

Mackenzie

The thunder woke her before her alarm did. Her dad had taught her to notice the difference between thunder coming from the east versus the west.

Western thunder always rattled her windows.

Glass shook in its frames, jolting her to a sitting-up position. Her alarm clock squawked: *beep beep beep!* It was 10:30 p.m. She slapped it silent and slipped out of bed, stepping into her house slippers before she stole out her bedroom door.

R-r-r-ummm-ble!

Her windows rattled again. Mac ignored the racket and crept down the hall to her baby brother's room. This had become her nightly vigil. Sometimes Mom looked after him, but whenever Mac could, she shouldered the burden of making sure Hiram didn't sleepwalk out of the house again.

Her poor mom needed the rest.

Hiram's pattern had become familiar: he dropped off around 9:00 p.m. and if he was going to sleepwalk, he'd rise sometime between 10:00 and 11:00 p.m. Mac got up every night Hiram spent at home and kept an eye on him for this dangerous half-hour, sitting outside his door and reading the latest *Goosebumps*. She was halfway through *One Day at HorrorLand* before it occurred to her something was missing.

Hiram's snores.

The kid usually sawed some serious logs, but not tonight. Mac jumped up, opened his door, and ran to his bed, which *appeared* to be full, but when she ripped back the covers, she found a pile of clothes arranged in a vaguely Hiram-esque shape.

Never should've let him watch Escape from Alcatraz, she thought.

She threw open the window, admitting a rush of freezing air. A dusting of snow covered the ground, revealing the faintest sign of footprints.

"Oh, my God," she whispered, lunging across the room to Hiram's desk, where she found his backpack missing.

He'd snuck out on purpose, the little shit.

Before she knew it, she was plunging down the stairs, rounding the corner to the master bedroom. The door was ajar. She inched it open and was about to speak—but didn't. Her mom had fallen asleep sitting up against the headboard, wearing the same clothes she taught in all day. A paperback novel was splayed open in her lap, her bedside lamp shining in her face. She was soundlessly and motionlessly asleep. Mac felt a surge of love for her.

I can take care of this.

She was about to close the door when she noticed something. Dozens of photos of Deak covered the walls, showing him on his many adventures in the Peace Corps—building schools, coaching basketball, digging trenches for water. He looked bearded and manly and happy as hell.

But there were no photos of him and Mom together.

Mac shut the door and let her mom sleep.

Justin

He hunched over his map, making notes and sketching in details: his house, which he drew with remarkable fidelity, right down to the retaining wall and cliffside. Next he turned his attention to the rest of the map, which he'd begun the previous night.

After an incredibly vivid dream.

To the right of his house, he'd drawn a wooded glen that surrounded a small depression. In the middle sat a rectangular structure.

He wrote: *Shipping container? Crate? Mobile home?*

Under that, he wrote: *ARE THEY HERE? How do I get here?*

Rusty jumped onto the back of his chair, by now his regular position. Justin regarded the map. He noted the position of the rectangular structure relative to his cottage. In the space between them, he drew two large wavy lines.

Outside, thunder rumbled.

Hiram's Journal

Sometimes I look back on this night—the night I almost found Justin Johnson—and think, "Wow, that could've gone either way."

But then, I guess I could say that about everything that happened in '89 and '90.

By this point, I'd figured out when Mac held her nightly vigil outside my door, so I set my alarm for half an hour earlier and stuffed it under my pillow so she wouldn't hear it through our house's paper-thin walls. Once outside, I made for the woods, complete with an exploration pack that included a flashlight and a monkey wrench, my sense of weaponry clearly influenced by the movie *Clue.* I was freezing my substantial ass off after five minutes, but I was determined to find Itza Linda, find the traincar, and open its attic.

Where's Skelton's victims were.

My dad's voice echoed in my mind: *There's another train.*

I didn't know what that meant. Had Skelton somehow stolen a traincar from the park? Was the traincar I saw in my dreams merely a representation of a traincar that was located somewhere else? I had to find out.

I was deep in the forest now, following my map closely. To the northwest was the town windmill, creaking and whining in spooky circles. Mountain noises rustled and whistled. Trees sighed, leaves crinkled and crunched. In the distance, a bobcat screeched. Holiday decorations cast a welcome-warm glow over the tree line, but they also hid the stars, which I used to navigate.

No matter; I had my trusty compass and a No. 2 pencil.

"Let's see," I muttered. "Where am I?"

Thunder rumbled to the west, accompanied by strangely low-hanging dark clouds. Snow was coming, I hoped. I could handle getting caught out in snow; freezing rain, not so much. I checked my map, remembering the words that had popped into my head the other night:

Who says that wouldn't work in the real world?

I'd been thinking about my dream, where I tore my map and it tore a hole in the earth. But this was different. I wasn't trying to *escape* the Plaid Man but *find* something. Still, I took care to judge my position relative to the windmill and made a few notes on my map. If my calculations were correct, the traincar would be due southeast from my current position. I set off at a lumbering lope, confident in my cartography but still contending with a nagging thought:

It wasn't there last time.

It wasn't. The traincar had only been there when I was dreaming.

So what're you gonna do, man? Go there, fall asleep in the freezing cold, and hope you dream about it again?

I didn't know, but I kept running. I had to find those kids.

Justin

R-r-r-ummmmble!

Rusty leaped from the easy chair, landing nimbly and scampering to the door, where he gave Justin a grumpy look. Justin stood, map in hand, and went to stand in the doorway. Dark clouds were gathering to east, while a sharp winter's wind cut through the trees and threatened to extinguish his fire. The map flapped in his hand, so he pocketed it.

"Looks like a snowstorm, Rust. Better get inside."

For once, Rusty obliged, slinking back in with a quick stop to mark his legs. Closing the door, he walked to the retaining wall. More clouds gathered, but there was something strange: they were so close to the earth. It looked less like a storm and more like a pitch-dark fog was washing into the forest on the rolling wave of a powerful wind. The plane of his bird feeder's water stood at a steep, rippling incline. One of his lawn ornaments (a sculpture of a woman holding an ecstatic ballet position) toppled over with a *crash*. He jumped.

And the black clouds kept gathering in the woods ahead.

Justin opened his front gate but hesitated, suddenly wishing he had neighbors. He pushed down his fear, calling it irrational. To his right, a light clicked on.

A light in a wrought-iron lamp-post.

His real estate agent, full of fairy-tale references, called it the Narnia lamp-post. It turned on and off at the same times every day, connected to some forgotten civic grid.

He walked toward the storm clouds.

Mackenzie

Mac was swifter than her little brother, she knew, but the problem was, she didn't know which way he'd gone. All she had was a dim memory of a few months ago, when he sleepwalked out of the house and said he saw that monster guy.

The Plaid Man.

She pulled her peacoat tighter and ran down their street toward the little forest trail Hiram was always taking. At the head of the trail, she stopped, her eyes widening at the sight of the storm clouds gathering over the woods; only they didn't seem to be gathering *over* so much as *within* the forest ahead.

What kind of storm is that?

Fear for her brother's safety took her. She was running and calling Hiram's name without even knowing it.

Hiram's Journal

There it was, the wooded glen where I'd last seen the traincar. I almost tripped into the broad depression in the glen's middle, but I caught myself and teetered to a stop at its rim, map in hand, wind kicking through the trees, the black clouds sinking lower and lower into the trees until they weren't storm clouds but a deranged kind of inky fog.

I was easing my way down into the depression when something shook against my leg. Reaching into my pocket, I produced the source: my compass. I held it—*tried* to hold it—but it quivered hard enough to render my hand a blur, its needle spinning into a silver smear.

"What the hell," I muttered, looking up—and that's when I finally saw it. The clouds gathering ahead were shot with streamers and sluices of white-bright light. The lightwaves whipped back and forth, sparking familiar memories. *What does this remind me of?* I thought. Images surged through my mind: a lamp-post by a cliffside, a gate bearing a strange dragon's-head symbol, and a powder-blue cabin with an A-frame overhang.

Crunch. I'd stepped in stones. There was a circle of them—black stones, dark and shiny as onyx. Crouching, I took one up; it was hot to the touch and magnetic to the eye. *These weren't here last time.* I couldn't stop looking at it. Lightning flashed overhead, flickering off the black stone, which I dropped. That's when it occurred to me. Looking closely at the black stone gave the same view as what was ahead of me: shimmering darkness.

That's what I was reminded of—water.

The darkness filling the forest wasn't clouds but some kind of *fluid*. But how could that be? How could millions of gallons of black water be flooding the forest without washing everything away?

A small voice in me whispered, *What if it isn't water at all?*

Another voice asked: *Who says that wouldn't work in the real world?*

Even though I knew it was a terrible idea, I marched ahead, straight into the shimmering darkness.

Justin

Snow fell in sharp bullets. They stung his face as he pressed into the woods, moving closer and closer to the wall—because that's what it looked like now, a shimmering black *wall*—his eyes wide, his map safe in his pocket. Somewhere deep inside, he sensed something shake against his leg, but the map was his pocket's only contents. He raised a forearm against the incoming snow-freeze, gritting his teeth and scared as hell but intent on finding out what was happening on his mountain that night.

Someone was screaming.

"*What?!*" Justin screamed back. His ears were trained to the tone: someone was in trouble.

The voice, a young woman to his ears, shouted back, but he could only make out snippets:

"*Cot . . . rittro . . . it!*"

"*Who's there?! Where are—*"

He stopped when he saw it: a shape, swimming in the darkness ahead. Was it someone struggling? Someone in need of help? He didn't care about the danger; he simply sprinted ahead.

Mackenzie

"*Hiram, get out here, you little shit!*"

Her thighs burned as she pushed herself into a massive headwind that had her holding her snow cap to her head and clutching her coat shut. Icy daggers rained down on her; she couldn't fucking *believe* her baby brother was out in this mess. They were going to have a serious talk, assuming they both got home alive.

No, don't think like that, Mac. You know you're both—

"Holy shit," she whispered.

It shimmered before her, a massive wall of inky water that seemed to stretch to the stratosphere. It was the black fog she'd seen before, only it had never been fog but rather this . . . *stuff.* She froze, hugging herself against the storm, which had worsened into a mix of snow and sky-falling slush. Surreality settled over her.

What was she looking at?

What *could* she be looking at?

Her eyes crept upward, expecting to see the same grid she'd seen in her dream library, but instead her eyes lit on a quivering shape in the middle distance.

A chubby shape.

"Hiram!"

Hiram's Journal

The wall wasn't a wall but a dim and fuzzy boundary. You didn't feel yourself pass through anything; instead, as you walked farther and farther into the black water, the fainter else everything became. It was like someone was lowering the opacity on existence.

But my surroundings weren't featureless. Amazing sights flashed past me: oceans and mountains and deserts and tundras. I flew past cities and coastal towns, I caught glimpses of strange hallways to nowhere, and I sensed the happy comfort of hearths and homes. I was walking through molasses, each step carrying me into deeper and deeper darkness.

Wait. What's that?

Something was taking shape ahead, something square. Was it a house? I pushed myself onward, even though it was getting hard to breathe. (Though who knew if that was a side effect of the darkness or my fat ass?) After a few more steps, the shape racked into focus and revealed it wasn't just one shape; it was two:

A house and a man.

I was in a dream, running with feet that couldn't move and yelling with a voice that wasn't mine:

"Hello? Who's there?"

Justin

The voices from the darkness were competing with each other. One was incomprehensible:

"Kemmo faxang wholo!"

The other sounded like a boy:

"Hello? Who's there?"

Even stranger, both voices rang a bell. Justin stopped, surrounded by the black water, and squinted, trying to bring the shape into focus.

Who is that?

The girl's voice sounded again:

"Holo axalo ug!"

Justin shouted: "Hey! Do you need help?!"

A moment passed before the boy responded with the last words he expected to hear:

"Mr. Johnson?!"

The shape came running forward, awkward and plodding. When it got close enough for him to see, Justin had to stifle a scream.

Hiram's Journal

It was him, the man himself—Justin Johnson. Somehow I knew it, so I ran into the thickening murk as fast as I could, bringing the incredible sight into view: some kind of quaint Snow White cottage, and near it was a sight that took my breath away:

A wrought-iron lamp-post, straight out of Narnia.

My previous vision flashed before me: the strange dragon's-head symbol, the lamp-post, and the cabin with the A-frame overhang.

But that's not an A-frame cabin up ahead, I thought. *Why did I see one in my vision?*

I could worry about that later. For now, I needed to get his attention.

"Mr. Johnson?!" I yelled.

Justin

The kid had no face.

It emerged from the forest, dressed in a kid's wintertime clothes and covered with snow. The kid looked heavyset, with red hair . . . and nothing but a blank, flat expanse of flesh where his face should be. Snow fell harder and harder. Justin almost bolted, but something held him in place, some unseen force or deep intuition that what he was seeing was no threat.

The girl yelled again: *"Pumv hoo-lo!"*

Justin ignored her, instead focusing on the boy's non-face, which was slowly fading into view. Features sprang from the flat flesh: a pug nose, chubby cheeks, a pair of kind eyes.

He'd seen this kid before. But where? He searched his memory and was about to remember when he saw the creature.

"Oh, my holy God," Justin whispered.

The creature reared up from the earth—about a dozen yards to the boy's left—shoving aside the black water with massive limbs the size of redwoods. It floated for a moment and morphed into a recognizably humanoid shape before it slammed silently into the earth. Somehow Justin knew this thing, big as it was, was designed for stealth. It lumbered closer and brought its face into view.

Its plaid face.

Mackenzie

Mac had seen footage of whales emerging from the sea; they looked like they'd been fired out of something, shooting skyward, surrounded by graceful waves.

If the earth were an ocean, this thing shot out of it like a whale.

It was *enormous.* She flashed on any number of fairy tales about giants as she watched it take shape above. The black water submerged everything in sight, rendering the scene dim and indistinct and blotting out the stars but still admitting snow, which spat and showered on her in freezing sheets. The creature split into dozens of floating spheres and blobs, reconstituting itself into a human shape—two arms, two legs, and a head—before it slammed to earth without a sound.

And about a dozen yards away from her baby brother.

A grown-up man's screaming voice floated through the night, but Mac could barely make it out:

"Gid! Evolve solo!"

The giant creature must've heard it, because it swiveled its head toward Hiram—and opened a whole new world to Mac.

It had a plaid face.

The rest of its body was a swirling, paisley watercolor; a fractal madness of blues, purples, reds, yellows, and oranges. As its body took on a more human shape, so too did its "clothes": darker colors covered it from its neckline to its wrists and ankles. But its face was undeniably plaid.

Suddenly all of Hiram's weird stories about his dreams made sense, came to life, and felt true. Shame shot through her for an instant—shame at not believing her brother—but it was quickly banished by terror and resolve. Before she knew it, her feet were churning though the thick darkness and she was screaming:

"Hiram! Behind you!"

Justin

"Kid! Over there!"

He slapped his thigh, looking for a gun. It was an old instinct, and he cursed himself for not keeping it around. No matter, Justin Johnson lowered his shoulders and ran for the little boy, ignoring the danger posed by the giant creature, his legs a blur, his mind hell-bent-intent on saving this kid.

Suddenly, the calculus changed: the girl was there.

She seemed to pop into existence to his left, summoned by some grim but friendly deity, her intent same as his: save the kid! Weird words floated across the black water: *"Fo-hicked ugh!"* They were closing in on the chubby kid when he surprised them both by hurling a rock at the creature's face. It soared skyward, the stone did, at least thirty to forty yards—*Nice arm, kid*—and connected!

But instead of reacting in pain, the creature's entire head burst apart in a massive black cloud shot with multi-colored lightning-bolts of red, blue, and yellow hue. It took a step toward the kid, its feet shapeless horrors, its hands a thousand bristling willow-branches capped with talons. The sight must've shocked the kid, because he staggered back, arms spinning, and fell right into the girl's arms.

The Gold Rush.

The words sprang to mind, sure as sunshine, and he remembered where they'd all met: in the old, abandoned gondola station. Before he could speak, though, the girl—*What was her name?*—yanked her brother back into the black water, where they both winked out of view.

Leaving him alone with the creature.

Hiram's Journal

"Wait, wait! We have to go back and help him, help Mr. Johnson!"

Mac was wrestling me back and out of the black water, pulling and shoving me along.

"He can take care of himself!" she screamed as the snow-slush showered us harder and harder, sharp as knives now, each a white-cold cut to the flesh. Through the black water, I could faintly make out the shapes of the Plaid Man and Justin. They both stood perfectly still for one endless moment before the Plaid Man reached up to its inhuman face and—

—CRASHHH!

Mac and I slammed to the ground, splashing in a puddle of slush, blinking into the sudden moon-glare that bathed us, because the black water was gone. Whatever it was, it had vanished, taking Justin and the Plaid Man with it.

"Noooo! Oh my God, no! Justin! Mr. Justin! Oh, no!"

Mac hugged me close. "It's okay, it's okay, it's okay."

"No, it isn't! We have to help him!"

Justin

The kids were gone, but the monster remained.

Justin Johnson stood in the sprawling darkness that surrounded his home and faced off against the giant. It regarded him, tilting its head as if curious.

"Stay away from those kids," Justin said, steady as she goes.

In response, the giant reached up to its face and sank its thousands of willowy fingertips into the bloody latticework that was its flesh—and pulled. Justin grimaced in horror as the creature tore off its own face, the expanse of flesh still connected to its head by hundreds of gory filaments. Hidden underneath was something flat and shiny:

Glass. A television screen.

Light flickered from within its massive skull, illuminating the screen with eleven flashing letters:

IDESLESSTWO

IDESLESSTWO

IDESLESSTWO

Justin frowned in confusion.

How did it know about that? he thought.

And it vanished; the creature, the darkness, the freezing snow and rain, everything. It all vanished in a head-spinning instant, leaving Justin standing alone on a quiet winter's night in the mountains. Something snapped, and he spun on a heel, ready for a fight, but it was only Rusty scampering over. Dazed, Justin crouched to pet the cat, only to quickly stand back up when freezing water seeped into his shoes; his pajamas were soaked. On a hunch, he pulled out his map.

It was soggy-wet and falling to pieces.

Mackenzie

She had no time to argue. They were cold and soaked and had to get home before their mom woke up. She hoisted Hiram to his feet, but he was apoplectic, pulling something out of his pocket and waving it wildly in the air.

"No, no! There has to be a way to get back to him. I-I uh I made notes, here, look!"

He proffered the map, which she waved away.

"We gotta get home, buddy, before . . . before . . ."

"Before what?" he asked before realizing she was gaping in horror at something behind him.

Hiram's Journal

I didn't want to turn around, but I had to.

When I did, the world un-seamed. Thousands of willowy fingers were prying open a slash-cut in reality. It hung in the sky about twenty feet overhead, this dark slash, growing wider and wider as the Plaid Man's thousands of fingers pulled it open.

For some reason, I was feeling petty.

"D-do you believe me now?"

"Hiram. Shut. The fuck. Up."

With limbs as long as a sycamore, the Plaid Man writhed its way out of the hole, which was surrounded by a miasma of spectral black ink that glittered with blinding-black star specks. His skin—if you can call it that— had been a multi-colored soup until now, a trippy paisley pattern, but now it was coalescing back into his blue suit, his complexion returning to the Freddy Krueger look I'd seen before. His head bore a plaid pattern where his face should be; the pattern-section shifted forward like a single tile and transformed into a patch of flannel that was secured in place by staple after staple that blinked into existence, one at a time, and lanced into his face with audible *clicks*. He'd been shrinking, too, the Plaid Man, until he stood at roughly eye level with us.

Whereupon I shit you not, he *curtsied* to us.

"I cain't reveal what ain't real," he said with Skelton's voice, rising from his curtsy and reaching for his plaid patch, which he tore off to reveal an old-school throw-switch. He cranked it down and—*KRAZZZZKTT!* Lightning flashed and licked from his head. I was fully thunderstruck, my voice little more than a wheeze.

"Uh I think it's time to—"

But Mac was already pulling me along.

Mackenzie

A nightmare chased them through a burgeoning blizzard. As they ran,

Mac looked to see the Plaid Man moving like a flip-book with pages missing, quantum-leaping from one location to the next; sometimes hiding behind a tree, sometimes inches behind them, sometimes a hundred feet in the air, all the while howling with the voices of a thousand horrors.

"I cain't reveal what ain't real."

"We're off limits, okay? You and me, we're off limits."

"I'da done tore up the map by now."

"Mother-*fehhker!*"

Mac fell back a few steps to grab her brother, who was sucking wind and lagging.

"C'mon, you got this, you got this! We're almost there!"

Trees closed in around them as the forest thickened. It was harder going, but the change in terrain encouraged Mac; it meant they were close. The West Chim windmill creaked immediately over the tree line—*almost there*—and they burst from the woods onto their street, both of them billowing sweaty steam. The freezing rain had become a proper blizzard sometime during the chase.

They stopped. And breathed. And watched the woods.

Nothing emerged.

Some Washington Irving-esque rite had bound the Plaid Man to the forest, at least for now. Mac, out of breath, patted her baby brother's shoulder.

"Come on, goofball. We need to talk."

Hiram's Journal

I was sitting in Mac's room, waiting for her. We'd made it home and changed into dry clothes, whereupon she told me to wait in her room. Something clattered in the hallway, followed by Mac backing in her room with the extension phone in hand, the cord stretched to the limit. She cradled a phone book under her arm. After kicking the door shut, she sat with her back against her built-in desk, eyes downcast.

"Did you know that would happen?" she asked.

"Uh what? No. No way."

"So you haven't been going out in the woods and almost getting lost in a . . . I don't even know what to call that."

"The black water? No, that's the first time I've seen it."

"But it's not the first time you've seen the plaid guy."

"The Plaid Man. No."

She finally looked up. "Hiram, I can't let you go in those woods again."

"Uh don't, uh don't you want to know why I'm going out there?"

"Okay, why?"

"I think Lenny Skelton hid those kids, the ones he . . ."

Barely audible: "Murdered."

I nodded. "Yeah. I think he hid them out there."

"In the woods?"

"No. Well uh, yes, kind of. I think there's a magic traincar out in the woods. You can only get to it a certain way. I think all the kids are there."

"What does that mean, a 'certain way'?"

"I don't know. That's what I'm trying to figure out. When I was dreaming, I was able to find it, but when I woke up, it was gone. I think maybe you have to be dreaming to find it?"

Mac sat thinking. I was worried she was about to tell me I was nutso, but she surprised me.

"Okay."

"Okay? Okay what?"

"I'm sorry I didn't believe you."

"They didn't believe Lucy, either."

Mac frowned.

I smiled. "In *The Lion, The Witch, and the Wardrobe?*"

"Right," she said with a nod. "I don't know *what* exactly's going on, but I know there's something happening in the woods. And I think I know why you want to find the kids. To help Mr. Johnson."

I nodded. "I keep thinking about their moms and dads and brothers and sisters. It's not fair, what happened to those kids. It's not fair, what their families have to live with. It's not fair that they blamed it on Mr. Johnson. It's not fair that Auntie Hanna had to quit. It's bull—" I stopped short.

"You can say it was bullshit. That's what Auntie Hanna called it."

"It was bullshit. He should get his job back. So should Auntie Hanna."

"Auntie Hanna chose to leave her job. And Mr. Johnson's doing fine. He got all that money from the park. He doesn't need your help."

"Then why did the map take me to him?"

Mac didn't have an answer for that.

I asked: "You remember, don't you?"

"Remember what?"

"What happened tonight. Sometimes grown-ups can't remember. Like in that book about the clown."

"I'm not a grown-up, dummy. I'm about three years older than you."

"But you remember everything, right?"

"Yeah, I remember every minute of it. And did you actually *read* that book? It was, like, a thousand pages long."

I gave a quiet laugh, nodding. "Yeah, I loved it. Gave me crazy nightmares."

"Same here. Great book. We should probably be taking notes from it."

"Do you think Mr. Johnson remembers what happened?"

She thought, shrugged. "I don't know. But I *am* worried about him." She indicated the phone and opened the phone book to the *J* section. "Let's call him."

Justin

Justin plodded back to his cottage, the remnants of his map in hand, his mind swirling at what he'd just seen. Rusty was waiting for him at the door, marking his legs and purring.

"Hey, Rust. Anything interesting happen?"

He practically staggered across the room and flopped in his easy chair. The door stood open, admitting a freezing breeze. His head lolled back, his eyes slipping shut for a moment before he sat up with a snort, shaking his head and glancing around the room. Rusty lingered in the doorway, prompting him to hop up with a chuckle.

"Left the dang door open," he muttered to himself as he waved Rusty inside. "Come on, Rust."

He returned to his seat with a puzzled expression, sat for a moment staring at the fire, then turned on his television. The image made him wince.

It was Skelton, being interviewed again on that damn tabloid show.

He left it on mute with closed-captioning, picked up the phone, and dialed.

"Hi, Momma? JJ again. Yeah, I know it's late. No, no—everything's fine. I just . . . well, something happened tonight, and . . . well . . . remember those dreams I had as a kid? I'm having 'em again. And, Momma? I don't think they're . . . they're . . ."

Text on his television silenced him:

SKELTON EXECUTION SET FOR MARCH 15, 1990.

"March fifteenth."

He flashed on the letters the Plaid Man had shown him:

IDESLESSTWO

"March fifteenth. The ides of March. Less two." He realized he was whispering and gave a theatrical jerk of his head, saying into the receiver: "No, Momma, I wasn't talking to you. Yeah, I remember why that date's so important to us."

March thirteenth. A date that would live in infamy for Justin Johnson.

Skelton appeared onscreen. Stark white-on-black words, some of them misspelled, spilled across the screen, screaming at him:

SKELTON: JENNY'S WON OF THE LUCKY WONS, U NO THAT RIGHT?
INTERVIEWER: WAT DO YOU MEAN WON OF THE LUCKY ONES?
Justin unmuted the TV. Skelton's voice was a knife in his mind:

"Jenny, see—I didn't get to *keep* her. That's the trick of it, neighbor. If you keep 'em, you get to stay and sneak around. And as long as them *[beep]*ing cops don't find the rest, I can keep sneakin' around."

"What do you mean when you say 'sneak around'?"

Skelton's expression fluctuated between joy and abject terror.

"Someone showed it to me."

"Showed you what?"

"The pathways between the pathways, the shuttle-zone between the lodges, the lurkway between the happy place and the sad. It's where the floor's jagged and everything's made of icing."

"What are you talking about?"

"See, there's only so much room through them white and pearlies—them Gates of Saint Peter—only so much room. The Good-Lord-God-A'mighty told me it was plumb too crowded up there. He told me I could sneak around as long as I kept a few little'uns from gettin' their wings."

Justin's chest was heaving, his sobs instant and uncontrollable. He held the receiver away from his face. Rusty jumped in his lap and started grooming his beard. He did it every time Justin cried, which was a lot these days. Justin muted the television and pressed the receiver back to his face.

"Nah, Momma, I'm fine. What I was trying to tell you is . . . I think those dreams I used to have were more than dreams."

The closed-captioning read: *SKELTON: IVE GOT MY NEW FAN TO THANK FOR THIS WON I SEE HIM I'M GOIN TO WAVE AND SAY HIGH.*

Justin turned off the television. "I think something's coming down the line, something big. And I think it's gonna happen on Ides Less Two. I don't know what." He sat silent. Nodded. "Yeah." His voice grew more resolute: "Yes. I remember what you said: 'Sometimes it is required you do awake your faith.' Yes, ma'am, I know you played that part in community theater. I bet you tore it up. Okay, thanks again for talking, Momma. I miss you so much."

He hung up and brooded for a long while. After the fire had flickered out and Rusty had fallen asleep in his lap, he took another sheet of paper from his side table and drew a compass rose on it.

It's a start, he thought as he rose and went to bed, letting Rusty in with him. He shut his door.

Silence settled over his home. Nothing stirred for hours.

Until his phone rang.

But Justin didn't hear it.

Hiram's Journal

"But we don't know his number. We don't even know where he lives. And it's late."

"I know, but at least people will be home. We can start here. If he doesn't live around here any more, maybe we can ask Auntie Hanna." She dialed the first number and handed me the phone. "You mind doing the talking?"

"Me? Why?"

"Your voice already cracked. You sound like a grown-up."

It was ringing. My throat was constricting. "Uh what am I supposed to ask?"

"Ask for Justin Johnson."

I hung up the phone. "What about my stutter?"

"Oh, I didn't think of that. Let's try some practice runs. Try saying 'Is Justin there?'"

"Uh is Justin there, uh is Justin there?"

"Now keep whispering that until someone picks up. Okay?"

I nodded. She dialed again. The receiver buzzed.

"Busy."

"Okay, let's try the next one."

Mac dialed. It rang. A woman answered.

"Hello?"

"Is Justin there?"

"Who may I ask is speaking?"

"Uh . . ."

Mac whispered: "His brother."

"His brother."

A pause, then: "He doesn't have a brother. Who is this?"

I slammed down the phone.

"Why'd you hang up?" Mac asked, throwing up a palm.

"She said he didn't have a brother! I didn't know what to say."

"Yeah, we should've made up a script."

"I think we should wait and call Auntie Hanna tomorrow. Maybe she knows how to find him."

"Okay. You sure you're okay going to bed? You were pretty freaked out in the woods."

I nodded and spoke the truth: "I don't think he's in danger, at least not tonight."

"Me neither," she said with a tired smile. "All right, goofball, let's get you to—"

RIIIIIING.

We stared at the phone like it had come to life.

"Who'd be calling this late?" Mac asked.

RIIIIIING. The sound echoed through the house.

"I don't know."

RIIIIIING.

"Answer it!"

I did, my hands shaking. "Uh hello?"

"Is this about those kids?"

It was the same woman as before. Her voice was loud enough for Mac to hear.

I covered the receiver. "What should I say?"

"Tell her yes."

Uncovering the receiver, I whispered: "Yes."

The woman let loose with a long, exhausted sigh. "We must get ten calls a week from you freaks. Telling us it was Justin's fault those kids are dead. *Well, this isn't his house. That's some other Justin. So stop calling goddammit!*"

"I'm sorry, I'm sorry," I said, already in tears. I was about to hang up.

"Wait, wait. Don't you *dare* hang up, not after you rousted me outta bed this time of night. You're going to do something for me. I already traced your number, and if you don't do what I say, you're going to get in serious trouble."

By this point, I was holding the phone between our ears. My hands were ice, my blood pumping and boiling with fear. Who *was* this lady, and what was she going to do to us?

Mac spoke: "What do you want?"

"I want . . . to tell you a joke."

"What?"

"Don't you like jokes?" She was screaming: *"Answer me!"*

"Yes, yes, we like jokes!"

"Here's the joke," she said, her voice suddenly deeper and lower. "What's the tastiest dish?"

The temperature dropped fifty degrees. Her voice had changed. That much I knew. It sounded layered, like a remix of three or four different voices.

"H-huh?" I said.

"Huh? Huh?" She made a guttural sound, the kind you make when you're making fun of a stutterer. "Can't you even *talk,* you little shit?"

Mac: "Hang up."

The woman was screaming, her voice *fritzing* out like she was being broadcast through a faulty speaker.

"Wha—zzzzkkkt—t's the tast—zzzzkkkt—iest dish? Zzzzkkkt!"

"I don't know!"

Mac was yelling: *"Hang up, hang up!"*

Now the woman was gone, replaced by the same horror from my dreams: *"IT'S KIDS! KIDS ARE THE zzzzkkkt TASTIEST DISH zzzzkkkt HAHAHAHAHA!"* It was Skelton and Trent and the Plaid Man, all screaming as one through the phone: *"THEY'LL NEVER GET TO HEAVEN, AND zzzzkkkt IT'S ALL YOUR FAULT! Zzzzkkkt! YOU'RE DEAD ANYWAY! IF YOU KEEP DRAWING MAPS, YOU'LL ONLY MAKE IT WORSE! YOU'RE DEAD, YOU'RE zzzzkkkt DEADzzzzkkkt!"*

Mac wrested the phone from me and slammed it down. The Plaid Man's screams lingered in the air like a solar afterimage.

"We've got to help those kids," I said.

"You're fuckin'-A right we do," Mac said before she rose on a pair of shaking legs and went downstairs. She returned, closing the door quietly.

"It didn't wake Mom." She sat. Took my hand. We were both crying. She wrist-wiped away some tears and said, "Did you hear what he said?"

"They'll never get to heaven," I said. "I think they're stuck here."

"They can't be stuck. That's not how it works."

"How do *you* know how it works?" I asked. "We don't go to church. It could be anything. What if it's *all* made up, what happens after we die? Or what if someone like Skelton can just make it up as he goes?"

"You're right. I don't know what happens after we die." She cried even harder, so hard she had to pause for breath. "But we can't leave them out there. I know that now. It's just . . . we have to be careful. *So* careful. I can't put Mom through this again."

I frowned, shook my head.

Mac's tears slowed. She said: "I keep forgetting you don't remember him much."

"Oh. Dad."

"Yeah."

I thought. "Should we keep trying to call Mr. Johnson?"

"No, let's ask Auntie Hanna about him," she said. "I don't want to call another wrong number and get *him* again. What you need to do is keep working on your map."

"But the Plaid Man said . . ." I trailed off.

"If we keep drawing maps, we're dead?" Mac said with a firm nod. "Yeah. Fuck him. I'm not scared of him. Well, I *am* scared, but that's not gonna stop us. I think the maps are the key to finding the traincar. And those kids."

"I do, too," I said, taking out my map. "But I don't understand why this map . . . well, why it did what it did."

Mac smiled, indicating the compass rose. "That's really good, Hiram. Have you been practicing?"

"No, I didn't draw that, Lee—" I stopped, looking closer at the map. "Lee drew it. Oh, my gosh, what if that's it?"

"What if it's what?"

"What if . . . I dunno . . . what if two people have to work on the same map for it to work?"

"But it *didn't* work. You didn't find the traincar."

"I know, but it still opened up a magic portal to Mr. Johnson's house."

Mac nodded, deep in thought. "Maybe you're right. Have you told Lee about any of this?"

"No, I was worried . . ."

"What?"

"I was worried it'd be too dangerous."

Mac gently socked my shoulder. "It *is* too dangerous, ya goofball. But . . . I think we need the help."

"So are you gonna tell Dawn?"

She nodded. "I think we have to. You're hanging out with Lee tomorrow night, right?"

"Yeah, and you're going to that big party at Soddy Farm? Oh, I mean, you're spending the night at Sabrina's house?" I smiled.

"Yeah, thanks for not blowing my cover. If I'm gonna be out all night, I always tell Mom I'm sleeping over somewhere so she doesn't worry."

"That's a good idea. I'll have to remember that once I'm old enough to drive."

"If we live that long."

Hanna

The former Sheriff Blackledge lived in a sculpture of glass and wood near the highest crests of the Smokies. A sweeping, single-floor, open-layout masterpiece, it could've been designed by Frank Lloyd Wright or tucked away in the trendiest enclaves of Southern California. It was accessible only by a single switchback road that narrowed directly into her driveway, which was flanked by all manner of hippie paraphernalia: goofy-looking windmills, lawn ornaments, and tchotchkes.

A small guest house stood next to hers, its windows aglow with warm, golden light. Hanna had been intending to rent out the cozy one-bedroom bungalow, but she kept putting it off. For now, she'd set up a bohemian teahouse in it. Ornate brass side tables adorned with stained glass sat among comfy Papasan chairs, while a star-shaped light hung overhead. She sat in a Papasan in front of the guest house, wearing linen pajamas, sipping coffee, and watching the sunrise.

The previous night's storm had filled her sleep with nightmares of a factory spewing blood and fire. She'd sprung from bed at one point and almost dialed her sister but decided against it.

Jumping at shadows again, Hanna. You know better.

But somehow, she *didn't* think she knew better. Something was happening in the Smokies, and she was afraid it had to do with Skelton. His interview the night before had deeply disturbed her, even though they'd finally set the date for his execution. She generally opposed putting people to death, but for Skelton, she'd make an exception.

But what did he mean about his new fan? And what was all that talk about sneaking around?

Her cordless phone *beep-beep-beeped*. She answered it to some familiar voices.

"Hi, Auntie, it's Mac and Hi."

"Well, hello there, you two. What can I do for ya?"

Mac: "Sorry to bug you so early. We wanted to ask you about Justin Johnson?"

"Oh? What about him?"

"Is he . . . okay?"

An image from her previous night's dreams flashed before her: Justin Johnson standing in that same factory of horrors, but he wasn't standing; he was *flying, floating* among a series of hovering platforms, like little sky-islands. Normally, Hanna would've written off the dream as simple surrealism, but the makeup of the hovering platforms deeply disturbed her.

They were hewn from skulls and bones and bits of gore, as if someone had crafted them from the sorry remains of so many hundreds of victims.

An impulse to tell a strange kind of unfiltered truth struck her—she wanted to say that Justin *wasn't* okay, that he was in danger . . . but she decided not to.

After all, what could she tell them? That she'd dreamed he was in trouble?

"Honey, I'm afraid I don't know much about Mr. Johnson. All I know is he got a lot of money in his civil suit, and he moved out of town."

"He did?" Hiram asked. "Do you know where?"

"Why? You wanna send him a letter?"

"No," he said, his voice quieter. "We were just worried about him."

Mac added: "Did he leave a phone number?"

Hanna hesitated. From her pocket, she produced a scrap of paper that had Justin's name written on it.

And his phone number.

Well, it wasn't *his* number but the number for a bar near his house where she could leave messages. Hanna didn't like lying, but she occasionally stretched the truth for the greater good.

"He didn't leave his number, kids, because he doesn't have a phone."

"He doesn't?" Mac asked. "Why not?"

"I think because he'd like to live out his days in peace and quiet." She shifted gears: "I'm sure he'd appreciate you being so worried about him. You're good kids. But he's a grown man. Let's leave him be."

A pause, then Hiram mumbled: "We understand, Auntie. Thank you."

Mac: "Thank you, Auntie Hanna. Love you."

"Love you, too, kids."

She hung up and sat for a long time, wondering whether she'd done the right thing . . . and whether her dreams last night had been more than dreams.

Mackenzie

Mac pored over a pair of maps: one a fold-out atlas of the east Tennessee region, the other one of her own making. She'd cleared away her clay and plasticine and overlaid her sketching paper onto the atlas. It was Friday night, and both she and her brother were going out into the wild—where the Plaid Man might be waiting.

Hiram came in with his coat and snow cap draped over an arm. He was ready to go.

"Hey, what are you working on?" he asked.

She presented her map to him. "What do you think?"

Without looking at it, he said: "Why are you drawing a map?"

She shrugged. "We don't know how the magic works. Maybe two people need to work on the same map, or maybe we need more than one map. Plus, I wanted to show this to Dawn tonight and see what she thinks."

"Does she know a lot about this kind of thing?"

"I don't think anyone knows anything about this, but Dawn's really smart. She's just kind of shy about it."

"Why?"

"Because being smart isn't cool? She got teased about it all the time in elementary school, so she got contacts and changed her hair. You do what you gotta do to get by."

"Yeah, I guess I do that kind of thing, too."

"We all do, but trust me, it's worse for girls."

"Got it. Uh so you want to show this to Dawn and see if she has any ideas?"

"Yeah. What do you think of it, map-master?"

Hiram smiled at the nickname and looked over her map, his expression shifting between an impressed grin and exasperation. Her map was drawn to scale and accurate to the last detail, but she'd added in bunch of goofy "girly" details: all the trees looked like poofy clouds and bore heart-shaped fruit, while M-shaped birds flapped in the distance. There were no fewer than three rainbows arcing from one cluster of clouds to another. A title spanned the top that read: *MAP OF WEST CHIMNEY TOP AND VICINITY, INCL. DIZZY PINES TRAILER PARK AND THE OLD SODDY FARM.* She'd dotted all the i's with hearts, of course.

Her brother fidgeted. "This is really cool, but I don't know if maps are supposed to have all these hearts and rainbows and stuff."

"Why not? What are maps *supposed* to have?"

"Uh I don't know—a compass rose?"

"I drew one in right here." She'd drawn a set of four interlocking hexagons that indicated the cardinal directions, adding a little heart overlaying the middle and a fluffy cloud rolling behind it.

"Oh, I see. I guess it's okay. Gosh, that looks really cool." He took out his map and looked forlornly at it.

"Yours looks great." She tapped his drawing of their house. "Why'd you include the Office?"

"I don't know," Hiram said. "I . . . I can't stop thinking about it."

She nodded, a strange look on her face. "Gotcha. Well, Lee's a really good artist. He made a lot of improvements."

"Yeah, maybe that's it." He got quiet. "Maybe you have to be a really good artist for it to work."

"You mean like this?" she giggled and added the most girly-looking unicorn she could conjure to her map. It had a rainbow mane and big, dewy eyes. Hiram waved his hands in outrage.

"But, but—wait, c'mon. That's not supposed—there are no *unicorns in the Smoky Mountains, Mac!* That's an, uh, an ana-uh—anachron—"

"Anachronism?"

"That's what I said," he said with a quick shake of his head, an old tic. He was red-faced as usual.

"I don't think you're using that word right, but check this out."

She stopped his complaints by sketching in a slew of new details: a pond, which she highlighted in varying shades of blue, as a well as a small cabin at Soddy Farm.

Hiram's eyes got big. "Oh, wow. That's pretty cool. What's this?"

He indicated the little cabin.

"Oh, that's a little shack they've got at Soddy Farm," Mac said. "Been around since the Civil War, I think. Dawn and I used to hang out there."

Hiram looked at her map and frowned. "Hm. The cabin's a little too close to Dizzy Pines, but this is really good."

"Yeah, I ran out of space," Mac said, noticing Hiram's sad tone. "What is it, goofball?"

"Oh, it's dumb. It's just that . . . I felt special. Being the first one to draw a magic map. And my maps aren't even any good."

Mac took his shoulder. "Hey. This is special for everybody. And it took a lot of nerve to go out in the woods the way you did. You wanna know something else? I get the feeling we're not the first ones to stumble onto this stuff."

"Yeah, you're probably right," he said, reaching for her colored pencils. "Mind if I borrow these for a second?"

"Go for it."

He pulled up a little stool next to her and set to work, his tongue sticking out slightly. Mac smiled at his effort; he was referring to her map and recreating all her details: the pond, the trailer park, the little cabin. He was doing a pretty good job of it, too.

"Nice work, goofball. You're a better artist than you think. You drew all that and didn't even trace. Just keep practicing, and you'll get to be as good as Lee."

His chubby little cheeks reddened with pride. It was one of her favorite sights.

"Thanks, I will. I promise," he said. Mac stood up to get ready, but Hiram tapped a blank spot on his map. "Do you think we should add it to our maps?"

"What?"

"Mr. Johnson's cottage?"

She thought, shook her head. "Auntie Hanna said he moved away. I think it might be too dangerous to try and draw a map to him."

"Well, if he doesn't have a phone, and we don't know his address, how are we going to get in touch with him?"

Mac shrugged. "Maybe we don't."

Hiram nodded and went to go pack the rest of his stuff, but he looked disappointed; as if her answer wasn't good enough. Mac suspected it wasn't.

After all, hadn't the map sent them to help Mr. Johnson?

Hiram's Journal

Dizzy Pines Trailer Park sat on the outskirts of West Chim, off a dirt road that had no name other than a cryptic mile marker that designated it as *Route 0*. Dozens of trailer homes, some single-wide, some double-wide, sat scattered among low-hanging trees. A dusting of snow covered the ground from the previous night's storm.

Their double-wide was covered with handsome faux-wood vinyl siding. A wooden wraparound deck expanded its footprint and bore several reclining lawn chairs and outdoor tables. Framed cross-stitch patterns hung on the outside of the trailer. (A cool touch; I'd never seen artwork hung *outside* a house before.) The patterns were the usual Southern fare—*BLESS THIS HOME, JOHN 3:16*—while another depicted the letters R and G interlocked like an Ouroboros. A beat-up old Volvo was parked out front, next to some kind of miniature motorcycle, a helmet hung from its handlebar.

Lee and his mom, Sandra, were waiting for us when we pulled up in the Sentra, Mom giving them some friendly honks. Sandra wore her usual uniform: mom jeans and that green fleece. Lee was bouncing in place, holding a stack of notepads and other art supplies. A superstitious part of me wonders now if he knew what was in store for us that night.

We got out. Mom and Sandra hugged.

"I *love* your place!" Mom said, disengaging from the hug. "Did you build this porch yourself?"

"My Hank did before he passed."

"I'm so sorry. I've got a serious case of foot-in-mouth disease."

"It's all right," Sandra said, turning to us. "Hi, buddy," Sandra said. "So glad you could make it over. Lee just talks and talks about you."

Lee made a mock-mortified face that I think he practiced in the mirror.

"Mother, please. You're embarrassing me." But he was smiling his ass off.

Mom nudged me. "Why don't you two go inside. Sandy and I wanna catch up."

That struck me as strange. Hadn't she been looking forward to having the house to herself? But I took the hint and headed inside, my knapsack slung over my shoulder. Lee bowed and waved me inside.

"Right this way, my good sir."

"Thank you, sir," I said with a salute, trying to get in the spirit of things. Inside was an eighties and nineties wonderland: wood paneling, cushy couches and easy chairs, half a dozen Thomas Kinkades, framed silhouettes of Lee and Dawn, a poster from the 1982 Knoxville World's Fair, more embroidery, bronzed baby shoes, and the centerpiece, a massive collection of salt-and-pepper shakers in a wall-mounted hutch. A kitchenette took up about a third of the main room, separated by a small bar/oven-range island, while the rest of the room was dominated by the biggest TV I'd ever seen. There were two bedrooms, one at each end of the trailer. Sandra had ceded them to her kids, electing to crash on a couch in the main room. Bedding lay folded on the couch's arm alongside a stack of books.

Lee flomped down onto the couch, only to spring back up, run over, and open his fridge.

"Would you like something to drink, Admir—I mean, Hiram?"

"Yeah, I'd love something."

Slam. Sandra was back inside, a lit cigarette in hand.

"Levi David Dockery, can you get your mother a beer and Ms. Corrie a Mr. Pibb, please?"

"Yes, ma'am!" Lee rooted around in the fridge, which was packed with an encyclopedic selection of sodas in an array of cans and bottles: Coke, New Coke, all the Fantas, something called "Beverly," Cheerwine, Mr. Pibb, Vernor's, and others.

"I'll take a Coke, thanks." I wrinkled my nose. "Is my mom staying over?"

"We're just catching up, dear," Sandra said as she accepted the drinks from Lee. "You two play your games while we chat."

She went outside. Lee was opening up a box of Girl Scout Tagalongs that got my mouth watering. I forgot about the weirdness of my mom staying over for the time being and moved a stack of books so I could sit. One book's cover was packed with unusual symbols and glyphs that dimly reminded me of New Age-y stuff I'd seen on TV.

"Mind if I get the festivities underway?" Lee asked.

"Go for it," I said, bending my ear to the conversation outside.

Sandra: "—would go weeks at a time without seeing him when he was on the road."

The gigantic TV fired up with a wall of blocky video-game text: *MASTERMINDER HOME EDUTAINMENT PRESENTS THESEUS'S LABYRINTH OF TERROR.* Lee fiddled with the Masterminder's controller, which was a beast: a panel about the size of an iPhone with about a million buttons. (I found that astonishing; the Atari only had one, the Nintendo two!)

"Wow, this is *rad*," I said.

"Let's begin." He pressed a button and brought up a new screen, a blocky rendition of a castle on a coastal shelf. Underneath the castle sprouted a network of small rooms, each stacked on top of each other. "Each one of those is a level in the dungeon we must traverse." More text spilled out across the screen:

THE GREAT GREEK HERO THESEUS MUST FACE THE LABYRINTH OF DAEDALUS. EVERY NINE YEARS, SEVEN ATHENIAN BOYS AND GIRLS MUST ENTER THE LABYRINTH TO BE EATEN BY THE FEARSOME MINOTAUR. BUT THIS YEAR, THESEUS HAS VOWED TO END THE MINOTAUR'S REIGN OF TERROR.

"That's cool," I said. "I knew about Perseus from *Clash of the Titans,* but I've never heard of Theseus."

"Indeed. All the Masterminder games include educational facts and puzzles. They provide cover for the violence and more occult elements."

Mom's voice drifted in: "—did you find out? He just up and told me one day."

My knapsack fell open and from it spilled a change of clothes, my graph paper . . . and my map.

"Are you making notes?" Lee asked, indicating the graph paper. The screen changed to a first-person display of a dungeon. "I'd like to make maps of all the levels. I think they're randomized, but I'm not sure."

"I'm on it, Admiral," I said, taking up a pencil, but before I could write anything, he pointed in horror at my graph paper.

"What on earth is that?!"

"Uh, graph paper?"

"We can't use that, no, not at all!"

He ran to his room and returned with a stack of graph paper unlike any I'd seen; it was made up of hexagons instead of squares.

"Okay, this is *way* better," I admitted as Lee took a ladder down to a deeper level and faced off against a few monsters rendered in blocky but evocative graphics. "How have I never played this?"

"I thought you had a Nintendo Entertainment System, or NES, aka the Super Famicom, as it was known in Japan," Lee said. "Don't you have *The Legend of Zelda?*"

"I won't get any new games until Christmas," I said.

"Well, we have dozens," Lee said, leaning back so he could kick open a custom cartridge-holder that was overflowing with Atari 2600 and Masterminder games. I looked on with awe. Lee got on with the game, killing monsters and collecting treasures, and gasped when he encountered a special kind of door. Most doors in *Labyrinth of Theseus* were blue, but this one lit up bright yellow.

"Great Scott," he whispered.

"What happened? What's wrong with that door?"

"Those are magic gates. There's some kind of really powerful monster protecting it. We're not strong enough to fight it yet."

"Is there a way around?"

"We can simply walk around the dungeon until we reach the other side, but our best chance is to acquire armaments that can match the creature's might. There's also an enchanted tome that will enable us to teleport through walls."

My mission to recruit Lee was quickly fading into the misty mayhem of kid-dom. As I made notes, I accidentally jostled Sandra's stack of books, knocking one into my lap. It was the one with all the weird symbols: *Mastery of Occultopsychic Phenomena* by some lady with a really long name.

Where have I seen that name before?

"Hey, guys!"

We both jumped. It was our moms, standing in the doorway. Sandra swept over and gathered up her books, the smell of cigarettes following her.

"Sorry for the mess!" she said. "It gets pretty cramped in here sometimes."

Mom said: "We're going to Kay's Kastle for ice cream cones. Do you want anything, Lee?"

Sandra shoved her books into a shelf on the far wall, pausing to wave her palm in front of them and snap her fingers. That done, she smiled and pointed at Lee.

"Let me guess: hot fudge sundae?"

Lee jumped up. "I'd love one, my lady!"

"Done and done, then," Sandra said. "Hiram, how about you? Banana split?"

Mom cut me off: "He doesn't want that, do you, sweetie?"

I wanted a banana split more than anything, but I simply nodded.

"We'll be back in a bit," Mom said.

They left, the misfiring of Mom's Sentra fading into the distance. I was still fixated on the treat I wouldn't get when I noticed Lee standing beside me. He was holding a gallon of ice cream.

"We have leftover Mayfield-brand ice cream, if you'd like."

This is another of those moments I often remember. Everyone gave Lee grief for not being able to pick up on other people's feelings, but he could read me easy-peasy.

It was time.

I smiled. "Nah, it's okay. But can I show you something?" I pulled out my map of the area, but I couldn't bring myself to say anything. I tried to imagine telling him that magic was real and an ancient evil was menacing the Smokies (and my dreams), but I was so sure he'd think I was playing a prank on him. I already couldn't bear the thought of hurting his feelings.

He said: "You look . . . upset?"

I nodded. "I want to tell you something, but I don't want you to think I'm playing a prank or making fun."

He shrugged and said simply: "We're all admirals here."

"Okay," I said, whipping up some courage. "I think I can draw magic maps, and I need your help to draw a better one."

The only sign that he'd heard me were his eyes, which changed density slightly as he processed my words.

"Lee?" I asked.

He blurted: *"CooooOOOooooool!"*

Mackenzie

It was as bright as a football game and about as loud. Billy Bones had been as good as his word, getting the keys to the old Soddy Farm, which had been abandoned for years after Marshall Soddy decamped for greener pastures. The party emanated from a central ring of cars and pickups, some of which had their engines running and lights on—blazing KC lights were the favored illumination—while competing musics blared from an array of sound systems large and small. A few pop-up shade structures stood here and there, interspersed with tents and tons of lawn furniture. Christmas lights dangled between trucks and tents, blinking merrily.

Dawn had her license, so she volunteered to drive everyone over in her mom's Honda CRT hatchback. She slung it into a space next to Randall's beater pickup and jumped out, hooting. Mac emerged, clown-car-style, with Sabrina, Becky, and their other friend, Jarra. As always, *Dawn-n-Gresh* had coordinated outfits but had opted for slight variations: both wore jeans over a unitard—"I wanna look sporty!" Dawn had insisted. Dawn opted for a heavy winter coat and her usual pigtails, while Mac elected for a dorky-looking patchwork vest, an attempt at being fashion-forward.

Everyone spotted friends and squealed. Dawn pulled a lingering Mac toward the fun.

"You need a drink, Gresh!"

"Okay," Mac said reluctantly. *I need to get Dawn alone so I can explain what's going on.* "Hey, Dawn—"

"Randall!" Dawn shouted. *"Girls! Here! Need drinks!"*

Jarra spotted another phalanx of cars arriving.

"Oh mah *gawd,* I think it's the Knox High football team," she said.

Everyone turned to look. Becky confirmed the intel by jumping in place, squealing, and wagging her finger.

"Everyone act cool," Sabrina said.

Randall finally arrived juggling an armful of beers. A pleasant-looking longhair, he had dropped out of Polk High in the mid-eighties but never left the region except to follow Phish for a few months. He wore the usual uniform: knit hoodie, slowly dreadlocking blonde hair, and jeans three sizes too large. His belt jangled with tools and his prized possession, a tiny tank of nitrous oxide.

"Ladies!" Randall said. Becky sidled over to him and played with his hair.

"Why didn't you come and say hi?" she said. "I thought I was your favorite."

"Aw, sorry, Becky! You're always my favorite." His penance complete, he distributed the beers and offered a balloon of nitrous, which the girls declined. He scampered off in search of more trouble while the newly-arrived cars disgorged the Knox High footballers, who charged cheering into the party like an ear-splitting student-body-left.

"Hi, hi!" Jarra called to them.

"Hey, girl," one of the guys, a good-looking skill player, said as he passed.

Jarra pretended to swoon into Sabrina's arms. They both busted up laughing. Beers were cracked everywhere, some of which exploded, prompting more laughter.

Dawn called: "Yo! Randall! Is whatzizname coming tonight?!"

Randall came dutifully running over. "Gotta be more specific, Dockery. It's kicking in."

"Oh? What didja take? Acid? Shrooms?"

Randall blinked owlishly. "Yes."

Mac giggled. "Better talk fast, Dawnie."

"Are those kids from Cherokee coming over? I was hoping to see that fella Jimmy."

"You mean Jimmy Bryant?" Becky asked. "He's dreamy. But you better get outta my way if he comes."

Dawn rolled her eyes. "Yeah, whatever, Becky. I'm gonna be the one having his babies," she said, chugging her beer. "Whadda you say, Gresh?"

"Would I have Jimmy Bryant's babies? I don't think so. I might wanna—I dunno—get to know him first?" She walked over to Dawn. "Hey, Dawnie—"

"Oh, I'd get to know him, all right," Dawn said with a laugh.

Randall suddenly pointed into the distance.

"Check it ooooooout! New arrivals!"

Several sets of headlights swung across the farmland, skidding to a stop and producing a few dozen more kids, but one car caught Mac's attention: a bulky BMW that roared onto the property blaring Steely Dan's "Reelin' in the Years." It skidded to a stop, leaving grooves in the grass.

Mac's face fell. "Oh, no."

Her voice was unmistakable: *"Somebody beer this biiiiiiitch!"*
It was Kaitlyn and Jason.

Hiram's Journal

Lee took to it immediately.

"Explain the mechanics to me as best you can."

"Honestly, we don't know much. All I know is I discovered the traincar at a certain point in the woods near my house, but I was dreaming. When I'm awake, the traincar's gone. Last night I tried to get back to the traincar by following my map—" I stopped because Lee raised his hand.

"I know you don't like to be interrupted," he said, prompting a big smile from me. I hated being interrupted, but I'd never actually told him. He simply intuited it. He continued: "If the traincar hadn't been there before, why did you think it would be there last night?"

"I don't know. I thought I might've made a mistake when I wrote down the traincar's location, or maybe . . ."

"Yes?"

"Well, I thought maybe if I went out there and went to sleep, it would appear."

He nodded. "I see. That's extremely hazardous, exposing yourself to the elements in that manner, though I follow your logic, unusual as the circumstances may be. May I ask: let's say you manage to find this traincar, what happens?"

"I think Lenny Skelton has trapped the souls of his victims here on earth, and they're in that traincar."

Lee's brow furrowed. "I don't know if I believe in such things, but recovering his victims' remains is an undertaking I might describe as holy. That he's kept them is . . ."

"Evil."

"Yes," Lee said, barely above a whisper. "But when you went out last night, something unexpected happened?"

"Yeah, some kind of magic portal appeared that led to Mr. Johnson's house."

"Justin Johnson, the former police officer and security guard, yes?"

"That's the one."

"Were you able to speak with him?"

"No, because the portal was . . . unstable?"

"Like a wormhole, perhaps?" Lee said.

"Right!" I said with a jab of my finger. "It was . . . well, I'm not sure how to describe it. An ocean of black ink crashing through the woods."

"Fascinating."

"And there was a monster from my dreams chasing us."

"A monster? What kind of monster?"

"A man with a plaid face. The Plaid Man. He's some kind of shapeshifter, and he can speak with all kinds of different voices."

Lee nodded. "I'll have to do some research. Various tales from folklore describe such entities."

"Aren't you scared? I mean, to try and find Mr. Johnson? We might run into the Plaid Man again. In fact, we probably will."

"I'm terrified. Make no mistake. But this is a matter of great and grave importance. My resolve is strong."

I swear, something about Lee made my chest swell. He made me stand up a little straighter and doubt myself a little less.

"I'm with you," I said.

Lee nodded. "Question: Why would a portal have appeared leading to him, specifically?"

"I think it's because he wants to find the traincar, too, and he needs our help."

Lee looked at my map and frowned in thought. "Have you considered the contrary?"

"Huh?"

"Have you considered that he doesn't need your help, but rather we need his?"

My face got hot. I was embarrassed again, the feeling comparable to how I felt when Mac dressed me down about Lee. I felt selfish and stupid and short-sighted. Of *course* Justin didn't need our help; he was a grown man with his own life. Why would he need help from a dipshit eleven-year-old kid? I almost gave up right then and there, suddenly certain that I would, in all my grand stupidity, get someone hurt.

Luckily, Lee happened to spot something that changed the course of the evening . . . and our lives.

"What's that?" he said, pointing out the window.

We headed outside and around the back of the trailer. Low-slung fences subdivided the properties. They had a few neighbors in their section of the park, plus a small toolshed.

"What am I looking at?" I asked.

"This," Lee said, walking over to the toolshed.

"What about it?"

"I've never seen it before in my life. It shouldn't be here."

Dawn

Dawn hated to admit it, but she had a bit of a temper.

As soon as that rich bitch Kaitlyn Sutton came traipsing out of her big, fancy BMW, Dawn felt *sure* that Mac had gone behind her back and invited her. Dawn couldn't *stand* her; she was so pretty, so confident, so rich. She strode their way wearing a purple-and-red dirndl skirt under a knee-length leather coat with fluffy lining. Round sunglasses completed the look, which recalled Janis Joplin in her heyday, and which rankled the hell out of Dawn.

What a poser, she thought and immediately felt an impulse to leave. She reached for her keys but stopped; she was already feeling tipsy from chugging that beer, plus she was everyone's ride. She resolved to sober up and leave as soon as she could.

But then she saw the tall dreamboat from the Mystery Mansion.

Dawn had met Kaitlyn but not her brother. Seeing him again in this context threw her for a loop. Memories of Jenny and her funeral competed with her irrational crush on this guy. Mac had said he was a big bully, but Dawn saw something sad in him. Christmas lights hanging from a jacked-up pickup cast his frame in a sparkling cloud of wintertime dream-light. He wore the same Tennessee Volunteers windbreaker with jeans and a flannel button-down. Dawn dimly realized that Becky was tugging her sleeve and feeding her another beer.

"Dawnie! The Cherokee boys made it, and guess what—Jimmy Bryant's here! Wanna race me for him?"

"Who?" Dawn asked, cracking the beer. She was about to make a move on Jason when *her* voice shattered her reverie:

"I said, *somebody beer this biiiiiitch!*" Kaitlyn screamed. On cue, a beer shot over her head, missing it by inches. She ducked, flailing her arms about. Standing straight, she yelled: "Shit, dude! Y'almost fuckin' killed me!"

"Sorry!" came Randall's answer in the distance.

Wish you'd aimed lower, Randall, Dawn thought, instantly feeling guilty for it.

Kaitlyn didn't miss a beat. She propped a hand on her hip and jabbed a finger at Randall.

"Hey, you know what? It's all right, man!" Another beer zipped over her head. She dove to the ground, yelling, *"Fuck, dude!"*

Mac came to her rescue: "I've got this one, Randall!"

She ran over to Randall's group, who were gathered around a truck bed that bore a keg and a shitload of coolers, all packed with ice and cans of cheapo beer. Dawn approached Kaitlyn, who was pulling herself up. It was the closest they'd ever been and the first time Dawn noticed her scar.

Wow, it's right under her eye. I wonder how that happened?

Kaitlyn continued to theatrically dust herself off, mugging for the crowd.

"No, please! Hold your applause!"

"What're you doing here?" Dawn asked.

Mac ran back and handed beers to Kaitlyn and Jason. "Yeah, same question, Kaity."

"*Nuh*-thing gets by Kaity Sutton, superbitch. When big bro and I heard you'd absconded to a party most miraculous, we just had to crash and make sure you had a good time."

Jason grunted and headed into the darkness.

"You didn't have to do that," Mac said.

"Ain't you gonna introduce us?" Dawn asked.

"Kaitlyn Sutton, my dear," she said, adopting her hammy English persona. "How'd you do?"

Dawn assumed a mock-impressed look and said: "Wow, are you from England?"

"No, I'm not from *Eng-land*, dumb-ass!" she said with a cackle. "I'm from round the bend and down a-ways. Second slut to the right 'n' straight up your butt! Jase and I wanted to drop in and make sure our sweet lil sister-to-be was having a good time."

"I knew you was kiddin', asshole," Dawn said, her gaze following Jason's retreating form. "What's with him?"

"Oh, he's in a shitty-ass fuckin' *bad* mood tonight. No idea why."

"I like bad moods," Dawn said, setting off in pursuit.

Kaitlyn adopted a prim Julie Andrews accent: *"Dawnie and Jason, sittin' in a tree!"*

As she chased after Jason, Mac asked Kaitlyn: "Who told you about this party?"

Mackenzie

"Who told you about this party?"

Kaitlyn sipped her beer and made eyes with some boys. "I thought you'd want me here, lil sis."

"It's not that I *don't* want you here, it's just—"

Kaitlyn's voice was a siren: *"What's a girl gotta do to get fucked up at this hootenanny?!"*

Randall appeared like a genie being summoned.

"Did someone say 'get fucked up'?"

Kaitlyn twined her fingers, clowning around and acting like an old lady. "Good, sir, you look like you've killed a few brain cells in your time. My fellow sluts and I would *very* much like to get . . . how did you say . . . *fucked?* And what was that second word? *Down? Fucked down?* Can you help us?"

"I think Looney Balls brought some shit!"

"That is *outstanding.* Well, please tell Mr. Balls that *Misseseses* Sutton and Gresham (and associates) would be obliged for the most mind-blowing acid he has on hand." She addressed Mac: "You in?"

Mac shrugged. "I think I'll pass. I'll catch you later, Kaity."

Kaitlyn caught her arm. "Girl, you can't let me look at the Grid all by myself."

Mac's heart skipped a beat. "The what?"

Kaitlyn clownishly spat out her drink. "Why, Mackenzie Sluttington Gresham the Third, am I to understand you've never seen the almighty *grid?*"

"Little Ms. Goodie Two-Shoes ain't never done anything!" Becky said.

Mac shot Becky a nasty look. Kaitlyn's eyes bugged. She flexed her arms like a pro wrestler. *"Awwwww yeahhhhhhh* Mac is gonna see the *Grid!"* She waved away Randall. "Off with you now!"

"On it!" he yelled, running off, chanting: "Grid, Grid, Grid, Grid!"

Mac was suddenly contrite. "Hey, sorry if I was rude. I was just hoping to catch up with Dawn tonight."

Randall, in the distance: "Grid, grid, grid, grid!"

Mac spoke in a hushed tone: "Have you seen it?"

Instead of responding, Kaitlyn wrapped her arms around Mac and Becky and whooped up an impromptu bastardization of "Islands in the Stream" in which she swapped out all the lyrics for profane counterparts. She added to Mac *sotto voce:* "—c'mon, it's your favorite, *all together now!"*

Dawn

She followed him, nervous to approach and yet unable to stay away. He lit a cigarette and walked down by the pond, where he sat on a small wooden bench and smoked. In the distance, Kaitlyn was bellowing a bastardized version of "Islands in the Stream." Jason produced a crumped-up paper and took a few notes. Dawn lingered in the darkness on the party's outskirts and tried to summon the courage to say hi. Her decision was made for her when she stepped on a stick: *snap!*

Jason whirled around: "Shit!"

He stuffed his paper away. Dawn took a few steps forward.

"Sorry! I didn't meant to sneak up on ya."

"It's okay."

Dawn hesitated a moment before asking: "Is anyone sitting—"

Kaitlyn screamed an especially dirty variant of the original lyrics to "Islands in the Stream."

Jason screamed: *"Shut the fuck up!"* Then, to Dawn: "What'd you say?"

His voice rang in her ears. "Is, uh, anyone sitting here?"

He shrugged and scooted over. Dawn sat and looked at the water. Music floated over, including Skynyrd, Allman Brothers, Guster, Widespread Panic, Toad the Wet Sprocket, and Kaitlyn's profane "Islands in the Stream." Christmas lights cast a rainbow haze across the water.

"S'pretty."

"I guess."

"Uh, your sister's that girl Kaitlyn?"

Jason looked at her. It wasn't a kind look.

"You figure that out all by yourself?"

Dawn's brow darkened at the jab, but she pressed on.

"You play football?"

"Used to. Hurt my knee. My dad wants me to go back to it, though."

Silence. Dawn was about to leave when she noticed streaks on his cheeks. She knew what they meant: he'd been crying.

"Are you all right?" she asked.

He puffed his cigarette. "Why wouldn't I be?"

"I heard about what happened with you. In the park, with that guy. Skelton."

Jason didn't move, but the terrain shifted. Dawn knew it. All sound seemed to drain away.

"You think what everybody else thinks?" he asked. "That I'm a coward?"

"I thought it was real brave."

"It wasn't. That girl." His voice cracked. "That poor girl."

"Yeah, Jenny. Her and me were friends."

Jason's face snapped over, his expression some unreadable mix of horror and sorrow.

"You were?"

"We used to do everything together. Then she moved five miles away in second grade. I went to Polk, she went to Sevierville Central. It was only five miles, but it was like she moved to another city. I ain't even told my friends at Polk I knew her. I don't know what they'd say."

"I'm . . . I'm so sorry."

"I went to her funeral. It was real beautiful."

That hit Jason in a deep and painful place. "I'm . . . I'm sorry I didn't go. I figured they'd yell at me."

"Why? It wasn't your fault."

"You shouldn't be saying that. I'm the one who got her . . ."

"It wasn't you, it was him."

Beep, beep, beep! An alarm sounded on Jason's wristwatch. He checked the sky, squirming in his seat like his blood had turned to snakes.

"Listen. Can you just. Please. Leave. Me. Alone. I've got . . . *things* to do."

Dawn almost got offended, but her empathetic nature kicked in.

"I'm sorry. For what happened to you."

"I'm the one who should be sorry."

Dawn opened her mouth, but Kaitlyn's gonglike voice blasted across the scene:

"Where's my aciiiiiid?!"

Off her look, Jason managed a smile. "Go on. Have fun."

She nodded, standing. "Say hey later?"

He shrugged. She lingered for a moment and ran off to join her friends. Out of the corner of her eye, she caught him pulling out that same piece of paper.

Hiram's Journal

We circled the toolshed like it might attack us, both of us taking tentative steps, me with an eye on my map.

"Maybe a neighbor put it up and you didn't notice?" I asked.

"That seems unlikely," Lee said. "The craftsmanship is incredibly solid. In order for someone to have built a structure like like this without us noticing, it would need to be pre-fabricated."

I looked closer. "Wow, check this out." Carved into the base was a date: *1857 AD.* That's when it hit me. "Lee, I think I've drawn this exact cabin." I indicated my map. "I drew this earlier. Mac drew it on hers, too. This cabin is located out at Soddy Farm, but . . ."

"It's appearing here, as well."

"Because I drew it?"

Lee nodded. "Perhaps that's one of the rules? If you draw something on a map, it must appear?"

"Yeah," I said, lost in thought. A distant part of me wondered why Mac and I hadn't drawn the A-frame cabin from my vision, but I ignored the question for now. "Maybe that's why we couldn't get to Mr. Johnson's last night. I hadn't drawn his house on my map."

"Admiral, if I may posit a course of action: In *Masterminder Home*

Edutainment Presents Theseus's Labyrinth of Terror, there are specific markers and gateways that lead to different realms. A ladder leads you to the next floor, a gate leads you to the next room."

"Got it. So?"

"What if it's not enough to simply draw Mr. Johnson's house on your map? What if the magic calls for greater ceremony and a more specific intention?"

I looked at my map and nodded. "We need to draw a gate."

Mackenzie

Randall came galloping back, followed by Dawn, who arrived back from the pond, where Jason lingered. Randall held a plastic baggie of various goodies, including smaller baggies of white powder, various pills, some colorful stamp paper, and an eyedropper vial.

"Yo!" Randall said, shaking the baggie. "Looney Balls came through!"

"Thanks, Looney Balls!" Kaitlyn called.

Looney Balls's voice floated over: *"Raise hell!"*

Dawn rejoined the group next to Mac, who fidgeted, wondering simultaneously how she was going to get Dawn alone long enough to talk to her and also how to ask Kaitlyn about the Grid.

I thought we were the only ones who had seen it, Mac thought, though she had the feeling that the magic bubbling up in the Smokies belonged to everyone, not just her family. Kaitlyn whipped out a Gucci wallet and doled a wad of cash to Randall. Dawn stepped in, her brow creased, pulling out her own wallet.

"How much is it per hit?" Dawn asked.

Randall: "Ten bucks a drop, so—"

Kaitlyn jostled Dawn out of the way, shoving her money in Randall's hand.

Winking at Dawn, she said: "I got this, sweetie." Pinpricks of red appeared on Dawn's cheeks. Mac inwardly cringed. Kaitlyn gave another twenty dollars to Randall. "Make sure that the good Mr. Balls gets a tip, won't you, lad?"

"Oh, wow, you got it!" He took off.

Dawn pulled some cash from her wallet and put it in Kaitlyn's hand.

"I can cover my own," she said.

"Your money's no good here," Kaitlyn said, dropping the money to the ground before she addressed the girls: "Now, who wants to get a little breezy, and who wants to go to the moon?"

In the distance, Looney Balls got his tip: *"Raise hell!"*

"Just a little breezy, thanks," Becky said.

"One drop for you, then," Kaitlyn said. Jarra and Sabrina both opted for a single drop in their beers. Kaitlyn got to Mac and held the dropper over her beer.

"Will this help me see the Grid?" Mac asked.

"One drop might not be enough," Kaitlyn said.

Becky agreed: "Yeah, I gotta dive pretty deep if I wanna see the Grid."

"What *is* it?"

"The Grid?" Kaitlyn said with a shrug. "Beats the hell outta me."

"It's a neurological phenomenon," Dawn mumbled as she picked up her cash, prompting an astonished look from Kaitlyn.

"Ex-*cuse* me, sister? Are there some brains inside that ditzy little head of yours?"

"I ain't ditzy," Dawn said. "I just don't shoot my mouth off all the time like *some* folks."

Kaitlyn covered her mouth in mock-shock. "Why, goodness gracious. Are you talking about lil old *me?*"

"Knock it off, Kaity," Mac said. "Give me a drop and a half. I don't wanna get sick, but I wanna see it."

"Then a drop and a half it shall be," Kaitlyn said, her words seeming to summon Randall from the ether. He popped up in the middle of the crew and proffered his beer.

"Five for me, thanks!"

Kaitlyn assumed her hammy English persona: "Everyone, please note that clear communication is key to a positive acid trip. To wit, Randall here is telling us he doesn't have any plans for the next fortnight." She gave him his drops.

"Gettin' fucked *uuuuuup!*" Randall shouted and ran off.

Kaitlyn gingerly administered Mac's dose and turned to Dawn.

"How about you, Mary Lou?"

"One for me thanks," she said, her gaze steely.

Oh, God, am I gonna have to break up a fight? Mac thought. *I need Dawn's help.*

But maybe Kaitlyn knows about the magic, too?

Ever since the night at Ober Gatlinburg, Mac and Kaitlyn had been getting to know each other fairly well, much to Dawn's chagrin. Kaitlyn contained multitudes; around others, she was always putting on a show, assuming goofy accents and clowning around; but one-on-one, she was surprisingly kind, even though she always had a big mouth. She'd even sent Mac a care package filled with snacks, beauty supplies, and a note:

Call me if you need anything and hang in there. — Kaity

Mac liked her. Dawn would always be her first and best friend, but she wanted to be friends with Kaitlyn, too, and frankly, she needed a friend at her new school.

Dawn's head snapped around. "Huh?"

"What is it?" Mac asked.

Kaitlyn giggled. "Already kicking in, girlie?"

Randall's voice floated over again: "A black eye and then I fell in a haze."

Dawn checked over her shoulder, looked back, and shrugged. Kaitlyn got a devilish look.

"The farm's haunted!" she cackled. "Mac, you gonna join us and see the Grid, or what?"

Mac downed her beer and crushed the can.

"Let's go for a walk."

"Let's scorch my board!" Randall said in the distance.

As they all headed into the darkness, Kaitlyn yelled: "You might wanna sit down, Randall! Sounds like it's kickin' in pretty hard!"

"Hey, what's that?" Sabrina said, pointing at a sparkling something in the distance.

"I say we go investigate," Kaitlyn said.

They all struck off into the night. Mac felt a sudden stab of anxiety.

Sidling up to Kaitlyn, she said, "Do you think I took too much? What if I freak out?"

"You won't freak out, lil sis," Kaitlyn said. "We're here. All of us, and we'll look after you. Relax and watch the trees." *R-r-r-r-r-rrrumble!* Clouds were starting to roll in. Kaitlyn leaned in to whisper: "Pretend like it's a train. The thunder. We're at a train station, waiting for our ride. That's the Transcendent Express, heading our way. All we have to do is stay true and wait."

"Waiting for our ride. I can do that."

They were headed toward the sparkling light when another, familiar voice, came from behind:

"Gresh?"

Mac's heart boomed. She turned. It was sweet Dave Shuler.

"Uh, hi, Dave," she said, dimly aware she'd used one of Hiram's stuttering hacks.

"Got a sec?" Dave said.

Mac's chest felt tight, but Kaitlyn bailed her out:

"Walk with us, neighbor!"

Hiram's Journal

R-r-r-r-r-rrrumble!

As dark storm clouds rolled in, we teamed up on my map. Thinking back across my favorite places, I thought of the Gold Rush and its magic gate from Christmasville to the North Pole. I sketched the basic outline of an archway. Lee filled in the rest of the details, including Mr. Johnson's cottage, which I described to him as best I could.

"Where do you think the gate will appear?" I asked. "I mean, assuming it does."

"The map isn't precisely to scale, but I tried to situate the gate immediately inside the forest to the north of the park." As a final touch, he added a strange symbol to the keystone, a blue glyph that depicted two snakes eating each other's tails entwined around a dragon's skull. My mind reeled.

I had seen this symbol before. *But where?*

Plaid! Why don't you tell me about the time you and your SEAL team had that mission in the Persian Gulf.

At the Gold Rush. The day we met the Suttons. When Mom called Trent "Plaid," I'd had a vision of this symbol, along with a cabin with a powder-blue A-frame overhang . . . and something else.

What was that third vision? We didn't have time for me to search my memory banks, so I pressed on, pointing at the strange symbol.

"What's that?"

"It is an *ourobuck,*" Lee said. "In *Masterminder Home Edutainment Presents Theseus's Labyrinth of Terror,* the different ourobucks tell you what you can expect on your current level. A blue ourobuck signifies magic, mystery, and most important: help. Blue mazes include some of the most powerful weapons and spells in the game. I am, in essence, invoking the most benevolent magicks I can muster to guide our way safely."

"Can I add one more thing?" Off Lee's nod, I sketched in an arrow-shaped road sign that read *THIS WAY TO JUSTIN JOHNSON'S HOUSE.* I shrugged. "Figure it couldn't hurt."

"I concur."

"Let's do this."

Lee ran to grab a pair of flashlights, as well as his trail bike, the little motorcycle I'd seen parked beside his trailer.

"Your torch, milord!" he said, presenting me with a flashlight.

"Are we riding that thing?"

"It can seat two," he said. "If we are to enlist Mr. Johnson's aid, I feel that time is of the essence."

"Okay, but go slow," I said and climbed on.

He fired it up and roared out, me screaming all the way.

Mackenzie

What am I going to say to him? He's so nice, and I'd hate to hurt his feelings.

Dave Shuler tagged along with Mac and her friends as they strolled down toward the old log cabin. Off to their left—roughly eastward—was the pond, where the cherry of Jason's cigarette smoldered and left little streaks across Mac's vision. Blazing starbursts filled the sky, glimmering behind an encroaching cloud-cover and casting double-rainbows everywhere. A few campfires flickered in the distance, surrounded by dancing, carousing kids. The earth swam before Mac.

"Pretty crazy party, huh?" Dave asked.

"Mm-hmm," Mac said, taking one deep breath after another.

Randall's voice floated over again: "Guess gone wry way?"

Dawn looked around again. "Weird."

"What is it?" Mac asked.

"Oh . . . it's nothing," Dawn said, but Mac had an idea what it was.

"Sounded like your baby brother," she said, prodding Dawn. "Weird, huh?"

Dawn gave her a funny look but nodded.

Kaitlyn escorted everyone down by the log cabin, comically shading her eyes to get a better view at whatever was sparkling in the distance.

"Right this way, druggies!"

They congregated around the cabin, Mac taking up a spot next to its dedication, *1857 AD*. Mac slipped her map out to check it only to have it ripped from her grasp by a sudden wind accompanied by the unmistakable *vrooom* of a motorcycle engine. The wind kicked around everyone's hair and clothes. Jarra's headband got blown completely off. Kaitlyn spun around with a slightly deranged smile.

"Okay, *that* was fuckin' de-*men*-to! I'm gonna go for a walk!"

Kaitlyn went jogging off into the darkness, finally giving Mac a moment's peace with Dawn.

If only Dave hadn't crashed the party.

"Your sister cain't dole acid worth shit," Dawn said. "Everything's going all topsy-turvy."

"She's not my sister. And you're still my bestie-bestie."

Dawn's eyes were downcast. "If you're transferrin' to that school, you know your mama's marrying him."

The thought of having to live with Trent made Mac's stomach seize, but she dismissed the anxiety and tried to focus on her mission.

"Dawnie, do you believe in magic?"

Her best friend wrinkled her nose at her. "Huh?"

Becky suddenly whooped. Sabrina added a "whoa," while Jarra simply spat out her drink, but unlike Kaitlyn, Jarra really was surprised. Dave pointed.

"Do y'all see that?"

Kaitlyn came running out of the darkness, panting. "Guys, guys, guys! Look!" At that moment, heat lightning flashed through the clouds, illuminating thousands of fiery capillaries, all of which snapped together into a familiar honeycomb pattern: the Grid. Mac took Dawn's hand.

"There it is," Mac whispered.

Kaitlyn stopped before them, hands on knees. Mac released Dawn's hand and took Kaitlyn's in hers, saying: "I'm glad we met."

"Yeah, great, glad it's kicking in," Kaitlyn said, taking her shoulders and guiding her gaze across the field. "Do you see what I see?"

Everything was swirling into a paisley pattern, the trees talking, the clouds whirlpooling together. Mac's world was the sound of her breath and the peering scope of her eyes, which struggled to focus on the sparkling something-or-other they'd all spotted earlier. The shape grew as it approached, seeming to bounce its way toward them. It was an animal of some kind, galloping on four legs. When it came into their light, an awestruck silence settled over the group. The horse glowed a remarkable shade of purple, its mane bright gold.

It also had a single horn.

Tears welled in Mac's eyes. "I know you."

Kaitlyn stroked the creature's mane, giggling. Becky, Sabrina, and Jarra all gathered around.

"Remind me to thank Mr. Balls for that acid," Kaitlyn said.

"She's beautiful," Dawn said, her voice thick.

Dave inched his way toward the unicorn. "Uh, girls?"

"What is it, Dave Shuler?" Mac said.

"Are y'all seeing a unicorn with a gold mane?"

"You bet we are," Sabrina said.

"Cool. That's really cool. Because so am I, and I didn't take anything."

Everyone's eyes bugged out.

Kaitlyn: "What. The Living. Heck. Is happening?"

Hiram's Journal

We slashed between trailers and toward the tree line beyond the park, darkness enclosing us as we rode. I would've felt ridiculous doing this if not for the old cabin.

That has to be part of the magic, I thought. *How else could it have appeared there?*

Lee hit the brakes, almost throwing me off the bike. I was ready to gripe at him when I saw it.

My sign.

It had a rudimentary look about it, as if someone had taken a child's drawing and made it real, but all the same, there it was. The text was even in my handwriting: *THIS WAY TO JUSTIN JOHNSON'S HOUSE.*

"I guess we're going the right way," I said.

"Admiral, look." He pointed into the woods, where something glimmered.

We took off again in pursuit of the glimmer. It emerged from behind a bank of trees as Lee wheeled the bike around a curve. He parked, and we dismounted, clicking on our flashlights and approaching with great care. Ten feet tall and hewn from stone, the gate was nothing but a stone archway; there was no door or portcullis.

It was an almost perfect match for the gate from the Gold Rush.

"Look," Lee said, shining his light on its base, where moss grew. "It has every appearance of a ruin, as if it's been here for decades. Remarkable."

I nodded and shined my light on Lee's ourobuck, which looked like it had been carved from blue marble. Sapphires glittered in the snakes' eyes.

"It worked," I whispered. "And look at this." I produced my compass. The needle was spinning.

"Yes, indeed it appears to have—"

The sound shook our inner ears; a subwoofing *vummmm*, it came from within the gate, which suddenly filled with rippling yellow light.

"Whoa," I said. "What does that mean?"

"A yellow gate in *Masterminder Home Edutainment Presents Theseus's Labyrinth of Terror* signifies a threat."

"But your blue ourobuck is up there," I said. "Doesn't that mean it's safe on the other side?"

"Although I appreciate the benefit of the doubt, Admiral, this world you've introduced me to is entirely new and wondrous. I have no idea. How did you come to know of it all?"

"I dreamed about it."

Lee shook his head. "My dreams only involve me showing up at school in various states of undress."

"A little too much information there, Admiral."

"Point taken, but the fact remains: there may be danger on the far side of this gate. We're taking a risk if we proceed. May I ask—why not simply call Mr. Johnson?"

"Me and my sister tried that."

"My sister and I tried that."

"You and Dawn tried to call Mr. Johnson, too?"

"No, you said it wrong. It's 'My sister and I,' not 'me and my sister.'"

My shoulders slumped. "We're never getting girlfriends." Lee and I met eyes and smiled sadly. I mumbled, "Sorry. Just kidding." Steeling myself, I added: "Lee, I think we should try it. I don't think we can find those kids without his help."

"I agree."

We walked through the gate. Golden light engulfed us.

Mackenzie

"What. The Living. Heck. Is happening?"

Kaitlyn had spoken, circling around the unicorn, gently stroking its mane.

"Is this a gag?" Dawn asked.

Dave: "Yeah, Did someone paint this poor thing to glow in the dark?"

They approached the unicorn, which at a glance resembled a normal horse, but on closer examination had a lot of unusual details. Its eyes glistened like a *My Little Pony* cartoon, while its legs were about a quarter-length too short. Mac checked her map again, puzzled. Her unicorn was white with a rainbow mane, while this one was purple with a gold mane.

"Huh," she muttered loud enough to draw Kaitlyn's attention.

"What're you looking at?" she asked, stepping over.

"Nothing," Mac said, stowing the map and pointing skyward. "The Grid."

Incidentally, the Grid was still there. Mac sighed. Dawn was suddenly there, hooking an arm around her.

"Gresh, I'm glad you're finally seein' the Grid."

"Me too," Kaitlyn said.

Mac: "What . . . *is* it?"

"It's a collective neurological phenomenon," Dawn said, giggling. "Some folks see spiderwebs, some folks see crisscrosses. We see the honeycomb."

"But it looks like it's really *there,* just like this unicorn." Mac passed her fingertips over her map. "Dawn, Kaitlyn, there's something I need to tell you."

"I am *freaking out here, people,*" Dave yelled. "Where did this horse come from?!"

Kaitlyn: "It came from the Grid, dum-dum!" Then to Mac: "What was it you needed to tell us, lil sis?"

"It has to do with the Grid." Her confidence fled her. "It . . . it—"

WHOOP! The siren blasted across the farm, spooking the unicorn, which vanished into the night. Kids scattered, their scrambling panic highlighted in flashing red and blue. Headlights slanted this way and that as engines roared, several of 'em, all of them belonging to the West Chimney Top PD, who were on the case and busting the holy hell out of Billy Bones's big bash.

"Shit!" Kaitlyn yelled, hurling her drink into the dark. Mac started backpedaling as Sabrina, Dawn, Becky, and Jarra all turned and high-tailed it for their cars, Becky and Jarra taking Mac by the arms and carrying her part of the way before she shook herself loose, pulled an about-face, and sprinted along with everyone else toward Dawn's Honda.

"Can you drive, Dawn?!"

"Hell, no! I cain't hardly even walk! The ground feels like fuckin' marshmallows!"

Kaitlyn shouted: "I have a brother named Jason!"

Mac: "We know!"

"He might not be fucked up yet! I'll go find him. Where do they keep brothers?!"

Mac and Dawn rolled their eyes. They reached the party, where scores of frantic kids were tearing down Christmas lights and shoving coolers into truck beds. A few cars tore out only to get cut off by the advancing phalanx of police cruisers. Exhaust fumes, mud, and dirt flew everywhere, accompanied by misfiring and roaring engines. A voice boomed from the lead cruiser's loudspeaker:

"NOBODY! FUCKING! MOVE!"

The voice was heavily accented, hailing from deepest Appalachia or maybe north Alabama. The lead cruiser was bouncing their way, caroming over rocks and old tree roots, the voice's owner leaning outside his window, radio-receiver in hand, like he'd just arrived from Hazzard County. He wore a ten-gallon cowboy hat that bristled with peacock feathers. Doffing the ten-galloner, he trumpeted:

"MY NAME IS BEAUFORT DAVIS COLQUITT, AND I'M HERE TO BREAK UP THIS PARTY!"

Hiram's Journal

It worked.

There was no black water, no intermediate netherspace, and most important: no Plaid Man. We passed through the gate and emerged onto the same scenic cliffside I'd seen the night before. Mr. Johnson's cottage stood before us, his curtains drawn. The cottage overlooked a broad valley that cradled a pair of lakes that reflected twin suns.

Suns. It's still daylight here. He must live pretty far away.

"Is this it?" Lee asked.

"Yeah. I can't believe it. And look." I pointed up.

Lee nodded. "I doubt this is the Smoky Mountains, but I can't quite place where we are. To the west, for certain. The climate is much more arid than the Smokies. Shall we?"

We headed to the front gate, where Lee parked his bike. I paused, looking around.

Lee: "What is it?"

"I dunno," I muttered. "Seems like . . . something's missing." I cast my mind back over the last few weeks but couldn't put my finger on what was troubling me. I felt like I was trying to remember a dream that was slipping away. Lee read the concern on my face.

"Should we abort?"

I shook my head. "No, but stay frosty." I opened the gate, which felt slippery. "Ah, beans. Watch it. Paint's wet."

"Thank you," Lee said as he sidestepped his way through the gate. I bent down and wiped my hand clean on the grass, but it only seemed to make it worse; now my hand was covered in red paint and grass stains. Lee was waiting by the front door. As I approached, Justin threw back his curtains, a huge smile on his face.

I waved. "Mr. Johnson! It's me, Hiram Gresham!"

Justin snatched the curtains shut. I joined Lee on the front porch. The main picture window had a stained-glass detail I'd seen before: snakes and tentacles all coiling around a train locomotive. I heard my dad's voice again:

There's another train.

"He seems nice," Lee said.

"Yeah, he's really cool," I mumbled, fixated on the stained-glass window. "Lee, have you ever seen that—"

Cre-a-aak! The door opened to reveal Justin Johnson himself. He wore pajama pants, a robe, and a T-shirt with some faded writing I couldn't make out.

"I know you," he said.

"Yeah, it's me! Hiram Gresham. We met at the Gold Rush park a while back, the day that . . . well, the day Skelton got caught."

Justin stared at us. Then smiled. Then stopped smiling. Then waved a finger at us.

"I know you," he whispered, as if confirming his suspicion. He glanced at Lee's bike. "You brought a motorcycle."

"Oh, it isn't much more than a trail bike, sir," he said, offering his hand. "Greetings. I'm Levi David Dockery."

Justin reached out with a robe-clad arm. The sleeve of his robe looked like it had been sewn shut, but his hand snaked out of it. They shook.

"Hi, Lee. I'm Justin. Do you know what today's date is?"

"Today's date? It's December fifteenth, sir. Friday."

"December," Justin said. "Decemberrrrr."

He hadn't released Lee's hand. I peeked inside; it was pitch black.

Oh gosh. He must've been sitting in the dark all by himself.

I asked: "Mr. Johnson, is something wrong?"

"No, no. Nothing wrong."

"Sir?" Lee asked. "May I have my hand back?"

Justin's jaw dropped. "Oh!" He released him. "Ha ha, sorry about that, Lee. Old man doesn't know his own strength! Ha ha!" When he laughed, it sounded like he was saying the word "ha" over and over. He addressed me: "Now, why would you ask if I was feeling okay?"

"Uh I noticed you'd been sitting in the uh dark," I said, my stutter ramping back up. I figured he'd be depressed, but I didn't think he'd be this far gone. He seemed manic.

His smile flickered. "I guess I have been feeling a little blue. A little down in the dumps. They've asked me before. And I have to say, I've been feeling a little dreary! Give me one moment, guys, and I can give you some ice cream."

Slam! He shut the door so hard it jostled plaster loose from the outer walls and made us jump.

"Well, at least you might get the ice cream you wanted, when all is said and done."

"Great."

From inside: *"Come on in, guys!"*

We shared a look. I opened the door with my clean hand, wiping the grass and paint off on my pants. The inside was cozy as heck: Everything was arrayed around a single cushy easy chair, which was accompanied by a side table. Both faced a fireplace, next to which was a big-screen television. A kitchenette, separated by a small bar, took up the far corner of the room and stood next to his bedroom door. There were no Christmas decorations, though.

Maybe he doesn't celebrate it. None of my business.

Justin stood behind the bar, fussing around in the kitchen. The refrigerator door stood open and emitted a cloud of glowing mist that rolled around the floor and concealed him up to his knees.

"Come on in, don't be shy! Have a seat wherever. 'Make yourselves at home,' as they say."

Lee and I inched closer. The room's only light came from the fridge. Dozens of photos covered the wall next to his bedroom door, but I couldn't make them out. Justin back-stepped from the bar and opened his freezer.

"What flavor do you boys fancy? I've got chocolate, vanilla, strawberry, rocky road, and rainbow sherbet."

Lee spoke first: "None for me, sir! My mom's bringing me Kay's Kastle later."

"Well, that's okay! How about you, young Hiram?"

I glanced at Lee. We mouthed *Young Hiram?* to each other.

"Uh vanilla's fine," I said. "Mr. uh Johnson, it's okay if you're sad."

Slam! We jumped. Justin had practically rammed his fridge's two doors shut. He scooped ice cream into a bowl.

I continued: "After everything you've been through, I'd feel sad, too. But I think there's a way you can get your old job back. But we need your help to do it."

"What if I don't *want* my old job back?" he asked, holding up the bowl. "Chocolate syrup?"

"Oh, I understand. I guess I might not want my job back, either, if I'd been treated like you had. But even if you don't want your old job—" (I responded to him, distracted) "—Oh, uh sure. Chocolate syrup. Even if you don't want your old job back, there's still a way to help Skelton's victims—"

"*Extra* chocolate syrup?!"

I jumped again. He'd shouted the question. Not asked, *shouted.* I scratched my brow in thought and flinched when something glittered next to my eye. I'd wiped something shiny onto my eyebrow that was catching the light.

"Uh sure, extra chocolate syrup . . . Still a way to help all those—"

"Hiram?" Lee whispered, pointing at me. "You have gold paint on your brow."

"Extra chocolate syrup it is! Hershey's is my favorite."

"Paint?" I turned on my flashlight and shined it on my hand. It was covered in gold paint.

Justin was still carrying on: "Hershey's! That's a brand you can trust!"

"What the heck?" I muttered, rubbing my fingertips together. It looked like sand bonded with luminescent glue, or maybe even a fancy mustard, the kind with the really big seeds. But the color, although yellowish, wasn't quite gold but—

"*Brass.*"

Lee looked over. "What was that, Admiral?"

I spun back to the front door. The doorknob had a smear on it; a *handprint-shaped* smear.

My handprint.

More than that, though, the handprint had left a divot in the metal, as if I'd pulled off a chunk of it.

Justin prattled on: "Did you know that my favorite band is from Jacksonville and Hershey's chocolate is available in more than sixty countries around *the whole entire world?*"

"Lee, look," I hissed.

He frowned. "What happened to the doorknob? Is that paint?"

"No, it's not paint. It's *brass.*"

"*What?*"

"Ice cream's almost ready! Whaddaya boys jawing about over there?"

I swung my flashlight around and lit up Justin's wall of photos.

Everyone was faceless.

A memory reared up before me, my sister's voice: *I'm sorry I didn't believe you.*

They didn't believe Lucy, either, I had said in response. It was the night of the black water, when we almost reached Mr. Johnson's house, and when we tried to call him but got the Plaid Man instead. I was referring to Lucy from *The Lion, the Witch, and the Wardrobe.* What was the first thing she saw in Narnia?

"A lamp-post," I whispered.

That's what had been troubling me outside. There was no lamp-post.

"Admiral?" Lee whispered. He and I met eyes and started backing toward the door. Justin presented my bowl of ice cream like a golden chalice.

"This is, if I may say so, the most deliciously delicious bowl of ice cream I've ever made."

Mackenzie

She didn't think she could hate Colquitt more than she did, but he proved her wrong.

Colquitt strutted down the line of kids, sticking his flashlight in their faces. A three-inch-wide belt held a clutch of peacock feathers to his Stetson, the buckle a giant pewter monstrosity that depicted the faces of Stone Mountain and made sure Colquitt's every move was overseen by Davis, Jackson, and Lee. Mac remembered Colquitt's face from the news. He lived with a constant smirk, his eyes twinkling with the knowledge that he was always one step ahead, the deck stacked in his favor.

They corralled most everyone down by the old cabin: Mac, Dawn, Becky, Sabrina, Jarra, and Kaitlyn. They didn't see Jason, but his Beamer was still there. Colquitt was attended by about a dozen other cops, all of whom bore similar smirks—except for one guy. Mac's eye was drawn to him, this other cop; he stood apart, ignoring Colquitt's antics and warily scanning the property for threats. In contrast with Colquitt, who sported a barrel chest that stretched his shirt buttons to the max, this guy was fit, with cords of muscle popping out along his forearms and neck.

He was good-looking, too. Mac thought he could be on TV.

Colquitt got to Mac and blasted her retinas with light:

"Have a lookee here, missy," he said with a chuckle. She winced and squeezed her eyes shut. He guffawed. "Where's your glasses at, missy?"

"Glasses?"

"Looks to me like you got your pupils dilated. The last time *my* pupils were as big and wide as yours, the eye doctor had to dilate 'em to be sure I didn't have glaucoma. Family history, y'see. Oh, do you have a family history of glaucoma?"

"No, sir, I don't . . ." Mac trailed off, her eyes bugging out.

The unicorn was back.

Colquitt shared a shit-eating grin with his colleagues.

"Little missy's seeing stars, by the looks of it! Whadda you think, Baird?"

Another cop, presumably Baird, chortled. "Looks that way, boss!"

"How about you, Baywatch?"

Colquitt shined his light on the good-looking cop, who wasn't amused. Baird prodded him.

"Hey, Baywatch, boss asked you a question. Hard of hearing?"

"The name's Webb, and I heard him fine," the good-looking cop, Webb, said. "Thought I saw something, boss. All clear."

Colquitt boomed laughter. "Baywatch thought he saw himself a wendigo!"

Laughter all around.

Mac pointed. "No, look!"

Colquitt rolled his eyes. Oldest trick in the book. He turned, looked straight at the approaching creature, and wheeled back toward the kids.

"Oh, my holy God!"

Hiram's Journal

That's when it dawned on me. Since we'd arrived, Justin had been moving strangely.

He had never *turned away* from us.

He'd only ever looked at us head-on, from the moment he opened his curtains to when he opened the door to when we came inside. When we came inside, he was already in the kitchen, facing us.

"Mr. Johnson, can I ask you a favor?"

Lee whispered: "Let's go."

Justin: "First come grab a seat at the bar, enjoy your ice cream!"

"We will in a second, sir. Can you do me a favor and turn to the side?"

"If I may, Admiral, I think we should abort the mission."

Justin's eyes got round; not wide, *round.* His lips curled away from all of his teeth, upper and lower. When he spoke, his lips didn't move. His voice emanated from the ceiling.

"Now, why would a smart young boy like yourself ask such a strange, strange, *strange* thing of a grown-up?"

"Uh can you do it for us, please?"

"We should abort, Admiral."

"Now, why would a smart young boy like yourself ask such a strange *fucking* thing of a grown-up?"

The only sound was our breathing. Justin slung the bowl into the sink like he was inbounding a soccer ball—*CRASSSSH!* It shattered, splattering ice cream everywhere.

"Fine!" He screamed the same way Trent did outside Dr. Eldridge's office. We flinched. He came around the bar, but when he moved, he didn't bob with the natural gait of someone walking; he *floated.* He came into our light, and we both gasped.

The cottage's floor was melting into his legs.

He didn't have feet or knees but rather two cylindrical columns that faded in a fine gradient from his pajama bottoms into the floor. As he moved, his lower legs flickered to match whatever surface he was standing on: when he stood on carpet, they were carpet; on wood, wood. His smile grotesquely spread across his face until it touched his ears. He looked like his head had split in half.

"Hershey's! That's a brand you can trust! Shame you didn't want your ice cream, Hiram! You really coulda put one over on your bitch mom, ya stupid, *DISGUSTING FAT FUCK! HA HA HA HAHAHAHAAA!"*

"Admiral!"

I screamed: *"Turn to the side!"*

Cackling, the thing that looked like Justin rotated to the side, revealing that he was wearing a *shell* of Justin that covered only his front. His true form was a familiar horror of scar tissue and charred, red flesh.

Lee: "Admiral, if the front door is locked and we die in here, I may not invite you over again."

Suddenly, *fwoomp!* The thing that looked like Justin grabbed fistfuls of its chest and tore away its shell to reveal the *him,* the *it,* the *thing,* the *creature*— the Plaid Man. Its voice came from everywhere:

"Who's the new snack?!"

We simultaneously screamed: *"FUUUUUUCK!"*

Our actions were instant and comical; we ran into each other, both of us grabbing the doorknob, which for one insane instant I thought was locked but nope! It came off, the whole shebang, knob, doorplate and a chunk of the door itself, all of which melted in my grasp like ice cream—or maybe icing—under a propane torch.

The Plaid Man was yelling laughter: *"HA HA HA HA!"*

I grabbed Lee's elbow and yelled: "Not over but *through!*" On a hunch, I shoved him straight through the door, which exploded apart like a hundred layers of icing. I clambered through the hole, the Plaid Man's claws swiping at my rear. We crashed onto the front porch, which splattered under our weight. The whole world was a bizarre kind of pudding-icing glop that was hot to the touch, like it had just come out of an oven. We struggled to our feet, slipping and sliding everywhere, and plunged up the front walk. A glance over my shoulder revealed that not only was the entire house melting, but *the entire fucking world was melting.* The sun was a dripping yellow inferno, the clouds sagging and seeping groundward, the mountains boiling away.

We reached the front gate just as the Plaid Man burst from the house cackling, his gait an insane jitter because all his joints were reversed, his face a latticework of gore from his gushing staple-wounds.

I hollered: *"Juuuuuump!"*

We leaped over the fence like fucking action heroes.

Mackenzie

Colquitt's eyes were still gogging. He stepped closer to the unicorn, raising a trembling hand.

And he walked right through it.

Bursting into laughter, he said: "Look, look, fellas! It's . . . it's the Yellow Submarine! There she blowwwwws!" The unicorn shivered apart around Colquitt like mist and reconstituted itself directly before Mac and the gang. Colquitt was shining his flashlight out across the farm, but another flashlight beam swung toward Mac and passed straight through the unicorn.

Webb's.

Frowning, his eyes scanned the area in front of Mac, like he was trying and failing to focus on something. The rest of the cops were following Colquitt's schtick:

"If I didn't know any better, I'd say we got us a whole passel of glaucoma patients. If I shine this light—" (he indicated his flashlight) "—in alla yall's eyes, am I gonna see the same big ol' pupils as I saw in missy's there?"

The unicorn vanished once more into the night. Mac kept an eye on Webb, who squinted, shook his head, and turned his attention back to watching the land.

Could that guy Webb see the unicorn? Mac thought. *It's like he could* almost *see it, but none of the other grown-ups could.*

Colquitt waved his flashlight. "Open 'em up, kids. I'm your eye doctor tonight."

In the distance, a motorcycle's engine revved.

Hiram's Journal

The world was a wet canvas smeared by the hand of a giant.

Lee gunned his trail bike through the rapidly melting fantasy world we'd stumbled into. Trees sagged and toppled over like massive columns of icing. Sheet after sheet of sopping-wet icing-earth shot out from the bike's tires as we rode and dodged around dissolving terrain. Overhead, the sun was plummeting to the earth like a massive, sweating sphere of slop. All color was draining from everything, leaving behind a bizarre *reverse*-version of the world, with a stark-white sky and a smear of black ink instead of a sun.

And always, always, always, the Plaid Man was gaining.

"HIDY HIRAM STAMMERSTONE! DEAD, DEAD, YOU'RE ALREADY DEAD! LITTLE LEE PEED HIS PANTS! DEAD, DEAD, YOU'RE ALREADY DEAD! HA HA HA!"

"Step on it!" I screamed.

"Hang on! It's getting slick!"

"There it is!"

Our gate, thank God, was still standing and swimming with that same spectral golden light. The bike's rear end fishtailed through the liquefying non-earth, but Lee kept us steady enough to zoom through the gate.

We made it out of whatever reverse, bizarro world we'd stumbled into, but we weren't safe yet.

Behind us—*boom!* The gate exploded into a million pieces as the Plaid Man smashed through it, his suit once more melting away into fractal soup, the remnants of our gate fading away into the air.

Lee was a veritable motocross champion, slaloming around trees and making jumps over little creeks. Behind us, the Plaid Man's body sprouted two extra arms and legs; he chased us like a gigantic spider, his face bleeding sheets of red tears as he skittered over hill and dale. The bike's engine sputtered and misfired, forcing Lee to hunch over, his forearms shaking as he struggled to maintain control.

"The wheels!" he yelled. "I can't control it!"

Icing-slop was flooding the bike's innards and coating its tires with glistening slickness. The engine made an awful, cracking howl before the bike's rear shot out from behind us, spinning us in a full circle—

"Looook ooooouuuuut!"

—right into the old Civil War cabin, which we smashed into, flying through its back door, skidding across the floor, my coat coming off as we flipped end over end out the front door, where voices screamed, lights flashed, and our inner ears popped from a sudden change in altitude. We skidded to a stop, and I realized the flashing lights were *police* lights. Someone swung a flashlight toward me. I raised a hand to block it and brought a pistoning silhouette into view, a line of people, all jostling to get a better look. I blinked into the glare as voices familiar and strange spoke:

"Who the Sam Hill is that?"

"Did you see where they came from?"

"Came outta goldurn nowhere!"

"Lee?!"

A stocky figure advanced from the silhouette and kneeled before me.

"Hiram?"

It was Mac.

We were at Soddy Farm.

Mackenzie

It exploded between them. Splinters flew and exhaust spewed from the cabin, a sudden magical momentum hurling Mac and Dawn to the ground in opposite directions. Everyone else staggered apart, covering their ears or eyes before gawking in astonishment at the two new arrivals, who came to a skidding stop a few feet before the cabin, a steaming trail bike still chugging away next to them, its headlight flickering out.

Colquitt swung his flashlight around. "Who the Sam Hill is that?"

Baird was looking right and left. "Did you see where they came from?"

"Came outta goldurn nowhere!"

Dawn awkwardly pulled herself up and yelled: *"Lee?!"*

As if in a dream, Mac kneeled before her baby brother. She looked him over, then back at the cabin. The door was miraculously still intact, if a little splintered. The cabin's interior was dark. Mac looked back.

"Hiram?"

Voices shouted and murmured all around. Someone cracked a joke about everyone being high. Lee sat up.

"Greetings, sister." He gawked around. "Goodness. One small leap."

Dawn: "Lee, what the fuck are you—"

The cops were in disarray, running about, shouting, pointing this way and that. Hiram patted his chest.

"Jacket's gone," he said.

Vummm-m-m-m came a thrum that squeezed your diaphragm and pinched your inner ear. A blinding light, bright as the sun, blasted from the cabin. Hiram forearm-shielded his eyes and screamed:

"Shut the door!"

Nobody moved, but that same chucklehead cracked the same joke about everyone being too high. Even Colquitt stood there like an idiot, while Webb gaped into the cabin like he was looking at the burning bush. Hiram lunged to his feet and slammed the door shut.

One of the cops muttered: "That's the reason."

Mac touched Hiram's shoulder and whispered: "I know how to—"

Bang! The cabin's door bowed outward. Everyone backed away. That same guy was joking about everyone being high. Colquitt was screaming at his team:

"How'd y'all miss a coupla kids on a goddamn moped?!" Turning his attention to the cabin, he yelled: "Knock it off, whoever you are! We know you're in there! Come on out and join the party with the rest of your buddies!"

Silence. Someone whispered: "Reason."

Bang! The door bowed outward, dust and plaster raining from the overhanging roof. Everyone flinched. Colquitt's face, heretofore either smug or angry, took on the slightest hint of confusion. Hiram patted his chest and checked his pockets.

"Shit!" he yelled, running to Mac and urgently whispering: "Give me your map."

"Why?"

"I lost mine. Uh just *give it!*"

She did. Hiram pulled out a pencil and erased the old cabin.

Ba—silence. The banging stopped mid-*bang*. The light inside faded. Jason chose that moment to come running up.

"Kaity! What's going on?!"

Colquitt swung his flashlight over.

"Grab that tall drinka water, wouldya, Baywatch?" He redirected his ire at the cabin, which he approached slowly, calling: "Whoever you are! There's no point in trying to hide—"

That same whispering voice: "Reason."

"—we got ya surrounded, kid." Silence. Colquitt jerked his head at Baird. "Open that door and draw your sidearm, just in case."

Webb took Jason's elbow and said: "Hang tight here, son."

"Kaity," Jason hissed.

"Hi, Jason," Kaitlyn said, smiling dreamily. "You're my brother, whose name is Jason."

That same joke again: "High reason."

"Huh?" Jason said.

A cop standing in the darkness next to Webb and Jason had made the joke.

Webb nodded. "Yeah, that's why she's so spaced out all right."

Baird whipped open the door and jumped back, weapon drawn. Everyone angled their gaze inside. Baird turned to Colquitt, holstering his weapon and stepping back over to the kids. He ushered Hiram, Lee, and Mac over with the others.

"All clear, boss."

That same random cop spoke again: "High reason."

Colquitt looked incredulously at Baird. "Whaddaya mean 'all clear'? Looked like a goddamn Q-beam shinin' outta there!" He went inside the cabin and shined his flashlight around.

Lee whispered, "Admiral, mental note: In the real world, a yellow gate also signifies *monster.*"

"No shit, Admiral." Hiram tapped Mac and said: "I think I know how to get to Mr. Johnson's house."

Mac smiled, her pupils the size of dimes. "I think I do, too." She took a really deep breath and whispered: "How. Did. You. Get. Here."

Dawn leaned over: "That's what I wanna know!"

Kaitlyn was still in a dream world: "Say hi to your friend, Jase."

"High reason," said the random cop again, inching forward. His outfit jumped out at Mac, who frowned. The rest of the cops were wearing their usual beige and brown uniforms, but this guy was wearing all white. Baird and a few other cops joined Colquitt in the cabin, their flashlights whipping this way and that, occasionally flashing across the man in white. His face blinked into view, revealing yellow teeth and a grime-covered complexion.

Another flash: He was wearing a name-tag.

Another flash: His name-tag displayed numbers, about ten random ones.

Another flash: His eyes lit up, one of them big and round as a moon.

"High reason," he said, smiling with cracked, yellow teeth.

Webb finally noticed the guy, who he stared at for a full five seconds before he shoved Jason behind him, pulled his gun, and screamed to wake the dead:

"Freeze! Put your hands up! Put 'em up now!"

Colquitt stumbled out, yelling: "What the fuckin' hell's going on?!"

Webb backed away from the man in white: *"Move slowly, get on your knees!"*

The man in white stepped into the light cast by the cops' flashlights. The kids all made an arc, with the man in white at its focus. His chest heaved, his smile pulsing in size with his breaths.

He was excited.

Colquitt turned stark white. He instantly dropped to a crouch, weapon drawn, his voice breaking in a shriek:

"Don't you fuckin' move!" He waved frantically at the kids. *"Get back! Get back!"*

Another cop arrived from a random part of the farm with Randall in tow.

"Got a rabbit here, boss! Caught this one tryin' to—"

Colquitt screamed: *"James pull your gun the situation's changed the situation's changed oh my fuckin' Christ the situation's changed—"*

The man in white struck like a snake, snatching one of the kids from the crowd, who screamed.

"Oh, my God oh no let me go!"

Jason: *"Kaity!"*

Everyone was standing in still shock, slack-jawed, eyes gogging at the sight of a man in a white prison jumpsuit pulling one of the kids into the darkness, a massive arm coiled around her neck. Mac's altered mind made a few connections. Voices called from distant somewheres, trying to tell her what to do—*Protect Hiram, he's in danger*—but she remained motionless, the primary question of the evening still perplexing her:

Who is this man in white?

It was her brother who answered for everyone, her sweet baby brother who had discovered how to draw magic maps, her sweet baby brother who was now covering his mouth with one hand and pointing with the other, his voice hoarse from all-out terror:

"Skelton. Skelton. *Skelton!*"

The name and its awful attendant meaning spread like wildfire through the crowd, who reacted like someone said a nuclear missile was inbound; they shrieked, screamed, cried out, and ran in every direction, ripping themselves free of whatever cops were holding them and pelting into the dark.

But Skelton, Leonard Shane "Lenny" Skelton, the Blue Ribbon Killer, maintained his grip around his captive, a young woman Mac recognized; recognized because she knew they were destined to become sisters, this Janis Joplin-looking cut-up.

Mac was wailing: *"Kaitlyn!"*

Webb: "God a'mighty, boss, you see who that is?!"

"*Shut up, Webb!*" Colquitt yelled, stepping forward. "*Skelton, let her go!*"

Skelton looked at Jason. "Hi, Jason. Good to see you again." You'd think they were old friends.

Kaitlyn blubbered: "*Ohmigod ohmigod ohmigod.*"

Skelton's face seized: "*EVERYBODY SHUT THE FUCK UP!*"

Everyone did. Wind blew. Bonfires flickered and guttered in the distance. Colquitt's brow sparkled with sweat.

"Skelton, we can work this out. Let the girl go, and—"

"This girl's got thirty seconds to live."

Kaitlyn sobbed. Skelton's bicep flexed and exerted a savage vise around her neck. Her face turned red.

Colquitt yelled: "Ain't gotta be that way!"

Webb: "Boss, we gotta—"

"Shut the fuck *up*, lemme think—"

"Twenty-*six*, twenty-*five* . . ."

Skelton continued his countdown, inching his way toward the cabin door with Kaitlyn in tow.

"Jesus God almighty, Skelton, if you—"

Skelton: "*I'd move away from that door, hoss!*"

Colquitt obeyed, his hands shaking so bad he was practically waggling his gun. He stumbled on a tree stump but righted himself. Skelton backed his way toward the door, almost done:

"Eleven, ten, nine, eight, *seven, SIX, FIVE!*"

Kaitlyn's face was tearslick and drawn with terror: "*Help me, pleeeeeasssseeee!*"

Jason: "*No! Don't!*"

Skelton barked his final two numbers: "*TWO! ONE!*"

Two things happened at once: Colquitt made a run at Skelton, and Skelton slung Kaitlyn into him. She crashed into his arms—and he turned positively feral, screaming, "*Get the fuck off me*" and hurling her aside, his Stetson falling off to reveal a gleaming bald head. Kaitlyn smashed into Dawn, and they both went toppling over a tree stump into an outcropping of rocks beside the cabin. They hit the ground hard and both screamed in pain.

Skelton slammed the door.

Virtually all the kids rushed to the girls' aid. Hiram and Mac kneeled next to them. Dawn was holding her ankle, basically unhurt, but Kaitlyn's right forearm was bent at an awful angle, broken. She cradled it, hyperventilating in shock. Dawn sprang to her feet.

"We need help! She's hurt!" On a hurt leg, Dawn kneeled by Kaitlyn and comforted her. "You're gonna be all right, Kaity. Don't move your arm."

Webb ran over and screamed: "Boss! These kids, they're hurt!"

But Colquitt was in a world of rage:

"SKELTON! SKELTONNNN! GET OUTTA THERE! We've got you surrounded!" He wheeled on his men: *"GET ME THE FUCKING BATTERING RAM!"*

Whoom! Flames erupted inside the cabin, licking from under the door and around the shutters. Webb grabbed a couple other cops. Colquitt lowered his gun, his jaw slack.

Skelton squealed: *"Help me help me help meeeeee!"*

Webb ordered the other cops: "Help these kids outta here!" He hefted Kaitlyn into his arms and carried her to safety among a mass of kids—Hiram and Mac included; Mac, who was helping a hobbling Dawn—who all rushed away from the fire as the rest of the cops closed in, Colquitt at the fore.

His voice was gone, his eyes vacant: "I thought, I thought I saw a light."

What emitted from the cabin wasn't earthly, wasn't real, *couldn't be* real, because how could someone cry for joy while howling in anguish? The sound brought instant tears to Mac's eyes, the image of Jenny's mother suddenly frank and crystalline in her mind's eye. Skelton's screams reminded her of that moment, and she burned with a deep hatred of him for it. Her gaze drifted across the crowd and landed on Jason, who stood in the dark, his face blank, a wad of paper crumpled up in his hand.

The cabin collapsed. Skelton was gone.

Hiram's Journal

It was only the three of us: me, Mac, and Lee sitting in a narrow hallway in the West Chim Police Department, awaiting our fate. Dawn and Kaitlyn were both at the hospital, along with Jason. We faced a line of windows looking in on a room full of police cubicles, as well as the police radio command center. Officers filed to and fro, some in plainclothes, some in uniforms. Mac sat with her arms crossed, slumped halfway down her seat, while Lee and I sat, heads downcast.

Mac leaned over. "You two okay?"

"Yeah," I said. "I've just never heard someone scream like that."

"Yeah," she said. "I saw a unicorn."

Lee whispered: "And we saw the cabin."

"The one I drew?" Mac asked.

I nodded.

Mac leaned back, eyes wide. "Wowwwwww."

"Can you please focus?"

"I *am* focused. It's just that something magical is happening."

"Well, to be *perfectly* accurate, we're not sure if it's magic or simply a form of science we don't yet have the cognitive capacity to understand."

"Lee," I said.

"Right. Sorry. Yes, it may very well be magic."

Mac asked: "Why did you erase the cabin from my map?"

"I think whatever we draw on our maps . . . happens?"

Mac nodded. "You drew our neighborhood and Soddy Farm and Lee's house. So did I."

"Then you added the cabin to your map."

"Then *you* added the cabin to *your* map."

Lee: "And then it appeared over by my house. The cabin."

"And when you crashed into it, you popped out over at the farm."

"So did the Plaid Man."

Mac looked frightened. "That's who was banging on the door?"

I nodded. "I thought if I erased the cabin from my map, it would . . . make the portal go away somehow. I don't know. But I lost my map."

"How'd you lose it?"

"I lost my jacket. It was in my pocket."

Mac made an *oh, gosh* face and hooked an arm around him. "You *did* lose your jacket. You must be freezing."

Hiram hugged her back. "I'm okay, thanks. So that's why I asked for your map."

"And you were right," Mac said. "Once you erased it, he disappeared. But how did you run into him in the first place?"

Lee started speed-speaking: "We were playing *Masterminder Home Edutainment Presents Theseus's Labyrinth of Terror,* which features magic gates, yes? So I think the admiral, Hiram here, got the idea to draw a magic gate to Mr. Johnson's house."

I smiled. "That was *your* idea, Admiral, but thanks anyway."

Some officers walked by. We sat in silence until Mac held up a palm. "*And?*"

"We went through it," I said.

"And we met Not Mr. Johnson."

Mac shook her head. "What does that mean?"

"It was the Plaid Man, not Mr. Johnson," I said.

Lee: "Tell her the rest. Tell her about how everything melted."

Mac sat back, freaked out. "Don't mess with me. I'm too high for this shit."

"We're not messing with you," I whispered as another officer walked by. "We drew a gate on my map, and it took us someplace that *looked* like Mr.

Johnson's house, but it wasn't."

"What do you mean it *wasn't?*" she asked.

"It was . . . fake," Lee said.

"The cottage was fake?"

I said: "No. Everything. Everything was fake."

"It was a made-up world."

Mac's eyes looked like dinner plates. "And you ran into the Plaid Man again?"

"Yes. And he was wearing a disguise."

"He was disguised as Mr. Johnson. It was like he was . . . wearing his skin."

Mac's jaw flexed. "I don't know who I hate more—Skelton or the Plaid Man."

"Or Colquitt," I whispered.

Mac nodded. I don't think I'd ever seen her so pissed off. She swallowed and gathered herself.

"So why were you able to . . . well, to teleport from Lee's place to Soddy Farm, but when you tried to go to Mr. Johnson's, you ran into the Plaid Man? Didn't you and Lee both work on your map?"

Lee's eyes filled his coke-bottle lenses. "Oh."

We looked at him and said: "What?"

"We drew a gate on Hiram's map, but you didn't draw one on yours."

We both sat back. I nodded.

"It takes two."

Mac took my hand. "Yeah. Once we draw two maps, the magic happens."

Lee: "That is my current hypothesis."

I said: "But our gate still worked."

Mac: "Except for the part where it took you to the evil lair of a supermonster, it worked great." She chuckled. "You guys need to show me that game *Labyrinth of Tarbo*."

Lee corrected her: *Masterminder Home Edutainment Presents Theseus's Labyrinth of Terror.*"

"Terrence."

"Terror."

"Marmalade."

"Mac," I said, elbowing her. "Quit foolin.'"

"Was she kidding me?" Lee asked.

"Yeah, a little," Mac said. "Sorry."

"No, it's okay. I just want to remember it for later. Hmm."

I said: "There's still one thing I don't understand."

Mac cocked an eyebrow and quoted *Clue: "One* thing?"

I followed suit: "'Flames, flames, from the sides of my face'!"

We broke into giggles. Lee's tone was a portrait of patience:

"Admiral? May we get back on track?"

"Sorry," I said. "What I don't understand is this: If you need two people to draw two maps with the same stuff on 'em to make the magic work, then what happened last night with all the black water?" I turned to Lee and added: "The unstable wormhole I told you about."

"Right," Mac said. "That *sort of* worked."

I said: "But I don't understand why it worked *at all*. You didn't draw a map."

Now Mac was the one figuring things out: "What if someone else did?"

We both looked at her. Nodded.

She smiled. "Mr. Johnson must be drawing a map, and he must've included some of the same details as your map, Hi."

Lee broke in: "Do you think . . ."

"What?" Mac asked.

"It's stupid."

"We're talking about magic maps and unicorns, Lee," Mac said. "Nothing's stupid."

"Understood. I was thinking: Hiram and I drew a portal on our map, and it led to the Plaid Man. Last night, you accidentally stumbled into the black water, which was a kind of portal. Perhaps you and Mr. Johnson both drew the same map, and he drew a portal on his."

I asked: "But what could he have drawn that would've caused that black water? And why did his portal even work *at all*?"

Lee's eyes narrowed in concentration. "I don't know."

Mac: "Maybe some people can draw stuff on their own, and it'll work? I drew that unicorn, and it came to life, but . . ." She trailed off.

"But what?" I asked.

"It didn't look exactly like the one I drew."

"Perhaps that's an element of the magic," Lee said. "If you add an element to a map by yourself, some chaotic principle governs it. Mr. Johnson drew a portal by himself, and it summoned the black water. You drew a unicorn by yourself, but it didn't precisely match your vision."

I frowned in thought. "I *think* I follow you."

Mac: "We'll figure it out. But here's what we know: Unless we've *all* worked on our maps and drawn the exact same stuff, we shouldn't try to use them to teleport anywhere."

"All?" Lee asked. "Who else would be drawing maps?"

Mac shrugged. "Why can't all of us draw maps?" Her voice dropped as her eyes got distant; some other voice spoke through her: "I think the more maps, the more powerful the magic. We're stronger together."

We basked in that joy for a moment before I practically yelled: *"Shit."*

"What's wrong?" Mac asked, checking the hallway to make sure no one heard.

"If we were working on a map with Soddy Farm . . . and Skelton teleported there . . ."

Lee gasped slightly. "Oh, beans."

Mac nodded. "Skelton must've had a map, too. That's how he appeared at the farm."

"It's far worse than that," Lee said. "Skelton not only had a map, he *knows about* the maps. He knows about the magic."

Mac's eyes widened. "And if he was able to appear at the farm . . ."

I finished her thought: "He might've been able to disappear, too."

Mac leaped to her feet and flagged down the first cop she saw, a movie-star-looking guy we'd come to know as Officer Holton Webb. He was rushing down the hall with some folders tucked under his arm, his face about as haggard as a matinee idol's could look. Mac blocked his way.

"Sir, sir!"

He tried to brush past her with: "Honey, you need to take a seat and keep drinking water."

"No, Skelton escaped!"

He stopped, pivoted our way. "Yeah, we know—"

"No, I mean he escaped into the fire!"

Webb looked ready to pass out on his feet, but he mustered some compassion.

"Honey—"

"Don't call me honey!" Mac shouted. "You have to go look!"

I was ready for Webb to tell my sister to shut up, but he absorbed her words and looked her in the eye. This guy was all right.

"I'm sorry I called you honey, young lady. But . . . we got him."

"You did?"

"Yeah. Keep a lid on it, but we're waiting on dentals to come back."

I asked: "Dentals?"

"Dental records. When someone gets burned up so bad we can't . . . Well, the only way we can get an ID sometimes is by looking at the victim's teeth."

Mac glared. "He's not a victim."

"Right, sorry. The person who died. Point is: he's gone." He put a hand on her shoulder. "You're safe. You're all safe, and they're tending to your sister at the hospital."

"Oh! She's not our sister," Mac said. "Not yet, anyway. Is she okay?"

"Doc said it was a clean break. He was able to set it just fine. Want me to take you over there?"

"No, thanks. Our mom asked us to wait here."

"That's Ms. Gresham, you mean?"

"Yes, sir."

"Got it. She's a nice lady. And let me tell you something about Ms. Kaitlyn: She's a very brave and lucky young woman. She's gonna walk outta there tonight. And . . ." —he whispered: "I'm sorry." He nodded over his shoulder through the glass, where a red-faced Colquitt sat fuming. An older police officer was screaming at him. "I'm sorry about him. Colquitt. Fuckin' embarrassment to the force, you ask me; pardon my French."

"If I may," Lee said, raising a finger. "Why is he your superior, then?"

Webb shrugged. "Knows all the right people."

The older officer stopped yelling at Colquitt and called: *"Webb! Get in here!"*

"Gotta git," Webb said, producing a business card from his pocket. "Here's my card. If y'all ever need anything, give me a call, day or night."

Webb headed into the cubicles. Mac sat, staring at the card.

I asked: "What did you mean 'into' the fire?"

"Huh?" Mac said.

"When you told him Skelton escaped, you didn't say he escaped *from* the fire. You said he escaped *into* the fire."

"Yeah. I figured he drew a magic portal from his jail cell to the farm and another one from the cabin to . . . I don't know where. But I guess he didn't."

She burst into tears. Doors swung open down the hall and admitted Mom, Trent, Jason, and Kaitlyn, who was wearing an arm cast. Sandra escorted Dawn, who loped along on a crutch with a wrapped ankle. Lee jumped up and ran to her.

"Dawn!"

They all hugged, but Sandra kneeled and took Lee's shoulders.

"Levi David Dockery, what on earth were you doin' out there?"

Dawn: "That's what I wanna know. The farm's about ten miles from Dizzy Pines. Did you ride all that way?"

"Um," Lee said, averting his eyes.

Trent saw Mac crying and kneeled before her, putting on a weird, toothy grimace. I think the huge asshole was trying to be fatherly.

"Sweetie! What—"

"DON'T FUCKING CALL ME SWEETIE!"

He recoiled. I prepared myself for an explosion, but Mom belayed it with a touch of his shoulder. She had a strange look that in retrospect, I now recognize: it's the look she normally would've had *after* yelling at us. Normally, if Mac had lied to her about where she'd be, and I suddenly turned up on the other side of town at a big-kids' party, she'd be furious. But Skelton out-flanked her anger. The fact that we'd all had a near-miss with death made her forget how pissed she'd normally be with us. Funny how that works.

Instead, she muttered with a weird rictus grin: "I'm going to *kill* you. I'm going to *kill* you."

Mac: "Mom, I know I said I was spending the night at Dawn's, but—"

Mom bared her teeth an instant and shook her head once.

She hissed: "Later."

Kaitlyn smiled. "Hey, losers."

Mac stood and hugged her. "You okay?"

"Yeah. I'll be back in black inside of six weeks."

Mac hugged Dawn next. "Hey, bestie."

"Hey," Dawn said, choked up.

Sandra: "I swear. I want to sue the sumbitch who did this to you."

"Well, you can't rightly sue a dead man, can you?" Trent asked.

"Not him," Sandra said, giving him a look so withering I almost laughed. "The cop who broke her arm and almost busted my little Dawn's ankle. The way she told it, that officer, Colquitt, threw Kaitlyn to the ground like a bag of trash and—"

"*Bo!*"

Trent's siren-like voice silenced Sandra. Bo Colquitt emerged from the cubicles beaming at Trent.

"Well, I'll be a goddamn motherfucking sonofabitch, as I live and breathe— Trent Sutton! Plaid!"

Trent's nickname made my stomach lurch. Kaitlyn shrank from him. All the air drained from us. Trent pumped Bo's hand and hugged him.

Of course these two assholes are friends.

"Heard you saw some action tonight," Trent said.

"Finally got that sick fuck. Put him down myself. You shoulda seen it! He was beggin' for his life!"

Kaitlyn snorted. Dawn and Mac shared a look that said *bullshit.* Mom seemed to go into stasis.

Sandra, however, got in Colquitt's face: "Would you watch your language?"

His lip curled, his eyes narrowed, he shook his head slightly. It was the same look you'd give a pile of garbage.

"Excuse me? Ma'am, you're going to want to watch *your* language with—"

"You broke her arm. You almost broke my daughter's leg."

Somehow, Colquitt hadn't noticed us, much less remembered our role in the evening, but when he recognized Kaitlyn, he slowed his roll.

"Your daughter's lucky to be alive, ma'am."

Trent broke in, giving Colquitt a hearty pat on the back: "You're *all* lucky to be alive. You should all thank Officer Colquitt for his bravery in the line of fire when you get a chance. Bo?"

It was like he was handing off a microphone. Colquitt gave him an annoyed look but continued blabbering:

"Uh, thanks. Yes'm, your children—your daughters, everyone—they was *all* in the middle of a serious, high-stakes takedown of a *murder*-one, *death* row, public-enemy-*number*-one inmate on the loose. She's lucky she escaped with only the broken arm, and she's lucky me and my boys, my boys in blue were there. All of us put our lives on the line every day of the *live*-long day so she can go home with nothing but a broken arm." He addressed Kaitlyn, his voice weirdly loud, like a clueless tourist speaking the wrong language: "You're going to be. All. Right. Little darling."

Kaitlyn was shooting eye-bullets. I hid my smile. Trent started pumping Trent's hand again.

"Thank you for putting yourself on the line." He addressed us: "And guess what? We've got some good news to announce!"

Mac and I stopped breathing and met eyes. Our look said *Oh my fucking God, no, no, NO.* Dawn and Lee looked horrified, too, but Sandra's face betrayed nothing; it was pure blank, pure void, like someone had switched her off.

Trent extended a hand to our mom: "My love? Wouldn't you like to tell everyone?"

She cleared her throat. "We're getting engaged."

Blood pounded in my ears. No one said shit for a moment until Colquitt started braying:

"Well, I'll be a sonofabitch! Fuck me, man! Engaged *again?* After I done tole you once was enough for any man?"

He offered his hand for another down-home fist-pumper. Sandra lowered her head and gathered her kids.

"We gotta get home," she said on her way past Mom.

Lee whispered to us: "We must reconvene soon."

"You got it," I whispered.

Dawn loped along, turning to linger. She waved.

"Nice meeting you, Jason!"

He ignored her, staring at the floor. Dawn slowly lowered her hand and left with her family. Colquitt slapped Trent's back.

"Couldn't happen to an unluckier sonofabitch twice! I'll be praying for ya,

Plaid!"

It occurred to me that Trent was a widow. I hated Trent's guts, but even *I* thought Colquitt was being insensitive.

I guess assholes only know how to speak asshole.

Trent wrapped one of his ten-foot arms around Mom, who accepted his embrace but seemed to lean away from him as he prattled on: "And I wanted to make one small correction: We *got* engaged. Got, as in I popped the question tonight—on the way over here, in fact!—and she gave me the green light, God bless her." He smiled wolfishly at me and Mac. "Gonna be some changes. Some big changes. All of your lives just took a turn for the better, kids."

Later that night, Mac and I were in a guest bedroom at Auntie Hanna's house, me lying in the bottom of a bunk bed, her sitting on the floor, her back to the bed. Hanna had invited us over to spend the night in peace and quiet, and "So she could keep an eye on us." Trent worked it out with Colquitt to let us all go home without being questioned. Now that Skelton was dead, there wasn't much point.

"I think it's because they want to protect Colquitt," Mac whispered.

Auntie Hanna's house was big and rambling with lots of wood paneling, big windows, and cushy furniture. It felt like a little mountain lodge. We wished we could always live there.

But now we were destined to move in with Trent.

Like usual, we left our door cracked so we could eavesdrop on Mom and Auntie Hanna.

I whispered: "Are we going to have to live with him? And Jason?"

Mac nodded. "We'll be in a bigger house, at least."

"Yeah. I wonder if I'll ever find Itza Linda."

"It's a what?"

"Oh, Sorry. Itza Linda. It's what I call the place with the magic traincar."

"Where Skelton hid those kids."

"Yeah."

Mac's voice was steely: "We still have to find it."

"Even though he's gone."

Mac frowned, looking doubtful. "Even though . . . he's gone."

Mom and Auntie Hanna's voices floated in. We hushed up.

"Well, I'll be," Auntie Hanna said. "When's the date?"

"March thirteenth."

A pause, then: "Where did this come from?"

"He's good to me." Mom's voice dropped: "Don't you dare judge me."

"Can I judge my sister positively for making a choice that's right for her, *if* that's what she's doing?"

"That's what I'm doing."

"You know you can always come to me for money."

"I'm not marrying him for his money. I think I love him."

"Huh. I guess . . ." Auntie Hanna trailed off.

"What?"

"It's just . . . he doesn't seem like . . . the kind you'd write about in the danavreece."

I sat up quickly. The bed *creee-a-aked.*

Mom, instantly: "Hey! Close that door and go to sleep!"

Mac slammed the door. "Nice work, goofball."

My head was full of colliding ideas. I thought of Justin, of how he'd crossed paths with Skelton twice. My heart hurt for him; thinking of his pain brought tears to my eyes and a strange image bubbling to the surface of my imagination: Justin and Skelton were two points on the same map, a *shifting* map, and they were growing closer and closer together.

"Mac, I think we have to figure out how to call Mr. Johnson."

Mac turned around. "Have to? Why?"

"I think he's the only one who can draw a portal to Itza Linda."

Her brow creased. "Why him?"

"I think it's because of what he's lived through. What Skelton's put him through. Something like that. I think he can find Itza Linda even if he doesn't know where it is." I blushed. "I know that sounds dumb."

"It doesn't sound dumb. I get it. And I think you're right. I don't know why you're right, but I think you're right. But can you do be a favor?" She shook my leg and smiled. "Get some sleep."

I did, wondering how I was going to call Justin Johnson.

Two weeks later, we'd call each other.

Let me explain:

Since I was six, I snuck downstairs every Christmas Eve to look at the tree. We always kept all our presents hidden until the night before, when my mom would go out and arrange everything under the tree. She put so much love into it, making little hand-crafted tags for each of presents, built from felt and twine and time. Most of the gifts were from one member of the family to another, but a few—the biggies—she kept in reserve. Those she marked from Santa.

I recognized her handwriting. But I appreciated the gesture. Part of me wondered why she didn't want to take the credit for the coolest gifts. Part of me thought about how distant and withholding she was and wondered if it was simply another way for her to martyr herself. Another part of me— an older part of me—came to see that as you get older, you give less of a shit about that kind of thing: credit, praise.

At least some people do. At least she did. I think.

Christmas Eve was our last night as a family.

This story is about the end of one family and the beginning of another. The family of Deacon, Corrie, Mackenzie, and Hiram Gresham had one last night together. Deacon had died, survived by his wife and two loving children. Corrie was now engaged to Trent Sutton, whose own wife, Marie, had died. He had two children, Jason and Kaitlyn.

We would join the Sutton family in March, but my family's true, final form was still being forged in the crucible of the events of 1989 and 1990.

To be clear: This was not going through my head at the time. What was probably going through my head was something more like, "I sure hope I get my Nintendo Whasamadoodles" or "I sure wish I was eating some boogers." You don't think very deeply when you're eleven.

But a part of me knew something was rounding the corner like the train from Susie Schuppe's Smoky Mountain Gold Rush. Part of me also sensed, like my sister did, that Skelton had a few more tricks up his sleeve. Because that's right, motherfuckers. Skelton didn't die in that fire, and I was due to meet him in person in a matter of months.

But that's all coming up later. For now, let's enjoy this totally quiet, completely non-insane Christmas Eve in front of the tree. We tucked the tree by the stairs in front of the walk-in closet, which is also where Mom always hid our presents. I sat on the stairs and enjoyed the quiet. God, we were a loud family.

I must've sat there for half an hour before I heard it.

"—dunno how I feel—*zzkkt*—"

It came from the closet. The voice was familiar, but not the one I was expecting to hear.

"—they said they found—*zzzkktt*—"

I eased my way past the tree, my big belly knocking off a couple of ornaments, and entered the walk-in closet.

"—said they found his—*zzzkt*—teeth and matched the dental records—"

Who is that? It isn't Dad. But I know that voice. And who is he talking about?

But I knew. Who else would he be talking about? After the Soddy Farm incident, the whole dang country was talking about it. Colquitt was being hailed as a hero, of course, even though he almost got my sister and my friend killed.

Huh. I called Kaity a friend. I guess she is. Kind of.

I hated Jason, but I had to admit, Kaitlyn was growing on me. She was a pain in the ass sometimes, but she kept surprising us with her kindness. She saw me drawing one time and got me an eraser called Artgum. I'd never heard of it, but it was the best eraser I'd ever used in my life. We were over at their house, and she slipped it into my pocket and whispered, "Here ya go, Michelangelo," then cut a loud, raunchy fart. She could make me laugh so hard.

The voice spoke again: "—but I don't know. That man was nothing if not—*zzkt*—wily."

I rounded the U-bend and brought the old radio into view. Mom had padlocked the pocket door to the Office; part of me was disappointed I'd never get to explore it again.

The voice spoke again: "Right, right. You're right, Momma. The West Chim cops said they brought in someone to ID his remains, too. I know, I know." He paused. "Why you gotta come at me with all this logic? Just kidding. Nah, I appreciate it." (pause) "Yes, I've been thinking about gettin' back out there again. Lay off. I'll date when I'm ready. It's just hard to meet the right . . ." (pause) "Aw, don't worry, Momma. I'm fine. I'm even thinking about fostering another cat. It's just . . ." (pause) "It's just that this guy kept me up nights. "Yeah, yeah. I know you're right, Mom. JJ can rest easy now that he's gone."

JJ? I thought.

"It's just that . . . I can't stop thinking about that night, the way he slipped away. Those parents, they had him surrounded. It was like . . . it was like he *vanished.*"

I spoke on a hunch: "Mr. Johnson?"

"Aaaaugh!"

Justin

Justin Johnson held his phone like a viper ready to spit venom: at arm's length in a trembling hand. He gaped at it for a moment before slowly bringing it back to his face.

"Who's that?"

A familiar voice responded: "Huh? Is this Mr. Johnson?"

Justin lowered the phone. "I'm losing it."

"Wait, wait! Don't go!"

"Who is this?"

Hiram's Journal

"Who is this?"

"It's Hiram. Hiram Gresham?"

"Hiram . . . the kid from the park?"

"Yes, sir. Uh and do you remember seeing me the other night?"

"Jesus—you mean that was you? I wasn't dreaming?"

"Yes, sir."

"Are you okay, little man? There was that . . . thing out there, too."

"Oh, the Plaid Man? Yeah, we got away from him. We keep bumping into him, though. He even dressed up like you one time."

"What does that mean?"

"Well, I think some people can draw magic maps, and we sort of tried to draw a magic portal to your house, but it—actually, never mind. I don't know how long this connection's going to last. Mr. Johnson, I need you to draw something on your map, right now." There was a long silence. "Mr. Johnson?"

"How'd you know I was drawing a map?"

"Oh, well—because we were drawing maps, and Lee and I rode a motorcycle through a cabin, although I guess it was more of a moped and—"

"Are you trying to find the box?"

"Yes! Yes, we are. Only it's not a box."

"No? What is it, then?"

"It's a traincar. A caboose? Like the ones people ride in?"

He sounded fascinated. "A traincar. Huh. From where?"

"I think it's from the Gold Rush park. I think it's the caboose from their train."

"But they searched the park."

My dad spoke in my mind: *There's another train.*

"I think they had an extra one that Skelton stole and moved somewhere."

"He stole an entire traincar? How?"

"I don't know."

"Do you know where it is?"

"Kinda? I got there in a dream once, but whenever I try to go back to the same place, it's not there."

"I don't know what that means, kid."

"Sorry. I think there's only one way to get to the traincar, it's through the maps, and we think you're really good at drawing portals."

"Why do you think that?"

"It works like this: Two people have to draw something on a map to make it come to life, but you drew a portal by yourself, and it worked. We think you need to draw the portal to Itza Linda."

"And then go there?"

"Yeah."

"Because that's where they are."

"The kids. His victims."

We sat in silence for a long time. I thought I'd lost him.

Justin

By this point, Justin Johnson had stood up and crossed to his mother's photograph of him in *A Few Good Men*. He'd tucked the phone under his arm, the cord trailing to the receiver, which he'd shouldered to his face. He looked wistfully at the photo, then across the other photos detailing the triumphs of his formative years: touchdowns and starring roles, clowning around at parties and hugging his friends.

The kid's voice came again: "Mr. Johnson?"

He walked outside, still in the same position, still with the phone tucked under his arm. Rusty slinked along next to him, occasionally marking his leg. Outside on his front porch, he sat in his lawn chair. Rusty ranged out to the middle of his yard and sat, scanning the trees, his usual vigil.

"Mr. Johnson?"

He figured his last encounter with those kids was a dream. How could it have been anything *but* a dream? A giant monster? Black water crashing through the trees before vanishing instantly?

Magic maps?

There was no avoiding it. Justin had to look, had to acknowledge, had to lift the phone and see the truth. There was no cord. There never had been. He was talking into a dead phone.

He had always been talking into a dead phone.

"Mr. Johnson, are you—"

"This is a dream," Justin whispered.

"No, wait!"

He hung up, stood, made kissing noises to summon Rusty, and went inside. He set the phone, which he'd bought for three dollars at a swap meet, back on the side table. Rusty got on his hind legs and batted his hand. Justin obliged by crouching down to give him more pets. He lifted Rusty into his arms. His cat usually got grumpy when picked up, but he tolerated it as Justin carried him into the bedroom, where he stretched out.

"It was only a dream," he said.

But if it was, then why did you hang up the phone?

Hiram's Journal

The connection ended. I idiotically fiddled with the dials for a minute before giving up. I was inching my way past the Christmas tree when I saw Mom sitting on the stairs. Panic struck me! Funny how your mind works as a kid. I was trying to wrangle magic forces to my will in aid of Skelton's countless victims, yet here I was, terrified my mom was about to bust me for peeking at my presents.

"Oh, my gosh! Hi, Mom! I wasn't—"

"It's okay," she said, patting the stair next to her. "Come on over here."

She was holding her diary, the danavreece. I eyed it as I sat.

"Merry Christmas," she said. "Y'know, normally around this time, I'd be sneaking out for a smoke, but Trent helped me quit."

We'd begged her to quit so many times, only for her to ignore or yell at us. It simultaneously saddened and annoyed me that Trent got her to do it in a matter of weeks. I set the feeling aside for now.

"Merry Chirstmas to you too." I nodded at the danavreece. "What do you write in there?"

"Nothing much. It's my dream journal."

"Uh have I heard you call it the 'danavreece'?"

She gave me a funny look. "Didn't think you'd ever heard that."

"Is that part of yours and Dad's secret code?"

She nodded. "It means 'diary.'"

"Danavreece. Cool word."

"Thanks." She nodded at the tree. "I love this time. Before the chaos."

"Me too. I never told you, but I sneak down here every year."

She chuckled. "Yeah, I know."

"You *do?*"

"I know every creak this house makes. You're about as sneaky as an elephant."

The mild jab hurt my feelings for reasons I couldn't articulate.

"Oh. I didn't mean to ruin anything."

She gave me a squeeze.

"Aw, sweetie. I didn't mean anything. I just know this house better than you do. I should—I've lived here longer."

"Are you going to miss it?"

She thought for a moment. "No. Wanna know something? I hate this house. I have for a while. This house has never . . . liked me. It's prickly. Mean.

The floors yell at you. I've always tripped over the jamb into the first-floor bathroom. The dryer's never worked right, not any of 'em. My bed's broken not once, not twice, but three times. *And* your dad died here, or outside."

"Are you looking forward to moving into Trent—Mr. Sutton's?"

"You can call him Trent."

"Do I have to call him Dad?"

"I don't think so, but maybe we can ask him that. And I think we'll like the new house fine. I know you will."

"Why?"

"Your room is *huge*. C'mon, sweetie. Got a big day tomorrow."

She stood, but I said: "Mom, why didn't you ever take us to church?"

She thought. "I don't really believe in any of that stuff. I figured if either of you wanted to look into it, you would." She paused. "Do you want to start going to church?"

"No, it's just . . . I was wondering if people can get stuck on their way to heaven. Can they?"

"That's one for the philosophers. Night."

She left me sitting there.

"I don't know what that means," I whispered.

Mackenzie

Mac had long since gotten over her childlike excitement for Christmas. As soon as her head hit the pillow on December 24, she was unconscious until her baby brother shook her shoulder. She lurched awake, snorting and mumbling word salad. In her confusion, she felt suddenly sure she was back at Soddy Farm and that it was Skelton waking her, not Hiram.

"Who izzit? Who izzit?!"

"It's me, it's me."

Her vision cleared in tandem with her waking nightmare; it was only her baby brother.

"You were really asleep," he said. "I knocked for five minutes before coming in here."

She checked the time: 1:30 a.m. "What's the matter?"

"I just talked with Mr. Johnson."

"What?" she asked, leaning forward. "How? Did you get his number? Did Auntie Hanna—"

"We called each other. Through the old radio in the walk-in."

She hugged her knees to her chest and shook her head. "Wow."

"Yeah."

"What did you talk about?"

"I tried to tell him about Itza Linda and how we need his help to find it, but he said it was a dream and hung up."

"I thought you said you were talking on the radio?"

"*I* was, but he was on his phone."

"Auntie Hanna said he didn't have one."

Hiram opened his mouth to say something but appeared to change his mind.

"Maybe he has a toy one? Or a prop? He used to do plays, didn't he?"

"Yeah, I guess that's possible."

"So what do we do? Can we call him back? Can you try the radio again?"

She thought. "Auntie Hanna said to leave him alone. I think she's right."

"But . . ."

"What?"

He hung his head. "Nothing. I guess you're right."

Hiram's Journal

Christmas morning mayhem. Mac crammed presents into a big plastic bag while I slapped paper around a last-minute gift on the kitchen table. (My godawful wrapping jobs were the stuff of family legend.) Mom was talking to herself as usual, fretting over a platter of Chex snack mix cooking in the oven.

"Come on, come on," she muttered.

I couldn't stop thinking about the previous night's magic . . . and why I'd concealed part of it from Mac. Justin had been pretending to talk with his departed mother, but when Mac asked me about his phone, I withheld the secret.

Why didn't you tell her?

At the time, I had no idea. I felt really bad for him, and although I wasn't an especially emotionally intelligent kid, part of me felt like I'd be betraying a confidence. Plus, I was still confused by what my elders were telling me.

Auntie Hanna said we should leave Justin alone.

Mac said he didn't need our help.

But the magic kept putting us in touch. We came close to talking on the night of the black water, and we had actually spoken last night.

Surely that meant *something*.

RIIIING. We had two phones, one in the living room and one in the kitchen.

Mom said: "Can someone get that?"

Mac and I looked at each other, waiting for the other to blink. I jokingly shook my fist at her, and she relented, jumping up to get it. I kept wrapping.

"Hello?" Mac said before she fumbled the phone, her eyes bugging. "Hi, it's for you." She lowered her voice: "Better get it in the living room."

I frowned and ran in to get it. "Hello?"

"It's Justin."

The morning sun chose that moment to burst above the windowsill, blinding me. I blinked, nearly dropped the phone and tried to answer, but my lungs were empty. A weird grunt rattled out of me.

"You there?" he asked.

My breath returned. "Hi. Yes, I'm here."

"Is this Hiram?" Muffled voices chattered behind him. Was he at a restaurant, maybe?

"Yes, sir, this is Hiram."

"I need to ask you something, and it might sound weird."

"It won't."

"Okay. Did we . . . talk last night?"

"Yes."

Mom called: *"Chex mix is readyyy, Hirammm, let's goooo."*

"Just a second, Mom!" Into the phone: "You still there?"

"Yeah, I'm here. Last night, you were asking me about drawing maps?"

"Yes. We think we need you to help us draw a map to get to Itza Linda."

"Itza—" he stopped, paused. "Don't try to call me again."

"Wh-what?"

"Skelton's dead, and . . . kid, I'm sorry, but I need to be done with that part of my life. I don't want to draw any more maps."

"Are you sure?" Silence. I added: "Mr. Johnson, can I ask you a question?"

Mom: *"Hirammmm Trent's here he's gonna drive youuuu and Mac overrrr."*

"Okay, Mom, just a second!" To Justin: "Do you have a phone?"

Pause. "No."

"So last night, you were pretending to talk to your mom?"

Another pause, this one longer. Quietly: "Yeah."

My lower lip curled as tears welled up. "Gosh, I'm so sorry you lost her. I bet she was really nice."

"Hirammmmmmmm."

I ignored her and waited, praying he hadn't hung up.

Finally, he said: "Yeah, she was. Did you . . . well, were you pretending to talk to someone?"

"I hear my dad talking out of the radio sometimes."

"Did you lose your dad?"

"Yeah."

"I'm sorry. I bet he was really nice, too. Sorry I can't help you, kid. Merry Christmas."

Click. He was gone. I stared at the phone until I realized Mac was standing before me.

"What did he say?" she asked.

"I guess you and Auntie Hanna are right," I said. "He said he doesn't want to draw any more maps."

There are primordial feelings you have as a kid that you can't process until you're older. After I spoke with Justin that morning, I felt one of those things. At the time, I was (of course) crushed that he didn't want to help draw more maps, but I also felt a strange kind of envy.

He really missed his mom, but I couldn't say the same about my dad.

I just didn't really know him. I knew his shadows, his echoes. I knew my mom's stories about him; about how they lived in Puerto Rico for two months learning Spanish, about how they met volunteering at a homeless shelter in Sedalia; and I knew what he looked like. Her bedroom was a shrine to him, his face everywhere. I had memories of him from before I could even really make memories.

But I didn't miss him.

Justin

The first blush of morning, the same soft orange as a popsicle, seeped over the mountains. A Chevy Bronco came rumbling up the mountain path and parked. Justin Johnson emerged in his house robe, which he'd worn on his trip into town. His friend Beverly had been kind enough to let him into her bar so he could use her phone. His brow furrowed as he crossed to the retaining wall that enclosed his house. The lamp-post stood nearby, its light still active and emitting a faint buzz. A mailbox stood by his front gate, rusty from disuse. (He had to get his mail in town because no postal carrier would brave the switchback road.) He opened it to reveal a pack of cigarettes and a plastic lighter. He'd quit ages ago, but he still kept a pack around, mainly to prove he didn't need them.

From his pocket, he produced his map and re-read his notes about that strange, rectangular-shaped structure he'd felt compelled to draw:

Shipping container? Crate? Mobile home?

An impulse arose in him to cross out those words and write, *Traincar from the Gold Rush park.* With a *click,* the lamp-post extinguished. The moment passed. Justin took the lighter and set his map on fire, dropping it in a steel bucket that sat under his mailbox. He went inside.

Even though he never got mail delivered to his house, Justin had still put his address on his box in stick-on letters. They read:

JUSTIN J. JOHNSON
236 BARNABY PASS
FORBES, OREGON

Hiram's Journal

Getting to the Suttons' house was like getting into NORAD. I'm exaggerating, but it was behind no less than two locked gates in the fanciest neighborhood in town, Signal Hills. I'd met one or two rich kids who went to Montmarnass, and they all lived in Signal Hills.

Now we did too.

Today we'd call Trent's house a McMansion. Huge white columns lined the front, while the front lawn was perfectly manicured. Equipment from Trent's landscaping business packed the four-car garage, all of it new or near-new: lawn-mowers the size of cars, gleaming chrome chainsaws, leaf-blowers, hole-diggers, log-splitters, and more. Other trophies of Trent's wealth stood by: a jet ski, a four-door pickup truck that bore the logo *SUTTON LANDSCAPING & TURF.* The backyard was about the size of a football field and covered in shade. It looked like it'd be fun to play in. I was already updating my mental map of the area to figure a path through the woods from here over to Dizzy Pines.

Inside was downright palatial, if a little *nouveau riche.* Faux marble made up all the countertops. Hardwood floors ran everywhere. All the glass was crystal. Their Christmas tree was fifteen feet tall and sat in a two-story atrium through which a staircase coiled leading up. Mom and Trent crowded into a loveseat (barf) while Mac grabbed a chaise and I sat on a small couch.

Trent screamed: "Kids! They're here!"

Jason's voice, from above: "Be right down!"

I inwardly cringed at seeing him again but brightened a bit with what came next:

"Just a second!" Kaitlyn yelled. "Takin' a shit!"

She gave a ditzy giggle. Mac and I stifled laughs. Trent looked like he was about to blow a gasket.

"Maybe a little too much information, Kaity!"

Kaitlyn strode in, wearing jammies, her arm in a cast.

"Hey, dipshits!"

Trent: "Hey, wanna watch that mouth?"

"Sorry, Pops," she said, plopping on the chaise. Prodding Mac, she said, "Hey, sis."

"Where's Jase?" Trent asked.

"He was jerking—" Kaitlyn course-corrected off Trent's look: "He was being a real jerk, lemme tell ya!"

Mac and I cracked up. Mom blushed under Trent's scowl.

"That's really not funny," she mumbled before joining the fun.

A new voice: "Hi."

We all hooted in surprise. It was Jason, who seemed to magically appear at the foot of the stairs. The scare made us laugh even harder.

Mom got a case of the giggles: "Oh! I didn't hear you come in! Oh, my goodness! How long have you been standing there?"

"Not long."

He sat by me in that way bullies did, without the slightest acknowledgement of my presence. Mom kept laughing.

Kaitlyn: "Yeah, we can never hear sneakypants here. He's always coming up on me unawares."

I told Jason, "Merry Christmas." I think he said "thanks" but Mom was laughing too loud for me to hear.

Mom, still laughing: "Goodness. Goodness. Deacon, Mackenzie, Kaitlyn, Jason, Trent—*Hiram*. Hi. Hi. Hi."

Trent's face fell. "Honey?"

"Hi. Hi. Hi. Can you get your mother . . ." She trailed off, falling limp, her head coming to rest on his shoulder.

"Corrie?" he said with urgency.

She sprang to life, as if activated: "That must be a magic trick, the way you snuck in here, Jason!" Hopping to her feet, she headed for the back of the house. "I'm heading to the kitchen. Anybody need anything?" Without waiting for a response, she turned, stopped. "Kitchen." She stood in the doorway to the back of the house, swaying.

Trent stood and pointed. "It's through there, sweetie."

For a moment, she wore the unmistakable expression of someone looking at a room full of strangers.

"Thank you. Um. Sweetie." Suddenly, she yelped: "*Trent!* My goodness. I think my blood sugar dropped!" She leaned and held a hand to her mouth as if imparting a secret to me: "That's where you get it from, sweetie. Us and our hypoglycemia!" Her eyes went dark and blank, her voice dropping an octave: "We'll all have a part to play in the park." Then in a harsh whisper: "The candle." She bounced—literally bounced—and brightened, addressing

Trent: "Can I trouble you for a glass of cold, cold orange uh juice? You know, I could never say that."

By this point, Trent had taken her arm to escort her.

"What's that, honey?"

"Orange. Uh. Juice. I can't say it. Doesn't roll off the tongue. I have to say one word, stop, say the next. Orange. Uh. Juice. I think that's sad." They were gone.

A wide-eyed Kaitlyn leaned over: "What the fuck was that?"

Mac: "I don't know. That was—"

"Does she, like, *have* something?"

I said: "I don't know."

"She's never acted like that before," Mac said.

Kaitlyn: "What did that mean, that weird stuff she said about the park?"

Mac: "I didn't hear what she said."

"She said we'll all have a part to play."

It was Jason who'd spoken. We all looked at him.

He added: "In the park."

PART THREE
FOR EVERYONE WHO COULDN'T BE HERE

Hiram's Journal

We believed Skelton was dead, but in our hearts, we knew it wasn't true.

Three months later. March 12. Three days before the day Skelton would've been executed, my mom married the biggest asshole I ever knew.

The dreams about the traincar hadn't stopped.

I hadn't dropped drawing maps.

We stopped trying to call Justin Johnson, though we'd soon have no choice but to reach back out to him.

But life went on—until Skelton spoke to us.

"You're fulla shit!"

My sister's voice, laughing: "Keep your voice down!"

Mom married Trent at the same place she married Dad, Zonder's Lodge. It was the one concession she got from him in the planning. Located smack between West Chim and Gatlinburg, Zonder's was a series of small cottages all arrayed to either side of a babbling brook that led into an endless forest. Late-afternoon mist shrouded the Smokies as sunsetting light slanted through the mist and scattered across the scene in diffuse, golden glory.

The ceremony was over. I wandered through the crowd in my itchy rented tux, dodging through the legs of Trent's enormous family. Everyone was there, including the Dockerys and Auntie Hanna. The reception unfolded on a broad patio that overlooked the brook. Mom and Trent were holding court at a stand-up table.

Mac's voice was coming from a cottage just to the side of the patio. The door stood open, pot smoke wafting out. I went to investigate but stopped when I saw something I recognized.

A locomotive.

The cottage had a picture window with a stained-glass inlay: a locomotive covered with coiling snakes and tentacles. I'd seen this image twice before: once in my dreams, painted on the side of Skelton's traincar. The second time had been at Not Mr. Johnson's cottage. The Plaid Man's simulacrum of his cottage had a stained-glass window with the same depiction.

There's another train.

I shivered but pressed on, stopping in the open doorway. Jason and Mac sat inside with three other kids, a mean-looking rich kid in a pinstriped blazer and two other girls I didn't recognize. They all passed around a joint and took no notice of me. More smoke slipped out under the bathroom door, which was closed.

"You really landed a punch?" the guy asked Jason.

"If I hadn't, I wouldn't be here today, Commerce."

That guy's name is "Commerce"? What kind of name is "Commerce"?

One of the girls, who had close-cropped black hair, cooed. "Wow! That must've been so scary!"

"I'd have been peeing my pants!" said the other.

"So what was it happened *exactly*? Set the scene for us. Walk us through it."

Jason pulled on his joint.

"Okay, so Jenny snuck me in there to show me around."

"To show you around," Commerce snorted. *"Riiiight."*

Kaitlyn emerged from the bathroom, holding a huge bong, which she passed to Mac. She was healed, though her forearm bore a permanent divot from the cast. She spotted me and gave me a big, goofy conspiratorial wink.

"Right, so she takes me up there for a look around," Jason said.

"I heard she was a *huge* slut," Commerce said.

Girl One: "She *was*. *Ohhh* my God!"

Girl Two: "Yeah, total ho."

Kaitlyn and Mac looked at each other and curled their lips in disapproval. Jason's expression remained neutral.

"There was one main room hidden behind the ride," he said. "We hung out in there, smoked up, looked around. There was this access hallway she wanted to check. Said she'd never seen it. That's where he was."

Girl One, the short-haired brunette: "Holy shit."

"He was wearing a ski mask. A plaid one."

My heart boomed. Why, of all the details Jason could've chosen for his bullshit story, would he pick a plaid mask?

Girl Two: "Oh, my God."

"He'd gotten in behind us somehow. He had a crowbar."

Commerce: "Is that when he hit you?"

Jason shook his head: "He came at us, swiped at me a couple of times. I swung, missed, swung, got him in the jaw. He dropped the crowbar, came running at me."

Girl One: *"Shiiiiiit."*

"I was all set to tackle him, but I tripped and rammed my head into a beam," he said, snapping his fingers. "Out cold! When I came to, she was gone."

Girl Two: "Ohmigod, wow."

Commerce dropped his gaze and shook his head with a scoff. "Yeah."

"Scariest fucking day of my life," Jason said.

Commerce looked up. "Until the night at the farm huh?"

Silence. Jason's fists closed. Commerce had him, and he knew it.

Jason: "Excuse me?"

"See, what I don't understand is: If you were all John Matrix with big-bad Skelton that day, why'd you freeze up like a pussy the night at the farm?"

More silence. More. Jason's jaw clenched, his face reddening. He looked at us with an inscrutable expression. He was almost *smiling.*

"I wasn't *expecting* him."

Commerce frowned. Another voice joined us:

"Uh that's not what you told us."

Hoo boy. I'd gone and opened my big mouth. Every head swiveled toward me. An evil grin spread across Commerce's face.

"Is that right, dude? What *did* he say?"

I ignored him and addressed Jason: "You shouldn't be telling stories. You told us you didn't remember anything."

My sister stood on wobbly legs and made an attempt to get me out of the room.

"Hey, some other time, okay?" she said, but I already had a head of steam:

"Were you lying? Were you *lying, Jason?*"

Commerce took a pull and said: "Maybe you need to call the cops and change your bullshit story."

Jason sprang to his feet, and the room seemed to shrink. Mac reflexively put herself between me and him.

"*Shut the fuck up!*" He leaned around Mac to wave a finger in my face. "We're *brothers* now, y'little shit. *My* dad's *your* dad, and I'm gonna tell him you were gonna call the cops on his *son.*"

"Do we need to?"

Her drawl was unmistakable. We turned to behold Hanna Blackledge standing in the doorway, wearing a killer blue pantsuit and generally looking unimpressed.

Jason sneered: "Oh, look. It's Quitters Incorporated. How's it going, Quitters Inc.? They got you shining Uncle Bo's shoes yet?"

She touched my shoulder and gently guided me out of the room. Stepping in next to Mac, she jerked her chin at everyone else.

"Rest of you, scram."

Commerce and the two girls jumped up, all of 'em sharing smirks and whispers and jibes.

"Ohmigawd, look at her."

"Looks like a man."

Commerce grabbed a half-drunk beer from the floor and took the girls under his arms on his way out the door. As he passed Hanna, he looked her dead in the eye and said, "Thanks for your service, officer." Under his breath, he added: *"Killer."*

They left. Jason moved to leave, but Hanna shifted her bulk into his path. It was like an I-beam slamming into place. He crossed his arms. Jason had the advantage in size, but Hanna didn't look intimidated.

Jason: "You gonna lecture me about drinking?"

"No. Was gonna ask if you need these." She held up a vial of eye drops. "You're looking pretty red in the eyes, son. How many you had?"

Jason deflated a little. He rubbed his eyes and yawned in a way that reminded you that, for all his bluster, he was still a kid.

"I dunno," he said, taking the eye drops. "A few."

Hanna smiled wryly "I *bet* you had a few. Kaity, you mind opening that window? Your folks paid a handsome security deposit on this place; don't want 'em losin' it because one of these rooms smells like a head shop."

"Sure," Kaitlyn said, cracking a window. Hanna pulled out a seat for Jason.

"Why don't you have a seat and collect yourself before you go back out and face the crowd?"

He sat and put in some drops while Hanna soaked a washcloth with cold water and handed it to him.

"Thanks," he mumbled.

Hanna crossed her arms and leaned against the wall. "You kids all right?"

Mac shrugged. "I guess."

"C'mon now—don't lie to your auntie. Y'all been through a lot. Are you all right?" Silence. Hanna sucked her teeth and added: "I dunno about alla y'all, but I've been having nightmares about . . . everything we've been through."

Mac and I shared a significant look.

I asked: "Uh what kind of nightmares?"

Everyone, Jason included, looked at her.

Slowly, she said: "They were gonna kill him three days from now. March fifteenth. I keep having dreams about it. Something goes wrong. He gets loose again."

"But he's not going to."

"No, he's not going to." She paused and whispered: "Because he's gone." She shifted gears: "How's your mom?"

Mac answered: "She's . . . okay. We go sometimes and sit with her when they do the . . ."

She tapped the inside of her arm. Hanna nodded.

"That's good. Our cousin Sally went through that when we were in high school, and it's brutal. Go as often as you can." Hanna un-leaned from the wall and theatrically sniffed. "Okay, then. Still smells like the 'Dead played a few sets in here, but it'll do. C'mon, no more hiding from the grown-ups. Everyone wants to see your smiling faces."

We all filed out. Jason headed toward the brook, taking out a small notebook, while Kaitlyn bade us farewell and headed off in search of another drink. Mac and I lingered with Auntie Hanna. Mac headed back into the party.

"Bye, Auntie Hanna!"

"See you later, girl," Hanna said before turning to Hiram: "You better run along. Your aunt's gonna pull an Irish exit."

I stopped her cold with a question: "Why didn't you fight that other kid?"

Hanna

It was a world of mixed messages.

Hanna Blackledge, former officer of the law, had just let some snot-nose, silver-spoon jerk call her a killer. Why *hadn't* she done anything?

"That's a fair question. I think I'm a little old to be picking fights with teenagers. See him over there?" They looked across the party, where Commerce has donned a pair of sunglasses. He was sitting on a guardrail overlooking the brook, mugging and cracking jokes with those two other girls. "I'll be honest: I'd love to go over there and shove him in the water." Hiram giggled, his chubby cheeks turning a happy shade of red. Hanna added: "But I might get in trouble with the law if I did."

"But aren't we supposed to stand up to bullies?"

Hanna's eyebrows rose. "Yes, but sometimes, you've got to let their bullshit slide. You can't fight every fight. Trust me, if you ever have to get in a fight, you'll know."

Hiram lingered, pulling at his lip. "Um."

"What is it, Hiram?"

"Mom said she has seven more sessions before she's done with chemo."

"Okay."

"Is it . . . like, you do a bunch of sessions, and then you lose a number?"

This was basically word salad, but Hanna summoned her patience: "Lose a number?"

"Yeah. She said she's at number four. If she does all these sessions, will she go down to stage three?"

Hanna assumed the look of bone-deep grief that only the old can feel for the sweet, ignorant young.

"It doesn't really work like that, sweetie. It's more like—you do those sessions, and maybe stage four lasts a little longer."

"Oh."

Turning to leave, she said: "Love you, kidd—"

"Auntie Hanna, I've got one more question."

She sighed. "Shoot."

"Is stage five worse?"

"There isn't a stage five."

They stood in silence until a new, extremely loud, voice jolted them:

"HEY, EVERYBODY, THANK YOU SO MUCH FOR COMING WHO WANTS SOME CAAAAAKE?! IS THAT HANNA BLACKLEDGE I SEE SKULKIN' IN THE BACK? COME ON DOWN AND GET SOME CAAAAAKE!"

It was Trent, standing on a small stage, waving around a tumbler of something brown and screaming into a microphone. Hanna cringed and shook her head.

"Almost made it."

Hiram's Journal

"Oh, I'm sorry!"

But she was already smiling and heading back into the party. I felt like I'd committed a faux pas. (I didn't know what "Irish exit" meant at the time.) Social rituals confused me; they still do. I was still trying to figure out what social cue I missed when Jason spoke behind me:

"You got a pen?"

I jumped. "Whoa! Scared me!"

"Yeah, I can tell. You got a pen?"

Even though Jason had bullied me at every opportunity, I was still thrilled at the prospect of doing him a favor, however small. I fished around in my pocket and came out with a pen—but hesitated.

"What?" he said, his expression the flat anger you get from a bully forced to deal with a victim.

"This is a Pilot Precise V7," I said to the same flat stare. He didn't even look like he was breathing. I added: "I've only got three."

"Good for you," he said, snatching the pen from me and giving my hand a painful shove; he almost jammed one of my fingers.

"Uh you-y-you you uh gonna give it back when you're done?"

In slow motion, he stopped and turned. He shook his head, his lips curling; the same look Colquitt gave Sandra.

"I forgot to tell you the good news: everyone knows about your new name now."

"Huh?"

"*Huh? Huh?* What're you, deaf? Are you fucking *deaf? Huh?* I'm talking at a normal volume. If you were a cool person and not so fucking stupid, maybe we wouldn't have to repeat ourselves all the time. Honestly, maybe you wouldn't have that stupid fucking stutter. It's really annoying and really hard on all of us to deal with you. We talk about it all the time."

Looking back, I see this now as the filthiest of lies, but at the time, the prospect that my family had been talking about me behind my back felt true and horrible, and hearing it from such a big, cool, powerful kid ratified it. He controlled my world in that moment. My lips were quivering, my eyes welling up. I didn't so much hate myself for showing weakness as I was terrified to give him more ammunition. I was right to be, because the next words out of his mouth stand among the cruelest ever said to me by anyone, anywhere, ever.

"Wow. Look at you. One little poke, and we see what you're made of. Is that all it took, me telling you the truth about how everyone feels about you? You've really got something *wrong* with you. Don't worry. We'll get you some help. You're stupid, and you're fat. *Really* fat. It's okay, though. Being fat doesn't necessarily mean you're a bad person. It's just . . . kind of a strike against you. If you want to be cool, that is. Maybe you don't!" He put his hands on his knees so he could whisper in my face: "Now, I'm going to say this *one* more time, so make sure you're paying attention, because if you don't, then we'll know for sure that you're a stupid pussy. Tell me you're paying attention, or you're a stupid fucking pussy."

"Uh I'm . . . I'm paying attention."

"It's okay. I told everyone for you, including all the girls. They think it's a really cool name for you. See?"

He straightened and waved at the two girls from earlier. They merely waved back, but in my current mental state, they appeared to be pointing and laughing at me.

Jason hammered me: "Remember your name, Wimpy? Remember your name, Wimpy? Remember your name, Wimpy?"

Incredibly, I tried to slap him. He dodged it. My attempt at a slap was barely more than a wave, but it still took all my fortitude to summon it. When it failed, and I saw the same flat, hateful emptiness in his eyes, my legs carried me away. I stupidly thought it was a time to fight. I guess I was wrong.

I never got the pen back.

Mackenzie

Everything smelled new and scary.

Mackenzie Gresham stood at the end of Montmarnass Academy's cavernous new gymnasium. It had been completed only a month before she and Hiram enrolled at the school, the oldest and most prestigious in Smokies. Their home smelled new and scary, too, with its perpetually waxed floors and newly-installed carpet.

Home and school both smelled foreign and frightening.

She stood in the gym among a couple dozen other girls around her age, all of them wearing leotards and facing a wiry woman with chiseled features and close-cropped gray hair. She strode, always on the balls of her feet, and examined the girls with the most jaundiced of eyes. Her uniform described a lifetime in the studio and on the dance floor: leotard, torn T-shirt, sweats, and a pair of scuffed-up ballet slippers. She stopped before a fold-out table that bore a banner.

It read: *SISTERS OF ATHENS TRYOUTS TODAY!*

She barked into a bullhorn: "Girls! Form a straight line! We shall start with some pliés!"

Mac and the girls scrambled to the far wall and took up their positions, each gingerly holding a guardrail. Mac's body felt unwieldy, uncomfortable, and too big for her leotard and leg warmers. (She'd insisted on wearing them in honor of *Xanadu* even though they'd fallen out of fashion.) All the other girls were slender and nimble—and much shorter than her. She felt like a giant stomping around a village swarming with prettier, more confident girls.

But she was determined. Swallowing a lump in her throat, she did her pliés and waited on Ms. Olivia's next commands.

"Very good!" Ms. Olivia said, screaming into the bullhorn at point-blank range. "We shall now move on to the tryouts. There are two stages: personal dance and the choreography test. Your personal dance will tell us something about who you are. The choreography test will tell us if you can follow directions, execute moves, and become a Sister of Athens!" She addressed a terrified girl in a French braid.

"Ms. Weston! Please help Mrs. Johannsen with the music."

French Braid Girl, Weston presumably, scampered over to help Ms. Johannsen, who wore inch-thick glasses and a leotard over an ancient yet wiry body. She took notes while Ms. Olivia screamed orders. Weston thumbed through a stack of cassette tapes.

"Who's first?!"

Ms. Johannsen: "MS. HUNTMICHAELLLLL." She didn't need a bullhorn.

A girl with short, black hair, Kimber Huntmichael, ran out to the middle of the court and limbered up. Mac recognized her from the wedding as one of Commerce's flunkies. Ms. Olivia clapped, bringing everyone to silence.

"Position one!" she barked. Kimber assumed an initial balletic pose. Ms. Olivia yelled: "Music!"

Kimber soared, her moves confident, her routine polished. It would've fit in at any dance conservatory. She ended her routine on the floor, perfectly folded in half, her fingertips touching the tips of her fully extended toes. Everyone clapped. Ms. Olivia managed to look both pleased and furious.

"Very good, Ms. Huntmichael! You may leave the floor! Who is next?!"

"MS. GRESHAMMMM."

All eyes swiveled to Mac, who was limbering up her legs when an unexpected sight stopped her cold:

A smiling Kaitlyn, watching from the mezzanine. She leaned cross-armed against the railing and waved.

"Kick some ass, Gresh!"

Mac covered her face, blushing, but she was glad to have at least one fan in the house. Ms. Olivia, incensed, screamed: *"Silence from the mezzanine, if you please!"* Turning to her underlings, she added: "Music!"

At first there was only silence . . . until a killer chord roared followed by a quietly driving riff that kept building and building. A voice familiar to any outcast or freak drawled the opening words to "Time Warp" from *The Rocky Horror Picture Show*. Mac slung one of her massive legs in the air, a perfect kick, and rocked and rolled her way through a high-energy routine she'd worked out with Kaitlyn, who'd encouraged her to do something different.

"All those Sisters of Athens bitches are *très snobbeee*," she said in a goofy French accent. "Broadside 'em with something they're not expecting!"

As soon as Mac heard about the Sisters of Athens, she wanted to be a part of it. They performed once a month for the school, all while getting to travel around the Southland. Some of them even got to apprentice with real dancers from New York! Plus, they were all pretty and popular—something Mac stopped being as soon as she left Polk.

Mac ignored everyone and focused on her routine. She'd run it a hundred times in their massive new backyard, all while Kaitlyn snuck drinks and yelled directions from a set of lawn furniture situated a hundred yards away from the house—and Trent. Winter had eased into an early, humid spring, bringing with it the never-ending chirrups of cicadas and the sweet aura of honeysuckle that seemed to flow from the Smoky Mountain mists. Mac and Kaitlyn forged a new friendship that spring, one that would soon be put to the test by the horrors that were to come.

When the famous chorus kicked in, Mac's legs launched her skyward, her arms spread, her body suddenly weightless. She hadn't missed a step yet.

"Hold music!"

Mac twirled through several more moves before realizing she'd been cut off. She stumbled on her own feet and came crashing down on her outstretched palms. Struggling to her feet, she saw only Ms. Olivia's back.

"What?" Mac muttered.

Kaitlyn was already clapping and screaming, *"Way to go, Gresh!"*

Ms. Olivia jerked her chin at one of the girls, indicating Kaitlyn. "See that she's removed."

One of the girls went running across the gym, but Kaitlyn had already skedaddled. A door slammed above.

Mac approached Ms. Olivia. "Um, I wasn't done."

"Who is next?!" she barked. Mac tried to protest, but French Braid was already handing over her *Rocky Horror* cassette. "Ms. Gresham, you may leave." She didn't even look at her.

"But what about the choreography test?"

"Fuck off, cow."

It was like someone had smacked both of her cheeks, hard. The words cleared her sinuses and brought the world into horrible, crackling focus. Whoever had spoken had done so at a normal speaking voice. Instinctively, Mac sought aid from the teachers, but they both ignored her. If anything, they looked pissed off that she was still there. Mac looked to the rest of the auditionees only to find more cruelty. Some of the expressions verged on sympathy, others were nasty, but all of them said, *You should leave.*

Ms. Olivia: *"Who is next?!"*

"MS. BERTRANNNND."

Mac trudged off the court, head hung.

"Cow."

Her head snapped up to instant eye contact with Kimber, who was smirking.

She ran from the room in tears.

She was still crying when she entered the Montmarnass rotunda, which sat at roughly the center of campus and served as the hub for each of the school's wings: humanities, sciences, athletics, and administration. White columns lined the room's perimeter, punctuating a sweeping three-hundred-sixty-degree view of the Smokies.

Her shoulders heaved as she staggered in, stopping just outside the gymnasium. Inside, the next girl's music started up, something from Bach.

Why did I listen to Kaitlyn's stupid suggestion? She railed at herself, but another part of her knew her audition music wouldn't have mattered. She came from West Chim and wasn't thin or pretty. That's all that mattered to Ms. Olivia.

"Um, excuse me?"

She jerked to attention, horrified that someone saw her crying. Before her was a delivery guy, maybe thirty years old, white with buzzed hair, wearing a brown uniform. He read from a clipboard and tucked a long white box under his arm.

"Oh, sorry. Didn't mean to bother you. I've got some flowers here."

"You can take it to school reception, that way."

She pointed, but the guy was already shaking his head. "No, the instructions said to come right here, to the rotunda, and deliver these flowers to a guy named Mackenzie Gresham. He's got some kind of audition today?"

"Oh, yeah, that's right. It's tradition here."

"What is?"

"All the girls get flowers on Valentine's Day and their birthday," Mac said, adding a shrug. "And tryout days, I guess."

The delivery guy cocked a dubious eyebrow. "Hm. Okay. That's kinda weird. What if no one sends 'em any flowers?"

"Then they don't get any."

"That sounds shitty."

"It's really shitty."

"Well, I guess a guy's getting flowers today 'cause these are Mac's. You know who that is?"

Mac regarded the box, frowning. "It's not a guy. It's me. And guys can get flowers, too, ya dumbo."

"Oh! Sorry again, I guess. Then these are for you," he said, offering the box. She took the box. "Sorry I called you a dumb—"

The exit door was already swinging shut, the guy gone. *Weird,* she thought as she opened the box. Inside was a standard arrangement of springtime blooms—pink roses and tulips—but Mac's gaze stopped on a decorative seedpod. It had a thousands little holes, all in a hectic pattern that made her skin crawl. She imagined the same pattern of holes opening across her forehead and winced, her dread instant and primal. She turned the pod's face away and flipped open the bouquet's card.

"Fucking Trent," she whispered only to audibly gasp. The card wasn't from Trent. It bore no signature, only four words written in a childlike scrawl:

tHaNKS fOr tHe MAP

Crunch! The sound's origin was a mystery until she saw the crushed seedpod in her hand. She'd ripped it from the bouquet, which now lay scattered across the rotunda. The exit door was still swinging open and shut, admitting a breeze that caught on a ribbon that had heretofore bound the bouquet.

A plaid ribbon.

The words were insane howls: *"Pum'v sellupp. Pum joow te kot pit signaxatulo bel zaxat!"*

Mac nearly fell over, she backed up so fast. Standing in the doorway was the delivery guy, transformed: His back faced her, his head flipped a hundred and eighty degrees and shaved clean to reveal thousands of tiny holes that covered every square inch of his exposed flesh. The holes slithered in horrific tandem, forming into a makeshift maw that spoke again:

"Pum joow te kot pit signaxatulo bel zaxat!"

But by then, Mac was already gone. She left her flowers behind.

The delivery guy, who looked normal again, frowned in confusion.

"All I said was, 'I need a signature for that.'"

Hiram's Journal

"I am your spaniel!"

That line always made me laugh. I was hunched over my notebook in the back of Montmarnass's black box theater, where I was an assistant stage manager for the spring production, *A Midsummer Night's Dream*. Our Helena and Demetrius were in the middle of the epic first scene of Act Two. The drama director, Mr. Andre, crouched on his haunches at the foot of our thrust stage, his fingers twined, his brow furrowed in comical concentration. You'd think he was directing the Royal Shakespeare Company.

The theater had become my new home. Note that I don't say "home away from home" because our *home*-home didn't feel like home anymore.

Trent stiffed us. We didn't even get our own bedrooms.

Home was a hell peppered with shouting matches between our folks, emotional abuse doled out by Jason, and various sundry bullshit. The only respites came when we—and by "we," I mean myself, Mac, and Kaitlyn— retreated to the farthest reaches of the backyard to clown around, put on shows . . . and draw more maps.

Kaitlyn surprised me. She was a pain in the ass sometimes—she'd cut you down you with a body-shaming joke—but she was always giving us sweet little gifts. She bought me the biggest, most expensive secret guide to *The Legend of Zelda* she could find. She worked tirelessly with Mac on her audition routine for that dumb dance squad. She took us to as many movies as we asked for; anything to get us out of the house and away from Trent. We had to have seen *Batman* six times already.

She also drove us to half of Mom's chemo sessions, always silent, always ready to let us cry when we did, which was often.

As I took lines notes on *Midsummer,* I added details to my new map. I lost the other one the night of Soddy Farm, so my new map focused on it: I drew in every detail of the farm I could remember or look up. My new map was a masterpiece of detail, with concentric topographical lines, a to-scale sketch of the old cabin, and Xs marking where Mac first saw her unicorn and where we believed Skelton first emerged. I added questions:

WHAT IS HE PLANNING?

DOES IT HAVE SOMETHING TO DO WITH MARCH 15?

We knew he was still alive. We just *knew* it. And he had been scheduled to die on March 15. All of us had circled the date on our internal calendars; something bad was going to happen. We'd bet our lives on it.

"Hi!"

We all whirled toward the door, where a sweaty, leotard-clad Mac was panting. My name was still confusing, so a bunch of the drama kids responded ("hello," "hey," "hi") in return. Mr. Andre stood to his full six-foot-seven height and hung his head—the moment had been ruined. Our Helena, a catty junior-year girl, jumped up from her "spaniel" pose and brayed:

"You ruined our rehearsal!"

Mac ignored her and beckoned me over, hissing: "Hiram! Get over here!"

Mr. Andre sighed. "Take five, everyone." Crossing to Mac, he added: "Hello to you, Miss. Is there anything we can do for you?"

I liked old Mr. Andre. He had to juggle a lot of big personalities as the drama teacher, and he did so with aplomb. He was also looking at my sister with compassion, which I appreciated. Most adults got annoyed with you when you were upset.

Mac finally noticed him. "Oh! Hi, Mr. Andre. Sorry to barge in."

"I see you're still in your leotard. How'd your tryout go?"

"Shitty, thanks. I gotta ask my baby brother something."

My face turned red: "I'm not your baby—"

"Whatever, just come on!"

If Mr. Andre reacted to her casual profanity, I didn't see it, but it amused the hell out of me. Mac had changed over the last few months, and I admired her for it. She yanked me outside, where other kids were heading back and forth, some in sports uniforms (soccer and lacrosse), while others were headed for meetings for the yearbook or literary magazine.

"Mac, Mac! Hold up! What's going on?!"

"Look."

She handed me a small card. Someone had scrawled on it:

tHaNKS fOr tHe MAP

My reaction was instant: I slung it to the ground.

"What the hell?" I whispered. "Where'd this come from?"

"Someone sent me flowers. This was the card. And the flowers were tied with a ribbon, dude, a *fucking plaid ribbon.*"

"Oh, no," I said, looking around in case the Plaid Man jumped out from a corner. "What does that mean?"

"It means Skelton's back," she said.

"Hey, guys!"

We jumped, turned to see the huge asshole striding our way.

"Ugh," Mac muttered.

"Trent," I agreed.

"I bet they loved that song, right?" Trent chattered away. "Kaity says it's one of your favorites."

"Oh. Yeah, they really liked it," Mac said, summoning some courage: "Trent, did you—"

"Dad."

"Right. Did you—"

"Let's hear it for the old man."

My jaw was clenched before I realized it. Trent was keeping his tone light, but the temperature in the G-Wagon was ticking up and up. Mac was dogged, though:

"When you got me the flowers, did you—"

"Come on. Humor me. You don't even gotta mean it."

"I don't *want* to. When you got me the flowers—"

"—JUDGE MILLSAPS HAD SENTENCED SKELTON TO DIE THE DAY AFTER TOMORROW—"

It boomed from the truck's thermonuclear sound system, the radio news. We jumped, ready for a trademarked Trent explosion to accompany it, but he threw us a curveball.

"IT'S FINE IF YOU DON'T WANNA CALL ME DAD, BUT IF YOU'RE NOT, THEN *SHUT UP* SO I CAN LISTEN UNTIL WE GET TO YOUR MOM."

"Hey," Mac said. *"Hey, I had a question!"*

He turned the radio up. I had to cover my ears. Mac sat, red-faced and glaring.

"—ON THE IDES OF MARCH, MARCH FIFTEENTH, BUT HIS EXECUTION WAS UNEXPECTEDLY FORESTALLED WHEN HE STAGED A DARING ESCAPE FROM THE TENNESSEE STATE PEN THAT BAFFLES LAW ENFORCEMENT OFFICIALS TO THIS DAY. THEIR ONLY CLUE IS THIS AUDIO RECORDING FROM AN INTERVIEW WITH KNOXVILLE'S OWN W-O-K-I NEWS."

"Y'AIN'T GONNA HEAR ME, AIN'T GONNA SEE ME, BUT I'M GONNA SLIP BETWEEN THE LODGES AND BACK TO THE FARM, MARK MY WORDS."

The radio announcer continued: "THOSE WERE SKELTON'S LAST WORDS TO ANYONE BEFORE HE INEXPLICABLY APPEARED AT A PARTY OF LOCAL HIGH SCHOOLERS LATER THAT NIGHT . . ."

Mac was gaping at me. She mouthed, *The Farm?*

Justin

Forbes was a sleepy hamlet tucked in the mountains of eastern Oregon. It was close to nothing and convenient for no one. Little more than a cluster of stores and restaurants around one intersection, the town was home to a variety of folks. Some, like Justin, were trying to escape their pasts, while others were longtime locals and fussbudgets. Justin had few illusions about moving to a place like this—small towns in the north gave quarter to about as many bigots as down south—but so far, he liked it.

He'd also found a regular watering hole, Beverly's Bar, named for a burly local woman who'd taken over a nearby hotel some years ago. She was rarely seen in her namesake pub, but whenever she visited, she always had a kind word for everyone there. Her husband was a kooky-looking redhead with a kind face who never said a word but only looked at Beverly with hearts in his eyes.

Justin spent many an evening there, joking around with the barkeep, a guy named Tony Hubbard, who was one of the only other Black folks in town. He was a curious reflection of Justin, slight where Justin was musclebound, with horn-rimmed glasses and prematurely graying temples. They'd bonded over a shared love for *Coming to America* the night Tony showed up wearing a McDowell's T-shirt.

Growing up in east Tennessee was tough, especially for a kid like Justin, who liked sports fine, but he *loved* movies, theater, and comics. As a kid, he used to play superheroes with his friends, but whenever he tried to play a hero, his friends—all white kids—told him he couldn't.

"You can't play Superman. He's white."

"Batman's a white guy. You can't play him."

"You can play the bank robber."

One day his momma came home from work with Justin's weekly bag full of comics. She dropped by the Dollar General every payday to pick up a bunch for her little guy, but this time when Justin dumped them out, one jumped out at him: *Green Lantern.*

He was Black.

Justin must've stared at that comic for ten minutes. He'd flipped through so many TV channels, read so many comics and books, and simply looked everywhere to find a Black hero, and here he was, a member of the Green Lantern Corps. A member of the Justice League. His name was John Stewart. He fought alongside Superman and Wonder Woman. He was a Marine and an architect. His momma was a community organizer. Part of Justin felt deep delight and pride, while another part of him was annoyed at his friends for bullshitting him.

Coming to America filled him with pride, too, because it was the first time he could remember going to the movies and finding the theater full of Black folks, and in east Tennessee, no less. That, and it was hilarious. After seeing it, Justin refused to call McDonald's anything other than "The Golden Arcs," which was the exact opening gag he pulled on Tony.

"I am *dying* for some Golden Arcs, man!"

Tony had apparently forgotten what shirt he was wearing that day, because he stared owlishly at Justin for a few seconds before cracking up. Justin and Tony had amassed an extensive catalogue of inside jokes so quickly that Beverly liked to say they each had half of the same magic amulet.

On the evening of "Ides Less Two," two days before Skelton's scheduled execution, a knapsack-toting Justin slid into his regular booth at Beverly's, which combined the woodsy dark coziness of an Irish pub with a boxing gym: bodybuilding memorabilia hung everywhere, including a signed photo of Lou Ferrigno and a speed bag. There were also tons of movie posters (*Plan 9 from Outer Space, Romancing the Stone, Who Framed Roger Rabbit, Trading Places, Back to the Future, Beverly Hills Cop*), and an Indiana Jones pinball machine that Justin had played to *tilt.* Tony waved at him.

"Hey, J, what's up, man? Your usual?"

"Yeah, Tone. Thanks. How you holding up?"

Tony pulled a quick pint and walked it over with the bar's cordless phone. His T-shirt for the evening was *Calrissian Tibanna Gas Mines of Bespin.*

"Same old, same old. Hey, how come you don't have a phone?"

Justin shrugged. "Let's say I like the charm of distance." He tipped his glass. "Thanks, brother. Won't be long."

Tony smiled. "No rush."

Justin pulled a notebook from his knapsack and opened it to a page packed with notes. He dialed a number from memory. A woman's voice answered, a nice old white lady.

"Hello?"

"Mrs. Glenn?"

Her voice brightened: "Is this Justin?"

"Yes, ma'am, it is. Just doing my monthly check-in. How are you?"

"Oh, I'm all right. What I want to know is: How are *you?*"

"Me?"

"I know what time of year this is for you."

"Aw, Ms. Glenn. It's no big deal. I—"

"It is indeed a big deal. It's one of the first things that brought us together. This date."

"March thirteenth."

"Two days before the ides."

"The day when . . ."

"Yes. And the day when . . ."

Justin closed his eyes. "Momma had her accident."

"What do you call this time of year? 'Justin's Depression Christmas'?"

Justin smiled wryly. "Yeah."

"Are you doing anything to make the Christmas season shorter this year?"

"Now, wait a minute. *I'm* the one who's supposed to be taking care of *you.*"

"Justin Johnson, you take care of me quite enough. The care packages, the calls. The kindness. It's meant so much to me and the other parents. I worry about you this time of year. I know how hard it is. What're you doing to take care of yourself?"

"Well. I guess . . . I guess there *was* one thing."

"Tell me."

"I met this family. Families, actually. Their kids."

"Oh? In Oregon?"

"Uh, yeah. Sure. In Oregon. Let's say that. Or nearby. It's a great bunch of kids, and they were . . . working on something. An . . . art project."

"That sounds nice. I know you have a background in the arts. So you're helping them with their project?"

"I . . . was."

"You were? Meaning you stopped?"

"Yeah."

"I see. May I ask why?"

"It . . . it brought back a lot of bad memories."

"I understand."

"But—they're a great bunch of kids. You'd like 'em. One of them, this little guy, loves to draw. I bet he's going to be an artist someday."

"I imagine he will," she said, her tone shifting: "Oh! I just remembered. Your mother left something at our house ages ago."

"She did? What?"

"It's . . . uh, well, I'm not rightly sure what it is. It looks like a disk? For a computer, perhaps?"

"A computer disk? She never had a computer."

"Well, regardless, it belongs to you. May I send it to you?"

"Sure, thanks. But how about we talk about *you* for a minute? Anything you need? Groceries? Books? Oh, how's the subscription to *The Times* treating you?"

"It's fine, Justin. And I'm fine. I lit a candle for little Jamie and finally rented out his room." She didn't speak for a moment. "They say time heals all wounds. It doesn't. We put his things in storage today—toys and books and games and clothes—and I thought about the last time I saw him . . . and it felt as awful as it did that night."

Silence. Justin listened.

Mrs. Glenn continued: "But I couldn't look at his room anymore. Gerald held my hand, bless his heart, and helped me close the door to the storage room. We walked a step at a time back to the car and drove home. I thought he was holding it together, but then he missed the turnoff to our house. We parked on the side of the road and had a good cry together. But we made it home."

"Ms. Glenn, I'm so sorry."

Her tone assumed the slightest air of a kindly schoolmarm: "Justin Johnson, I do hope you're saying you're sorry for my loss and not implying you had a hand in it." When he didn't answer, she continued: "The only person who bears any fault is Leonard Shane Skelton, and rest assured, he will face a heavy reckoning before our Lord and Redeemer." A door slammed on her end. People chattered indistinctly. "The other parents are here. We're having a cookout. Talk to you next month?"

"Talk to you next month."

"I'll put that package in the mail tomorrow."

She hung up. Justin sat looking at the phone for a moment, then collected his things, stood, and walked the receiver back to Tony, who met his look with concern.

"You okay?"

"Yeah. Thanks again, Tone. See you tomorrow."

They clasped hands. Tony looked like he wanted to say something, but Justin left before he could.

Dusk was settling over sleepy Forbes. Beverly's Bar stood at the corner of Castle and Main, the only two streets in town. Justin stood, knapsack over his shoulder, and inhaled deeply.

The air smelled sweet in the mountains.

It's what brought him back to the Smokies from New York, and it's what lured him to eastern Oregon after the lawsuit. He yearned for peace, quiet, and that sweet, sweet air.

Ding-ding-ding!

The bell hung over the bar's next-door neighbor, Junebug Jubilee's Arts & Crafts. One of the town's numerous old-timers was walking out with a bag full of oil paints and a canvas under his arm. He gave Justin a friendly nod and walked toward the sunset.

"Ides Less Two" was almost over, and nothing had happened; nothing, that is, except the crushing sadness Justin felt at the loss of his mother. His mother was an amazing woman, tough and smart, but she could be distant and opaque.

Like every parent, I guess, he thought.

His last visual memory was of her struggling up a small hill to her old apartment in West Chim. It was little more than a gentle slope, but for her old knees, it was Everest. She was wearing her favorite blue dress, a relic from her days living in Delaware. Sometimes Justin wondered what he would've done if someone had told him that was the last time he'd see her alive.

They spoke once more before her death. He was traveling through the mountains on a trip to Alabama and stopped at a pay phone to check in on her. Their connection was intermittent, her voice muffled and faint, like she was calling across a foggy expanse.

"I'm on my way to Birmingham," he had said.

"You're going to burn something?" she asked, her voice fading away. The exchange gave Justin the shivers when he thought about it; its eeriness, its unlikely surreality.

March 13 was the day she died.

She seldom drove, and the cold math of it all kept Justin up nights. The one time she decides to run down to the store, she's gone. Her birthday was October 28. *That* day usually came and went without incident. Sometimes he even forgot it entirely.

But not Ides Less Two, March 13.

Ides Less Two left a blast radius across his internal calendar, a dark spot from late February to early April during which he struggled to function, his attention wandering, his mind always drawn to the thought of her walking up that hill or getting in her car that last time. It was Justin's Depression Christmas.

Ever since meeting Mrs. Glenn and her support group, Ides Less Two had taken on extra meaning, too.

More on that later. For now, know that Justin Johnson was bracing for impact as he stood on the corner outside Beverly's Bar that March 13, 1990. The previous Christmas, after his run-in with that monster in the woods, he had predicted that something big was coming down the line. Even though he'd stopped drawing maps, his prediction hadn't changed.

He didn't know *what* was coming, but he knew it was *some*thing, and he knew it was bad.

He faced the art store.

It was time to prepare for battle.

Ding-ding-ding!

Hiram's Journal

She wrote in her danavreece in a room full of people doing their sessions. We had all been expecting a hospital, but Mom said it was just a place to sit. And that's what it was. The clinic sat on the same river-brook as Zonder's Lodge and thrust out over the water. Windows wrapped around the room, giving sweeping views of the Smokies to the patients, who sat in two rows of chairs, facing out. Tall lights stood in the corners, casting a soft glow across hardwood floors.

Mom's chair—she always took the same one—sat near the nurse's station. It was the coolest easy chair I'd ever seen. It reminded me of a first-class airplane seat, with comfy cushions, a pull-out table, and a tiny television unit with headphones. A rolling module, kind of like an IV unit, sat next to each chair, dangling a tube. For some people, the tube was connected to their chest, while for Mom, it was linked to her arm. The therapy had darkened her veins over time; red and dark brown threadlines snaked and zig-zagged down her arms. A few veins even turned dark on her legs. Dark rings curled under her eyes, her cheeks sunken.

Mac and I sat in our usual tense silence, trying to read. She'd asked us to sit with her but persistently ignored us. Looking back, I understand why, but it was tough to handle at the time.

I tried to break the ice:

"Did you write down any cool dreams in the danavreece?"

Mac: "How'd you know that's what she called it?"

"I know *some* stuff."

Mom: "I told him last Christmas morning. It was one of my last presents for you."

Silence settled over us. Mac was working her mouth the way she did when she wanted to say something, but Mom's sheer presence shut her down. She made us disappear again, like she could.

Mac finally spoke: "Mom . . ."

"Honey, I'm really tired. Just a few more minutes and we can leave."

"I have a question."

Mom went into lockdown, a mode she adopted when she absolutely, positively did not want to talk about something. She called the nurse: "Excuse me? How much longer do I have?"

Mac kept at it, though: "Why did you—"

A male nurse walked over. "You all right, Ms. Gresham?"

"Gresham-Sutton. Yes, thanks, I'm fine, but—"

"Why did you marry Trent?"

Mom addressed Mac without looking at her: "Dad, honey. He's your dad."

"You told us we could decide whether we wanted to call him Dad."

"No, I didn't," Mom lied, then addressing the nurse: "Can you adjust my unit, speed it up? I forgot how to do it."

Fidgeting around, she dropped her diary to the floor. I was the only one who noticed. While the nurse tried to deal with my mom, and Mac tried to extract an explanation from her, I picked it up. It flopped open to a page that included, I shit you not, a hand-drawn map. A really cool-looking map, I might add. I always forgot that Mom was a talented artist.

It depicted everything from Pigeon Forge to West Chim to Gatlinburg. For some reason, the location of the Gold Rush park was marked with a giant candle.

Snatch!

The diary was gone, replaced by Mom's burning-furious eyes. My throat closed, my chest seized, and all my bodily systems shut down in the instant panic that always overtook me when I incurred Mom's wrath. Her anger usually hit the lower registers—she'd freeze you out—but sometimes she'd ignite, and God help you when she did.

"You do *not* look at this. This does *not* belong to you. It *does not. Do you understand me?*"

I'd lost the ability to talk, so I nodded. Bad idea.

"Don't nod, use your words."

Some deep-seated survival instinct made me choke out: "Uh sorry. Won't look."

She wheeled on Mac: "You've never once asked me how I was doing or what I was feeling or what my life was like and *now, now*, all of a *sudden*, out of the *blue*, you're gonna be what Toni and Pepper and Willie and Hanna couldn't be?" Her eyes narrowed. "You're going to be my *friend?*"

The nurse practically shouted: *"Ma'am?"*

Our breathing—Mom's labored, mine hitching, Mac's a faint wheeze—were the only sounds. Everyone was averting their eyes. Mom suddenly touched her lips, a small sob seeping out. It relieved some tension. People sent over empathetic looks. Looking back, I can't even imagine the stress she was under, the pent-up anger and grief she was feeling. Her generation largely ignored mental health; certainly her family did. Her parents, both drunk belligerents, fucked her up beyond all recognition. She had almost none of the tools needed to contend with her feelings, her vast stores of disappointment and regret. That she managed to raise us amid all her heartache is a triumph of the highest order.

But she was a difficult person, and there are some things I struggle to forgive, even though I still love her. I can hold these competing feelings, the love and the anger, the grief and the grudge.

The nurse smiled kindly. "Got some good news. You're done for today."

Mom sob-laughed. "Oh! Look at me, blubbering. Hormones again. Your mom's getting old, guys. Ha ha!" Mom took our hands as the nurse removed her port. "I'm sorry."

Mac: "Mom, it's okay. This is hard."

"I know it's hard. *I'm* the one who's doing it. But it's not okay. I shouldn't have gotten so angry. You're both asking me questions I can't answer. At least . . . not yet. Hiram, I can't show you the danavreece yet. I will, promise." To Mac she said: "About Trent . . . I've got my reasons. You don't get to know what they are. They're mine. I want them to be mine. I need some things to be mine, mine, only for me. I need to keep one or two things to myself. Okay?"

Mac nodded. She was crying, too.

Mackenzie

She held two cards: the note from Skelton and Officer Webb's business card.

Mac and Hiram shared a room in Trent's house. It was fairly large—each half was larger than their original bedrooms in the old house—but it still needled them that Trent kept a whole other room to himself for his study. As they became closer friends with Kaitlyn, they spent more and more time in her room, which they both thought was the coolest. (She had a corner bedroom and a million books.)

No one had ever set foot in Jason's room. Not even Kaitlyn, at least not since she was nine.

Mac and Hiram had peaceably collaborated on splitting up the room, which was a mishmash of Masters of the Universe and various movie posters (*Indiana Jones and the Temple of Doom, The Goonies*) from Hiram, heartthrobs and her own selection of movie posters from Mac (William Zabka, Tom Cruise, *Romancing the Stone, Stand By Me*), as well as a sweet She-Ra poster their mom had scavenged on the same dumpster-diving expedition that got them Hiram's prized *Return of the Jedi* poster.

Hiram slipped in, trying (and mostly failing) not to make any noise. He sat next to her, holding his new map. They were silent for a time, each of them trying to read the energy in the room, both of them balancing something on the tips of their tongues. They spoke at once, stumbling over each other's words, and stopped.

Mac smiled. "You go first."

"No, it's okay," Hiram said. "You can go ahead."

"It's fine. I want to hear your idea first."

"It's not an idea. It's *ideas*."

"Mine too," she said.

"Got it," Hiram said with a nod. "I think we need to go back out to Soddy Farm. And I think we need to tell Kaity. Everything. Honestly, I think we should've told her sooner. I really like her."

Dimples dipped into Mac's cheeks. She had their mom's smile, and it always gladdened Hiram's heart.

"That's exactly what I was going to say," she said.

Hiram let out a long breath he'd been holding in. "Really?"

"We can trust her. And I think we need her. She's really brave and tough. Go get her."

Hiram stood and opened the door. Kaitlyn was standing there with a glass to her ear and an *Oh, shit, I'm busted* gawk on her face. Lowering the glass, she shaded her eyes and said, "*This* isn't my bedroom!"

Mac smiled. "Wanna come in?"

Kaitlyn was wearing jammie-pants and a ringed T-shirt with an iron-on photo of her dressed as an Old West bar wench, age eleven. He shut the door and they all sat down. Mac started to speak, but Kaitlyn held up a hand.

"Is this about Soddy Farm?" she asked. Hiram and Mac nodded. She continued: "I mean, I kinda heard you mention Soddy Farm when I was eavesdropping, but you—" (she pointed at Hiram) "—*appeared* there that night."

"Yep," Hiram said.

"Was it . . ." Kaitlyn stopped and let loose a semi-frustrated sigh. "Magic? God, if you two are pranking me—"

"It was magic," Hiram said.

Kaitlyn's expression in response was nothing short of reverent. The weight of the moment settled on her heart, but there was still a spark of doubt in her eyes, some leftover rustlings of rationalism that any sensible kid would have. Mac and Hiram were telling her the Earth had a ring system, her house extra rooms, the laws of physics extra entries; Kaitlyn took a moment to absorb these new truths.

"Thank you for telling me," she said. "Thank you for trusting me."

Mac liked her more every moment.

"You bet. We need you."

Kaitlyn nodded, a tear running down her cheek, and whispered: "Thanks. So," she added in a normal tone: "What's the deal, what's the plan?"

Mac prodded her baby brother. "You tell her, map-master."

His cheeks took on that happy shade of red. "We can draw magic maps."

Kaitlyn's eyes got big. "Whoa. Okay."

Hiram started picking up steam: "We can draw magic maps, but they're . . . tricky. We need to draw more than one, and they have to match for them to work."

"We think," Mac added.

"Right, we think," Hiram said. "We think there might be people who can draw stuff *on their own* and still have them work. Mr. Johnson—"

Mac broke in: "Hiram—oh, sorry I interrupted—but let's tell her about Mr. Johnson later."

Kaitlyn raised her hand. "What do you mean by 'work'? What happens when the maps *work*?"

"Oh, gosh," Hiram said. "Sorry, right. When we draw stuff, they . . . appear."

"They happen," Mac said. "We can make magic things appear."

"Like unicorns?" Kaitlyn asked.

"Like unicorns," Mac said.

Kaitlyn shook her head and whispered: "So that wasn't the acid."

Hiram: "And we can create portals to different places."

Kaitlyn nodded. "That's how you and Lee got to Soddy Farm that night." It wasn't a question. "Huh. When did I . . ." She got lost in her thoughts, her gaze growing distant.

Mac: "What is it?"

Kaitlyn shook her head. "Nothing. Déjà vu."

"Okay. Well, yeah," Hiram said. "We . . . uh, well, we kind of accidentally created a portal from their house to the farm."

Mac: "Tell her about Skelton."

Kaitlyn's complexion grew pale. She said nothing.

Hiram said: "He's back. And I think he's figured out how to get into the place between places."

"The lodges," Mac said.

Kaitlyn frowned. "The lodges?"

Mac: "Skelton called it that on the radio, the place between places. Lodges. I started calling them that in my head."

Kaitlyn: "But what are they exactly? Do the portals lead to the lodges? Do the unicorns come from the lodges?"

Mac shrugged. "All of the above? I don't know for sure, but I think there's a magic world right next to ours, and the maps can help us . . . see it. Access it."

"Channel it," Hiram said.

Kaitlyn: "Got it. So if Skelton can get into these lodge places . . . that means he can draw magic maps—um, he can draw magic maps—um, um, um—" Her words got sucked down her throat, her chest heaving, her eyes glazing over and staring at nothing. Hiram looked back and forth.

"What's wrong, what's wrong?"

"Kaity?" Mac said, her voice even. "Kaity? We're here. You're safe."

Kaitlyn sat back, touching her chest. Blinking her eyes open, she wheezed: "That was super drama-queen-y of me, guys. Sorry about that!"

Mac touched her hand. "You weren't being a drama queen. That night was terrifying. You have every reason to freak out."

Hiram: "Kaity, are you okay?"

Kaitlyn waved away the concern. "Me? Never better. Five by five. I had a little panic attack is all."

"Oh," he whispered. "I'm really sorry."

Mac: "You don't have to come. I wouldn't blame you."

"Girl, no force on earth could keep me away. Every kid in the Smokies has nightmares about Lenny Skelton. If he's back, and if someone showed him how to draw his way off of death row, we've got to do something. We can't let him draw any more maps."

"Or steal them," Hiram said, handing Kaitlyn the note. "Mac got that today. Someone sent her flowers."

Kaitlyn squinted. "You're telling me he's got one of your maps?"

"Yeah. He got mine at Soddy Farm. I had it in my coat. I lost it when we, uh, when we teleported from Dizzy Pines to the farm."

"Give me a second. I'm trying to catch up. If Skelton can draw magic maps, and you need more than one map for the magic to work, and he has one of your maps—"

"He's even more powerful than he was before."

"Shit," Kaitlyn said. "So what does that mean?"

Mac: "We think he somehow teleported from death row to the farm . . . and then from the cabin . . ."

"To somewhere else," Kaitlyn said. "But where?"

"We don't know," Hiram said. "Maybe someplace on my map. But we need to find out."

Mac: "That's why we have to go back out to Soddy Farm."

Kaitlyn sat for a moment, her eyes downcast. Her right forearm had a slight curve from the break; it had been a spiral fracture. Her hands were shaking, but she flexed her jaw. She looked up.

"I am a really fucking shitty artist. But I want to help. I want to draw a map."

Mac and Hiram met eyes.

Mac nodded. "Let's move."

Hiram's Journal

My sister and I made eye contact—and an instant pact:

Kaitlyn was in.

Mac nodded. "Let's move."

We were fucking Navy SEALs. I sprang to my feet—well, more like *jiggle-bounced* to my feet—while Mac lunged under her bed and pulled out a plastic storage drawer packed with art supplies. Flipping it open, she passed a pad of paper to Kaitlyn.

I cooed. "That's Strathmore four hundred! That's the good stuff!"

Kaitlyn smiled and cocked an eyebrow. "You sure you wanna trust me with this?"

For a moment, I thought she was razzing me. She wasn't; she was in dear, sweet earnest. I snatched a variety of drawing implements from the drawer: colored pencils, tubes of gauche, and an Artgum eraser, all of which I crammed into my backpack.

"You're darn right we do," I said, then to Mac: "Do I need to *study?*"

I drenched the last word in significance. She nodded, and I stole into the hallway.

Mackenzie

Kaitlyn frowned at Hiram's exit. "Where's he going?"

Mac ignored her, pulling out a Masters of the Universe-themed walkie-talkie. It resembled a rectangular section of green stone wall that bore a sword and shield. The shield's face served as the speaker-receiver. She squelched the walkie and spoke:

"Joan Wilder to Vicki Vale, come in Vicki Vale."

The answer came: "Um, this is Dawn, how can I help you?"

"Codenames, Dawn! I mean, Vicki! Codenames!"

"Oh, shit, right! This is Ms. Vicki, how can I help you?"

"We need transpo, stat."

Lee

Dawn sat bolt upright in her bed, holding the counterpart to Mac's He-Man walkie-talkie. Lee sat on the floor reading the "Puzzler to Roy Raymond" issue of *DC's Who's Who*. She jostled him with her foot.

"We gotta move."

Lee turned. "Did they send up the Bat-Signal?"

"You heard Mackenzie on the walkie! Now git!"

He had indeed heard Mac, but there was a protocol, and it needed to be followed.

"Only if I have confirmation that they sent up the Bat-Signal."

"Yeah, they sent up the Bat-Signal," she whispered. "Just git a move on! I'll be out in a minute!"

"Very well," Lee said, a tumbler falling into place in his mind. He opened her bedroom window, climbed out, and crept around the trailer, pausing to peek inside. Their mom was on the couch, talking on the phone and flipping through a book.

"Everyone loved you at the meeting," she said. "You're ready."

Grief management for Ms. Gresham, perhaps? Lee thought, noticing the book, a leather-bound antique volume he'd never seen before. He was about to get a better look when light suddenly burst from the right.

Orange light.

Overhead, the stars plummeted earthward and presented him with a strange, divine vision. The stars performed a wonderful dance and arranged themselves into the vertices of a connect-the-dots drawing. *Is that some manner of house?* Lee thought, squinting at the lights. His suspicion was confirmed when threadlines of light sprang from the dot-stars, connecting them and slowly sketching out a luminescent orange cottage. It was cozy and small, fit for one person, with a surprise: mounted to its roof were a pair of plasma cannons that would've looked right at home on the Death Star.

"Lee! I need a hand!"

Dawn was clambering out her window wearing black sweats. Lee turned, and his vision was gone. With a shrug, he went to help her. She handed him his own black hoodie, which he donned. The trailer park was humming with a pleasant evening's buzz of chattering televisions and conversations. A few lights switched off as early-shift folks bedded down. Around the side of the trailer sat Lee's trail bike alongside Dawn's sixteenth-birthday present:

A red four-wheeler that bore the roaring lion emblem of the Thundercats on its fuselage.

Lee had admired his sister's kind cunning in asking for it. After the incident at Soddy Farm, the four of them—he, Dawn, Mac, and his co-admiral—had grown closer and gone on many adventures in the woods around West Chim, but as Hiram didn't yet know how to ride a bicycle, Dawn talked their mother into giving her a method of transport for him. Lee had acquired the Thundercats sticker by eating twenty boxes of Corn Pops in record time and mailing in the proofs of purchase. The delight on his friend's face had been worth the tummy-aches.

They wheeled both vehicles up the gravel path that led to the main road, mounted their steeds, and fired 'em up. Headlights cut through misty darkness. They were off.

Hiram's Journal

Cr-r-eeeak.

I froze. Every house, even fancy ones, had their quirks—creaky floorboards and rusty windows. I knew every loud spot in our old house, but I was still learning this one. Happily, all the floors were hardwood, which gave me one advantage: I could slide around on my socks. As I slid, my sock got caught on something sticky. I lifted my foot; it was a piece of shiny masking tape. Huh.

Dropping the tape, I slid to the end of the hall, where a pair of doors awaited. A Union Jack covered one door—the forbidden entrance to Jason's room—while the other sat ajar, Trent's study. The master bedroom was downstairs, where Mom was on the phone:

"Are you sure I'm ready? Is there any more reading I should do?"

I eased the door open to reveal a sanctum of studded leather, dark-finished wood, and books that never got read. His desk was a blackwood block that hulked in the corner, covered with green library lamps and stacks of papers that detailed his business. (Mac and I had a running gag that we had no idea what he did for a living.) Track lighting ran along the ceiling and cast a warm glow. It felt like a hotel room.

Man, this house is nice.

I still wasn't used to living in a mansion, and I still couldn't believe dumb-ass Trent kept a whole room for himself. Speaking of the huge asshole, I paused and listened.

Snoooooore.

He was sawing logs downstairs, presumably next to Mom, so I proceeded with the plan and crossed to his fifty-foot-long desk. Set above the drawers was a check-signing panel, which I slid out. Taped underneath was a series of numeric codes. He changed them every week, crossing them out one at a time.

This week's was 31240184.

I recited the number to myself a few times, replaced the panel, and snuck back out.

We were the least-sneaky trio in history.

Cr-r-a-aaack!

Mac and I glared at Kaitlyn, who had hit the creaky stair. She threw up her hands.

Mac whispered: "I thought you knew this house."

"I do," Kaitlyn said. "Just not every square inch of it."

We reached the landing where our Christmas tree had stood. Mom's voice floated out from the house's rear, where she was in bed next to the World's Biggest Asshole.

"What was that name again?" she asked. "Really? *Cleopatra?*"

We padded into the kitchen. All of us had thrown on night-time outfits: flannels and hoodies and sneakers with backpacks. A small keypad was mounted next to the back door. I entered the code: 31240184.

Click!

"Jeez, this house is loud," I whispered. We all waited, listened, but Mom kept chattering away while Trent snored. Mac and I nodded at each other and stole outside. Trent's house was the only one around for miles, so we didn't have to worry about nosy neighbors, but all the same, we heel-toed it to the garage, leaving a nervous Kaitlyn behind.

Mac whispered into the walkie: "We're out. What's your twenty?"

"Incoming," Dawn said.

"Got it," Mac said. "Meet you at the Castle."

Kaitlyn scampered over on tip-toes, eyes wide: "Castle? Castle? What castle?"

Mac jerked her head at the woods.

"C'mon, got a bit of a walk ahead of us. We gotta hurry. Kaity, grab your bike."

Dawn

The Castle was a hike, but they had a need for speed. They rode up a huge incline—at least half a mile up—before coming to the crest and bringing a spectacular, sparkling view of Gatlinburg and West Chimney Top into sight. Off to the right was a dangerous ravine webbed with rusty gantry-ways and catwalks. Local rumor held that the ravine used to house an old revival theater that a disgruntled employee had blown up. No one knew what really happened, but it was the common ancestor of countless tall tales around the area.

They paused on the hillcrest—and the sky ignited for Dawn.

Stars overhead reconfigured themselves into precise geometric patterns—interlocking hexagons and squares and triangles and octagons—and shone a bright-blazing orange. That same orange light rose from the horizon, casting a distant structure in sudden silhouette:

An observatory.

The giant domed structure existed in no part of the Smokies she knew. With its telescope retracted, it stood on a floating island of earth that was bathed in waves of mist that broke against its spectral shores.

Then it was gone.

"Sister? Are you all right?"

Lee was waiting. She nodded, dismissing the vision as a trick of the light, though it reminded her of her hallucinations at Soddy Farm.

Maybe I had one of them acid flashbacks?

They rode over the crest, past the ravine, and down a small embankment until the terrain flattened out and carried them past a mountain-brook that was starting to burble again after sitting dry for the winter. Past the brook stood an expanse of sycamores and pines, evenly arrayed like columns. Mist floated through the treetops and caught their headlights like passing star-specters. In the distance, they spotted three flashlights bobbing and slashing about. Lee slowed to let Dawn catch up.

"They seem to have brought a third compatriot," he said. "Who do you think it is?"

"Oh, I've got a notion," Dawn said, her stomach clenching slightly. She figured they'd invite Kaitlyn along one of these nights. For the most part, she welcomed it, but a part of her mourned the loss of *Dawn-n-Gresh.* They'd been best friends since they were seven, but when this rich, pretty girl bulldozed her way into Mac's life, she had to give up part of that connection. *Kaitlyn* was now her best friend, too. Dawn had lost count of how many times she'd invited Mac over, only to have her decline so she could hang out with

Kaitlyn in that huge backyard of theirs, clowning around, sneaking drinks, and practicing with her rubber-band gun. Oh, sure, Mac invited her over all the time, but their step-dad treated her like she was stupid just because of her Southern accent. (Plus, Dawn knew how he treated his kids. He was a monster.) Their clubhouse, which was where they were headed, was the last special thing that they, and *only* they, shared. Dawn knew she'd eventually have to give that up, too, but it still made her yearn for those days down by the lakeside cottages, even though she knew that was silly.

You give up stuff as you grow up, she thought. *That's part of growing up.*

Another part of her wondered if Jason had told Kaitlyn her secret: that she had known Jenny Miles. Dawn had been bracing for Mac to ask her about it ever since Soddy Farm. She assumed Jason would tell his sister; after all, didn't siblings share secrets?

I guess they don't ever talk, she thought. *But Dawn, why haven't* you *simply told them yourself?*

Dawn's answer to that question existed not in words but in a mass of feelings, some clear, others indistinct. She'd told Mac about her old best friend before, but never by name. She hadn't been able to muster the nerve to say hello to Jenny in the Mystery Mansion that day, and she still wasn't sure why. Besides her family, no one knew she'd attended Jenny's funeral, and she'd asked Lee to keep it to himself, especially after what happened to Kaity at Soddy Farm.

Lee called: "The Castle is in sight!"

Their headlights danced across the petrified leg of an ancient leviathan planted in the deep Smoky Mountain woods: Radagast's Oak. Lee had chosen the name from *The Lord of the Rings,* naturally, and bequeathed it on the great tree, whose massive trunk split into half a dozen mighty limbs that could easily bear their weight. They needed no ladder, as the oak's gnarled trunk provided natural footrests. A bicycle rested against the tree.

Dawn and Lee rode up, parked, and dismounted, already shining flashlights at the newcomer, who was climbing off her own bike and giving a shy smile.

Hiram's Journal

The only thing more awkward than two people fighting are two people trying to be *really polite* to each other. That was the vibe between Dawn and Kaitlyn. They'd bonded the night of Soddy Farm—crossing paths with Skelton and Colquitt had that effect—but Dawn never fully warmed up to Kaity, no matter how many times Kaity got them booze with her fake ID or paid for their trips to Blockbuster.

"Dawnieeeeee!" Kaitlyn said, comically excited and offering a high-five. "Great to see ya!"

"Yeah, you too," Dawn said cooly, ignoring her high-five.

Kaitlyn's smile flickered. Turning to me, she whispered, "Don't leave me hanging."

I high-fived her. She winked and gave me a big thumbs-up.

Dawn indicated the tree. "We goin' up?"

"We're going up," Mac confirmed, climbing up to where a pair of tree limbs made a V-shaped nestle-point that cradled the coolest damn treehouse you ever saw:

Castle GrayCrystal.

We'd discovered it on one of our expeditions into the deep forest. Somehow, an old Tilt-A-Whirl car got lodged in that nestle-point, its back resting against Radagast's broad trunk. Over the next month, we gathered scrap metal and wood to build the Castle, using the Tilt-A-Whirl as the first wall. Dawn had masterminded the construction—she had dreams of being an architect— and we'd all contributed the detritus from old toys: I'd contributed in the walls from a Masters of the Universe-themed plastic clubhouse (they looked like green stone bricks), while Mac had added the She-Ra version of same (dark pink stone bricks). Dawn and Lee both contributed scrap lumber from around Dizzy Pines. Old Lady McIntyre from trailer forty-seven donated a dryer door, while Mr. Jerry-Jerry in trailer two gave us the frame from a jon boat that Dawn had chopped up and used for both the floor and roof. The Castle had spread along the V created by those two branches, giving it a wedge shape like a Flatiron building. The screen door from Horn's Superette (grabbed by me and Lee when it closed) was its gateway, held shut by a small combination padlock. Mac climbed up, opened the door, and let us in.

Inside was paradise. At least for a bunch of sad kids.

That wedge shape enclosed a two-tiered treehouse, complete with the Tilt-a-Whirl at one end and a full restaurant-style booth at the far end, overlooking the front window. We'd snatched the booth after the Pizza Hut down by Pigeon Forge burned down, and—*holy shit*, was it an ordeal getting it up there. Pulling it off took our combined efforts: Mac's strength, Lee's cunning, and a madcap night where we "borrowed" one of Trent's gigantic pickup trucks from his landscaping business. (We half expected him to be the kind of stickler who'd count the miles on his odometer, but he never noticed.) The front windows (frames finished in a patchwork of colors with a smattering of stained glass) we'd discovered during a trip to the dump. A fraying old easy chair sat against one wall, flanked by bookshelves packed with board games and comic books. The Castle had been accruing posters and knick-knacks since its christening via purloined Southern Comfort back around Valentine's Day. There was the usual assortment of fun movies (*The Empire Strikes Back, The Monster Squad*) with some more R-rated fare (*A Nightmare on Elm Street 3: Dream Warriors, Friday the 13th 3D, Terror Train, The Terminator*) and oodles of classic movies Lee had contributed (Howard Hawks's *The Thing, Dracula, Psycho*). One wall was reserved for target practice and held both a dartboard and a bullseye for Mac's rubber-band gun. Action figures and dolls (yes, I know they're the same thing, as Mac was constantly reminding me) stood everywhere: Masters of the Universe, Barbies, Transformers, Thundercats, BraveStarr, and a few G.I. Joes (Lee had contributed his pride and joy, Snake Eyes). Dawn had brought over a bunch of classic toys, wonderful little tin robots and wind-up cars. Mac and Dawn had also taken it upon themselves to snap Polaroids of us at every opportunity, so every free inch of wall-space was covered with shots of us goofing around, reading comics, or playing games.

Sometimes the back of our huge backyard wasn't far enough away from Trent. Looking back, I chuckle at the hours of back-breaking work we put into a treehouse we only used for a few precious years . . . but I'm glad we did. That place was awesome, and it was worth it.

We were worth it.

We all climbed in ahead of Kaitlyn and waited. She pulled her way in and immediately stopped, slack-jawed at the Castle's *pièce de résistance*: the view. Radagast's Oak overlooked all of Gatlinburg, Pigeon Forge, and West Chim. A dazzling spread of lights and mists and starshine all gleamed and glittered through the front windows. Kaitlyn took in the rest of the place, her eyes falling on a sign that hung from the far wall. It read:

CASTLE GRAYCRYSTAL: HEADQUARTERS OF THE LODGE WHISPERERS.

"The Lodge Whisperers, huh?" Kaitlyn asked. "I like it. Boss name. Lets 'em know you mean business." She dropped into a goofy martial arts pose. "It's like, don't fuck with the Lodge Whisperers, or we'll kick ya in the nards."

We sat in pleasant silence for a moment before Dawn stared giggling. Her giggles turned into guffaws, and Mac and I joined in. Poor Kaitlyn looked a little hurt—she usually wasn't the butt of the joke—but she rallied, ripping off some silly kicks and punches that belonged to no martial art on this earth.

Only Lee wasn't laughing. He stepped in front of us, arms akimbo.

"*If I may have your attention,*" he said, slightly annoyed. "What is the mission?"

"Yeah," Kaitlyn said as she flomped onto the easy chair. "You want me to tell him?"

Lee was glaring at her. "Um, excuse me, Ms. Kaitlyn, but—"

Dawn: "Lee, it's all right."

Kaitlyn gave a confused look around. "What'd I do?"

Lee: "That's Dawn's chair."

Kaitlyn sprang up like the chair had an ejector. "Oh, I'm sorry!"

"Kaity, it's all right. You can sit—"

But Kaitlyn was already shaking her head. "No way, José." She crossed and sat in the booth. "I like this seat better anyway. Love this view—*hey!* I can see Trent takin' a shit!"

"Gross!" Mac said, laughing.

A begrudging smile crept onto Dawn's face. We all sat—Mac and I in the booth across from Kaitlyn, Lee grabbing a fold-out camping chair.

"Thanks, Kaity," Dawn muttered. "And I've got the same question: What's the mission?"

Mac presented the note that came with her bouquet. Dawn and Lee reacted with horror.

"What means this?" Lee asked.

"It means Skelton's back," Mac said.

We explained everything to them. We told Kaitlyn about the Plaid Man and our close encounters with him. I explained how I'd spoken with Justin Johnson through the radio in our old house. (But I didn't tell them he'd been pretending to talk with his mom.) We told them our theory that Skelton had gotten help to draw his own map to teleport from death row to the farm and then from the farm to somewhere else.

They looked frightened, freaked out . . . and brave.

"Who do we think helped him?" Lee asked.

"No idea," Mac said.

Kaitlyn raised her hand. "Hey, am I the only one who thinks we should go to the cops?"

Barely audible, Dawn said: "And tell 'em what? That Skelton's back, and he's got magic maps?"

"Right," I said. "Plus, I don't want that jerk Colquitt knowing about any of this."

"Even if he wasn't a total asshole, I don't think he could see any of this stuff anyway," Mac said. "I don't think grown-ups can. Except . . . What about that other cop? The . . . y'know, the nice one."

Kaitlyn pounced: "Why, Mackenzie Sluttington Gresham the Third! Are you talking about the handsome and hunky Officer Webb?" She cackled.

Mac blushed. "Yeah, yeah, yeah, he's kinda good-looking. I guess. If you're into that sorta thing."

"You wanna touch his buns," Kaitlyn said.

Laughing, Mac threw a Nerf football at her. "Would you knock it off?!"

Kaitlyn caught the ball, smiling. "Sorry, sorry, sorry."

Lee raised a finger. "There may be another grown-up who could help us."

All of us except Kaitlyn nodded.

"Who?" Kaitlyn asked.

"Justin Johnson," I said. "He can draw magic maps, too."

An astonished Kaitlyn said: "Well, we need to ask his help, don't we?"

I shook my head. "He said he doesn't want to draw any more maps."

We let that reality sink in.

"We're on our own," Mac said.

Looking back on this moment, those words hit me even harder.

We're on our own.

We had parents, teachers, and confidantes in our lives, and yet the horrors facing us that spring of 1990 felt too terrible, too unbelievable, too *big* to share with any grown-up. As heartbreaking as that was, I can't even blame us. So many of our parents were dead, gone, abusive, or simply MIA.

When there's no one at home, you build a family of choice.

I love the movie *Stand By Me,* but when I was little, I found it so strange that those kids forged such strong friendships. I figured it was a product of the era. The fifties were a tougher time, right? So kids were forced to grow up faster. Now I know I was wrong about that.

It doesn't matter *when* you grew up. It matters *how* you grew up.

In *Stand By Me,* or its origin novella, *The Body,* do you remember the main kid, the Wil Wheaton character? His dad hated him, and his brother was dead. Trent and Jason hated us, and our dad was dead. Lee and Dawn's dad was dead. Kaitlyn's mom was dead, and her dad was an asshole. Justin Johnson's mom was dead. Our mom was MIA.

Somehow that part was the worst.

I can't blame my father for dying, but I *do* blame my mom for letting Trent and Jason ride roughshod over us. It's like she wasn't even there. Again, I can't imagine how hard it was for her; her depression, her disappointment. Her illness. Looking back, I remember she told us "I love you" every day, but I don't know if she actually *liked* us.

It doesn't matter when you grew up. It matters *how* you grew up. It matters if your parents got their shit together before they had you and if they continued to keep it together after they had you.

It matters if they love you.

It matters if they like you.

I hold these competing feelings: the love and the anger, the grief and the grudge.

Kaitlyn invoked the voice of Peter Venkman: "So whadda we do?"

"We go back out to Soddy Farm," I said.

Mac: "And we find his portal."

Kaitlyn: "But how? If he knows how to use this magic—"

Lee interrupted: "It's far more likely to be a form of super-science or extra-dimensional slippage we simply don't understand yet."

"Yer watching way too much *Star Trek*," Dawn said.

"I am watching precisely the right amount of *Star Trek*."

Kaitlyn rolled her eyes. "You two are adorable. If Skelton knows how to use the extra-dimensional science stuff, how are we going to find his portal?"

The rest of us looked at each other.

Lee: "We draw maps."

"Yeah," I said. "We drew a gate that led into the Plaid Man's world. Maybe we can draw one that shows us Skelton's portal."

Kaitlyn, incredulous: "Will that work?"

Lee shrugged. "It sounds strange and unusual but not any more strange and unusual than what's been going on."

"Are we really doing this?" Dawn asked. "Sneakin' out to the Farm and into Skelton's *lair?*"

"I think we have to," I said. "If we don't, he won't stop."

Lee suddenly looked terrified. "Admiral, you didn't draw Castle GrayCrystal on your map, did you?"

"No, that was months ago. We hadn't even found Radagast's Oak yet," I said.

Kaitlyn snorted. "You nerds named this tree after that random wizard from *The Lord of the Rings?*"

Mac smirked. "If you're so cool, how'd you know it was from *Lord of the Rings?*"

Kaitlyn stammered: "I—I—I'm gonna put my head on my desk." She did so but shot me a sly wink.

I giggled, then asked Lee: "Why did you want to know if I'd drawn the Castle on my map?"

"Well, it's only a hypothesis, but I fear that if Skelton has your map, he could conceivably draw a portal leading into any landmark you drew on it."

Mac nodded. "You're right. He probably can."

"Lee," I said, my chest suddenly cold. "I didn't draw Castle GrayCrystal, but

I *did* draw Dizzy Pines."

Silence. Lee nodded. "In how much detail did you draw it? Did you include our trailer number?"

I thought. Hard. Shook my head. "No. I didn't draw any of the trailers."

Dawn: "He don't even know who we are anyway. Why would he come after us specifically?"

Lee nodded. "Still, it's another reason to be cautious. Let's institute security measures around our house and take every step to prevent Skelton from acquiring any more maps. If he can amass more and more maps, he may become too powerful to stop."

I exhaled harshly. "That might actually be true."

Mac: "We'll help you with the security, too."

Kaitlyn's breathing grew ragged. "Hey, there's no chance Skelton has a map with our house on it, right?" She swallowed with a grimace. Mac touched her hand.

"No. At least not from us."

Kaitlyn released a pent-up breath. "Okay. Good to know." She rapped the table with her knuckles. "Listen, I love this plan. I'm excited to be a part of it. But let's say we *can* create a gateway into Skelton's extra-dimensional lodge zone, then what?"

Lee asked: "Lodge zone?"

"That's what Mackenzie Sluttington there calls 'em," Kaitlyn said.

Mac nodded. "Skelton called it that on the radio, 'lodges.'" She asked me: "Are you thinking what I'm thinking?"

"We seal him in," I said. "That night at Soddy Farm, Mac and I had both drawn the old cabin. When I erased it, it stopped the Plaid Man."

Lee: "Even if we can do that, he's most likely created more portals."

Dawn: "Lee, I think you're right, but if we can find out where his portals go, maybe we can lead the police to him, Officer Webb maybe."

"Or Auntie Hanna," Mac said.

Auntie Hanna. I'd forgotten about her, like I did sometimes.

Maybe we're not entirely on our own.

Silence. Faint traffic noises—bleating horns and revving engines—floated up from below and were swallowed in the murmurs and moans and mournful chimes of forest-wind and birdsong.

I whispered: "This sounds like the scariest thing in the universe."

"What's scarier?" Mac asked. "Making sure he goes to jail or leaving him out there to hurt more kids?"

Kaitlyn made a fist. "Easiest question I ever heard. Nothing's scarier than that."

Lee: "As of tonight, we're the only thing standing in his way."

"If he gets another kid, I couldn't live with myself," I said.

"Me neither," Dawn said.

Kaitlyn: "What do we do if we run into him?"

Lee: "We have armaments." He reached under the booth and pulled out a foot chest, which he opened to reveal a stack of aluminum baseball bats and some other melee weapons. For armor we had some bicycle helmets, a couple of leather jerkin costume pieces, an aviator helmet (mine), and a set of tiny football pads, all of which I fished out of the Polk High dumpster before we left. Lee had a custom-built set of He-Man armor reinforced with heavy cardboard.

We suited up.

"Lee?" Dawn asked. "Would you like to give the order?"

Lee dropped his tiny voice into his chest and gave us his best Peter Cullen: *"Autobots! Transform and roll out!"*

We poured out of the Castle. Kaitlyn, Mac, and Dawn jumped onto bikes, while Lee mounted his trail bike and motioned me toward the four-wheeler.

"You've got the Thundertank, as usual, Admiral."

Dawn: "Ain't you ever gonna learn to ride a bike?"

"Oh, I dunno," I said. "Do I have to?"

Mac: "Yes, you have to. You've just never had anyone to teach you. Grampa Blackledge taught me. Took me an hour to get the hang of it." She wheeled over, broad-shouldered and six inches taller than everyone else, and chucked my shoulder. "C'mon, we'll do it together. Maybe this weekend?"

"Okay," I said, gloomier than I meant to.

Kaitlyn called: "Ooh! Ooh! I can help, I can help! And don't worry about it, squirt. I still eat shit all the time, and I never really figured out how to turn left. It'll be fun." She snapped her fingers. "Oh, I forgot to tell you—" She farted loud enough to spook the birds above us and rode away cackling. "Let's go not get serial-murdered!"

Mackenzie

They were out without permission and riding through the east Tennessee mountain mist on their way to high adventure.

Lee's trail bike moved as confidently as if it were mounted on rails, slaloming around trees, jumping over hillocks, and skidding down embankments. Hiram brought up the rear on the Thundertank, his headlight illuminating the path for the girls, who huffed and puffed on their bikes but kept pace.

Clouds scudded across the moon as the forest closed in around them, the sycamores giving way to tightly-packed pines that hemmed in their path to a single-file trail.

They were armed and ready to do battle with whatever evils lay ahead.

Mac wore one of the leather jerkins and had slipped a strange-looking wooden gun into her belt, a single-action pistol that fired heavy-duty rubber bands. Carved into its grip was a small depiction of Mac as a child.

Hiram wore the football pads—the closest he'd ever come to being an athlete—with forearm guards and an aviator's helmet, goggles, and the monkey wrench. For the first time, he'd elected to leave his compass behind.

Dawn wore a bicycle helmet, a jerkin, and carried an aluminum baseball bat.

Lee elected for his reinforced He-Man armor, to which he added an off-roading helmet with a headlamp. His armament: a lead pipe.

Kaitlyn, the rookie, wore the other leather jerkin and carried no weapon that any of them could see.

From above, they were five fireflies skittering through the forest, slashing this way and that, leaving streaking trails of light. They emerged from the woods into a narrow band of flatland. A fence sat a few paces ahead and stretched a mile in either direction. Lee guided them to a break in the fence large enough to admit the Thundertank.

They had reached the farm.

At night and empty, it felt alien and menacing. Mac felt eyes following them from the trees, though she knew there wasn't a house around for miles. A few errant beer cans lay here and there, along with random bits of garbage. She made a mental note to come back out and clean up. The ground dipped and tossed Mac's stomach into her throat. The dip led them down past the pond where Jason had hung out with Dawn.

I wonder what they were talking about?

Past the pond, the ground rose again and carried them to their goal.

The cabin.

They all parked and dismounted, gathering around its charred ruins. Their flashlights revealed nothing but ash and blackened wood. Kaitlyn looked disappointed.

"Is it invisible? Can we just walk into it?"

Dawn shook her head. "Naw. I think we need to draw our own."

"I agree," Hiram said. "Our maps need to match."

Dawn indicated the ruins. "And we need to draw it here. *Right* here. If Skelton's portal was here, there oughta be some . . . I dunno. Leftover magic. A residue."

Lee: "A residual ion trail, perhaps."

Kaitlyn stroked her chin. "A residual nylon trail. Yes, *gooooood.*" She winked at Lee. "Just kiddin' ya, Mr. Spock."

Lee's chest positively swelled. "Thank you for calling me that."

"You bet," Kaitlyn said, pleasantly bemused by his reaction. "Okay. Let's draw some magically magical fuckin' maps. How's this work?"

Hiram unslung his backpack and distributed art supplies to everyone. He had drawn a new map of the area, while Mac still had hers from before. He produced a road atlas and laid it out.

"The more accurate the map, the stronger the magic," Hiram said. "Try to follow this atlas as close as possible. Trace if you need to."

Mac added: "But make it your own. Add details that make you smile."

Kaitlyn got to work. "Have *all* of you done this before?"

The other four exchanged shy glances. And nodded.

"Really?" Kaitlyn asked. "What did you do?"

Dawn shrugged. "Nothing big. Me and Lee made a gate that took us from one side of Dizzy Pines to the other."

"Why not anything bigger?" Kaitlyn asked, showing her map to Lee. "How's this look, big guy?"

"Quite good," Lee said, adding: "After the night of Soddy Farm, we all agreed to curtail our trips to the lodges."

Hiram: "Uh yeah, after it looked like Skelton was gone and—" (his voice hitched) "— Mr. Johnson said he didn't want to draw any more maps, there didn't seem to be much of a point."

Mac: "And every time we do this, we run the risk of attracting the Plaid Man."

Hiram: "Oh, by the way—Lee, did you find anything in your research?"

"Yes, several leads," he said. "Our mother has many such books on occult legends. The Plaid Man may be the modern manifestation of the Mothman or the Bell Witch. Both were seen around Appalachia, and yet . . . the Plaid Man feels different. More research is needed."

Kaitlyn smiled. "You guys have been busy. Sounds like fun."

Her expression was a mixture of joy and sadness that Mac knew well. Kaitlyn was happy to be with them that night, but she still felt left out. The last few months had been a blast with Dawn, Lee, and her baby brother.

Hiram was right, Mac thought. *We should've told her sooner. That house is just as bad for her as it is for us. And she's so brave and tough.*

Dawn, bless her heart, picked up on Kaitlyn's feelings, too: "Oh, we was mostly busy building Castle GrayCrystal. I pretty much forgot about the maps for a while."

Kaitlyn nodded. "You forgot about the maps . . . until today."

Mac: "Until today."

Hiram stood. "Are we ready to add the gate?"

"Yep," Dawn said, standing. "I ain't much of artist. What kinda gate are we drawin'?"

"Admiral?" Hiram asked Lee.

Lee stood, hands on hips, looking simultaneously silly and badass in his makeshift armor. He paced around the cabin, looking it up and down before returning to their side.

"Admiral, should we recreate our efforts from the night we met Not Mr. Johnson?"

Hiram nodded. "That's a good idea. That gate didn't *work* exactly, but the magic certainly did."

Dawn: "What kinda gate did y'all draw?"

"We depicted that fanciful gate from Christmasville," Lee said.

Mac: "You mean the one that leads to the North Pole?"

Hiram: "Yep, that one. Mac and Lee are the best artists. They should draw it first."

Mac smiled. "That's really nice of you to say."

Hiram shrugged. "It's true."

"If I may object," Lee said. "Ms. Mackenzie is a far more skilled artist than I."

Mac smiled. "Lee, how about we say it's a tie?"

"Very well."

"Why don't you go first?" Mac said.

"The honor is mine," he said, squatting down to draw the gate, which he presented to everyone.

Kaitlyn's eyebrows hopped. "That's really good." She pointed at the green ourobuck he'd drawn on the gate's keystone. "What's that?"

Hiram squinched an eye shut and spoke like a pirate. "It means there be monsters ahead!"

Lee: "So take care and watch out for the Minotaur!"

They cracked up. Kaitlyn assumed a mock-terrified face but didn't say anything. Mac appreciated her discretion.

She's trying not to tease them so much when they're having a good time, she thought. *That's really sweet.*

Dawn sighed. "Why are y'always so strange?"

Mac: "It's a symbol from that video game, right, guys? From *Labyrinth of Terror?*"

Lee intoned: "Yes. From *Masterminder Home Edutainment Presents*

Theseus's—"

"—*Labyrinth of Terror*, got it."

Kaitlyn: "You guys are the biggest bunch of ner—uh, *brainiacs* in human history. I love it. But you still haven't told me what that thingamajig is."

Hiram: "It's an ourobuck. In *Labyrinth of Terror*—*"

Lee broke in: "*Masterminder Home Edutainment Presents Theseus's Labyrinth of Terror.*"

"Right, right, Lee," Hiram laughed, adding: "In that game, different color ourobucks mean different things. Green means you're entering a dangerous maze."

"A maze filled with supernatural hazards," Lee said. "A maze that might even hold the dreaded Minotaur."

Kaitlyn blanched. "Why'd you draw *that?* Don't we want an oodlefuck—"

"Ourobuck," Lee corrected.

"Don't we want an ouro-whatever that'll be one hundred percent safe with zero monsters?"

Lee, quietly: "We're trying to access the realm of a monster. We need to call on appropriate magicks to accomplish that."

Kaitlyn absorbed his words. Nodded. "Understood. Now we all draw the gate on our maps?"

"Correct."

Hiram added: "But remember: add something to make it your own."

The simple sounds of blissful productivity settled over the scene: scribbles and sketches and false starts and rapid erasings. Kaitlyn chewed her pencil.

"I'm not trying to make the rest of you feel bad, but Hiram gave me Strathmore four hundred paper, so mine'll have *extra* magic. No big deal."

Everyone smiled but kept working. Moments later, they all looked up. Mac checked everyone's maps.

"I think these look good," she said.

"I *know* they look good," Hiram said as he raised a shaking finger.

On cue, the moon emerged and shined on the cabin—only it wasn't the cabin anymore.

Hiram's Journal

Somebody page Steven Spielberg, because shit just got magisterial.

The cabin had reconstituted itself into the gate we'd all drawn. Imagine piles of ash and charred wood sculpted to look like a stone archway capped with one of Lee's ourobucks, but instead of blue marble, this one was rendered in jade: two snakes devoured each other, forever entwined around a dragon's skull with emerald eyes. Dust-motes sparkled in a nimbus of moonglow that enshrouded the gate.

We all approached it, noting our contributions:

"I added the portcullis and moss," I said.

Suddenly, a set of girly eyelashes sprouted from the dragon's brow, making me instantly grumpy.

"Uh who added *those?*"

"Those're mine," Mac said smiling.

"Come *on*. Monster eyes don't have *eyelashes*. Well, maybe if they're girls."

"Hiram, *you* have eyelashes, ya goofball," she said.

"Oh, right," I said.

Lee chimed in: "Eyelashes are also crucial on any planet with particulate matter in the atmosphere. They help keep our eyes clean."

Kaitlyn slapped me on the back. "Hear that, big guy? Particulate matter!"

"Oh, right," I said, but I dug in my heels, pounding a fist in my palm: "Regardless, we're veering further and further away from true period *detail* for magic gates." *Bloop!* The magic actually made a *bloop* sound in concert with a light bulb (complete with pull-cord) that protruded from the keystone. I was outraged: "Who the heck added this?!"

"That's mine," Dawn said.

"You know that's uh an, uh, anach—uh—anach—"

Mac: "Anachronism."

"That's what I said."

"Got it, goofball. And hey, you used it correctly that time."

Dawn raised her palms. "I thought we might need to see our way back."

I relented. "Oh, okay. Shoot, that's a good idea."

Blazing green light suddenly emanated from the ourobuck. Threadlines of verdant flame carved a series of hexagons into the dragon's forehead, followed by what appeared to be an anthropomorphic octopus tentacle.

Mac prodded Kaitlyn and said: "I assume that's yours?"

"Yeah, the tentacle's from the game *Maniac Mansion*," Kaitlyn said. "I played the hell out of that on our old Apple II." Kaitlyn indicated Mac's map and added: "And I dig your compass rose. The hexagons. I wanted to pay my respects to the Grid."

As before, Mac had added a rendition of the Grid to her compass rose.

We all waited.

"Nothing's happening," Kaitlyn said. "Oh, shit, did I screw it up?"

I shook my head. "Uh you didn't screw anything up. Oh." Something occurred to me. "Dawn. I think I'm about to get an idea." I stood under her light bulb, made a goofy face, and scratched my head. Smiling, she pulled the cord: *click!* I raised a finger in a *eureka* gesture.

Vummm-m-m-m came the same thrum that pressed on your chest and made you squint. A spark ignited at the gate's center and spread, flooding it with shimmering amethyst-purple light.

"Whoa," Lee said.

Mac nodded. "I think we *all* need to add something for it to work. Like eyelashes and light bulbs."

I stared at the light. "Admiral, what does a purple gate mean in *Theseus's Labyrinth of Terror?*"

"There are no purple gates in *Masterminder Home Edutainment Presents Theseus's Labyrinth of Terror.*"

Even though what Lee said was basically nerd gibberish, it scared the shit out of everyone. What happened next scared us even more:

Our gate started melting.

It sweated away thousands of rivulets of magic ooze that collected at its base like wax. Everything we'd drawn boiled away, slowly revealing *another* gate underneath that was so stomach-turning in appearance we averted our eyes. What came into view was an archway of crumbling red brick overlaid with steaming sheets and fragments of viscera and gore. A demented infestation of vessels and veins slithered and coiled through the bricks, seething with the pulse-beats of a dark and distant heart. Like our gate, it bore a keystone, but instead of an ourobuck, this one depicted the face of a slumbering young woman wreathed with a prize ribbon.

The young woman was Jenny Miles.

It nearly struck the strength out of us, that sight.

Wind rustled through distant treetops. Someone swallowed a lump in their throat. A sob escaped Dawn, who covered her face.

"I knew her," she said, grimacing with grief.

Mac touched her heart. "You did?"

Dawn nodded. "Long time ago. She was my bestie-bestie. Before you."

Lee hugged her. They remained arm in arm.

Mac's lips were quivering. "Oh, my God. I had no idea. Why didn't you tell us?"

Dawn shrugged. "A lot of reasons. Her and me lost touch when we was little. And after everything that happened to you all, it just didn't feel right. Gresh, you and Kaity saw Jenny's mom the night she died. Kaity, the night of the party, he almost—I can't even say it. And Jason. I talked with him that night. He blames himself for what happened. I know y'all don't like him, but you should know that. After all that, I didn't think I had any right to feel so sad."

Mac: "That's so not true. I'm sorry you thought you couldn't tell me. I'm so sorry I wasn't there for you. I'm sorry I wasn't a better friend."

The sound of scraping metal drew our attention. Kaitlyn was unscrewing a flask. She took a pull.

"Dawnie, I'm sorry, too. And let me tell you something: this is not a competition to see who Skelton's terrorized the most. Not on my watch. Trust me, when it comes to *that* bullshit, there's enough grief and and pain and love to go around for everyone here."

"But you and Jason—"

Kaitlyn shook her head. "After we get home tonight—and we're *getting* home tonight—I'll check in with shit-for-brains. You let me worry about him. For now, we're gonna worry about *you*, girl. I'm so sorry you lost your friend. That must've hurt so much, I can't even imagine. I'm sorry you've had to carry that grief on your own. It's not right, and if I have anything to say about it, it's going to change."

Dawn tried to say "thanks" but broke down in tears. Without a word, Mac hugged her. We all hugged her. Skelton's evil had touched us all, distantly and personally. Kaitlyn raised her flask.

"I hate that I know this, but Lenny Skelton has killed eight kids. I was almost number nine. This is for everyone who couldn't be here. This is for Jenny."

Kaitlyn passed the flask around, and we all drank. I coughed for a full minute but pulled myself together. I hefted my wrench.

"Stay frosty, everyone."

We entered the gate.

And nothing happened.

"What the hell?" Kaitlyn said, looking around. "We didn't go anywhere!"

Each of us had stepped out of shimmering purple soup into what appeared to be Soddy Farm, but eagle-eyed Lee noticed the difference.

"It *did* work," he said, stepping halfway into the gate. He leaned back and forth, his upper body appearing and disappearing. Waving us over, he added: "Come look."

I imitated his actions, and sure enough, when I leaned to the other side of the gate, the mountains around us noticeably shrank.

"You're right, Admiral. The mountains have changed."

Everyone else checked, too.

"Where do you think we are?" Kaitlyn asked.

"Still looks like the Smokies to me," Dawn said, forearm-wiping her tears. She cleared her throat. "Mountains are all worn down. We're in the

Appalachians, at least. Maybe a little farther north?"

"Really wish I had a sextant," I mumbled.

Lee wasn't satisfied. "There's something else. Something not right. Look at Sagittarius."

He pointed skyward. We all looked. Kaitlyn shoulder-bumped Dawn.

"Do I gotta be the one to tell him we don't know where Sagittarius is?"

Lee pursed his lips impatiently. "You can see the haze of the Milky Way. Sagittarius lies over the center of our galaxy. But it's off by several degrees."

Kaitlyn gawked. "How do you *know* that?"

Dawn was nodding. "You're right, Lee." To Kaitlyn, she added: "And he knows it because he's a genius."

"As are you, sister," Lee said with a bow.

Dawn and Lee explained how to spot the four bright stars that composed Sagittarius, and sure enough, they were nowhere near the haze of the Milky Way. Mac crossed her arms and peered into the distance, where there was a dark tree line. Our surroundings were looking less and less like Soddy Farm.

"Where are we?" Mac said. "Another planet?"

She shined her flashlight at the forest, and we all reacted at the sight: Dawn gasped, jaws dropped, and Lee touched his heart in surprise.

The trees looked like they were underwater.

Dawn walked over. "Hiram, is this what y'all saw that night? The black water?"

I shook my head. "No, that water was dark, almost o—op—uh—"

"Opaque," Mac said.

"That's what I said. Uh opaque. This is different."

Kaitlyn asked: "You and Mac saw the black water the night you saw Mr. Johnson, right? I mean, the *real* Mr. Johnson?"

"Yeah," I said.

"Didn't you say something about him being good at drawing stuff?"

"Yeah," Mac said. "Usually you need more than one person to draw something, right?"

"Right," Kaitlyn said, smiling. "Because magic maps are real. And awesome, I might add."

"Ha ha," Mac said, cocking an eyebrow. "We think Mr. Johnson can draw portals by himself, and they'll work."

I added: "We're pretty sure the black water was one of his portals."

"Why'd it look like black water?" Kaitlyn asked. "Why not a gate or a door?"

I shrugged. "We don't know."

Lee: "But more important to our current predicament, *this* effect isn't localized to the forest." He shined his flashlight all around. "It's everywhere."

He was right. All around us, the view was swimming slightly, as if the world had gone a little slippery.

"Sagittarius is out of the place, and the world's underwater," Kaitlyn said. "I think the gate worked."

"But is this Skelton's lair?" I asked.

Lee pointed. "The effect is more dramatic in this direction."

Where Lee was pointing, the forest roiled as if submerged in ocean waves.

"We gotta see what's in there," I said.

We'd only taken a few steps when the earth started shaking.

Kaitlyn

A part of her still didn't believe it. She figured she got too stoned over at stupid Kimber Huntmichael's lake house. She'd jolt awake with a snort in a pool chair and have a good laugh about it all.

But the instant they made a move toward the forest, everything shivered to pieces.

It was like the world had been built from gigantic geometric blocks of earth and grass and trees. All around them, tens of thousands of these blocks retracted into nothingness. Some were hexagonal, some octagonal, some square. Everyone screamed and grabbed at each other for help and support. They collapsed to the ground in a heap of howls and tears. Once retracted, the massive slices of earth left behind nothing but diving darkness.

And a pathway.

Behind them stood the purple gate back to Soddy Farm, while ahead stretched a single grassy pathway that floated in endless space.

Kaitlyn found herself holding Dawn in a viselike hug; she'd been standing near the edge of one of the retracting sections and was teetering for a delirious moment before Kaitlyn grabbed her and pulled her safely to the ground.

"You okay?" Kaitlyn asked.

"I think I mighta peed myself some, but yeah, I'm all right. Thanks for grabbin' me."

Under her breath, Kaitlyn said: "I'll never let you fall. Any of you." It was a big admission, a declaration of allegiance she'd been whipping up the nerve to say to everybody, but she wasn't ready to do it yet. The rest of them completed each other's sentences and could read each other's minds. They were a superhero team with a cool-ass name. Kaitlyn knew Dawn was envious of her friendship with Mac, but to Kaitlyn, there was no comparison. Mac and Dawn had an *actual* friendship, built on trust and love and years spent together. Kaitlyn was the newcomer, the flavor of the month, the interloper who could afford to buy them a good time.

She had also been a total bitch to Dawn at Soddy Farm, but when Kaitlyn got hurt, Dawn's first instinct was to help her. Now that Kaitlyn knew Dawn had lost a friend, however distant, to Skelton, she felt even worse about her behavior that night.

Kaitlyn had never been more terrified than she was at that moment. She was even more frightened than she was when Skelton grabbed her, because if Skelton killed her, so what? She was one person. She wasn't important. She wouldn't be missed.

Now she had a family to worry about.

Family, Kaitlyn thought as they all stood up. *I didn't even mean to use that word, but that's what they are: my family. And I have to protect them. I don't care how fucking scared I am.*

Hiram, his aviator's helmet all cockeyed, cast an awestruck look around.

"Wow. Wow. *Wowww.* It's like it came to life." He addressed Mac: "The Mystery Mansion."

"What do you mean?"

"The last room, right before the ride ends. After you go through the Most Intense Dimension. The Space-within-Spaces?"

Mac thought, nodded. "The floor."

"I concur," Lee said.

"Y'know, that ain't exactly what *concur* means," Dawn said. "'Concur' means you agree with 'em but maybe for a different reason."

Lee's eyebrows raised. "So it does. Thank you, sister." To Hiram and Mac: "I agree. This recalls the ride's final chamber so accurately it must have been purposeful."

Kaitlyn sidled over. "What're you weirdos talking about?"

Hiram: "The last room in the Mystery Mansion *looks like this.* It's one pathway floating in outer space."

Lee: "I don't know if this is outer space so much as some kind of undefined nether-void."

"Right," Hiram said. "But what does that mean? Did the people who built the Mystery Mansion know about the magic maps and the lodges?"

No one had an answer. They all marveled. Kaitlyn prodded Mac.

"Is this the first time you've seen something like this?"

She nodded. "Yeah. Not even close."

Kaitlyn was terrified but also had to stifle a smile; she was glad to be around for a first. Part of her regretted Jason's absence, but she also knew how much her new step-siblings couldn't stand him. (And she couldn't blame them.)

"But where the heck *are* we?" Dawn asked.

"The lodges," Lee said.

Hiram: "The place between places."

"Skelton's place," Mac said. "He could be anywhere."

They lingered on their next decision until Kaitlyn broke the silence: "We're going forward, right?"

Lee clicked on his headlamp. "Yes. If this is how he gets around, we should figure out where he's getting around *to*."

He headed down the pathway. Everyone else followed. Kaitlyn cast glances at Mac and Hiram, who were bringing up the rear. Light gleamed ahead. The pathway connected to an octagonal platform, from which sprouted three more pathways, all shrouded in darkness. The ground slowly faded from grass to cobblestone. The moment they stepped onto the octagonal platform, the other pathways suddenly illuminated. Lee shook his head.

"Fascinating. The maze seems to be revealing itself."

Kaitlyn: "Maze?"

Lee gestured around. "Doesn't this seem like a maze to you?"

Hiram: "But what *is* this place?"

Kaitlyn suddenly went pale. "Shit. What about Plaiddy?"

Mac fielded that one: "The Plaid Man? Frankly, fuck him. He doesn't scare me. Skelton is the one who . . ."

Her voice faded into a hiss that emanated from the back of her throat. Her eyes gogged, her mouth stretched in horror—and she was gone, pelting down one of the newly-illuminated pathways. Hiram tripped and fell in pursuit.

"Mac! Wait!"

Kaitlyn hefted him to his feet. "Easy there, squirt!"

Dawn and Lee joined the chase, rushing down the cobblestone pathway, their advance flanked by pitch-dark void, their rapid-fire footfalls emptily echoing in the endless expanse. As they ran, the pathway continued to illuminate one section at a time, as if some unseen figure was activating panels of lights overhead, one after the other. When they caught up with Mac, she was standing before another gate—this one filled with red light— that bore a familiar sight on its keystone:

Kaitlyn's freshman yearbook photo.

Mac pointed at it in horror and wheezed: "It's hideous, it's hideous."

The words punched Kaitlyn in the gut. Freshman year had been one of the worst of her life. Mom died. Dad fell off the wagon and started treating her and Jason like his personal punching bags. She snuck out at night often enough that he installed their current security system.

Freshman year was also when she lost the thread with Jason.

They'd been so tight up to that point; tight enough where she thought she could pull him back from whatever brink he was approaching. But once Dad turned into . . . whatever he was now, she gave up on him.

She gave up on her own brother.

And now this fat bitch was saying her yearbook photo was hideous.

Before she knew it, Kaitlyn was shouldering her way past those two-bit white-trash hayseed friends of theirs and jabbing her finger in piggy's face:

"Shut your fucking mouth, you fat pig bitch!"

Mackenzie

The icon stared at her with a million squiggling eyes that made her scalp crawl. She was mumbling something about it being hideous when Kaitlyn suddenly came crashing through the group, waving a finger in her face.

"Shut your fucking mouth, you fat pig bitch!"

Kaitlyn's nostrils were flaring, her cheeks splotchy red, her lower teeth bared. Mac didn't usually back down from a fight, but she dropped back a step just to give the stupid, privileged shrimpy bitch some space.

"Ohhhh, what's wrong, Kaity? Your forget to bring enough booze to get blind-drunk? Your Daddy not hit you enough?"

Hiram lunged between them, frantic: "Hey! Stop saying that stuff!"

Dawn was jumping up and down: "He's right! He's right! There's something wrong with this place!"

All Mac heard was ocean noises. "The only thing *wrong* is this rich bitch's ugly *face!*"

"I hear you sneaking downstairs at night to eat all the ice cream, piggy," Kaitlyn said. "I can hear you snorting—*snort, snort—auuugh!*" A swift shove to the chest cut off Kaitlyn's insults. She fell on her ass, but it wasn't Mac who'd shoved her; it was Dawn. She'd interceded and was standing between them, arms extended, palms raised . . . and eyes closed.

"Close your eyes and answer me! When y'all looked at the keystone, what did you see?"

Kaitlyn was panting. *"What?"*

Mac's face slipped from rage to panic for a crucial instant. "Ohmigod, she's right. Close your eyes, everybody! *Close them!*"

They did. Their breathing echoed. Finally Kaitlyn spoke.

"It's my freshman yearbook photo. You said I was hideous, Mac. What the fuck?"

"What?" Mac said. "It's not a picture of you. It's that disgusting seedpod Skelton sent with my bouquet."

Kaitlyn

Kaitlyn, eyes still closed, climbed to her knees. "Are you serious?"

"I would never call you hideous, Kaity."

Kaitlyn held her own face in horror. "Oh, my God. I'm sorry I said all those things. I can't believe I said all those things. You're so pretty, and I've been envious since the moment we met."

Mac flared: "Are you making fun of me?"

Kaitlyn stood and dared to open her eyes. Her yearbook photo was still there, but now it was staring at her with a wolfish rictus grin and empty eyes. Shame settled over her like a coat filled with bricks; her shoulders sagged under it. This place was casting a spell on all of them, and she'd succumbed to it instantly.

But when she thought back across the last six months, her shame deepened. Mac would never call her hideous, but Kaitlyn *had* called Mac fat.

Pig.

Tons of fun.

Wide load.

And she wasn't under any enchantment then.

Mackenzie was one of the coolest, strongest, bravest people she knew, and she'd shit on her like she did everyone; everyone who was prettier, everyone who was smarter, everyone who intimidated her—which was everybody, when she thought about it. She and Mac had become friends, but Mac had never confronted her about her name-calling. Kaitlyn had simply dialed down her obnoxiousness as they got closer and closer, though she'd never apologized.

And she *had* heard Mac sneak down to the kitchen at night to eat.

Trent and Corrie subtly shamed both Gresham kids about their weight all the time. Corrie would actually make rich desserts that she'd offer to Kaitlyn and Jason but not her own kids. Both of them were so cool, and it made Kaitlyn feel rotten that their own mother could be so mean to them.

And now she'd blown one of Mac's biggest secrets to her whole gang.

Nice fucking job, Kaity. No wonder no one likes you.

Dawn appeared next to her and whispered: "Make it right."

Although she'd resigned herself to being unliked and unloved, Kaitlyn was determined to correct this one, terrible mistake. She propped a hand on her hip and forced a laugh.

"I mean, *project much* Kaitlyn? *I'm* the one who sneaks ice cream at night. Sorry I bullshitted you all. That wasn't cool." She realized she was crying. "And I am so sorry I said all those things. I was being a real See You Next

Tuesday."

She presented herself for a hug. Mac's face was still drawn in sorrow, her lips trembling. But she nodded and hugged her back. When they disengaged, Mac held up a hand to block the sight of the seedpod.

"I saw the seedpod. Kaity saw her freshman year photo. What did everyone else see? And what's inside this gate anyway?"

"I think I know," Dawn said quietly.

Dawn

The rules of this place were strange and fluid. For Kaitlyn and Mac, the keystone image had brought out old angers and resentments. For Dawn, it brought her back to her saddest day in recent memory.

When Mac told her she was changing schools.

She hadn't even *really* told her. They were getting a buzz on in Randall's basement, and Mac had said she was going to miss clowning around with her in Mr. Evanston's homeroom. She'd known for a while she was changing schools and hadn't summoned the nerve to tell her.

That's how Dawn knew what was inside the gate.

She didn't see herself and Mac in Randall's basement. No, what she saw was a grainy Polaroid of that ill-fated Brownies camping trip. Their troop had ridden a flotilla of jon boats out to a small island on the Tennessee River. The hollow remains of an old mansion stood near a Civil War-era cemetery. They'd all planned to camp on the beach, but a rainstorm had sent them scrambling back to the mainland.

It was the first time Dawn suggested they be "bestie-besties."

Jenny had, to Dawn's young mind, only recently vanished from her life, and she missed her so intensely she was still crying herself to sleep sometimes. Mac helped assuage that grief. As they bailed their boat and squealed with laughter, Dawn suggested the alliance, and Mac readily agreed. Seeing that day presented in sudden, perfect fidelity didn't make Dawn angry, but it did tell her what was on the other side of the gate. She jerked her head, leading the way.

"Come on, everybody. But turn your flashlights off before we go in."

Hiram's Journal

What I saw on the keystone confused me until we got through the gate.

The school-time smells of chalk, dust, and floor wax hit us as we passed through the red gate and emerged into the Montmarnass Academy rotunda, empty and eerie at night. Dawn had led the way, and when she passed through the gate, she had to open the glass door into the rotunda. It now stood open and swirled with red light through which we could dimly see Skelton's lair.

Dawn looked around. "Nice school. It's nicer than Polk."

Mac: "What did you see, Dawn?"

"I saw us as kids. On that Brownie trip."

"When we got rained out."

"Yeah. I know we still hang out, but I miss you."

Mac nodded. "We're always going to be bestie-besties."

A complicated array of expressions passed across Dawn's face, but she said nothing.

The keystone showed me Trent's stupid Mercedes truck, the G-Wagon, but not with him at the wheel. No, I saw Mom driving it. She always insisted on driving it when she took us to Montmarnass. Mac and I hated it.

One day, Mom had to pick me up in the Sentra, and I was late getting out of rehearsal. When I finally got out, the Sentra was leaking smoke, an old belt in its engine shrieking. Mom was red-faced and humiliated. On the way home, she yelled at me about how I'd embarrassed her. I asked her why she didn't just turn off the car. Her face seized in response, and she started silently crying. Five full minutes passed like that before she whispered:

"One day, I'm going to make you so proud of me."

I really had no idea how her mind worked.

Changing schools was tough on all of us, and it highlighted differences that were largely meaningless. Mac and I grew up with a little more money than Dawn and Lee, but not that much more. (The only person who ever thought those differences meant anything was me, Mr. "I Don't Think I'd Know How To Play A Masterminder Video Game," and that's because I'm a dumb fucking moron.) We came close to losing our house at one point, and by all accounts, Mom pissed away her inheritance.

But when she started dating Trent, everything changed. It shouldn't have, but it did. I remember Trent bragging to Lee about how much that stupid Mercedes truck cost, and I felt like such an asshole. Montmarnass was a great school and a challenging one—trust me, I nearly flunked out more than once. Going there afforded me all kinds of opportunities . . . but I didn't *earn* those opportunities. They were only presented to me because that huge asshole Trent made a lot of money. Guys like me are a dime a dozen.

Turning to Lee, I asked: "What did you see?"

"Nothing," he said, immediately addressing Mac: "Is this where you received your bouquet?"

"Yeah, but what does it mean? Was that Skelton who delivered the flowers? It didn't look like him."

Lee's dodge troubled me, but I set it aside and said: "I think Skelton had already created the portal, so when the delivery guy was standing in the doorway, it made him look different."

"That makes a weird kind of sense," Mac said. "But why would he sneak into Montmarnass?"

Dawn: "To look for his next target." She was already on her way back out: "We gotta check them other gates."

Lee

That night in Skelton's Labyrinth of Doom—that's what he was calling it in his head—Lee's primary mental epicycle was focused on helping and protecting his friends. When he saw the Montmarnass keystone, he knew immediately that the imagery was bespoke and specific to them all. Another epicycle spun up to process his feelings about what he saw, because he understood its significance instantly.

It was him, alone.

He sat in Mr. Tucker's homeroom class by himself. No Admiral Hiram Gresham, no Danny Sizemore, no Christy Hodges, no one. He had the classroom to himself. Unlike the others, whose images all conjured a range of unpleasant feelings, Lee's filled him with peace.

Mostly.

He had never imagined himself being alone at school, but when the keystone showed him as such, he realized that deep down, a part of him was still hurt by Hiram's put-downs, bullying, and snobbery. He adored Hiram, but a tiny voice inside him asked, *Why? After everything he did to you, why?*

They all followed Dawn as she ran from the Montmarnass gate back to the octagonal intersection. She ran full pelt down another hallway that illuminated in tandem with their movements. When they reached the next gate, which shimmered with the same red light, Lee had already guessed what the keystone would present him:

The admiral. Hiram.

Only he wasn't himself. He was staring into Lee's eyes, his brow knit, his teeth bared in a cruel smile. Next to him was the hulking Danny Sizemore, leaning down with a palm cupped over his ear. Hiram was whispering something to him. Lee didn't need a word balloon to know what Hiram was saying. He had heard it himself. It was months ago. Hiram tried to sit with Danny at lunch, and to win his favor, he called Lee a "stupid, four-eyed weirdo-dork." The insult made Danny roar with approval. He let Hiram sit with them that day, but when he tried to sit with them the following day, he pretended like he'd never seen Hiram before.

Hiram didn't know Lee had overheard him. The lunchroom was unbelievably loud, but Lee had ears keen enough to single out one voice from a chorus. He'd never told Hiram he overheard him. He intended to, but he simply hadn't gotten around to it. Once again, that tiny voice inside him asked, *Why not speak with him about it now? No time like the present.*

"May I have everyone's attention, please?"

They all looked at him in various states of upset and confusion, their moods no doubt in horrible flux from seeing the new keystone. Tears were streaming down Dawn's cheeks.

"What is it, Lee?"

"Just as the Dark Lord Sauron smelt a shard of his own soul into the One Ring, so too did Skelton endow this labyrinth with his boundless evils and deviltry. Listen to me: The feelings we're feeling are true and real. We all have a lot to talk about, I suspect." He paused and balled his fist like Yoda did in *The Empire Strikes Back*. "But not on the terms of this evil place, no matter how terrible it makes us feel."

"Lee?" The admiral had spoken. "Can I still say I'm sorry now? I think I know what the keystone's showing you."

"Apology accepted, Admiral. It's okay."

Hiram stepped over. "No. It's not okay. I really blew it. We can talk more later, but I want you to know that. I let you down."

Another epicycle spun up, one dedicated to processing his feelings of grief. It mostly lay dormant, this epicycle. Usually it sang pyrrhic tones and direful dirges, like it did when his father died or when he overheard the admiral insulting him. Strangely, that night in the Labyrinth of Doom, its music was baleful, yes, but it was also bright. It shone and it shivered, it sang and it keened, weighing in equal scale delight and dole.

Kaitlyn broke the spell by making a few armpit farts.

"I don't know about *you merde*-heads, but the keystone's showing me being a total bitch to Dawnie here, so I'm gonna go out on a limb and say it leads us straight into Polk High."

Hiram's Journal

Kaitlyn was right. The gate led to Polk High, but it didn't lead to the entranceway or a hallway. Kaitlyn was the first through the gate, and she immediately banged into something plastic, the sound distorted as it echoed back through the gate's barrier.

"Come on in, the magic's fine!" she called. "But take it slow."

We all took tentative steps through the red light and emerged into the school's trophy case, cramming ourselves into a space between the 1971 state basketball runner-up trophy and a mass of medals for the now-defunct swimming team, nixed these ten years after funding cuts. The space was so tight that I was still hanging halfway into Skelton's lair.

"Why'd he create a portal here?" Mac asked. "Kaity, can you get it open?"

Kaitlyn slid the glass door open, and we all stepped into Polk High's main foyer, right inside the front doors. The sudden change in smells hit me—Montmarnass had been around longer but most of its buildings were relatively new; the spoils of having a twenty-five-million-dollar endowment, I guess. Polk smelled like chalk dust and feet . . . and trees. The surrounding forest contributed to the sensory experience more than I remembered.

Dawn, her brow knit, scanned the hallway. "So he's targeting kids from Polk, too."

"Of course he is," Mac said. "But why the trophy case?"

Lee, pointing at something, said: "Here's why."

Glued to the inside of the glass was a small scrap of paper that bore a message written in the same scrawl as Mac's bouquet card:

Feeling blue? Come to the I-75 rest area for a pick-me-up.

We all grimaced in disgust and horror.

Mac: "Oh, my God, that's creepy."

I asked: "How did no one notice this?"

Dawn: "I don't even think that was the point. I think he enjoys showing off his powers."

Lee had spun to scan the rest of the foyer. "You're right, sister. Look."

We crossed the room and climbed a few stairs to a landing where everyone posted all their announcements. More of Skelton's little glued-on messages were scattered everywhere. Some were specific calls to action:

Angry at Mom and Dad? Come down to Milhouse Park Saturday morning to share your feelings.

Siblings making you crazy? Come down to the Enchanted Caverns parking lot to vent.

Others were more cryptic—but still familiar:

WE'RE WATCHING YOU RIGHT NOW AND ALL THE TIME

IT'S A PLEASURE TO WATCH YOU

SHE'S CRYING BECAUSE SHE'S UGLY

I WATCH FROM THE FOREST, I WATCH FROM THE TREES, I WATCH FROM ABOVE

"Wild guess, but I bet he left these all around Montmarnass, too," I said.

Lee: "From what I've read about Skelton's previous crimes, this wasn't a part of his modus operandi."

Dawn: "Neither was leaving a Polaroid of his victim—until he started doing it."

Mac: "That's why he did it." We all looked at her; she continued: "To confuse Auntie Hanna and Mr. Johnson. When we all found Jason in the park, they came *so close* to shutting it down, but those weird messages threw them off the scent."

"I think you're right," Dawn said, still staring at the messages. "Gawd, I actually noticed some of these at school and didn't think anything of 'em."

"He's showing off, like you said," I told Dawn. "That day at the park, he was playing music in a mask."

Mac shuddered. "I remember that. God."

I was already heading for the gate. "I bet that's where the next portal leads."

I led the way to the next gate, my mind dancing with the image of a girl.

The keystone to Polk High had shown me the face of a girl, but not Christy Hodges. No, the face I saw was another girl, Jaclyn Sneed. Danny Sizemore had tricked me into thinking she liked me back in fifth grade. I still remember how amazing it felt to think a girl liked me and how awful it felt when I asked to sit next to her at lunch, and she laughed at me. Someone had pulled a similar trick on Mac when she was in sixth grade, but I never heard all the details.

We all tromped back to the octagonal intersection and down another pathway; this one terminated in another gate. As with the others, red light swirled within it. The keystone showed me the mask Skelton had worn while singing. I turned to the others with a nod.

"This must lead to the Gold Rush. What do you see?"

"Jenny," Lee said, then to Dawn: "Though I didn't know her as well as you."

Dawn: "That's who I see, too. She's wearing her princess costume." To Mac: "How about you, bestie-bestie?"

Mac smiled. "I see Mom with Trent. Kaity, how about you?"

"I see the big shit-for-brains. With Jenny."

"Fascinating," Lee said. "Where did this magic come from? And how is it reading our minds?"

Kaitlyn stepped halfway through the gate and waved us in. "Hey, you know what happens when you assume, right? Ya look like a fuckin' asshole. Let's make sure this leads where we think it does."

We passed through the gate and emerged in a dark hallway. To our left was a wall filled with Polaroids.

Peering down the hall, I said: "Yeah, this is the park. The old gondola house."

Kaitlyn prodded Lee and said: "Hey, none of these went to your trailer—to Dizzy Pines. At least there's that."

Dawn smirked. "You can call it a trailer park, Kaity."

Kaitlyn nodded. Mac walked up toward the gondola house and looked back.

"Do you think he had a magic map that day?" she asked.

For some reason, everyone thought I'd know the answer. I didn't . . . and yet I still had a hunch.

"I don't think he did. In fact, I don't think he did until the night of Soddy Farm."

Lee: "Admiral, if memory serves, Skelton vanished the night Justin Johnson almost caught him. Wouldn't that suggest he had a map then?"

I nodded. "Yeah, I guess it might, but . . ."

Mac: "What?"

I shrugged. "I don't know. Something about that night doesn't add up."

"You don't gotta tell *me* twice," Kaitlyn said before raising her palms for attention. "Hey, Whisperers. There's one more gate, and I'm starting to get the feeling we've been here too long. I don't wanna sound like a bossy-pants, but—" Lee's hand appeared over her mouth. She flinched backward, surprised at the contact. "Lee, what the—"

Barely audible, Lee rumbled: "Dot, dot, dot. Dash, dash, dash." He indicated the gate. "Don't you see it?"

The gate, a swirling red vortex, was blinking. Up to now, it had shone a bright, classic red, like a turbulent pool of Kool-Aid, but now its color shifted ever so slightly toward pink—and it was following a familiar pattern:

Dot, dot, dot. Dash, dash, dash.

I whispered: "SOS."

Mac: "Why is it doing that?"

The idea flashed before me, and as wild as it sounded, I blurted it out:

"Dawn's light bulb. Someone's using it to signal us."

"But it's gone," Dawn said. "How could someone be using it?"

Mac was already hustling us through the gate, hissing: "We'll figure that out later. *Move.*"

I always thought cold sweat was one of those clichés they put in books, but I broke into one the instant I saw that gate flash. My skin crackled as we sprinted back to the octagonal intersection. Mac gripped my forearm.

"Look. The gate."

A dark shape shimmered into view in the entry gate, the one back to Soddy Farm, like a blob of ink soaking into a dry page. Strangely, all the other gates were blinking SOS but not the entry one. Our questions came in rapid-fire succession:

"Who's doing that?"

"What if he notices the other gates?"

"What if he's trying to *trick* us?"

"Who even knows we're here?"

Mac grabbed me and Lee and shoved us into Dawn and Kaitlyn, hustling us down the final pathway, the one we'd yet to explore—but there was no place to hide. Whatever power lit these pathways was shining a blinding light down on us.

"Shit," Kaitlyn hissed. "He'll be able to see us."

The shape was growing darker and more distinct every second. Mac peered over the edge of the pathway. "Look, look." She waved us over. The pathway had the slightest bit of a shoulder, a slanted embankment that descended about ten feet before vanishing into darkness. She dropped to her rear and scooted down the embankment, kicking loose bits of earth and gravel that tumbled off the pathway and into sheer nothingness.

"Are we sure this is gonna work?" Kaitlyn said, her eyes locked on the entry gate.

I pulled her down. "No time to test it; we've gotta move!"

Dawn and Lee followed suit, all of us searching for footholds in the ever-loosening earth. For a terrible moment, I thought we were screwed—that the mysterious overhead light would lead Skelton straight to us—but it worked. The instant the last of us, Dawn in this case, slid off the main pathway, the light extinguished.

Just in time, too, because Lenny Skelton himself emerged from Soddy Farm.

And he was singing a song about a certain horse named Paul Revere.

Yep, the monster was singing *Guys and Dolls*. We all linked arms and braced our feet against the pathway's shivering edge, our every heartbeat and tremble dislodging dirt and gravel into eternity.

What if he sees it falling? What if he finds us? What'll we do?

His footfalls padded, then clicked as he moved from grass to cobblestones. They grew louder and louder: *click, click, CLICK, CLICK, CLICK* until he passed right over us, heading for the final gate, humming *Guys and Dolls*. As he walked, those strange overhead lights illuminated the walkway until he reached another gate, only this one was locked tight with dozens of overlapping portcullises. He stood about ten yards away. If we craned our heads, we could barely make out what he was doing. He wore a flannel button-down—plaid, naturally—and chinos with hiking boots, all of which looked relatively new. From his pockets he produced a pair of maps: one was drawn on heavy-stock sketch paper with colored pencils, the other on college-ruled notebook paper.

"He's got my map," I whispered. The rest of the gang nodded.

Skelton held up both maps—and released them. They floated in space, flanking the gate, and glowed from their middles, like a pair of flashlights were shining behind them. The portcullises clattered open, each sliding back in a different direction, revealing another red gate. Skelton passed through.

And I sprang into action.

"We've gotta keep it open," I urgently whispered, waving everyone along. I sprinted as fast as my chubby legs could carry me to the gate, where the portcullises were already sliding shut. Mac protested.

"What if he hears us?"

I ignored her, slid to the ground before the gate, and wedged my monkey wrench in place, holding one of the portcullises open, but there were *dozens,* all of 'em closing rapidly. *Slam!* Lee was there, wedging his lead pipe in place diagonally and stopping a few more.

Dawn's voice came: "Stand back."

We jumped out of her way. She gave the gate a quick glance and slid her aluminum baseball bat in place across the rest of the portcullises, its tip dipping into the red swirl of the gate itself. She propped a foot on the gate's edge and pulled the bat like a lever. Mac slid in behind her, grabbed the bat, and added her strength.

"C'mon, everybody, help!"

We all pitched in, slowly pulling the portcullises open. They locked into place, letting the wrench and lead pipe clank to the ground. All of us froze in fear, waiting for Skelton's horror-show face to appear from the swirling red light, but nothing came. Dawn wedged the bat in place as best she could and propped her hands on her hips.

"Are we doin' this or what?"

"I don't know," Mac said. "What if we get trapped on the other side? It's not like these portculli are real."

Lee: "No, the plural of portcullis is *portcullises.* It's a Middle English word, so you pluralize it by adding an S or, in this case, ES." He scoffed. "Adding an I to pluralize a word is an old misconception. It's 'octopuses,' too. Now, if we were speaking Latin on the other hand . . ."

God, I loved Lee. We all smiled. Mac said: "Got it, Lee. Thanks for the language lesson. But are we doing this or not?"

Lee said: "It would be a shame to travel all the way to the moon only to stay in the landing module."

I agreed: "This was never going to be safe. We're never going to convince any grown-ups he's still alive unless we know where he's hiding out."

Dawn nodded. "I think we've gotta do it."

"Agreed," Kaitlyn said. "But what about the SOS?"

Mac: "We'll worry about that later. For now—forward."

We looked at each other, steeled ourselves . . . and entered the gate.

Mackenzie

Her bravado was entirely invented, though she knew that was true for all of the Lodge Whisperers.

The far side of the gate held new terrain. They emerged onto a rocky embankment that formed a U shape behind a building shrouded in darkness about twenty feet below and ahead. Past the building was a small parking lot; beyond that a state highway. Behind them stood the forest, while all around rose the familiar gentle slopes of the Smokies.

Although Hiram had been the first to discover the magic maps, Mac felt the mantle of leadership falling to her. Lee always looked to his sister for guidance, and Dawn was too shaken by everything to handle it. Kaitlyn was the oldest but also the greenest. It was up to Mac.

They were her soldiers now.

"Hold it," Mac whispered. "These rocks are making noise."

Everyone held their position, scanning the area.

"Where are we?" Dawn asked.

Lee was pointing up. "I don't know, but look at the sky."

It looked like two halves of existence had been fitted together. A visible line demarcated the world along the same plane as the gate, only the line wasn't straight. It was—

"The Grid," Mac whispered, prodding Kaitlyn. "See it?"

She looked up and nodded. "Holy shit."

Interlocking hexagons and geometric shapes composed the line that joined the two halves of existence, the boundary twinkling like an endless string of stars. Dawn shook her head in wonderment.

"Whadday'all think this means?"

"No idea," Hiram said. "Do you think we're still in the Smokies?"

Lee nodded. "Yes, but even farther away. Perhaps to the north?"

"That road looks familiar," Hiram said. "But what building is that?"

Overhanging trees blocked the down-shining light of the full moon. Mac jerked her chin forward and looked for secure footholds on her way down. Hiram trailed immediately behind her, followed by Lee, Dawn, and Kaitlyn. They made their way to the right, slowly climbing down until they brought the building's profile into view. They all crouched on the rocks. Clouds shifted overhead and released a shaft of light.

Hiram's breath hitched in response. Mac took his shoulder.

"What is it?"

"I've seen this building before."

Hiram's Journal

Six months ago, the night we first met Trent, Kaitlyn, and Jason, Mom had said these words:

Plaid! Why don't you tell me about the time you and your SEAL team had that mission in the Persian Gulf?

Those words sparked a series of three visions, three oracles:

First was the Christmasville gate leading to the North Pole, only this one was capped with a symbol I now knew as an ourobuck.

That was the gate Lee and I drew, the one that led to Not Mr. Johnson, the Plaid Man's lair.

Second was the wrought-iron lamp-post standing by a cliff.

I saw the lamp-post near the real Mr. Johnson's house.

The last image I had been waiting to see. I thought I might see it the night of the Soddy Farm party. Instead all I saw was the old Civil War cabin. But when the moon revealed Skelton's hideout, the trifecta was complete. The building was a cabin with a powder-blue A-framed overhang. More tumblers fell into place in my mind:

Spaces create shapes.

Shapes hold secrets.

My two maps of the Gold Rush park depicted the Mystery Mansion with a secret attic. I'd even labeled it *Secret Attic*. That secret attic was where Jenny Miles met her fate, and now I was looking at an A-frame cabin with almost the same silhouette.

Neurons misfired, and my mind jumped to another image: the dream I had outside the Wal-Mart last December. In my dream, Skelton's traincar had *grown* a little A-frame attic, its roof bursting like a wooden bubble, and now I was looking at an A-frame cabin with almost the same silhouette.

The Mystery Mansion. The traincar. This cabin.

They were all the same shape.

Spaces create shapes.

Shapes hold secrets.

Skelton's singing voice warbled out from the cabin and froze our blood.

Kaitlyn: "Think we should go look, see what road this is."

"Ain't no way I'm walkin' past that man's house," Dawn said.

Lee: "I don't think it would help. Look at the building's facade."

We did. It took a moment—our eyes were still adjusting to the increasing moonlight—but the sight was familiar: everything looked like it was swimming.

I said: "It's like we're underwater."

Dawn: "I keep askin' this, but—*What does that mean?*"

Once again, everyone looked to me like I had the answers. I was close to making the connection, but Mac was a step ahead:

"Hiram, is it anything like your maps? The way the new Mystery Mansion was built over the old gondola house? They had the same shape."

I frowned in thought and actually squinted; the moon was positively *blazing* overhead.

Finally, I nodded. "This is an illusion."

Kaitlyn leaned over. "Guys, I'm not gonna lie: I'm a little tipsy. Catch me up."

Lee shaded his eyes from the moonlight and said: "Skelton not only created that network of pathways to connect various locations, he also shrouded this very location in an illusion."

Off Kaitlyn's baffled frown, I added: "This whole place is in disguise." I indicated the cabin. "That cabin isn't what it looks like. Skelton built his own illusion *over* wherever this is."

Lee added: "There's something else . . ."

"What?" I asked.

He shook his head. "There's a reason why certain things look like they're underwater. But I don't know what the connection is."

Kaitlyn nodded. "Got it, Lee. But if we're gonna bring your Aunt Hanna out here—"

"Or Officer Webb," Mac said.

"Or your boyfriend, right," Kaitlyn said with a wink. "If we're gonna bring them out here, we need to be able to find this place in the real world, without the gates. We need to figure out where *here* is."

I pulled out some paper and started to sketch Skelton's hideout.

Mac: "What're you doing?"

"Spaces create shapes. Shapes hold secrets." I indicated the hideout. "There has to be a building *shaped* like this one somewhere in the Smokies. If we find it, we find Skelton."

Dawn blocked the moonlight with her hand. She shook her head. "That'll take forever. What're we gonna do, drive all over the Smokies lookin' at every building?"

Lee: "I have a more troubling hypothesis." We all looked to him. "Skelton has disguised this location, yes?"

"Right," I said, then slapped my forehead. "Oh, beans."

"Indeed," Lee said with a nod.

Mac: "What, what?"

Lee: "Even if we were to return to this location in the real world, Skelton himself wouldn't be there."

I was squinching one eye shut because of the moon. "He'd be hidden inside the in-between place."

Mac nodded. "So we *have* to draw a gate."

Dawn's jaw dropped. "Guys—"

I said: "Maybe there's a way to draw a gate that a grown-up can see—"

Dawn grabbed mine and Mac's shoulders and said: "Don't move."

Instant stillness took us, our skin tingling, our senses on high alert. My back was to the cabin, and I imagined Skelton having somehow teleported behind us, wielding a knife over his head like Michael Myers.

I whispered: "Is it him?"

"No, it's the moon," Dawn said, nodding skyward.

All of us craned our heads but had to squint into the glare. It looked like a blazing white disk at first, but as my eyes adjusted, its surface took on an unfamiliar pattern; *unfamiliar* because it's not one I expected to see on the moon. Instead of splotches and craters, *stripes* were sinking into its surface like a latticework of canals. First one set of stripes, then another, then another at a slightly different latitude—

"Oh, shit," I whispered.

They weren't stripes. They were *plaid.* Mac lurched to her feet.

"We have to—"

The moon exploded silently. I'm not kidding. But it didn't fly to pieces like Krypton meeting its end; no, only its lower hemisphere blew. It burst open like a massive pumpkin full of streamers and confetti that were millions upon millions of grotesque tendrils that coiled and spawned and wriggled and writhed together to construct a torso, arms, and legs until the Plaid Man was hulking over us, big as Galactus, a Lovecraftian Colossus of Rhodes. Poor Dawn couldn't help what she did next.

She shrieked.

Dawn

Their description always sounded silly to Dawn.

A man with a plaid face? she had thought at one point. *Come on.*

But when the Plaid Man materialized in the sky over Skelton's hideout, the stresses and horrors of the past six months crashed down on Dawn. Her higher brain functions went into a super-hot hard-freeze, leaving her with nothing but instinct, nothing but animal reaction.

And honestly, it felt good for her to let loose.

She'd been bottling up so much since Jenny was killed. Their mom had been acting more and more distant, disappearing to her weird club meetings or spending half the evening on the phone with Ms. Corrie. As she shrieked, Dawn distantly registered that hands were grasping her shoulders and trying to shake some sense into her.

"Dawn, Dawnie!" Mac said from a million miles away.

Hiram was waving his hands in Xs, the universal gesture for *shut the fuck up!*

But her mind was offline for the moment. Somewhere close by but far away, a voice stopped singing *Guys and Dolls* and a door slammed. Rough hands hoisted her off the ground and bore her at a hectic, rocky run toward the gate.

"Hey!" came the voice of a cheerful devil. "Don't move!"

Hiram: "We!"

Lee: "Are!"

Mac: *"Dead! Runnnn!"*

The devil's footfalls were the stuff of nightmares, the sound of a pursuer you could never escape, clambering across the parking lot and crunching onto the rocky embankment with alarming, unstoppable speed. Kaitlyn, heretofore seemingly unarmed, produced a can of mace and brandished it.

"Fuck you, dude!" she screamed.

The devil was undeterred: "I like those weapons!"

Kaitlyn's mace *poofed* into glittering bits, her eyes popping wide in shock that was soon overshadowed by an actual, massive shadow. A skyscraper-sized leg was stepping over the mountains, its end still a mass of tendrils that were slowly constituting themselves into a foot. Dawn dared a glance back: the shadow blotted out the devil—except for his glass eye, which glinted in the ambient moon-glare—and the devil paused, his gaze tracking upward.

His voice was hushed reverence: "It's a sight to behold."

The Plaid Man's response shattered the heavens and halved their hearing: *"I HUNGERRRRRR."*

The gate was growing closer and closer as they ran and ran, the remnants of Dawn's baseball bat little more than a sparkling cylinder—*He can make our weapons vanish,* she thought, her cerebral cortex slowly coming back online—and now the portcullises were sliding shut again, dozens of them, one after the other, inexorably sealing their doom until the impossible happened:

Light burst from the gate.

It blinded them, the light, before fading to reveal the silhouette of someone holding a thick bar that was about five feet long capped with two cartoon hands.

Yes, *cartoon* hands.

The hands looked like they had been penciled, inked, and painted. They gripped either side of the gate and pushed the portcullises back.

Who is that in the gate?

Their eyes recovered from the light burst, bringing into view a living cartoon character. Orange neon lined his ribbed leather jacket and pants, which blinked and clicked with inlaid readouts and keypads. He was a walking, talking, Saturday-morning-cartoon computer, a lantern-jawed, cyberpunk hero animated by Don Bluth, his blonde hair buzzed on the sides and cut with punk stripes. Orange wraparound sunglasses encased his head and glittered with rapidly updating heads-up displays.

Dawn's panic subsided at the sight of him, for she'd never seen anyone handsomer.

Or taller.

He's even taller than Max Stanford up in Knoxville.

"Oh, my God," came Kaitlyn's stunned voice. "Is that you, shit-for-brains?!"

Indeed it was.

It was Jason.

Hiram's Journal

Remember when I said visiting the Mystery Mansion was like going into a Saturday Morning Cartoon? Well, now that was happening *for real* as Jason frantically waved us into the gate, which he was holding open with an animated wedge capped with articulated, animated hands whose knuckles had gone white from the effort.

"Run! Run!" he yelled, his voice booming like it had been mixed and enhanced in a studio; he sounded like every Saturday-morning hero I loved: Spike and Hot Rod and Lion-O and Matt Trakker and Flint all rolled into one. Some unseen wind kicked his locks of blonde hair, his movements

comically exaggerated like Space Ace or Dirk the Daring.

THOOOOM! The Plaid Man's foot, massive as a hundred-foot-wide redwood, smashed into the earth behind Skelton's hideout, sending a rippling shockwave through the illusion, giving us a fleeting glimpse of the reality underneath:

The hideout's overhanging roof wasn't powder blue but a deep burgundy.

Where have I seen that roof before?

The impact sent us all toppling to the ground at Jason's feet. He tapped a few buttons on his forearm and activated an array of orange lasers that insta-sketched a new animated implement: a luminescent orange shoulder-mounted bazooka.

Skelton's voice rang out: *"I can feel your breath, my little—"*

ZAM! Jason's shoulder-bazooka blasted Skelton in the chest. He reeled backward and crashed to the rocky embankment. Kaitlyn hugged her big brother.

"Jase?! How did you—"

The Plaid Man bellowed: *"I HUNGERRR!"*

"No time!" Jason yelled. "C'mon, I've got my car back at the farm! Let's go go go!"

A shadow expanded over our heads, blocking the stars and the Plaid Man's moon-face: he was raising his foot to crush us. We all hurled ourselves into the gate just as it came crashing down like a fucking avalanche.

We weren't safe yet.

Jason deactivated his shoulder-bazooka and yanked the double-handed wedge out of the gate. The Plaid Man retracted his foot to reveal Skelton sprinting toward us. The portcullises screeched shut just as Skelton slammed into them. He sucked his yellow teeth at us, his good eye gogging, a wild wail ripping out of him: *"Who's your friend?!"*

"Fuck you!" Kaitlyn yelled.

"Never mind him!" Jason yelled. "Follow me!"

He took off back up the pathway, lights igniting overhead as he ran, his form leaving a slight animated wake. I pulled Lee to his feet while Dawn was helping Mac to hers, Kaitlyn in the rear, and we all sprinted in pursuit of Jason, the portcullises screaming back open behind us.

"Might as well about-face into my arms!" Skelton cackled. "Ain't no escape!"

We loped through the octagonal intersection and ran, ran, ran for the gate back to Soddy Farm, but it was no use: Skelton, somewhere behind us, had cast a spell that created *another* portcullis, this one lined with bloody barbed wire, but as it started to clatter shut before us, Jason activated a jetpack (the same luminescent orange as the bazooka) that blasted him forward. He trailed a pair of jet streams to the gate, where his lasers sketched out an animated tire-jack that held it open. He turned to us, reactivating his bazooka, which fired three more times. A triplet of cartoon missiles streaked over our heads, scoring three concussive hits. Skelton screamed. Looking back, I saw Skelton dangling off the pathway, clawing at the disintegrating earth. Ahead, the portcullis audibly strained against Jason's magic tire-jack, which bowed from the pressure. Behind, an earth-shattering *kaboom* signaled the incursion of the Plaid Man into Skelton's lair.

"Oh my fuckin' God, look!" Dawn screamed.

The gate to Skelton's lair exploded in a slinging starburst of stone and dust and gnarled steel, leaving behind a shimmering hole in existence through which the Plaid Man pulled himself, his massive body squeezing through the tiny opening like toothpaste from a tube. As he passed through the gate, he shrank to about thirty feet tall, his legs long and willowy and jointless. He loped down the pathway to where Skelton dangled—and he helped him up.

When I saw that the Plaid Man and Skelton were apparently allies, I felt suddenly sure Jason was about to ditch us.

But he didn't.

He waited for us all, shoving us through the gate one at a time. Once we were safe at Soddy Farm, Jason ducked under the gateway, the magical barrier transforming him from cyberpunk cartoon hero back to jeans-and-warmup-wearing teenager like a three-dimensional cinematic wipe. Faint wisps of steam rose from his eyebrows as a slight sunburn faded from his skin. All that remained of his superhero-self outfit were a pair of strange-looking glasses that he doffed and pocketed.

Holy shit, I thought. *Those are his 3D glasses from the Mystery Mansion!*

Jason's tire-jack vanished, letting the portcullis slam shut—just in time for a familiar, shit-eating voice to shatter our sense of triumph:

"Gotcha! Hold it right there!"

Flashlights blasted our eyes. Police lights spun in the distance.

And Bo Colquitt had us dead to rights. Ugh.

"Well, well, well! Lookit what we done caught!"

A half-dozen other cops stood nearby, an astonishing number to bust a bunch of kids. Had Jason ratted on us? Couldn't be—Colquitt almost got Kaitlyn killed. But none of that mattered, not with the gate right behind us. It was still there in its grotesque, industrial glory, all red brick and steaming viscera.

No, it's more than steaming. It's bubbling.

The gate's facade was heating up for some reason—*Maybe because of all the magical activity?* Regardless, the sheets of vessel-shot flesh covering it bubbled and popped like cracklings on a campfire stove. All of us wiped sweat from our brows or tugged at our shirt collars.

Jason looked at the gate in horror.

"No! No! You gotta let us—"

Colquitt, who was wearing a police duty coat, got in his face: "Gotta let'cha what, son?" He slung Jason into the arms of a waiting cop, whom we all immediately recognized: Officer Webb. He was also wearing a coat.

Mac and I met eyes; she'd noticed him too.

Colquitt prattled on: "Mercy me, but when I got a call sayin' two whole houses-fulla kids up and went missing, I said to myself, 'Bo, surely there cain't be *four* kids out 'n' about in the middle of damn near nowhere . . . but *five?*'" All our eyes were locked on the gate. It was then that I noticed the light bulb.

Dawn's light bulb! It's back!

Colquitt: "Them dipshits I get, but you, son? You? Your folks're in one heckuva state, you runnin' out like this."

The portcullis slowly slid up. Jason looked terrified, but he gathered himself and executed an arcane gesture: with his palm facing down, he balled his fist, flipped his hand upward, then flipped it back down and extended his fingers.

Dawn's light bulb vanished. But the portcullis was still rising.

All of us discreetly sidestepped away from the gate. At first it was empty, but soon enough, a dark figure appeared in the gate, grinning his mad grin.

Colquitt: "Your daddy's one of the finest men I know."

Mac and I held hands. Lee, Dawn, and Kaitlyn followed suit, squeezing each other's hands so hard they turned white.

Colquitt paced around: "Your daddy's upstandin' and brave . . ." And he walked *right through* Skelton and the gate like they were mist. (Indeed, everything magical appeared dimmer and slightly transparent.) Somehow, Skelton's huge grin got even bigger. He took a deep breath and bellowed:

"I DONE TORE UP THE MAP, LAWMAN! HA HA HA! I DONE TORE IT UP!"

All of us winced, but Colquitt carried on like he hadn't heard, because he hadn't.

". . . and nothing if not the most headlong, ambitious fella in the state, and when—"

Another voice: "Boss?"

Colquitt spun: "What is it, Baywatch?"

My heart leaped. All eyes turned to Officer Webb, who was doffing his coat, his brow glistening, as he shined a flashlight through the gate. He was frowning and squinting in Skelton's direction. A confused breath escaped him. Dropping his coat to the ground, he forearm-wiped sweat from his brow and stepped toward the gate—to the confusion and amusement of the rest of the cops.

Barely audible, Mac whispered: "I don't know if he can see it, but he can *feel* it."

Colquitt propped his hands on his hips and whooped. "I think Baywatch is seein' things, fellas!"

They all laughed. We didn't. We were frozen in stark-fucking-terror as Skelton extended his forearm beyond the gate's boundary, the gesture lending his arm some opacity—and revealing it instantly to Webb, who audibly gasped. The rest of the men were laughing too hard to notice Skelton take a swipe at the back of Colquitt's head.

Webb hissed: *"Boss! Look!"*

At the same instant Colquitt spun around, Skelton retracted his arm, leaving a puff of magical mist in his wake. It looked like Colquitt was peering straight into Skelton's eyes, but all the cop did was smile and shake his head.

Turning around: "Might need to get them eyes checked, Baywatch—"

Mac hissed: "Oh, shit."

He was there. Not Skelton, the Plaid Man. He appeared over Skelton's shoulder wearing his dark blue suit and tie and laid a hand on his shoulder. Skelton's eyes bugged at his touch; we could practically feel the electricity. The Plaid Man leaned over and whispered in Skelton's ear, raising one of his scar-tissue-covered hands to point.

At Webb.

Skelton nodded and whispered: "He can see." Skelton backed away from the gate and hooked his thumb at the Plaid Man. "Him and me, we're coming together soon. But first blood'll be Saturday night." The portcullis slammed shut, and the gate vanished.

A few dozen yards away, a flashlight bobbed into view.

Another cop called: "Ain't no other kids, boss!"

Webb still looked troubled: "Boss . . ."

Colquitt glared: "What is it, Webb?"

Webb pursed his lips and relented. "Nothing."

Satisfied, Colquitt faced Jason: "Trent raised himself a better man than this, son." Walking away, he yelled: "Throw 'em in the paddy wagon!"

Mackenzie

They were morose as shit, sitting in a familiar scene: the West Chimney Top police station.

The whole gang was there: Hiram, Mac, Dawn, Lee, Kaitlyn . . . and now Jason. Officer Webb, aka "Baywatch," had deposited them in the same hallway where they'd sat months earlier after Skelton's magical appearance. Everyone had the same questions on their minds:

How had Jason found out about them? And how had he figured out how to draw maps?

Mac expected Kaitlyn to interrogate her brother, but all she did was sit there, arms crossed, nibbling her lip and frowning. She was lost in thought, so Mac prodded Hiram.

"Ask him," she whispered.

"Me?" he said, shaking his head. "He hates me."

"I don't hate anybody, kid," Jason said.

Hiram, emboldened by the night's adventures, flared: "Uh don't call me a kid, you big jerk."

Slam! At the far end of the hall, Corrie, Trent, and Sandra entered. Jason sprang to his feet.

"And I've been drawing maps longer'n you. *Kid.*"

The rest of them gaped at each other, too baffled to respond. Trent, meanwhile, was already raging. Wearing pajama pants and a winter coat, he stalked toward us, shoulders hunched, fists balled, face a livid purple-red.

"You wanna *explain to me—*"

Jason walked right past him: "Not now."

Trent pivoted in pursuit, his sneaker squeaking on the linoleum.

"Not now? Not *now? Hey, I'm talking to you—*"

He shoved Jason in the back, a move that shocked everyone—even Hiram, Mac, and Kaitlyn. They'd seen this kind of violence around the house but not in public. Sandra covered her mouth, and even Corrie, who usually found a way to ignore Trent's bullshit, squeezed her eyes shut. The shove sent Jason staggering out the side door into the parking lot. All the kids jumped up and ran outside into the crisp spring night. They cast a nervous glance at the moon before turning their attention to the scene Trent was causing.

Lee approached Sandra and whispered: "Mother, I can explain—"

"Just git in the car," she said.

Dawn tapped Mac. "Gotta go. Call me?"

Mac nodded, already miserable. The Dockerys loaded up and rode off while Trent kept at it:

"You have ANY IDEA HOW WORRIED WE WERE? Did you take

everyone out there? HUH? *ANSWER ME!"*

Jason had bowed his head, his brow knit, his shoulders slumped. It was a posture of beleaguered submission, something he did to weather Trent's ghoulishness. Mac had lost count of how many times she'd seen him do it around their house. Sometimes it worked, and Trent's attention would wander back to sports, or Corrie, or drinking, or railing on about this or that ethnic group, but sometimes it only stoked his flames even higher—like it did that night. Trent planted his palms in Jason's chest and launched himself forward like he was trying to topple a brimming bookshelf. Jason reeled back.

Trent advanced, bellowing: "I GO UPSTAIRS FIND EVERYONE'S ROOMS EMPTY AFTER WHAT HAPPENED LAST TIME YOU DISAPPEARED DON'T YOU GIVE ME THAT LOOK THAT LOOK SAYS *FUCK YOU, DAD, FUCK YOU—"*

Another voice: "Hey."

Trent whipped toward the sound with a grunt.

It was Officer Webb . . . and he was laughing.

Holton

Holton "Baywatch" Webb loved OODA.

Observe, Orient, Decide, Act.

He learned the OODA loop when he was earning his trident. It was the foundation of his close-quarters combat training, the four stages of an engagement. The key to getting the upper hand was disrupting the loop in your opponent's mind.

Especially if they were bigger than you.

Holton Webb had been trained in violence of action, and in a pitched battle, he was pretty sure he could take Trent Sutton. *Pretty* sure. Big guys like him either had a glass jaw or were well-nigh invulnerable. So he went to Plan B:

Disrupt his OODA loop.

Holt was practically slapping his knee, he was laughing so hard. An observer might think he and Trent knew each other and that Holt was picking up a previous conversational thread. He hooked a thumb at the station, waving at Trent and giggling.

"Oh, man, Trent, you're not gonna believe it!"

Trent's expression was a familiar one to Holt: that of a beast distracted. The miserable son of a bitch looked like a werewolf standing on its hind legs, hunched over its prey. Light from a streetlamp lit Trent's pupils a movie-monster red, his lips glistening with spittle, his nostrils spewing steam.

It was time to strike.

Holt approached Trent and laid a hand on his shoulder; a gesture at odds with the latter's intensity. Holt acted like Trent was laughing, too, and not trying to pummel his own son.

"Y'know, me and the boys had a bet, and we were hoping you could settle it for us. Got a minute?"

He escorted Trent across the lot to the side of the building, where Trent's breathing slowed. He crossed his arms.

"What bet did you need settled?"

Boy, he ain't too bright, is he? Holt thought. "I was there that night. When they brought Skelton in. Gatlinburg PD called in a few of us from West Chim." Trent, finally glomming onto the ruse, nodded. Holt continued: "I ain't never seen evil like him. Not before, not since. I get it. I get why you're so worried. If a man like Skelton can sneak outta state pen with no one the wiser, who *else* might be out there?"

"This going somewhere?" Trent growled.

"I know you and Bo go back a-ways. But if you can't keep your kids safe, I'm gonna have to call the county."

His big, stupid face fell.

"They—they—those little shits, they snuck out after I fell asleep—I don't KNOW how—"

"Maybe the question ain't *how* but *why*," Holt said and paused, remembering something he'd heard around the station. "I'm talking to you man to man here. SEAL to SEAL."

Trent's face, which had been burning bright red, got pale *really* fast. "You're a SEAL?"

"Yes, sir. BUD/S class one nine eight. Which were you?"

"Which what?"

"Which BUD/S class?"

Trent stammered: "Uh, well, that was—we weren't supposed to—they told us—"

"Listen, we're lettin' everyone off with a warning. But y'heard what I said?"

Trent clammed up and turned to leave, but jerked to a stop. His coat sleeve puckered from where Holt had caught him in an iron grip. Trent was big, but the wisp of a wince on his face told the story: Holt's grip hurt.

"I need to know you heard me."

"I heard you."

Holt held on for another couple of moments—mainly to demonstrate he *could*—before releasing him. Trent yanked his arm away and stalked back over to his family. Jason hadn't moved, his eyes downcast, his shoulders slumped.

"Get in the fucking car," Trent said.

Jason was six foot seven, but he looked two inches tall.

I've been there, big guy, Holt thought. *Stay strong.*

Mackenzie

The Union Jack hung over the forbidden sanctum.

They had ridden home in sheer misery but bursting with questions. The instant they got home, Jason retreated to his room. The rest of them waited until the shouting downstairs subsided—Trent found a way to blame Corrie for what happened—before they snuck down the hall and did something none of them had done, not even Kaitlyn:

They knocked on his door, lightly, ever so lightly.

"What?"

Hiram gave his sister a look that said *Now what*? She moved aside the Union Jack and opened the door. His room was tucked into the corner, with a slanted ceiling. Posters (mostly Tennessee Vols stuff along with some Cindy Crawfords and Kathy Irelands) covered the wall, as well as another flag: a red cross on a white background. Bookshelves lined the walls, packed to overflowing with mass-market paperbacks and tons of comics, mostly Marvel: *Thor, Daredevil, X-Men.* Three or four video game systems lay jammed under his bed: an Atari 2600, an Intellivision, a Masterminder, and a ColecoVision. He had no less than three old computers: an Apple IIGS jammed under his bed, an Amiga on his work-desk, and something called a ZX Spectrum jammed into the space between the bed and the wall. Sheets of clear plastic lay next to the Atari, covered with weird, arcane maps, drawn in pen. Various sports equipment lay everywhere: a lacrosse stick, a basketball, some old football cleats.

Jason sat on his bed, hugging his knees.

Mac: "Can we sit down?" He shrugged. She whispered to Hiram: "Shut the door."

He did. Hiram and Mac sat, but Kaitlyn picked up the basketball and remained standing.

"How long have you been drawing magic maps, Jase?" she asked.

He finally looked up. "Years. My whole life. I can't think of a time when I didn't know about them. The first one I drew led from my closet in the old house to the backyard. I still have it." He leaned over, fished around in a drawer, and produced a yellowing sheet of broad-ruled composition paper, the kind used to practice penmanship in first and second grade. Jason had drawn a rudimentary map of their old house with one important addition: a thick black line connecting his bedroom with the backyard.

A label read: *SECRET TUNNEL.* His young handwriting was perfect.

Kaitlyn's face bloomed with the astonishment of rediscovered memories. "Can I see?" she asked.

Jason hesitated but handed over the map, whispering, "Careful."

Light shone through the paper, which was as soft as an ancient parchment.

"You drew this when you were when?" Kaitlyn asked, her eyes flicking back and forth.

"Five or six."

Kaitlyn looked up. "I've drawn this map, too." She shook her head. "God, that's why I was having déjà vu earlier. You asked me to draw another map. I remember. I don't know how or why, but I remember. I was in my room, and you told me you could draw better than I could, so I tried to prove you wrong."

Mac: "But how'd you find out about the magic in the first place?"

"I dunno," Jason said before addressing Hiram: "How'd you find out about it?"

Hiram's eyes rose in thought. "I dreamed about it."

Jason nodded. "I think I did, too. Did you see Mr. Pajamas?"

"Who?"

"The guy in the suit with the pajamas on his face."

"Oh, you mean the Plaid Man? Yeah. I dreamed of him. And the traincar."

"Traincar?" Jason asked.

"There's a traincar in the woods somewhere, we think."

Mac: "It's where we think Skelton's hidden them. His victims."

Jason: "Where in the woods is it?"

Hiram shook his head. "We don't know. I only found it once, and I was dreaming. We think there's a way to find it through the maps. We think it's hidden in the Lodges."

"The whats?"

"The Lodges."

Mac: "It's what we call the place between places, where the maps go."

Jason slipped off his bed to the floor, where he picked up a sheet of glassine. It was covered with a maze. He actually smiled. "Oh, you mean the Sneakaround Network. That's what I call it. What you oughta call it."

Hiram's face said, *Why didn't we think of that?* "That's a pretty cool name."

"Thanks. The Plaid Man's a pretty cool name. I think I'm gonna start calling him that."

Hiram was so happy he got flustered. Mac knew the feeling and felt instantly defensive and dubious. She'd had bullies pay her kindnesses before only to have them turn around and hit her with even more cruelty.

"Hey, wait a minute. Hiram, don't say another word," Mac said before addressing Jason: "How'd you know we've been sneaking out?"

Kaitlyn: "Yeah, inquiring minds."

Jason: "You guys are as subtle as a fuckin' tropical storm going outta here. You're lucky Dad's drunk and your mom's sick, or you'd have been busted."

"Um," Hiram began. "Can we turn into cartoons, too?"

Jason was suddenly fixated on the glassine. "That's hard to do. It's harder than creating a dungeon."

"A dungeon?" Mac asked.

"Those floating pathways."

Hiram looked at Jason like he was a superhero.

"You can do *that,* too?"

"Yeah. But it's tricky."

"Oh, okay."

Mac's heart broke at the sight of her brother's disappointment. Kaitlyn redirected the conversation by passing Jason the basketball. He caught it and immediately had it spinning on his index finger.

Kaitlyn: "Hey, big bro—Why'd you draw a tunnel out of here anyway?"

Jason passed the ball back, his brow darkening. "Why do you think?"

"Right," she said. "Howcome you never told me?"

"Why would I?"

Kaitlyn passed the ball back. "Maybe *I* would've liked to tunnel the fuck outta here sometimes."

"Sorry," Jason said, catching it.

Mac: "What made you follow us tonight?"

"I heard you talking about going back out to the farm. And I was curious how you beat the security system."

Hiram: "Uh he—I mean, Trent—uh he keeps the passwords taped under that slide-out thingy in his rolltop."

"Nice. But this house creaks like a motherfucker. I'll show you my Sneakaround Network in here."

Kaitlyn: "There are two Sneakaround Networks?"

"Well, there's just the one," Jason said. "But I kinda pretend like the one in here is part of it. Let me show you." He stood, crossed to the door, and opened it. Placing a finger to his mouth—*shhh!*—he opened his bedroom door and clicked off the hall light. "See? Look at the floor."

A glowing green constellation illuminated across the top floor and down the stairway.

Kaitlyn shook her head. "Holy freakin' hell. I'm always finding those bits of tape."

"Yeah, I stole some from the drama nerds," Jason said. "Glows in the dark. Those are all the safe spots. You can walk there and the floor won't creak." He closed the door and sat. Hiram sat back down, but Mac went and stood next to the flag. Kaitlyn passed the basketball back to Jason.

"You guys are getting good with the maps," he said, tossing the ball back to Kaitlyn. "The way you made Skelton's gate appear was boss. I've tried that kind of thing but never made it work. I'm better at . . . creating things."

Mac fiddled with the flag, frowning. Something about this wasn't right. Didn't add up.

Kaitlyn bounced the basketball between her hands. She addressed Hiram and Mac: "Hey, didn't you guys say Mr. Johnson was really good at creating portals?"

"Yeah," Hiram said.

Mac didn't answer. Something was on the tip of her tongue, taunting her. She lifted the flag, peeked behind it—and stopped breathing.

Jason: "What kind of portals can he make?"

Behind the flag was an airbrushed poster that was completely out of place in Jason's room. The rest of the room screamed "meathead jock," but this poster spoke of childlike wonder. It looked like something Hiram might like, frankly. It also depicted something Mac had seen before, firsthand.

A unicorn.

And not just any unicorn, but a purple one with a golden mane, the very same one she saw at Soddy Farm the night Skelton appeared. Her mind made distant connections and told her a terrible truth. It sounded outlandish, but she had to say it:

"You let Skelton out."

Hiram's Journal

Jason seldom looked scared. He'd looked terrified the night of Soddy Farm, and he sometimes betrayed fear when Trent was laying into him, but by and large, he was stone-faced, his feelings buried deep under the hundred layers of cardiac scar tissue all abused kids build up.

But Mac's words turned him stark white.

"What?" he said.

R-r-r-riiiip! Mac tore down the the white flag, revealing an airbrushed poster of a purple unicorn.

Mac pointed at it. "You drew this. You drew this that night, didn't you? You were drawing a map that night, a map for Skelton. *And it had this unicorn on it.* You were the one who showed him how to draw maps. Weren't you? *Weren't you?"*

Jason's silence was confirmation. The basketball stopped in Kaitlyn's hands. Her expression was smack dab between compassion and rage.

"Why?" she whispered.

Jason grimaced. Swallowed. Coughed. Clenched his eyes shut. A moan rose from his gut and reverberated through his pursed lips. He shook his head once, twice, and kept shaking it slowly. A tear dripped on his lap with an audible *tap.*

This image has lingered with me over the years.

I probably think of it once a week. I *hated* Jason, and yet in that moment, I felt such urgent empathy for him. I also thought of how awfully Trent treated him. He was monstrous to all of us, but Jason got it the worst. It was no excuse for how Jason treated me . . . but that night, I was able to put myself in his shoes for the first, slightest moment. His next words were strangled:

"Far nee."

"What?" Kaitlyn asked.

"Fenny. For Jenny."

"What *about* Jenny?"

"I . . ." he trailed off, his eyes darting this way and that. "He . . . *did* something in my mind."

A hush fell over the room. A whisper from Kaitlyn broke it:

"Jase, what does that mean?"

"I'm going to kill him." We all started in response, but before anyone could speak, he pressed on: "Started writing him fan letters in jail. Told him I was one of those serial killer superfans. I helped him draw his first map. Figured if I could get him out to Soddy Farm, I could take care of him. But he didn't appear where I thought he was gonna—"

It hit him hard as a cannonball: *smash!* The basketball flew bullet-fast, hurled overhand by Kaitlyn at point-blank range. It caromed around the room, knocking over a bedside lamp and casting us all in a horror-movie under-shadow. Jason clutched an instant gusher of a bloody nose, wailing.

But Kaitlyn's wails were louder: "ARE YOU OUTTA YOUR FUCKIN' MIND?!"

The violence summoned the old Jason we all knew and feared. He roared to his feet in a stark-dark rage, but Kaitlyn had another trick up her sleeve: a can of mace.

"Sit the *fuck* back down or I'll empty this whole can into your face, I swear to God."

"Why do you have *mace?*"

"Why don't *you* have mace is the question."

"*What?*"

Mac: "I thought it vanished?"

"Keep a backup mace in your vanity, this bitch always says." To Jason: "Back in your seat, little boy." Jason, his face a red-hot beacon of hatred, sat on his bed, holding his nose. Kaitlyn railed at him: "You're telling us you let a psycho loose so you could try and *kill him* but wound up almost getting all of *us* killed instead. He broke my fucking *arm*, man! And we saw her mom that night. Dawn's friend. Jenny. Her mom. We saw her." She was crying now. "They *had* him, man. They had him locked away, and now he's loose again."

Jason rubbed his nose. "When you say it like that. What was even *your* plan tonight? Go out and get killed? If I hadn't followed you, you'd be worm food."

Mac: "We were gonna try and lead the cops to him."

Jason nodded, wincing. "Not such a shitty idea. Seemed like one of 'em could almost see the magic, right?"

Kzzzzzzt! Our walkie-talkie squelched back in mine and Mac's room. Lee's voice rang through the house:

"Joan Wilder and Ironhide, come in!"

Trent yelled from downstairs: *"Hold it down!"*

Jason waved us away. "Go get it before the stupid fuck comes up here."

"Okay, okay," I said, already running out the door. I was back moments later with the walkie in hand. "Panthro, it's Ironhide. What's up?"

"Ironhide, listen to me: go get your Encyclopedia Brittanica and turn to the page for *circuits*. Oh, and I think we need to break into your old house."

Mackenzie

Hiram jumped up, but Jason stopped him.

"I've got an encyclopedia under my bed." He pulled out the C volume and opened it to *circuits*. "What're we looking for?"

Hiram set the walkie-talkie on the floor and looked over the entry for circuits. Mac leaned over to talk:

"Lee? It's Mackenzie. What's going on?"

"Hello, Mackenzie. I heard some other voices in the room. With whom am I speaking?"

"Uh, the same people as before, Lee. Me, Hiram, and our steps, Kaity and Jason."

Silence. The walkie crackled, but Lee said nothing.

Hiram: "Lee? I've got the page for circuits open." Silence. "Lee?"

"I'm not saying anything while he's there."

Jason frowned, looking put-upon. "What's he talking about? I saved your asses tonight."

"Hiram, have you told them what he said to you? All the things he's said?"

Mac's heart boomed. She knew Jason bullied and abused Hiram. Hell, he bullied and abused just about everyone around him. But the tone of Lee's voice told her the situation had changed, the terrain had shifted. They were barreling toward a reckoning. Mac and Jason had almost come to blows the first night they met; she'd done her best to avoid him—and to help Hiram avoid him—but there was no stopping what happened next.

"What did you say to him?" she asked.

"I don't even know what you're talking about. What did I say?"

"It's nothing," Hiram said. "He didn't say anything."

Mac: "No, I want to hear this. Jason, what did you say to my brother?"

Jason couldn't even remember. He threw up his hands.

"I don't know, *Hiram?* Why don't you *tell* us?"

Hiram's cheeks were quivering.

"Uh I can't—can't remember."

Lee's voice blasted: "He called you Wimpy. He said he'd break your face. At the wedding, he made you feel really stupid for stuttering. He asked if you were deaf, he called you a stupid pussy, he said if you were a cool person, people wouldn't have to repeat themselves all the time. He called you fat. He said it was really hard on everyone to have to deal with you. When you started crying, he said, 'Look at you. One little poke, and we see what you're made of.'"

The only sound was Hiram's sobs.

"Jesus," Kaitlyn said, glaring at Jason. "What the hell is wrong with you?"

Lee pressed on: "He also said—"

Hiram yelled: *"Stop stop stop stop stop stop!"*

Jason, after everything that had happened, everything he had *already* admitted to, actually had the fucking temerity to smirk.

"I didn't say that. You're remembering it wr—"

It crunched this time: *wham!* Silently, Mac had taken up the basketball. She slung it, full-force, into Jason's stupid, smug face. He reeled back.

"JESUS! STOP THROWING BASKETBALLS AT MY FACE!"

Kaitlyn screamed: "How about *you* stop being such an asshole?!"

"Hey, I didn't say *any* of that! The little shit made it—"

A shadow cut him off. Mac stood over him, fists shaking. Jason had her beat by several inches and almost a hundred pounds, but she'd grown a lot over the last few months. She was five-ten and close to one hundred and seventy pounds, almost all of it muscle. She spoke quietly and evenly with a slight quaver that was the product of blood-deep rage, not fear.

"I don't care how big you are. I don't care how tough you are. I don't care how mean you are. If you ever say something like that to my brother again, you will get in a fight. You might kick my ass, but I swear to God Almighty you'll know you'd been in a fight."

Kaitlyn stood next to her. "Ditto what she said. I should mace you on principle."

Jason's eyes narrowed, and for two or three seconds, the energy of violence rose in the room.

But Jason looked both girls in the eye—and shrank.

"Can someone hand me a towel?" he mumbled. "My nose really hurts."

Kaitlyn: "How about you promise you're gonna be cool from now on?"

"I don't even know what that *means!* I don't remember—"

Kaitlyn waved the mace in his face. He recoiled.

"Hey, *hey!* Get that away from me!"

"It's an easy promise, big bro! Repeat after me: 'I Jason Shit-For-Brains Sutton . . .'"

"I, Jason Sutton."

"Jason *Shit-For-Brains* Sutton."

"Jason Shit-For-Brains Sutton."

"Do solemnly swear to be cool to my rad step-sibs from henceforth and forevermore, et cetera, et cetera."

"I swear to be cool. I swear." Silence. Jason really started to cry now. "I'm sorry I said that stuff, Hi. Sorry I was so mean to you. I'm really sorry. I got nothing. No excuse. I'm just really sorry. You deserve better. From anybody. But especially someone who's supposed to be your brother."

Hiram was crying so hard he could barely speak. "Thanks."

Mac sat and hooked an arm around his shoulder, an old, comfortable pose. "Hey, c'mere, kid."

That got a smile out of him: "You're like three years older'n me."

Jason continued: "And I'm sorry for . . . for letting him out. I . . . I just can't stop thinking about Jenny. How it was my fault."

Kaitlyn crossed her arms, gaping. "Your *fault?* Hey, shit-for-brains: this is no one's fault but his, Skelton's. *He's* the monster. But you fucked up. Bad. And now we have to make it right. The cops think he's dead. We gotta fix that."

Silence. Dawn's voice fritzed over the walkie:

"Are folks gettin' maced over there?"

Everyone looked at each other. Their eyes were all red and puffy from crying. Jason was bleeding like hell, and they still had the encyclopedia open to the page for *circuits* for some reason. Laughter welled up quietly at first, then burst forth merrily.

We just might be able to pull this off, Mac thought, though she had no idea what "this" was.

She would in the next few minutes.

Kaitlyn

Lee spoke: "I'd still mace him, to be safe."

Kaitlyn picked up the walkie: "Don't worry, Lee. I just might."

Jason moaned. "Can someone *please* get me a towel?"

Mac was already headed for the door. "I'll get some ice, too."

In that moment, Jason suddenly looked like he was ten again—small and confused. He gingerly touched the sides of his nose, wincing. Kaitlyn sat next to him.

"Here, shit-for-brains. Let me have a look." She checked him out. "I think you're fine. Doesn't look like it's broken."

"You guys don't know what it was like growing up with him."

Kaitlyn smiled wryly. "You had, like, a three-year head start on me, dude, but I got it just as bad. I still do."

Hiram: "Why is he so mean?"

"His mom was a drunk," Kaitlyn said. "Her dad was aggro. I dunno."

Jason added: "Shit rolls downhill, I guess."

Mac returned with a Ziploc full of ice and a towel, which she handed over. Jason lay back.

Kaitlyn prodded him. "Turn over, dumb-ass, or the blood'll run into your lungs."

"Right," he said, flipping over and pressing the ice to his face, which was already blackening.

Mac crossed her arms and leaned against the wall.

"Can I ask—Why have you two never called the cops on him?"

They looked at each other and shrugged.

Kaitlyn: "Uh . . . the rest of our family sucks and I don't wanna wind up gettin' raised by the state?"

"I'd do it just to put the fear of God into him," Mac whispered.

Jason: "It'd only make things worse. Trust me. I still remember the first time I talked back to him. Fucker must've lay in wait a whole week before he cornered me out in the hall. He did a helluva job telling the doctors how a five-year-old got a concussion. I figured the secret tunnel was my ticket outta here. Too bad no one else cares." He sat up. "Are . . . uh, your friends still on?"

The walkie crackled: "These are operatives Vicki Vale and Panthro. My given name is Levi David Dockery. Jason, are you listening?"

Jason smirked and opened his mouth, but Kaitlyn squeezed his forearm and shook her head with a stern look. He accepted the silent rebuke but rolled his eyes. He seemed repentant a moment ago, but the old Jason was still rearing his ugly head.

"Levi, this is Jason. I'm listening. Go ahead."

"Jason, do you know what happens to oathbreakers?"

"Uh . . . no, Lee, I don't."

"They wind up on the Paths of the Dead. You'll be trapped under a mountain with a bunch of other jerks like you, *forever*. I expect you to hold to your oath if I'm going to share this intelligence with you."

Something shone suddenly bright in the hallway. Kaitlyn squinted into its brilliance, her senses slowing dramatically until time stopped. She blinked, stunned at the image: the world was on pause. Everyone in the room was frozen in place. Under the door blazed a sheet of hot-white light. She stood, taking care not to jostle anything, and crossed to the door, which she opened.

Outside was the Grid.

She knew it was "Grid" with a capital G now. Outside the room were nothing but two endless planes of hexagons, their segments and vertices all glowing orange. All was silent until rock music burst forth from every direction, loud enough that she covered her ears. The twin hexagonal planes reconstituted themselves into a pair of music speakers that blasted a triumphant, major-key power-anthem. It was no rock song she'd heard before, and yet its beauty brought tears to her eyes.

She beheld a universe of music.

Turning around, she found everyone in the same poses—everyone except for Jason. He had split in twain, his twin selves vibrating at fantastic speed. Kaitlyn squinted to get a better look at the two Jasons. One bore a cruel expression, laughing at Lee. The other looked like . . . well, he looked like he was in church, or at someone's bedside, or listening intently to someone unburdening themselves.

The other Jason looked reverent.

But the first Jason still existed; the one whose cruelty and bitterness would win out. Kaitlyn lowered her hands and willed the music to play louder and louder. She didn't cover her ears, no matter how much it hurt. She directed all her love and strength at Jason, playing the music of the Grid louder and louder.

Until the first Jason was no more.

The first Jason gone, the second Jason stopped vibrating. The music stopped, too. The only remaining sign of the noise was the encyclopedia: one page stood straight up. Kaitlyn stepped across the room, gently lowered the page, resumed her same position on the bed, and squeezed her brother's forearm. Time resumed its normal pace, but it had somehow backed up a few moments. Lee repeated himself:

"They wind up on the Paths of the Dead. You'll be trapped under a mountain with a bunch of other jerks like you, *forever*. I expect you to hold to your oath if I'm going to share this intelligence with you."

Jason closed his eyes.

Kaitlyn released his forearm, secure in the knowledge that he was on the right path.

Hiram's Journal

"They wind up on the Paths of the Dead. You'll be trapped under a mountain with a bunch of other jerks like you, *forever*. I expect you to hold to your oath if I'm going to share this intelligence with you."

When Lee said those words, I had another of my visions. I could swear that Kaitlyn's eyes glowed a sudden bright orange. Even weirder, she seemed to blink out of existence for a millisecond, like she'd been deleted from a single frame of film. I figured I was imagining things when I noticed that the encyclopedia was open to the entry for Cincinnati.

Something had flipped it back a page. But what?

My confusion was cut short by Jason's voice: "Lee, I swear to you and to everyone here: I will hold to my oath. Thank you for giving me this chance."

His voice had changed, and we all noticed. There wasn't the slightest hint of sarcasm or sneering. He was talking to an eleven-year-old kid on the other side of a He-Man walkie-talkie, but his voice carried the air of solemn pronouncements and ancient rites.

Lee: "Very well. Hiram, are you looking at the page for circuits?"

I flipped the page back. "Yep."

"May I please draw your attention to the example schematic. You should see notations for diodes, switches, relays. You see them?"

"We see 'em."

Dawn: "Just *tell* 'em, Lee!"

"All in good time. Do you see the long circuit along the right side of the schematic?"

Mac: "Yep."

"Do you see the two wavy lines halfway along the circuit?"

My brow creased. "Yeah. What do those mean?"

Jason answered for us: "It's a caesura, or an axis break. I loved those Radio Shack kits when I was little."

Lee, sounding very happy with himself, said: "That is correct. Those wavy lines mean the circuit is actually much longer in reality, but they couldn't show all of it, so they *leave out* part and put in the caesura to tell us they took something out. You know where else they do this?"

Holy shit. "On maps."

"On maps. I wasn't with you the night you saw Mr. Johnson—the real one, not the Plaid Man—but I think I have an explanation for the black water that ties into what we saw tonight at Skelton's hideout. What if Mr. Johnson can draw portals on his own, and on the night of the black water, he was drawing a map—and he inserted a caesura to indicate the great distance between his home and the Smoky Mountains?"

I leaned back. "He can draw portals, so the caesura *became* one."

"The reason why you saw all that black water is because you were walking through a caesura."

"Because he doesn't live in the Smokies anymore. He's really far away now."

"Correct," Lee said.

Jason: "Lee, that's really good. I think you're right. You said the 'real' Mr. Johnson. As opposed to a fake one?"

"Yeah, we wanted to try and find him, so when we were playing *Labyrinth of Terror—*"

Lee: "*Masterminder Home Edutainment Presents Theseus's Labyrinth of Terror—*"

"*Masterminder Home Edutainment Presents Theseus's Labyrinth of Terror,* yes, Lee had the idea to draw our own magic gate to him."

"But it didn't work, did it?" Jason asked.

"No."

"Yeah, same with me. I can't draw gates solo, but I can draw weapons and armor pretty well on my own."

"And unicorns," Mac added.

"And unicorns."

Lee continued: "Right, yes, but more than that: The night of Soddy Farm, Hiram and Mac both drew the cabin, and it worked as a portal. When you saw him that night, you said it looked like an ocean of black water was crashing through the woods. Tonight, Skelton's hideout also appeared to be underwater, but it wasn't as dark."

Mac: "Everything around Skelton's hideout was a *little* wavy tonight. Does that mean his hideout is *kind* of far away?"

Dawn's voice crackled: "That's what we was thinkin'. The farther away someone is, the harder it is to draw a portal to 'em."

Lee: "Point of fact, that was Dawn's epiphany, not mine. Though I appreciate her trying to share the credit."

Jason wore an astonished half-smile. "So Justin—Mr. Johnson—he lives, like, on the other side of the country, and he drew a portal on his own. And it worked. *Wow.*"

Lee: "If we're to somehow draw a portal to Skelton's hideout that a grown-up can see, we need his help."

I was already shaking my head. "He said he doesn't want to draw any more maps."

"Hiram," Mac began quietly. "We may not have any choice but to call him."

"But you said he doesn't need our help," I said, knowing it was a dodge. A deep-seated instinct to protect Justin welled up in me. "He said he wanted to be done with this part of his life."

Lee, quietly: "Admiral, do you remember what I said the night we met Not Justin Johnson?"

"Yeah. You said Justin didn't need our help, but that we need his."

"Do you think we can do this without his help?" Lee asked.

I closed my eyes. "On Christmas Eve, I talked with him, with Mr. Johnson."

Dawn: "We know. You told us."

"I didn't tell you everything. He has a phone, but not a phone line. He was pretending to talk with his mom when he got through to me." I paused. "His mom died."

I opened my eyes.

Mac's eyes had welled up with tears. Kaitlyn had covered her face.

Jason hung his head. "I'm so sorry."

Mac nodded. "I feel awful."

"Gosh, Hiram, that is so sad," Dawn said.

I said: "I didn't tell you because I didn't want to tell one of his secrets."

Mac nodded. "No, you did the right thing."

"He's had such a hard time," I said. "I don't feel right asking any more of him."

"Then we don't," Jason said. "We tell him Skelton's back. And that he's threatened that cop Saturday night. He deserves to know that, right?" Jason looked to me. When I nodded, he continued: "If he wants to help us, great, and if not . . . well, we'll find another way."

Mac: "Shouldn't we tell Auntie Hanna first? I mean, Skelton mentioned

Webb by name."

Lee: "Did he, though? He noticed that Webb has some ability to perceive the magic, but he only said, 'First blood will be Saturday night.'"

Mac: "I think it's a pretty safe bet he's going after Webb. Maybe we should call him now. Skelton could've been lying about Saturday night. I've got Webb's card."

"Do you think he'd believe us? Or your aunt?" Jason said. When Mac didn't answer, he continued: "I think Mr. Johnson's our best shot. He's the only grown-up we know *for sure* who's seen the magic."

Mac touched my hand. "How do you feel about that?"

Something about it didn't feel right. For some reason, my mind kept wandering back to an image I couldn't remember, a book. *The author had a really long, weird name. What was the name? I'd seen it before . . .*

The memory faded. So I nodded.

"Okay," Mac said. "Lee, what did you mean when you said we have to break into our old house?"

"We need to recreate the exact conditions of the admiral's last call with Mr. Johnson. On your old radio, in your walk-in closet."

Jason gave a thumbs-up. "Piece of cake. I've got the keys to our storage room. That's where the radio is." To Mac: "Does your mom have the keys to your old house?"

"Yeah," Mac said. "I think I can sneak 'em out of her purse."

Kaitlyn: "So do we need to, like, rent a U-Haul to move that thing, or what?"

"Nope," Jason said. "We can create a dungeon. Like Skelton's. We'll connect all the locations we need to hit and be done in no time."

We all fell silent. Lee spoke next: "Extraordinary. How is that accomplished?"

"Maps," Jason said with a shrug. "You draw one map with the locations you need connected, then you draw another of your dungeon. That's why I've got these." He held up the sheets of glassine. "Easier to make sure they overlap properly."

Kaitlyn: "And you did this with Skelton? You created a dungeon?"

Jason nodded.

"Shouldn't you, y'know, *stop him?* Can't you tear up your map so he can't sneak around anymore?"

Jason hesitated. His answer was barely audible: "It wouldn't matter."

I asked: "Why not?"

"I already destroyed my map. He must have found someone else to draw one with him."

"Who would do that?"

Jason shrugged. "No idea. But his dungeon isn't going anywhere." He picked up the walkie. "Lee, you said something about drawing a portal to Skelton's hideout that grown-ups can see. What did you mean?"

Lee: "We believe that Skelton has created a *double* of his hideout in the Sneakaround Network. Even if we were to find the exact location of it in the real world—"

"—he'd be hidden in the Sneakaround Network," Jason finished. "Got it."

Lee: "Even worse than him being hidden would be the control he would have over the space."

"What do you mean?" I asked.

"Imagine if you were standing in a space Skelton controlled. It would *look* normal to you, but he might be able to open a pit underneath your feet, or attack you with a magic weapon."

Mac: "So we find his hideout, get Mr. Johnson to draw a doorway into it. Then at least we could *see* his hideout, right?"

Lee nodded. "If my hypothesis is correct."

I added: "*If* Mr. Johnson wants to help us."

Everyone stopped. Dawn asked: "What if he doesn't want to help us? Do y'all think we can make a portal for grown-ups on our own?"

Mac: "One thing at a time. First we need to call Mr. Johnson, and in order to do that, we have to get the radio out of storage and put it back into our old house."

Lee: "And then after that, we have to figure out where Skelton's hideout actually is."

Dawn: "And hope to heck Mr. Johnson will help us draw a doorway into it before Skelton goes after Officer Webb."

Clap, clap, clap, clap. Kaitlyn was giving us her best John Bender slow clap.

"Big bro, aren't you glad you gave the most dangerous killer in America the keys to *Narnia?* Way to go, shit-for-brains." She addressed us all: "Guys, I wanna congratulate everyone for coming up with the most psychonuts-bizarre-ass-stupid-fuckin' plan in the history of psychonuts-bizarre-ass-stupid-fuckin' plans. But even if you were gonna *do* all this, you'd have to figure out where Skelton's hideout is *before* Saturday night. And you can't."

"Yes, we can," Mac said, producing Skelton's note. "Look."

She flipped it over. The back read:

STEMS 'N' STAMENS FLORIST—BLUE RIDGE SUPERMALL

Kaitlyn snatched the card.

"Well, I'll be a son of a *gun.* Nice work, little sis. I guess we're going to the mall tomorrow!"

Kaitlyn

She sat holding her big brother's hand in the quiet night, Kaitlyn did. She hadn't heard him, but after the intensity of the evening's events, she knew he needed some words of love and knocked on his door. His bedside clock read 1:15 a.m. His face was bright and slick with tears, in addition to the shiner they gave him.

"I can't stop thinking about that day," he said. "What I did wrong. What I should've done."

"There was no 'right' way. You should never've been put in that situation."

"Yeah." He cried harder. "I can't believe I said all those things to him. To Hiram."

"I can," Kaitlyn said quietly. "You've said worse to me."

Jason sat up, toweling away tears. His nose still trickled blood.

"I have?"

"You don't even remember, do you?" When he didn't say anything, she continued: "You used to wait for me to get home and yell at me for being fat."

"When was this?"

"I was in seventh grade, you were in tenth, just started to drive. Remember how I used to take the bus because Dad was too busy? They had to drive all the way up here and let me out at the foot of our driveway. I used to walk up the hill staring at the ground, praying you'd still be at school. Because I knew if I saw your car in the driveway, that meant you were home and I was about to get screamed at for being fat. I stared at the ground because I hated staring at your car on that long walk up the hill, knowing I was about to get it. Fucked me up something good."

"I'm so sorry I did that. You were just a kid."

Kaitlyn had summoned an untold amount of empathy for her brother, but his bullshit was still infuriating.

She flared: "We're *still* kids. We're *both* kids. *You are not a grown-up. You are not a father figure. You are a stupid shit-for-brains, just like me.* And you did a *lot* of things to me. I told you *one.* I could sit here and tell you a *thousand.*"

"Got it," he said quietly.

"We can see the Grid now. *I* can see it. And I know we're in a better timeline. It's not your fault Trent's an asshole or that Skelton's a monster. But everything that happens *after* that? That's on you. This is where your destinies diverge. Tonight. There are two timelines. One of 'em ends with you angry and alone and wondering where all your friends went . . . and the other starts tomorrow. At the stupid fucking mall."

Jason lowered his head, steeled himself . . . and smiled. It was a smile she hadn't seen in years; the smile he *used* to smile before Trent destroyed him. Kaitlyn had resigned herself to never seeing that smile again, but it was still in there, lurking around.

He nodded, resolute. "Okay. I'll start now. Thanks for knocking on my door."

"Anytime. Love you, shit-for-brains."

"Love you, too."

*PART FOUR
THE SMOKY MOUNTAINS*

Hiram's Journal

"Man, I'd hate to see the guy who *lost* the fight!"

Trent was hanging on Jason like they were drinking buddies, his massive arm wrapped around his neck tight enough to turn his son's face red. Jason had, to his credit, pulled some minor shenanigans to explain away his asskicking of the previous night, slipping away to school early and blaming his bruised face on a fight. All of us—me, Mac, Kaitlyn, Jason, Trent, and Mom—were walking across a million-acre parking lot toward the Blue Ridge Supermall.

That's right everyone. It was more than a mall . . . it was a supermall.

Trent: "You sure I can't call the headmaster, get that kid thrown outta school?"

He mimed punching someone, prompting Jason to wriggle free.

"Nah, it's fine, Dad."

"You sure I can't get his name outta ya?"

Kaitlyn stepped between them, hooking her arm through Jason's.

"Trust us, Pops, Jason kicked his ass so bad, he's had enough."

She winked at us. All of us, Jason included, stifled a laugh. A spark of joy united us as we approached the mall's front doors. The Blue Ridge Supermall sprawled across the mountainside and three terraced levels. It looked like a massive, neon-glimmering staircase, a bubblegummy idol to capitalism, community, and teenage fun. To the west, the topmost turrets of the Mystery Mansion peeked over the tree line, the tracks of the Wow-Zo roller coaster coiling around it. Farther beyond twinkled Ober Gatlinburg. It was a blazing orange dusk in the Smokies, the weekend was just getting underway, and the sky was the limit.

That's how part of me felt.

Another part of me knew that the eighties were over, which meant a part of my childhood was, too. The mall was still bustling, but one of the stores had already shuttered, an orange FOR RENT sign marking its demise. Next fall was ninth grade. I could get a learner's permit. I'd have to start thinking about college soon—

My thoughts of the future slammed into a roadblock:

Tonight.

Tonight, after the movies, all of us would face off against Lenny Skelton. I was terrified, but we had a powerful and unexpected new ally in our battle: Jason. He knew of mysterious sorceries we all wanted to learn. None of us knew that the night wouldn't unfold the way we expected. We thought had one last evening together to have fun.

Mollified by Kaitlyn's story, Trent pulled out a wad of cash at the front doors. He shoved a bunch in all our hands. I think he gave me fifty bucks; it was the most money I'd ever held in my life.

"Uh what am I supposed to do with this?"

Trent's shrug was like a mountain range shifting. "Eh, go blow it on your video games or your *FernGullys* or whatever. Have fun!" (I'd asked for the cartoon *FernGully: The Last Rainforest* the previous Christmas. When I unwrapped it, Trent looked at me like I was a space alien and asked, "Is that a video game?")

"Ooooh! Thanks! I wanna play *X-Men!*" I started running inside, only for Mom to yell:

"Wait, aren't you meeting your friends?"

Jason smiled. "Yeah, isn't that egghead friend of yours coming? And his . . . uh, sister?"

Kaitlyn's eyes twinkled at the way Jason brought up Dawn, but she kept her mouth shut and pointed inside.

"Hey, I think I see Dawnie now!"

Inside, the eighties were giving way to the nineties. Big hair and distressed denim shared fashion floorspace with neon colors, rimmed-black *Blossom* hats, and stylish, primary-color suits. A few T-shirts bearing the likeness of Susie Schuppe peppered the scene, as the mall sat less than two miles from the park and often caught its overflow. A massive video arcade called Emerald City stood on the right, while on the left was a movie theater playing a murderer's row of 1990's best: *Total Recall, Die Hard 2, Ghost, Gremlins 2: The New Batch,* and our movie of the evening, *Back to the Future III.*

Sandra, Dawn, and Lee were indeed there, Dawn having dolled herself up with lipstick and eyeshadow (and a jumper with tights underneath), while Lee was, for some ungodly reason, wearing neon from head to toe: fluorescent green jams, a neon-orange tie-dye T-shirt with Link from *The Legend of Zelda,* and a kooky pair of asymmetrical sunglasses straight out of *Mannequin.* The look stopped us all cold; we weren't sure if he was putting us on.

"Hi, Lee!" I said.

"Sup." He gave me an upward nod.

Kaitlyn, bless her heart, turned away to stifle a laugh, while Jason tucked his hands in his pockets and smiled warmly.

"Good to see you, Lee. I like your outfit."

"Thanks," Lee said. "Good to see you cats, too."

Kaitlyn turned back and offered Lee a high-five, which he accepted.

"Lookin' good, Joe Cool!" she said, her smile growing when she saw Dawn.

"Dawnie. I like the new face."

In Jason's presence, Dawn was already blushing. "Aw, thanks, Kaity."

Sandra, wearing her green vest like always, nodded at Mom.

"Cor."

"Sandy."

Trent cleared his throat and hooked his thumb at an Applebee's. "Think you kids can stay out of trouble while your mom and I grab some caddy margs?"

Dawn's eyes popped wide. "Oh, yeah! Ain't we gettin' makeovers?"

Mac frowned. "Do we need makeovers?"

"Why Mackenzie Slu—Gresham-Sutton the Third, we *always* need makeovers. C'mon, ladies."

Mom called: "Don't forget! The movie's in an hour, then dinner at the Olive Garden!"

Kaitlyn yelled: *"Dibs on all the breadsticks!"*

"Silly, they give you as many as you want," Dawn said.

"And *they're all mine mwa-ha-ha*—just kidding you can have one. Follow me, ladies!"

They whispered amongst themselves and ran giggling into the mall. Jason nodded his head forward, beckoning us.

"C'mon, guys. I've got an idea."

He strode inside, huge and confident and drawing looks from all the pretty girls. Mom and Trent were already gone, but Sandra lingered.

"Pick you up after the movie?" she asked.

"Yes, Mother. I love you."

Something caught my eye. The purple pin on her vest caught some neon, illuminating its engraving, the letters ETSOSD. I'd seen the icon before, but I couldn't remember where. I was about to ask her when a kind voice interrupted me:

"Hey, buddy!"

It was Jason, standing with Lee and smiling. I turned back to Sandra only to find she'd gone. With a shrug, I ventured into the mall with my friends.

Mackenzie

"And *they're all mine mwa-ha-ha*—just kidding you can have one. Follow me, ladies!"

As soon as the girls were alone, Kaitlyn elbowed Mac and said, "Do we *need* makeovers? You almost blew our cover, girl! We established a code over the walkies last night!"

Mac slapped her forehead. "Oh, sorry!"

Dawn: "I still kinda want a makeover, though."

"Oh, you don't need one," Kaitlyn said to Dawn's visible pleasure. "Mac, you got the card?"

They ran giggling past a Waldenbooks, a Tape World, a Suncoast, a Spencer's Gifts, a No Guarantees, and many more, the three of them all huddled together, peering at Skelton's strange card. They were a trio of competing styles: Mac in her usual denim jacket and jeans, Kaitlyn channeling Alicia Silverstone from *Clueless,* and Dawn in her all-black jumper with trademark pigtails. They were rounding a corner when a shrill laugh broke their conspiratorial reverie.

"She should *not* be wearing that!"

Mac corralled her friends behind a pink-neon-lined fountain that smelled of petrichor. Coming around the corner was a pretty, dark-haired teenage girl wearing her own *Clueless* suit and flanked by a retinue of uniformly dressed toadies. They were pointing and jeering at a girl in line at Orange Julius who was wearing overalls.

"Ugh. Kimber Huntmichael."

Kaitlyn: "More like Cuntmichael."

Dawn prodded Kaitlyn. "Language, Kaity. That ain't nice to say about a girl, don't matter how mean she is."

Mac waved them down another raised pathway lined with polished wood handrails. "C'mon. She's been making my life miserable ever since I tanked dance tryouts."

She ran up the pathway, the other two girls scampering along. Kaitlyn was shaking her head.

"You nailed that audition, girl. Those dumb old biddies weren't ready for your awesomeness."

"Thanks, Kaity," Mac said, peering ahead. "I think it's this way."

They circled around Kimber's gang, dashed past Globe of Gaming, and arrived at a section of the mall whose atmosphere was strangely at odds with its overall eighties/nineties gleam. A single hallway, it was themed to look like a mishmash of turn-of-the-century New Orleans or Victorian London. Wrought-iron railings and fencings ran everywhere. Even the pay phones were old-fashioned handle-and-speaker models. A single lamp-post sat at the entranceway. Hanging from it was a street sign:

MISBEGOTTEN AVENUE, the I in "Misbegotten" a stylized fleur-de-lis.

The hallway dead-ended in a mall entrance/exit. Orange light washed over the hall, giving it a subterranean feel. Dawn almost rolled her ankle on something.

"What the heck?"

It was set of train tracks. They ran the length of Misbegotten Avenue and terminated at the doors. Dark-finished wood paneling fronted every store, including their destination, *STEMS & STAMENS*, the name burn-etched into its wood frontage. A wrought-iron trellis arched over the entrance. The girls crept in to discover a veritable jungle of blossoms and foliage. It felt less like a florist and more like a greenhouse. As they passed under the trellis, a gust of wind kicked through their hair. Somewhere in the distance, a train whistle sounded. They all made eye contact.

"You hear that?" Kaitlyn asked.

Dawn: "I sure did. Last time we heard something like that—"

"Hiram and Lee came smashing out of the cabin at Soddy Farm."

Once inside, the sun seemed to vanish, supplanted by a louring darkness that emanated from the plants themselves. The girls pressed their way inward. Photos and memorabilia lined the walls: photos of dozens of young women, all attended by an ever-changing honor guard of flowers. Mac pushed aside a palm frond to reveal a counter and cash register.

"Hello?"

Rustling from the back heralded the arrival of the shop's proprietor, an old man, bald on top, with a strip of sandy gray hair he'd grown into a ponytail. He wore glasses with yellowing lenses and nose-grips that were green from age. His outfit was a sweat-stained T-shirt and a pendant that depicted a man with his arms raised in celebration.

"Help you girls?" he asked, his nose a moonscape of pockmarks deep enough to give Mac the willies.

Silence. The girls fidgeted before Kaitlyn nudged Mac in the rear.

"Mister, can you tell me who placed this order?"

She handed over the card, which he looked over.

"Hm. Can you tell me where this one went?" he asked.

"Montmarnass Academy. The rotunda."

He looked up and stared at them with solid white eyes.

"Westy highkint ah where to flandon."

Mac instinctively grabbed her friends' arms. "What?"

A blink, and the old man's eyes were normal again.

"I said, was it for a young lady's birthday or somesuch?"

Unblinking, Mac released her friends' arms. "Yeah."

"But you don't know who it's from?"

"Nope."

Dawn: "And we really need to find out."

The old man's eyes narrowed. "Y'all are in *sooo much trouble.* I think I'm gonna run you in. Got you a secret admirer, huh?"

Mac's stomach turned. "Uh . . . yeah. That's exactly it."

He returned the card. "I don't reveal my customers' addresses, young lady, especially not if they're a well-meaning young man trying to show his affections."

Kaitlyn rested her forearms on the counter.

"Hey, uh—sir? This guy might not be so much of a secret admirer as a creep who's stalking her. Can you give us a hand? This guy might be a weirdo."

He took off his glasses, leaving behind two livid red divots in his nose. The density of his eyes shifted.

"*Half*way to *Se*vierville," he said with the cadence of a mild oath, like *Well, I'll be damned.* "You serious about that, young lady?"

Mac nodded. "Might be, yeah."

From under the counter, he produced a phone.

"It's my decision, then, that this is a matter for the authorities. In fact, one of my best buddies is the cap over there, Bo Colquitt, he—"

A wake of fluttering foliage marked the girls' hasty exit.

Hiram's Journal

A neon sign reading Globe of Gaming stood over the gates to Paradise. It was the size of a Blockbuster Video but instead of movies, it was packed with video games for every platform. Atari 2600 titles, including the first round of new games since the Crash of '83, covered one wall. Games for the Nintendo Entertainment System, Sega Master System, and Atari 7800 lined dozens of other shelves, while standees for the Super Nintendo and Sega Genesis promised the next generation of digitized mayhem.

But Jason bypassed all those shelves for the back of the store, where several shelves held a dazzling array of games for personal computers: *King's Quest* and *Police Quest* and *Space Quest* and *The Bard's Tale* and *Might & Magic* and *Wizardry,* as well as games with strange titles like *Zork* and *Akalabeth.* I spotted Kaitlyn's professed favorite game, *Maniac Mansion,* which featured a kooky cast of characters that reminded me of us. One was a big, good-looking blond guy in sunglasses, another was a supergeek (Lee and I would have to duke it out for that one) while another was a punk-rock-looking girl with wild red hair and a spiked collar.

I bet she was Kaitlyn's favorite.

Hands on his hips, Jason was scanning the "new releases" shelf. Lee stood next to him and imitated his stance.

"Hey there, cool cat. You were talkin' about an idea?" Lee asked, sounding stilted.

"Yeah. Or half of one."

"You know what they say, Daddy-O: half of an idea is a hundred percent better than no idea."

Daddy-O? What the heck is wrong with Lee?

Despite of (or because of) Lee's weirdness, Jason smiled. It suited him. "Good call, man. Ah! They've got it!"

He picked up a game called *Ultima VI: The False Prophet*. Lee, no kidding, held his head in joyous shock.

"Oh, my goodness! The new *Ultima!* Oh, my goodness!"

I guess a new *Ultima* game was enough to disrupt Lee's "cool guy" act. Jason crouched and hooked an arm around his shoulder so they could read the game box together. Against all odds, I watched my best friend bond with my former worst enemy. I'd never seen Jason so unironically happy about something. He was gawking at the game with a huge, dorky smile.

Lee shook his head. "Wow! Lord British has really outdone himself."

I inched forward, not wanting to cramp their style.

"Uh what's that? I don't know those games."

Jason waved me over and showed me the box. "Oh, these games have been around since the seventies. Really innovative. Part four was impossible but cool. Loved part five. See these guys?" He indicated an illustration that depicted a knight in shining armor standing triumphant over the prone form of a blood-red gargoyle. The gargoyle cowered, holding its taloned hands up in supplication. "They're threatening the kingdom, but . . ."

He trailed off, his eyes growing distant.

"But what?" I asked.

Jason's gaze drifted to the shelf for Masterminder games. He slowly walked over, as if in a daze, and picked up a title from the new releases:

Masterminder Home Edutainment Presents Labyrinth of Terror: The Dragon of Smoky Mountain.

"Hey guys have you heard of—"

But now Lee and I were the ones freaking out:

"There's a new Labyrinth of Terror *game for the Masterminder?!"* I shouted so loud Jason flinched.

Lee took off his *Mannequin* sunglasses and joined in: "I've been dying to play this! With this, Shigeru Miyamoto's *Legend of Zelda*, and Warren Robinett's classic Atari *Adventure*, we're seeing the birth of a whole new genre: the action RPG."

Jason: "That's really cool, Lee, but I hadn't told you my idea yet." He flipped over the box. *Dragon of Smoky Mountain* took place in two modes:

an overworld and an underworld, both shown on the back of the box. The overworld was a map of a fantasy realm with forests, mountains, and rivers. The hero's house stood on one side, Smoky Mountain on the other.

But it was the underworld, the *dungeon,* that blew my mind.

The hero—a rudimentary stick figure—ran through a series of hallways, his pathway the only light on the screen. One pathway connected to an octagonal intersection, while another dead-ended in a small square room.

Just like Skelton's dungeon.

"Look at this," Jason said, pointing at the *Ultima* box. The spectacular graphics were more detailed than *Smoky Mountain* by several orders of magnitude, but they shared a common visual motif: one scene depicted the heroes exploring a dark area. Their torches lit their path in a series of geometric shapes. I looked up in astonishment and was about to speak when Lee came running over holding Atari *Adventure.*

"I see it, Jason," he said, presenting the box. Just like *Ultima VI* and *Smoky Mountain,* the hero's path in a dungeon was depicted as a series of geometric shapes I recognized.

"Jason, were you tracing the maps from *Adventure* on your sheets of glassine? The ones I saw in your room?"

"Good memory," he said. "Yeah, I couldn't figure out those dungeons, so I mapped 'em out by tracing them off my TV screen. It's where I got the idea to use the glassine to create dungeons in the Sneakaround Network."

Lee: "Jason, if I'm intuiting your intent correctly, you're suggesting that because these games resemble the magical dungeons of the Sneakaround Network, they may hold other clues, as well?"

"I guess that was my idea, yeah, but there's more. I think that these games are sending us a message . . . from the Grid. And I think they're more than messages."

I nodded. "The Mystery Mansion. The last room—it looks like a dungeon in the Sneakaround Network, just like all these games do."

Lee: "Does that mean someone encoded a message into these games? Or that someone encoded a message into an amusement park ride? Who would do such a thing?"

"I don't know," Jason said. "But I don't think we're alone in this. And I do think we need to play these games." He headed for the cash register. "Lee, if it's okay with you and your mom, this one's on me."

"Oh." Lee blushed. "I don't think I should. Maybe you could get it for the admiral, and I could come over sometimes?"

Jason nodded. The Suttons were used to throwing their money around, but *this* Sutton was learning you couldn't always do that.

"Right, got it. That's a much better idea. But you've gotta help me rebuild my Amiga, deal?"

"You, sir, have a deal." Lee offered his hand. Jason squared shoulders with him, bowed slightly, and shook his hand like he was meeting the president. His eyes glistened. I touched his arm.

"Are you okay?"

"I'm fine. I'm just trying to see the Grid a little better."

Suddenly: *"Dudes!"*

We all wheeled toward the door, where Mac, Dawn, and Kaitlyn were running in.

Kaitlyn

The boys were in nerdvana when they arrived, all of them checking out a bunch of games. Jason and Lee were shaking hands for some reason. The image brought joy to Kaitlyn's heart.

"What's up?" Jason asked.

Hiram: "Did you get the address?"

Kaitlyn stopped, winded. "No. And you're not gonna *believe* why. Dawnie, tell him."

"Creepy old guy at the florist stonewalled us, and he—" (she lowered her voice) "—was *possessed*."

Jason: *"What?"*

Kaitlyn looked at both girls. "I wasn't the only one who saw it, right?"

Hiram: "Saw what?"

"His eyes," Mac said. "They turned white for a second. And he said . . . something."

"Gibberish," Dawn said.

Hiram's eyes got wide. "Itza Linda? Gedda Brusha?"

Everyone stared at him.

"Hiram, are you okay?" Mac asked.

"Yeah, no, I'm fine. Did the flower guy say any of those things? That's what I keep hearing in my dreams."

"Oh," Kaitlyn said. "No, he said something about the west? 'Western hijinks' or something."

Dawn added: "And something about landing?"

"Regardless, it was *super* fuckin' weird," Kaitlyn said.

Mac: "And he wouldn't give us the address."

Kaitlyn: "So we told him Mac was being stalked—"

Dawn: "And he said it was—" (she lowered her voice to imitate him) "—'a matter for the cops.' He was gonna call that asshole Colquitt!"

Another voice: "Can you guys hold it down, please?"

It was a Globe of Gaming employee doing his best Eddie Deezen impression: thick glasses, bad haircut, and a nasal voice. Kaitlyn's reaction was instinctive and instant:

"Why don't *you* hold it down, Melvin?"

The kid blanched at the insult. Lee crossed his arms. His voice was clarion-clear:

"Hey. Don't call him that. We don't call people names."

Lee's hyper-neon outfit made him look like a living traffic pylon. Normally, Kaitlyn would be razzing him about it, but his use of the word "we" derailed her. *He meant me. He's including me. I'm a part of the "we"!* She also noticed the games: *Ultima VI, The Dragon of Smoky Mountain,* and *Atari Adventure.*

"Holy fucking shit," she whispered before addressing the employee: "Um, sorry for being a bitch. And sorry for calling you a Melvin. I don't know if you know it, but you're really cute. We'll hold it down."

The employee blushed and smiled a dimply-delighted smile. "Oh. Uh, thanks. Jeez. Let me know if you need anything."

Kaitlyn snatched the games. "We need to *get. These. Games.*"

"I gotta play more nerd shit," Kaitlyn said.

They were stationed by a mall fountain, some sitting on a bench, others sitting on the fountain wall. Jason stood over everyone, his foot propped on the bench. Pink and blue neon splashed across everything, while the food court chattered nearby and sent over the decadent aromas of Sbarro pizza, Wetzel's pretzels, Häagen Dazs ice cream, and whatever the hell Petro's was.

The boys explained their hypothesis that the Grid—or whatever controlled the Grid—was encoding messages into games and books and theme park rides—and dreams. Hiram recounted how his dad loved *A Wrinkle in Time* and wanted to name him after Buckaroo Banzai.

"Both are stories about people traveling a long way using magic or super-science."

The stories—and connections—kept coming. Mac revealed her visions: seeing the Grid at school and seeing that library in the Mystery Mansion. Hiram noted that he'd seen the Plaid Man in the same place where Mac had seen her library. Kaitlyn told them about her vision of the Grid and its beautiful rock music. Dawn told them about the observatory, and Lee described his plasma-cannon-outfitted cottage.

All eyes turned to Jason.

"Was that you, big bro?" Kaitlyn asked.

Hiram: "Yeah, these all sound like those magic things you could make inside the Sneakaround Network."

He shook his head. "My power constructs? Nope. I followed you guys sometimes, but I can't create those in the real world. That must've been the Grid talking."

Mac nodded. "Got it. Well, if we're going to pull this off, we'll need all the help we can get." She addressed Jason: "We're gonna have to draw a gate that leads in here, to Misbegotten Avenue."

She pointed at the strange hallway, which lay a few dozen yards away.

Dawn: "There's even a fleur-de-lis we can use as a symbol for the keystone."

Lee: "That's incredibly well conceived, sister."

Dawn: "Yeah, I figured our keystone symbols can go on being normal stuff and not magic spells that make us wanna kill each other."

Kaitlyn whooped with laughter to Dawn's delight. The noise drew some looks from the folks in the food court. The gang clustered closer, slightly embarrassed but smiling.

"Sorry for being a spaz," Kaitlyn said. "That was a good one, Dawnie."

Jason leaned closer. "Got it. So we're busting into that flower joint?"

"That's right," Dawn said. "Our plan to call Mr. Johnson just got a little more heist-y."

Mac: "Are we going to do this all tonight?"

Dawn: "I think we gotta. Skelton said he was going after Webb tomorrow night."

Lee raised a finger. "Dudes, I maintain that his words were vague, but we must proceed as if he was telling the truth. Admiral, what do you think?"

Hiram cocked an eyebrow at Lee's use of the word "dudes," but simply said: "Yeah. We gotta do it tonight."

Kaitlyn: "Looks like I'm gonna have to grind my Ritalin into your pasta tonight, kids."

"Please do not do that," Mac said.

"Oh, I'm totally kidding." She mouthed to Hiram and Lee *I'm not kidding.* Everyone giggled—except for Jason. Blood had drained from his sunken cheeks. Kaitlyn hadn't noticed until now, but he'd lost weight over the past few months; an unhealthy amount.

Hiram: "But what about what Skelton said? That stuff about him and the Plaid Man 'coming together'?"

Mac touched his shoulder. "One thing at a time. Let's make sure he gets busted."

Hiram nodded. "So how's this gonna work?"

"We'll build a Smoky Mountain."

No one expected it to come from her, but come from Kaitlyn it did. Everyone looked at her and smiled.

"Cool name," Hiram said.

"Much better than calling them labyrinths of doom," Lee said.

A little bit of color returned to Jason's cheeks. "Yeah. And it's way better than 'dungeon.'"

Mac: "So we're doing this? We're gonna build our own dungeon—I mean, Smoky Mountain—that connects all these locations: the mall, the storage room, and our old house?"

"Yep," Jason said, his voice shaking. "We'll need the make the call first and hope we can get to Skelton's house in time. Once we get the address, we can add a pathway to his hideout from our Smoky Mountain."

Hiram: "We'll need better weapons."

Mac: "And armor."

Lee: "And our armaments must be immune to *Skelton's* magic. Jason, I suspect you have the ability to craft such wonders?"

His face turned white again. "Guys, this is gonna be dangerous. I think—"

A shrill voice cut him off:

"Hey there, Rocky Horror!"

Screeches of laughter shattered their mood. To everyone's dismay, it was Kimber Huntmichael and her crew, all of them sipping Orange Julius and shooting nasty looks as they strutted over. They stopped a few yards away and arrayed themselves around a food court table like a cruel bunch of Charlie's Angels.

"Oh, Mackenzie, I spoke with Ms. Olivia, and she said she'll give you another tryout."

Kaitlyn was about to blurt a comeback, but she stopped when she saw the look on Mac's face. It was one of naked, desperate hope. Mac laid bare her soul in front of everyone, her tough-girl defenses undone with one sleazy lie.

"Really?" she asked quietly.

"Yeah . . . if you drop about fifty pounds, cow!"

They all cackled. Mac's face scrunched up in advance of tears, but suddenly, arms engulfed her. Hiram hugged her. Jason hugged her. Lee hugged her. Dawn hugged her.

But Kaitlyn didn't.

No, she was already marching across the way, where Kimber and her mean-girl friends were still cackling and jabbing fingers at her.

"Oh, look!" Kimber cooed. "Daddy's little punching bag! Nice makeup on that shiner, slut!"

Splooooosh! It happened in an instant upsplash of glittering orange smoothie. Kaitlyn smacked the drink right into her smug-smirking face.

Sputtering mad, Kimber said: "You fucking—"

Kaitlyn shoved her in the chest and sent her flying back into the table, which toppled over and brought some of her toadies down, too. Her face a rictus of rage, Kimber tried to stand, only to slip 'n' splatter floorward in her Orange Julius. Kaitlyn advanced on her.

"I'd make you apologize, but she doesn't need an apology. Mac's too fucking cool for the likes of you. And y'know what else? I'm not a slut. I'm a *huge* slut. And? *And?* Y'know what *else?* I've seen the Grid, motherfuckers. We're gonna make a Smoky Mountain, call our friend, bust a bad guy, and while we're there, we might even kill the Humungus."

Lee called: "The Minotaur!"

"*Thank* you, Lee. Yes, the Minotaur."

"The Humungus was the villain in—"

"—in the *Road Warrior*, thank you, Lee!" She pulled a can of mace and addressed the mean girls: "'Cause y'see, the Minotaur is the big bad in *Masterminder Home Edutainment Presents Theseus's Labyrinth of Terror*. He's got a plaid face and a shit attitude, and when we find him, I'm gonna empty this can of mace right into his stupid plaid snout." She'd built up a head of steam. The mean girls were gog-eyed. Some folks in the food court moved tables. "If you ever bother my girl Mackenzie Sluttington Gresham-Sutton the Third Esquire again, you're gonna hear from me."

Hiram stepped forward. "And me."

Lee stepped forward. "And me."

Dawn stepped forward. "And me."

Jason stepped forward. His voice was hushed and hoarse: "And me."

Kaitlyn hooked her thumb at them. "You're gonna hear from the Sneakaround Gang. Toodles, bitches. I'm gonna go eat an entire basket of breadsticks. *And then belch.*"

She wheeled and ran to meet her friends, her family, her crew, her gang, who set off at a brisk jog to the movie theater, laughing and hugging each other all the way.

Dawn: "I take it back. She *is* a See You Next Tuesday. Sorry, Lee."

"For her, I think I can make an exception."

Everyone laughed—except Jason, who lagged behind, hands in his pockets.

Hiram's Journal

The movies were the closest I'd ever get to church. We all crowded into the cushy pews with our sacraments (popcorn and candy and Cokes), laughing and smiling. Even Trent seemed jovial; the caddy margs must've taken the edge off. Mom had allowed me and Mac a small box of popcorn and Milk Duds (to share, of course), while the other kids had loaded themselves down with Twizzlers, Whoppers, Peanut M&Ms, and more. Trent was inhaling a hot dog (which he held, I shit you not, like a hammer). Kaitlyn had opted for a Mr. Pibb and Hot Tamales combo. Only Jason wasn't snacking.

"Hey big bro," Kaitlyn said, elbowing him. "Aren't you getting anything?"

Trent leaned over: "Gotta keep up your strength for next year's football team, fella! Chow down!"

He shook his head and took a seat at the end of our group and next to Mom, who sat next to Sandra, Lee, and Dawn, followed by Kaitlyn, Mac, and me. The pre-show music was a succession of movie scores. Mac and I were settling in to play our game of "guess the score" when someone tapped me.

"Hiram?"

Sound vanished. Time slowed. I recognized her voice immediately.

Christy Hodges.

She'd somehow gotten even prettier in the last few months. Her black hair was in a French braid that rested on her shoulder. A blue vinyl jacket was zipped up to her neck. Mac was prodding me.

"She said hi."

"Uh hi, um . . ."

"Christy?" Christy said, smiling.

"Christy, right."

"I can't believe you didn't remember my name!"

Of course I remembered her name. I had been stuttering.

"Gonna get me another!" Trent said, popping up. He'd somehow finished his jumbo-sized hot dog in less than thirty seconds. "Now, gang, we've got *perfect* seats, so don't move!" He headed up the aisle. I looked for an escape route, but I had no choice but to do the thing I most feared:

Talk to a girl.

Yep, nothing scared me more than girls; not Skelton, not the Plaid Man, not Trent, or Colquitt. I didn't know what to say, so I fell back on an old standby: apologizing for my presence.

"Oh, uh . . . uh sorry."

"Aw, it's okay. How have you been? Heard you're up at the fancy school now."

"Uh fine, thanks. The work's really hard."

"Yeah, I heard you were failing out."

I was half mortified, half flattered: "You . . . *heard* something about me?"

Yet another new voice: "Hey, Hiram!"

Only this wasn't a voice but *voices,* the voices of two men who had called out to me simultaneously. At the end of the aisle stood both Mr. Tucker, my old homeroom teacher, and, of all people, Dr. Eldridge, my therapist. They wore their usual attire like uniforms: Tucker in one of his many purple flannels, Dr. Eldridge in his tweed coat, though a pair of horn-rimmed glasses had joined the ensemble.

Huh, I didn't know they were friends, I thought; naively, of course.

Mom said: "Oh hello, Bill! And ...?"

Mr. Tucker extended his hand. "Greg Tucker. I used to have Hiram for homeroom."

Mom smiled in recognition. "Oh, my goodness. Of course. So sorry I didn't remember you."

"No problem," he said. "It's been a while." He indicated the theater row. "So sorry to bother you, but would you mind scooting down a seat?"

The theater was already packed. There were two available seats on our row: one at the end . . . and one between me and Christy. Mom stood up instantly.

"Of course, no problem." She waved to us. "Can we all scoot down a seat?"

All of us blanched; not because we didn't want to sit next to them, but because we all knew how Trent would react when he got back and saw we'd moved seats against his orders. I, of course, was terrified to sit next to Christy.

Jason spoke first: "I don't think that's a good idea. Can't they split up?"

"I think they want to sit together, honey," Mom whispered.

Jason's eyebrows rose as he did the math. "Oh, I get it." He chewed on silent words. "But I don't we should."

Dr. Eldridge frowned and sized up Jason, who was wearing his usual combo: a Tennessee Volunteers warm-up, Brooks Brothers button-down, jeans, and Air Jordans. They'd never met until tonight.

"Why not?" Dr. Eldridge asked. "It's one seat."

Some folks had started staring. A few of them smirked, sharing whispers and pointing at the two men. Mom was already blushing. She was a weird pain in the ass, yes, but not a bigot.

"Honey," she said, glowering at Jason. "It's not a big deal, and they'd really like to sit together."

Jason sat silent, not looking at the men, who were both getting angrier.

"Are you saying you don't want to sit next to us?" Mr. Tucker asked, barely audible. I wanted to intervene, to explain to them that Jason was changing for the better and our dad was an asshole . . . but I couldn't, and I also couldn't blame them for getting pissed. Looking back, I know now that they had to put up with so much bullshit every day.

If they only knew.

Jason, for his part, was staring into space, his eyes getting wider and wider.

Jason

He was looking into the face of evil.

He stood in the emergency exit, casually holding it open. He could've been standing on the front porch to his own house, letting the breeze in. He wore a plaid flannel—the same pattern as Mr. Pajamas—and jeans. He'd replaced his usual glass eye with a more realistic-looking one, and he'd spackled over his scars with stage makeup.

He looked like anybody. He looked like nobody.

If anyone had taken a closer look, they might've thought he *looked* like him, but they would've dismissed it as a trick of the light. After all, hadn't he died in that fire?

Jason scanned the crowd. No one even noticed the guy standing in the doorway. Was he even there?

His question was answered when a couple of kids came sneaking in through the emergency exit, an old gag Jason used to pull to sneak into R-rated movies or skip out on paying. They gave the face of evil a smile and a wave.

"Thanks, dude!" one of them called.

And he nodded to them, the face of evil did, like he was just another patron. Jason's breath was a high-pitched wheeze, his throat cinched tight as a pinprick.

That's when the face of evil waved.

He gave Jason a finger-dancing wave, like he was adding the final flourish to a piano concerto.

"Honey?"

She was a million miles away, his step-mother, the sweet, strange woman who married his monster of a father. Trent met her when his company sent him to deliver a donation to her small elementary school. She was four years a widow, him two years a widower. His dad could charm the scales off a snake, but he had no need of those skills with her. She insinuated herself into their lives in a matter of days. She was nothing like Mom, like Marie. Marie laughed readily and could put the skids on Dad's worst impulses.

Marie actually knew Dad in the *before* times; before he turned into a monster.

Once, Marie found Jason on the floor of their foyer, covered in glass. Trent was asleep somewhere, his rage sated. Jason asked her if he was always like this. She said there had been a time when he never even raised his voice, not once, not to anybody.

But he changed.

Marie died before she could tell Jason why.

It was one of those family mysteries lost to the storms of time. He could never ask his dad why he changed, although Jason suspected there was no good reason why; as much as it pained him, he suspected that his father was simply born bad, and after a time, bad blood always will out.

"Honey?" his step-mother asked. "Are you all right?"

Jason's vision was a shimmering blur. He blinked away tears and shook his head clear.

The face of evil was gone.

He took his step-mother's hand and smiled, his eyes rimmed with red. The gesture was awkward, what with him sitting and her standing. He stood and smiled.

"I'm fine, Mom."

She gave a faint sigh. He knew she liked it when he called her "Mom." The two men turned to leave, but Jason waved them down.

"Sorry for being so rude, guys," he said before turning to the Sneakaround Gang. "Can you all scoot down one?"

Hiram looked like he'd asked him to take a dive off a thousand-foot cliff, but he moved down nevertheless. The two men, smiling, settled into their seats. Jason sat back down next to his sister, who was so brave and tough, and bumped shoulders with her.

"Love you, Kaity."

She frowned at him, still a little red-faced from the fracas earlier.

"Did you hit your head?" she asked curtly. "You look weird."

"Nah, I'm fine. I just wanted to say I love you."

"I love you, too, shit-for-brains," she said with a smile, then turned her attention to Mac, who had asked her something. Jason beheld them, his new friends, his new family, his new gang. His chest swelled. He realized he had been clenching his jaw and forced himself to relax.

Bad blood always will out?

Not tonight it won't.

Dawn

"Can you guys scoot down one?"

Everyone stood and moved down a spot. Dawn leaned in to whisper to Lee:

"I meant to ask, what's with the outfit?"

Lee shielded his mouth with the back of his hand: "I'm trying to fool everyone."

"Fool everyone how?"

"Into thinking I'm cool."

Dawn gave him a sad, loving look.

"Lee, you *are* cool."

"No, I'm not. It's okay. You are, though, and I figured, 'She plays pretend, maybe I can, too.'"

"Pretend? What're you talking about? How do I play pretend?"

"You act like you're not smart when you are."

She nodded. "I guess that's true, but let me show you something." She called: "Hey, guys! Do you think Lee is cool?"

Everyone was buried in one conversation or another, but all of them stopped and answered instantly:

Mac: "Of course."

Kaitlyn: "What kinda question is that? He's the coolest. Gimme a hard one next time."

Hiram: "Uh darn right."

Jason leaned forward: "Don't let anyone tell you different."

The two moms remained silent but watched their kids heap praise on Lee with kind smiles. Sandra touched her nose, pointed at him, and mouthed *Love you.*"

Lee looked like he could fly.

"Thank you, sister."

Hiram's Journal

"Can you guys scoot down one?"

Jason looked like he'd seen a ghost, but I was too busy shitting my pants to worry about him. We all moved down. Christy smiled as I sat.

"Mind if I sit here?"

"Looks like you've got to."

"Just out of curiosity, how'd you hear I was flunking out of Montmarnass?" She gave me an eyebrow-raised smirk, scoffed, and pointed at Lee. I blushed and whispered: "Lee? He said I was failing out?"

"He said you wanted to come back to Polk so you could sit next to me."

My response was instant and truthful: "I didn't say that."

Her face fell. She whined: "You didn't? Why didn't you want to sit with me?"

I looked around the theater, wishing I could be anywhere else. I was enthralled to be next to her while also humiliated for reasons I couldn't describe. Dimly, I registered that Mac was eavesdropping on us. Christy shrugged out of her vinyl coat—revealing a plaid dress underneath. My stuttering ratcheted up to maximum.

"Uh uh *haaave* you been wearing that this whole time?"

She snickered at me.

"Aw, you're cute. You should come out of your shell more often." Her tone dropped into a minor key: "You still drawing those maps?"

How did she remember that?

"What maps?"

"Those treasure maps. I seen you drawin' 'em in geometry." She giggled. "Didja bury treasure somewhere?"

Mackenzie

I don't like how she's treating Hiram.

She felt it, the contempt, sharp and clear and as soon as Christy asked her baby brother why he didn't want to sit with her. Mac knew the trick—she'd seen Becky pull it at parties. A guy they liked would arrive. She'd wait for him to come around. When he did, they'd ask, "Why didn't you come over and say hi?" It was a quick and easy way for her to put a guy back on his heels.

Come to think of it, Mac didn't like Becky that much.

But she had other worries. After Dad died, there was so much she had to keep track of, and tonight, she had to watch out for her whole gang, including Kaitlyn, whom she prodded.

Mac asked: "Hey, you all right?"

"Yeah. Why? Do I not *look* all right?" Kaitlyn caught herself. "Sorry. I'm still keyed up after our face-off with Kimber See-You-Next-Tuesday-Michael."

"I . . . Listen, I'm glad you did what you did . . . I mean, I'm not saying I'm mad about it, but . . . uh, has anyone ever said you might have some anger issues?"

"Anger issues?" She cocked an eyebrow. "You sure you wanna be asking me about anger issues after you almost picked a fight with my brother?"

"That's a fair point, but—" Giggles derailed Mac's response; her mom and Sandra were leaning close and sharing secrets. Light glinted off Sandra's triangular pin; Mac frowned—*Where have I seen the letters ETSOSD before? Is that a support group? Is Dawn's mom in AA or something?*

Kaitlyn was talking: "—protective of you."

"Huh?"

"I was saying I've gotten really protective of you guys. I'll never let you fall."

Mac stopped puzzling over Sandra's pin to absorb Kaitlyn's words, as well as the look on her face; her features were usually sharp—she was pretty in a severe way—but they'd softened in tandem with her admission, her eyes glowing with kindness. Mac touched her hand.

"Thank you for saying that. But I'm two years behind you. You'll be outta here soon. I'm not gonna be able to run off to college so fast. And I can fight my own fights."

Dawn called to everyone: "Hey, guys! Do you think Lee is cool?"

The gang answered in the resounding affirmative to Lee's visible happiness. At the same time, Trent arrived back with two more hot dogs and the biggest Coke Mac had ever seen.

Kaitlyn smiled. "Okay. I promise not to mace Kimber. Too much."

Mac: "Thanks, and . . . thanks for sticking up for me." She leaned in and whispered: "No one's ever stuck up for me before. For either of us."

"Really?" Kaitlyn asked with some surprise. "Not even your Mom?"

Mac shook her head. "Nope."

"Well, those days are fuckin' *over*. Wanna know something else? I don't think I'm going to college."

"No kidding? Why not?"

Another voice, bright and happy, shot across the room:

"Hi, Gresh!"

Mac's emotions quantum-leaped from delighted to despondent in a heartbreaking instant. It was sweet Dave Shuler who had called to her, of course, standing on the far side of the theater with his arms full of popcorn and candy . . . and a cute girl. She wore a neon-red pencil skirt with a denim jacket, her hair scrunchied into a side-pony.

It was Becky, of course.

Mac forced herself to smile and wave back. Kaitlyn watched the exchange and was about to speak when Mac's mom leaned over.

"It's all right, sweetie. You're too busy for him anyway."

Trent frowned at the two men before visibly counting the seats with his fingertip. The lights lowered, sparking cheers across the theater. Hiram muttered something, while their mom went back to whispering with Sandra. Kaitlyn prodded her.

"You're a thousand times cooler than she is."

"Oh, I know," Mac said. "He can date who he likes, but . . ."

"Why'd it have to be her?"

Mac nodded and smiled wryly.

Trent boomed: "Hey! What happened?"

Kaitlyn rolled her eyes. "Ugh."

Hiram's Journal

"Those treasure maps. I seen you drawin' 'em in geometry." She giggled. "Didja bury treasure somewhere?"

Dr. Eldridge, my therapist, rarely gave me advice. He was sphinx-like, spending most of our sessions nodding, asking me how I felt, and dodging questions.

But he *did* give me one piece of advice: trust my gut.

"If something doesn't feel right to you, Hiram, there's a good chance it's not right."

I hadn't noticed until this moment, but Christy wasn't sitting with anyone. Next to her was an empty seat, followed by another family that could've been hers, I guess, but why would they leave an empty seat? I was about to ask her when Dawn called:

"Hey, guys! Do you think Lee is cool?"

As often happened, I wanted to speak first, but my stutter bumped me back a few spaces in the queue, behind Mac and Kaitlyn.

"Uh darn right," I said, turning back to find Christy gone. I looked around the theater and found no sign of her. Leaning over, I tapped the next person down the row, a middle-aged couple. "Excuse me, Mrs. Hodges?"

She looked over and smiled. "I'm sorry, dear?"

"Are you Christy's Mom?"

Her brow creased. "I don't know any Christy, young man. Do you need help?"

I leaned back, my skin crackling cold.

"Uh no, thank you, ma'am."

She smiled and returned to her evening. Voices chattered all around me. Were they friends? Foes? Scanning the theater turned up no clues, except for the emergency exit door, which swung open and shut. Had Christy snuck out that way?

Was that even Christy?

"Hi, Gresh!"

It was that Dave Shuler guy, on a date with one of Mac's old Polk friends. Couldn't remember her name. I wanted to tell Mac about what happened, but she was busy whispering with Kaitlyn while dumb-ass Trent had returned with a shitload of food. Mom whispered something to Mac while Trent was counting the seats in the row. The lights lowered.

"Oh, thank God," I muttered, hoping Trent wouldn't cause a scene.

No such luck: "Hey! What happened?"

Corrie looked over. "What is it, sweetie?"

"We had perfect seats! I went out for two minutes, and we moved halfway down the goddamn row!"

Trailers started playing. Someone yelled, "Sit down, man!"

Trent ignored him: "Why'd you guys move down? I told you not to move!"

Dr. Eldridge half stood: "Mr. Sutton? They moved down so we could sit together."

"Am I talking to you?" Trent shouted, hunching over, his pupils a pair of flickering rubies.

"Oh, my God," Kaitlyn said.

Mac leaned over and whispered to Lee and Dawn: "I'm so sorry."

Jason looked like he was trying to melt into his chair. Mom touched Trent's hand.

"Can you lower your voice?"

Kaitlyn: "Dad, just sit down. It's not a big deal."

"I said *not to move!*"

"We moved *one* seat," Kaitlyn yelled. "Who cares?"

From the back: *"Down in front, asshole!"*

Animated words spilled across the screen: *BLUE RIDGE SUPERMALL PRESENTS: A WEEKEND OF NIGHTMARES,* followed by a booming narrator: *"We're celebrating Halloween early at Blue Ridge Supermall with a marathon of everyone's favorite villain: Freddy Krueger!"*

A supercut of Freddy's greatest hits splattered across the screen. Freddy turned a kid into a cockroach, another kid into a meatball. In part three, *Dream Warriors,* a group of kids fought back, including a punk-looking girl with spiked hair and a nerdy kid who turned himself into a wizard.

Huh. Reminds me of Maniac Mansion, I thought.

The projection of Freddy's sweater cast red-and-gray stripes across Trent's face.

"Get up!" he yelled at the two men.

"The movie's starting," Mr. Tucker said. "We're already sitting here."

"Not anymore you're not."

Dr. Eldridge got to his feet. He was smaller than Trent—most everyone was—but he was stocky.

"Excuse me?"

From the back: *"Kick his ass, man!"*

Another guy: *"Sit the fuck down!"*

Kaitlyn: "Dad. The movie's starting. It's no big deal. We can see just fine."

Mom hissed: "Would you *please just sit.*"

Somehow, that got him to back down. Fuming, Trent jostled his way past the the two men and took his seat.

"Halfway down the goddamn row," he muttered loud enough for everyone to hear.

Sandra whispered: "Cor, would you like to step outside, get some air?"

Mom said nothing, but Trent sure did:

"No, she's fine where she is."

Dr. Eldridge muttered something to his date; something I couldn't make out:

"Fleed so far."

I grimly nodded to myself. *I sure would like to flee from this asshole.* All of us sank into our seats, the heat of Trent's casual cruelty having melted us. All of us had been looking forward to this one last respite before tonight's battle royale, and he'd ruined it, like he ruined everything.

But then the movie started.

The familiar, magical chimes of Alan Silvestri's score played, followed by a title card:

SATURDAY NOVEMBER 5, 1955 — 10:03 p.m.

All was well with the world . . . at least for those couple of hours. I'd been dying to see what happened to Marty after he got trapped in 1955. What unfolded was one of my favorite childhood memories. As I got older, I came to appreciate *Back to the Future Part II* and its middle-chapter-in-a-trilogy mayhem. Ditto for *The Empire Strikes Back.* But as a kid, I liked emotional payoff. I liked closure.

I liked endings.

This story is about the end of one family and the beginning of another.

I didn't know it, but my family was going to end sooner than I thought.

Dawn

Usually, the Dockerys wouldn't shut up. On any other night, a trip back from the mall would've filled Sandra's Volvo with happy chattering as they traded tales of the evening's adventures. After dinner that Saturday night, they rode in silence, Lee in shotgun with Dawn stretched out in the back.

"Can we turn on some music?" Dawn asked.

Sandra flipped on the radio and cycled through stations. A newscast fritzed in and out:

"—reports of a mysterious figure menacing a Pigeon Forge neighborhood—"

Lee and Dawn looked at each other in alarm as their mom landed on a rock station that was just putting on Phil Collins's "Another Day in Paradise." The kids realized she was crying.

"Mom? Are you okay?"

"I'm sorry. I hate it when I cry around you two. I just don't understand why she married that sonofabitch, sorry for swearing."

Mackenzie

Once again—and like it often was—the truck was a prison. It was a prison of Trent's own making, his rancid rage poisoning everything. They rode in silence, the lot of them: Corrie up front, with Jason, Mac, and Hiram in the back, and Kaitlyn in the boot.

Trent slammed the horn and screamed.

"You guys moved halfway down the fucking row! Just admit it!" He yelled loud enough to sting their ears, but no one answered. He ranted on: "I asked you a question, and I expect a prompt and honest answer to it!"

Mac mumbled: "It was one seat, Dad."

Trent's red eyes flashed in the rear-view mirror: "*Oh!* Ms. Uppity finally fucking decides I'm good enough to call Dad, but she fucks it up with a *bald-faced lie.* We were right in the middle, perfect seats, no obstructions, and you just rolled over when some bullies told you to move. And then when that prissy little shit mouthed off at me, *I got no backup from my own fucking family—*"

Mac stared at her mom, who sat in silence and let Trent scream and scream.

Why doesn't she say anything? Why did she marry this monster?

Jason took Mac's hand. Another hand slid over her shoulder, Kaitlyn's from the back, and squeezed. In turn, Mac took Hiram's hand. Jason squeezed her hand and mouthed, *I'm sorry.*

Hiram's Journal

He didn't stop screaming the whole way home. He didn't stop screaming all the way up our driveway. He didn't stop screaming as we marched into his gigantic, stupid fucking house.

"Well, hey — it's fine. It's FINE. This is how it is now. You don't have my back, I won't have yours. Next time you need my help, hit the bricks, pal, and fuck you all."

Mom sighed. "Can we go to bed, honey?"

It happened in a few flashes of motion. He wrenched her arm behind her back and shoved her against the wall. Mom made sounds in her chest but couldn't speak. Reflexively, Mac hugged me, while Jason and Kaitlyn stood in wide-eyed silence. Trent ground his teeth.

"Okay, okay, okay. Calm down, calm down. You're sick, remember?"

Lava flowed in my veins, I was so angry. My eyes bugged out. I leaned back and forth rapidly, juking, like I was head-faking my dad. I must've looked ridiculous, but it was where my indecision trapped me. I wanted to attack him. I wanted to punch him and kick him and pound on him. I wanted to gouge his eyes out.

But I was too scared. He was so big and so strong.

So I did nothing.

I think about this moment a lot, every detail recorded in one-hundred-percent, high-definition fidelity. The house lights were off, leaving us with only slanting moon-rays from the skylight. Light and darkness sliced up Mom's face in alternating bands. Her expression was surreal: shock and pain and betrayal alongside a deep boredom. Part of her—and all of us—were somehow surprised yet not surprised that he had escalated this far.

Certainly Jason and Kaitlyn weren't surprised.

Mac's voice was a harsh whisper: "She's . . . she's sick."

Trent: "Kids, tell her she's hurting your feelings."

He sounded casual, like we were hanging out. Despite the effort he was putting into pinning her, he didn't sound out of breath. He could've been at a baseball game or relaxing in his big, stupid fucking backyard.

Jason: "Dad—"

"Tell her she's hurting your feelings. Tell her to apologize for not having my back. I think I deserve an apology."

"Mom, you're hurting our feelings."

We all looked at him. Jason had said it to the floor, his shoulders slumped in shame.

Mac, her face slick with tears: "What?"

Trent: "Could you say that a little louder, Jase?"

"Mom, you're hurting our feelings," Jason said louder.

Trent looked over, his eyes glinting with triumph. "Now everyone say it."

Silence, except for Mom's labored breathing.

"SAY IT!"

He'd let loose with one of those "span the Grand Canyon" screams again. We all jolted in response. The lava in my veins froze to stone. My heart grew harder that night, and it never softened again, not even to this day. Legions of people had it worse than we did, but we would've made the podium. Monsters lived among us. Their faces weren't plaid. They didn't leave a body count. They enjoyed the full support of the cops. They got away with everything.

I was babbling: "You're hurting our feelings, you're hurting our feelings, you're hurting our feelings, you're hurting our feelings . . ."

Mac clenched her eyes shut: "You're hurting our feelings."

Kaitlyn, in a dead drone: "You're hurting our feelings."

Mom wheezed: "I'm sorry I hurt your feelings."

Trent released her so fast she bumped into the wall. She turned around, her face wet with tears, and assumed a strange smile.

"Well, at least I won't have to worry about my hair for much longer."

She mussed it up, forcing a laugh, and trudged to the bedroom, Trent in tow. *Click.*

He had hurt us, but he made us apologize to him.

Jason sat on the stairs, holding his head. Kaitlyn sat next to him.

Mac: "He was *hurting* her."

"I know," Jason said.

"She's sick," I said.

"I know."

Does it still count as an apology if you're under duress?

Mac: "Why'd you say it? Why did you tell *us* to say it?"

"Because it's the only way I know to make it stop." He looked up. "Because I'm not as brave as you. I'm not as strong as you."

Does it still count as a betrayal if you're under duress?

"You learn shortcuts," Kaitlyn said. "Tricks. Hacks."

Jason was sobbing: "I promise one day you'll be proud of me. I promise."

My ears tingled. Mom had said the same thing months ago.

Mac hugged me. I squeezed her back so hard she sighed. Jason looked up, his face bright with tears, and swallowed. His next words came out eerily calm:

"Hey, I've got some presents for you guys. Wanna see 'em?"

"Presents?" Mac asked.

"Yeah, come check 'em out." He stood and walked silently up the stairs, lurching from one side to the other. I realized he was walking on his bits of glowing tape. Halfway up, he paused and pressed a finger over his lips. "Walk on the tape."

Kaitlyn started stomping up the stairs. "Why? They're not asleep, Houdini."

He stopped her. "You know how he gets. One creak, and he might come back out here to scream at us." He lowered his voice: "Please."

Kaitlyn rolled her eyes but relented. "Okay, okay. Let's see these presents."

We walked up, taking care to hit every bit of glow-tape. I got a little dizzy on the fourth or fifth step, but it passed. It worked, too—we made the passage upstairs in silence. Jason led us down the hall, where he held up the Union Jack, allowing us passage into his room. We filed in, and I sat on the bed. He shut the door. Kaitlyn crossed her arms.

"Jase, what's going on? What gifts are you talking about?"

Jason stood before the door, head hung. Silence extended for at least ten seconds before I noticed it:

We were underwater.

At least that's how it *looked.* The room swam as if in a heat mirage.

Springing to my feet, I yelled: "Guys! Guys! We're not in the house any—"

Jason balled his fist, flipped it up and down, and extended his fingers—the same arcane gesture he'd executed at Soddy Farm last night. The ceiling and floor split apart into hundreds of geometric slices before retracting away as if a vacuum had opened around the house.

We stood in empty space.

All that remained was a floating island that held Jason's bedroom—or a representation of it. The details of everything had blurred and blended together into an impressionist watercolor.

Kaitlyn shouted: "Jase! What are you—"

He executed another arcane gesture, and a luminescent orange cage materialized around us. Jason stepped forward, still crying but steeling himself for the task at hand.

"Lee was right about Skelton's hideout. If he's hidden it in the Sneakaround Network, he'll have total control over it. If you walked into his hideout with your eyes open, he could do whatever he wanted to you. Just like I have. All I had to do was trick you into walking the right path. You have to create a gate from the *outside* in order to see all the magic."

"The glow tape," Kaitlyn said. "Jase, what is this? What're you doing?"

From his pocket he produced a small purple burlap pouch lined with glittering gold-and-red threads.

"I've been working on these ever since I found out you discovered the Sneakaround Network. To Hiram, I gift—"

Mac: "Let us out of here!"

They were shouting, but I kept my voice steady: "Jason, why are you doing this?"

"Because I lied to you."

Kaitlyn: "What're you *talking* about?"

"When I told you I wanted to kill Skelton."

"What is that supposed to—" Kaitlyn broke off, her face stretching in a sorrowful mix of terror and grief. "Oh, sweet Jase, don't. Don't. It's not worth it."

Mac gave her a baffled look: "What does he mean?"

Kaitlyn: "God, god, god, don't leave me."

"It's okay," Jason said. "I don't want it anymore." He paused. "Want him to kill me. Because if he killed me, he could keep hurting other people, other kids. Like Jenny. You guys don't have to do anything. I'll take care of everything. I'll save Officer Webb and make sure he catches Skelton. I've got my own plan to do it."

"Jason."

Kaitlyn's voice had dropped to a low whisper. Jason couldn't meet her gaze.

"Kaity—"

"I love you. You don't have to do this. We can do it together."

"No, we can't. I know that now. I'm not worth it. I don't deserve to be happy. I don't deserve anything. The best I can do is try and fix everything I've done." He plunged his arm into the pouch all the way to his elbow. He seemed to fish around inside before pulling out a footlong hatchet. "These gifts weren't easy to make, but they'll come in handy when you follow me. But I'm begging you—*please don't follow me.*" He presented us with our gifts, pulling them out of the pouch one after the other, Mary Poppins-style. "For Mackenzie, the hatchet, which can cut no tree of this world."

"Jason, stop this. You're scaring us."

Next he produced a small, gilded sextant. "For Hiram, the sextant."

It had a satisfying weight. I marveled at it. "How'd you know I needed a sextant?"

"I didn't, but I happened to be working on one," he said. "When I overheard you say you wanted one, I went ahead and finished it up for you. *This* sextant does so much more than simply chart the stars. You'll discover all its uses in time." Next was a gleaming black cylinder about two feet long. "For Kaitlyn, the Scepter of Chaos, an umbrella to cover you in times of sorrow."

She shook her head. "Keep it. Let's do this together."

"If you don't take it, it'll vanish."

Her resolve faltered; she took the staff. "Didn't have time to whip anything up for Dawnie and Lee?"

"If I act fast enough, they won't need anything." He turned around and executed another series of arcane gestures, his hands sketching a succession of rapid-fire shapes. His bedroom door shivered apart into tens of thousands of letters and numbers and symbols, all rendered in glowing Courier, before reassembling into another gate. He turned to address us: "That was a good trick with Skelton's gate, but it's an easy one to counter." He snapped his fingers, and the ASCII characters turned red. "You won't be able to access my gate. And don't follow me. Don't try to stop me."

"How the hell're we supposed to *follow* you when we're locked in here?!" Mac yelled.

"The cage will fade after I leave." He reached into his pockets and tossed Kaitlyn a set of keys. "I know you'll try. But don't. This is my mess. I'll clean it up. But if you *do* try to stop me—" (he smiled warmly) "—good luck. I love you."

"Jason?"

He stopped and looked at me.

"What is it, buddy?"

"Even if you can pull this off, they'll still be out there." I could barely say it: "His victims. Their remains. This won't save them."

He closed his eyes. I honestly think he'd forgotten about them all. All eight of them, hidden away from their families by that monster. Looking back, I think my appeal almost changed his mind; almost spared us the horrors of that night. But something in him resisted and kept him on course.

"I'm sorry," he said and back-stepped into his gate, which vanished in a sparkling cloud of crimson Courier characters.

Kaitlyn

She knew exactly why he'd left the keys.

The instant his gate vanished, their cage dissolved like icing under a propane flame. Jason's room solidified, snapping from "impressionist" back to its normal appearance. Kaitlyn turned to the gang and brandished the keys.

"We gotta move. I'm gonna *kill* him when we catch him, but at least he left us a clue."

"What clue?" Mac asked. "What're those keys for?"

"Our storage room," Kaitlyn said. "Which means he's not going to try and call Mr. Johnson." She lurched over to his desk and yanked out a few sketch pads and pencils. "We need to start drawing our maps *right now.*"

Jason

He'd built his Smoky Mountain over the past few years. Every night, he'd set his alarm and labor over his maps. You needed at least two people to draw maps to make it work, so Jason found secret confederates. He'd slyly ask friends at school to help him on his art projects, telling them to add in details here and there. Once he even offered to assistant-teach a middle school class.

At school, he was a superstar.

At school, he was the nice older kid who always pitched in, who volunteered to help Ms. Millson clean the art studio. All he asked in return was her help painting a makeshift atlas of the area.

Jason had many maps. He'd amassed at least a dozen different ones over the years, each of them in a different style—one in colored pencils, one in pure graphite, one in gauche, one in oils. But his favorite was his master map, which combined all those media. He'd recruited help from three different people for that one: Ms. Millson, Tommy May in middle school, and even his sister.

Yes, he'd kept the very first map she'd drawn.

It was the one that included the tunnel from his closet to the backyard. He'd kept it hidden away all these years, occasionally adding details to it. When Dad met Corrie, he found out the Greshams' address and added their house. He had found ways to get others to add details to her map, too. For a collaborative collage assignment in art class, he slipped Kaitlyn's map underneath some cardboard through which he'd cut a small window. He directed his classmate to add details to what would wind up being Dizzy Pines.

All of those steps were overkill, of course. He knew that. You only needed more than one map and more than one artist.

Usually.

For some reason, certain people never added any magic to the maps. Jason had yet to figure out why. It wasn't a function of their artistic skill or personality. It was something else. Perhaps it was connected to belief? Like, if you were the kind of kid who believed in bullshit like Santa Claus, you could draw the maps? Hiram, Mac, Dawn, and Lee clearly all had the ability. They'd accidentally generated a small portal between Dizzy Pines and Soddy Farm, but they'd need help with their magic weapons.

The neigh of a horse preceded the *clickity-clack* of hooves on brick. Jason's unicorn trotted up like she always did. He'd spent years crafting her, this imaginary beast. Her appearance at Soddy Farm had been unplanned. He occasionally created "bubbles" at the ends of his Smoky Mountains to let her run loose for a while, one of which sat at Soddy Farm. He'd forgotten to close it at the worst possible time.

It didn't matter. All that mattered now was saving Officer Webb and putting Skelton away.

He emerged from his ASCII gate onto a single floating pathway, this one dark red brick. He paused, taking it all in. He'd spent years building this place, but he'd never really made use of it. He had built it using his two most powerful maps: his and Kaitlyn's originals.

If I have to draw a portal into Skelton's lair, surely these will be powerful enough.

He ran down the pathway and stopped.

He wasn't alone.

In the distance floated what appeared to be a moon, but of course Jason knew it was no moon.

"The Plaid Man," he whispered.

Half a million "miles" away floated his disembodied head, slowly rotating, his face casting a beam of light across the endless void. Jason froze. Waited. The beam of light swept across something in the distance.

Another Smoky Mountain.

Huh. So they all occupy the same space, he thought, keeping a wary eye on the Plaid Man. The beam of light swept this way and that . . . but didn't land on Jason's Smoky Mountain. Certain of his safety—at least for the moment— Jason pulled out his 3D sunglasses and put them on. Lightning encircled his feet and surged up his body in a three-dimensional cinematic wipe that transformed him from regular Jason to *Turbo* Jason, his animated self. His 3D glasses morphed into his cyberpunk smart-glasses, while his clothes remolded themselves into his ribbed leather techno-speedsuit. Punk stripes etched themselves across his temples, while his sandy blond hair flashed a sudden lemon-yellow; perfect for Saturday mornings.

As unseen winds kicked through his hair, he jogged down the pathway. It met an octagonal intersection that sprouted a few more floating pathways. He knew exactly which one to take and pelted down it, the overhead lights illuminating in concert with his movements, until he reached a gate that bore a familiar symbol as its keystone:

A fleur-de-lis.

Hiram's Journal

"Be *super* careful drawing your maps! They've got to match up perfectly."

It was cartographical mayhem. Hexagonal graph paper lay strewn alongside boxes of crayons, colored pencils, paints, and chalk. Kaitlyn was Scotch-taping extra paper to her map, adding space for all the locations we needed to visit, while Mac and I opted for glue sticks.

Mac prodded me and said: "Is there enough glassine to cover all our maps?"

I scrambled across the room and rifled under Jason's bed. Thankfully, a full pad of glassine slid out. I yanked out several sheets as Kaitlyn handed me the Scotch tape—we were a perfect team.

"So? Where are these going to go?" Kaitlyn asked.

"The mall for one," Mac said. "Misbegotten Avenue."

"Right," I said as I taped glassine together. "We need Skelton's address."

Kaitlyn: "What if Jason gets it first?"

"We can't worry about that," I said. "We've gotta follow the plan."

"Got it," Kaitlyn said, turning to me. "Is this how we build the Smoky Mountain? We just . . . *draw* it on this plastic stuff?"

"I guess so," I said, falling silent for a moment to work. "Hey, can I ask you guys a question?"

"Shoot," Kaitlyn said.

"Do you know much about girls?"

They shared an amused look, given the circumstances.

"Uh, last I checked, we might know a thing or two, squirt."

"Well, uh in the movie theater. I saw Christy Hodges."

Kaitlyn finished her sketch of the mall and shot me a delighted grin.

"Why, Hiram Stud-Muffin Gresham the Second! Do you have a lady friend you've been hiding from us?"

If I could've blushed harder, I would have. Shaking my head, I said: "Uh no, uh no. I mean, I think she's pretty, but—"

Mac rescued me. For once, getting interrupted was welcome: "Yeah, I heard you talking."

"I don't think it was her."

"What do you mean?"

"She uh disappeared. And she was wearing plaid."

Kaitlyn looked up from her map. "Oh, shit. Whadda you think that means? Is Plaiddy trying to manipulate us?"

It's a testament to how much Kaitlyn had earned our trust that I said: "I don't know, but I don't know if I ever want to talk to girls again."

They shared another look, this one a mix of empathy and sadness.

Mac: "Can I tell you something, honestly?"

"Sure."

"I don't know if that was her or not, but I didn't like the way she was talking to you. I don't think she was being very nice."

Kaitlyn smiled wryly. "I think I caught that. The ol', 'Why didn't you say hi to me?'"

"Exactly!" I said with a wave. "I felt awful. I just don't know if, y'know, dating or having a girlfriend's for me. Mom says I'm too busy, anyway."

Mac: "She says that to me, too, y'know."

"Yeah?"

"Hiram, I want you to know that just because someone is pretty doesn't mean they're automatically nice, or smart, or worth any more than you."

Kaitlyn touched my hand. "Except me, of course." She winked.

I smiled. Mac continued: "And I *also* want you to know that just because one girl was mean to you doesn't mean all girls are mean. Okay?"

"Okay, I get it," I said. "I just think it'd be so cool to have a girlfriend."

"Sure it would! But having one or not having one doesn't make you any better or worse of a person. You're you, and you're great."

"Thanks. There are kids at school who have girlfriends and go out on dates, and I just figured I was doing something wrong."

Kaitlyn shook her head. "Jesus, you're like, eleven. You're not doing anything wrong."

"Nope," Mac said. "And I want you to know: we don't bite. We've got hopes and dreams and fears just like you."

I nodded. "Got it. And—" (I lowered my voice) "—were Dr. Eldridge and Mr. Tucker there . . . um, together?"

"Uh-huh," Mac said. "You know that's okay, too, right?"

"Of course! Why wouldn't I?"

Kaitlyn chuckled, her eyes flashing wide. "Oh, maybe because Trent's a huge, bigoted asshole?"

Mac nodded. "Yeah. You know he keyed your doctor's car, right?"

"Oh." My eyes got wide. *"Oh. Keyed my car."*

"Huh?"

"I heard him in the theater. He said 'he keyed my car.' Trent's a jerk. Sorry, Kaitlyn."

She patted my back. "No apology necessary, squirt. Are your maps done? Mine is."

The girls checked and compared their maps. I handed mine over. Mac stacked them together and held them up to the light to make sure all the key locations lined up. She nodded.

"Looks good," she said, setting them flat and laying the taped-together glassine over them. I was about to start drawing but hesitated.

"Should maybe one of you do this?"

Kaitlyn squeezed my shoulder. "Nah, squirt. I trust ya."

Mac gave me an approving nod.

"Okay," I said. "We'll put the entrance at Castle GrayCrystal." I drew a gate over Radagast's Oak. "What should the keystone be?"

"That's a no-brainer," Kaitlyn said, sketching out a stylized symbol that depicted two interlocking letters, S and G, both shaped like extended hexagons. "The Sneakaround Gang."

"The Sneakaround Gang," Mac said with a nod.

"The Sneakaround Gang," I said as I sketched in the keystone. "Okay. We start at the Castle."

Kaitlyn: "Then the mall, then the storage room."

I sketched a single path away from the Castle, then a hub. From it, I added paths to the mall, the storage center, and finally our old house.

I added: "Then we'll move the radio back to the house."

"Right," Mac said. "We call Mr. Johnson and hope he'll draw a portal into Skelton's hideout."

"Then we go get your boyfriend," Kaitlyn said.

"This isn't the time for jokes," Mac snapped.

Kaitlyn held up her hands. "Hey, this might be our last night alive. If I'm gonna go out, I wanna go out laughing."

"Got it, got it. Sorry I lost my temper. But we're not gonna die." She checked her pockets. "Oh shit."

My head snapped up. "What?"

She was already charging out the door. I jumped up and followed, both of us skipping silently along Jason's glow-tape. In our bedroom, Mac rifled through her drawers and checked under her mattress before turning to me, her face a portrait of panic.

"I don't have it," she hissed.

"What?"

"Webb's card! We don't know his address!"

At that instant, my walkie crackled: "Panthro to Ironhide, come in Ironhide!"

Jason

He executed an arcane gesture, and the gate opened to reveal a direct view of Stems & Stamens.

Which was locked up tight with a sliding steel door.

"Dammit," Jason muttered.

Jason paused, checking for the Plaid Man. He was little more than a pinprick of light, having floated many millions of miles away. Turning his attention back to the flower shop, Jason produced his maps—his, his sister's, and the glassine sheet that depicted his Smoky Mountain—and with a few taps on his wrist-mounted keyboard, a pair of orange lasers sketched out an easel. He laid the maps on it and pulled a pen from his breast pocket. The maps included most of the area.

Including Officer Webb's apartment.

He pulled out his business card, which Jason had nicked from Mac's room the night before, and confirmed the address. Next he sketched out an *addition* to his Smoky Mountain. To the end of his current gate, he added a small bubble of extra space. In response, the ground shook slightly as the shimmering plane of his gate rushed forward and enveloped Stems & Stamens in a translucent dome of glimmering blue light.

It was the same trick Skelton had pulled to conceal his hideout—to expand his Smoky Mountain.

With the taps of a few more keys, Jason activated his shoulder-mounted bazookas.

And fired.

Hiram's Journal

I grabbed the walkie. "This is Panthro!"

Lee's voice fritzed: "What's the plan, Admiral? We expected a call an hour ago. There was word on the radio of a menacing figure down in Pigeon Forge."

Mac and I met eyes. She said: "That's got to be Skelton."

Dawn: "Everything all right over there?"

Mac: "We'll tell you later," she said, pulling me out of the room. "Change of plans. Jason took off without us."

We ran back to Jason's room, where Kaitlyn was frantically waving us in.

"Get in here, get in here!" she hissed.

Dawn: "Whadda you mean Jason took off?"

Mac: "He's gonna try and do it all himself. He stole Webb's card, too."

She passed the walkie to Kaitlyn. "We're flying blind, girlfriend, and we need transpo."

I grabbed the walkie. "Smoky Mountain currently under construction with three seeds: me, Kaitlyn, and Mac."

Lee: "That should be plenty of magic. I assume the entrance will be at Castle GrayCrystal?"

"Affirmative," I said. "Assuming our maps worked."

"They'll work," Lee said. "I have faith. Let's motorvate!"

Dawn

"Let's motorvate!" Lee said, jumping to his feet in Dawn's bedroom. He'd changed out of his neon-fluorescent outfit into all-black. They gathered their nighttime gear. Lee grabbed the walkie. Dawn crept to her bedroom door and inched it open, peeking in on their mom, who was already asleep on the couch, a book open on her chest. Dawn turned to Lee and nodded.

"She's down for the night," she said, suddenly hesitating.

"What is it?" Lee asked.

Frowning, Dawn whispered, "Cleopatra?"

"What did you say?"

"Nothing," Dawn said. "Let's get a move on."

He opened the window—just as their mother stirred.

"Kids?" she called, her voice fuzzy from sleep.

Dawn closed her door. "Dammit, we gotta stall."

Jason

It worked. All that remained was a heap of gnarled, smoking steel. Jason hopped over it and ran behind the counter, hoping to hell no one heard the explosion. He rifled through the cash register and several Rolodexes before he found the order sheet.

L. S. — Delivery to Montmarnass Rotunda

Home address:

2568 Enchanted Caverns Drive

Sevierville, TN

"Oh, my God, of course," he whispered, already running back over to his orange easel and thinking, *Enchanted Caverns is that old roadside attraction up near Sevierville. Skelton's hideout had the same A-frame roof.* At his easel, he produced a fold-out atlas of the area—and stopped. Lee's words came back to him:

We believe that Skelton has created a double *of his hideout in the Sneakaround Network.*

This was uncharted territory. If Skelton had somehow concealed Enchanted Caverns inside the Sneakaround Network, Jason had to be careful. If he created a gate that led directly into Skelton's realm, he'd be at a disadvantage. Skelton would be able to control what he saw, just like how Jason had been able to control what the gang saw back in his bedroom.

He needed to create a path to Enchanted Caverns, but he would have to put his gate far enough away to make sure he was *outside* Skelton's realm.

But how far? A hundred feet? A mile?

And what if Webb can't even see the gate into this place? Do I really need to draw a pathway to Enchanted Caverns?

He was about to omit the pathway when he caught a glimpse of the Plaid Man in the distance, scanning the Sneakaround Network like the Eye of Sauron. Jason couldn't have told you why, but he went ahead and added Sevierville—and the Enchanted Caverns attraction—to his maps, followed by adding a new path to his Smoky Mountain on the glassine overlay. He set his gate a full mile away, and for an icon, he added a prize ribbon. Next he drew the details for Officer Webb's apartment, which he labeled with a badge icon.

With a few arcane gestures, he closed the gate to Misbegotten Avenue, made his easel vanish, and sprinted back to the octagonal intersection.

Where he waited, his breaths echoing.

Come on, come on.

He had broken the rules. He had drawn on both maps instead of collaborating. That wasn't how the magic worked. But he had spent *years* teaming up with others—including an unwitting Kaitlyn—to build out these two maps. *Surely* he had endowed them with enough magic to let him cheat *just a little.*

He was about to give up when the ground groaned. A sound like a massive door *cree-e-ee-aaaking* open shook his Smoky Mountain, heralding two new additions: a pair of red brick pathways blasted forth from the octagon, snaking through empty space before terminating in two new gates—one for Officer Webb, one for Skelton.

It had worked. And if Jason could add to his Smoky Mountain on his own, maybe he'd be able to draw a portal into Skelton's hideout on his own.

Maybe they wouldn't even *need* Mr. Johnson's help.

He ran through Webb's gate and emerged from a utility shed into a small parking lot, his appearance returning to normal with an electric crackle. An array of brown-wood, blocky, seventies-style apartment buildings stood nearby, fronted by a backlit sign that read *FALCONCREST APARTMENTS.* The buildings' hallways ran along the outside. Now all he had to do was convince Officer Webb that Skelton was still alive and that he had mastered some kind of dark cartographical sorcery.

Jason checked Webb's card. "Apartment Two-C, building four," he whispered, jogging toward the complex and around buildings one, two, and three. Building four came into view along with its second-floor hallway.

Where a dark figure was approaching apartment Two-C.

Jason lowered his head and ran as fast as he could.

Kaitlyn

Hiram came running back into Jason's room with the night's security code.

"Got it," he said. "Let's go, and don't forget the gifts."

They all crammed their maps, gifts, night-time gear, and art supplies into backpacks before they scurried down the stairs, following Jason's sneakround network to move silently. At the back door, Hiram punched in the code: 7427624. The door beeped, but he didn't move. Kaitlyn gave him a small shove.

"What's up, squirt?"

"The numbers," he muttered. "Something doesn't feel right." He thought. "Seven four two . . ."

Mac pulled him outside. "We can figure it out later. Got a long run ahead of us."

Hiram shook his head. "I think Trent's been spelling words. With his codes. Seven four two . . ." His eyes popped wide. "Pharaoh."

Kaitlyn had scampered to the corner of the house. She turned and waved them along.

"That's great, big guy," she stage-whispered. "But we gotta keep moving."

They ran up to join her, Hiram still looking puzzled. "Pharaoh. Egypt."

Mac wheeled the girls' bikes out of the garage. Left behind was one of Hiram's Christmas presents, a bike of his own, which he had stubbornly refused to learn to ride. Mac and Kaitlyn climbed on theirs, clicking on their headlamps. They were about to take off, but Hiram was still lost in thought. Mac wheeled around and took his shoulder.

"What's wrong?"

"Pharaoh. Pharaoh. What was the name of that book?"

Jason

The hallway bounced before him as he ran, his vision bright red, his knee throbbing. His instincts had fully taken over, his fear of Skelton lost in the haze of battle. Skelton was about to knock on Webb's door. *God, what is he going to do to him?* No time to think, because Jason was already grabbing Skelton's shoulder—*What's that smell?*—and wrenching him around. He was in disguise, of course, dressed as a pizza guy, and he'd even thought to bring a prop. A cardboard box flew open, complete with a steaming-hot pie, which spun and splattered to the ground.

"What the *fuck, dude?!*" Skelton yelled, his voice a shrill shriek.

The door flung open. Webb stood there wearing, of all things, a train conductor's uniform, complete with a striped cap.

"What in the living hell?" he yelled.

Jason's chest heaved, his battle-rage having blacked out his senses. He had been ready to do the unspeakable to protect Officer Webb—but there was no need.

It wasn't Skelton lying on the ground before him.

It was just some kid wearing a delivery uniform.

Jason's blood turned to ice.

"Oh, no," he whispered.

Lee

They walked out to the main room, where their mom was rubbing her eyes.

"Hey, guys. I heard the walkie-talkie in there. You and the Greshams playing a game?"

She slipped a bookmark into her night's reading, a leather-bound volume she set on a side table. Lee froze. An epicycle spun up, one Lee didn't immediately recognize. The Da Vinci-esque mechanism that emerged from his consciousness was flaking rust, creaking, and groaning with disuse. Hundreds of brass and bronze workings screamed into action, delivering up a projection from his past, a vignette-ringed movie reel that flickered to life.

It was a memory—one his mind felt was important enough to *keep* but not quite important enough to *keep fresh.* The memory depicted a portrait of a wide-eyed woman with frizzy hair, a cross between the Bride of Frankenstein and Dr. Emmett Brown. She wore a triangular pin on her smock that bore the letters ETSOSD.

The same pin his mother wore.

A plaque on the picture frame identified her as *DR. CLEOPATRA VON WIZARDO-SORORA.*

Who was the author of the very book their mom was reading.

Lee stepped over to the side table and took up the book: *Mastery of Occultopsychic Phenomena.*

I've seen this portrait before.

In the Mystery Mansion.

Lee opened his mouth to speak, but Dawn beat him to it:

"Mama, what's this book?"

She gave her a funny look. "Oh, it's just some weird old book my mom gave me before—"

Knock, knock.

They all jumped. Lee dropped the book: *whump!* Dawn gasped at the added noise. Lee and Dawn gaped at the door. Their mom was already walking over to it.

"Now, who in the dickens is knocking at this hour?"

Holton

He'd cleared his evening to rebuild the Old West.

He was three months past a rough breakup, and model trains had filled his off-hours with painstakingly wonderful work. As a kid, his Grandma Maxwell always built the most beautiful miniature holiday villages. She built a new set every year and gifted one of the buildings to Holt and his three siblings. To their astonishment, Grandma Maxwell personalized the cottages for each one of them, riffing on the same themes every year. The eldest child, Jimmy, received the biggest buildings—usually a bank or department store— while their sister Nance, as the sole girl, got a succession of different churches. Holton's big brother Davey, as the black sheep, received bars and speakeasies.

Holton, as the youngest, usually got toy stores and candy shops.

But he was always envious of Davey's bars.

He'd packed every free square inch of his tiny apartment with train tracks, hills, buildings, crossbucks, switches, water towers, and mountains. Over the years, he'd asked his siblings to donate some of their Christmas cottages to his collection. Grandma Maxwell had chosen an Old West theme for Christmas 1976. Davey had just sent over his '76 bar—in this case, a saloon—one of Holt's favorites. Jimmy got a bank, Nance a lovely little one-room church, and Holt a schoolhouse, a thematic deviation that delighted him. The four buildings even fit together into a sort of play set. Jimmy and Nance had already gifted theirs to Holt. Davey's saloon completed the set.

He was about to install it but hesitated, lingering on its every detail.

It's like having a little bit of Davey here. It's like having a little bit of them all here.

That's when the shouts came, followed by a crash.

"What the *fuck, dude?!*"

Holton yanked his door open to reveal a beleaguered delivery kid on the ground, pimply-faced and blushing. His shirt read *MELLOW MUSHROOM*. The pizza lay in shambles, one slice stuck to the outer wall, while hulking over the kid was a six-and-a-half-foot blonde teenager wearing 3D glasses for some reason. His face rang a bell.

"Do I know you, fella?"

"I'm Jason Sutton," he said, fumbling off the glasses. "Trent's son?"

Holt's eyebrows rose. "Trent—you mean Bo's friend?"

The delivery kid stood, dusting himself off. "Anyone curious about *me?!* What the hell's your problem, dude?"

Jason produced his wallet and pulled out a hundred-dollar bill.

"I am so sorry about that, man. Will this cover you?"

The kid beamed. "Holy shit, dude. Thanks." To Holt: "Mister, you want a replacement pie?"

Holt shook his head, his gaze locked on Jason. "No thanks. Sorry about the trouble."

As the delivery kid ran off, Jason took Holt's shoulder.

"Officer Webb, you need to come with me. *Right now.*"

Holt didn't move. "Are you all right? Has he been . . . well, has he been hurtin' you?"

"No, no—it's not that. Well, it *is* that, but there's something worse going on. I need to take you somewhere, no questions asked, and have you arrest someone. There's lives at stake, people in danger."

Holt doffed his conductor's cap. "Arrest who?"

Dawn

"Now, who in the dickens is knocking at this hour?"

She touched the doorknob. A male voice spoke:

"Sorry to bother you, ma'am. Just taking a quick survey."

Dawn's skin crackled and sparked with reactive energy. The man outside had dropped his voice into his chest, but she'd forever recognize his register. Lee took her hand and squeezed. The world transformed into a nightmare where she couldn't speak.

"Mom," she said, barely more than a whisper.

Sandra inclined her ear. "Isn't it awfully late, sir?"

Dawn cleared her throat. "Mom." It was audible, at least.

"One second, sweetheart." She addressed the man outside: "Sir?"

Lee spoke, his voice a bleat: "Mother. Don't open that door."

She turned to them. "Why shouldn't I—"

BANG! The door jolted inward. Lee activated the walkie-talkie.

Hiram's Journal

I finally shook out of my stupor and ran alongside the girls into the woods. Usually they'd be walking their bikes but not tonight. They weaved back and forth to slow their pace so I could keep up.

"I swear, are you *ever* gonna learn to ride a bike, Hi?" Kaitlyn hissed.

"Aw, give me a break!" I said. "We've been pretty busy with all these magic portals and serial killers and stuff."

My walkie squelched and blasted Lee's voice: "HIRAM HIRAM MAYDAY MAYDAY!"

We all stopped immediately, the girls dismounting their bikes and running over next to me.

"Lee?!" I yelled. "What's—"

"IT'S SKELTON HE'S HERE HE'S—"

Slam. It was unmistakable, the sound: a blunt instrument met flesh and bone. The walkie thumped to the floor. Women screamed—Dawn and Sandra. Fabric rustled, followed by more thumping as someone took up the walkie again. I hadn't breathed in ten seconds. I was too terrified, because if I took another breath, this horrible night would have to continue.

If I took another breath, I'd have to find out what happened to the Dockerys.

The walkie sprayed static in a caustic heartbeat until hell rumbled forth:

"Well, hello there, little sumpty."

Blackness encircled my vision. I must've swayed, because Mac steadied me. My knuckles were white around the walkie.

"Skel . . ." I stuttered on the letter T.

"Left me a choice of three snacks here, three top-prize specimens."

I actually lost a few seconds of memory here. One moment, the girls were flanking me, the next, I was charging forward, toward nothing, shaking my fist and erupting: "—YOU FUCKING HURT MY FRIENDS! DON'T YOU HURT THEM DON'T YOU—" Mac hugged me, halting my harangue. I was sobbing. The devil's laughter wafted from the walkie:

"Such a fine spirit in you, son. Blue ribbon caliber, born from them strong bones." His voice dropped a few octaves. "*You're already dead.* Alla y'all. Six feet and wormfood, less'n you turn back now. *You're dead* unless—unless—my toll is one. That's the price for another Christmas, another birthday: one of these three fine, strong specimens. I know not which one I'll pick, but say your goodbyes now, because they're already gone."

Click. Silence. Nobody moved.

Mac grabbed me by the shoulders: "Hiram, we—"

I turned on a heel and sprinted back to the house.

Jason

"Arrest who?"

Jason weighed his options: he could tell the truth now and risk getting the door slammed in his face, or he could string him along. He chose the latter.

"I can tell you later, but you've got to come with me first."

Webb scratched his head, regarding him.

"Where would be be going?"

BRRRRIINNGGGG! Webb's phone blared. Jason's eyes flicked to it.

"Eventually Sevierville."

"Eventually Sevierville? What's that mean?"

BRRRRIINNGGGG!

Jason twined his fingers, pleading. "Trust me. Please. I know this sounds crazy, but—"

"Does this have something to do with that night at the farm?"

"Yeah. Something to do with the farm."

BRRRRII—click! Webb's answering machine picked up.

"You've reached Holton Webb. I can't take your call at the present time, but please leave a message, and I'll call you back." The machine started spinning. Jason's eyes were locked on it, which recorded nothing but silence.

Webb: "Tell you what. Seeing as how you done messed up my Mellow Mushroom—"

Jason pointed. "Aren't you gonna get that?"

Webb shook his head. "Prank caller. Asshole's been at it all night. Let's—"

"I've got him." Click.

Webb turned toward the machine, but Jason had already taken hold of his arm, pulling him out.

"*Whoa!* Son, leggome!" He yanked his arm free. "I'm coming with you."

"You are?"

"Son, you don't strike me as the pranking type. You're not, are you?"

Jason shook his head.

"Relax, son. Let me get my sidearm."

Moments later, they were crossing the parking lot toward Webb's Camry, but Jason grabbed Webb's arm and guided him over to the utility shed that held his gate back into the Sneakaround Network.

"Can you look over here for me?" he asked.

Webb shrugged and said: "Sure." Jason opened the shed, releasing a blast of shimmering blue light. He looked at Webb expectantly, but all he did was put his hands in his pockets. "What am I looking at here, son?"

"Damn," Jason muttered. "Can you do me a favor and try walking in here?"

Webb's eyebrows rose, but he shook his head in doubt and walked in. When he passed through Jason's gate, it faded away, leaving only the shed. Webb raised his palms.

"Son, I done asked if you were the pranking type."

"It's not a prank, but we need to drive to Sevierville. *Now.*"

Mackenzie

"Hiram? Hiram?! HIRAM!"

Caution was a laughable memory. She didn't care if she woke that monster back home with her screaming, she had to catch her baby brother, whose courage had apparently deserted him at the moment of truth. She and Kaitlyn had already lost sight of him as they ran back toward the house. Kaitlyn smacked her shoulder.

"Where the hell's he going?!"

Mac ignored her and kept calling: "Hiram! Hiram, it's okay! It's okay if you're scared! It's—"

Ding-ding-ding! Hiram was herking and jerking and swerving and listing back toward them.

On his bike.

Despite the horrors of the moment, the girls smiled. Kaitlyn applauded.

"Way to go, squirt!"

He shot past them, finally steadying himself, and made a swooping clockwise circle to turn left into the woods.

Mac called: "Castle GrayCrystal is the other way!"

"I know! We're going to the Dockerys'!"

Dawn

Her vision had been reduced to twin pinpricks of light. They shimmered—through tears, presumably—before slowly expanding to reveal a sideways big-screen TV, its screen smashed in. It was sideways because Dawn lay sprawled on the ground, blinking her way back to consciousness, her temple throbbing.

Her memory was coming back online in fits and starts.

He'd hit her on the head. That much she knew.

But *who* had hit her on the head? And where was she?

Home, Dawn. You're at home. That's your TV.

She lay on her side, her arm extended under her head as a makeshift pillow. Rolling onto her stomach, she struggled to her elbows. When she turned her head, fiery lightning shot down the side of her body and made her hiss in agony. Something hot ran into the corner of her mouth. Blood.

Blood.

Saturday night.

First blood will be Saturday night.

"Lee," she rasped. "Mom. It's Friday."

The statement was nonsense borne from head trauma, but it demonstrated that her brain was still working, and moreover, that her thoughts were increasingly coherent and converging on the truth:

Skelton lied. Lee was right. He lied about Saturday night, and he lied about who he was going after.

"Mom!" She'd hoisted herself to one knee, using her forearm to lever herself upright, her other hand swiping at the kitchen island countertop. Her scope of vision had expanded to encompass most of the room. Bookshelves lay toppled, TV-dinner tables overturned, windows smashed, papers fluttering. The refrigerator stood open and emitted ghostly-glowing fog. The walkie-talkie lay nearby. She grabbed it.

Someone groaned in the kitchen. A woman.

"Mom!" Dawn yelled with a wince, lurching to her feet. She staggered around the kitchen island to find her mom lying halfway in the fridge, blood pooling around her head.

She moaned. "Put your toys away, kids. Time for . . ."

"Mom! Hang on—I'm calling for help!" Thankfully, the kitchen phone was still intact. Dawn snatched it off the wall and dialed 911. It rang and rang and rang. "Come on come on come on . . ."

An operator answered, a woman: "Nine-one-one emergency response, what is your address?"

"Yes, this is Dawn Dockery over in Dizzy Pines trailer park, right off mile marker zero on West Chim Access Road, number twelve. We need an ambulance and the cops! Lenn—"

Something rustled outside. Dawn clammed up.

"Ma'am? Are you in danger?"

She whispered: "I think he's still here. Send the cops, now."

Something thudded against the trailer. The operator was still talking, though Dawn barely heard her. She was saying something about how the cops weren't needed.

"You're fine," the operator said.

"What?" Dawn hissed. "There's someone here. I need help."

She must've switched with someone, because now a man was talking: "See, we don't waste valuable city resources on poor trash like you."

Shadows flashed by the window. Dawn crept toward the front door, the phone cord stretching behind her.

"What're you talking about? It's . . . it's Lenny Skelton. He's still alive, and . . . he's got my brother."

Another voice. It was Colquitt. "Now lissen here, you stupid dumbfuck redneck whore." He let loose with an unearthly, grinding howl. *"NO ONE'LL*

BELIEVE YOU HA HA HA!" She knew the voice. It belonged to the Plaid Man. *"HE'S ALREADY DEAD GIVE UP NOW WHILE YOU STILL HAVE A—"*

Cra-a-assssh! She'd ripped out the cord and slung the phone through their picture window without realizing it. Her mother moaned.

"Dawn, is that the DWP? Tell 'em to go around . . ."

Ohmigawd! The door! The door!

It hung on a hinge, halfway open, swinging slightly and casting shifting shadows all around. Dawn was about to leap through the shattered window when—*whang!*—the screen door slammed inward and admitted her friends, Mac, Kaitlyn, and Hiram. She fell to her knees, sobbing.

"Oh, thank God thank God thank God he busted in so fast, got Lee, hit me so hard then Colquitt was the Plaid Man on the phone and I-I-I-*I'm just so scarred-d-d-d."*

Kaitlyn had already knelt and presented her flask. Dawn took a pull and hugged her.

Mac was looking around the trailer. "It's okay, Dawn, it's okay—we're here! Oh, God, your mom! Hiram, help!"

The Gresham kids ran to the kitchen, where Dawn's mom was sitting up. Mac helped her to her feet.

"Ms. Dockery? Ms. Dockery? You okay?" She looked around and called: "Lee? *Lee?!"*

Sandra mumbled: "Hi . . . hi, uh, Mac? Kaitlyn? Hi? Is that you? Where's Dawn? Lee?"

Kaitlyn ducked into one of the bedrooms and came back, shaking her head. "Empty." She sidestepped everyone and ran into the other bedroom, yelling: *"Lee! Where are you, buddy?!"*

Sandra met her daughter's gaze—and her face fell in dark realization. "Where's Lee?"

Kaitlyn emerged from the other room. "He's not here."

Mac: "Oh, my God."

Dawn touched her injured head and grimaced. "He got him. Oh, God in Heaven, he got him. What's he, what is he, is he—"

Mac steadied a swooning Sandra, who said: "Lee? Where is he? My word, my word. Who was that at the—Where is Lee? What happened?"

Dawn looked around, bleary-eyed but increasingly coherent. A moment's hesitation preceded a collective decision: tell the truth.

Which Dawn told: "Mama, it was Lenny Skelton."

Sandra's mouth closed. Her jaw clenched. Mac had wet a washcloth, which Sandra accepted and pressed to her forehead. As the washcloth slowly turned red, Sandra scanned the room, her eyes at first flinty with focus but quickly fogging up again as her voice slurred:

"But . . . my cross-stitch, my word . . . he . . . he died in that fire . . . at the farm."

"He didn't," Mac said.

Sandra turned over a TV table and shifted papers and books around.

"He didn't?" She winced, still casting her gaze around the room. "Where is it? Where *is* it?" She swooned and collapsed to the ground. The girls rushed to her. "But where did he take Lee? Is he hurt? Is he okay? Where is my son?"

"We don't know, but we're gonna find him," Kaitlyn said before addressing Hiram: "Phone! Call an ambulance!"

Hiram ran to the kitchen phone to find only a cord dangling from the wall. "Uh where's the phone?"

Sandra indicated the bedroom. "There's another in Dawn's room."

"Don't!" Dawn yelled, running over. "I done did. It was him."

"Who?" Hiram asked, eyes wide.

Dawn glanced at her mom, then back. She whispered: "Him. The Plaid Man."

Hiram turned white. Kaitlyn ran over. "You sure, Dawnie?"

"Sure as shit and sunshine, I am," Dawn said. "We can't risk callin' the cops. And we gotta get Mama to the emergency room, *now.*"

Sandra was still fussing around the room. "Where is it . . . ?"

Kaitlyn nodded. "Okay, so no more phones. I can drive Dawnie and her mom to the hospital while you guys hustle over to Castle GrayCrystal."

Mac shook her head. "I don't want us to get separated."

Hiram: "We can draw a portal from the hospital to our Smoky Mountain. We just need to add the hospital to all our maps."

Kaitlyn slapped him on the back. "Hiram, you're a daggum Rhodes scholar. Let's do it."

Hiram raised his hand to object about something, but they were already headed for the door. Kaitlyn crossed to Dawn's mom.

"Ms. Dockery? We're gonna take you in. You with me?"

Sandra was waving her away. "Where is it?"

Hiram stuttered: "Uh uhh *uhhh* what about—"

They all ignored him for the time being. Dawn pulled her mom along, saying: "We can find it later, Mama. We gotta hurry! We gotta help Lee!"

They all ran outside, Hiram holding out his map and waving it around, still stuttering. Sandra made a weak swipe behind her.

"But it's important," she whispered.

Hiram's Journal

Every second was an emergency, and it shut down my ability to speak. Kaitlyn helped Dawn and Sandra into their Volvo, while Mac climbed on her bike, and I stumbled around, stuttering and waving around my map. As Kaitlyn slammed herself into the Volvo's driver's seat, I wheeled over, stammering out syllables. Kaitlyn finally picked up on my distress.

"What is it, squirt?"

"Uh *uhhh uh*-give—uh we need your map! We need to add the hospital to it, then Skelton's lair, and then we'll need to add both of those to the glassine!" I held up our master sheet of glassine, which had presumably already generated our magical, extra-dimensional floating dungeon.

Our Smoky Mountain.

"You sure that's how it works, squirt?" Kaitlyn asked.

I nodded, my eyes wide. "Yes, all the maps need to match *precisely* for the magic to work!"

Mac, straddling her bike, waddle-walked over.

"What's the hold-up?"

Kaitlyn: "The big guy wants to take my map. No way I'm handing it over."

"But we need to add more stuff to it," Mac said, turning to me. "Right?"

"Uhhh yeah."

Kaitlyn leaned out. "What if *I* need to add my own path somewhere?"

"Uh that's not how it works."

"You sure you know *everything* about how it works?"

I rifled through my memory banks in a frantic search to come up with one, ironclad set of rules for how the magic worked, but I couldn't. So I shook my head.

Kaitlyn touched my hand. "You've got your maps, Dawnie and I got ours. We'll be on the walkies and make sure we're drawing them as close as possible. Besides, aren't we gonna ask Mr. Johnson to do the same thing? It'll be enough."

Mac leaned in. "Hiram? I think she's right. And we *have to get going.*" She addressed Kaitlyn: "Hit it."

Kaitlyn fired up the Volvo. "So—we're going to the hospital, drop off Momma Dockery—"

I said: "We're going to the mall first to try and find Skelton's address—"

"You'll draw us a gate into the Smoky Mountain—"

Mac: "Then over to the storage facility to get the radio and *then* over to the old house."

"Oh, that reminds me," Kaitlyn said, handing over the keys to the storage room. She put the Volvo into gear but hesitated. "What if we can't find Skelton's address? What if Jase beat us to it?"

"We'll figure something out," Mac said. "Let's go!"

Mackenzie

They raced through the woods. Even with everything that had happened, Mac still found the energy to feel delight for her baby brother.

"When the hell'd you learn to ride a bike?"

"Once I figured out Trent's security code, I snuck out at night and taught myself!"

"Good for you!" Mac said. "Sorry I never got around to teaching you."

"Aw, it's okay! It was worth the skinned knees." He pointed ahead. "Here we are!"

In a clatter of colliding metal and jangling bells, they dumped their bikes and stood staring up at the treehouse.

"We made this the entrance to our Smoky Mountain." Mac said, indicating the door. "What if it didn't work?"

"Then we've got a long night of riding ahead of us. And I still haven't figured out how to turn left on this thing."

They climbed up, and before they even opened the door, Mac noticed something new.

"Look," she said, pointing. Carved into the wood over the door was their SG glyph.

Their keystone.

They shared a quick, hopeful smile, and Mac opened the door.

Kaitlyn

After setting a new land-speed record between Dizzy Pines and West Chim General Hospital, Kaitlyn and Dawn stood in the reception area fending off a well-meaning nurse who kept trying to examine Dawn's head injury. A bleary-eyed Sandra sat in a wheelchair nearby, the whole scene bathed in fluorescent light.

"Honey, we're processing your mama, but you took a pretty nasty lick yourself." The nurse turned and called: "Can we get a doctor out here?" Turning back to Dawn, she added: "Did someone do this to you? Do you need someplace to stay tonight?" Her eyes landed on Kaitlyn's scar. "Or you, honey?"

A couple of burly orderlies ran out. One took command of Sandra's wheelchair and started rolling her in. In response to the nurse's question, Dawn shook her head.

"We don't need someplace to stay."

Sandra vanished into the emergency room behind a pair of flapping doors. The nurse escorted them into the ER right after. They all stopped inside a bed cubicle with the curtain open.

The nurse lowered her voice: "It's all right if you can't tell us right away." She pointed at another nurse: "Can you call the officer on duty, tell him we've got an assault?"

They recognized the next voice instantly: "An assault? Where at?"

Oh, shit, Kaitlyn thought, meeting the gaze of a wide-eyed Dawn. Down the hall, a familiar figure rounded a corner, just doffing a rimmed campaign hat that bristled with peacock feathers. The nurse jogged down the hallway, waving him down.

"Sheriff Colquitt! Thank God you're here, these two girls—"

She turned back to find the girls gone.

Hiram's Journal

Blinding light greeted us, accompanied by a distant, buzzing hum. Swirling blue fire filled the entranceway, while our keystone emitted a laser of blue light that shot through the woods. We stepped in and emerged into the treehouse. For a terrible moment, I thought it hadn't worked, but then I remembered Skelton's Smoky Mountain—the way everything looked normal immediately inside the gate. I squinted to get a better look.

As I expected, everything before me was swimming.

I prodded Mac. "Wanna bet what happens when we take a step forward?"

She took my hand. "Let's do it together."

With a single step, the world shivered to pieces. The ceiling shot skyward, while the walls subdivided into thousands of smaller geometric shapes before zooming away into nothingness. Only the floor remained, stretching forward over infinite, diving darkness. The pathway's composition reflected the raw materials—and sheer love—that went into Castle GrayCrystal. It was a patchwork of hardwood and weathered bricks that alternated between dark green (from Castle Grayskull) and a deep pink (from the Crystal Castle). In the distance floated brass wall fixtures that glowed with spectral orange-yellow light.

But that wasn't the coolest part of our Smoky Mountain. The coolest part was the *shelves.*

A series of bookshelves (about three feet high) lined the pathway like a makeshift guardrail, presenting us with our armor and weapons. Mac pulled on her leather jerkin and slipped her rubber-band gun into her belt, while I strapped on my football pads, forearm guards, and aviator's helmet.

Kaitlyn's, Dawn's, and Lee's armaments all remained. I gave them a worried look.

Mac touched my shoulder. "They'll be along soon."

I gritted my teeth and nodded. We both raced forward, our way flanked by even more shelves, all of them packed with memorabilia, action figures, dolls, toys, and hundreds of photos from all our lives. We noted dozens of little details:

"There's that Man-E-Faces figure you lost when you were five!" she said.

"Aw, there's a picture of you and Dawn in Brownies, when you tried to ride out to that island," I said.

"There's a photo of Dad. Wow, he was handsome."

Both of us stopped at a photo of Mom. It was her senior portrait from Gatlinburg Central. She wore a black formal dress, her hair "Donna Reed" perfect.

She looked happy.

She looked fucking gorgeous.

She looked like Mom.

"Weird," Mac said. "I've never seen this one before. I wonder why she never showed it to us?"

I pulled her along. "We can ask her later. C'mon!"

We arrived at the hub, overhead lights activating in tandem with our movements. For some reason, our Smoky Mountain's hub wasn't *oct*agonal but *hex*agonal. Ours also included a column that rose from the hub's center. Eight podiums, each a different height, featured all of us as superheroes.

No kidding. *Us.* As superheroes.

Lee wore medieval chain mail and carried a shield that bore a stylized heart icon. Dawn also wore armor, but hers hailed from the fantastical worlds of comic books—rich details adorned her armor and helmet like a blue-and-gold labyrinth. She wielded a massive battle axe, and her helmet's visor was a pair of metallic lightning-bolts that met over her brow. Mac's statue wore a medieval thief's robe, while I was dressed in a steampunk-inspired military uniform, complete with an aviator's helmet, epaulets, and a bandolier. Kaitlyn, strangely, held no weapon and wore her normal clothes. Mac pointed.

"You look a little like that red guy from that weird cartoon."

"Oh, you mean Necron 99? From *Wizards?*"

She nodded, frowning. "I wonder where these outfits came from. Did

Jason make them? And why doesn't Kaity have one?"

"Why are there extra podiums?" I asked, indicating the empty podiums. "Who's supposed to go in these three extra spaces?"

Mac shook her head, shrugged, then snapped her fingers. "Wait! What about our weapons?"

We unslung our backpacks, reached in—

The world had flipped sideways. When I touched my gift, the sextant, I might as well have grabbed a live wire. Electricity blasted through me and laid me flat. I lost a few seconds; when I came to, all I saw was the endless darkness above.

But the darkness wasn't empty. Something blighted the darkness, a distant filament of light.

Groggy, I sat up, rubbing my eyes. Mac's gift had the same effect, and it must've burned her skin somehow because her flesh looked bright pink.

"Mac," I said with a hoarse voice. "Are you okay? There's something up—"

Mac's appearance shut me up. She'd sat up and was rubbing her temples, but she'd transformed. Her street clothes were gone, replaced by a suit of armor. Weirdly, she wore the gleaming, futuristic armor Dawn wore in her statue . . . but that wasn't even the coolest part.

Her skin wasn't pink.

It was *paint*.

She'd transformed into a living cartoon—just like Jason.

Mackenzie

Blackness engulfed her the instant she touched her gift. Her next sight was a closeup of the ground. Up close, she could see that everything inside their Smoky Mountains was composed of trillions of tiny hexagons. Sitting up, she half expected steam to be rising from her flesh.

Her flesh.

Oh, my God, she thought, looking at her hands; her hands, which weren't her hands anymore, but bright blue gauntlets adorned with hundreds of delicate, interlocking golden details like the circuits of a microchip. Something weighed on her head, and she found she was wearing an ornate helmet.

The same helmet Dawn wore on her statue.

"Mac," came her brother's voice. "Are you okay? There's something up—"

He gaped at her with gogged eyes that would befit Roger Rabbit. Like her, he had transformed into a cartoon, but unlike her, he seemed to be wearing his "correct" outfit; he wore a pseudo-military jacket with epaulets, a bandolier, plus an aviator's helmet. All were the cherry red of a Saturday-morning cartoon. They both stood up and approached each other in astonishment, each holding their weapon: Hiram the sextant, Mac the axe. Mac shook her head.

"I guess when we get a weapon, this happens," she said.

Hiram had already noticed the discrepancy in outfits. "But you're wearing Dawn's armor. And the axe looks different on her statue. Why?"

Mac shrugged. "No clue. Maybe when we catch Jason, he can explain, but for now, we've got to keep moving."

"Wait." Hiram stopped her, pointing up. "Do you see that?" It looked like an airport runway, a filament of light that sparkled in the undefined distance. "What do you think it is?"

"No idea," she said, shaking her head. Her animated hair swayed back and forth like two-dimensional crimson paper cut-outs.

Suddenly: *Rummm-vum-vum-vum-vum-VUM.*

The axe started vibrating as hard as a paint mixer. Mac staggered back a few steps, holding it with both fists as it transformed into a massive, golden-hilted battle axe with a blade as long and razor-sharp as a scimitar.

"Whoa," Hiram said. "Why'd *that* happen?"

"We don't have time to puzzle this out," she said. "We've got to get to the mall."

"And we need to add an entrance from the hospital into here," I added.

"Right," Mac said, taking off at a loping, Don Bluth-esque sprint down the floating pathway, not noticing that the endless darkness around them wasn't *completely* empty. If she'd paused a moment to search the space more carefully, she would've seen not only the filament of light Hiram saw but also *other* distant filaments. Even stranger, if they'd looked closer, they might've noticed that the darkness *itself* had taken on some texture; it bristled and fluttered, the movements catching the occasional shaft of light from those distant filaments.

If they'd looked closer, they might've thought the darkness looked like trees.

Maybe even a forest.

Dawn

Colquitt's voice, along with his running footsteps, followed them from behind:

"Wait! Girls, wait up! Someone stop those two girls!"

They sprinted down the hall, which was thankfully empty, and ducked into a hospital room. Curtains were drawn around the beds. Dawn swept them open and found the room unoccupied. After locking the outer door, she waved Kaitlyn into the bathroom.

"Come on, come on!"

They quietly shut themselves into the dark bathroom. Outside, Colquitt's boots clomped past.

"Dammit, where the Sam Hill'd they go?" he muttered as his footfalls faded.

Kaitlyn pulled out their walkie and squelched it.

"Guys? Guys?" she whispered. "We're gonna start adding to our maps. We need an exit outta here, stat." Her only response was static. "Damn, we're outta range."

"Or they're already in our Smoky Mountain." Dawn smiled. "Must not get much reception between dimensions."

Thrummm-m-m-m. The walkie started to vibrate wildly. They gaped in astonishment.

"What the holy fucking shit is happening?" Kaitlyn said.

Hiram's Journal

We sprinted through our Smoky Mountain, our every motion exaggerated and amplified. Mac's animated avatar retained her bulky, powerful build, adding to it a perpetual swirl of fairy dust that accentuated her every action. Each of us held our magical gifts close as we ran.

Jason said this sextant does more than simply chart the stars, I thought. *What did he mean?*

"Here we go!" Mac said, pointing to a wooden arrow sign that read *THIS WAY TO THE MALL!* When she pointed, golden dust *poofed* around her hand, while her voice resounded like it had been remixed in a magical animation studio. "God, I hope we can find that address."

We reached the gate, a stone archway bearing a keystone marked with a fleur-de-lis. It opened as we approached.

Mackenzie

Like a three-dimensional cinematic wipe, the gate stripped them of their magic and transformed them both back into their regular selves. Hiram's sextant (which he hooked to his belt) looked roughly the same, while the battle axe shrank back down to a humble hatchet as they entered the mall.

And froze.

"Oh, shit," Mac whispered.

Red-and-blue lights washed over the scene in a revolving pulse. Outside, dozens of police cars were parked alongside a fire truck and an ambulance. A half-dozen cops and firemen stood right outside the mall's doors, flanking an old man Mac immediately recognized: the owner of Stems & Stamens. He'd clearly just been rousted from sleep, wearing a robe, the remnants of his white hair a frizzy mess. He fumbled with a ring of keys.

They were there for a clear reason: someone had bombed the mall.

Stems & Stamens had been reduced to a pile of smoking wreckage. Its night-time guard door lay splayed open like a snarling maw of blackened steel fangs. Black scoring streaked all around the store's entrance. Small fires flickered here and there.

"Did Jason do this?" Hiram whispered.

"I think so," Mac said. "But how?"

Mac pointed. "Look." A few yards away from their gate stood another one, rendered in the same red ASCII alphanumerics they'd seen before. Interlocking portcullises blocked the opening. "That must be Jason's." She ran over and shook the portcullises. "Locked. But maybe there's a way we can—"

Down the hall, a key clicked into place. The cops and everyone were about to enter. Mac turned and pushed Hiram back through the gate, the movement transforming them both back into their fully armed and animated magical selves. Voices reverberated through the swirling blue light:

"I heard the explosion clear across town!"

"Stay calm, sir," one cop said.

As soon as they were both in the Smoky Mountain, the portcullises closed. Mac was already running back toward the hub, yelling, "C'mon! We've got to get to the storage room!"

"Okay, but how are we—"

Thrummm-m-m-m came a magical thrum in tune with the sextant, the gleaming, animated sextant, which rattled and *rummed* and *thrummed* and shook itself clean off his belt, clattering to the pathway and perilously close to the edge, where Hiram went scrambling after it, stumbling over his own boot-clad, Saturday-morning feet, his walkie-talkie getting yanked out of his backpack by an unseen magical force that drew it and the sextant together like supercharged electromagnets: *clack!* Once fused, the walkie squelched and crackled . . . and spoke.

"What the holy fucking shit is happening?"

Hiram, beaming, grabbed the walkie-sextant combo and yelled: *"Kaity?!"*

Hiram's Journal

"Kaity?!"

Her voice came back, loud and clear: "Squirt?! Is that you?"

Mac ran over, her eyes cartoony wide. "Is that them?"

"Yeah!" I said, jumping up and handing her the device. The two objects hadn't merely stuck together; they had *merged,* combining details, form, and function. The sextant's degree-measuring arc served as its antennae, while the walkie's body—a simulacrum of Castle Grayskull's green-stone walls—was now shot through with silver and gold details. The sextant's small telescope was mounted over the walkie's receiver.

Mac: "Kaity? Dawn? Are you at the hospital?"

"Yeah, and fuckin' Colquitt's after us," Dawn hissed, her voice muffled like she was cupping a hand over the receiver. "We gotta draw a portal outta here *right now.*" I made eyes with Mac, my expression saying *I hope this works.*

Mac and I produced our maps, along with the glassine overlay, and spread them out.

Dawn's voice crackled: "How'd the Smoky Mountain turn out? Does it work?"

We shared big, conspiratorial smiles. "It works better than you can possibly imagine," Mac said. "There are even a few surprises. Dawn, I actually have a gift for you." She'd slid the battle axe into a scabbard mounted to her back.

"Gift?" Dawn asked, sounding intrigued in spite of her stress. "What kinda gift?"

"Later," Mac said. "Let's get to work on these maps."

Kaitlyn

I'll never let them fall.

It was a promise and an oath. They were her family now. If anything, the Dockerys and the Greshams felt even more like her family than her real family did.

Except maybe Jason.

Sweet Jase, what happened to you? Where did you go wrong?

She grappled with those questions and all their unknowable implications as they worked on their maps, adding one detail at a time, double-checking their work at every step. Dawn had said she wasn't a good artist but was being humble. She added the hospital to her map in a few confident strokes, while Kaitlyn basically had to copy her work to keep up.

Dawn and Lee are freakin' geniuses, Kaitlyn thought with admiration and awe. *I'm lucky to be friends with them. I'm so lucky they all let me into their lives. And if anything happens to Lee, I'll kill Skelton myself.*

"Okay," Dawn said, taking up the walkie. "We're done. Now what?"

Hiram's voice boomed back: "I'll add the hospital to the glassine. That should add it to our Smoky Mountain." Dawn turned down the volume.

"Hiram, y'all sound funny. Are you all right?"

Mac answered: "We're fine. But . . . well, we'll explain once you get in here. Hiram, are you done?"

"Yep," he said. "I've added the hospital."

Kaitlyn and Dawn peeked out of the bathroom door. Nothing had changed. They were still locked into the empty hospital room. A small window on the door looked onto a long hallway that was perpendicular to the room. Stepping out of the bathroom, Kaitlyn took the walkie from Dawn.

"Hey, squirt—"

Clomp, clomp, clomp! The girls both lunged to the floor under the door's window as Colquitt passed by and *clomped* down the long hallway, exchanging words with another cop.

"I think it's Trent's kids," Colquitt said, his voice fading. "They got loose again, goddammit."

After he was gone, Kaitlyn said: "How do we find the gate?"

"I think I know how," Dawn said, jumping up to grab a pen from a bedside table. "Draw it on here, on the doorjamb. The keystone." Into the walkie, she added: "You copy that, guys?"

Kaitlyn stood and nodded. "You're a genius. Gimme that pen."

She sketched the stylized SG glyph. Blue light blazed in her face. Blinking, she backed away from the door. The door-window seemed to be looking down at a swimming pool on a perfect summer day. Blue light shimmered. Before she knew it, Kaitlyn had taken Dawn's hand.

"Did it work?" came Mac's voice.

"Sure as shit and sunshine," Dawn said, opening the door.

Dawn

Blue light swam before them. Dimly through it moved the shapes of the two cops, Colquitt and Baird, who rounded a corner and pointed their way.

"*You two! Stop!*" Colquitt screamed, sprinting toward them so fast his hat fell off.

Kaitlyn's hand felt good. To Dawn's lack of surprise, it felt soft as silk. "High-class hands," her mama would've called them. In her peripheral vision, Dawn noted the slight bend in Kaitlyn's forearm from where Colquitt had broken it. *She's got a lot of grit,* Dawn thought and immediately flashed on all the folks she'd had to bid farewell to over the years.

Her father.

Jenny Miles.

Dawn-n-Gresh.

The cops were drawing close, and as they ran, Colquitt's face un-seamed in a latticework of criss-crossing gashes that bled red and blue, staining his face plaid with gore.

"WHY RUN, BITCHES? YOU'RE ALREADY DEAD AND THIS! IS! HELLLLL!"

Dawn's heart turned to ice, and yet Kaitlyn's presence steadied her, as did the knowledge that her friends awaited her on the other side of the gate. Somehow, she knew that a showdown with the Plaid Man was coming, but for tonight, he and his taunts seemed like petty nuisances.

Lee was in trouble. Jason was in trouble. Dawn had to do right by them.

And Jenny.

She glared into the Plaid Man's face.

"I HUNGERRR!" he wailed.

"You ain't that scary," Dawn said as they stepped through the gate.

Colquitt

Colquitt and his partner, Bubba Baird, crashed into the hospital room only to find it empty.

"What the hell?" Colquitt muttered, throwing open the bathroom door to also find it empty. It was supposed to be his night off, but because Captain Myslinski still had him in the doghouse for the Soddy Farm thing, he got stuck watching the hospital.

Moments earlier, when they were sprinting down the hall, he realized he recognized them from that night. Seeing them again opened a pit in his stomach because those bitches had caused him such trouble.

But there was something else. As they sprinted, Colquitt could've sworn the room was flooding with fire.

Shimmering blue fire.

Baird leaned back into the hall and looked both ways. Nothing.

"Boss, I seen both them girls in here. They gotta be around somewhere."

Colquitt, shaking his head in bafflement, was already storming into the hallway. He barked into his radio: "Radio, this is Colquitt working West Chim General. I wanna put out an APB on some teenagers, and get me Trent Sutton on the horn. I think I just saw his daughter."

Hiram's Journal

We followed another arrow sign that read *THIS WAY TO THE HOSPITAL.* Only moments before, another path had sprouted from our hub, snaking through the endless darkness until it stopped, a new gate springing forth from it, bearing our chosen keystone: a red cross. The portcullises opened as we approached, but behind them was nothing.

No magic blue light.

Just more darkness.

That's when Kaitlyn's voice came over the walkie. Dawn's idea to draw a keystone on the doorjamb must've worked, because blue light flooded the gate and immediately disgorged Kaitlyn and Dawn, who both started to hug us but stopped short, their expressions caught between joyful and thunderstruck. Kaitlyn deduced the cause of our appearance right away.

"Ohmygod this has to do with our gifts, doesn't it?!"

I yelled: "Kaity, wait, wait—*don't!*"

Too late. She plunged a hand into her backpack and exploded in a ball of lightning that slung her to the ground. We both ran to her. Somehow, she was still conscious. Tiny lightning-bolts flashed from her hair and licked in little circles around her arms and legs.

But besides being a cartoon, her appearance hadn't changed.

Standing, she looked herself over, frowning. "Why didn't I get a Halloween costume thingy?"

"Does that do something?" Mac indicated the billy club.

Kaitlyn's eyes rose as she searched her memory. "'For Kaitlyn, the Scepter of Chaos, an umbrella to cover you in times of sorrow,'" she muttered before giving us a knowing grin. "Jason's a meathead, but the guy loves his comics. Thor's alter ego carries an umbrella, and when he needed to transform, he—"

She dropped to a knee and slammed the club's end into the ground. Lightning licked from its tips. As she stood, the scepter lengthened to six feet and sprouted from its end a ram's skull wreathed with an ankh. More lightning swirled around her, slowly outfitting her in a leather halter and pants, all of it lined with fishnet. Her hair stood in a spiked mohawk, while black lipstick and eye shadow gave her face a stunningly severe sculpt. Steel-toed platform boots completed the ensemble. Like us, she was a cartoon, but unlike us, her edges weren't smooth but slightly *pixelated,* as if she'd walked off a computer screen.

She regarded her new look—and got a little choked up. "In my dreams, I'm beautiful and bad. Wow, Jase, thank you." She touched her lower eyelid. "Do . . . do I still have my scar?"

Mac looked. "Yeah. Do you—?"

"Oh, yeah," Kaitlyn said. "Good or bad, it's all a part of the art."

Now Dawn was the one feeling left out. "Aw. Those are so cool. Did he . . . Uh, did Jason—"

Mac took her hand. "Follow me."

We all ran to the hub, where the girls fell silent at the sight of our statues. Kaitlyn's had transformed to match her current appearance.

"We look fuckin' rad," Kaitlyn said, her voice bearing a slight digitized undertone. Dawn's breathing hitched. She was on the verge of tears. Kaitlyn added: "Dawnie, he's gonna be fine."

"You don't know that."

"Yes, we do," Mac said. "And we're going to get this done." She brought Dawn to her statue and presented the battle axe to her. "Jason said he made this for me, but I think it's meant for you."

Dawn looked it but shook her head. "Why would the statue show *me* with it when he made it for *you?*"

"The Grid," I said. All heads swiveled to me. "I think the Grid is speaking to us through this place. And it somehow knows who should get what."

"But what about Mac?" Dawn said. "What'll she do without a weapon?"

Mac produced her wooden gun, which was loaded with a heavy-duty rubber-band.

"I'll be fine, Dawn," she said, offering the axe. "You deserve this. I think Jason meant for you to have it, even if he didn't know it."

Kaitlyn stifled a smile. After a moment's hesitation, Dawn nodded and grinned slightly. "Maybe I oughta sit down? Seems like these gifts pack a punch."

We all nodded. She sat and accepted the axe, which blasted her flat in a burst of thunder and lightning that flashed into the distant darkness. Tornadoes of electricity encircled both Mac and Dawn—or should I say *Dawn-n-Gresh*—as the power transferred from one to the other, the gleaming armor disassembling into a trillion tiny bits and flowing around Dawn, where they reassembled themselves a piece at a time: gauntlets, skirt, breastplate. The last detail to coalesce was her helmet's visor, which materialized in a flash of gleaming gold. Like us, Dawn had transformed into a cartoon.

But to our surprise (and delight), Mac hadn't changed back entirely. Her outfit had morphed back into her street clothes with the leather jerkin, but she was still a cartoon. She patted herself down.

"Huh! I guess we get to keep a little bit of the magic." She smiled. "Fine by me."

Dawn was already rushing down the path to the storage room.

"Ain't no time to celebrate! Keep movin'!"

Holton

He always wanted to see what was inside Davey's saloon.

Holton Webb parked his Camry where the kid told him to, a full mile away from the attraction. He strapped on his shoulder holster and nestled his Glock in place. They walked along an empty state highway that held the eerie energy of expectation. Power lines hummed and crackled. Holton's mind was abuzz with new possibilities and strange outcomes. The big kid was persuasive—*there's lives at stake, people in danger,* he'd said—and Holt tried his best to take folks at their word.

Especially when his instincts told him something was wrong.

Jason held out a hand. "Stop here."

Holton did. The kid produced two hand-drawn maps that were rendered in loving detail on paper that had to be ten years old. They were drawn in half a dozen different media: graphite, oils, watercolor, and more. Whoever had drawn those maps had lavished them with as much care and detail as his mom did on their Christmas cottages. The big kid added something to both maps. Holt peeked over his shoulder. It looked like he'd drawn an archway on both maps, or a kind of gate. He added a portcullis to both, followed by a little emblem at the top of each gate: a tiny prize ribbon.

He looked up, muttering to himself: "Please, please, please."

"What the heck are you doing?"

"Damn," Jason whispered. "We *do* need him." He strode forward, stowing his maps, but Holt stopped him.

"Son, I've only got so much patience in me. What's happening here?"

"It's not a simple answer."

"I'll take a complicated one."

The big kid steeled himself. Holt knew the look: he was afraid he wouldn't believe him. But when he spoke, the batwing doors of Davey's saloon swung open and gave him a glimpse of dark wonders within.

"Lenny Skelton's still alive. He's in Enchanted Caverns, and he's kidnapped someone I . . . someone I love."

Holton absorbed his words. Nodded. "Okay."

"You believe me?" The look of astonished gratitude on the poor kid's face broke Holt's heart. He looked like no one had taken him at his word in years.

Holton nodded. "That was him on my phone, wasn't it?"

"Yes."

Holton winced. "It never felt right, the way he went. Those dentals—they were all that was left. That's it. I seen house fires before, and they're hot . . . but they ain't hot enough to make a whole man disappear." He headed forward, but now Jason was the one stopping him.

"It won't be what you expect when we get there."

"Meaning what?"

"It's . . . well . . . "

"This another complicated answer?"

"Yeah."

"Give me the basics."

"Skelton's in there, but he'll be hard to . . . hard to see."

"Fair enough. What else?"

"It'll be dangerous. There'll be . . . traps."

"My Uncle Estes used to booby-trap his front lawn to keep G-men away. I think I can handle it. Let's go."

"Wait," Jason said, reaching into his pocket to produce a thick piece of sidewalk chalk. "I need to do something."

Colquitt

Fucking kids think they can prank Beaufort Davis Colquitt, huh?

Baird braced himself against the dashboard as Colquitt downshifted and floored it, the police cruiser fishtailing around a corner toward the police station, siren wailing and lights flashing.

Baird: "Boss, you think we need the lights and all that? Ain't no one broken any laws."

"Shut it. Tell me you didn't see that in the door."

"The door?"

Colquitt glared. "That *fire* in the door. That *blue fire*."

Baird shook his head. "I didn't see nothing, boss."

The radio squawked: "Sheriff, I've got Trent Sutton on the line for you."

"Put him through."

He'd been drinking, his vowels heavy, his consonants soft: "Bo! They're gone! All gone!"

"Now, Trent, buddy, stay calm. I think I saw Kaity down at West Chim General. What do you mean they're *all* gone?"

"You saw Kaity?!"

Colquitt suddenly doubted his memory. "Well, I—I *think* I did! Now, listen, bud: stay calm and give Wanda a description of all four. She'll get an APB out on all of 'em. I'm on my way!"

Hiram's Journal

Passing through the gates felt uncanny, like your whole body was a tongue making contact with a nine-volt battery. The transformation from cartoon and back also left a perceptible scorch across your skin, a temporary sunburn that quickly faded and left wisps of steam rising from your hair.

We were moving so fast, our magic sunburns hadn't even had time to fade before we had our old radio loaded up and rolling back into our Smoky Mountain.

"Go, go, go!" Mac yelled, waving us back into the swirling blue gate, which had opened in one of the storage center's cinder-block walls. Finding the radio was easy, as Mom had left it at the front of the room. Dawn procured us a dolly, and within moments, we were sprinting through the gate and clattering across the pink-and-green bricks of our Smoky Mountain, all of us crackling from our magical transformation back to cartoons.

"Where's the pathway to our old house?" Mac called.

I pointed. "There!"

Yet another arrow sign guided us toward *THE GRESHAMS' OLD HOUSE.* As we ran, Kaitlyn noticed one of those weird filaments of light.

"What is that?" she asked.

"Dunno," Mac said.

Dawn gave us a look. "Y'all can't tell what that is?"

"No," I said, huffing and puffing. "You can?"

"Yeah, it's another one of these things. Another Smoky Mountain."

We all stopped and squinted into the distance. It looked like a hectic, coiling sidewalk floating in the endless expanse, a tangle of ribbons made from brick and cobblestone suspended in space. Like our Smoky Mountain, lights glowed above the walkway like streetlamps through fog. There were others floating even farther away, but one in particular seemed to be within striking distance.

I shook my head, astonished. "Do you think we can get to it?"

"Would we even want to?" Kaitlyn asked. "How do we know that's not Skelton's?"

Mac: "But what if it's Jason's? Sure would speed things up if we could catch him in his own Smoky Mountain."

We rattled down the pathway to another gate. Its keystone was mine and Mac's childhood silhouettes, which Mom had drawn herself.

Dang, she was so talented. As the portcullises rattled open, I reflected on my choice of words:

She was *so talented. Why'd I use the past tense?*

Mac jerked her chin at the gate. We pushed the radio in and emerged into our old house's living room, the walk-in just ahead and to the right. Our lights swept across the scene: a room empty except for some dust bunnies, a *FOR SALE* sign in the front window. Steam rose from our sizzling hair as our magic sunburns faded. As we rolled the radio into the walk-in, Mac indicated the new hardwood floors.

"They pulled up the carpet," she said.

They'd done a lot more, too, replacing the wood paneling with wallpaper and the chintzy old fixtures with track lighting. Kaitlyn tipped the dolly up so we could roll the radio off it. Mac and Dawn gripped the radio's sides and slid it around the U-shaped turn and under the stairs.

"Is this where it went?" Dawn asked. "Under here?"

"Yeah," I said. "As far under the stairs as you can push it."

For a moment, I thought the house smelled different, but it occurred to me: this was how it had *always* smelled. It took us being away from it for a few months for me to really smell—and see and hear—our old house again. The walk-in's popcorn ceiling reminded me of the surface of the moon. A crack snaked across it like a dark lightning-bolt. I'd never noticed it before. Had it always been there, like the Office?

Mac nodded. "Okay, it's in."

All heads turned to me, and that's when I noticed it.

"Look," I said, pointing. Flashlights and headlamps brought Dad's old movie poster into view, mounted to the slanted ceiling under the stairs: *The Adventures of Buckaroo Banzai Across the Eighth Dimension,* with its collage of images, including a computer monitor covered with a latticework of spidery orange lines.

Our eyes went to it immediately.

"The Grid," someone said. It didn't matter who. We were all thinking it.

Mac touched my hand. "How's this work? Do we just turn it on?"

I nodded and clicked the radio's power knob to *ON*. Nothing happened, of course, because it wasn't plugged in, and the house had no electricity anyway. My mind kept circling back to the way I thought about Mom moments before.

She was so talented.

Was.

Mom rarely asked us about ourselves, and when she did, it was little more than an excuse for her to talk about herself. I used to joke that she was a "five-worder": she'd ask you something, you'd say five words, and then she'd start talking. She was a bottomless pit of stories about her past, most of them orthogonal to her experiences with Dad:

I was this close to getting my master's when I met him. If I got my master's,

I could've stopped teaching elementary, maybe moved up to high school and worked on a PhD over the summers. I could've been teaching at Northwestern by now.

She constantly imagined a parallel world where, instead of marrying Dad, she pursued her own dreams, her own life. It wasn't lost on either of us that in that parallel world, Mac and I didn't exist. In *this* world, the one where she married Dad and had us, she thought her old life was over. So did we, because that was how she spoke of it.

But to this day, I think Mom sold herself short. Mac and I would eventually grow up and leave the house. She was only thirty-three when she had me, and if I moved out at eighteen, she'd only be fifty-one. I'm almost fifty-one today, and I can assure you, I don't feel like my life is over. On the contrary, I feel like I'm just getting started.

On that fateful Friday night in 1990, hunched under the stairs of our old house, our headlamps casting shafts of light that glittered with dust, I looked at that old movie poster . . . and into the Grid. What I said next may have been out loud or only in my head. Like I said, I get those mixed up sometimes. What mattered was that I thought of Mom in the present tense.

"Mom is so talented." And: "Good on you, little buckaroo."

Krzzzzkt!

Lee

When the door to their trailer burst open, all Lee could think was, *How did he get our trailer number?* The question faded into the darkness of lost memories once Skelton struck him over the head. After that, all was swirling blackness except for occasional flashes:

His mom and sister unconscious.

Books and papers flying around their trailer.

The world turning upside-down as he was lifted into a fireman's carry.

Red flashes of light.

His head throbbed. Consciousness was returning slowly, bringing with it sounds and sensations. Water dripped and echoed. A cool breeze carried the faint scent of sulphur.

I must be underground somewhere. Enchanted Caverns!

When he opened his eyes, blood ran into them from a gash across his cheek. He tried to wipe it away but found he was suspended upside-down. Strange hands gripped his ankles, but nothing appeared to be holding him. He floated, his hands held behind his back by another pair of unseen hands. Another gash on his head dribbled blood in echoing *patter-pat-pats*.

His view stained with a crimson vignette, Lee found his supposition correct: he was in Enchanted Caverns. He'd come here on a field trip in grade school, and he vividly remembered this chamber. He floated above a small mesa, about ten feet in diameter, that rose from an underground pond. Man-made lights shone from the bottom like headlights through a dense fog. A rainbow array of stalagmites and stalactites surrounded him like a set of menacing mandibles.

This is right inside the main entrance, he thought. *So I'm close to the surface. At least he didn't take me too far underground.*

He cleared his throat. "Hello? *Hello? I need help! Help meeeee!*"

The caves answered: *"Help meeee help meeeee."*

He appeared behind him: "I'm proud of you, boy."

Lee yelped. Heat warmed the back of his head, moving around to the side in concert with the devil's thundering footfalls. He wore a plaid flannel button-down and jeans. One of his eye sockets sat empty like a tiny maw. The scent of cheap after-shave surrounded him. From his back pocket he pulled a washcloth and wiped Lee's brow clean. Lee flinched away from his touch, but he gripped his scalp, his fingernails digging into his cheeks like talons.

"I was tryin' to send ye henceforth, but you took that blow I delivered and kept on tickin'. Blue ribbon, for sure, once I get done here tonight." He released his face and stood straight, glancing around casually. "How long till your friends 'n' neighbors show up, d'ya think?" Silence. "I figger they'll be along any minute now, less'n they forgot about you." His toothy smile was a line of crumbling tombstones pockmarked by acid rain. "Funny how y'all fell for it. Me goin' after that piggie." Silence. "Well, sit tight now, little Blue Ribbon. I'm gonna go claim what's mine."

"My friends—" (his voice cracked) "—will save me. Would you like to know why?"

"Yes, I surely would."

"Because they're fearless."

Skelton bent over like he'd taken a punch to the gut. But he was only stifling laughter, patting his stomach in glee. He relaxed and let his mad gales ring forth, a staccato song from the underworld, and as he laughed, the world melted. The glowing pond bubbled away, revealing endless darkness underneath. Skulls and bones materialized all across Lee's little stone mesa, which was suddenly a floating sky-island. The walls divided into thousands of geometric shapes and retracted away to nothing, revealing more endless black. All around floated a scattering of more small sky-islands.

Next to Lee, some of the bones shifted around, forming a perceptible square shape. That square rose from the ground on a column of bones.

Skelton crossed over and knocked on it twice.

From nothing appeared a familiar sight: a book.

Mastery of Occultopsychic Phenomena, by Dr. Cleopatra Von Wizardo-Sorora.

He took it up and paged through it. "That night under the bleachers was an accident, when your boy JJ Flash almost caught me. Didja know that? Dumb fuckin' luck that someone left one of them gates open. I near-about tripped into the damn thing. Found myself in one of these places. The *in-betweens.* There warn't but one pathway, and it popped me out somewhere near Pigeon Forge, in the backyard of my next prize, as happened. They caught me soon after, but I never forgot that night, and I never stopped tryin' to get back into the in-betweens."

He stopped at a certain page. "Lucky for me, your friend, Mr. Tall and Dark, reached out to me in stir and showed me the way." Skelton plucked three folded pieces of paper from the book and held it up.

They were three hand-drawn maps. One he recognized as Hiram's, another he figured to be Skelton's.

But the third was Lee's.

Skelton continued: "Thanks for this. Your friend told me: more maps, more power. Took a few weeks to plan it all out, adding the gates to the farm, picking the perfect night to break out. Didn't count on the piggies showing up, but that was a nice little cherry on top, having an official audience for my grand exit." He turned the book upside down so Lee could see. It depicted a specter with a million faces, each a different color, each of them slightly overlapping like a satanic Venn diagram. Lee had read this very page in his research, but it had escaped his notice because the creature's face wasn't a match.

But from a distance, the illustration did indeed look plaid.

The creature was named *THE FACELESS ONE, ORIGINAL EVIL.*

Skelton tapped the illustration. "Your boy, the tall drinka, introduced me to the in-betweens, but the in-betweens introduced me to *him.* He spoke to me. Asked me about my prizes."

His prizes. The kids. His victims. Their remains.

Skelton carried on with his unholy litany: "My prizes, be they first, second, runner-ups, or honorable mentions. They're the kindlin' for the flame that keeps me burnin'. This man, the Faceless, told me I done good, and then he told me where to find this here book. He said *some* lazy little boy left a gate open the night of my grand escape. Said this lazy little boy opened a gate right next to his trailer."

The portal from Dizzy Pines to Soddy Farm. The old cabin. That's how he found us.

Skelton continued: "He told me we needed it."

"For what?" Lee whispered. "My mother has many unusual books. Why is that book so important?"

Skelton shook his head, *tut-tut-tutting* him. "Ain't you ever wondered *why* your mama had all them strange tomes, little sumpty?" He leaned forward and whispered: "For what's to come *next*." He came closer, his voice lowering. "This is it for you. Tonight's the night. You didn't even make it to a dozen on this green earth. I'mma shuffle you off and store you away in the attic."

Voices floated down: "Where do you think he is?"

"I don't know. He could be anywhere. Maintain noise discipline."

Jason! And Officer Webb! They made it! But—oh no!

Skelton had already slammed his paw over Lee's mouth. He screamed and screamed, all for naught. Skelton stuffed a rag into his mouth and wrapped his head in Duck tape. Turning away, he executed an arcane gesture that brought a sketching easel into existence. He produced his three maps and flipped them into the air, where they floated, glowing from within. The easel held a piece of glassine that must've depicted his Smoky Mountain, including the hideout.

"So y'all found my hidey-hole, didja? Well, we'll haveta do something about that, won't we?"

He bent over and added something to the glassine. Lee craned his neck to see but Skelton blocked him. Suddenly, the earth shook . . . and shook . . . and shook. Lee swung from his ankles like a pendulum. Skelton executed another gesture, and a skull-and-bones pathway sprang from the mesa, stretching upward until it terminated in a pair of glass doors. He gave Lee one last evil smile and headed up the new pathway.

Lee closed his eyes.

And prayed.

Justin

Calliope wouldn't stop sitting on his map.

"Cal, give me a break, girl."

Justin Johnson had had to move his new art project to his kitchen table to accommodate all the paints and pencils and chalk he'd bought at Junebug Jubilee's. His map had spread across several sheets of hexagonal graph paper—a little voice had suggested he get it—and on that Friday night, his new foster cat, a tortie he'd named after the muse of epic poetry, kept setting her substantial rear end in the middle of his work. Rusty, meanwhile, was fully conked out in his lap, purring like a motor. Justin nursed a glass of red wine.

"What'd that kid call it?" he muttered before raising a finger. "Right."

He'd sketched in the mysterious traincar in the woods near the Greshams' old house, but now he labeled the area *ITZA LINDA*. That done, he reviewed his work. His map included every important location he could think of that was connected to Skelton:

Soddy Farm.

Polk Middle-Senior High.

West Chimney Top Police Department.

Montmarnass Academy.

The Gold Rush park.

Rusty stirred in his lap, which he began to knead. Justin gave a slight hiss.

"Watch the claws, Rust." He pushed Calliope back off his map, prompting her to slink around and head-bonk his hand. He added in the home of Maggie Vaughn, Skelton's last victim, down in Pigeon Forge, followed by the homes of each of his victims. He labored over his map's every detail, shading in each house and tree, each river and brook. He cycled through media depending on what his instincts told him; some places he drew in pencil, others he painted in oils. Some locations came to him in surges of intuition:

The Greshams' old house. When he looked up their address, he lingered on their phone number, feeling the urge to call that sweet kid back.

"Hiram," he muttered.

He'd added in Dizzy Pines trailer park, followed by Trent Sutton's mansion. (He maintained a subscription to the West Chim Weekly, where he'd seen Corrie Gresham's marriage notice to the huge asshole.) Another location had presented itself the night before, an array of blocky buildings that he labeled *APARTMENTS?*

That Friday night, as he gently fended off the affections of his cats, Justin added one final location: Enchanted Caverns, the old roadside attraction. Calliope set a paw on his hand and was instantly asleep. Rusty rested his chin on the table and continued purring before suddenly giving Justin's hand a nibble.

"Rust, you keep that up, I swear I'm gonna pitch you in the street."

He seemed to take the rebuke seriously, because he fell instantly asleep with Justin's hand between his fangs. Both his hands held captive, Justin smiled and glanced over at his phone.

It was still unplugged.

Beverly's was open, but he'd already had a couple of glasses. It'd be risky to make the drive—the road down was a switchbacked nightmare—but something told him he might have to. He extracted his hands and stood, carefully setting Rusty in his seat. Heat-lightning flashed outside, casting the shadow of a beer-fermenting tank on his far wall, the design on his home's stained-glass window. Lightning flashed again and again, creating a shadowy zoetrope across his wall, and in his buzzed mental state, the fermenting tank looked a little like a locomotive charging across the inside of his house.

If he put on some coffee now, he could sober up in half an hour and get to Beverly's by eleven.

Unless . . .

—computer disk—

He frowned at the invasive thought. He had no idea why, but Ms. Glenn's words of the previous afternoon came to mind: *It looks like a disk? For a computer, perhaps?*

"Why would Momma have had a computer disk?" he whispered.

It sounded like someone was trying to jump-start a rotary-dial phone: *Krzzzzkt—BRRRRINNNG!*

The noise drove him back a few steps in surprise. He glanced around, wondering if his doorbell had malfunctioned, before he noticed steam rising from his phone.

His *disconnected* phone.

Justin stepped forward, his movement accentuated by another flash of heat-lightning. Rusty appeared by his side and marked his leg.

"Did you hear that, Ru—"

It was louder this time: *Krzzzzkt—BRRRRINNNG!* The phone jolted clean off the side table and *bang-clanged* to the floor. Rusty hissed and padded over to bat at it. Calliope was still asleep on his map; it was her only defense. The receiver had fallen off. Steam poured from both ends.

But that wasn't all that poured from the phone.

There were voices, too:

"Mr. Johnson? Are you there?"

Jason

They inched their way into the lobby, Webb having picked the lock.

"Probably lose my badge for this, but if Skelton's back, it'll be worth it."

Scattered stone composed the floors, while wood paneling covered the walls and were hung with dozens of photos of the natural wonders that lay within: Fat Man's Squeeze, subterranean lakes, and caves with as many colors as a rainbow. A gift shop sat empty to the left. A pair of double doors waited ahead.

Webb looked around, drawing his sidearm. "Maintain noise discipline."

"Huh?"

"It's Special Forces talk for 'be quiet.'"

"Oh. My dad was Special Forces."

Webb snorted. "He wasn't Special Forces."

Jason gaped at him and absorbed the truth. His dad had woven all manner of tall tales about his time in Special Forces, telling anyone who would listen about people he'd saved, missions he'd carried out. "He made it up."

"A lot of guys do. They do it to look tough, impress women."

"I wish I was surprised."

"I hope I'm not outta line saying this, son, but your dad's something of an asshole."

"You're not out of line. You're totally *in* line."

They crept forward, step by careful step.

"Where do you think he is?" Webb asked.

"I don't know. He could be anywhere. Maintain noise discipline."

Webb smiled. They reached the far side of the lobby. He was about to open the double doors into the attraction when the ground shook them off their feet. Jason awkwardly dropped to a knee, while Webb fell onto his rear. Sitting up, he shook his head.

"Had to be at least a four point five. Hadn't felt one around here since the seventies."

Jason, still on one knee, looked around with a tense jaw and gleaming eyes.

"I don't think that was an earthquake."

Lee

Lord in Heaven above, I try not to ask You for things. I know that's now how You work. You don't have the time to concern Yourself with the petty concerns of one of Your creations, and besides, You don't barter. You don't trade a prayer for a favor.

But I need to ask You for something tonight.

I need to ask You to help me warn my friends.

I ask for nothing in return, and indeed, I welcome the sacrifice of my life in Your name, O Lord. It has been a great honor to exist in one of Your creations. Leonard Skelton, whom I consider little more than a malformed afterthought in Your creation, suggested that only getting to live eleven years would be a tragedy.

Lee shook his head in contempt.

He knows not Your glory, O Lord, for he hails from a realm beyond Your grace, a realm of shrieking nothingness, a realm of the unspeakable. My eleven years have been a gift. I exalt in gratitude.

I offer my life for theirs, such as it is, O Lord. Amen.

His prayer complete, Lee let his muscles go limp. He'd been crafty enough to ballon his cheeks when Skelton gagged him, which left him with a bit of slack. He strained his tongue hard enough to bring tears to his eyes, pushing and pushing against the fabric until he'd forced it all the way out. He closed his mouth, the fabric trapped between his lips and the Duck tape, and twisted his neck until he'd pressed the tape against his shoulder. Sharp pain shot down his spine as he struggled, but after a moment, he'd pulled the tape down far enough to be able to breathe.

Breathe . . . and scream.

Jason

Webb gave a disbelieving look around. "Well, what the hell *was* it, then?" He waved away Jason's answer. "Let me guess—It's complicated?"

A child howled from within: *"IT'S A TRAAAAAAP!"*

Jason sprang to his feet. "Lee! *Lee! Hang on! We're here!"*

Webb pressed his back to the wall by the door. "Who was that?"

"Lee Dockery," Jason said, pressing his back to the door's other side.

Lee screamed again: *"IT'S A TRAAAAAAP!"* And his voice sang so clarion-clear that it shook the foundations of existence; the world quivered and quavered before Jason, parting like a curtain for a few crucial moments and giving him a glimpse of how it *really* looked:

Skulls and bones composed the floor, all of it shot through with veins and bits of gore and viscera.

But the *darkness* was worse.

Jason and Webb had, by the most fantastic of luck, managed to avoid plummeting to their doom. They stood on solid ground, but inches away from them both was sheer, diving darkness. The drop-off's horrible proximity prompted Jason to lunge over and pull Officer Webb to the floor with him.

"Hey!" he yelled. "What gives?!"

"Don't. Move," Jason said, his eyes stark-shocking wide. He was on the highest of high alerts, taking in every detail of Skelton's hideout that Lee's enchanted wail had granted him. He flash-memorized the layout of the lobby, although he knew the knowledge would cease to be useful beyond this room, inside the caves themselves.

Inside the caves was unknown territory.

Whump! They both blinked and squinted. Someone had activated the lights. A recorded narration droned from above: *"Welcome to Enchanted Caverns, the largest underground lake in the eastern United States!"*

As the narration continued, Jason stood and hefted Webb to his feet. The lobby's appearance had returned to normal, but he closed his eyes and brought up his internal map. Webb struggled in his grip.

"We gotta—"

"Don't move. Trust me. Don't move, or you'll fall."

Webb looked around. "Fall? Fall on *what?"*

Webb's heels were inches away from an endless abyss. For the first time that night, Jason regretted his strategy. They *needed* Justin Johnson's powers to reveal the magic to grown-ups, and frankly, he should've worked with at least one of the Sneakaround Gang on a gate into Skelton's hideout.

If he'd done that, then at least *he* would be able to see everything.

Jason's eyes welled up. He'd really fucked up. *Again.* He was about to give up when he remembered that he'd left a pathway to Enchanted Caverns in his Smoky Mountain, along with a special message.

And that gave him hope.

It gave him hope because he also remembered his gift to Mac, the axe. If she learned how to use it properly, she'd be able to find them, even without an address.

Jason loosened his grip on Officer Webb and said: "Remember what I said about booby traps?"

"Yeah," Webb said, still freaked out and glancing around.

"Let's just say that *I* can see 'em, but you can't."

Webb met his eyes with an expression of dumbfounded disbelief that slowly faded into resignation. He nodded, swallowed, and wiped sweat from his brow.

"Lead the way—"

It appeared from nowhere and cracked against his head with terrible speed. In the instant before it appeared, Jason perceived a slight change in the colors of the walls behind Webb. The color-change formed a familiar shape: that of a man. The man-shape swung something heavy that flashed into view as it smashed across Webb's skull and dropped him to the ground.

From nothing, the man-shape walked forward through an invisible barrier, taking on opacity and assuming a form that Jason knew from his nightmares. Even though Jason had six inches and a hundred pounds on him, he sank to his knees, his mind filled with the ocean roars of terror. He held up a hand in a futile effort to defend himself. Brandishing a two-by-four, Skelton stepped closer, giving the unconscious Webb a look of pity.

"Such a shame. He ain't like you." Skelton tilted his head. "Ain't you remember what happened? That day at the park? No? I gave her a good lick, and her light went out like *that,*" he snapped. "Dead before she hit the floor. Denied me my fun, she did. It's better when their light's still on. But you? When you saw me, you yelled, 'Hey!' After I gave you your first lick, you kept hollering somethin' *fierce,* haw haw! 'Stay away from her!' And the *second* lick? Haw, that one rattled your marbles. You just moaned after that." He let loose with a keening wail in mockery of Jason's misery. "But you kept comin', because you got them strong bones. Blue ribbon caliber, beyond any shadow."

"No, no, please—"

"Last time, I said you could fly. You and your friend are gonna fly together." Skelton swung and blacked out the world.

Colquitt

"Bo!"

He wore pajamas, sneakers, and the stench of booze. Colquitt stood next to Wanda, their gray-haired radio officer, who sat before a bank of monitors, tapping away at a keyboard. Two other cops trailed after Trent, having failed to keep him out of the main precinct room. Colquitt rolled his eyes and held up his palms.

"Trent, now stay calm—"

Wanda: "Boss, we're getting strange reports from all over the county. Jimmy Ford called in a break-in over at Dizzy Pines about an hour ago."

"Let me guess," Colquitt said. "The Dockerys?"

Wanda sat back, surprised. "Yeah."

Trent: "The Dockerys? *Sandy* Dockery? Her kids are friends with ours. What does she know?"

"Hush a second, bud," Colquitt said with a wave. To Wanda: "And when you sent EMTs, the place was empty?"

"That's right, Sheriff. How'd you know?"

"Because I saw her at the hospital. *And* your daughter, Kaity, I think," he said, nodding to Trent. Back to Wanda: "You said you had other reports?"

"Yessir. Someone over at Falconcrest Apartments said his kid saw some tall drink of water skulking around the place, sneaking into the power shed."

"Jason!" Trent shouted. "We've got to go find him!"

"Hold your horses there, Sutton!" Colquitt yelled. He loved Trent like a brother, but even *his* patience with him was waning. He addressed Wanda: "Falconcrest. Ain't that where ol' Holt Webb lives?"

Wanda nodded. "Yessir, it is. But there was something else."

"What?"

"The kid said he saw some kind of electrical fire down by the power shed. Said he saw, and I quote, *blue fire*."

Blood drained from Colquitt's face. His barrel chest strained against his buttons with each heaving breath. He doffed his hat and stared into it. Wanda leaned over in concern.

"Boss? You still with us?"

Trent grabbed his elbow: "What would Jason be doing with one of your officers?"

Colquitt yanked his arm free and replaced his hat. "I dunno, hoss. You tell me. You're the one who just lost a houseful of kids."

"I didn't *lose a houseful—*"

"I don't got time for this!" Colquitt yelled before addressing Wanda: "Get an APB out on Webb's car. I'm gonna head over to Falconcrest and canvas the place."

"I'm coming with you," Trent said.

"Yeah, you better. Maybe your kids can explain what the hell's going on tonight."

Justin

The receiver was still steaming when Justin kneeled and put it to his ear.

"Kid? Is that you? Hiram?"

"Yes, sir."

"Why are you on my phone?"

"Um . . . uhhh . . . Did you get a new foster cat like you were talking about?"

Several other voices broke in: "*Hiram, jeez!*"

"*Get the lead out, man!*"

"Sorry, sorry! Sheez! Mr. Johnson, I know you said you didn't want to draw any more maps, but . . ." Static crackled. When he spoke again, his voice broke: "Mr. Johnson, oh God, I'm sorry, I just—we're just so scared and . . . and . . ."

Justin didn't realize he had stood up.

"Kid. What's the matter?"

Hiram's Journal

The radio's dial radiated golden light that under-lit our awestruck faces. Everyone's headlamps and flashlights cast a lambent lattice across the scene. We all hunched under the stairs in the spreading silence of an empty house.

"Skelton's back," I said.

A beat. "Damn."

Dawn spoke: "Mr. Johnson?"

"Yeah? Who's this?"

"Sir, this is Dawn Dockery. He's got my little brother, Levi David."

"Oh, no," Justin whispered.

Mac rested a hand on the radio, the other on my shoulder. "Mr. Johnson, this is Mackenzie Gresham, Hi's sister. He's got our brother, too. Jason. Or we think he does. Our sister Kaitlyn's here."

We met eyes with Kaitlyn, who smiled and mouthed, *Thanks* before adding: "Mr. Johnson, I—" Her grief silenced her. Usually when people burst into tears, their face clenches or they grimace. By contrast, Kaitlyn's face relaxed utterly as tears streamed down her cheeks. Her words came haltingly, buoyed by determination and love: "I wish I could say we're not a bunch of crybabies over here, but it's been a really fucking shitty night. A really fucking shitty year, frankly. We need your help."

I hooked an arm around Kaitlyn. "We need you to draw a map."

Mac took my hand. "The best map you've ever drawn."

I was about to speak, but Dawn held up a hand. "Mr. Johnson, this is Dawn Dockery. What I'm about to say is important, and I mean every word: if you're done, we understand. *I* understand."

"Yeah," Kaitlyn said, taking Dawn's hand. "If you need to be done with this part of your life, we understand."

"We know we're asking a lot," Mac said.

Only the occasional crackle of static broke the silence under the stairs.

I whispered: "Mr. Johnson?"

Justin

"Mr. Johnson?"

He held his mother's gift, the photo of him in *A Few Good Men.*

JJ's big night! Love, Sue. AYF. read her inscription.

The phone lay on the side table, emitting one final wisp of steam. Rusty was still eyeing it. Justin brought the photo over and, scooping Rusty into his lap, sat. He took up the phone.

"Where do you need to go?"

"*W-What?*" came Hiram's ecstatic response. Justin smiled in spite of everything.

"Yeah, guys. I don't quite understand how this all works, but I think you said I'm good at drawing gates? Where am I drawing it *to?*"

"That's the thing," Hiram said. "We don't know."

Dawn: "Actually, we do."

Dawn

Mac gaped at her. "You *do?!*"

"Yeah," she said and pulled out a small booklet, the instructions for *Masterminder Home Edutainment Presents The Dragon of Smoky Mountain.* "Am I the only one who read these?"

"Wait, what?" Hiram said. "You read those?"

"Yeah! Y'all said the Grid was encoding messages into games and stuff, so I read every word." She handed the instructions to Kaitlyn and pulled out the hatchet. "And I think I know what this is for. Here, follow me back into our Smoky Mountain, and I'll show y'all."

Hiram: "Wait! Someone needs to stay here to talk to Mr. Johnson." He added in a whisper: "He sounds really sad."

"I can hear you, kid."

"Oh, sorry!"

Mac prodded Hiram and said: "I think we'll be able to stay in touch. The sextant?"

"*Oh!*" He shouted loud enough that everyone jumped. "Sorry. I just got excited."

They all ran back out to the portal. Hiram pulled out the sextant and walkie-talkie. Outside their Smoky Mountain, they'd separated, but as soon as they passed back through the gate, they fused together again, all while they transformed back to cartoons in a firestorm of electric crackles. Dawn stowed the battle axe in a scabbard mounted to her back.

Hiram squelched the device. "Mr. Johnson, do you read me?"

Justin's voice came back with an echo: "Loud and clear, kid."

"*Wowww!*" Hiram coo'ed.

Justin chuckled. "Where are you? Is this more magic stuff? Sounds like a cave."

Dawn called: "You ain't far off!" She stopped. "Look up there."

She pointed up at the other Smoky Mountain, which lay several hundred "miles" away in the enchanted space. Mac stepped over.

"How do we know it's his?"

Dawn motioned to Hiram. "Can I see that?"

He handed it over, and with it, some of its animated effects. Epaulets, ribbons, and a bandolier assembled themselves across her armor, while a pair of goggles popped out of her helmet. Dawn looked through the eyepiece and found its range was limited to a few hundred feet. Disappointment and panic rose up in her, but she thought back to her premonition of the other night. Riding through the hills toward Castle GrayCrystal, the Grid had presented itself to her and shown her something.

An observatory.

It stood on a floating island of earth, surrounded by mist and clouds.

Dawn wasn't religious like her brother and mom. But the events of the last few months had opened her up to the possibility—if not of God, then of planes and realms parallel to and beyond their own.

I don't know if I believe in God, but I believe in the Grid.

"*This* is my observatory," she whispered as she peered through the telescope. Orange light flashed in it before clearing away to reveal a powerful look across the divide. If she'd been standing in California, she could've counted the stitches on a flag waving in New York. Strangely, the space *between* the two Smoky Mountains didn't seem to be empty; it had a texture that swayed in an unfelt breeze, like a closet full of coats next to an open window.

Or a forest full of trees, Dawn thought.

But more important, she could see that the other Smoky Mountain included a gate marked with a fleur-de-lis. She returned the sextant to Hiram, nodding to the others.

"That's his, all right," she said, pulling up her battle axe.

"Dawn, what're you doing?" Mac asked. "And what's up with those instructions?"

Kaitlyn joyfully pounded the Scepter of Chaos into the ground, her mohawk waving. "Oh *shit,* Dawnie! You win Nerd of the Year for cracking the code!" She showed everyone the booklet, which she'd opened to a page that read, *OBSTACLES ON YOUR QUEST TO THE SMOKY MOUNTAIN.* She read aloud: "*The magic AXE can cut through any tree, no matter how large, opening up new pathways on your quest to slay the dragon of Smoky Mountain.*"

Hiram: "Oh, cool! Gosh, I can't wait to play this with—" he stopped, looking up with glassy eyes.

"Hey," Mac said. "We're gonna save him. We're gonna save everyone."

Dawn pointed at us with the axe. "Including the others."

Hiram nodded. "All the rest. His victims."

"Where'd you say they were, Hiram? Itza Linda?"

"In the attic of the traincar in Itza Linda."

"Then this," Dawn said, raising the axe, "is the next step on the Quest for Itza Linda."

Mackenzie

But Dawn did nothing. She lowered the axe, her shoulders shaking.

Mac touched her. "Are you okay?"

Light flashed across Dawn's armor. "Lenny Skelton's got my brother. No, I am not okay. But we've gotta keep moving, and we cain't give up." Her voice boomed: *"STAND BACK!"*

When she swung the axe, the emptiness became a forest—a *black* forest, rendered in dark television static. Dozens of branches flew right and left as Dawn slashed her way forward, the dark static fading away upon contract with the pathway. She hacked and cut, her teeth grinding, the battle axe shrieking like a chainsaw played through a faulty speaker. With each slash, she advanced a few more feet, seemingly out over nothingness, and yet underneath her ran a pathway of black grass. Mac waved everyone along.

"Let's go!" she called as they all fell into a single-file line behind Dawn. Mac beamed at her friends: Kaitlyn in her badass punk gear, Hiram as a post-apocalyptic assassin, Dawn leading the way in her otherworldly blue-and-gold armor. She looked at her rubber-band gun and felt underwhelmed. It had been a stocking stuffer from her mom a few years ago. Dad had carved it for her while hiking the Appalachian Trail but had forgotten to give it to her. It lay in a drawer for years until a particularly cash-strapped year forced their mom to scour the house for gifts. It turned out to be one of Mac's favorite gifts ever. He'd carved a cartoony little drawing of her face into its grip. The depiction had faded over the years, the handle growing smooth and shiny from love and repeated usage.

But in spite of the crisis, she felt envious of everyone else's treasures. She had prickly feelings toward Jason, but she was still disappointed the axe hadn't been meant for her.

Will I get my own gift? she asked herself, feeling guilty for wanting something so silly.

Colquitt

"I've covered your ass for years, hoss, but I can't cover it forever. I don't know what you're doing back home, but you need to really start crackin' the whip!"

Lights blazing and siren blaring, the cruiser zoomed through a red light.

Trent nodded. "Yeah. You're right. Those little shits. Always mouthing off. It's their mom. She's too soft with 'em. Too soft. I'm gonna bring the hammer down. Hard." His voice darkened. "Those fucking little shits. Show them to cross me. Show them to—"

The radio squawked: "Sheriff, Fisher called in, said he might've seen Webb's Camry heading north on Veterans toward Sevierville. Let me get you the plates."

Holton

It was a game of *Don't Touch the Lava* come to life.

Webb regained consciousness moments after Skelton dragged Jason into the caves. Blood trickled from his ear; *not a good sign.* He struggled to his knees but froze when he remembered the kid's words:

Remember what I said about booby traps? Let's just say that I can see 'em, but you can't.

He had passed through the batwing doors into Davey's Christmas saloon, and it was terrifying. Holton dropped to his hands and knees and felt his way across the lobby. He almost ran into the caves, but he knew he needed a very specific kind of help if he was going to venture in there.

He needed people who understood whatever magic was bubbling up in the Smokies, and that meant kids.

Part of him felt ridiculous for . . . well, for believing in magic, but when he set his hand on nothing, he believed in it all. Because that's what happened: Holt set his hand before him, but it disappeared into the floor up to his elbow. Gray mist—the same color as the scattered stones—puffed around his forearm. Eyes gogging, he retracted his arm and felt around until he found a solid pathway to the front door, where he pulled himself upright and shoved his way outside. He worried that he might hit another invisible drop, but he gambled on Skelton's mischief ending at the front door.

Voices welcomed him outside. *Young* ones.

A girl yelled: "Holy shit! Look!" Four kids came running over, all of them dressed for Halloween. He recognized the girl who yelled as Jason's sister. *What was her name? Kaitlyn?* She held some kind of staff, although his brains were so rattled that he couldn't seem to fully focus on any of them.

"Help," Holton wheezed. "I need help."

He collapsed to his knees. Another of the kids, a powerful-looking girl, kneeled next to him.

"Ohmigod, he's hurt really bad."

He flashed on the dressing-down she gave him the night of Soddy Farm. *Mackenzie. That's her name. Good kid. Doesn't take shit from anyone.*

He shifted to a sitting position, hooking his thumb at the building.

"They're in there."

A sweet-looking kid, a heavyset redhead, kneeled next to Mackenzie.

Right, they're siblings, Holton thought warmly. The kid looked bookish and kind. He wore an aviator's helmet and held a sextant for some reason. *Hiram, that's his name.*

"Is it Skelton?" Hiram asked.

"Yeah. He got Jason. I guess you got his message. But he's not alone in there. Skelton got someone else, a little boy. Lee."

"My brother," said another young woman, pigtailed and wiry, her eyes puffy from crying. Like her friends, she looked ready to go trick-or-treating, clad in a medieval jerkin and holding a hatchet. She strode toward the building. The others ran to stop her.

"Wait, Dawn, wait!" Hiram yelled.

The short one, Kaitlyn, added: "You can't go in there!"

Holton hefted himself to his feet and padded along in pursuit.

Dawn wheeled on them: "Why *not?!* He's *my* brother, not yours. Besides, I've got my axe. Gotta be good for something."

Hiram blocked her. "It's not enough."

"Get outta my way!"

Webb staggered toward them: "He's right. Skelton's got it—got it booby trapped. And he . . . he can . . ."

He swayed. Mackenzie and Hiram moved to catch him. Suddenly, the little guy's walkie-talkie crackled.

A man's voice, an adult, spoke: "Let me guess: Skelton's got magic powers, too?"

"Who's that on the walkie?" Holton asked.

The voice responded: "Justin Johnson, former West Chim PD. Who's this?"

The kids gawked at the device like it had lobsters crawling out of it.

"Uh, this is Holt Webb from West Chim police. Is this *JJ Flash?*"

"Yeah."

"Hell, I remember you, man. You lit up Brentwood Academy back in the day."

"Yeah, that's me." He sounded annoyed.

Hiram: "Mr. Johnson, can you *hear* us?"

"You can call me Justin, kid."

Holt: "Is this one of those new cellular phones?"

Mac: "Why is it working? Jason's gifts only work inside the Sneakaround Network."

The kids all spun toward the building and backed away from it.

"Oh, shit," Kaitlyn said. "If that's working, then we're in the Sneakaround. We're in Skelton's hideout."

"The what?" Holton asked.

Justin's voice crackled: "Same question. What's the Sneakaround Network?"

"Wait," Hiram said. "I wasn't in the Sneakaround when I talked with you on the radio. Maybe the magic works differently for that; for talking and messages."

Mac nodded. "Yeah, and if we were in the Sneakaround, wouldn't we be cartoons?"

Holton rubbed his brow. "Kids, what the livin' heck is going on?"

They all exchanged looks that converged on Hiram.

"There's an enchanted place we can access," he said.

"We call it the Sneakaround Network," Mac said.

Kaitlyn: "We can draw magic maps."

Mac: "Create magic weapons."

"Basically, magic is real," Kaitlyn said.

Holton nodded. "Strange as it sounds, that's the only thing that makes all this add up. But Miss," he addressed Dawn, "your friends are right. Y'all don't wanna go in there. The floor . . . I can't even rightly describe it. There are pits you can't see. Booby traps."

Dawn: "He's got a hideout in the Sneakaround Network. And he controls it. That's why you couldn't see anything."

Hiram walked toward the road. "And we need to be *outside* the Sneakaround when we draw our gate into his hideout, or we won't be able to see it."

Mac: "Do you think that's why Jason put his gate so far away?"

"Yeah," Hiram said, nodding. "But I bet he couldn't make a gate into his hideout."

"Because he was alone," Kaitlyn said, a picture of grief. She covered her eyes. "God. I can't believe he thought he had to do this alone."

Mac wrapped an arm around her and said: "So Skelton's got them both in there, and his booby traps are invisible to us. Fuck."

Justin's voice crackled: "Guys, the clock's ticking. Are we drawing this gate or not?"

Hiram nodded. "We've got to get farther away. If we're inside the Sneakaround, our gate won't work."

Holton frowned. "JJ—I mean, Justin, if you're helping out, why ain't you here?"

"I live in Oregon."

"*What?*" He gawked at the walkie. "This here's a dang toy you could get at Kay-Bee. Ain't no way you're more'n half a mile away."

"I live in Oregon, I'm speaking into a disconnected phone, and that is a magic walkie-talkie."

Kaitlyn was already running toward the road. "More things in Heaven and

Earth, Holtacio! *Let's go!*"

Hiram's Journal

"Mr. Johnson—uh I mean, Justin, are you ready to draw, sir?"

We'd sprinted a half-mile up the road and spread our art supplies on the shoulder. A nearby streetlamp lit the scene a jaundiced yellow. Everyone took up their favorite implement: pencils for me, chalks for Kaitlyn, gauche for Dawn, and a combination for Mac.

Justin answered: "Ready. Got my atlas out in front of me. All I need's an address."

I checked the road. "We're on Veterans, just south of Enchanted Caverns, by mile marker nineteen."

"Got it."

Webb leaned over. "What's going on?"

"You said Skelton had booby-trapped the place, right?" Kaitlyn said, her voice undercut by a crackle from the power lines.

"Yeah, and it's all invisible."

"Well, we're about to pull back the curtain."

Mac added: "We can't make his traps disappear, but we can at least make it so we can *see* them."

"Kids, don't you think we should call the cops?" Holton asked.

The power lines hummed louder, almost drowning out Dawn's protests: "*No!* No cops!"

"Don't call Colquitt," Mac said. "Just trust us."

Kaitlyn spoke into the walkie: "Justin, how's that map coming?"

"Coming along fine. I'm drawing my gate and keeping it simple. Imagine the St. Louis Arch."

I said: "Oh! We all need to add something to our maps. It helps if we all add our own little detail to the gate."

Snap! A spark flew from the transformer above. The streetlamp flickered.

"Oh, okay," Justin said. "What're you adding?"

"I'm adding a picture of one of the magic books from *Labyrinth of Terror*. It's Lee's favorite weapon."

Webb managed a smile. "That's a really good drawing, fella. So, you put a little bit of yourself into each map?"

Mac nodded. "That's exactly right. I'm adding a picture of Dad."

"Gosh, that's really good," I said, looking over. "Dawn?"

"I'm adding Lee's glasses. He thinks they're ugly, but I think they make him look really cool. Kaity?"

"Oh, the usual." She'd sketched a can of mace. "Just in case we need extra."

"Justin, how about you?"

A brief pause, then: "I'm writing my mom's name, Sue. Hope that's okay. I don't really know how this part works."

"Of *course* it's okay. That's a great thing to add, shucks."

Kaitlyn elbowed me. "Aw, you said 'shucks' and you meant it."

I suddenly felt naked. "Wait, what's wrong with saying shucks?"

"Nothing," Mac said before adding: "So, what's the keystone?"

"Keystone?" Justin asked.

"Each gate needs a keystone with an icon that tells us where it's going to lead."

Kaitlyn: "Last time we used an ouro-badoodle."

"Ourobuck," I said.

"Right. That worked pretty well."

Mac shook her head slightly. "I don't know. I don't think that'll be powerful enough."

Justin: "I guess it's gotta be a prize ribbon, huh?"

We all shared a look and nodded.

"Yeah," Mac said. "Adding mine in now."

Dawn and Kaitlyn took a few more moments to finish their drawings. We all stood, compared our maps . . . and waited. Holton leaned in.

"Is something supposed to be happening?"

The streetlamp flashed a sudden blinding bright. I shielded my eyes and said: "There should be a gate."

Mac: "A gate into Skelton's hideout."

Snap! The transformer spat another several sparks, all of them raining down like drops of lava. Another shot skyward—*and bounced off something.* It hit the boundary of a dome far overhead, electrifying it and bringing into view a hexagonal grid, only this one was red instead of orange.

We all met eyes. I screamed: *"Oh, shit! We're inside his Smoky Mountain! Run! R—"*

We all took off running at a mad dash, but it wasn't enough: the Grid blazed with crimson light as the heavens and earth subdivided into geometric slices and rocketed away, leaving behind a single floating pathway. From above, an angled, translucent wall—like the cross-section of a foggy glass honeycomb—shot down with enough force to crack the earth's crust and send us all crashing to the ground.

The Smoky Mountains were getting stranger every second.

The last time we infiltrated Skelton's Smoky Mountain, we'd seen a similar wall. It carved up the world along the same plane as his gate. A wall also enclosed *this* Smoky Mountain, its boundary marked by a moat, twenty feet across, that sank into darkness and spread to either horizon.

And we were on opposite sides of it.

"Hiram!"

Mac, Kaitlyn, and Webb, as the fastest, wound up on the far side of the moat, while Dawn and I were stuck on the floating pathway inside the hideout. Now that Skelton had dropped the facade, electricity crackled and swirled around us as we both transformed back into our Saturday-morning-animated selves. (The sextant and walkie fused back together, too.) Behind us, the forest started to wilt and wither as blood flooded the moon and cast the countryside in a louring pall that was the same dark red as an angry scab.

Holton

The night of Soddy Farm, he *knew* he'd seen something.

It was an animated horse, but only its *outline*. It shimmered in and out of view in concert with the clouds' movements. Moonlight revealed the magic horse's outline to Holton, whose mind leaped back, as it always did, to his big brother's enchanting little Christmas bars.

Standing before a chasm that had suddenly opened, Holton thought with fondness of Davey's 1976 bar. That year, their Grandma Maxwell had decorated their cottages for both Christmas and the Bicentennial. Red, white, and blue banners hung from Davey's saloon, which had a little rooftop deck (lined with garlands, natch) that Holton loved, but even cooler was where the saloon was *located:*

It sat on a cliffside.

His grandma had painstakingly carved hundreds of details—a single branch that held a bird's nest, the suggestion of a river far below—and for years, Holton had begged Davey to give it up. He'd only relented this year.

Now, standing before a magic moat, Holton felt like he was holding one of his grandma's creations again, examining its every detail, marveling over her craftsmanship. It felt like he was holding his family close by, close to his heart of hearts.

But he felt unsettled, too, a feeling that dovetailed with his memories of the night of Soddy Farm. Before him shimmered the suggestion of a *boundary*, a *filter* that tinged everything a hellish shade of red.

"What the Sam Hill just—"

Hiram screamed: "You've gotta go, get help! Go get Auntie Hanna!"

The kid sounded slightly digitized, like his voice was fritzing out of a faulty speaker, while his and Dawn's shapes were surrounded by faint outlines—

like hand-drawn sketches—much like the magic horse he'd seen at Soddy Farm. Hiram seemed to be wearing faux-military regalia, while Dawn wore some manner of strange medieval armor. Holton flashed on the music video "Take On Me," where the people slipped into an animated world.

Even weirder: Hiram and Dawn appeared to be standing on a single pathway that was flanked by sheer, black nothingness. Holton squinted but couldn't quite bring it all into focus; the visions—the kids' strange costumes, the floating pathway—flickered on the edge of his comprehension.

Mac ran up next to Holton and called to her friends: "What're you gonna do?! We can't just leave you alone!"

Hiram's He-Man walkie proclaimed: "They're not alone."

Vum-vum-vum-VUMMMM!

Hiram's Journal

Black ink exploded from nothing.

It started small, a single drop, and expanded into a whirling pool of gleaming darkness. A shape emerged, taking on color and detail as he emerged onto mine and Dawn's side of the moat. He wore a light coat, jeans, and hiking boots. I can only assume he figured he might have to make this move and dressed for the occasion.

It was Justin Johnson.

Across the moat, Webb, no kidding, slapped his forehead.

"Holy Mary mother o' God."

I was instantly crying. Everyone was. We all jumped up and down, yelling: *"Justin!"*

Dawn and I moved to hug him, but he waved us off, clamping a hand over his mouth. Running over to the pathway's edge, he bazooka-barfed into the abyss with a *"BBBLLLAAAARRGHGH!"* He leaned back, forearm-wiped his mouth, and pointed at the gate.

"Holy shit! You kids actually walked *through* one of those things? Felt like I just rode the Mind-Bender backwards at a hundred miles an hour!" He caught his breath and smiled. "*And* you're . . . cartoons?"

"Yeah," Dawn said. "It's hard to explain."

"You don't need to." He opened his arms, and we ran to him. His embrace was strong enough to crack our ribs and made me feel sure and safe in a way I'd forgotten was possible.

I was bawling: "I'm so glad you made it. Thank you for coming. I'm so scared."

He released us, shaking his head. "I should've come sooner. And hey, I'm scared, too." He faced the magic wall and waved. "Is that Mac and Kaitlyn? And Holt? Hey, man, glad you could make it!" His voice hitched. "It is so good to see you guys."

Webb approached the wall. "What the hell *happened* to you two?!"

We all exchanged looks in hope. Justin did, too.

He said: "Did it work?"

"Mr. Webb!" I called. "What do you see?"

Leaning back, Webb took in the scene. He spoke with reverence: "Y'all are standing on a road over darkness and perdition. The land's turned into a nightmare. You turned into drawings. And . . . 'The moon shall be as blood.'"

Mac touched his shoulder. "You can see it?"

Webb nodded. "I don't think I understand what I'm lookin' at, but I see it."

Mac looked at me and said: "It worked."

"But I don't understand," Dawn said. "Justin made his gate *inside* Skelton's hideout. Why'd it work?"

Kaitlyn: "Who knows? Who cares? I mean, how the hell did Skelton make his hideout so freakin' huge in the first place?"

"Maps," Dawn whispered. Looking up, she added: "He's got Lee, so he got his map."

Mac: "More maps, more power."

Vum-vum-vum-VUMMM! We all backed away from Justin's portal, which opened like a camera shutter, giving us a view of his front yard. Another voyager leaped through:

A black cat.

It bounded into Justin's arms with a *meow.*

"Rusty?! God-dang it, man! Get back in there!" He tried to toss him back through the portal, but he leaped onto my shoulders and wrapped himself around me like a scarf. Another cat, a tortie, came into view through the portal. Justin waved his hands back and forth. "Cal! Don't come over here! Stay! *Stay! St—*" The tortie flomped onto its side, asleep. The portal closed. "Oh, *thanks,* Cal. Rust, I guess you're coming with us."

From the far side of the chasm, Mac shouted: "No you don't!"

Justin cocked an eyebrow. "Whadda you mean? We're doing this. Kaity, Mac, you're going with Holt to get your aunt, right?"

"No, not you—I'm talking to *him.*" Mac pointed at me. "Don't go in there without us. Wait for us to get help."

Dawn: "We don't got *time* to wait."

Webb muttered: "Am I dreaming?"

Justin called: "Trust me, man: This is the most awake you've ever been. Now, c'mon, get moving! Go get help!"

Mac was still fixated on us: "It's too dangerous. Please. Wait for us."

Justin, Dawn, and I shared a conspiratorial look. I crossed my hands—and my fingers—behind my back. The other two stifled smiles.

"I promise."

Mac gave me a dubious look before turning to the others. "Mr. Webb? Where's your car?"

"Back this way," he said, still in a daze.

"I'll drive!" Kaitlyn yelled. They took off running. As soon as they were gone, all three of us turned and started walking.

"What," Justin said after a while. "We're not gonna wait?"

Dawn pulled her battle axe and gave it a few practice swings.

"Are you kidding? It's boring out here."

"I agree," Justin said as we brought the parking lot into view. The sight ahead made our hearts boom. Looking back, I think Justin's portal was powerful enough to neutralize the magic concealing Skelton's hideout.

But will Auntie Hanna be able to see it? Mr. Webb already seemed to have *the vision. Will she?*

No time to worry about that. Before us was Skelton's mind writ large. He'd transformed Enchanted Caverns into an industrial nightmare hewn from blood, brick, and bone. Totems of his unthinkable evil adorned the A-frame roof, including the face of poor Jenny Miles. Each face was wreathed with a prize ribbon.

"Goddamn," Justin said. "That's Millie Albright, his third victim. Cody Tucker. Maggie Vaughn, the last one he took. There's not a deep enough circle in hell."

Dawn took a couple of steadying breaths. "I dunno, guys. He's got the— whaddaya call it? Home-town advantage?"

"Home field," Justin said.

I shook my head. "Look at us. Justin's portal worked. We're cartoons. And we've got our weapons. I think our magic works just as well in *his* lair as *ours.* It evens out."

"Besides," Justin said. "We're already here. Be rude not to say hi."

Mac's voice crackled over my walkie: "You guys better not be going in there."

I switched it off. Rusty *mewed* around my neck.

We went inside.

Hanna

"Auntie Hanna! Auntie Hanna!"

Pulling on her night coat, Hanna Blackledge opened her front door to a sharp-cold breeze and a view of three familiar faces. A car sat running in her driveway, its headlights blasting her face. The girls, Kaitlyn and Mackenzie, wore what looked like Halloween costumes, but it was Officer Webb's attire that put an icepick in her heart.

He was strapped. She spotted the shoulder holster immediately.

"What in the—" she said, as she stepped onto her front porch. "Holton? What in God's name are you doing here? And armed? And Kaitlyn? Mackenzie? What's the matter?"

The girls looked to Webb, who stood dumbfounded for a moment before he steeled himself.

"Ma'am, I dunno how to tell you this, but—"

She had a vision: *A factory of nightmares, spewing blood and fire. Justin Johnson standing on a floating platform crafted from human remains.* In tandem with her premonition, heat-lightning flashed across the sky, giving her view of a *second* premonition: an execution chamber—an *empty* one. Skelton had been set to die two days from now.

March 15. The Ides.

"It's him. Isn't it?"

They all looked at each other.

Webb nodded. "Yes, ma'am. He's back."

Hanna suddenly realized who *wasn't* there.

"Sweet blue Jesus. Little Hiram. And Jason."

Kaitlyn: "He's got Dawn and Lee, too."

"There's more," Mac said. "Mr. Johnson's here."

Hanna's surprise extended. "Johnson, as in *Justin* Johnson?"

"Yes."

"Him and his cat," Kaitlyn said.

"Well, thank God for that," Hanna said, turning to head back inside.

"Wait!" Mac said. "Where are you going?"

"To get my gun."

Hiram's Journal

Shoulder to shoulder, we eased our way into his hideout's lobby. Dawn held her battle axe broadsword-style. I kept my sextant at the ready, not sure if it had any offensive capabilities. Justin had only his fists, but for him, those were probably enough.

"Watch your backs," Dawn whispered, her armor reflecting the chamber's unholy crimson glow.

Scattered stone floors and wood-paneled walls melted like icing to reveal crumbling red brick interspersed with skulls and bones. Immediately inside the entrance stood a display with dozens of brochures for various attractions all over the Southland. We were about to pass it when something caught my eye.

"Guys, wait," I said, taking a closer look at a pamphlet for the Gold Rush park. Its cover depicted a Drew Struzan-style showcase of the park's attractions: the Slamwinder, the Burning Mine, and of course, the Mystery Mansion.

"What's up?" Justin asked.

"The park's been closed for months," I said. "Why would they still have brochures for it?"

Dawn leaned in and whispered: "Let's move. Forget the brochures."

Time telescoped. Dawn's words had opened a door in my mind that looked back on my first dream about the Plaid Man, when the very radio we'd used to call Justin Johnson spoke with my father's voice:

Gedda brusha. Trap. Trap. Itza linda adda.

Forget the brochures.

Gedda brusha.

Gedda brusha. Get the brochures. Trap. Trap.

"Hiram, we've gotta keep moving," Dawn said.

I nodded, but on a hunch, I grabbed brochures for both the Gold Rush and Enchanted Caverns. Rusty hopped from my shoulders onto Justin's. As we inched forward, the floor melted away, leaving only a single floating path that spanned the lobby from the front entrance to the doors leading into the caves.

"This might sound weird," Justin said. "But I think I'd feel better if I were a cartoon."

"Want my sextant?" I said. "I think if you have a magic weapon, it turns you into one."

"Nah, that's okay, kid. I'll be—"

He pitched forward like he'd missed the last stair. Instinctively, we both clawed at his shirt, catching fistfuls of it, but his bulk carried us all crashing to the ground. He landed with one leg bent underneath him, one seemingly severed at the hip. Our arms appeared to be severed at the shoulders, too, ending abruptly at the floor.

Justin had stepped into an invisible pit.

"Shit," he hissed as he heaved himself up and out of the opening, his leg sliding back into view like a magician's illusion. Dawn ground her teeth as she helped him up and out.

"He tricked us," she said. "He made us think we could see everything, but we can't."

"My portal didn't work, did it?"

I shook my head. "No, it did. Mr. Webb can see the magic now. You made that happen."

We all stood. Justin's jaw flexed. "Is that gonna be enough, though? How are we gonna get in there if we don't know where to walk?"

"Hang on," I said, bringing the sextant to my eye. I hoped it might give me some kind of magic sight, but the room looked unchanged.

"Can you see anything?" Dawn asked.

I shook my head, but something caught my attention: the brochure for the Gold Rush. Using gold ink, someone had drawn on it in almost *impossibly* delicate detail. Millimeter-thin lines sketched a path through the park, from the front gate through Hootin' Hollow, Christmasville, and Statuary Row before terminating in the middle of the Mystery Mansion. The final touch was a clear outline that highlighted the old gondola house's attic.

"Check this out," I said, holding it for them to see.

"I don't get it," Dawn said.

"Is it maybe the path we should follow to get through here?" I indicated the lobby.

Justin shook his head. "I don't know. That doesn't seem right." Rusty head-bonked his chin. He made eye contact with him and raised an eyebrow. "Hmm." Setting him down, Justin produced a small bag of treats and held one up to Rusty, who immediately went on his hind legs, batting at his hand.

"What're you doing?" Dawn asked.

Justin ignored her and said: "Rusty, go get it!" He tossed the treat across the room, where it landed by the entrance to the caves. Rusty padded across the room in an intricate, spiraling pattern, stopping only for the occasional sniff. He stopped at the door and wolfed down the treat as if nothing about the world was strange or out of control. To Rusty, he was merely negotiating some slightly unusual terrain. After a moment's pause to bathe himself, he faced us with his tail curled around his paws.

"Did anyone catch that path? Because I sure didn't," I said.

"I got it," Justin said, his tone darkening. He led us across the room slowly, and as we walked, I realized Rusty's pathway was actually *writing*; cursive writing to be exact.

"Justin, is this a message?" I muttered: "JJ's big night . . ."

Dawn finished: "Love, Sue, AYF. Aw, was that from your mama?"

"Yeah," Justin said.

"What's AYF stand for?"

He didn't answer. We reached the door, where Justin scooped up Rusty. His brow kept clenching, his expression fluctuating between grief and anger.

"What is it?" I asked.

"Does this mean Skelton's been in my house?" Justin asked, petting Rusty. "That message was private."

Dawn's response was steely with confidence: "They're not the only ones out there."

"Meaning what?"

"We're not alone in this," she said. "It ain't just us versus Skelton and the Plaid Man."

"The Grid," I said. "The Grid's got our backs."

Justin frowned, his brow troubled. But he nodded.

We went in.

Colquitt

Colquitt floored it, bringing up his internal map of everything between West Chimney Top and Sevierville. There wasn't much besides some old churches. Kids sometimes vandalized the gravestones, but that didn't feel like what was happening tonight.

Something *else* was afoot; something strange.

They came up behind a gray sedan. Colquitt recognized the plate numbers instantly.

"That's them!" he yelled, pointing. "And ain't that your little one at the wheel?"

Trent bared his perfectly straight and stark-white teeth. "She's gonna be sorry. She's gonna be so sorry she crossed me. She's not gonna fucking believe it. She's not gonna fucking believe how much I can fuck her up." To Colquitt: "Faster, faster! Pull up alongside!" His voice deepened into a guttural drone: "Things are gonna be different. Really different. We're gonna have rules and order and everything's going to have its place. Starting with that mouthy little fucking bitch."

Dawn

She'd run every scenario, every horrible outcome, but it didn't matter. Whenever she tried to imagine a timeline where one or both of them didn't make it, a black wall slammed down in her mind. To Dawn, those futures simply weren't possible.

She *willed* her future to include Lee and Jason.

Past the double doors, a hallway awaited them. Justin dropped Rusty, who led the way on a roughly straightforward course. Skelton's realm, as frightening as it was, also seemed unstable: the floating bone pathway flickered in and out of sight, giving them glimpses of wood-paneled walls and scattered stone floors.

But the *faces.*

Floating in the endless dark were dozens, *scores* of sorrowful faces, each one wreathed with a prize ribbon, and each one moaning. The combined effect reminded Dawn of singing a sad hymn in church.

"Sweet baby angels," Dawn said. "Kaity said she was almost number nine, but I think there's more."

"Itza Linda must be more crowded than we thought," Hiram said. "Justin, do you recognize any of—"

Justin's jawline trembled. Dawn took his shoulder.

"You know it ain't your fault, right?"

"Yeah. It's just . . . not fair. Sometimes it feels unfair that I get to be here when they can't."

"Justin, it's not fair, but I'm so glad you're here," Dawn said.

"Me too," Hiram said.

Justin brought his tears under control and hugged us. "I'm glad you're here too. I'm glad we're all here."

Rusty came padding back to mew at them. After sharing a brief grin, they followed him to a stone gateway that fully encircled the floating pathway. Its keystone was two words—*ALL ABOARD*—while a pair of stone statues flanked the gateway, floating in space. Golden light glimmered just inside the gate.

"Huh," Hiram said. "Narcissus and Echo."

"You're right," Dawn said. "Ain't these statues from the park? The Gold Rush?"

"Yeah," Hiram said. "But why would Skelton put 'em here?"

They approached the gate, bringing into view its far side, where clinging to its walls were hundreds of little chintzy Christmas cottages, all of them glowing from within. Each one was marked with a name and a date: A savings and loan was marked *Jimmy 1971,* a church with *Nance 1983,* a speakeasy with *Davey 1988.*

"Look," Dawn said, pointing at a little toy store. "It says, 'Holton, 1984.'"

Justin: "Holton? These are his?" A whistle shrieked, heralding the arrival of a model train that chugged around the gate's circumference. Justin's eyebrows rose. "Hiram, let me see that brochure again."

"Sure," he said, handing it over, but Justin also absentmindedly snagged his magic sextant-walkie device and blasted himself back ten feet up the path in a cyclone of lightning and smoke.

"*Justin!*" the kids yelled, running over. Justin shook his head, dazed, but he'd somehow remained conscious—and on his feet. As with the transfer of the battle axe, Hiram was still animated but wearing his street clothes, while Justin was now his own animated version of Necron 99 from *Wizards*. He wore a burgundy duster coat, aviator helmet and goggles, and reams of military medals, epaulets, and regalia. Blinking, he regarded his new appearance with a smile.

"Is there any way I can choose my own outfit?" he said. "I mean, this is cool, but I always wanted to be . . ."

"Who?" Hiram asked.

He shook his head. "Never mind." Justin peered through the sextant and looked it over, muttering to himself, before he looked up. "I know where Itza Linda is. It's not in the woods. It's in the park." He indicated the map. "It's in the Mystery Mansion, in the attic of the old gondola house."

Mackenzie

Police lights ignited behind them. Kaitlyn, who'd offered to sub in for the injured Webb behind the wheel, jolted in her seat but made no move to pull over. Hanna gaped at her from the passenger's seat.

"Are you going to pull over, young lady? That's a police officer behind you."

Mac grabbed her shoulder. "Do *not* stop this car!"

Hanna gaped. "*Excuse* me, young lady?"

Mac looked back. "Oh shit, it's Colquitt. And he's got *Dad* with him."

"Great," Kaitlyn said. "We've got the all-Smoky Mountain asshole convention in hot pursuit."

The cruiser pulled into the opposing lane and roared up beside them. Trent leaned out of the passenger window, his hair a mad-kicking mess, his nighttime robe flapping, his eyes pinpricks of blood, his arms a pair of massive trunks swiping at them.

"*PULL OVER! PULL OVER! IF YOU DON'T PULL OVER YOU'RE GONNA FUCKING REGRET IT!*"

Colquitt's voice blasted over his PA system: "Pull over to the side of the road *now!*"

Sweat sprang out across Hanna's brow. "Kaitlyn, if you don't stop this car—"

Mac: "Don't do it. If we stop, they're dead."

"I know!" Kaitlyn yelled as she stepped on the gas.

Hanna looked to Webb for support. "You on board with this, Holton?"

Dazed, he said: "I saw revelations that woulda made St. John himself weep. Those kids have put their lives on the line, same as they've put a bit of themselves into those maps they drew. Something wicked and strange is afoot in these hills. It's a night for improvisation."

Hiram's Journal

It *wasn't* fair.

That's what I thought as Justin showed us the enchanted brochure of the Gold Rush, indicating the glowing path that led from the front gate to the Mystery Mansion.

"This was looking us in the face the whole time," he said.

All I could think about were those kids.

And Mom.

Auntie Hanna said Mom doesn't have much time left. She was around before I was . . . but now I'm going to be around when she isn't. Justin's right, but not about himself. It's not fair that I get to be around when they won't.

"I don't deserve to be here." I might've said that part out loud, or I might've thought it. Like I said, I get those mixed up sometimes. Justin gave me a strange look—*Did he hear me?*—but didn't respond, instead simply returning the brochure and sextant and hustling ahead, hot on Rusty's tail. The "Necron 99" look transferred back to me, while Justin remained animated but wearing his street clothes. The pathway snaked through endless darkness, while in the deep distance floated the faces of Skelton's victims. Under our feet, multivarious shades of gore and bone spelled out familiar phrases:

TO JJ ON HIS BROADWAY DEBUT

LAST ONE THERE'S A WACKO

DON'T LET ANYONE TELL YOU DIFFERENT

DAWN-N-GRESH 4-EVA

Each one stabbed our souls and laid us bare. How much *did* Skelton know about us? And *how?* Had he found ways to spy on all of us, or was the Plaid Man able to read our minds and deliver intelligence to him? We raced ahead, Rusty bounding over the occasional invisible barrier or drop-off, until the pathway ended precipitously and brought a remarkable sight into view:

An array of floating islands, each of them built from brick, bone, and blood. All of them bobbed slightly amidst an endless ocean of emptiness and black. In the deep distance floated more sorrowful faces singing an endless dirge that lent the space a rumbling undertone.

Dawn pointed. "There they are."

Floating suspended by their ankles were Lee and Jason, both of them bound. Jason had transformed to his animated self but was only wearing street clothes. Lee was still his normal self.

"Well, it's a sight to behold."

He floated over, the devil did, on his own little sky-island, arms crossed, surrounded by five floating maps, all of which glowed from within. One I recognized as my original map of the West Chimney Top area, while another was the one Lee had drawn tonight. The other three, though, I didn't recognize. One map, Skelton's I presumed, was crudely drawn with a ballpoint pen on yellow college-rule paper.

The fourth and fifth had to belong to Jason and some other kid. They were *gorgeous*. Both must have taken years to create and made use of several different mediums: ink, paints, gauche, chalk, charcoal. They included multimedia elements, too. Little cardboard cut-out houses dotted both maps, alternating with multi-colored Legos and even some Lincoln Logs. One included some girly details like hearts and rainbows—and a little octopus tentacle.

Oh, no. That's Kaitlyn's old map. The one she drew when she was little. He must've kept it all these years.

The sight of their maps simultaneously warmed my heart and froze my soul, because for all the love Jason must've poured into them over the years, that meant Skelton had harvested that much more power for himself.

Rusty arched his back and hissed. Skelton's eyes flickered, I think, in recognition of our appearance.

Oh, no. He already has three of our maps. What if he gets his hands on one of our weapons? Will we be able to stop him?

Skelton: "If it ain't JJ Flash, hero of Gatlinburg and everyone's favorite momma's boy. They brought you outta retirement for one last jaunt around the gridiron, huh? One last curtain call? Just think. If you'd let them good folks take care of me, you wouldn't be standin' here right now." Justin said nothing. Rusty growled. Skelton addressed me: "How about you, little sumpty? Didja get my flowers?"

"Yeah," I said. "You sent 'em to my sister, you freak."

"Hee *heee*. Aw, you jealous? Ain't no thing, little buckaroo—" (I quietly gasped at the familiar turn of phrase) "—all them flowers was for alla y'all, thankin' you for the maps. I done liberated me three, one from you, Hiram Stammerstone, one from the Cowardly Lion, and one from Little Lee Peed His Pants. With all these maps, ain't no one ever gonna catch me again."

Dawn launched herself skyward before we had a chance to react. She was a soaring angel of blue-and-gold chrome that flashed across the expanse, her legs superhumanly strong, a member of Leonidas's 300 by way of Jack Kirby, her battle axe drawn above her head in anticipation of a brutal slice that she brought down through the middle of Skelton's head.

"*Dawn, no!*"

He exploded in a radial geyser that sprayed ectoplasmic icing everywhere, leaving Dawn crouched on the sky-island with her axe lodged in the ground and covered in imaginary ooze.

Justin

I need a weapon of my own, Justin thought the instant Dawn leaped. Once her attack failed, the sound of applause drew their attention to the right, where Skelton stood on another sky-island backed by a strange portal. Justin had heard the kids talk about different kinds of gates—archways with portcullises, that kind of thing—but this one was little more than a glowing ring of rippling red light. Floating in the darkness over it was a wooden A-frame roof that Justin recognized immediately.

That's the attic of the old gondola house in the Gold Rush park.

"Secret attic," Hiram whispered.

They locked eyes. Nodded.

Skelton continued: "Yer magic's good, little missy, but I'm holdin' court." His five maps rotated in a shifting, overlapping pattern behind him, like a ghoulish aura. On the other side of the gate stood a dusty, cobwebbed shelf packed with jars, chests, urns, and small boxes, each one inscribed with a name: *Millie, Jamie, Cody,* and others.

Justin prodded Hiram and said: "That's it."

Hiram nodded. "Itza Linda."

Skelton continued: "And now you're all here. With me. Y'know, my biggest mistake was with little Jenny? Snatchin' her in that park." He hooked his thumb through the gate. "On the one hand, it's a perfect place to snatch kids because their parents ain't paying no mind, but on the other hand, it's too fuckin' hard to extricate yourself with a kid in tow. Too hard to shut 'em up without killin' 'em. And why would I wanna walk outta Disney World with a dead kid when *my* Disney World is having a live kid back where I can do what I like with 'em? Just like now."

His maps paused for a moment as he executed an arcane gesture—crossing his arms in an X before bringing them apart—and behind us, the pathway leading out disintegrated, millions of bones and skulls raining into the darkness below. Skelton walked forward, seemingly about to pitch into the abyss, but with each step, all of those falling skulls and bones flew over and reassembled under his feet. His pathway carried him toward the small sky-island that held Dawn. The faces in the distance moaned louder and louder.

"See my collection there?" He indicated the cremains, stepping closer to a bright-blushing Dawn, who was struggling to free her axe from the floor. "They're my holy-soul, my power-point, my solar-center, the crux and the fulcrum that keeps *me* here and *them* from reachin' topside of the Hightower."

Justin looked at Hiram and saw recognition in his eyes. They'd both heard that word before, *Hightower,* but what did it mean? It didn't matter. He was getting closer to Dawn every second.

Skelton continued: "Seems a shame to keep 'em stuck here in the in-between, the Sneakarounds, here Midgard-side, trapped in ether and amber . . . but I cain't take any chances any more'n I can take just any child. Jenny had a stout heart, but she didn't have them strong bones like our sweet Jason here." With a wave of his hand, he sent his quintet of maps flying over, where they danced in a recurring helix around Jason. "Him I'll keep. Take his head, make my bread." A few hundred more bones completed his pathway. He was mere feet away from Dawn.

Justin leaned down to Hiram. "I think I can jump it. Hand me the sextant."

"Why?"

"Dawn's got magic powers with the axe," Justin whispered. "Maybe I'll get some from the sextant."

Dawn stopped struggling and released her axe. Dropping to her knees, her armor faded away, leaving only her cartoon self. She trembled, still covered with icing-ectoplasm, raising her hands in defense. Jason and Lee screamed through their gags. Hiram slipped Justin the sextant, transforming him. An aviator helmet materialized on his head, while a burgundy duster flumped to the floor, all in a whirlwind of animated electricity. Skelton must've missed it, because instead of reacting, he simply produced a small purple pouch lined with gold-and-red threads. Hiram winced.

"Oh, no."

"What is it?" Justin whispered.

"That's Jason's magic pouch."

From the pouch, Skelton pulled a strange, retrofitted tool: an awl soldered with various implements of cutting and shredding, rusty and crusted with black-dried blood. A bicycle chain dangled from its end. Until then, he'd been smiling and smirking, but now his face fell slack, like someone had let all the air out of him. His remaining eye stared into eternity, stone-dead. His words had no effect.

"This here's the grismal," he said, pronouncing it *grizz-mull.* He droned, his words echoing through the chamber, underscored by the faces of his victims. "Made it myself from my daddy's leftovers. Jason's worth it. But the resta y'all? Little Lee Peed His Pants? Ditzy Dawn Don't Know A Thing?" He faced Justin and Hiram. "And you two? JJ Turntail Got Blood on His Hands? Little Hiram Stammerstone Cain't Talk A-Tall? It ain't yer fault. Y'all ain't got them strong bones. So yain't nothing. To me. Nor anyone else. That's why your parents don't love you. Because you don't matter. Because you're nothing. Because you're worthless. They won't even miss ya. At least them'uns on my shelf get to stay this side of the Hightower, but when I finish with you? You'll be nothing."

He seemed to forget about everyone.

No one moved until sirens saved their lives.

They sounded from above, faint from passing through a hundred feet of earth and however-much extra-dimensional void. Energy flooded back into Skelton's body. His eye twinkled, his lips curled. He faced Justin and Hiram. With a flick of the grismal, a luminescent red hexagonal grid-wall appeared in the air between them.

"Better not try that jump, hoss." He executed another arcane gesture, seeming to scoop up his current path and throw it across the room like a carpet runner. It coiled through the space until it terminated at the exit doors. His five maps flew over and circled around him like electrons. Skelton addressed us as he walked: "I'm gonna go outside. And I'm gonna kill someone. Don't know who yet. Maybe it'll be someone you love, maybe it won't." He paused and bared his teeth. "Wanna know the number? The *real* number? I killed thirty-seven human beings to date. Next time you see me, it'll be thirty-eight."

As he was about to reach the door, Justin spoke.

"Hey. Happy birthday."

That seemed to scramble Skelton's circuits: "Say which?"

Justin returned the sextant to Hiram and transformed back into his standard appearance.

"Not yours. Jamie Scott Glenn's, born today, March thirteenth, 1977." He whispered: "Ides Less Two." Aloud: "He was your seventh victim. At least he's presumed your seventh because we never found his remains." Justin dimly registered that Hiram had taken his hand. His voice hitched, every vowel quavering: "I memorized everything about those kids. Birthdays, favorite subjects in school, their hopes and dreams. I know 'em cold. I talk with their parents sometimes. I know Jamie's really well. They started a whole support network for folks who'd lost kids. They exchange letters, meet a couple times a year, share stories. Did you know, after I met you, Skelton, did you know . . . I stopped believing in angels. I did. Because how could they exist in a world that had you in it? How could angels exist in a world that would take Susan

Lauren Johnson away from me? But when I met Ms. Glenn, and I saw how much she reminded me of my momma, I remembered: just because we can't always see 'em doesn't mean they're not always there. I checked in with Ms. Glenn just yesterday. Asked if she needs anything. She never does, but I keep asking. After all, she's an angel."

He swallowed and continued: "You wanna know something, man? Ten years from now, no one's gonna know your name. Or your fucking number. I get it. It's all about that. Get your name in the history books next to a big one. John Wayne Gacy killed this many, Ted Bundy that many. But you? Ten years from now, no matter what, I swear by God and Sunny Jesus, it's gonna be like, 'Lenny Skelton? Who the fuck is that?' And this . . . this place? This unholy temple? My friends and I, we're about to turn it to dust. And your victims? Every one you stole from us, every last one, we'll remember their names. We will celebrate them. We will mourn them. We will sing their sorrow down the ages. But you? You're done. We're about to delete you from the record. You best get right with it, because starting today, you're about to inherit the fuckin' wind."

Skelton spat. "I'd think twice about that, big man, because I'm gonna take all that matters to you to help my ascendance. Her remnants, the shadowcast, smiley's secret, and JJ's big night—all of it."

He vanished up the pathway. The instant Skelton was gone, his magic wall and the gate to Itza Linda both vanished. Justin cleared his throat to hold off an onslaught of grief.

Steeling himself, he said: "We've got to go to Itza Linda."

Dawn nodded. "Those sweet baby angels. They need us." She finally freed her axe and hurled herself over to Jason and Lee's sky-island, where she severed whatever magical force was holding them bound and airborne. They fell to the ground in a heap. Lee jumped to his feet and hugged Dawn.

"Dawnie, Dawnie, Dawnie," Lee said as they both sobbed. "Ohmigod, ohmigod, ohmigod, ohmigod thank you!"

Jason stood and dusted himself off. Dawn released Lee and crossed to him.

"I'm so sorry," he said, but his expression lightened at the sight of her. "Looks like I shoulda given *you* that gift."

Her face, locked in a tight scowl, softened one perceptible step.

"I guess we weren't good enough, huh?"

He shook his head. "I didn't think you'd need 'em. But I've got more gifts, don't you worry." From his shirtsleeve, Jason produced his 3D glasses. Slipping them on, he transformed into his animated cyberpunk avatar in a shatter-blast of electric wind.

Hiram called: "I thought Skelton had those! Didn't he steal your pouch?!"

"He did, and he got my maps, too, but I know some tricks he doesn't. Now, Lee, for your gift—"

"Wait, we need to warn the others!" Hiram said, squelching the walkie-sextant. *"Guys! Guys! Skelton's coming! Skelton's coming! And he has your maps!"*

An unexpected voice responded, his voice faint: "Who the Sam Hill is that?"

"Colquitt?" Hiram said.

"How'd *he* get here?" Justin said.

Webb's voice was next, screaming: "Get away from the—"

A wet *thud* sounded over the walkie, like a pumpkin being smashed. Silence.

Dawn: "That ain't good."

"We must help them," Lee said, pointing toward the exit.

Mac came crackling over the walkie: "Hiram! Or, Panthro, whatever—come in!"

"We're here," Hiram said.

"Skelton . . . oh, God, oh, God—he killed—Colquitt's dead. He killed him, and he's heading back your way!"

"Okay. God, god, god. I don't know what to do. He's too powerful." He deactivated the walkie.

Justin called: "Tell 'em to keep him away from here. We're going to Itza Linda."

"How?" Dawn asked.

"Through here," Justin said. "What do you guys call these things? Cloudy Mountains?"

"Smoky Mountains," Dawn said. "But that don't make no sense. There ain't no place else to go! How are we—"

Justin: "We'll figure it out! Just *tell them!*"

Hiram squelched the walkie: "Guys, you gotta find a way to keep Skelton away from here. We're gonna go save them. We know where Itza Linda is. It's in the attic of the old gondola house, but we've gotta go through his Smoky Mountain to reach it."

Kaitlyn came back: "Hey, what did you mean he had our—"

A car's engine roared over the walkie, followed by some unintelligible shouts.

Hiram asked again: "Guys, did you get that last message?"

Kaitlyn responded: "Yeah, but what was all that talk about our maps? I've got mine."

"There's another," Hiram said. "One you drew when you were little. Jason kept it. It's how he built his Smoky Mountains." Hiram smiled. "You drew a little tentacle on it."

Mac spoke next: "More maps, more power."

"Right. So uh be ready for anything. He might be too powerful to stop."

"Okay. We're on our way. We'll meet you at Itza Linda if we can."

"See you at Itza Linda."

The walkie went silent. Justin took Hiram's shoulder.

"They're waiting for us," Justin said. "Let's send them home."

Mackenzie

Tires squealed as two cars slid to a halt before a chasm. Webb's gray Camry stopped first, its doors swinging open to allow Kaitlyn, Mac, and Hanna to jump out. The former Sheriff Blackledge crossed to the chasm's edge, her jaw hanging wide. Colquitt's police cruiser fishtailed off the side of the road, nearly pitching into the opening. Kaitlyn and Mac ran over to Hanna.

"Careful, Auntie!" Mac called.

"How did this happen? An earthquake?" Hanna said, dazed. The magical boundary into Skelton's lair shimmered on the chasm's far side.

Can she see it? Mac wondered.

"Ms. Blackledge—" Kaitlyn began but stopped when Colquitt and Trent slammed out of the cruiser, the latter grimly fixated on Kaitlyn. She backed away from his hulking, storming advance, her face falling in terror, her hands held up before her. "Dad, Dad, Daddy—"

It was history before it happened: he pulled her into a grotesque tableau, wrenching her arm behind her back and bellowing: "WHEN WE TELL YOU TO FUCKING PULL OVER YOU PULL OVER ARE YOU FUCKING KIDDING ME."

His voice thundered through the woods and swallowed up poor Kaitlyn's pleas:

"Dad Dad Dad stop that's my bad arm arm oww armmm!"

Mackenzie "Mac" Gresham faced an inflection point. She suddenly thought of the movie *The Terminator* and how the futuristic killing machine would analyze its opponents' strengths and weaknesses. Her mind conducted similar calculations on the inhuman beast that called itself her step-father.

I could shove him in. Right now. But he's holding Kaity, and I might knock her in, too.

Colquitt seemed not to notice the violence but instead gaped at Webb and Hanna: "Holt? And *Blackledge*? Why're you all in Holt's car?"

It took a bleary-eyed Webb in tandem with Hanna Blackledge to stop Trent.

Webb put him in a headlock and wrestled him off her, while Hanna decided to get old-school and pulled her sidearm. *That* got Colquitt's attention.

He raised his palms. "Whoa, whoa, *whoa*, there old-timer!"

Hanna ignored him, her focus on Kaitlyn.

"You okay, sweetie?"

"He . . . hurt me," she said, but "hurt" sounded like "hut." *He hut me.* Kaitlyn cradled her wounded arm, her lips clenched and forehead wrinkled with pain and grief and tears. She looked and sounded like a toddler, helpless and confused, her tears flowing free and ready. The scar under her eye blushed an angry red.

Colquitt put himself between Hanna and Trent. "You wanna stow the smoke wagon, Blackledge?"

"*Smoke wagon?*" Hanna sneered, holstering her sidearm. "It's a *gun,* you mouth-breathing goon, and someone had to make a move before that fucking lunatic did any more damage."

"Damage?" Colquitt said. "I'm not the one who just led the cops on a high-speed chase *halfway to Sevierville!*"

Mac registered the familiar turn of phrase: *halfway to Sevierville.* She met eyes with Kaitlyn. They'd both heard those words back at Stems & Stamens. The proprietor had said it in the manner of a mild oath, Mac thought, like he was saying, *Well, I'll be damned.*

Trent wrenched himself free of Webb. "Get off me!"

Now that he was standing alone, Mac's skin crackled cold. Moments ago, she'd been ready to do the unthinkable; or she *thought* she was. Hanna's bulk suddenly blocked her view and broke her focus. They met eyes. Hanna shook her head, once and finally. Mac swallowed a sob.

My God, what has he done *to me?*

Kaitlyn padded over. Mac hooked an arm around her.

"Did you hear what he said?" Kaitlyn asked, still tearful. "The Sevierville thing?"

"Yeah."

"That guy at Stems & Stamens said something else," Kaitlyn said. "What was it? 'Western' something?"

"I can't remember. *Shhh.* We need to find a way across that moat."

Colquitt finally turned his attention to his friend.

"Hoss, I need ya to take a time out over here, okay? Take a second, catch your breath."

"But she—"

"*I got this one,*" he said. Trent crossed his arms and stood next to the Camry, steaming. Colquitt turned to Webb: "Holton, what the goddamn hell are you doing with this bunch?! *Them* I can believe would pull a stunt like this, but not you!"

Webb blinked, still loopy. "Bo, listen to me, there's something seriously wrong."

"What's *wrong* is this little bitch led a law officer on a high-speed pursuit across ten god*damn* miles!"

"Bo, there's someone up in Enchanted Caverns, and he's kidnapped some of these kids."

Colquitt looked at him with pity. "Aw, who's in there, Baywatch? Tell me."

Hanna stepped in: "Sheriff, I can't endorse my nieces' behavior tonight, but there's something you need to know. This might sound outlandish, but I have reason to believe Lenny Skelton survived and is holed up in Enchanted Caverns."

"What?"

Trent uncrossed his arms. "Hanna, is this a joke?"

Webb: "He must've found a way out of the fire that night. I dunno how, but he did. And he's got four kids captive."

"And Justin Johnson," Hanna said to Colquitt's amusement.

"Justin—as in, *JJ Flash* Justin Johnson? Thought we ran him outta town on a rail!" His tone dropped: "Woman, you ain't never liked me. Warn't no secret around the force."

"Can't imagine why."

Colquitt spun on Webb: "Is this because me n' the boys pranked you last Memorial Day?"

"Bo. I don't care about that, and we don't have the time for—"

"I'll decide what we've got time for!" he yelled, not noticing the dark, rippling shape that appeared on the other side of the magic barrier. It looked like a walking Rorschach blot. Kaitlyn gasped.

"Sheriff! Look!" She pointed at the shape.

Colquitt turned on her. "That's enough of mischief, missy!" He faced the chasm again. "We gotta get some emergency vehicles out here. There ain't been a trembler 'round these parts for years." The shape grew larger and darker. Colquitt mused: "Y'all are in *so much trouble*. I think I'm gonna run you in."

Mac squeezed Kaitlyn. "Ohmigawd."

Halfway to Sevierville. Y'all are in so much trouble.

The guy at Stems & Stamens had said both of those things.

Webb crossed to them and indicated the dark shape. "Is that who I think it is?"

"Yes," Mac whispered. "We've gotta—"

Hiram's voice crackled and blared from Mac's pocket: *"Guys! Guys! Skelton's coming! Skelton's coming! And he has our maps!"*

Colquitt spun, pointed. "Who the Sam Hill is that?"

"Bo!" Webb shouted. "Get away from the wall!"

"Wall? What—" He stopped, his mouth instantly decoupled from his brain, one eye rolling to white. Everyone stood stunned, processing the sight. Its swing had been nearly silent, the terrible implement that looped out of the wall with a faint whistle, hooked to a bicycle chain. A cast-iron arm capped with dozens of talons lodged in Colquitt's skull-crown with a sickening, wet *thudge.* His arms fell limp as his mouth jabbered on: "Westy highkint ah where to flandon—" The yank nearly decapitated him. It was like someone had hooked the chain to a speeding car.

Everyone finally awoke.

Kaitlyn and Mac screamed. Webb lunged but caught only empty air. Hanna fired twice, but both shots disintegrated into the magic barrier. It was all for naught as Colquitt's rag doll body flew across the chasm and slammed into its inner wall. His head hung from a few strands of sinew and spine that audibly rent as the iron arm reeled him up and through the glimmering barrier.

"Sweet blue Jesus," Hanna said. "How did—what was—he just vanished!"

Mac strode over, pulling her walkie: "Hiram! Or, Panthro, whatever—come in!"

Hiram answered: "We're here."

"Skelton . . . oh, God, oh, God—he killed—Colquitt's dead. He killed him, and he's heading back your way."

"Okay. God, god, god. I don't know what to do. He's too powerful." The walkie cut out for a few moments before Hiram returned: "Guys, you gotta find a way to keep Skelton away from here. We're gonna go save them. We know where Itza Linda is. It's in the attic of the old gondola house, but we've gotta go through his Smoky Mountain to reach it."

"Hey," Kaitlyn said. "What did you mean he had our—"

Spinning tires *roared* and scattered a buckshot-blast of dust and gravel across them all. Webb sprinted down the road after his own car.

"Hey! HEY! What the fuck, man?!"

He bent over, hands on his knees, panting. The women all ran over next to him, their faces cast red by the Camry's receding tail-lights. Hanna shook her head. Kaitlyn's expression was one of maximum betrayal.

"He left us. I cannot believe that sonofabitch. He *left* us."

Hanna took her shoulder. "But *I'm* not going anywhere."

Hiram's voice crackled: "Guys, did you get that last message?"

"Yeah, but what was all that talk about our maps?!" Kaitlyn asked. "I've got mine."

"There's another," Hiram said. "One you drew when you were little. Jason kept it. It's how he built his Smoky Mountains. You drew a little tentacle on it."

Mac bared her teeth. "More maps, more power."

"Right," Hiram said. "So uh be ready for anything. He might be too powerful to stop."

"Okay. We're on our way. We'll meet you at Itza Linda if we can."

"See you at Itza Linda."

Mac stowed the walkie and ran to the chasm. "But how are we gonna get across this thing?"

Hanna nodded. "I can take care of that."

Hiram's Journal

The exit was less than a hundred feet away, but it may as well have been a thousand miles. Justin and I were still stranded on a platform about fifty feet from Dawn, Lee, and Jason.

Dawn pulled her axe: "How are we gonna do this? There ain't nothin' around us."

She was right. Surrounding us were millions of square "miles" of endless darkness. Skelton's Smoky Mountain—the one we'd previously infiltrated—was nowhere to be seen.

"If this is his Smoky Mountain, there must be *some* way to get to the rest of it."

"Admiral, an inquiry," Lee said. "Why can't we simply draw a gate from here to the Gold Rush?"

Justin: "I'm new to this magic map stuff. Is that how it works?"

Jason's eyes flicked up and down. "I have no idea. Justin's powers are a wild card. But let's try. Justin, Dawn, Hiram—you all have your maps. Add Enchanted Caverns and the Gold Rush to 'em as fast as you can."

We took turns using each other's backs as makeshift easels, adding the details to our maps.

Justin looked up from his work. "What's the keystone?"

"A butterfly," Dawn said. "For Susie Schuppe."

"Done."

We waited for the gate to appear, but nothing happened. Jason balled his fists.

"Damn. He's got five maps now, including mine and Kaitlyn's. He's got total control in here. But we've got to keep moving. Lee, I've got something for you." Jason balled his fists and crossed his wrists before flattening his palms and using his hands to sketch a circle about three feet across. From nothing materialized a golden, round shield that bore at its center a black field emblazoned with a pearly-white heart. He presented it to Lee.

"Sorry I couldn't get this to you sooner, Lee."

"Uh hey, Admiral!" I called. "Better brace yourself! Those gifts pack a punch!"

Lee nodded and planted a foot behind him in a pseudo-martial arts pose as he accepted the shield. A ten-foot-wide sphere of lightning ka-*zammed* around him, knocking him to his knees. He was conscious but a little winded as he stood back up in his fully armed and operational *animated* self. He'd stepped right out of a *Dungeons & Dragons* campaign, with gold chain-mail armor, a bright red cape, and blue chain-mail sleeves and leggings. Gold boots completed the look. His glasses had lost their stems and instead floated a few centimeters over his nose, his pupils a pair of animated dots that darted around.

Jason was beaming.

It's a great feeling when people surprise you. I'd spent the last several months hating Jason, and in the last few days, he'd been working his ass off to make things right. The look on Lee's face after he turned into a cartoon didn't make up for all the mean shit he'd said to me . . . but it didn't hurt.

Dawn prodded him. "You should give it a name."

Lee weighed the shield and addressed Jason: "May I?"

"Of course," Jason said.

It came instantly: "I name thee . . . *COMPASSION*."

"Cool name," Jason said.

"My friends, there's something important I need to share," Lee began, but Jason cut him off:

"Lee, I'm so sorry, but can it wait? Let's get someplace safe first."

Lee nodded. "Quite right."

Jason tapped a few keys on his forearm to bring up his laser array. "Justin, Hiram! Let's get you over here!" The lasers sketched out a luminescent orange bridge between their platform and ours. Justin and I took a step forward but Rusty blocked our path, hissing.

"Rust, what gives, man?"

"Wait!" Dawn called, kneeling to pry a bone from the ground. She tossed it onto Jason's power-bridge.

And it fell right through. The bridge fritzed and flickered like a TV losing its vertical hold—and vanished.

Jason grimaced. "Damn. Why didn't that work?"

Ru-u-u-mmble. Another earthquake rattled the room. The floor underneath me and Justin started shaking. My feet sank into the mass of skulls and bones.

"Oh, shit," Justin said. "This isn't gonna hold. We've got to move!"

"But where?!" I said. "And *how?!*"

Mac screeched from the walkie: "He's gone he's gone oh God oh God he's gone—*move move! You're gonna fall!*"

Hanna

"Hold on!"

Hanna Blackledge hadn't been expecting to re-enact *Smokey and the Bandit* that night, but when she found a twenty-foot chasm separating her from the people she loved, she got behind the wheel of Colquitt's police cruiser, fired it up, and floored it.

"Auntie Hanna, are you sure about this?" Mac yelled, bracing herself against the dash.

Hanna had an answer to that question, but she didn't think this was the right time to tell everyone she used to drive stunt cars at monster truck shows around the Southland. As for that night's stunt, she'd noticed a part of the chasm's rim that rose at a slight incline; more than enough to launch them across the divide.

Which it did.

"Eeeeeyeaaaaaaghgghgh!—" —vumMMM! Their screams were swallowed in a sudden silence that enshrouded the car like a glove as they reached the other side. The car slammed to the earth and fishtailed for a few dozen yards before she brought it back under control and downshifted. Hanna squinted and blinked. Her eyes itched, as if she'd just taken a blast of pollen in the face, but she hadn't had allergies in years.

That's when she noticed the water.

All around her, the world looked *mostly* normal, except for one detail: everything was swimming.

Mac, who was riding shotgun, touched her hand.

"Auntie, do you see it?"

She brought the cruiser to a halt before Enchanted Caverns.

"I don't think I feel quite right in the head," Hanna said. "My vision's blurry."

Mac made eye contact with Kaitlyn in the back seat. Both of them stared at the Enchanted Caverns building with gawk-eyed expressions of deep horror.

Kaitlyn: "Your vision isn't swimming, guys. We're inside his lair."

Mac shook her head. "She still can't see it. Not all of it."

"See *what?*" Hanna said.

"Skelton's hideout," Mac said, climbing out. "We need to get—"

The pavement heaved up like a wave of water and smashed into the cruiser's door, slamming it shut and knocking Mac to the ground outside. Hanna screamed and jumped out just as another pavement wave rose under the car and lifted it skyward.

"Oh my God!" Hanna yelled, pulling open the back door. "Jump! Jump!"

They all leaped to the ground. An instant later, the pavement-wave closed like a fist around the car, crushing it in a massive fireball that knocked everyone to the ground.

Holton struggled to his feet. "Hanna, are you—*holy God A'mighty, it's him it's HIM.*"

He was pointing, but when Hanna turned, she saw nothing—

—except for a shape. Her vision continued to swim, but amidst the swimming moved a watery distortion in the shape of a man with what appeared to be a windmill spinning behind him. Hanna flashed on that silly movie about the alien that hunted Arnold Schwarzenegger. Hiram had begged to watch it when she had them over one weekend, and she had lovingly obliged. She enjoyed it more than she expected, and now she seemed to be living it.

"What in creation is—" she began, only for Kaitlyn to shoulder her aside, drop to a knee, and pound her billy club into the earth. Nothing happened. She pounded it again, the watery distortion slowly but inexorably approaching, and yet nothing happened. She stood, and for the first time, Hanna could detect a change in her appearance; a glowing *outline* surrounded her—as if some unseen, magical hand had sketched an entirely new appearance around her. In Kaitlyn's case, the magical sketch artist apparently thought she belonged at a Motley Crue concert; the faint outline of a mohawk floated above her head, accompanied by the suggestion of a leather jacket and platform boots. Kaitlyn faced Mac.

"The scepter isn't working!"

Holton sprinted past her so fast she spun around from the momentum. He ran pell-mell and hurled himself at the watery distortion.

The instant he made contact, Hanna's world inverted.

It was like some godly force had thrown a lever that transformed reality. The moon exploded an instantaneous livid red, while all around, every tree, bush, and plant wilted into black husks. Lightning flashed to either side, seeming to focus on the girls. The watery distortion—*oh, the movie was called* Predator, she suddenly remembered—flooded with color: Caucasian flesh tones, plus a plaid flannel and blue jeans. It wasn't an alien but a *man* that Holton had tackled to the ground, and the "windmill" Hanna thought she'd seen were actually five pieces of paper that orbited this new arrival like electrons.

But that wasn't all. There was Enchanted Caverns, too.

A jittering, creeping horde of industrial detritus—crumbling red bricks, barbed wire, and shrapnel—bubbled up from the ground and swarmed across the building, encasing it in a patina of industrial decay. Vasculature snaked out of every inch of earth and coiled around the building, every vessel and vein leaking blood in slippery sheets of gore.

All that was terrifying enough, but when Hanna saw the faces, she feared she might lose her mind.

Faces, sorrowful *faces* burst from the building's roofline like terrible blossoms, each one frozen forevermore in a silent, plaintive wail, and each one wreathed with a blood-spattered prize ribbon. She recognized a few of them, and in tandem with that recognition was the realization that the man Holton had wrestled to the ground was Lenny Skelton, and they had infiltrated his magic lair.

Hanna wailed: *"Skelllll-tonnnn!"* But when she pulled her gun, she found she was holding little more than a gun-shaped configuration of glittering dust. "God Almighty," she muttered, vaguely noticing that both Kaitlyn and Mac had assumed bizarre new appearances—*they look like cut-outs from my old Katy Keene comics.*

The girls' appearance didn't matter. All that mattered was helping Holton, who straddled Skelton, choking him with one hand while the other made futile swipes at the papers spinning around him. All three women prepared to bull-rush the two men, but in a flash of motion, Skelton whipped a purple burlap pouch over Holton's head.

And cinched it shut.

Someone screamed, everyone screamed. Holton's arms dropped to his sides. Skelton removed the pouch to reveal a body whose neck terminated in a perfectly flat plane of flesh. He kicked Holton's body aside and leaped to his feet, brandishing the laden pouch like a demonic Perseus.

"Five maps, one head, grind their bones, make my bread," he said just as an earthquake rattled the countryside and threw everyone off balance. Skelton's smile wavered, but he bared his teeth and shook loose the pouch's nightmarish contents. Everyone looked away. "They're all, all, all gonna fall, fall, *fall!*"

Mac screamed into her walkie: "He's gone he's gone oh God oh God he's gone—*move move! You're gonna fall!*"

Dawn

Justin and Hiram's platform wasn't the only one falling apart. Dawn and Lee braced themselves against each other as the ground shook.

"We've gotta move!" Dawn screamed. "It's all gonna fall!"

"But how?!" Jason said. "There's no place else to go."

Hiram was jumping up and down but couldn't say anything.

Justin finished his sentence for him: *"There it is!"*

He was pointing across the space. Dawn, Lee, and Jason all spun to see the rest of Skelton's Smoky Mountain floating about a half-mile distant and a few hundred feet above their current position. She whooped with relief.

"Where the heckfire did *that* come from?!"

Holton

Don't run to your death.

That was a saying around Coronado. As a Navy SEAL in training, Holton "Baywatch" Webb had heard it a million times. His instructors said the saying basically meant to stay calm and show restraint, even in the heat of the most intense firefight.

But there was another saying they taught them:

All in, all the time.

Those two sayings always seemed to be at odds for Holton. How could you be all in if you were always sitting back on your heels, thinking about every last move? How could you protect your teammates unless you acted decisively? Holton resolved the conflict between the two sayings with one of his own:

Run to your death.

Any time he jumped out of a Black Hawk or faced down a bad guy, Holton always planned to run to his death. Every time. He tried his best to live a life of integrity, to be kind to others, to stand up for the weak and the helpless. If he was being honest with himself, his adherence to that saying is what kept him unattached all these years. Women came and went, but there was some part of him that didn't want to leave anyone behind (besides his family) to mourn him. Of course, Holton forgot that when you live a life of kindness and generosity, you amass a veritable army of people who will mourn your passing.

For the past several months, Holton seemed to be acquiring a sixth sense. He was always spying strange sights that lay just beyond the boundaries of his perception:

The unicorn at Soddy Farm.

The bizarre heat that seemed to radiate from the remains of that old cabin.

The disembodied arm that took a swipe at Colquitt.

But when Justin Johnson came running out of a magic portal, the world came un-seamed and parted like curtains to reveal it all. Skelton had constructed a realm of unearthly terror, and he had poured all of his soul's white-hot hatefulness into it. The moon was a bleeding wound. The forest was dead. Enchanted Caverns was an industrial hell upon which Skelton had mounted the heads of his victims.

And Skelton.

He was dressed normally—flannel and jeans—but his face was just . . . *wrong*. He looked like he was wearing a mask of his own face, one that was contorted into a devilish rictus, his teeth like fangs, his eye alight with the smolder of the underworld. Around him spun five pieces of paper that Holton recognized as maps, including some that the kids had been drawing earlier.

But it was when Kaitlyn kneeled and slammed her billy club into the earth that Baywatch made a connection that spurred him to run to his death on that surreal night in March 1990.

"The scepter isn't working!"

It struck him momentarily dizzy, the realization. When he held one of Davey's bars or Nance's churches, his family felt close. Those maps were just as special, as magical, as *holy* as his mom's annual Christmas cottages.

They put a part of themselves into those maps, same as Mom put into our gifts.

As soon as he made the connection between the cottages and the maps, he knew what he had to do. By then he'd already tackled Skelton the ground.

If he has their maps, he must have a part of them.

If I can destroy the maps, maybe that will

Hiram's Journal

Justin and I scooted forward a few perilous steps as our platform shed thousands and thousands of more bones, Mac's previous words echoing in my mind: *he's gone.*

There was only one man up there. Officer Webb.

But we had to keep moving. Our platforms were almost gone. Dawn pointed at Rusty.

"Justin, can Rusty find his way over here?"

"Good call!" he said, producing the treats, but when he tossed one, it simply plunged into darkness. Rusty didn't move. "Shit!"

Our platform had almost completely disintegrated when Mac came over the walkie, her voice eerily calm:

"Hiram, we're gonna be okay. The sextant works now."

"What?" I said. "How do you—"

"Just look. If Skelton has your map, he has your powers."

I put the sextant to my eye—and the cavern lit up. Pathways ran *everywhere*, all of them coiling in strange shapes and words. I could make out partial phrases here and there—*it is so much fun; she will never be any; I think that's sad; the monster goes on*—but none of them connected with mine and Justin's platform.

"Mac, you're right! But how—"

Mac spoke again: "There goes Kaitlyn's."

Thunder rumbled overhead. Dust and stones from the *real* Enchanted Caverns filtered through the endless void and rained on us.

Jason: "Holy shit. What's happening up there?"

Lee marveled: "They must have found a way to destroy our maps."

Justin prodded me and said: "Let me look."

In the back of my mind, I wondered how they managed to destroy the maps, but I dismissed the concern and passed the sextant (and the Necron 99 costume) to Justin, who scanned the room and pointed toward a platform that floated about ten feet away.

"I think I can jump it," he said. "You'll follow me?"

"I can't jump that far," I said as a few more inches of our platform fell away.

"Sure you can! It's only a few feet."

"It's *way more* than a few feet!"

Dawn pulled up her axe. "I've got an idea! He don't got my map, and this lets me jump real far. Hiram! Catch!"

"No!" I screamed. No, I didn't scream; I *screeched.* My voice cracked in a shrill, humiliating wail that echoed everywhere. The world was falling apart around me. "I can't do it. I'm too *fat.*"

Jason took off his 3D glasses. "What? Buddy, that's not true. You're athletic as hell. Sorry I don't say it enough. You got this! You can do it!"

"You said it at the wedding. You said there was something wrong with me."

The memory was a black blot in my mind; a black blot that swallowed up all of Jason's good deeds and highlighted all his bad ones. He was nothing but his cruelty, nothing but his insults. I was crying so hard I barely felt the platform falling away under my heels.

"Why would you say that if you didn't mean it?" I said.

Across the divide, Dawn said: "What the hell is *wrong* with you?"

"Remember your oath," Lee said.

I was bawling too hard to see what happened next, but the world turned orange. Warm light engulfed me and lifted me in a soft cradle that faintly snapped and hissed with sparkle-cracks of lightning. I opened my eyes to see a glowing orange hand carrying me and Justin across the divide. Jason guided the hand with his laser-array, gently setting us both down. Justin marveled.

"I thought he had your map," he said. "How'd you know you could do that?"

"I think they destroyed another one, and I gambled on it being mine," he said.

Mac's voice crackled from the walkie: "Jason, you're back in business. We lost Skelton, but he's down to two maps. His Smoky Mountain's smaller, too."

"Less maps, less power," Jason said.

"Right," Mac said. "He's headed your way. We're trying to catch him, but you better hurry."

"Got it. See you at Itza Linda."

"See you at Itza Linda."

I deactivated the walkie. Jason turned to us and said: "Are you both okay?"

"Yeah," Justin said.

I nodded, still sniffling.

Jason kneeled before me. "I love you so much, man. I'm sorry for everything. I can't make up for it, but I swear to God I'm gonna try. I will not break my oath to you." The platform shivered under our feet. Justin handed the sextant back to me, while Jason stood and indicated Dawn's battle axe, asking: "You know how to use this, right?"

"Damn right I do," she said, slashing her way out of the darkness.

Mackenzie

"He's gone he's gone oh God oh God he's gone—*move move! You're gonna fall!*"

They couldn't look at his remains. All they could see was Skelton marching their way, the devil himself, his hands slashing out a series of arcane gestures, his magic maps swarming around him.

"Get behind us!" Mac called to her aunt, pulling her rubber-band gun only for it to dissolve into a cloud of sparkling dust. "*No!*" Mac screamed, her heart breaking at the loss of one of her dad's final gifts. Kaitlyn pulled out the scepter, and even though it was useless, Mac wished Jason could have enchanted Dad's rubber-band gun to protect it from Skelton's magic. She shook the thought out of her head, blinking into Skelton's oncoming heat; the maps were fireballs now, *comets* that swooped around him faster and faster until they were perfect, blinding loops of light. Mac kneeled to pick up a rock to throw when she noticed something:

Her rubber-band gun.

It was like a sand sculpture of her gun had been destroyed in the tide, only for entropy to reverse itself. Millions of sparkling particles reassembled themselves, all the way down to the little etching of her face. Suddenly, Kaitlyn was pointing and screaming:

"Look!"

They all squinted past Skelton's blaze at Enchanted Caverns—the *normal* Enchanted Caverns. Gone was the industrial nightmare, the barbed wire, the crumbling brick, all of it. At the same time, Skelton's maps slowed down enough for Mac to realize the tactical terrain had shifted.

He only had *four* maps, not five.

Mac's memories went into overdrive. Lee had said if Skelton kept getting more maps, he'd become too powerful to stop, but now he had lost a map, and his powers seemed to have reduced.

But what happened to that fifth map?

That's when she saw it. In his hand. Officer Webb's. Crushed in his fist was one of their maps. On it was an ornate compass rose that bore the hallmarks of Lee Dockery's artistic style. He'd added such a rose to Hiram's original map, the one he'd lost at Soddy Farm. Sisterly intuition slowed the passage of time to a mindful crawl. Dawn had been able to use the sextant to see. To *see*. Officer Webb had destroyed Hiram's map, and it had shattered part of Skelton's illusion.

Mac's mind connected a pair of critical dots.

Hiram's map. The sextant.

Kaitlyn's map. The scepter.

Sorrow sang from a distant depth of her soul in honor of Webb's passing and heroism. Her entire self ached with grief, but she set it aside.

Mourn him later. For now, you have to make sure he didn't die in vain. You have to save your family.

"Hiram, we're gonna be okay," she said into the walkie, her voice loud but steady. "The sextant works now."

Hiram responded: "What? How do you—"

"Just look." Mac said. "If Skelton has your map, he has your powers."

Kaitlyn's gift, the scepter, wasn't working. Skelton had one of her maps. Not her current one, but an older one; one she'd originally drawn for Jason, unwittingly granting him access to the Sneakaround Network for the first time. She'd drawn a *tentacle* on it, a bit of whimsy from that video game she liked. And now it was contributing to Skelton's power. Mac spotted Kaitlyn's map flying through the air, the tentacle rendered in crude, childish crayon. Mac took up her rubber-band gun. Hiram spoke again, his voice faint and distant:

"Mac, you're right! But how—"

Hers was a moving target that bizarre night in March of 1990, but so confident was she in her aim that she called the shot before she pulled the trigger.

"There goes Kaitlyn's."

Kaitlyn

Her map dropped like a clay pigeon, the shot having shorn it into a dozen pieces. Skelton's expression, a grotesque sneer of triumph, faltered. Kaitlyn kneeled and slammed the scepter into the earth. In response, the sky flashed a blinding white and delivered a bolt right through her. The ground shook everyone off balance. When the smoke cleared, Kaitlyn stood, clenching the scepter in both fists like a quarter-staff. An otherworldly light ignited inside the ram's skull and surrounded her in a hyper-flashing, electro-surging power storm.

"You don't have MY map anymore, motherfucker!"

She unleashed a blast of energy that could've flattened a forest. It was like a freight train of orange-and-purple fire that smashed into Skelton and slammed him into the side of the building, where he left a cracking divot and slid to the ground, his eyes closed. Another earthquake shook the land. A charred and smoking Skelton shook his head and pushed himself to his feet as the women advanced, Kaitlyn at the fore, her teeth bared, her eyes enwreathed with orange lightning.

"Get up, get up!" she screamed.

Skelton blinked his one eye open. To his side lay the remains of another map.

Jason's.

Kaitlyn recognized his style and handwriting immediately. She felt an instant's regret at its destruction but knew it was for the greater cause. His two remaining maps spun slowly around him. Kaitlyn moved to strike again but a sudden onrush of heat hit her from behind. They turned to see the boundary of Skelton's Smoky Mountain contracting like a massive wall of water. The girls wheeled on Skelton with triumph in their eyes.

"Less maps, less power," Mac said.

That's when Skelton surprised them all.

He ran.

The doors to Enchanted Caverns swung in the wake of Skelton's retreat. Mac squelched the walkie.

"Jason, you're back in business. We lost Skelton. He's headed your way. We're trying to catch him, but you better hurry."

Justin

Justin couldn't stop thinking about what treasure he wanted. He felt ridiculous thinking about it, given the circumstances, but the kids looked so cool in their magical Saturday-morning-cartoon costumes. He sort of dug Hiram's futuristic assassin look . . . but he wanted one of his own, and he had a pretty good idea what it was.

I wonder if Jason takes requests.

They all followed Dawn as she slashed her away across the darkness to another series of floating pathways, one that the kids had already visited, Justin gathered, but its appearance had changed. They plunged down the gruesome pathway, lights illuminating overhead in tandem with their movements.

"The Gold Rush is this way!" Dawn called, leading the way.

"Fascinating," Lee said as they ran. "The floors were cobblestones and grass during our last visit."

Jason: "More maps, more power."

They arrived at a gate that swirled with red light. Hiram prodded him.

"Justin, be careful when you look at the keystone."

Dawn turned, nodding. "It might show you something that'll make you angry."

"Or extremely sad," Lee said. "Everyone sees something different."

The keystone showed Justin a prize ribbon, but not just any prize ribbon. No, this one belonged to Jenny Miles, whom they'd found in the attic of the old gondola house that terrible night. Justin's heart seized, his lips curling in a grimace. Instantly, four sets of arms wrapped him up in love and kindness. He cleared his throat and leaned back.

"Thanks, guys. I'm fine. Let's keep moving."

Dawn held up a hand. "Should we, though? The ladies said he was headin' this way. He's down to two maps. I think we could take him."

Jason shook his head. "We're still in his Smoky Mountain. He's got the home-court advantage."

Dawn nudged him. "I thought it was home *field* advantage."

"That's football. Home *court* is hoops."

They shared a warm smile. Justin nodded at the gate.

"C'mon, guys. They're waiting."

Skelton had left the gate open—that was *one* break they caught—and they each passed through the red barrier into the hallway adjoining the old gondola house. Jason checked everyone's appearance.

"We're still cartoons."

Dawn nodded. "He's made this part of his hideout, too. Same as Enchanted Caverns."

"We're close to Itza Linda," Hiram said.

Passing the hundreds of Polaroids, they arrived in the gondola house, the air heavy with dust and spectral energies. Floorboards creaked and cracked. Someone coughed. Cartoon characters covered the walls: Wilbur Claus, the Nine Muses of the Holidays. A sign over the far door read, *THIS WAY TO OBER GATLINBURG SKY-GONDOLA*, LOWER STATION.

And a small door was set into the ceiling.

The door to the attic. The *secret attic*.

He'd disguised himself as a park performer that day, sneaking in behind an employee as they clocked in and insinuating himself among one of the live bands.

Justin reached up and pulled a string to open the door. A collapsing ladder extended to the floor before them. Justin stepped up to it and turned.

"Itza Linda was never only *one* place," he said, cradling Rusty. "It's wherever they are."

Dawn was crying. "Those baby angels."

Justin started to climb but hesitated. "Lee, what were you going to tell us before?"

Lee took a deep breath and pursed his lips. He spoke quietly.

"It can wait. Itza Linda is calling."

"Itza Linda is calling," Justin said, putting a foot on the ladder.

They all climbed up.

Mackenzie

He was fleet of foot, but his advantage was fading. With the destruction of three maps, Skelton's magic had ebbed enough to return Enchanted Caverns to its normal appearance—*almost*. The women rushed into the lobby to see a pair of double doors swinging shut across the room. Mac held out a hand to slow her aunt's headlong advance.

"He's getting away!" Hanna said.

"Holton said this place was booby-trapped," Mac said. "Kaity, think the scepter can help?"

"I don't know, but I'll try," she said, holding the scepter over her head. She whispered: "Light our darkest hour." Her staff illuminated from within and flooded the room with orange-and-purple light that brought into relief a labyrinth set into the floor. Mac thought back to the entrance foyer to the Mystery Mansion—*this is just like it*—except for one difference:

There were words.

Woven into the labyrinth were the words, *JJ's big night, Love, Sue. AYF.* Hanna slowly shook her head.

"Is this . . . Are these the powers and forces arrayed at your command?"

"They are," Mac said.

"And does Skelton command comparable forces?"

Kaitlyn fielded that one: "Fuckin' A right he does."

They scurried through the labyrinth.

"How long have you known about this, girls?"

Mac: "Hiram told me."

"Jason's known about it since he was little," Kaitlyn said as they reached the double doors. She lowered the scepter. "I think . . . I think it's a place for kids."

Mac nodded. "An in-between place."

"Where we can walk in, if we need to get away, to escape. If we're in pain. But he's corrupted it. Skelton."

"And he's not the only one," Kaitlyn said. "There's a monster that lives here."

"Monster?" Hanna asked.

"The Plaid Man," Kaitlyn said.

"Who's he?"

"We don't know. But he might show up."

"We've got to be careful," Mac said. "And we have to save them. Skelton's victims. We know where they are."

Hanna lips trembled. "Kids, I'm so sorry I didn't see. I can't believe you've had to carry this burden all by yourselves."

Mac: "Auntie, it's okay. You're here now. And they're waiting for us. We've got to move."

Kaitlyn

They'd left a trail of breadcrumbs. When they arrived in the caverns' first chamber, most of it had returned to normal, except for one entire wall that was missing. In its place was a view of endless darkness. Kaitlyn, armed with the most powerful weapon, led the way, lighting the path with the scepter. They reached a stone platform amidst a sea of stalagmites. A massive window opened onto eternity. About a "mile" away floated Skelton's Smoky

Mountain—and Skelton himself. He was practically raining sweat as he sprinted down the floating path. In the deep distance, he vanished through the gate to the Gold Rush park.

"We've gotta hurry!" Kaitlyn yelled. "Come on!"

Kaitlyn ignited the scepter once more and illuminated a pathway that led across the endless void. After sharing a nod with the others, she led the way out over sheer nothingness. Hanna's breath quickened with every step, but Mac took her hand to calm her. Kaitlyn led them through Skelton's Smoky Mountain, through the gate into the Gold Rush park, up the hallway to the old gondola house, and all the way to the ladder leading to the secret attic, where they paused. Hanna looked up, her face drawn in awe and sorrow.

"But . . . we searched the attic. It's where we found Jenny Miles. There was nothing else there."

"He moved them," Mac said.

Hanna nodded. "Then let's go put them to rest."

They climbed up.

Hiram's Journal

We should've known.

It was a ritual as well as a snare, our voyage to the secret attic, and Skelton had lured us there, picking us off, revealing our strengths and weaknesses, and finally arraying us all in the attic. When we climbed into it, we thought we'd found Itza Linda. Shelves and shelves of urns and boxes of remains surrounded us, only to vanish in a blink. We found ourselves frozen in a horrible stasis, trapped in stillness and silence, doomed to watch our friends climb the ladder into the same trap that hoodwinked us. The door in the floor opened and admitted Auntie Hanna, Mac, and Kaitlyn. We all screamed and yelled our warnings, but Skelton's magic was too much, even when it was reduced to the three maps that spun behind him.

His magic was too much because he had a new and powerful ally.

The Plaid Man.

When the last three had climbed into the attic with us, he revealed the scope and horror of his power. The walls raced away, leaving the eight of us standing on a lone platform: me, Mac, Jason, Kaitlyn, Dawn, Lee, Hanna, Justin. We floated in nothingness, facing off against Skelton, who floated in space before us, while behind him stood the Plaid Man as we'd never seen him before. He was naked, his arms crossed, his flesh a slithering, trypophobic atlas of the grotesque. Gory lattices criss-crossed his face.

But even more horrifying than his appearance was his *size*.

He was the size of a stellar nursery. Millions of light-years tall. His legs faded into the black void below. His sheer, mind-bending scale was enough to strike you dizzy. You couldn't look at it head-on; you had to squint and blink and avert your eyes, telling yourself, *Maybe he's not really there, maybe this is all a terrible nightmare.*

All that was bullshit, of course. He and Skelton were real and terrible, so packed with existence and reality that you wanted to scream and howl and wail and keen and moan and cry.

Skelton snapped his fingers. We unfroze, and true to form, we sprang into action. Kaitlyn let loose with a massive blast from her scepter; Dawn leaped forth with her axe; Jason constructed a luminescent rocket launcher and fired. Even Rusty hissed and sprang forward. All of our attacks disintegrated before reaching him. Dawn and Rusty were repelled back to their original positions, eyes rattling in their sockets.

Smiling, Skelton floated toward us and produced Jason's magic pouch. From it, he pulled a book I'd seen before, one that was covered with arcane symbols: *Mastery of Occultopsychic Phenomena.* I inhaled sharply in recognition.

"By Cleopatra Von Wizardo-Sorora," I whispered. "Lee, that's your mom's book."

"I know," he said. "That is the intelligence I was trying to relate."

"He done tole me to thank you," he said, jerking his chin at the Plaid Man. "Y'all got more spectral-spectacular skills than even *he* knew. He tole me tonight was first blood, and he revealed unto me the crucial keys I needed to unlock it all. One was the blood of He Who Kept the Spirit and the Sight." Skelton's gravestone teeth came out in a cruel simulacrum of a smile. "That was your friend Smiley. Second was this here tome. But there's a problem."

Skelton shook his head in mock disbelief and continued: "He cain't read it. All that power, and the Sentinel of the Hightower can't make heads or tails of it. But that brings us to step three: Your fancies. All them wonders most miraculous from the tall drinka there. Y'all done sussed out the connection between your maps and the presents, so you can probably guess that I'm gonna need one." His focus closed around me: "From little Hiram Stammerstone."

"Me?"

"We *could* just take 'em all," Skelton said. "But the Sentinel, the First, the Original, he said all he needs is your spyglass. Give us that, and y'all can go. Can live. Another birthday, another Christmas. Alla y'all. All you gotta do is drop it in Santa's sack here, and when you wake up, you'll be at home, smilin' and never knowin' any of this ever happened. Just toss it in, Hiram

Stammerstone, and you can go."

To my eternal shame, I stepped forward immediately and was ready to pitch it into the pouch, but Jason, bless his soul, stopped me. He smiled down from his towering height. I'd never seen him look kinder than he did in that moment.

"The fact that you're even thinking about doing it shows you're a good kid. But you know it's a trick, right?" he asked. When I nodded, he continued: "This is the worst night of our lives. But it'll be over soon. We're going to get out of here. And he doesn't get *jack shit*. You with me?"

I nodded, then looked Skelton in the eye and screamed: *"Go to hell! You'll never get this from me! Never!"*

Skelton sneered: "Aw. Brave little Sumpty Stammerstone and his beleaguered brethren, all of 'em sad and alone and hailing here from parts broken. You really think you've got a chance? Here? *In my home?"*

The word "home" reverberated through the endless void. In the far beyond, the Plaid Man uncrossed his arms, the motion blasting us with a scorching wind that blew our hair back. He suddenly *doubled* in size, his body blushing a deep purple as he grew larger and larger until his head and feet scraped the boundaries of existence. His light shone from anywhere and everywhere, brighter and brighter. A doomed silence reigned until a joyful sight drew our attention.

A butterfly.

It materialized from nothing and fluttered before us. Justin stepped forward, and his voice rang through the darkness.

"Y'know what one of my favorite movies is? *The Great Escape.* My friends used to razz me for it. It's pretty old-school, I'll admit, but man, I loved Charles Bronson in it. Felt like a kindred spirit, that guy. You wanna know why?" Justin held out a finger. "Because we're the Tunnel Kings."

The butterfly landed on his outstretched finger. All of us, all nine of us—Skelton included—plummeted through space. The intergalactically-huge facade of the Plaid Man shot upward as we fell through a shimmering black portal and crashed into the earth next to the chasm that had opened near Enchanted Caverns. We'd landed on the near side of the chasm, but we were now *outside* Skelton's hideout, the boundary having contracted in concert with the destruction of our maps. I knew Justin could draw portals on his own, but this latest trick seemed unbelievable until I remembered our maps:

We'd added the Gold Rush park to it, with a butterfly as the keystone.

Justin and Jason's powers had intersected in an almighty confluence of fate and fortune: Jason's keystone had assumed physical form, while Justin had sneakily added a portal from the Gold Rush to mile marker nineteen. The locations had been drawn on two maps; all Justin had to do was add a portal. Electricity wiped through us, returning us to our normal, non-animated selves. As our magical sunburns faded, we struggled to our feet, all of us winded and dazed.

Except for Hanna.

She'd never turned into a cartoon, so her voyage out of the Sneakaround Network was nothing more than a simple fall. Her instincts kicked in and set her storming at Skelton, who had turned an ankle on the way down. The maps lay on the ground next to him, smoking at their corners. Hanna yanked him up by his lapels and stuck her newly-reconstituted service pistol in his face.

"Don't you fucking move, Skel—"

WHOOP-WHOOP! Half a dozen police cars and emergency vehicles roared up, sirens screaming. Justin ran over and helped shoved Skelton to the ground in tandem with Hanna giving him a pistol-whip to the head. He hit his knees and twined his fingers behind his head. Silhouettes of dozens of men swarmed out of the cars, with a set of firefighters at the vanguard. They dropped a few planks across the chasm, securing them in place with a bolt gun. The cops followed, led by Captain Myslinski, who was accompanied by a surprising face.

Trent.

Jason snorted. "The stupid sonofabitch managed to do something right."

In the distance, purple light shone over the tree line. Myslinski paused, hand on his brow, and gaped.

"What the Christ is that?"

Ka-thoooom! Something exploded in the distance. Myslinski blinked into the violet blaze as he took in the rest of the scene: a bunch of kids wearing what appeared to be Halloween costumes, plus two former police officers. Justin approached the captain.

"Cap, I don't know if you remember me, but—"

"JJ Flash? Holy goddamn hell, fella, but what're you doing here?"

"Uh, I'd prefer it if you call me Justin Johnson, sir. And I need to report . . . well, a citizen's arrest."

Hanna stood by his side. "Same here, sir."

She hefted Skelton to his feet and shoved him forward. Myslinski practically gasped.

"My decent soul. Forgive us our trespasses."

A swirling conflagration of lights splashed a whirlpool of color around us: reds and purples and blues. Dozens of silhouettes dotted the scene, all while Skelton babbled:

"It's here. It's time. It's almost mine. It's here. It's time. It's almost mine. It's here. It's time. It's almost mine."

Myslinski nodded to a few of his men, who slapped cuffs on Skelton, taking him under his arms.

Justin said: "Sir? Bo Colquitt and Holton Webb didn't make it."

As the cops escorted Skelton to a squad car, Myslinski doffed his hat.

"Damn. *Damn.* Johnson, I'm gonna need a full statement from you. You too, Blackledge. And . . . from everyone. We need to know what happened here tonight."

That got Skelton going again: "What happened here? What *happened* here? What happened here is . . . something wonderful. Something—" The cops shoved him into a cruiser, cutting off his tirade. Lee had run over to collect the maps and his mom's strange magic book, but when he came back, his face was struck with fear.

"It's not here," he whispered. "*Skelton's* map is missing."

Auntie Hanna took note of us and addressed Myslinski:

"Captain, this may sound strange, but don't give Skelton access to any papers, pencils, pens—anything he can draw with."

Myslinski frowned but nodded.

Dawn stepped forward. "Sir, is my mama okay? We left her at the hospital earlier."

Myslinski's chest deflated. We could barely hear his next words:

"Honey, who's your mom?"

Lee stood by his sister and took her hand. After the evening's action, they were pretty much cried out, but they summoned a few more tears at the prospect that their mom had become Skelton's latest victim.

"Our mama's name is Sandra Dockery, sir," Dawn said.

Myslinski's eyebrows rose. "Kids, I'm so sorry. Ms. Dockery's in a coma."

Dawn gasped and covered her mouth. Lee wrapped her in a hug. We all stood by their side. A hulking tower came shouldering his way through the crowd: Trent.

"You guys okay?"

Silence. We all stared at him. Myslinski started to speak again, but Kaitlyn cut him off:

"My arm's hurt."

"Oh, right," Trent said. "Sorry."

Mac was next: "You left us."

"I . . . I needed to go get help. And I got it."

Another officer came over. I think his name was Baird.

"Mr. Sutton? We can give y'all rides over to the hospital, if ya need. We can take everyone's statements there." He gave me and Mac a look and added: "And you might want to . . ."

Hanna's brow knit. "Might want to what?"

Trent hooked his thumb at one of the cruisers. "We should head over, guys."

Baird made eye contact with Myslinski, who addressed Trent: "Mr. Sutton."

"We'll take care of it *later*," Trent snapped, trying to bull his way past, but both cops stopped him. Hanna grabbed Trent's arm, but he wrenched it away, turning on her with burning eyes.

"You *don't* touch me, woman. Not tonight. *Not* tonight. Not after . . ." His face melted as he dissolved in tears. For the first and only time in his stupid, fucking, pathetic life, Trent looked sorry. His entire frame shrank a full foot in sorrow and contrition. "I'm sorry."

"Sorry about what?" Hanna said, unmoved, and suddenly her words from the wedding came back to me:

There isn't a stage five.

"Mom," I whispered.

"What's wrong with Corrie, Trent?" Hanna said, her voice rising. "What's wrong with my sister?"

Myslinski and Baird lowered their gaze and turned to Trent. It was his job to tell us, and he couldn't even muster the courage to use the words. All he managed were a few strangled syllables:

"I didn't know."

PART FIVE
STRONG BONES

Hanna

It was about the size of a shoebox.

She carried it under her arm, strolling up the long driveway to her house, enjoying the view, the summer breeze, and a spectacular Smoky Mountain sunset. The happy sounds of activity—furniture being moved, books being shelved, the chatter of happy children—greeted her as she crested a rise and brought her house into view. A few dozen cardboard boxes and wooden crates sat outside her little guest house alongside some lawn chairs. The music of Stevie Wonder's album *Talking Book* floated out along with another familiar voice:

"Hey, you," Justin Johnson said, speaking into a cordless phone. "Yeah, I'm getting moved in fine."

Hanna paused at a respectful distance, propping the package on her hip. One of Justin's cardboard boxes was marked, *WEST CHIMNEY TOP SHERIFF'S OFFICE*. She smiled. In the aftermath of that terrible night, Hanna had taken every step she could to give Justin all the credit. Skelton's capture and return to death row had become national news. She swore to an affidavit that, while it stretched the truth, was true enough in *spirit* that she didn't mind the mild perjury. After that night, Justin said he wanted to come back to the sheriff's office.

Hanna made sure he came back as sheriff.

Into the phone, Justin said: "So when are we getting you out here?" He came outside and waved to Hanna with a smile, listening to the person on the other end. "Okay, okay. I get it. You can't just up and run. Fair enough." Rusty and Calliope both slinked out and marked Hanna's legs. She crouched down, wincing at the pain in her hamstring, and petted them both. Justin continued: "Hey, I've gotta run. Got company. Yeah, love you too." He hung up and tossed the phone on the lawn chair. "Evening, Ms. Landlady."

"I'll brook none of this 'landlady' nonsense," she said. "We're neighbors, plain and simple. I appreciate you helping me with the mortgage till you find a nice place of your own."

He nodded. "How long have you had this place, anyway?"

"Oh, since my parents died. They left it to me and my sis—to Corrie."

A silence settled over them, broken only by the sound of laughter rolling up the mountainside. Two kids came up into the front yard waving sparklers around: Dawn and Lee Dockery. Hanna waved.

"Hey, kids! Dinner's in about an hour, okay?"

"Thank you, Auntie Hanna," Dawn said, barely audible over the distance.

Lee stopped and saluted. "Greetings, Justin!" He'd adopted the practice after that terrible night in March. Hanna had happily volunteered to take them in until their mom woke from her coma. None of their family lived close by, but they were always sending care packages, plus a few dollars here and there. Lee ran inside, while Dawn seemed to trudge in his wake.

Justin gave Hanna a kind smile. "Glad to see 'em in good spirits."

"*He* is," she said. "At least he seems like it. But the rest of 'em . . ."

"They're resilient. And I think Lee just . . . processes things differently. Feels the pain in his own way. He'll work it out in his own time."

"We'll all have to work through what happened."

Justin nodded. "It was good of you to take them in."

Hanna shrugged. "It was an easy choice."

"How's she doing?"

"Sandy?" Hanna peered at the horizon. "They're not giving up, so I won't, either."

Justin nodded, then hooked his thumb at the guest house.

"You ever rented this place before?"

"Never trusted anyone to live this close to me, frankly." She paused. "Nice to have you back. The sheriff's office is in good hands."

"Thanks. I hope so. I missed it, if you can believe that."

"I can indeed." She weighed her next words. "Are you going tonight?"

Justin thought. "No. I've done my bit for king and country. I think I'm gonna head down to Knoxville, call up a friend, maybe watch some fireworks. But you are, right?"

"Oh, yeah. I'll be there. I don't really believe in it, but . . . for him? I'll sleep better knowing he's gone. They made me a temporary deputy so I could be the state's witness." She held out the package. "Oh, this just came for you. New mail carrier today. Nice lady, but she seemed out of sorts. Asked me which *hemisphere* we were in, if you can believe that."

The package had been forwarded from Justin's old place in Oregon. The return address read *MYRA GLENN, CLEVELAND, TENNESSEE.*

"Thanks," Justin said, his brow darkening.

"Everything okay?"

"Sure, sure. It's just . . . This is from Myra Glenn." He looked up. "Jamie Scott's mom?"

"Oh—one of his . . ."

"Yeah," he said, tearing it open. "She said my momma left this at her place before she died. Said it was computer stuff. A disk." Inside was a white cardboard container, the kind for cakes or pastries. He opened it to reveal a single plastic disk, blue, about three inches in diameter, and lined with concentric grooves like a record. It sat on a bed of crumpled-up paper.

"That doesn't look like any computer disk I've seen," Hanna said.

"No, it doesn't." He held it up. "What *is* this?"

Another voice called: "Hanna!"

A man clad in the powder-blue-and-white uniform of the US Postal Service was jogging up the driveway. Hanna's face fell in surprise.

"Rick?"

The mailman, Rick, tipped his hat and handed her a stack of letters.

"Sorry about the delay, Han," he said. "Got held up on my route." He noted Justin. "And is this your new tenant?"

Justin's brow wrinkled in confusion. "Yeah. Justin." They shook hands. Rick nodded and turned to leave.

"I thought you changed routes?" she asked.

Over his shoulder, Rick said: "Come again?"

"The new woman? Just came by? She said she was taking over for you?"

Rick slowly turned around. "Ain't no nobody replacing me. You're saying someone else came by here with mail?"

"Yeah," Hanna said. "A package."

Rick shrugged. "Must've been UPS or FedEx."

He left. Hanna and Justin looked at each other before instinctively backing away a step to check their respective sixes. Justin looked over.

"Uh oh, what's going on?"

"I don't know, but let's keep a wary eye tonight, Sheriff."

"You need backup?"

"Nah, I got it. Go have fun. I'll send his soul to hell."

Hiram's Journal

Before I was born, there was nothingness. A shrieking void. But history marched on without me. In that time, other people lived lives and made memories of a time I would never know. Now I had entered into the flip-side, a contrary-complementary time where *I* was having experiences that my mom would never know.

She had been dead for three months.

Although we still visited Castle GrayCrystal sometimes, we didn't dare venture back into the Sneakaround Network. Not with Skelton still alive. Not with the Plaid Man still out there. We'd resigned ourselves to lives of constant dread and drudgery.

All that changed the night Sandra Dockery woke from her coma. It was July 3, 1990, the *day of* Skelton's execution. That night also happened to be when we finally got to see what was inside the danavreece.

We sat in a strange place: the master bedroom. Trent never let us in here, but after clearing out the storage room, he finally got around to organizing (and disposing of) the last of Mom's stuff. He'd hefted an ancient cedar foot chest in from the garage. It had been one of Mom's most prized possessions and a chronicle of her life. In it she stored every award, honor, marriage certificate, deed, photo, letter, or knick-knack she'd collected over the years.

Trent hunched over an open dresser, sifting through the last of her clothes. A tumbler of something brown sat on the dresser nearby, while he wore the same pair of long-sleeve Brown University sweats he'd had on for a week. Sweat soaked through his armpits and the small of his back. He'd barely touched Mom's stuff over the last three months, what with the funeral, the memorials, and the near-constant flow of Suttons through the house. The only "good" thing about losing Mom was that it put the brakes on Trent's worst impulses. He drank more than ever, but thankfully, he had been spending a lot of time out of the house, and when he *was* at home, he usually drank himself to sleep before turning his attention to us.

Usually. Jason got the worst of it.

Piles of clothes, papers, and books lay everywhere. Mac and I teamed up on the cedar chest, pulling everything out to organize. Underneath an old framed photo of Mom in Fort Lauderdale, I found a stack of letters.

"What're all these?"

Mac glanced over. "Letters Dad—Deacon—sent Mom from Puerto Rico."

We'd both learned never to refer to him as our "first" Dad. Trent was our one and only father.

"I thought they lived there together?"

"Not after the miscarriage. Mom almost didn't join the Peace Corps with him. She changed her mind at the last minute."

My sister dropped that bomb like she was telling me the weather. A miscarriage.

"When . . . um, when was the uh miscarriage?"

She gave me a funny look, and for the hundredth time since March, I noticed the rings under her eyes, her hollow cheeks, her loss of affect. We'd all lost a step since that night, me included. Only Lee seemed the same, and the key word there is *seemed*. He and I would take long walks through the woods. We even spent the night in the Castle sometimes. One night, he pointed into the distance.

"I think I can see the ships departing the Grey Havens from here. I wonder if they have room for extra passengers?"

It broke my heart, but I knew how he felt.

In response to my question, Mac tapped a store of patience and energy. "About a year after you were born."

"I didn't know."

Mac frowned. "Really?"

"You never told me."

"I guess I didn't. Huh."

I thought about pressing her on it but decided not to. Not tonight. Part of our history was that miscarriage. I almost had a younger sibling. It was so much a part of my sister's history that she forgot I didn't know.

Just like the Office.

A whole room in our old house existed independent of my knowledge. My childhood home was literally *larger* for my mother and sister, because they knew about that room . . . just like they knew about the miscarriage. The world kept getting bigger without my knowledge, and it instilled me with a kind of retroactive dread, like when you realize you've been walking on a dangerous precipice without knowing it.

I felt the same way when I found the danavreece.

I moved aside a stack of Polaroids to uncover it, the very book she'd so jealousy guarded. I lifted it out of the chest like a holy artifact. Its binding was green leather, almost snakeskin, with royal purple lining. Mac's eyes lighted on it.

"Mom's diary."

"The danavreece."

He was so quiet we almost missed it: "It's yours."

Mac looked at Trent and said: "Huh?"

Trent sat on the bed, sorting through a stack of papers on his lap.

"I'm sorry. I forgot to tell you. It was in her will. She left her diary to you two."

"She did?" I asked.

"Yeah, and one other thing." He set aside the papers, stood, and rummaged through a dresser drawer until he came out with a small device, a bright red module about the size of two packs of cards stacked together. A small half-circle of clear plastic gave view to some kind of spinning mechanism inside. Two buttons sat on top: PLAY and STOP. He handed it to Mac.

"Oh, huh. This used to be mine."

"What is it?"

"It's one of those little record-player things. For storybooks?"

"Oh, yeah. I had one, too. Why would Mom give us one?"

Mac lowered her voice: "I'm more interested in why she gave us the davavreece." She jerked her chin at the door. "Come on." We rounded the

corner to the stairs, Trent close behind us. As we climbed up, he called:
"*Jase! It's time to go, buddy!*"

Hanna

Hanna Blackledge was in a unique position to know that the truth was stranger than the tall tales.

Despite Hanna's request that Skelton be denied access to writing implements, he'd been allowed to write his own appeals. He had to, because no lawyer would represent him. Even public defenders refused, filing special pleas to get out of it. Their pleas found sympathy with the court, which granted them all, despite the thorny constitutional issues they raised.

All of Tennessee was simply *through* with Skelton.

Clank. A deadbolt slammed home, and a set of prison bars—flaking green paint showing through with ghosts of rust—slid back, revealing an apparatus whose pop-cultural nickname wouldn't become a household word until the following Valentine's Day. Looking back on this night, during which Skelton played his one, final trump card from the grave, people would come to say he looked like that guy from *The Silence of the Lambs*. (Another local rumor held that Skelton's treatment may have even influenced the film's portrayal of Lecter himself.)

Hanna initially balked at the temporary deputization, but given that they were short-staffed, she wanted to help. (She also wanted to relieve Justin of the responsibility.) Plus, everyone had heard how Justin Johnson and Hanna Blackledge had collared the most elusive and terrifying serial killer in the Southland. In the years to come, there would be no fewer than five blood-spattered documentaries made about him, each sillier than the last, but all of them included various dramatizations of the night Enchanted Caverns exploded. One even starred a comely young TV actress who grayed her hair to play Hanna.

"She looks like she could be my daughter," Hanna groused, though everyone knew she was secretly flattered.

She'd declined a full duty uniform, instead opting for a denim button-down, khaki chinos, work boots, and a kevlar vest. As half a dozen guards rolled Skelton out of death row, she unsnapped her holster and rested a hand on her sidearm.

A buffer of ten feet surrounded Skelton. It was the closest anyone had come since he arrived back on death row in March. The rest of the inmates had screamed and pleaded and filed civil rights complaints to get away from him. All of Tennessee State Pen had heard the rumors about how he put a hex on his cell neighbor—a family annihilator named Elwood Chester Cartwright who'd taken out three generations of kin—to help him spirit his way off the row and over to Soddy Farm. Hanna knew that was only part of the truth. A detailed map of the area had indeed been found in Cartwright's cell, but neither of them would've known exactly *how* to draw them without the help of another person.

Jason.

And no one needed to know that.

That kid's done his penance, she thought. *And besides, who would even believe*—her blood froze instantly solid.

He was looking at her.

A half-dozen guards surrounded him. He stood on a human dolly-cart, tilted back slightly to roll. Two guards handled the rolling, both of them holding ten-foot rods capped with carabiners. Four other guards each held similar rods, two for his arms, two for his legs. A straitjacket bound his arms to his sides, dozens of chains and padlocks jangling around it. A clear plastic mask dotted with a few dozen breathing holes covered the lower half of his face.

Hanna flashed on Skelton's appearance outside Enchanted Caverns, the way he looked like he was wearing a mask of his own face, frozen in an evil leer. His mask's breathing holes formed a second smile over his real one, his bald head covered with livid open sores. (They'd shaved his head for the execution, but he'd already pulled most of it out, one fistful at a time, over the last week.) His breath fogged the mask in rapid-fire bursts, his pulse visibly throbbing on his neck.

"Dymarick," he whispered, causing all heads to swivel her way.

Everyone knew he was addressing her.

Hanna had rehearsed all kinds of responses. She knew she had to keep her voice steady if she spoke to him, and keep it steady she did: "Speak up. Or were those your last words?"

The guards paused. Skelton licked the inside of his mask and cleared his throat.

"Denied me my hat trick, this one did," he announced to the room. "Only got me *two* little piggies, Smiley and Mr. Cock of the Walk. Straw and stick, but Old Lady Grayhair denied me my brick." His remaining eye narrowed. "But I'll get'cha, don't you fret. I'm gonna huff and puff."

Hanna stood in the execution chamber proper. A curtained-off window stood across from the chair. Chipped green tiles covered every surface, a drain sitting between the chair and the window to collect blood and excrement from the condemned. (Death row inmates receive a plug to prevent such a mess, but sometimes they'd fail.) A priest and the executioner stood across the way, next to the warden, a squat man with a slate-gray flat-top. The six guards crowded into the room next to Hanna; this amount of personnel was unprecedented. You usually only needed two guards for one prisoner.

Not Skelton.

The guards manning his right side yanked him off the dolly. He staggered forward and fell to a knee. Everyone froze, waiting on Skelton to make a move. The rumor mill had churned out a never-ending chain of horror stories in the wake of Enchanted Caverns.

They say he's got magic powers.

He made Colquitt levitate before killing him.

They never found poor Holt's head.

Holton. Grief plunged a hot knife into Hanna's heart. True to form, sweet and humble Holt had never told anyone around the sheriff's office he was former special forces, so when word got out that Skelton had beheaded a former Navy SEAL in single combat, his aura grew and grew like a sludge-dark cloud over a factory.

And they *had* found all of his remains, she knew. *That* rumor pissed her off. As soon as Skelton's Smoky Mountain collapsed, the magic affecting Holt's body did, too. Gone was the flat plane of flesh that terminated his neck. In its place was what you'd expect—spilling sinew and gore—although the coroner had marveled over the "remarkably clean cut."

Back in the execution chamber, Skelton paused on his knees for a moment but didn't make a move, instead bouncing to his feet and into the chair, where he could only half-sit, the straitjacket constraining his movement. *Click, click, clank, CLANK.* The lead guard began the arduous process of unlocking him. They freed one limb at a time, immediately securing it to the chair with steel cuffs and several feet of Duck tape. A guard looped a length of rope around his neck to hold his head in place while another undid his mask with shaking hands. He jumped back the instant it fell loose. The other guard retracted the rope.

Skelton shrugged out of one half of the straitjacket. "Ain't no need for fear, hoss." He nodded at Hanna. "It's her and her scamps, the beleaguered brethren, what gotta worry."

Worry about what, Skelton? Hanna wanted to ask but didn't. He was just trying to scare her. They had him. He was being strapped into the electric chair after a decade-long reign of terror across the southeast. Still, something had been needling her for the last few months . . . something Lee had said that night. He'd been so insistent on getting their attention about something, but once they caught Skelton, he'd simply shrugged it off.

Hanna smiled at the thought of that brave little boy. They'd all been interviewed on the local news. Their shared story was that they'd been playing *Dungeons & Dragons* in the woods when they ran afoul of Skelton. It was a stretch getting the authorities to get on board with the narrative, but once again, Hanna endured some mild perjury to make it happen.

But still, something nagged at her. She shook it off and checked the time. The clock read 11:58 a.m. In less than two minutes, he'd be gone, barring a reprieve from the governor.

BRRRING.

The warden answered the wall phone, listened, hung up. He nodded to one of the guards, who knocked on the window. The curtains drew back—and took Hanna's breath away.

Trent and Jason were there.

Jason

Dad had said it was a "matter of honor."

They fidgeted in metal folding chairs, both gigantic men having folded *themselves* into the tiny space. Threadbare red carpet covered the floor, while those same green tiles covered the walls. The room was, at most, ten square feet and trapezoidal in shape.

A lot like the old gondola station, Jason thought with a shudder. Trent bumped into him, shifting around in his chair, the armpits of his suit stained dark black and leaking droplets of sweat. His face was bright red, his brow gleaming.

"Dad," Jason whispered. "You should really go to the doctor. You probably have the flu."

"I'm fine."

The curtains swept back to reveal the mad devil, finally corralled and strapped to the instrument of his doom. Jason's eyes snapped shut, but somehow seeing Skelton wasn't even what terrified him the most about the evening. No, what terrified him the most was the prospect of seeing Jenny's mom, but Ms. Miles had decided against coming. Some of the other victims' families made the trip. A few had even made personal appeals to Skelton to give up the remains of their children.

All he said was: "I cain't reveal what ain't real."

Jason crossed his arms and sat back, his eyes still closed. *Itza Linda,* he thought. *We never found it. He tricked us again. They searched every inch of Enchanted Caverns, the Gold Rush park—nothing.* The Suttons, Greshams, and Dockerys had even consented to having their own homes searched, even though Skelton had only visited one of them.

Still, nothing. No remains. No Itza Linda. No closure.

Skelton's words from that night echoed in his head: *They're my holy-soul, my power-point, my solar-center, the crux and the fulcrum that keeps me here and them from reachin' topside of the Hightower.*

Skelton was in league with the Plaid Man himself, and if he said their remains kept him "here," would electrocuting him even do any good?

It will. It has to.

Jason opened his eyes. Auntie Hanna was smiling at him, sending him strength his father couldn't.

The warden stepped forward.

"Leonard Shane Skelton, it is the judgment of the people of the state of Tennessee that you be electrocuted until you are dead for the murder of Jennifer Jane Miles. Do you have any last words?"

Someone hit the *mute* button on reality. All movement stopped. All breathing slowed.

Everyone took a breath . . . and listened.

Hanna

All he said was: "I'll say it again: I'm gonna huff and puff. Go on, warden, give me my communion."

The warden nodded to the executioner, who blindfolded Skelton. Other guards secured the final apparatus, including the saline-soaked sponge, and stood back. With another nod from the warden, they threw the switch—and unleashed a torrent from Skelton. The words poured out of him like someone was squeezing them out of his guts. Bloody mist attended their exit from his body, his remaining eye bursting down his cheek and boiling against his flesh. Lightning flashed around his head—Hanna half expected it to transform him into a cartoon—as he screamed gibberish through his final agony:

"Mil tunicaxa caxarodeniaxa dipso olit saxarvaxatel vous, saxanndo vous, axanimaxa voaxa, seris conklum ot axaoquiriflium baxaciaxank quew clux, jaxano mivaxamus viriaxa, vaxaggio—"

In the months to follow, everyone across the region would say they could hear Skelton die, but in truth, all they heard was the storm. The Great Red Spot of the Smokies, as it would come to be known, ignited that night.

But more on that later.

Hanna Blackledge touched her heart and resisted an impulse to put a bullet in Skelton's head; not only to end his life, but to stop whatever he was doing.

Another invasive thought hit her:

Lee, Lee, what did he say that night? About his mother's book?

She'd quickly forgotten about the book in the hectic weeks that followed, but as she watched Skelton convulse, she felt certain that whatever tongues he was speaking in weren't the rantings of a madman but specific sounds and syllables handed down from the Plaid Man: "*Tungol, jaxamio—olaxam, axad caxaptaxactaxam whec axanimaxafus mochlis rux eftonofloscot litu iluolo axalcom-com-com-COM—it's a sight to behold, look at it, look with me! Am I notorious? YES! He's there! He's asking! Beckoning me to the City of Flowers! We'll ride a red Cadillac and bear witness and despair at—*" His insides boiled up and out of his mouth, silencing him as he left this plane. Everyone grimaced, scuffling away to press themselves against the walls. His head lolled to the side, covered in steaming gore and filth.

The coroner didn't even bother to check his heartbeat.

Hiram's Journal

Jason's room had gone from being the forbidden zone to our sanctum sanctorum. We congregated there almost every night to study, play video games, trade stories, and goof around. We all still had nightmares and flashbacks because of everything we'd been through, but our newfound sense of love and community helped. Jason had left with Trent for the evening, but Kaitlyn joined us in a circle around the danavreece.

"Who's gonna break the seal?" she asked.

"Not me," I said. "Mac? Wanna do the honors?"

She nodded, and when she flipped it open, the contents of the first page broke our hearts:

You can't inter me in the Suttons' mausoleum.

Kaitlyn sat back. "Oh, shit. I'm so sorry."

Mom had asked to be cremated but had left no other living will or instructions for her death, so Trent interred her with the rest of his family. Mac and I looked at each other.

"Why wouldn't she tell us this before she died?" Mac asked.

I hung my head. "Why didn't we think to ask? Does that make us bad kids?"

Kaitlyn touched my knee. "That doesn't make you bad kids. Sometimes people just don't talk about this stuff."

I nodded. "We didn't talk about much. Well, *me and Mom* didn't talk about much." I was thinking of stuff like the Office, the miscarriage, and the danavreece, which Mac took up and started paging through.

"She and I didn't talk much either," she said. "Now, *Dad* and I were pretty tight. We talked about everything."

Mom's last days alive came back to me in a rush: her harsh words during chemo, the way she'd walked up the stairs after Trent hurt her. After he abused her. It occurred to me to cry, but after enduring the last year, my eyes felt dry. Instead of weeping, I'd just get a headache. I rubbed my brow.

"I didn't get to say anything nice to her before she died. I didn't get to say anything, really."

Kaitlyn: "Hoo boy, do I ever know *that* feeling, squirt. Me and Mom, we had a knock-down-drag-out before she died. Pretty sure my last words to her were 'Fuck you, you fucking bitch.' Then she was gone."

"Should *we* have a maw, maw, uh mawboleeum?"

Mac, still flipping through the danavreece: "Mausoleum."

"That's what I said." I gave my head a quick shake. "Is it weird that we don't?"

"We don't really have much of a family," Mac said. "There's us and Auntie Hanna."

Kaitlyn snorted. "Guys, trust me. It's not weird. It's weird that we *have* a mausoleum." She shook her head. "God, I still can't believe he made him go watch."

Mac nodded. "I know. He can always close his eyes."

"But he can't close his *ears*. Who knows what that monster'll say?"

I touched her hand. "It'll be all right. We'll take care of him."

Kaitlyn gave me a kind, brave smile as Mac paused on a familiar page; familiar to *me*, at least. I'd seen it at Mom's last chemo session, her map of the area that, for some reason, depicted a giant candle over the Gold Rush park. Various other locations were marked, including Enchanted Caverns, which she'd drawn in a different color ink, as well as all our houses. Leading from Enchanted Caverns to the Gold Rush was a path that followed no road or highway. It coiled through the countryside before slashing through the mall and terminating at the park.

At the candle.

"What *is* this?" Mac said, flipping to the successive pages, only to find them all blank. The diary's previous pages all included the expected entries about her life. Mac closed the book. "I don't know if I'm ready to read this yet."

"But she said it was for us," I said.

"Yeah, but—"

Through the window, it was like the sun exploded over the horizon for an instant, only to dive back behind the earth. The sky flared to life in a blinding blast, illuminating the countryside for hundreds of miles, all in tandem with yet another earthquake that shook me from a sitting position to my side. We all jumped up, ran to the window, and gaped in wide-eyed, quietly-sighing astonishment at a sight that would perplex scientists for years to come.

A storm had ignited over the Smokies—a storm of crackling red lightning.

The storm dropped no rain, instead swirling in a constant crimson whirlpool several miles away over a particular location. It's funny, looking back, I'm still surprised (and strangely delighted) at who figured out exactly where the storm was.

"Guys, that's over the park," Kaitlyn said. "That's over the Gold Rush."

Sandra

She slept amidst the tones of hearts at rest. The head trauma had been bad enough for them to induce coma, but she'd quickly slipped further and further away.

But no one gave up.

Dawn and Lee came to visit every other day, usually accompanied by their friends, their *new* friends, Hiram and Mac, and even Jason and Kaitlyn, who'd provided invaluable support during her slumber. Jason had even brought this amazing new color handheld video game for Lee to play. He had taken to saluting her son, too, and refused to accept salutes in return. Sandra had an awareness of this kindness, though she knew of no specifics where she was. Even though magic surrounded her, her current home was the purview of science and biology.

She was near death. She was near life. She was in between.

Like many others in her state, she had vivid dreams that made literal this metaphor. In Sandra's case, she was sitting high in the sky over her doublewide. Her height was the product of an elevated steel platform that her late husband Hank had added to the roof instead of their wraparound porch. Sandra sat in a lawn chair next to someone—she couldn't quite tell who—watching the sun set.

But something troubled her.

"What am I forgetting?" she kept asking her friend. "I'm forgetting it. Something important. Can you help me remember?" She kept standing with the intention to go down to her trailer and find what she'd forgotten, but she never did. She always lingered, high in the sky with her friend, because she didn't want to miss the sunset.

All that changed the moment Lenny Skelton died.

As his insides erupted out of him, Sandra's sunset bled a sudden and horrifying dark red, as if a trillion tons of dust had been heaved into the atmosphere. Clouds boiled across the landscape like redhot toxic waste, causing Sandra to wipe sweat from her imaginary brow.

"Is that what you were worried about?" she asked her friend, but for the first time since she found herself in this in-between place, Sandra could see her friend's face. At first, she was blocking it with her palm, but she lowered it to reveal a patch of plaid fabric that had been staple-gunned to her flesh. Staggering back, Sandra spun on a heel and leaped off the walkway, screaming in her dream:

"Diufoe vo Migiraxankom!"

And then she awoke.

She had no vision at first, her eyes having been shut for three months. Every muscle in her body screamed. Nurses had tried to keep them from atrophying but with limited success. Blinking, she waited for her vision to return and tried to find her bearings. She was in bed, she knew that. Was she at home? No, not at home. Didn't smell like home. She tried to move but found her limbs had been secured to her sides. *Have I been abducted?* Panic rose in her chest and sped up her breathing. She tried to speak but could only grunt. Something was in her mouth, a tube. Finally, a repetitive sound put her mind at relative ease:

Beep, beep, beep.

Heart monitor. Hospital. She was in the hospital. Had she been in a car crash?

No. Not a car crash.

He'd smashed their door right off its hinges, his strength surprising for his size. Lee had his toy walkie and screamed into it—*MAYDAY, MAYDAY*—and where was her cross-stitch? And the book? What about her cross-stitch? They'd missed something, some vital detail, and goodness gracious if it didn't start with her cross-stitch.

A familiar voice whispered: "I'm here."

Sandra's vision returned enough to let her see her friend's silhouette in the doorway. The silhouette checked over her shoulder before coming closer. She was a friend from far away who Sandra hadn't seen in a life-age. A Black woman, she wore her usual: a baseball cap, motorcycle jacket, and an armored kilt. A pair of goggles sat atop her brow. Her friend's hands were shaking, her gaze wide-eyed and strangely unsure for someone with her courage. Sandra understood why; these surroundings were doubtlessly unfamiliar to her.

But she had come immediately when needed.

Medical training from ages past guided her friend's hands, first removing her intubation tube, then her restraints, leather cuffs that bound her wrists and ankles. She sat on the bed and took her hand.

Sandra spoke in a hushed wheeze: "My word, my ward, my word. My cross-stitch?"

Her old friend shook her head. "The 'smiths said it was in the back yard."

Sandra thought. Realized what had happened. "It wasn't enough."

Her friend shook her head again.

Sandra pulled back her covers. "We need to—"

"We already broke the glass," her friend said, handing her the bedside phone. "Make the call."

<hr>

Hiram's Journal

<hr>

"What *is* that?" Mac said. "Some kind of tornado?"

BRRRRRRIIIIIIINNGGGGG! We all jumped. Jason had asked for his own extension, and it blared like a klaxon from the floor. Kaitlyn snatched it up. "Sutton residence." Her head dipped and her brow furrowed. She looked up, eyes widening.

"What is it?" I asked.

She tucked the phone to his chest and pointed. "Go get the cordless phone from my room."

Mac ran and brought it back. Kaitlyn held out his receiver, and we all listened in.

"Ma'am?" Kaity said. "Could you say that again for everyone?"

"Hello, kids."

I screamed and was immediately *shushed:* "Ms.—oh, sorry, Ms. Dockery!"

It was Sandra Dockery. She'd woken up.

"You're back," Mac said.

"Oh, gosh!" I said. "We need to tell you everything. Dawn and Lee are living with—"

"Hanna Blackledge," she said. "Yes, I know, dear. They're about to—" *Beep, beep!* It was call waiting. "Are you going to get that?"

"Uh no, Ms. Dockery," I said. "They can wait. How are you?"

"Yeah," Mac said. "How long have you been awake?"

She cleared her throat. Her voice sounded tinny and scratchy from disuse. "We can discuss that later. You probably want to see who it is."

All of us exchanged looks. Kaitlyn shrugged and toggled the receiver. "Who's there?"

A familiar voice answered: "Who's *there?* Who the heck answers the phone saying 'who's there'?"

We all smiled. Kaitlyn said: "Is this Justin?"

"Uh, yeah. Did I call into a party line or something? I hear a lot of voices."

"Hi, Mr. Johnson, I mean, Justin!" I said. "We're all here—me, Mac, and Kaitlyn."

"Oh, fantastic. Great to hear your voices, guys. I've got something important to ask—"

"Mr.—uh, Justin, I'm so sorry, but we've got someone on the other line, the Dockerys. Ms. Dockery's awake!"

A new voice joined the call: "Yes, we know, kids. Tell Sandy I say hi. This concerns her too."

"Hi, Auntie Hanna!" Mac said.

"Hi, sweetie," she said. "We had two questions: One, do you see that storm outside, and two, do you all have a book with blank pages?"

We exchanged looks. Mac said: "Uh, no, Auntie Hanna. I mean, I've got some new composition notebooks, if that's what you mean."

"That's not what I mean. It's a book you would have received tonight."

Mac took up the danavreece. "Trent gave us Mom's old diary, but—" She stopped upon opening it.

It was blank.

I took it and paged through it. "What the—Where'd it go? Everything she wrote? What happened to it?" Landing on the first page, I saw that the book wasn't completely blank. Mom's request remained:

You can't inter me in the Suttons' mausoleum.

Kaitlyn prodded me. "Did you switch out the pages?"

"No! I didn't—"

Auntie Hanna broke in: "Kids, no one swapped out anything."

Justin jumped in: "And they're not blank. Do me a favor: take a closer look at the pages. Do they have a kind of divot in them? Almost like a place where you could put a drink?"

Mac tilted the danavreece into the light, revealing a slight, saucer-sized depression that sank into each page.

"Yeah, there is," Mac said. "How'd you know?"

"Ask Sandy," Hanna said. "And while you're at it, can you ask her if she has any magic ink?"

Mac made an *are you kidding me* face.

Hanna must've sensed it: "No, I'm not kidding. Ask her."

We clicked over. I said: "Ms. Dockery?"

"Let me guess: That was Hanna Blackledge?"

"Yes, ma'am," I said. "And our friend Justin Johnson. He moved into her guest house."

"Yes, Dawn and Lee told me. That was expected and welcome."

Kaitlyn frowned. "This is startin' to freak me out."

Sandra's voice lowered. "Is that Kaitlyn?" Her tone was at odds with the evening's burgeoning weirdness. She spoke like she was addressing a favorite niece or grandchild. Kaitlyn actually blushed a little.

"Yeah, it's Kaity. Hi."

"Thank you for saving my life. All of you. And I'm sorry I've been quiet for so long. I'd been waiting for the sunset. But now I'm back, as the final page turns, and I'm ready to finish this."

Kaitlyn shook her head. "Ms. D, it's great to hear from you, but—What're you talking about?"

"To answer the question you were about to ask: yes, I have the magic ink. It's in the form of markers, as happens. But wait—don't click over just yet. We need to meet immediately."

"But Ms. Dockery, you only just woke up," Mac said.

"There's no time. Skelton has sprung one last trap, and he did it from the electric chair. You've probably already seen it. The storm."

My heart pounded in my ears. Danger bled from the world's pores. Gnarled fingers slithered around every door and under every window, ready to rip away our safety, which, if Sandra was telling the truth, had always been an illusion.

RATTLE-rat-rat-chug-chug-clank-CLANK. We all jolted and frowned in disgust. The automatic garage door was rolling up. We'd learned to fall into a deep stasis every time that sound rumbled through the house, because it meant *he* was home. Sometimes if he heard us chattering or playing, he'd come up and ruin our fun . . . but if we stayed perfectly quiet and still, sometimes he'd forget about us. His voice floated up:

"We're home."

Nobody moved. A door slammed downstairs, followed by a silence we knew well: Jason was following his personal Sneakaround Network through the house upstairs. He opened the door, his face drawn. Kaitlyn rose and hugged him.

"Are you okay?"

"I'm fine. It was horrible. But I'm fine."

Mac waved. "Hey, fella."

He doffed his suit coat and gave me a squeeze as he sat next to me. "Hey, guys."

Sandra spoke: "Is that Jason?"

Jason frowned, peering into the phone. "Ms. . . . Ms. Dockery? You're awake?"

"I am."

Jason sat back and rubbed his brow. "Guys, what is happening? Ms.

Dockery's awake? And did you see that . . . I don't even know what to call it. That *tornado* over the park?"

I asked: "Did Skelton do that?"

Sandra's answer was unequivocal: "No. Not him. Not alone. What fools we've been. We'd been looking in one direction, while—get over here. *Now*. Time is short. Bring everything: your mother's diary, *Mastery of Occultopsychic Phenomena*, the ink, all of your magic treasures. Lenny Skelton's not done yet, and we're the only ones who can stop him, the storm . . . and the Faceless One."

Dawn

Justin led the way down the hospital hallway, skulking out ahead a few steps. He'd worn his sheriff's uniform in case they got busted. Dawn noted each of her friends' bobbing silhouettes and felt such gratitude. All of them had come without hesitation, including sweet Kaitlyn and Jason, who had hung out with them so often while their mom was asleep.

A nurse passed across an intersecting hallway. Justin held up a fist like they were in an Army movie. She stifled a smile; not only at the silly gesture, but also because she knew she was about to hear her mama again for the first time in three months.

They all filed in. Auntie Hanna—they'd taken to calling her that—checked the hall and silently closed the door. Dawn crossed to her, tears welling up. The sight of her awake was initially more upsetting than she expected. Her mama had raised her bed-back to a sitting position. She seemed translucent and deflated; skin hung from her cheekbones, and her hair had faded several shades. Her eyes, previously a deep-dark brown, had turned beige.

But she was there. Dawn and Lee flanked the bed and each took a hand.

"You made it," Sandra said.

"Mama," Dawn said, crying.

Lee stood silent, his lips trembling, holding her hand with white knuckles, as if she might try to escape if he didn't keep hold. Hanna stepped over.

"Sandy. Good morning."

She smiled at the light joke. "Did everyone bring their materials?"

Justin held up the blue disk.

Mac and Hiram held up the danavreece and the small record player.

Finally, Sandra held up the magic markers and said: "Excellent."

Kaitlyn's teeth were bared in stress. "Ms. D, what's happening? What's that storm over the park?"

"We have a lot to discuss, but before we start, would anyone mind if we prayed?"

Justin smiled. "Love to."

Hanna shifted her weight. "You kids can, if you want. I'll take a step back, if you don't mind, Sandy."

"Of course."

Mac picked her lip. "Can I just listen?"

"Yeah," Hiram said. "Same here."

"Of course you can. You all can."

Jason gave a kind nod. "Thanks. I guess I'm not much for prayer."

Kaitlyn frowned in thought. "Is it weird that we've never prayed before dinner? Or like, at all?"

"It's not weird at all," Sandra said.

"Mother gives the best prayers."

Dawn added: "And we like to hold hands. Would that be okay with y'all? Even if you just listen?"

Everyone shared a smile or a kind look and joined hands. Sandra, Lee, Dawn, and Justin all closed their eyes, while everyone else kept theirs open.

Sandra prayed: "Heavenly Father, we thank You for the bounty we are about to receive. There are so many who go with so little . . . or nothing at all, and we thank You for our good fortune . . . and good friends."

She paused to catch her breath.

"We thank You for Hanna Marjorie Bohon-Blackledge, a good mother, a loving sister, a kind friend, and a brave officer of the law, though she's since been called to another path in Your service, O Lord. She gave comfort to her sister during her final days on this earth, and her love extends to her nieces and nephews, who now include another family of wonderful children, Jason Jeffrey Sutton and Kaitlyn Julia Sutton. I thank You, O Lord, for their bravery and selflessness. Kaitlyn's fast thinking and quick action saved my life in March, while Jason risked his own life to rescue my children, Levi David and Dawnstar Moonchild."

Everyone's heads swiveled to Dawn. Kaitlyn mouthed *'Dawnstar Moonchild?'* Dawn smiled and silently shushed them all, most of whom were already choked up.

All except Hiram.

Sandra continued: "We thank You, O Lord, for Hiram Deacon Gresham and Mackenzie Lynn Gresham, who both acted with bravery and selflessness last March in the rescue of me and my children."

She paused, then: "And finally, we thank You, Lord of Hosts and King of Kings, for Your son, Justin Joseph Johnson, who You've so kindly returned to us here in the Smokies. He has lived a life of service to the people of East

Tennessee and to West Chimney Top in particular. Without his bravery and sacrifice, none of us would be here today. We thank You for Your generosity, O Lord, even as we had to bid farewell to one of our own, Corrie Janine Blackledge, whom You saw fit to call back to Your light. We say this in the name of our Lord and Savior, Jesus Christ of Nazareth. Amen."

Dawn and Lee, on cue: "Amen."

Tears, happy and sad, abounded. Kaitlyn forearm-wiped her cheek and waved a finger around.

"I'm not crying, *you're* crying."

Justin touched Sandra's hand and said: "Thanks, Mrs. D."

"You will call me Sandra or Sandy, dear. You're family."

Hanna: "*We're* family."

Hiram raised his hand like he was in class. "Ms. Dockery, on the phone, you said something about a guy with no face? Who were you talking about?"

Sandra didn't answer but looked to Lee.

"We call him the Plaid Man."

"Quite right," Sandra said with a nod. "And we have only hours to stop him." She addressed Justin: "I think you have something to read to us?"

Justin gave everyone a confused look. "Read what?"

"The box you received today," Sandra said. "Open it."

Justin

He'd long since reckoned with the existence of magic, but somehow this trick astonished him the most. Justin opened the package to reveal not only the strange plastic disk but also an envelope inscribed in a hand he knew well:

To my little man.

"Momma," he whispered before addressing Sandra: "Where'd this come from?"

"Time is short," Sandra said. "You should read it. Aloud."

He unfolded the letter, addressed to *My little JJ,* and began:

"'Dear JJ—By the time you read this, I'll be back with your father. Don't grieve. I'm in a better place, here atop it all, looking down on you from behind the veil, beyond the Hightower. I hope you know how proud I am of you, of your accomplishments, of your bravery, of your compassion.'"

Hiram was so moved, he blushed. "Your mom sounds really cool."

"She was," Justin said, glancing ahead. "But here's where the letter gets strange: 'What I'm about to tell you emanates from a wellspring of magic that runs deep through the Smokies, as well as through the hearts and minds of children everywhere. We couldn't share it with you directly because that's not how we were told it works. You discover it on your own, by exploring, by discovering, by believing. You don't have to believe in God . . . I know you have your doubts. You only have to believe in the essential goodness of humanity. Which will be hard sometimes.'" Justin muttered to himself: "Tell me about it."

He kept reading: "'A group of us were brought together by powers beyond our reckoning to give aid to you and your allies in this, your final battle.'"

Kaitlyn: "Your mom knew about all this, Justin?" She corrected herself: "Well, *both* moms, including Ms. Dockery?"

"We did indeed," Sandra said.

"Then *why* didn't you—"

Sandra silenced her with a touch of her hand. "Answers are coming, and time is short. The storm is growing. Justin, keep going."

Justin continued: "'The hand of providence has guided us all, bringing our lives into contact at key moments. Western North Carolina and East Tennessee are groundswells for this magic. Some years ago, a dark sorcerer refashioned a revival theater into a place of bloodshed and heartache. His aim was to commit an act evil enough to defy description. He failed, but his magicks opened a hole in reality that admitted a faceless evil.'"

"Mr. Pajamas," Jason said.

"The Plaid Man," Dawn said.

Justin read: "'Every third confluential rotation, this faceless evil seeks a host. It once inhabited a being—" (he shook his head in astonishment) "—on the far side of the universe but was banished into oblivion until the acts of that dark sorcerer allowed it entrance to the place between places.'"

"The Sneakaround Network," Jason said.

"Shh!" Kaitlyn bopped his arm.

Justin held up a finger. "Get a load of this: 'Myself and the *East Tennessee Sororal Order of Spiritual Defense* met in secret lo these many years ago to defend the Hightower from threats terrestrial . . . and cosmic.'"

Kaitlyn looked like Moses having a confab with the Burning Bush. "What. Is going. On."

Outside, a bomb exploded; only it wasn't a bomb but a thunder-crack loud enough to shake dust from the ceiling and exert pressure on everyone's chests. We winced and covered our ears. Jason ran over to pull open the blinds. The storm had grown. Fully a mile wide, it churned over the park like a whirlpool of blood and lightning. Sandra sat up, her teeth set.

"Justin, keep reading."

"Yes, ma'am. 'When we learned of the threat this creature posed to our realm, we assembled a countermeasure, only to be undertaken in the darkest hour, when all hope had faded, and when—'" Justin paused to address them: "She underlined this part three times: '—if or when the Faceless One declared war on the ETSOSD.'"

"Declared war?" Kaitlyn asked. "What's that mean?"

Lee nodded at the window. "The storm. The Mystery Mansion. It is a place of great import and power, isn't it?"

Sandra nodded. "It is. And we have been such fools. After the night of Enchanted Caverns, we assumed the Faceless One had chosen Skelton as his new human host, and we enacted security measures to that effect, but the Faceless One out-thought us by simply electing to decapitate us. The Mansion is our secret citadel, a place where we've stored some of our most powerful magicks."

Jason smiled. "It's like a battery, isn't it? Or a sponge?"

"It is indeed. How did you know?"

Jason produced his 3D glasses. "These. I told you guys how my magic treasures take a long time to make, right? They usually take months. But not these."

Justin smiled in approval—and secret foreknowledge. He knew Jason had some surprises in store for everyone.

"That's really good, kid. Those had soaked up a bunch of magic from the Mansion, so they were basically ready to go, I take it?"

Bloody lightning cracked outside. Sandra broke in: "Time is short. Yes, the Mansion acts as a holding-place, a *capacitor* for the Order's magicks. We assumed the Faceless One had planned to merge with Skelton."

Justin: "And that's not possible anymore."

"Are we certain?" Lee asked. "Skelton's misled us before."

Jason shook his head. "Not this time. I saw what was left of him. He's being cremated tonight."

Sandra nodded. "In addition, Dr. Sorora took drastic measures to prevent such a calamity. She encoded in her book the unholy ritual to join the Faceless One with a human host."

"*Mastery of Occultopsychic Phenomena,*" Lee said presenting the book. It wasn't a question.

"Yes."

Kaitlyn: "Why'd she even write it down *anywhere?* Why not chuck it in the memory hole?"

"Dr. Sorora sealed the rite into that book, meaning it was the only copy of it anywhere. *Anywhere.* No one, not even someone who had performed the rite, would be able to perform it or recall it or write it down without that book."

She opened the book to the ritual in question, revealing pages covered in unintelligible glyphs and bizarre, headache-inducing illustrations.

"Fuckin' A—oh, sorry for swearing, Ms. D," Kaitlyn said before her eyes rose. She did some math in her head and added: "But Skelton got his hands on the book in March."

Sandra nodded. "And he memorized a *different* ritual, the Dark Rite to Destroy a Citadel of Light." She shook her head with a disgusted but wry chuckle. "The ritual is twenty pages and five hundred steps, with at least seventy components. In the few hours he held the book, he managed to commit every part of the ritual to memory, all while somehow enlisting aid from death row. We underestimated his cunning at every step."

Hanna: "So that's what he was saying."

Jason nodded. "That weird shit he was saying when he . . ."

"When he fried," Hanna said with a cold edge. Off everyone's looks, she added: "Skelton recited some magic words from the chair."

Sandra nodded. "This particular rite calls for innumerable human sacrifices, including that of the person carrying out the ritual."

Mac raised her hand. "Ma'am, I don't mean to, uh, criticize, but why didn't you keep it in a safety deposit box or something?"

"I thought the wards I'd placed on our home would fend off any attacks."

"Wards?" Justin asked. "You put a magic spell on your house?"

"I did, in the form of my cross-stitch pattern, as humble as that sounds."

Hiram: "Huh. You mean that thing that says 'RG' outside your house?"

"That is correct. I am the Revelation General of the East Tennessee Sororal Order of Spiritual Defense, hence the designation."

"Cool title," Jason said.

Justin's eyes fell in thought. "And my momma was a part of this? This Sororal Order?"

"She had been for some years. She was one of the greatest among us."

Justin smiled, somewhat wryly. His momma had always seemed like she had something going on behind the scenes. Her membership in an ancient order of magic moms barely even surprised him.

"What about our mom?" Mac asked, barely above a whisper.

Sandra nodded. "Corrie was one of our newest initiates. Mrs. Glenn and countless others were, too."

"But you said your magic spell didn't keep Skelton out?"

"We hadn't counted on a gate appearing so close. Our occultsmiths said it disrupted my ward."

Lee winced. "The cabin."

Hiram's shoulders sagged. "From Soddy Farm."

Kaitlyn cocked an eyebrow. "Did you say *occultsmith?*"

"Masters of the occult arts, like all of you."

Lee: "We're sorcerers?"

Sandra squeezed his hand. "In a manner of speaking."

Mac: "How long have you known about . . . well, us? About what we were doing?"

"We had some sense of what you were up to. We knew you'd all been visiting the Lodges, or—what did you call them?"

"The Sneakaround Network," Hiram said.

"I like that name," Sandra said. "But we don't have much time. Let Justin finish."

Justin nodded. "'This countermeasure is a weapon of last resort against the faceless evil. Deploy it only with great care and in tandem with at least one of our sisters.'" Everyone looked to Sandra. Justin continued: "'We have recorded this ritual in one of our *malleus mallefacara,* encrypting its contents with our deepest magicks.'"

"The danavreece," Hiram said.

"'You can decrypt it with a combination of implements, magicks, and devices provided by myself, Corrie, and our Revelation General . . . Sandra Divine Dockery.'"

Sandra: "I'm sorry I never told y'all about any of this. When I joined the Order, they swore us to secrecy. I never thought this day would come. None of us did. But it has. Skelton's forced our hands."

Hanna cleared her throat. "I'm sorry to interrupt, but I'm afraid I can't allow this to go forward."

Hanna

Hanna spotted the bruises when she identified the body. Over the years she'd seen every kind of injury from abuse or struggle you could imagine: handprints on biceps, slap marks, black eyes. In her baby sister's case, Trent had left his handprint on her arm. It was hard to miss, being the size of a fucking baseball glove. He'd also chipped one of her teeth, presumably when he struck her or pushed her against a wall.

Although she entertained all manner of dark thoughts about hurting him, she elected against doing him any violence herself.

That's what the bad guys do. Well, most of the time. Sometimes it's justified.

But in Trent's case, Hanna's weapon of choice wasn't violence but simple severance. She had been consulting with a lawyer to get the kids emancipated.

She knew they were miserable, and she hated them being there. Trent insisted he wanted to raise Hiram and Mac as his own. Hanna didn't care what he said. All she wanted was to get them someplace safe.

"We've already lost so many," she said. "I don't want to risk any more lives."

"Countless lives will be in danger if Skelton should merge with the Faceless One," Sandra said.

Hanna scoffed. "What was the name of your club? The *East Tennessee Sororal Order*? It's a big state. Find someone else to perform your little ritual."

"No one else is powerful enough."

"What? What kind of order is this, if you have to rely on a bunch of kids?"

Sandra shook her head. "We're not only relying on *them*. We're relying on you, too. And Justin. This magic emanates from the hopes and dreams and fears and sorrows of children everywhere. Most forget about it when they grow older, and yet these children here managed to forge friendships with you, Justin, and Mr. Webb. It takes a special soul and an especially broad manner of mind to hold on to those feelings. As children, we feel terrified, alone, confused, manipulated, condescended to. It takes daily, mindful care to hold on to those feelings into adulthood."

Hanna's anger had cooled a little, but she said: "If you knew about this magic, these *dangers,* you had no right to just leave it sitting around for them to find."

"Let me ask you a question," Sandra said, addressing the kids. "If we had reached out and told you to stop visiting the Lodges, would you have stopped?"

Jason, instantly: "Nope."

"No. You didn't stop visiting them even after you encountered the faceless evil—the Plaid Man—did you?"

"No," Hiram said.

"Why not?"

A silence extended. Justin broke it with: "I wanted to find them. Needed to. Skelton's victims."

"Yeah," Hiram said. "Us too. And . . . it was exciting. It was like . . . the Office."

Mac: "That old room behind the walk-in closet?"

"Yeah. When I found it, it felt like the world got bigger, more magical. But you and Mom already knew about it. I felt so stupid when I told you about it."

"Aw, Hiram. No reason to feel stupid. You just didn't know."

"Oh, I know. But it felt good to discover something. For *me* to discover something that I could share with all of you." He smiled at Jason and said: "Even though you already knew about it."

He shrugged. "It was a way out for me. To get away from Dad."

"Fuckin' A," Kaitlyn said.

Sandra smiled and addressed her kids: "And you two? Care to explain why you two put yourselves in harm's way?"

Dawn looked down, pleasantly frowning in thought. "Well, a lot of it was to help those kids. But . . . it was exciting, too."

"I see," Sandra said. "Levi David? Care to explain yourself?"

Lee spoke in perfect grammar, as if reading from a script: "Its appeal was tripartite; an opportunity to help those in need, a chance to explore the fantastic unknown, and also: a chance to expand my family."

Sandra sat up, her voice lowering: "There are so few who can even *see* the magic. Even less can master it. But you have. Hiram, Levi, our intelligence indicates you two actually created a portal *into* the Plaid Man's domain."

Hiram's eyes bugged. "How'd you know that?"

Sandra ignored him, her energy rising: "Justin, you created and traveled through a portal that led clear across the country. Jason, you're adept at creating magic weapons. All of you have created magic portals of varying degrees of power, and all of you have collaborated on creating *nexi profundi*—portals that link networks of portals." Her chest was heaving.

"Mom," Dawn said.

Sandra touched her forehead with a shaking hand. "Sorry. It's just that our adepts train for *years* to master what y'all have come to naturally. It's . . . it's remarkable that you've all become such close friends during this crisis."

"Yeah, I guess we're pretty badass, huh?" Kaitlyn said. "Pretty crazy how we all managed to meet."

"Where some see coincidence, I see providence."

"The Grid," Hanna said. She'd crossed her arms, her head hung in reflection. "Is that what you kids called it?"

"Yeah," Hiram said.

"Excuse me?" Sandra asked. "The Grid?"

Kaitlyn scratched her brow. "The Grid. It's—it's something we've seen when we've been . . . uh—"

"*High!*" Hiram blurted to an immediate rebuke from everyone.

"Shh! Shh!"

Jason checked the hall and wedged a chair under the door. Coming back, he wagged a playful finger at Hiram.

"Keep it down, buddy."

Sandra smiled. "Can someone explain, please?"

Kaitlyn assumed a mischievous grin. "Okay, okay, okay. I *may* have seen it while in a mental state that *some* would consider—" (she made air quotes) "—

high—Justinpleasedon'tarrestme. I also preemptively plead the Fifth, Sixth, and Eighty-Seventh Amendments. But we've *all* seen it. It's like a geodesic dome that covers everything. We see it everywhere when we use the maps."

"Sometimes even when we're not using them," Lee said. "Our collective visions?"

The kids recounted their visions: the observatory, the library, the cottage, and more.

Sandra nodded. "Ah. You're referring to the Hightower."

"Yeah," Justin said. "Skelton's mentioned it too. He said he's keeping all his victims on 'this side' of the Hightower."

"That's right."

Everyone looked at each other. Hiram was the first to speak:

"He was telling the truth, wasn't he? That they can't get to heaven?"

Sandra weighed her words. "He was. And in order to finally defeat Skelton and the Plaid Man, you'll need to find them. All of them."

Hiram's Journal

Once again, the universe got bigger—big enough to hold a terrible truth.

"Mama," Dawn said. "Please tell us that ain't so."

Auntie Hanna, who had been hanging her head, looked up with a dark expression.

"I don't believe in that kind of thing, Sandra. And I don't think it's much funny to joke about."

The sky caught fire. Lightning cleaved the night in twain, cutting a jagged path from the Gold Rush to parts distant. We squinted, flinched, and covered our eyes in response, the flash leaving ghostly-fading glow-marks on our retinas. Sandra nodded at the storm.

"I'm not joking. I wouldn't dare joke about such a serious thing. Your belief doesn't affect what is *true,* and regardless, consider this: he has desecrated their remains and profaned their names in death."

Auntie Hanna's chest deflated. Her brow darkened. "That's what he was saying? In that weird language?"

"It is an ancient tongue."

Justin looked back and forth. "Are you telling me he said that while he died?"

Hanna's lips curled, her eyes welling up. "He said their names . . . as a part of this?" She blinked rapidly, overcome with grief and rage, and stepped over to Justin, who had covered his eyes. She hooked an arm around him and squeezed.

Sandra: "Even if you don't believe in all of this, isn't that crime enough?"

Hanna thought. And nodded.

Sandra pressed: "It is the darkest of dark magicks, unholy and accursed, to keep them here. All those little ones. The Faceless One is the first evil, its malice predating what we know as existence. The fact that it has searched the universe for a lieutenant and chosen Skelton speaks to the untold depths of his depravity. *But* on the other side, the fact that it has singled out the Order for destruction speaks to our power. Hanna, I know you have your doubts, but we have surprising resources at our disposal."

"I have. I've seen it. I guess . . ." She went somewhere else for a moment. "I've never been able to stop believing in God, no matter how angry he made me. No matter how much he took from me. When he snatched away sweet little Corrie last March, I figured he'd taken enough from me. I guess I just can't believe he'd take so much from so many and ask so much from so few." She glared at Sandra. "And don't tell me he works in mysterious ways. These ways aren't mysterious. They're capricious. Mean-spirited. And they speak of a god who isn't all-powerful but who is barely clinging to his throne. So much so that he has to call on a bunch of kids and a tired old woman to stop the devil."

"Don't forget about me," Justin said. "Wannabe Broadway star turned small-town sheriff."

Hanna shook her head. "You too, Justin. You've done enough. You've *given* enough. I accept that the magic is real, but you all shouldn't be the ones to carry out this ritual."

A new voice: "Excuse me, but visiting hours are over."

A nurse stood in the doorway, a woman. I started to conjure a bullshit story to explain our presence, but Jason held up a hand to silence us. That's when I noticed it.

The door was still closed, the chair still wedged under it.

"Who are you?" Jason said.

The nurse flickered backward in time, like film running in reverse.

"Excuse me, but visiting hours are over."

Justin touched his sidearm, while Auntie Hanna reached for a gun that wasn't there. Sandra sat up.

"*Polorinquaxas,*" she said.

"Excuse me, but visiting hours are over. Excuse me, but visiting hours are over. Excuse me, but visiting hours are over." Her voice got quieter and quieter, all while color faded from her eyes, leaving them stark white. Her teeth lengthened into fangs. Her next words split our eardrums: *"YOU'RE ALREADY DEAD GIVE UP NOW."*

Sandra executed an arcane gesture: she raised her hand, balled her fist, and lowered it like she was closing a set of blinds, adding: "Close your eyes." We did. "This is a glammer. The Faceless One cannot hurt us here, outside the Lodges."

"You sure about that?" Hanna said.

"You may open your eyes."

The creature was gone.

Hanna shook her head. "I think I liked it better when shit didn't go bump in the night." She sighed. "Okay. I'm in."

"Thank you, Auntie," Lee said. "As am I. I would volunteer to do it."

"Me too," Dawn said.

Kaitlyn: "Kegger in the Sneakaround, bitches! And the Plaid Man's invited . . . *to his doom.*"

"Thanks, Auntie," Mac said. "We all chose to fight this fight a long time ago."

"Skelton picked this fight," I said. "He's a bully. A monster. I'm sick of being scared. And I hate that so many others had to feel so scared. I have nightmares about them. Their last moments. And their families. Never getting closure."

Justin remained silent but nodded. Only one of us hadn't answered: Jason.

Kaitlyn prodded him and said: "Big bro, are you joining the totally terrifying secret supernatural mission, or what?" His face had gone blank; *scarily* blank, like he was on the verge of catatonia. Katlyn took his hand. "Jase? Still with us?"

"This is my fault."

All of us reacted, shaking our heads or holding up our palms in protest. Kaitlyn hooked an arm around him. "This is no one's fault."

"I'm the one who let him out. I'm the one who showed him the maps. None of us would be here unless—"

"The world is bigger than you."

Sandra had spoken, her tone one tiny step sharper than before, although her expression was still the same mix of beaming and benevolent. Jason frowned and shook his head slightly.

"What do you mean?" he asked.

We all wondered the same thing. We'd all forgiven Jason . . . well, for a lot. Although we'd never spoken of it explicitly, we all knew his actions back in March stemmed not from a desire to hurt anyone but from a deep and twisted guilt. He blamed himself for Jenny's death, and he had done something terrible, but he had since dedicated himself to atoning for it.

But still, Sandra's rebuke was strange.

She nodded in acknowledgment of its strangeness and said: "Forgive my tone. I know you blame yourself for . . . for her death. And you carry incredible guilt for helping Skelton escape and for showing him the magic of the maps. But the world is bigger than you. Skelton's evil has no bounds. You weren't actually the first—or only—person to approach Skelton in the hopes of helping him escape."

"But I was the the first to tell him about the maps."

"Yes, but y'all aren't the only ones in East Tennessee who knows about them. There are others. The Order keeps a close watch over them, and many of them have felt Skelton's evil, first-hand or otherwise. Jason, Skelton's escape and alliance with the Faceless One was fore-ordained, and if you hadn't reached out to him, the Faceless One would've made sure someone else did. He would have discovered and exploited the power of the maps, no matter what. You made a terrible mistake, but it's time for you to join us with all your heart and all your soul."

"We *need* him," Lee said, quoting then-Admiral Kirk in *Star Trek: The Motion Picture*. We all nodded in accord.

"We need you, big bro."

"Yeah," Mac said. "It's time."

"Time to move on," Dawn said.

"Uh we love you, Jason," I said, and it was the right thing at the right moment. His eyes flicked toward me, glinting with a sudden, glowing gratitude.

"Okay," he said. "I'm here, heart and soul."

No one moved until Sandra spoke in a low whisper: "It's to be a race against Skelton through the Smokies to gather the components for our countermeasure."

Kaitlyn made a face. "Wait—say *exqueeze* me now? Race against *Skelton?* I thought he was fried dogshit."

"He's outsmarted us at every turn. We must assume he has a plan."

We all shared a look and a nod. Kaitlyn twined her fingers in mock supplication. "Please tell me we don't haveta round up, like, five hundred things?"

Sandra shook her head. "No, but they've been carefully hidden. Open the sacred text, the Zur-Vanadroz."

"The what?" Mac asked.

"The danavreece," I said. "I guess that's its real name."

We opened it, and Mom's words accused us:

You can't inter me in the Suttons' mausoleum.

Mac shook her head. "I *know* this had more writing in it. It was there earlier, before—"

She stopped and made eye contact with Justin, who held up his mom's letter.

"This wasn't there, either," he said before addressing Sandra: "I take it stuff like this was a part of this emergency countermeasure?"

Kaitlyn snapped her fingers. "Guys, chop-chop. Let's all admit that weird shit's gonna happen and we might not understand every last little bit of it."

"Precisely," Sandra said. "Turn the page and place the message-cipher in the divot. And play."

Justin's blue disk fit perfectly into the danavreece. Mac placed the red turntable module atop it and pressed *play* . . . and Mom spoke.

"Hi, kids. Surprised to hear me?" She paused. Room noises attended her speech: chairs shifting about, and strange voices, all women, speaking from another room.

Mac paused the record. "Where is she?"

"At one of our meetings. We changed locations every week."

Mac nodded and pressed *play:* "Before I say another word, let me make something clear: we were leaving. *I* was leaving. I'm sorry we stayed with him as long as we did, but at the time . . . I didn't know what else to do. I wanted security and a future for you, and I really did like him at first. He could charm the socks off you, trust me."

Mom paused, then: "I'm sorry. I'm sorry I wasn't a more loving mom. I'm sorry I was so cold, so distant. I'm sorry I never let you in. I'm sorry I kept up so many walls. When you get older, things get taken away from you. Your dreams die. The love of your life dies. And you wake up one morning, look around, and wonder where it all went. Last thing you knew, you were twenty-one and drinking beers on a patio on the Gulf of Mexico, dead-sure you were on your way to great things. Next thing you know . . . you're burying your husband and your youth's gone."

Pause. Kaitlyn mumbled, "Well, at least we have something to look forward to."

We all shared wry grins and smiles. Mom continued: "You'll understand when you get older. But none of that's important. What *is* important is this: I'm sorry. After I lost Deacon, I forgot how to be happy. I forgot how to make myself happy. I forgot to make choices that would help me be happy again. I *thought* I knew what I was doing, but I didn't."

Pause. "But then I met Sandy. And Mrs. Glenn. I wasn't able to meet Justin's mother, but you should've heard the ladies of the Order talk about her. You'd think they were Jimmy Olsen talking about Superman. I'm so sorry I never told you about all this, but . . . well, they're dead fucking serious about secrecy, pardon my French."

My sister and I both laughed. She was crying, although my tears had still abandoned me.

Mom continued: "If you're listening to this, it means your dear, sweet old mom has probably passed on. Sorry I went so fast, kids. When I got the diagnosis, I had to make a lot of difficult choices, and one of those was to help the Order immediately encrypt the danavreece. To keep it safe. We knew—" The record shorted out. Everyone looked at Sandra in a panic, Kaitlyn in particular.

"What happened? Where'd she go?!"

"Turn it over."

Kaitlyn theatrically slapped her forehead. "Oh, right." Some tension seeped out of the room.

I flipped it, and: "—the Faceless One was planning to move against the Order, though we didn't know exactly how. We thought he might try and merge with a human host—Skelton, most likely—or perhaps attack sweet Sandy, or stage some kind of assault. We didn't know for sure, but when we saw he'd mastered the Lodges, we knew we had to prepare our countermeasure. To begin the decryption, use the magic ink to reveal the first set of instructions on this page."

I took up the marker. "Uh does anyone mind?"

Everyone smiled. With each swipe, the marker brought luminescent text into view, as if the ink were blue lava.

But there was a problem.

"It's gibberish," I said. "Oh, no."

Jason crossed his arms. "Was there some other decryption tool we were supposed to bring? Hiram, your sextant, maybe?"

Hanna scoffed. "You're pulling this old lady's leg, right?"

"Uh, that's genuine frontier garbledeegoop," Kaitlyn said.

Hanna gave an astonished chuckle. "Sweet blue Jesus. This *is* some powerful magic. Hiram, keep at that marker. I'll read." She cleared her throat. "'When I learned of my fate, I volunteered to contribute . . . *myself* to this ritual. It was an easy choice, honestly. I spoke with your step-father about it, and he promised me he'd turn over my remains to you. We fought about it for hours. He insisted on burying me with his family, but I finally got him to make the promise. You must take my ashes and . . .'" She broke off and added: "Oh, dear."

Jason marched around the room. "Unbe-*fucking*-lievable."

Dawn: "He didn't give you yer mom's ashes, did he? Didn't he put 'em in his family's crypt?" She addressed Jason and Kaitlyn: "Well, in *your* family's crypt."

"Yeah, he did," Kaitlyn said. "Fuckin' asshole. Guys, I'm really sorry. There's no excuse."

Jason hunched over the foot of the bed, his fists planted in the mattress, fuming. Kaitlyn had crossed her arms and was shaking her head with a disgusted expression. Meanwhile, Mac and I mostly just looked puzzled. I couldn't speak for her, but as for me: as much as I missed her, I hadn't given much thought to her wishes. She'd never brought it up, not even when she was sick. I didn't cry when she died, and I didn't cry at her funeral. It wasn't because I didn't love her. It was because whatever mechanisms I had to process and feel grief had gotten smashed to bits over the last year. If asked, I couldn't point to any one event that caused this damage.

Maybe it was all the abuse from Jason and Trent.

Maybe it was living in terror of Skelton.

Maybe it was almost getting killed by Skelton.

Maybe it was all of the above.

Regardless, I was simultaneously touched and a little annoyed at Jason and Kaitlyn's reactions. She wasn't *their* mom, so why did they feel so sad? Of course, now I know it was because they'd come to love us so much.

I loved them, too.

"Uh it's okay, guys. We'll find a way to get her back. Auntie, I'll keep revealing, and you keep reading."

Hanna read: "'You must take my ashes and . . . inter them in Susie Schuppe's Smoky Mountain Gold Rush. Turn the page and play the next disk to find out why.'"

I did.

Mom spoke: "Hiram, you once asked me why we never went to church. I didn't know how to answer you at the time because by then, I'd already been working with the Order for a while. Sweet Sandy recruited me. And when I learned of the sheer scope of the Order's mandate, it upended my view of reality. There are powers and forces beyond our understanding, but I wouldn't call them God or the devil. More like gods and devils, heavens and hells, angels and demons, and—" (her voice faltered) "—some live with us, some of them we know first-hand, some of them live *within* us, some of them watch over us, protecting us . . . but they're not perfect. That's the problem. They fuck up about as often as we do . . . and that's a huge reason, maybe the main reason, why the Order exists."

Pause.

"Sorry, that was a long-winded way of saying I never took us to church because I never found a church that—I don't know what. That was big enough. That understood the stakes. That I felt could understand and embrace a group like the Order if they ever learned about it. But what I have to say next must be written."

The record ended. I decoded more of the magic ink, and Auntie Hanna read:

"'What I came to learn was that there are sacred spaces everywhere. Not just churches. And I know it's silly, but the Gold Rush is one of those spaces for me. I know that's sad. Why not a church, Mom? Why not the Grand Canyon or Niagara Falls or the Hanging Gardens of Babylon? The reason why is because it's one of the few places where I felt really happy after Deacon died. I felt happy with all of you, and I felt happy down deep in my soul in a way I rarely felt. When we prepared this countermeasure, the Order—Sweet Sandy in particular—asked me to name a sacred space where I'd want my ashes spread. I told them the Gold Rush. Specifically that one ride we liked—the Mystery Mansion? That was the first place where I kissed Sweet Sandy—' Oh, my."

Sandra was blushing, of course. Dawn beamed.

"Mama. I had no idea."

"It happened so fast. I'm sorry we never told y'all. It's just . . . well, it's just that we're in East Tennessee. It's harder here, and she'd already married that—" She caught herself and addressed Jason and Kaity: "Sorry. I didn't mean—"

"You mean 'that fucking asshole we call a father'?" Jason said. "It's okay. You can say it."

"Regardless. I'm sorry we never told y'all."

Hanna nodded. "Oh, I had some sense. But she played things pretty close to the vest. You don't owe anybody an apology."

Lee hugged her. Sandra held his shoulders and grinned.

"Hey there, Levi David. Thanks for this hug."

"You and Ms. Gresham made a formidable team."

"I'll say," Dawn said.

Mac: "It . . . makes a lot of other stuff make sense." She looked at me. "Y'know?"

"Yeah," I said. "Sometimes I think I didn't know her at all. Then other times, I feel like I know her really well? And that feels good, because there weren't many of those times. This is one of those really, really good times. You're so nice, Ms. Dockery. I'm glad she met you, and—" My tears, which had dried up for the last few months, came rushing back again. Mac hooked an arm around me.

"Aw, buddy."

"I'm sorry. I just wish . . . I just wish she'd had more time. I wish . . . I wish

I could've been friends with her."

"Me too."

Jason: "But . . ." When we all looked at him, he swallowed a lump in his throat. "Sorry. I didn't mean to butt in."

It was like a revitalized copy of his soul had taken up residence in him. He didn't just act and treat us differently; he *looked* different. He even *sounded* different. "Old" Jason spoke with a constant undercurrent of sarcasm. "New" Jason spoke softly. When you were speaking, he'd twine his fingers and relax his shoulders, looking you in the eye. He never interrupted me, no matter how much I stuttered.

Mac: "It's okay. What is it?"

"Maybe . . . maybe she's trying to be friends with you now. Maybe she's trying to be friends with you, and it's connected to something really important."

"And she's right about East Tennessee."

Justin had spoken, and even though Mom and Sandra had established a theme for the conversation, I had no idea what he was talking about. Hanna propped a hand on her hip and smiled.

"Was wondering if you were gonna say something."

Einstein here said: "What? What's going on?"

"Is he gonna move out here?" Hanna asked.

Justin nodded. "Yeah, he just needs to tie up some loose ends back in Oregon, at the bar."

I finally did the math. "Oh!" Everyone else stifled some good-natured giggles at my expense. "Oh, gosh, Mr. Johnson. I bet he's really handsome."

Mac rolled her eyes. "*Hi*-ram."

Hoo boy. The *ribbing* I've endured for this gaffe over the years!

Justin was smiling. "It's okay. Yeah, kid, he is. I think we're getting sidetracked."

"Quite right," Hanna said before reading again: "'It was the first place where I kissed Sweet Sandy, and it's where I want to be buried. But it won't be enough to simply inter my ashes there. The ritual will require several ingredients, but we couldn't risk including them all in this volume. We've hidden the information across West Chimney Top and Gatlinburg in places you know well. Some will be easy to acquire, others not so much. The next disk may be found in your collective fortress of solitude. Finally, I'll say this: Be bold and mighty forces will come to your aid.'"

I tried to decrypt the next page, but nothing happened. I kept scribbling and scribbling until Sandra stayed my hand.

"Oh, no," I said. "I thought there'd be more."

"There is," Sandra said. "But it's scattered across the Smokies, and time is short to complete the ritual. I've been entrusted with knowledge of two of its components: One is your mother's remains, and the other is something I believe you have, Jason."

"Me?"

"Yes, now let me see . . ." She produced a small notebook from her pocket. Kaitlyn: "Need magic ink for that, too?"

"No, young lady, I do not. Ah, here it is." She addressed Jason: "You came to the Order's attention for your skill at crafting portals, gates, throughways, *nexi profundi*, and especially *magic weapons*. You and Justin will need to jointly craft one before this is over, but for now, I need you to present your magic pouch of holding."

Jason tipped his head back and covered his face.

"Fuuuuuuuuuuuck."

"Don't you have it?" Sandra asked.

"I lost it. In Enchanted Caverns. Skelton took it from me."

"Can't you make another?" Kaitlyn asked.

"Yeah, in about three months. Those things are hard to make."

Justin leaned in. "I think I know where it is: his prison cell."

Hanna prodded him and said: "Think you can get us in there, Sheriff?"

"I don't know. The Feds came in, claimed jurisdiction. They're treating his whole life like a crime scene. But we'll figure it out."

We were all ramping up to spring into action. Lee was taking notes, Dawn had crossed to the door to check the hallway, while Mac and I were packing up the danavreece, magic marker, and the first disk. Jason double-checked his pocket to make sure he had his sunglasses.

"Anybody have any ideas about that clue? What's our 'fortress of solitude'?"

"Castle GrayCrystal," I said, realizing why it hadn't occurred to him:

Jason had yet to visit the Castle.

We'd invited him over and over, but he always demurred, saying, "That's your place, not mine." He was wrong, but I understood where he was coming from.

"Oh," he said. "I guess I'll finally get to visit."

Sandra raised a palm. "Wait. There is one more thing. Everyone gather around."

We did. Sandra held out her hands, palms down.

Silence. The recurrent crack and rumble of crimson lightning underscored Sandra's invocation:

"By the powers vested in me by the East Tennessee Sororal Order of

Spiritual Defense, I hereby induct you into our hallowed ranks, with all rights and privileges therein. We honor you. We celebrate you. We welcome you with these titles: Levi David Dockery: Cleric-Adept. Dawnstar Moonchild Dockery: Mountain-Master. Jason Jeffrey Sutton: Occultsmith. Kaitlyn Julia Sutton: Havoc-Wrangler. Hiram Deacon Gresham: Dreamweaver. Mackenzie Lynn Gresham: Grid-Runner. Hanna Bohon-Blackledge: Warrior-Sister-In-Arms. And unto Justin Joseph Johnson, we confer the title of *Captain* of the great state of Tennessee."

Justin's eyes welled up. He didn't so much smile as radiate maximum amounts of kindness and gratitude.

I prodded him and said: "Captain Tennessee. Pretty cool."

"Shh," Mac said.

"To you all we entrust this most holy of missions in defense of this realm against threats terrestrial and cosmic."

My memory of this moment has taken on a wholly welcome and lovely patina of myth over the years. If pressed, I would swear that Sandra's invocation had transformed us all into super-perfect, animated versions of ourselves. We were moving portraits of our shared love and bravery, each of us rendered in a different medium from moment to moment, fading from watercolor to oils to messy graphite sketches to wide-eyed Disney caricatures to halting (but charming) Saturday-morning superheroes. A golden vignette encircles my mental projection of this moment.

This story is about the end of one family.

Well, another one was fully formed and ratified in the fires of Smoky Mountain magic that night, and we had serious work to attend to. Kaitlyn nodded to Justin.

"Okay, Cap'n. What's the call?"

"Well, first . . ." He wrapped everyone in a hug.

"I love you," Justin said.

"I love you."

"I love you."

"I love you."

"I love you."

"I love you."

Someone was shaking our hug circle with sobs. We pulled back to see Jason crying uncontrollably. Kaitlyn wrapped him in a big squeeze.

"Hey, shit-for-brains. What is it?"

"I . . . I . . . I'm so sorry. I'm so sorry. Oh, God, I'm so sorry. I . . . I promise—I swear, I *swear* I won't fuck this up. I will be worthy of this." He cleared his throat and got himself under control. "Thank you. Everyone. I love you all so much."

"We love you too, shit-for-brains. Justin, what's next?"

"First, we need to head over to Castle CrystalLight to listen to the next record."

Lee raised a finger. "If I may, it's Castle *GrayCrystal*, sir. It's a portmanteau based on Castle Grayskull and the Crystal Castle."

Dawn prodded him and said: "Lee, be nice!"

But Justin was already laughing. "Hey, I got it, big man. Also, nice use of the word 'portmanteau.'"

"Thank you, Captain," Lee said with a salute.

I raised my hand. "Uh shouldn't we go over to the cemetery first? We know we're gonna need Mom's ashes, so shouldn't that be our first stop?"

Lee nodded. "The admiral has a point. And if Skelton plans to stymie our plans, we should acquire the most crucial elements first."

Sandra shook her head. "He doesn't know what is needed for our countermeasure. We encrypted and protected that intelligence every step of the way. But nevertheless, we applied one of our most powerful wards to her crypt. That is the sole advantage we have." Her eyebrows rose. "But if he's out there somehow, he'll be in the Lodges . . . and he'll be following you."

A silence fell over us. Kaitlyn raised a hand. "Everyone can relax! I just shit my pants in fear so no one else has to."

Justin smiled wryly and checked his watch. "Already ten o'clock. Getting late. Let's get to work on a Smoky Mountain."

Sandra shook her head. "You can't. The *nexi profundi* are closed."

"The Smoky Mountains are closed?" Jason asked. "You mean the Sneakaround Network's closed?"

"That's right," Sandra said. "The Faceless One has retaken the Lodges. The act was so violent that it destroyed Enchanted Caverns back in March."

Mac: "That purple explosion."

"That's right. His eye sees far and wide. It's too dangerous. You'll have to get around the old-fashioned way. At least at first."

"What's *that* mean?" Kaitlyn asked.

"Time is short. You'd better get going."

Justin

Following the kids' directions, Justin pulled his Bronco up a hill toward the massive oak tree they'd described. Sandra had remained at the hospital "to coordinate the resistance effort," whatever that meant, while Lee and Dawn sat in back. Jason drove Kaitlyn, Hiram, and Mac over in his Beamer, which he parked farther down the hill. Hanna drove over in her station wagon. The Plaid Man's storm continued its horrible spin over the Mystery Mansion, slamming it with the occasional bolt of lightning. Red light tinged the night sky. Headlights slashed, then extinguished as car doors slammed and hurried footsteps crunched through the forest on their way to their destination:

Castle GrayCrystal.

It had accrued some more details over the last three months, including a neon Coors Light sign the kids had liberated from the dump. Lee, bearing what appeared to be a garbage can lid over his back, led the way, chattering about the Castle's "extensive roots in classical and modern myths."

"I like to think of it as a minor outpost on the pathway of the Beacon of Amon Din."

They all climbed up into the castle, three of them newcomers: Jason, Hanna, and Justin. They were immediately impressed by the array of posters and action figures. Hanna nodded.

"Y'all really worked hard on this place."

Justin zeroed in on an action figure from the animated series *C.O.P.S.:* a burly Black man wearing a trench coat and sunglasses: Baldwin "Bulletproof" Vess. Justin took it up.

"Oh, I love this guy," he said to immediate approval from Hiram and Lee.

"He's the coolest!" Hiram said. "I like how he's a cyborg who can interface with computers. And he's really strong and loyal to his troops."

Lee nodded. "I personally like to think he's related to Victor Stone, aka Cyborg, founding member of the New Teen Titans."

Justin shared a significant glance with Jason and returned the figure to its place.

"That's a cool idea, Lee," Justin said. "You like to pretend that cartoon takes place in the same world as the *Teen Titans?*"

"Yes, Captain. I guess you could say it's a form of storytelling canon that only exists in my mind."

Kaitlyn and Mac were scouring the treehouse for the next disk.

"I can't find it," Mac said. "Where would they hide it?"

Hiram was headed for the door. "Uh I think I know." Opening it, he leaned out and plucked something off the exterior doorjamb: the next disk, this one red. "It's where the keystone was for our Smoky Mountain."

They all gathered around the booth at the far end. Hiram placed the disk into the danavreece while Mac played it.

A woman's voice spoke: "Hey there, little man."

Justin sighed. "Momma."

Everyone smiled. Sue Johnson continued: "Sorry I never told you your momma was a something of a superhero, but when they jumped me in, they said mum's the word or we'd put everyone in danger. I don't know when you'll need this, or when you'll be listening to it, but the Order's had its eye on you for some time now. You and a few other kids down in West Chim, but they're not sure yet."

Like Corrie, his momma was speaking from some kind of meeting. Voices chattered indistinctly behind her. Justin was sure he heard Mrs. Glenn and Sandra. As she spoke, he watched the disk run down. He had no idea that there was a recording of her voice; that there was more *of her* hidden away out here. Part of him was angry at the Order—and frankly, his momma—for keeping this from him, but another part of him knew that parents are puzzles, that they secret away special segments of their souls, and that he was lucky to be learning one of her biggest, most powerful secrets.

My momma was a superhero, he thought. *You're goddamn right.*

She continued: "I wish I could tell you about all this. When they told me how impossibly high the stakes were, I wanted to scream it to the heavens. I wanted to tell you everything, but the Order taught me: if you only have one arrow in your quiver, you wait for your best shot."

Pause. "Tonight, you're going to create a weapon. One that can only fire one shot. And you're gonna use it to take out the Faceless One. And honey, I wish I could say this would end evil for all time. It won't . . . but by God in heaven, we will strike a blow for those children. The Faceless One has vexed us since before it all began. Skelton has shattered so many families. Tonight we break 'em both in two, Skelton and the Faceless One. Here's what you'll need. Turn over the disk and continue."

Pause. Hiram flipped the disk. Mac was taking notes, of course.

"One of our members will volunteer to contribute herself to the ritual. This one calls for a statement of grief and a physical pledge of sorrow."

Hiram: "Mom's ashes."

"You will inter her remains in—" (Justin could tell she was smiling at this detail) "—the Gold Rush park. In the Order's secret citadel, the Mystery Mansion. You'll need to inter her remains in a certain room there. You'll know which one in time."

Pause. Sue continued: "I'm going to have to ask you to make a sacrifice, JJ. We all are, because this evil's not going down without a fight. I need you to bring something with you on this mission . . . something very special to you . . . and I think you know what it is. There's going to be a fire, when all's said and done, little JJ, and I need to ask you to put it in there. I signed it with my name because names are sacred, especially those of the ones we love."

Mac paused the disk. "Justin, do you know what she's talking about?"

He nodded. "Yeah. It's a photo from a show I did. It was the last thing she gave me."

Kaitlyn made a small moan of empathy. "Are you sure you want to give that up? Can't we ask the Order for another—"

"No. It's okay. I'm proud to contribute something to help stop that sonofabitch. Keep playing, Mac."

Sue continued: "Our oracular adepts foresee the need for an icon. He Who Kept the Spirit and the Sight is said to—" (she chuckled) "—build his own worlds? You'll need exactly two icons from his world, one of which is crucial. I'm not sure what this means but . . . a saloon?"

Mac paused the disk. "Anyone know what that means?"

Jason nodded. "He had a huge train set with all these little Christmas cottages. Like you'd put on a mantle? I got a look at it when I went over to his apartment that night. But I've got no idea where they wound up. I guess we'll have to call his family."

Hanna shook her head. "I know where they wound up. Over at Enchanted Caverns, in the lobby—well, in what's left of the lobby—there's a vigil set up for him. He was well-liked."

Justin nodded. "I bet he was. Mac, keep going. I'm wondering if we can pull this off without Jason's pouch."

Sue's next words were: "You're going to need a magic pouch of unlimited holding." Everyone groaned. She continued: "These elements will all contribute to a new map you're going to build to generate a final *nexus profundus.*"

Kaitlyn frowned. "I thought Mama Dockery said those were kaput?"

"Shh," Mac said. "We'll figure it out later."

Sue continued: "I'm told you'll have a master occultsmith in your crew. They will build a train, a locomotive, to carry you to your destination."

"What?" Jason said, waving his hands. "A train? As in *a full-size train?* It takes months just to build *one* treasure, and I need *stuff* to build them—clay or plasticine or a toy or something. You can't just make 'em out of nothing. It's impossible."

Justin took his shoulder. "Hey, take it easy, kid. We'll figure it out. They wouldn't ask us to do something unless they figured we could pull it off. Mac, keep going."

Sue spoke: "The Order has concealed the raw materials for such a locomotive in its citadel, the Mystery Mansion, hiding it in plain view."

Kaitlyn paused the disk, elbowed Jason, and said: "See, shit-for-brains? Whatever it is has been soakin' up magic juice for years. Oughta be a snap for a master cult-farter like you!"

Jason smiled but narrowed his eyes. "*Occultsmith.* 'Cult-farter'? That wasn't even *close.*"

"But is *this* close?" She gave him a pointed look before everyone reared back, laughing and grimacing.

Mac waved a hand before her face: "Gross, Kaity!"

Kaitlyn threw up her hands. "Don't look at me! *I'm* not the cult-farter!"

Justin opened a window and indicated the player: "Guys, focus! Keep playing."

Sue continued: "You will need to use the magic pouch to transport it from the Mystery Mansion to its dark companion, the citadel of Skelton and the Faceless One."

"Enchanted Caverns," Lee said. Everyone nodded in agreement.

Mac frowned. "But what do they mean by a locomotive hidden in the Mystery Mansion?"

Justin gave a slight hiss as a memory hit him. Hiram was doing it, too.

"There's another train," Hiram said, reaching out to touch Justin's arm. "We never saw your house. The one in Oregon."

Now Lee was getting in on it, his brow furrowing. "We didn't. We only saw the Plaid Man's projection of it."

Images flashed through Justin's mind: Heat-lightning. His cottage in Oregon. The stained-glass window. The lightning cast a shadow on his far wall, like a zoetrope or a flip-book. The shadow looked like a locomotive charging through his house.

Lee seemed to be reading their thoughts: "The Plaid Man's cottage had a stained-glass window. That window depicted a train locomotive."

Hiram was frowning. "So did one of the cottages where Mom married Trent. That hotel by the brook."

Whatever Justin, Hiram, and Lee had was catching, because now Mac was massaging her brow, lost in the depths of thought and memory: "Something in the Mystery Mansion *sounds* like a train."

Hiram: "Justin, at your cottage, the *real* one, what's in the window?"

"The shadowcast," Justin said, recalling Skelton's words. "That's what Skelton called it. He said he was going to 'take all that matters' to help his 'ascendance.' Her remnants, the shadowcast, Smiley's secret, and JJ's big night." He addressed Lee: "The window came from an old brewery. It had a beer-fermenting tank."

Lee cracked the code with a smile: "The Flambonium Airscoop Three Thousand."

Mac snapped her fingers. "That's it!" She made a *holy shit* face. "We have to *move* that thing?"

Justin: "So you think you can do it?"

"I'm not going to be able to do it without all of you, and I've never made anything as big as a train, but . . . yeah. We got this."

"Okay," Jason said, indicating the turntable: "Keep playing."

As the disk ran down, his momma's voice grew fainter and fainter: "Bring the ingredients there, to the Citadel of Evil, as well as the means to draw the greatest map you've ever made. You'll find the third and final disk along the way. Be careful. Be brave. And know this . . ."

Justin spoke the words at the same time as his momma:

"It is required you do awake your faith."

Awake Your Faith. AYF.

The disk ended. Lightning flashed and summoned an ominous rumble. Everyone waited in respectful silence for Justin to call their next move.

He spoke in a hoarse whisper: "Can I keep that?"

Mac nodded and handed it over, but Justin remained still. He seemed lost in thought, scanning the space. He leaned over, placing his palms on the booth table. He indicated the window.

"Anybody remember that Bugs Bunny cartoon, 'Fearless Freep'?"

Hiram's Journal

We all loved Justin, but we looked at him like he'd gone bonkers.

"What do you mean?" I asked.

Justin climbed onto the table, scooting the danavreece out of the way, and crawled to the window.

"How high up are we? About twenty feet?"

Kaitlyn leaned over. "You feeling all right there, Cap'n?"

"I'm fine, guys. It's just—we need to build a Smoky Mountain, and we need to build it now." He addressed me: "And I need your sextant."

Hanna: "I think I'm missing something here. Aren't we driving over to the jail?"

Justin pivoted around on his knees and shook his head. "They sent in a bunch of Feds from Atlanta. Every last one of 'em is a pain in my ass. They're about to throw Skelton's cell and store everything about a hundred feet under Quantico. Plus, Sandra said he might try to grab some of our stuff. We need to get in there and look *now.*"

I handed him the sextant. "So what're we gonna do?"

He jerked his chin out the window. "Ms. D said the Plaid Man's taken control of the Sneakaround. Fine. We're going to build the smallest Smoky Mountain in history. The entrance'll be down below. I'll jump and fly right through it." All of us were struck silent. Justin looked us all in the eye. "Hey. We got this. You heard my momma: 'awake your faith.' I have faith. I have faith I can do this."

Lee jumped onto the table with him.

"I'm with you, Captain. Might I suggest we place the gate a yard or two *away* from the tree so you can properly dive into it?"

Kaitlyn raised her palms. "Wait, wait, wait—you guys are fucking with me, right? Even by Sneakaround Gang standards, that's a psychonuts plan."

Justin was two steps ahead, giving everyone orders. "Jason, my notion is: we do what Skelton did. Y'know how he created a bubble of Smoky Mountain around Enchanted Caverns so he could use his magic? We do the same thing around his prison cell. That way, I'll be able to use Hiram's sextant to find the magic pouch."

I looked at Jason and said: "Is that how it works?"

Jason nodded. "Yeah, it can see just about anything magical, as long as you're in the Sneakaround."

"Listen," Hanna said, holding up her hands. "I can't believe it's gonna take the old lady in the room to remind y'all of the dangers in your magic plan, but: Back in March, didn't Skelton say he *wanted* the sextant? Sandra said he might find a way to . . . I don't know. *Get* at us. Disrupt our plans from beyond the grave. We have to assume he's still out there somehow. And now we're gonna bring him exactly what he was asking for?"

Justin nodded. "I'll be careful. I'll keep it close. Plus, Skelton's not the only one with some surprises. Jason? I think you have something for me and Mac?"

Jason nodded and unslung his backpack.

Jason

They all knew something was coming. Deep down, they did. It didn't matter that Skelton was on death row and nobody'd seen any sign of the Plaid Man in months. They knew a final reckoning was in store.

So Jason got to work on new treasures.

The more time you took, the better the treasure. He'd spent *months* on Hiram's sextant, endowing it with as many powers as he could. He liked to think of it as his own version of Doctor Who's Sonic Screwdriver. Lee's shield took less time because it had fewer powers, but they all required of him the same amount of love and care.

He started on his latest gifts within days of their last encounter with Skelton. Mac's came easy to him. They'd been spending more and more time together, learning about each other's likes and dislikes. Justin's, however, was a little more involved.

It was also his first custom job.

Justin had called him. The West Chim police were offering him the sheriff position, and if he was going to move back, he wanted to be ready for his next trip to the Sneakaround. That meant a magic treasure. Justin explained that he loved turning into a cartoon, but he also spoke frankly about how tough it was for him to find cool role models in pop culture. Most Black cultural icons were athletes, musicians, or rappers. He wanted a treasure that would be powerful enough to take on Skelton, but he also wanted it to be really freakin' cool.

"Like, if LL Cool J, Rico Tubbs, and Lando Calrissian teamed up on a magic treasure, what would they come up with?"

Jason had added his own contributions, of course, and had put the finishing touches on it only the night before. Now he was pulling it out along with Mac's gift. He laid them both on the table: a boomerang and a blue silk vest.

"For Mac, the—" Both gifts snapped together, drawn by a magnetic force. Jason chuckled and separated them. "Sorry about that. There's a lot of steel in Justin's gift, and Mac's works as a magnet, too." He cleared his throat. "For Mac, the boomerang-bow."

Mac took it in hand, her face aglow with gratitude. It was large, about four feet long, with red, white, and blue stripes that ran along its length.

Kaitlyn crossed her arms and leaned forward. "Jase, how about this time you don't play *Riddle Me This* and just tell us what they do?"

"Got it," Jason said with a smile. "Mac, this is both a boomerang and a bow. I might've taken inspiration from your sculpture of Terpsichore. Oh, and think of that cartoon you like. The one with all the swords and sorcery, where they get transported into a magical theme park ride. I made you a scabbard, too."

"Understood," Mac said, accepting both gifts, which she strapped on. They hugged. "Love you, Jase."

"Love you too," he said, presenting the vest. "For Justin, the vest."

Hiram smiled. "Oh, uh Justin, isn't that from your uhm Mystery Mansion costume?"

"Sure is," he said, climbing off the table. "Always liked how this thing fit."

Jason helped him shrug into it. "Also explains why this one was so much easier to make. It had soaked up a lot of good vibes." He raised his voice to properly announce the gift: "The vest will protect you in times of peril and provide a few tricks up your sleeve, too."

"Nice job, kid," Justin said. Our faces flashed a sudden blushing red from a lightning-bolt.

"Thanks, but let's be careful. I haven't had a chance to test either of 'em in the Sneakaround, so their powers might be unpredictable."

"I like unpredictable," Justin said. "Let's get to work on a new Smoky Mountain."

Hiram's Journal

We all guided Auntie Hanna through her first map, while everyone else touched up theirs, adding Tennessee State Pen to it. (Except for Lee, we'd all lost our maps back in March, but we'd been working on new ones. Somehow, we knew we'd have to.) To my utter lack of surprise, Hanna was a talented artist, using colored pencils to draw everything in flowing freehand. It was Lee who came up with a way to limit the size of the Smoky Mountain.

"Simple," he said, rolling a piece of glassine into a tube. He took all our maps and rolled them up, taking care to layer Castle GrayCrystal and Tennessee State Pen on top of each other. That done, he handed a magic marker to me. "Admiral, if it please you, find a small, flat stone outside and draw our collective glyph on it, the stylized SG that Ms. Kaitlyn—excuse me, Havoc-Wrangler—conceived."

I grabbed the marker and ran outside. I got lucky and found a suitable stone in moments while the others took one of the windows out of the Castle's prow. Wearing his new vest, Justin climbed onto the ledge. An eerie, bloody haze had settled across the Smokies. Fog rolled in from the south and hovered under the storm, hiding it in a semi-fluorescent mist that flashed and strobed and rumbled and roared. The rest of the gang came outside and gathered around a circle that Lee was drawing in the earth with a stick. Jason was strapping on a strange new belt. I'd seen him working on it over the last week.

"Is that a new treasure?" I asked.

"Nope," he said. "An old-fashioned protective measure. After all the bullshit with Skelton snatching our maps last time, I figured we needed a better way to protect 'em."

Built into the belt was a clear plastic tube. Once Lee had finished drawing our new Smoky Mountain, Jason slid all of our maps into it, except for the sheet of glassine that was going to generate our "miniature" Smoky Mountain. He locked it shut. My eyes got big.

"That's *really* cool."

"Thanks, buddy."

Lee stepped to the head of the circle. "Admiral, if you could present the keystone?"

"Aye aye, sir," I said, handing it over. Lee held it aloft.

"Captain, I am about to generate our Smoky Mountain. It leads straight into Skelton's prison cell. Ms. Blackledge was kind enough to provide a schematic of Tennessee State Penitentiary from memory. If my calculations are correct, you'll emerge from the ceiling. Your exit will be detectable with the sextant and should be on the floor. As soon as you've returned, we'll destroy the Smoky Mountain."

Kaitlyn cupped a hand over her mouth: "I still think this is *craaaa-zeeeee!*"

Justin shrugged. "You're right. It *is* crazy. And that's exactly why we're doing it. Awake your faith."

She nodded. "Awake your faith."

"Cleric? You ready?"

"Yessir," Lee said, kneeling to place the keystone. It was like he'd dropped a match into a ring of gasoline. Flame tore an instant circle in the earth that flooded with an unexpected color: white. We all leaned over. Our previous Smoky Mountains had all been dark, but this one was blinding bright and gave view onto an endless, blank landscape. An inkblot floated in the sky like an inverse of the sun. About twenty feet to our right, the "exit" gate opened in the ground.

"Holy shit," Jason said.

"Wowwww," Lee said.

Dawn simply nodded, while Mac and Kaitlyn covered their mouths.

Hanna remained on point, though: "It worked. Look." About thirty "feet" down into the Smoky Mountain floated another gate that looked into a prison cell: gray cinder-block walls, a steel commode, and a single cot. Lee *tutted* his disappointment.

"Curses," he muttered. "The gate isn't in the ceiling." He called up: "Take care when you pass into his cell, sir. You might crash into the wall."

Justin took a deep breath and dove through the gate.

Justin

The gate may have *looked* like it was thirty feet away, but it *felt* like miles. Justin dove from a Smoky Mountain night into a harsh, hellish day where he fell and fell and fell. The inkblot-black sun blasted the stark landscape with desert-like heat. All moisture vanished. The soundscape felt claustrophobic and empty, like he'd stepped into a soundproof chamber.

But worse were the voices—*and the view.*

The view he recognized. It was the Smokies, but an inversion of them. Gatlinburg and West Chim lay down the hill to his right, but their skylines had been replaced by jagged arrays of dark towers and parapets and ramparts. Spectral-dark creatures slithered and lurked all across the landscape. Murkiness swam around everything, as if the whole world were a newly-completed watercolor on a sopping-wet canvas.

The voices he also recognized. He'd only heard the Plaid Man speak once or twice, but he'd remember his voice forever. Trillions of faces—all of them criss-crossed with gore—crowded the sky, transforming it into a gruesome ocean. Justin's middle ear registered the kind of constant, low, recurring chant that would, after enough time, drive a person mad:

"Dead dead already dead dead already dead dead already dead dead already dead dead already."

On the plus side, though, was Justin's outfit. When he dove into the gate, electricity wiped through his body, transforming him into a Saturday-morning cartoon and outfitting him in a three-piece suit, tie, and a billowing cape. A pair of sunglasses sketched themselves into existence and completed the look just as he finally reached the other gate.

Lee had cautioned Justin against making noise as he landed in Skelton's cell, but he had nothing to worry about. Justin kicked his legs up and slid into the cell on one knee, his fingertips lightly touching the floor to keep balance. A quick glance revealed he was still a cartoon and still clad in Jason's treasure.

The animated series *C.O.P.S.* came a little after Justin's time, but he'd noticed Hiram and Lee watching it and smiled. It was your typical late-afternoon half-hour ad for toys, a goofy amalgam of *G.I. Joe, BraveStarr,* and *RoboCop* . . . but the team's leader was a Black man. He was smart and strong and everyone looked up to him. It wasn't much, but he liked that kids could turn on this show and see a Black man as a leader. (Even though the show's central conceit, the lionization of the police, troubled Justin in spite of his own career path.)

Justin, in all his years as a fan, had come to be a scavenger, and when you're looking for inspirations for a magic treasure, you do the best with what you've got.

He'd emerged in what was technically the rear of Skelton's cell, but it resembled no prison cell Justin had seen in his career, not even in solitary. After his fellow inmates' mass exodus, the state had worked with a team of specialists to contain him, clearing out some walls and building a triple-reinforced plexiglass cube in the middle of the space. Catwalks ran over top of the cube, while guard stations stood before and behind it. (Guards had to take an access hallway to reach the far side of death row.) The idea was to keep eyes on Skelton twenty-four hours a day.

It didn't work, because Skelton was Skelton.

In his final days, the man had *nested* in this space, tearing his furniture to bits, gathering papers and clothes and sheets, and piling everything into a corner, where he'd built a sort of burrow for himself. He'd crammed his desk into it, where he worked with no chair, hunched over under a canopy of sheets and papers and splintered wood. It looked like a cross between a child's sheet-fortress and a wasp's nest.

Justin surveyed the space. The boundary of their Smoky Mountain "bubble" shimmered just beyond the plexiglass walls, a dome enclosing a cube. Yellow emergency lights flashed from either end of the room, all of them mounted to orange-striped road barriers lined with yellow police tape.

But there were no maps.

He'd drawn none on the plexiglass walls, and if he had, the walls were cleaned by firehose-toting guards every day. Had Skelton found a way to draw a new map and collaborated with someone to transport his spirit from the electric chair into the Sneakaround? If so, then how . . . and more important, *who?*

There were no easy answers. Justin knew he'd need at least one other person to collaborate on maps with him, and to their credit, the staff at Tennessee State Pen had taken every step to deny him contact with the outside world. He'd never even spoken with a lawyer, because no one would represent him.

But there was still the Plaid Man.

What about him? Could he communicate with Skelton on death row? Could he have facilitated a connection between Skelton and an ally? They might never know.

Justin produced the sextant, which added epaulets, goggles, an aviator helmet, and a bandolier to his ensemble, and scanned the cell, not knowing what to expect. The little telescope revealed the gates they'd created: his entrance gate glowed on the wall, while the exit gate sat on the floor a few feet ahead. He scanned the rest of the room until—

There you are.

It was buried in his wasp's nest, the pouch was. An amorphous shape glowed through the scope, hovering a few feet off the ground. A moment's trepidation beset Justin as he contemplated entering the space; some deep-seated evolutionary instinct was telling him *danger, danger!* But he pushed the feeling down, lowered his head, and stepped inside. Even in his animated state, the stench was amazing. He'd built the nest around his commode, which had clogged up who knew how many weeks ago. No one had bothered to clear it, both because Skelton never complained and no one would dare go into his cell. Justin opened a drawer to reveal the pouch—and to summon a voice that was at once shocking and expected.

"Looks like them old biddies fed you some valuable intel."

Time dilated. Justin's sensory apparatus took in every detail. It was his voice, but he sounded distant and digitized, like he was speaking through a faulty speaker from the far side of a canyon. His vowels rasped and slurped wetly, too, like he was fighting off a chest cold. Justin kept his focus on the mission, pocketing the pouch and sextant and smashing his way out of his nest to bring him into view.

What stood in the cell—and blocking his exit gate—wasn't Skelton so much as an assemblage of memories *shaped* like Skelton. He wore the same outfit he'd worn the night he'd slipped away from Justin—a flannel and overalls— while his face was undeniably lifted from the previous March. He looked like he was wearing a mask of his own face, frozen in a perpetual laughing sneer. Dueling halos of red-and-purple light shimmered around his outline like a watery Venn diagram, revealing another bizarre truth:

He'd been dismembered.

Whether his dismemberment had preceded his cremation or welcomed him in the afterworld, Justin didn't know, but his arms, legs, and head floated a few millimeters away from his torso, admitting the occasional slitting slash of otherworldly light.

When he spoke, his lips didn't move: "Y'know, back on Ides Less Two, I almost went 'n' killed that grayhair you keep around. Figger'ed I'd send her packin' before I carried out the Sentinel's errand for the evening. But I spared her, left her here to shuffle in yer all's wake. And y'all ain't never shown no gratitude." Skelton appeared to be sweating heavily, but he wasn't; no, he had been *sculpted* from the same ectoplasmic icing they'd seen in the Sneakaround. Some unseen hand was holding him into a corporeal shape, invisible fingers constantly scooping and smearing drips of wax back into the shape of Skelton. He continued: "Lemme assure you: once me and the Sentinel of the Hightower've finished huffin' and puffin', we won't hurt ya . . . but if you don't give up that fancy right now—"

"Which one?" Justin asked. "The pouch—*or this?*" He shook open his trench coat to reveal that Jason's vest had coated his entire torso in solid steel that blinked and clicked with various cybernetic readouts and lights.

Skelton smiled. "Well, well, well. We got us an old-timey duel, don't we?" He closed his fists, seemingly around invisible triggers that fired an array of six or seven slippery tendrils that lashed across the space and closed around Justin's wrists and ankles.

Justin grunted and whispered: "Back off." The command activated a steel fist that shot out of his midsection and slammed Skelton against the cell's rear wall, where for a moment, Justin thought he'd finished him. His cybernetic steel fist *splattered* Skelton against the plexiglass wall like a shoe-heel smashing a gigantic, ectoplasmic insect, but within instants, those same invisible hands had started scooping and sculpting the goo and oozed back into Skelton, all of this shrouded by twin auras of red-and-purple light. Justin bounded over to the gate, where on the far rim, Skelton's face had reconstituted, floating on a puddle of gore. His laugh was an effervescent gurgle, like a sucking chest wound.

"Got you some new spectral-spectaculars." His floating face clenched. *"Levi David goes first and foremost,* JJ Turntail. Ya done condemned him." His spectral lungs hacked on his sopping interiors. His rage rose: "I'mma tell him you told me to trade his life for yours right before I spill his entrails into the Sentinel's waiting maw." The sculpting continued; his face rose from the puddle like a bubble. "The ones he eats go to hell, ain't no stoppin' it. He's a brimstone trifle for the Sentinel, he—"

"Shut up," Justin said, and from his trench coat sleeve emerged a hand-grenade. Pulling the pin, he shoved it in Skelton's mouth, gave him the finger, and dove through the exit portal.

Hiram's Journal

It was like someone had buried a trampoline underground. Justin shot out of the exit gate and hovered in the air for a moment. Something *thudded* down inside the Sneakaround and sent a small shockwave through our feet. The next instant, Lee snatched away the keystone while Jason tore the glassine in half. Both gates vanished. Justin landed on the balls of his feet and produced the pouch. We all cheered.

"That's one," he said, holding up a finger.

Lee ran over. "What did you see in the Sneakaround?"

"The scariest shit imaginable. If we have to go back in there, it's gonna be dangerous." He addressed Jason: "Yo! Nice work with this vest. The Inspector Gadget stuff worked perfectly against Skelton." Off our troubled reactions, he added: "Sandra was right: he's back. And he was waiting for me. He knows we're onto him, and he's powerful. More powerful than he was in March. We've gotta watch our backs and hit the gas."

Auntie Hanna, her arms crossed, cocked an eyebrow. "Can you humor the old lady here and make sure you still have the sextant?"

Justin held it up. "Right here. I kept it close."

Hanna uncrossed her arms. "What's our next move?"

"I think we've got to split up," Justin said.

This was the plan: Jason would drive me, Mac, and Kaitlyn home to get the key to the Suttons' mausoleum while Auntie Hanna and Lee would head over to the Mystery Mansion to get the flambonium locomotive, and Justin and Dawn would go to Enchanted Caverns to secure Officer Webb's little saloon, stopping at Justin's place along the way for his mom's photo. Everyone checked to make sure they had enough art supplies and glassine to create Smoky Mountain bubbles. Our rendezvous would also be our last stop: Enchanted Caverns.

Hanna objected at first: "I don't like us splitting up. Skelton could be anywhere. He *will* be anywhere."

Jason put on his 3D glasses. "Then we've got to make bubbles around every area where there's a treasure. My guess is if he's following us, he can't detect where we are unless we make a Sneakaround bubble."

"That's well considered, Occultsmith," Lee said. "So we'll generate our bubbles at the last possible moment. We must act with *surgical* precision."

Justin approached Lee and put a hand on his shoulder. "He said some nasty stuff about you, Lee, but I'm not gonna let him hurt you."

Lee shrugged. "That doesn't surprise me. He probably sees me as the weakest and most vulnerable of our troupe." Everyone immediately started shaking their heads. Dawn gave him a squeeze.

"That ain't true and you know it," she said.

The storm growled in the distance. Moaning wind summoned a chilly breeze that cut across our legs. "Oh, of course it's not true. Mother said that our sole advantage was the ward they'd erected around Ms. Gresham's remains. With respect, I disagree. Skelton has no honor. And he has no courage. That is our greatest advantage."

As always, Lee knew how to instill confidence and dispel doubts. But as we parted ways, I had to admit our next foe scared me even more than Skelton, because our next stop was home.

And Trent.

Lee

"Warrior Sister-in-Arms," Lee said as Hanna turned into the Gold Rush parking lot, "once we build a bubble around the Flambonium Airscoop, I suggest we build a tunnel straight from the Mystery Mansion to Enchanted Caverns. Goodness, this is quite the view."

Lee thought back to his visit to the science museum where he'd seen the models of epicycles. That same museum also featured an exhibit on the planet Jupiter. A semi-scale model of the solar system spanned the length of a main hallway, each step accompanied by artists' renderings of the different worlds. A painting of Jupiter's atmosphere always lingered with Lee. It depicted the imaginary view of a satellite plummeting through the gas giant's cloud cover.

Its caption read, *Artist's conception of a satellite falling through Jupiter's Great Red Spot, which is between 18,000 and 24,000 kilometers wide and could easily swallow the earth whole.*

Lee felt like that hapless satellite as they pulled up to the Gold Rush's front gates, which were chained shut. Skelton's storm, the Great Red Spot of the Smokies, roared over the park like a crimson maelstrom, sending down bolt after terrible bolt of red lightning. They climbed out and marveled at the sight.

"Like the very mouth of the Devil himself," Lee said, alluding to Gandalf's description of the Uruk-Hai's fearsome battering ram, Grond.

"That it is, Levi."

The park had been closed since Jenny Miles' murder and was still decorated for Halloween. They climbed out. Hanna grabbed a set of wire-cutters from her trunk.

"You can keep calling me Miss Blackledge or Auntie Hanna," she said as she snapped the chains. With an ominous creak, the gate swung open. Hanna returned the cutters to her trunk and shrugged into a kevlar vest, adding to it her shoulder-holster and pistol. Lee was wearing his He-Man armor like always, with Jason's shield, disguised in its earthly form as a trashcan lid, hooked to his backpack.

They hurried through the park, flashlights bouncing. Garbage had piled up in every corner, spawning trashy tumbleweeds that rolled by. Grafitti splattered almost every visible wall, most of it the expected profanity, but some was disturbingly evocative:

WE KNOW WHERE YOU ARE
SHE'S CRYING BECAUSE SHE'S UGLY
WHEN I GET THROUGH WITH HER
IT'S OPEN SEASON AGAIN

They ducked through Statuary Row, cut through Christmasville, and arrived at the Mystery Mansion, which thankfully hadn't been locked. Skelton's storm pummeled the building, its lightning lashing like bloody whips, each strike shaking loose shingles and rattling windows. Plaster dislodged from the walls and smashed to the ground in dusty clouds. A blinding flash split the night sky and spurred them both to cover their eyes. As their vision slowly returned, Lee could've sworn that a person was floating above the Mansion.

And not just any person. A *gigantic* person.

A megalith. A Lovecraftian Colossus of Rhodes, similar to how the Plaid Man presented himself over Skelton's hideout months ago. He was about to dismiss the vision as a trick of the light when Auntie Hanna prodded him.

"Did you see that?" she asked.

"A ... giant?"

"Like one of them Paul Bunyan statues you see on the road, but about ten times as big?"

Another lightning-bolt shattered one of the Mansion's windows.

"We haven't much time," Lee said, waving them inside.

Darkness and silence greeted them, broken only by the occasional squeak or scurry of a rat. Hanna and Lee crept through the halls, taking note of details they'd missed before. Lee paused at the portrait of Dr. Wizardo-Sorora and noted its details, including her title: Revelation General of the East Tennessee—the rest was scuffed out, but now he knew that his very own mother held the same station. His heart warmed with familial pride.

Hanna whispered: "Here it is."

Now that he knew what it was, Lee chuckled at himself for failing to notice it before. It looked exactly like a locomotive. Part of its sign had fallen off, leaving behind the letters lambonium Airsco p 300. The Order had soldered or hot-glued thousands of transistors, servos, diodes, vacuum tubes, and other assorted silliness to the locomotive's hull. Hanna turned to him and held up the pouch.

"So how's this work?"

Lee unslung his backpack and spread out their art supplies. They both still had their maps from last March, both of which included the Gold Rush.

"We need nothing more than a single gate with a bubble large enough to encompass the Flambonium device," he said to a snort from Hanna.

"Sorry, big guy. Ten years ago, if you'd told me this is how I'd be spending my retirement, I think I'd have stayed on the force." The joke cast a gloomy pall over Lee's excitement. Hanna detected it and course-corrected: "Just kidding. I wouldn't trade being here for anything."

He beamed and guided her drawing. Lee added a "breakout" box to their maps that depicted the room in detail. Both of them added gates in the same position—a few feet ahead—with the now-expected keystone of SG.

"Now all we need is—" Lee laid a sheet of glassine over both maps. "Are you ready?"

Hanna nodded. Lee drew a circle around the room, and light exploded everywhere.

Jason

He'd drunk himself to sleep again. They all huddled outside the master bedroom. His snores rumbled out, breathy and wet; Jason suddenly thought, *I wonder if this is what it sounded like when Bilbo snuck into Smaug's lair?* Hiram prodded him.

"Sounds like Smaug," he said.

Great minds, Jason thought with a smile. "Yeah, he does. Wait in the living room, guys. I'll come get you when I'm done."

Mac shook her head. "She's *our* mom. Shouldn't *we* be doing the talking?"

Jason took her hand. "I'm not good for much, but I think I'm supposed to do this. She's your mom, but this is my fight to fight." He looked between her and Hiram. "But I can't make you do anything. I'm asking to do this for you. Please."

Mac and Hiram exchanged looks. And nodded. Jason's eyes glowed with gratitude.

"Thank you."

They filed into the living room. Jason opened the door to a volley of grinding snores. Photos of his first mom, Marie, accompanied his creeping passage across the room. She was small, much smaller than Trent, and jaw-droppingly beautiful. Trent had unearthed dozens of photos of the two of them, scattering them about. The photos spanned a lifetime—as snot-nosed kids, as hell-raising teenagers, as college students (including a brief time spent apart), and finally as a married couple. They also told the story of Trent's descent. When he met Marie, his skin glowed and his eyes glinted with a cunning sharpness, but as the years wore on, dark bags grew and grew under his eyes, while his jowls sagged more and more. In spite of his massive size, he looked exhausted.

They'd taken one final photo before her death, a shot of her taking an awkward drink from a water fountain somewhere in South America. Trent had called it a second honeymoon, a last-ditch effort to repair their failing marriage. Jason and Kaitlyn both knew that if Mom had survived her illness, they would've split up.

His father spoke in his sleep: "What would I have done?"

Jason sat on the bed and jostled him. "Dad?"

Dawn

Enchanted Caverns was a ruin. As the Great Red Eye of the Smokies roiled over the Mystery Mansion, Justin and Dawn stopped at the bottom of the parking lot's sloping incline, Justin wearing his magic vest, Dawn armed with the battle axe. The attraction's front doors lay open and smashed, one door hanging from a hinge. Faint golden light flickered inside. Scorching darkened the roof and scattered-stone walls. Deep fissures in the earth snaked through the pavement. The remnants of a failed construction project lay strewn about: pylons and traffic barricades, plus a few bags of cement. They both produced their maps.

Dawn glanced over. "So all we do is add a little Smoky Mountain around this place?"

"Yep," Justin said. "Then I'll draw it on the glassine, and—" *Boom!* The instant he drew on the glassine, a blinding white dome blossomed and flash-expanded around the building, a stone gate embedded into its side. Its keystone depicted an eagle bearing an anchor and trident in honor of his service.

"You ready?" Justin asked. Dawn nodded, and they entered the gate. Dawn marveled at the sight. Enchanted Caverns stood before them, but it was rendered in hand-drawn, impressionist, black-and-white graphite sketches. Watery shimmers swam around the building's edges and roof, the kind of squiggly lines a cartoonist might draw to indicate the building was shaking.

It was colorless—except for the occasional distressing flash; *distressing* because every few seconds, one of Skelton's victims burst from the building's roof in vivid color, only to vanish the next instant. In that instant, they sounded a moan, each at a different register, transforming the building into an accursed organ that played Skelton's song into eternity.

"Son of a bitch," Justin muttered. With a snap of his fingers, his costume encased his hands in steel gauntlets, while a pair of mini-guns shifted into place over his shoulders. Dawn's eyebrows hopped.

"Jason done right by you," she said before jerking her chin at the doors. "Let's make this fast. He might already be here."

"Roger that."

They eased their way inside. Over by the gift shop stood a small shrine dedicated to Holton Webb. His high school senior photo stood amidst hundreds of candles and bouquets of flowers, as well as their target:

"There they are," Dawn whispered. Dozens of little Christmas cottages composed a makeshift wonderland village around Holton's smiling face. They both jogged over and knelt, carefully searching the shrine. "I don't wanna mess this up. He was so nice."

"Yeah, and brave," Justin said. "Ah. Here—" His face bathed in flickering candle-gleam, he lifted one of the cottages, an Old West saloon that stood on a cliffside. "I see a few other bars, but this is the only saloon."

Dawn took it in hand. "It's lovely." For the millionth time that year, she started crying again.

Justin sat back and waited.

She shook her head. "I'm sorry."

"Don't be."

"This has all been so much. I was so little when Daddy died. I barely even knew what was happening. Mom did her best to explain. But when Mom went into the hospital, I got ready to live without no parents." Her face suddenly fell. "Oh! Lookit me, goin' on and on, when you've . . ."

"Lost both my folks?" When she nodded, he continued: "Hey, it's okay. I get it. This year—this *everything*—has been a lot. Too much. If it were up to me, I'd wipe all of y'all's memories. No kid should have to go through what you guys have."

"Thank you. I wish I could do the same for you. I'm glad you're a part of the Sneakaround Gang. We wouldn't be here without ya."

He squeezed her shoulder and kept searching the cottages. "They said we needed one more, but which one?"

She scanned the village before landing on one bearing the inscription *Jimmy 1979*. It was a coal mine, with smokestacks, conveyor belts . . . and a strangely familiar A-framed roof. She held it up.

"Is it just me, or does this look like this place?"

Justin looked it over. Nodded. "Yeah. This has gotta be it. Stash it, and—"

He stopped short in response to Dawn's expression: her face had stretched in horror. A dark shape blocked the light from outside.

They weren't alone.

Hanna

A stone archway stood embedded in a dome of blinding white light. Hanna and Lee had agreed on a keystone: the emblem of the East Tennessee Sororal Order of Spiritual Defense, the triangular *ETSOSD*. They approached the gate, which was filled with glimmering black light. Inky black tendrils clawed and licked at the edges of their gate.

She started to move forward, only for Lee to step in her way.

"Auntie Warrior, please be warned that when you touch a magic treasure in the Sneakaround, the effect can be somewhat bracing."

"You're telling me I'm about to turn into a Max Fleischer cartoon?"

"Max Fleischer, he of the memorable Superman animated serials from the nineteen-forties?"

"That's the one," she said, marching inside. Lee scampered after her, an electric wall wiping through him and transforming him into his animated self, clad in medieval armor. The trashcan lid flashed solid white and morphed into his shield, Compassion. Hanna, meanwhile, was on her knees, the transition having knocked her off her feet. A swirlstorm of electricity encircled her, leaving behind an animated version of Hanna Blackledge with gleaming silver hair and big brown eyes. She stood and gave her head a hard shake. "Well, that'll clear your sinuses, won't it?"

They stood in a dome of light so bright they had to squint. Filaments of blackness snaked through the space. The flambonium engine sat before them, waiting.

She held up the pouch. "So, how does this—"

A deep *thrum* sounded from within the pouch, which doubled and tripled in size, growing and growing, its opening a yawning mouth that was about to engulf the engine when a familiar voice halted its growth and sent it rapidly shrinking back into Hanna's hand. Sitting next to the engine was a silhouette that slowly came into focus.

"Hey, Han."

"Cor?" Hanna said.

Corrie Blackledge Gresham sat before them, a couple of decades younger and wearing a Florida Gators football jersey. She sipped beer from a plastic red cup.

"Remember this day, Han? You came down to Gainesville to visit, and we sat on the front porch of that shabby old Victorian I was sharing with six other chuckleheads? I know you remember it, because your mind earmarked it as the last time Corrie was happy."

Everything she said was a brutal truth that shut Hanna down. Lee had taken something out of his backpack and was prattling on, but her entire world was zoomed in on her baby sister.

Corrie continued: "Everything fell apart from here. I gave up on school. Deak knocked me up. My dreams died, and later, *I* died, and it's one person's fault: yours. You could've saved me any time you wanted to, but you didn't, because you don't give a fuck about anyone but yourself." She shrugged and sipped her beer. "Never having kids while I pumped out two. Now, why don't you hand me that pouch? Make it easy on yourself."

Lee had raised his voice and was saying something about a ray gun: "—we all agreed that Jason should never construct a gun, because we don't believe in them, but we made an exception when Jason told us about the treasure he wanted to craft for you. We'd been hoping to surprise you with this under better circumstances, but Skelton forced our—"

Hanna spun on him: *"Lee, would you please be quiet?! I'm trying to listen to—"*

CR-AAA-AAAA-NNNNG! Lee's shield, Compassion, smashed into Corrie's face and rebounded back into his waiting hand. Hanna screamed; the blow had split her sister's head in two. She looked like a charred Venus flytrap, her jaws rent open at a grotesque angle, her tongue a black slug that whipped back and forth as her throat spewed oil slick against the top of the magic dome. The black sludge coated Not Corrie Gresham, whose flesh smoked and crackled as it boiled away, her exit accompanied by an ear-splitting shriek. Lee crossed to where she'd been sitting. All that remained was a small pile of black ooze. Lee crushed it under his boot and turned to Hanna.

"I beg your pardon for the outburst of violence, Auntie Warrior, but the Plaid Man's specters are so very tiresome."

Blue animated tears gathered in her eyes. "You saw Corrie, too?"

"No, I saw someone else." Lee squared his shoulders to her. "That must've been quite upsetting to see your sister rendered in such cruel fashion. I'm so sorry."

"Who'd you see? What did they say to you?"

He shook his head. "His lies aren't worth repeating."

Hanna realized she was clutching the pouch with both hands. Instinctively, she'd sensed that the specter wanted it, and in spite of her distress, she'd held onto it.

All of this magic stuff seems to come so easy to everyone else, but maybe I'm stronger than I think.

She turned her attention to Lee's gift. He was holding out a bargain-bin ray gun, a piece of cheap plastic junk lined with peeling stickers that depicted its electronic inner workings. A clear blue plastic cone served as its barrel.

"This is gonna knock your auntie on her keister again, isn't it?"

"Most likely, yes."

She accepted the gift, setting off another electrical firestorm that spun in a quick cyclone and outfitted her in a futuristic suit of armor. A burnt-orange breastplate covered her torso, while armored gauntlets and shin-guards materialized and clamped onto her forearms and calves. A shiny helmet popped onto her head and sprouted a retractable scope that slid out over her eye like a ruby-quartz monocle. The ray gun had transformed into a double-barreled cannon that attached itself to her gauntlet and snapped into place, ready to be deployed. After gathering herself, Hanna regarded her new look.

"You all made this for me?"

"All of us pitched in, yes. We didn't know if we'd need to return to the Sneakaround, and if we did, we wanted to make sure you were properly armed."

She held up the cannon. "I assume this isn't just for show?"

"No, ma'am."

"Thank you," she said, turning to the engine. "Now let's get this sucker."

The pouch yawned forth once more and swallowed the flambonium engine in succession of racking gulps. It looked like a snake slowly choking down a larger prey. As it swallowed more and more, the pouch gradually returned to its normal size. Hanna tested its weight.

"You'd never know anything was in here," she said. Lee got ready to tear the glassine in half, but Hanna stopped him. "Wait, won't this thing get big again if we're outside the . . . uh, the magic place?"

"Negative, ma'am. As long as it's inside the pouch, we'll be fine. We simply won't be able to get the flambonium engine *out* again unless we're in the Sneakaround." Lee tore the glassine, instantly dissolving the Sneakaround bubble and their animated appearances. To Hanna's astonishment, the locomotive engine was still gone. When she checked in the pouch, it was empty.

"Incredible," she said.

Lee tore out another sheet of glassine. "I'm going to create a passage between here and Enchanted Caverns. Can you please take out your map?"

Hanna touched his hand. "Levi, I don't think your Auntie Warrior's up for that. How about if I promise to drive like a mad banshee over there?"

"Deal. Let us make haste!"

Jason

He came awake with a grunt, drool glistening on his cheek.

"Huh? Wha—whaizzit?" Trent sat up. "Jase? What time is it? What's wrong?"

"I need to talk with you."

Trent held his head. A ceiling vent blasted them with cool air. Black sweat stains soaked through his pajamas, a classic red union suit that covered him up to his wrists and ankles.

"Can it wait till tomorrow?"

An empty bottle of Buffalo Trace sat on his bedside table. And an empty bottle of tequila. His head hit the pillow again, but Jason grabbed his shoulder.

"No. I need you to wake up. This is important."

Trent whipped to a sitting position, eliciting a gasp from Jason, and clicked on the bedside lamp.

"Fine. It's important. Tell me what's important?"

Jason's insides shriveled and dried up in the heat-blast of his father's dark mood, but he remembered the stakes and thought of his friends and family.

"It's about Mom. Hi and Mac's mom."

"Okay."

"We need her ashes."

Trent frowned and scratched his temple, his mind a malfunctioning computer.

"What do you mean you 'need' them?"

"They . . . they want to scatter them. Hiram and Mac do." He took a breath. "And we do, too. Me and Kaity."

His father clicked off the lamp. "Our family rests with our family. End of story. Good night."

Trent's breaths rasped and rumbled, hitting Jason's forearm with blazing heat. Silence extended between them until Jason crossed and turned on the overhead light.

His father reared: "Hey!"

"We're not done talking yet. This is important—"

"Turn off that fucking light. I've had a long night and—"

"This is important to them. This is about their mom."

Trent rubbed his brow, keeping a beady eye on his son. His jawline shifted, his mind worked. *Must've been a while since someone challenged him like this,* Jason thought. But instead of rising, his father merely lay back and put a pillow over his face.

His voice was muffled: "You're about to turn off the light. And I'm about to go back to sleep. And you're about to go to bed."

"No, I'm not. Get up."

Trent moved the pillow and sat up, his face a caricature of itself. His voice kept changing tones—one word too high, one too low.

"Feeling good about yourself, huh? Big boy now, talking back to your dad. How's it feel? Does it feel good, talking shit to your pop after he's just lost the second love of his life?"

"You never even asked them what they wanted to do with her remains."

"I didn't have to. They barely even fucking knew her. She said as much. I don't know if they even loved her as much as I—"

"Shut up! Yes, they did!"

Trent held his head. "Hold it the fuck *down.*" His bulk suddenly lurched across the room, his legs a tangle of redwood trunks, his torso a rushing wall. The surprise of him going from blackout-prone to charging bull was enough to move Jason away from the light switch, but the juxtaposition of their two bodies also served to highlight an important new reality:

He'd outgrown his dad.

He had at least two inches on him. Somehow the change had escaped Jason's notice over the last year, probably because Trent spent so much time off his feet, having farmed out most of his landscaping work to underlings. After flicking off the overhead light, Trent staggered around, only for Jason to take—and hold—his arm.

"We're gonna talk about this."

"This is going bad for you. This is not going well. This is going to end *very* badly for you."

"We're going out to the cemetery tonight to get her ashes. *Now.*"

"You know that pussy Webb stuck up for you."

Ice-water splashed across Jason's skin in a crackling wave. He said nothing and released his dad's arm.

Trent bared his teeth, knowing he'd drawn blood: "Yeah, one night last year when you little shits went wandering, he pulls me aside at the police station, tells me—*me*—that if I don't keep an eye on my kids, he was going to do something about it."

"Give me the keys or—"

"Or what? Or WHAT? You're gonna hit me? You've never stood up to me in your life, you little fucking coward pussy. Little pussy peed his pants when I showed you who's . . ."

Trent's eyes flickered; he'd glanced at something behind Jason. Sitting on a dresser were his keys, all of them.

They locked eyes. Trent raised a finger: "Don't you—"

Jason snatched the keys. "We're leaving."

Jason's father—who, truth be told, barely even felt like a relative anymore—exploded into him. Both men were human Goliaths who cast long shadows and took up inordinate space. The collision caused the bedroom door to bow outward. A crack un-seamed its middle and shed a few splinters.

Trent's voice was an inhuman howl: "YOU LITTLE SHIT TALK BACK TO ME MOTHERFUCKER YOU'RE NOTHING NOBODY NOTHING NOWHERE BETTER CALL NINE-ONE-ONE!"

What happened next was pure beast-mode brutality. The fight was over before Trent even knew it. Powered by a newfound righteous anger, Jason lifted Trent over his head. For a teetering moment, he held him dumbfounded and aloft. Jason seriously contemplated hurling him into the wall, but a quiet voice stopped him.

His sister's. But not Kaitlyn's.

"He's not worth it," Mac said.

The bedroom door had swung open. The rest of his family stood there, their expressions ranging from terrified (Hiram) to darkly impressed (Kaity) to intensely concerned and empathetic (Mac). The latter, Mac, had told him the truth: Trent *wasn't* worth it. He wasn't worth anything, much less the kind of soul-rending violence Jason was ready to dole out.

So he dropped him on the bed.

Unfortunately—or fortunately, depending on your point of view—Trent's mass caused him to carom off the bed and into Corrie's old vanity, which he smashed, the vanity's mirror shattering over him in a glittering cascade. Growling, Trent shook himself clean and stood, but by then, his son had already slammed the door.

"Better call nine-one-one, asshole!" Jason slid the key in the lock and snapped it off. He ran for the front door, holding the keys aloft like a prize: "Let's get the hell outta here!"

Justin

There wasn't one dark figure but *two.* Justin and Dawn both stood, the latter stowing Webb's little saloon in her backpack while the former drew his gun. Whispering voices rolled over them:

"Where is it?"

"There, there."

"Get back!" Justin shouted as he spun around to face two people, a man and a woman who were both so comically good-looking that there was no doubt in his mind: "Wait. Are you two related to Holton?"

One of them, a guy who looked like a slightly larger version of Holt, nodded.

"Yeah. Davey and Nance Webb. Aren't you Sheriff Johnson? Is everything okay?"

Justin started to conjure a white lie about why they were there but stopped. Nance, who looked like a female version of Holt, athletic with a kind face, was holding a bouquet of flowers and a few Polaroids. Standing in their Sneakaround bubble, they looked drained of color and dimension, as if someone had printed photographs of them on cellophane.

Justin deactivated his costume's weapons and motioned to Dawn, whispering: "Can I see the cottages?"

She nodded and produced them. The two siblings reacted, rearing back slightly, their eyes glazing over with the sheen of happy memories. Davey silently asked for them. Justin handed over the coal mine, which Davey held like the family heirloom it was.

"Aw, he always liked mine," he said. "I was kinda the black sheep, so I always got the strange ones: bars, saloons—sometimes a coal mine." He held up the tchotchke with a smile.

Nance leaned over slightly and pointed. "But what about the mans—the saloon?"

Something whistled across the soundscape. Nance had misspoken, and the first syllable she'd pronounced was unmistakably *mansch,* or the beginning of *mansion.*

Mystery Mansion, Justin thought, realizing that Davey's saloon bore a passing resemblance to the Order's secret citadel. Instinctively, he touched Dawn's arm, slowly drawing her back a step. Outside, Skelton's storm flashed and stained the dome of their Sneakaround bubble with a splotch of red that suddenly spat forth a pair of red tendrils that looped around the Webb siblings hundreds and hundreds of times, mummifying them and smashing them together into a gory, dripping mass. Justin reactivated his weaponry.

"It's him, it's him!"

The red mummy-mass quickly assumed a familiar shape, that of a man wearing flannel and overalls with a permanent devilish sneer slashing across his face, but instead of ectoplasmic icing, he had been sculpted from gore and viscera. Shards of bone and bits of brain and organ meat peppered his form, which seethed and pulsed with his racing heartbeat. As before, his limbs and head floated apart from his torso. He brandished the tiny coal mine in triumph.

"You're coming to the end of a dead end, my beleaguered brethren. Every bit counts. And now you're short." Dawn and Justin lunged forward, but he vanished in a splattery flash of bloody red light. Justin landed on his knees and slid to a stop, pounding the floor.

"Goddammit!" he yelled, jumping up. "We gotta get that coal mine back!"

Dawn was already running over to the shrine, where she grabbed another cottage at random, a haberdashery.

"We don't got time, come on!" she said, sprinting outside and back through their gate. Justin followed, both of them returning to their normal forms. Dawn threw open the door of his Bronco, adding: "The Order only said we needed the saloon, and we got that one. Besides, we don't even know what these thangs're for yet. Let's go!"

Hiram's Journal

The Suttons had all been interred in Gatlinburg Memorial Gardens, which sat down and off the main highway on an array of woodsy terraces. The cemetery's quaint and homely atmosphere stood in contrast to most of the

Suttons' public lives, which came across as chintzy and *nouveau riche.*

All of us shuffled down the slope, flashlights slashing and bobbing, Trent's keys jangling on Jason's belt loop, until we reached a small wrought-iron gate that stood open. A burned-wood sign stood to the side: *GATLINBURG GARDENS.*

Jason had been babbling most of the ride over: "Guys, I'm sorry you had to see that. I will never do something like that again. I swear."

"It's okay," I said as we jogged down a small set of scattered-stone stairs. Another terrace stretched out before us, about a hundred feet across, and gave view to the valley. Mist rolled by in dreamy strands of gray. Jason dropped back next to me:

"Hiram, buddy, it's *not* okay. I don't want you growing up thinking you should punch your way through every problem."

Kaitlyn pointed. "Hey, it's over here. Gawd, it's ugly." She ran over to elbow her brother. "He's lucky you *didn't* punch him. I *wanted* you to fuckin' body slam his ass. You missed your chance."

A miniature duplicate of the Parthenon emerged from the mist. We all gathered around the mausoleum, which was gilded with multi-colored faux marble: pink, green, and powder blue. The cemetery may have been humble, but this would've looked more at home in Las Vegas.

Jason shook his head. "He was drunk. I could've really hurt him."

Kaitlyn crossed her arms. "For all the times he's hurt us?"

"I thought about pushing him in."

Mac had spoken, her voice barely a whisper. Jason, who had found the key, slowly turned.

"Pushed him into what?"

"The moat around Enchanted Caverns. That night. When Officer Webb was wrestling with him." She paused. "Auntie Hanna saw me thinking about it. I've never felt so ashamed. I can't believe what he's done to us. We're not like him. We never will be."

My walkie-talkie squawked: "Sneakaround Gang, Sneakaround Gang! This is Justin Johnson, come in, come in!"

I grabbed it and said: "This is Hiram, go ahead."

"We blew it. We needed to get two of Holton's cottages, but Skelton got one, one we needed."

Dawn's voice floated over the walkie: "We don't *know* that!"

Justin relented a bit: "Okay, okay, we don't. But guys, he's out there, he's following us, and he strong. Goddamn if killing him wasn't his greatest wish. He doesn't even need our maps to beat us. Be ready for anything."

A car engine roared on the other side of the walkie. Doors slammed, followed by the voices of Auntie Hanna and Lee: "We got it! We got it!"

I smiled: "They got the train?"

"Yeah," Justin said. "Get over here with the ashes as soon as you can."

They clicked off. Jason faced the mausoleum. "Let's build this bubble."

Mackenzie

The keystone was simply her name: *Mom.* They all passed inside, transforming into their animated selves. The boomerang-bow had transformed Mac into the version of Terpsichore she'd sculpted—and got a C-minus on—in school: she wore an armored halter and skirt, a golden headband like Wonder Woman, and a pair of leg-warmers.

"I love it, Jase," she said.

He nodded, smiling, while his lasers sketched out an array of luminescent orange weaponry. Kaitlyn pounded the scepter to activate it.

"We'll keep watch," she said.

Inside was about seven to eight square feet of more gaudy marble. The name SUTTON covered one wall, the U rendered as a Roman V for some reason, while five rows of crypts covered the other wall. Some were steel drawers, while others were glass cabinets. Their bubble had drained the scene of color, leaving behind a jittery, black-and-white sketch.

"Mom," Mac whispered when she spotted a glass cabinet marked *Corrie Blackledge Gresham Sutton.* Trent's words from less than an hour ago echoed in her mind:

They barely even fucking knew her. She said as much.

True to form, their mom had requested a steel box, the same you'd use to count cash at a concert. Jason lowered his weaponry for a moment so he could approach the case, but when he tried to unlock it, the key froze in place just outside the keyhole, shaking in the air. He propped his other hand over it and pushed, only to summon a deep *thrummm* from within the crypt. His hands flew back, throwing him to the ground as the key shot across the space and lodged in the wall. Jason pushed himself to his knees, comically shaking his head.

"They weren't kidding about that ward," he said, standing to retrieve the key. He handed it to Mac. "I've got the feeling only one of you can do this."

He offered the key to both her and Hiram. He nodded to her: *you should do it.*

Mac reached out, thinking, *Did we know her? She hid so much from us. We didn't know she was in love with someone else. We didn't know she became a sorcerer.*

But Mac knew Trent's words were some of the same foul lies he always told. He liked to claim his territory and trample all over your boundaries. If you tried to resist, he gaslit you—or he simply hit you.

He's a monster. He didn't know her.

She held the key up, half expecting the lock to repel it, but instead, gold light shone from the keyhole, lighting everyone's slack-jawed faces with a dreamy underglow. The lock seemed to leak more light into the glass. Sparkling threadlines etched out a labyrinthine, runic glyph around the lock, which pulled the key into itself and turned. Jason and Kaitlyn stood behind Mac and Hiram, watching the door, weapons ready.

"Okay, sister," Kaitlyn said. "Grab it and let's go before *le grande merde*-head shows his ugly face."

Mac opened the crypt's door and picked up the box. What was hidden underneath reaffirmed to Mac that her step-father was full of shit.

"Look," she said, picking up another small plastic record-disk, this one yellow. "The last disk."

Their mother may have been distant and difficult, unkind and opaque at times, but she had, under cover of darkness, conspired with a team of heroes to save the world, and she had made every effort to let her kids know she loved them with the emotional tools and vocabulary she had.

In short, she did her level best.

They stepped outside on full alert, remaining in their bubble for now so they could fight back if Skelton appeared.

But he didn't.

Jason cursed. "Where the hell *is* he?"

Kaitlyn waved them toward the Beamer. "Who cares? Let's count our blessings and haul some ass!"

Hiram's Journal

We all drove over in a state of tense expectation, or in less polite language, in a state of perpetual *clench*. Every stoplight, every turn, every building, every corner held a potential trap or twist we couldn't see. Skelton had struck twice, scoring one win against us. Would it be enough to stop us? Would we *have* enough to stop him? The Great Red Eye of the Smokies had doubled in size over the last hour. More lightning rained down on the Mystery Mansion. Would we make it in time?

We had no choice but to keep moving forward with the plan. Once we arrived, all of us sat or kneeled in the sloping parking lot before Enchanted Caverns. I held open the danavreece while Mac played the final disk. All of us hoped to hear Sue Johnson one more time, but an unfamiliar voice spoke:

"Listen closely, champions."

Justin brightened. "That's Ms. Glenn! Myra Glenn. She's Jamie Scott's mom."

Jamie Scott Glenn. One of his victims. This is his mom.

"You know her," I said, thinking back to his words to Skelton in March. "You know a lot of the victims' parents."

Justin nodded. "As many as I can. Keep playing the disk."

Thunder rumbled as Ms. Glenn continued: "Skelton is our mirror, and the Lodges the pathway between our realms, one good, one evil. The Lodges are the midnight-twilight between them both, and at each end stands a citadel. By the time you hear this, you'll have already seen his."

Jason hooked his thumb at Enchanted Caverns: "That . . . place he built around it. That evil factory."

Ms. Glenn continued: "The passageway to his victims can only be accessed by constructing your own citadel, one of good that resides at the far end of the Lodges, deep within their spectral realm."

Kaitlyn winced. "Oh, shit. We have to go back in there?"

Lee shrugged. "Mother said we would have to venture back into the Sneakaround proper before the night was out, didn't she?"

Justin shushed them.

Ms. Glenn: "Although the Faceless One is like to a chaos having overgrown the Lodges, you must summon your greatest courage for one final mission: to cleave him in twain. From citadel to citadel must you thunder, astride a conveyance of your own making."

Pause. "Your journey must begin at Skelton's citadel, the Citadel of Evil, and it must end at your citadel, the citadel of kindness and courage, bravery and benevolence. You must draw your finest maps to create the citadel, for upon its threshold, between the icons of myth, will you fight your final battle against the Faceless One. It is there where you will deploy your weapon against him . . . and Skelton."

Pause: "You must inter our initiate's ashes in the Lodge-within-Lodges. Only then will both Skelton and the Faceless One be sealed away for all time, and only then will you finally reveal the location of his victims."

"Itza Linda," I said. "We'll finally see where it is."

The disk ended. Kaitlyn threw up her hands.

"That's it? We're just supposed to *know,* supposed to *intuit* what to do with the train engine and—What is it? Holton's little cottage things? Why do all these magic rituals have to be like fucking advanced calculus? If the stakes are so high, why not just *tell us exactly what we're supposed to do?!*"

Her panic level was rising. Jason hugged her.

Mac stood. "I think I know what we need to do."

She produced several sheets of something from her backpack: plasticine. I had always imagined clay coming in jars or cylinders, like Play-Doh, but Mac's plasticine came in sheets. They were little tubes, each the length and thickness of a pipe-cleaner, all of them arranged in squares the size of a piece of college-ruled paper.

"Everyone, lay out your maps."

We did. Lee's eyes twinkled.

"I think I see where you're headed, Grid-Runner."

Mac nodded. "Who has Officer Webb's little saloon?" Dawn produced it. Mac stacked everyone's maps, taking care to align all of West Chim and Gatlinburg's major landmarks. At one end stood Enchanted Caverns, while the Gold Rush park and the Mystery Mansion stood on the other. Mac peered into the saloon's little windows and muttered, "I think I can see the Space Within Space in there."

She sculpted a small mountain of plasticine and set it on the mansion's footprint. This small mountain served as the pedestal for Officer Webb's little saloon, which reminded me in passing of the Mystery Mansion.

Jason chuckled kindly. "Of course that's what it's for. It looks great."

Justin chucked my shoulder. "What did your momma say on her disk? About sacred spaces?"

"There are sacred spaces everywhere," I said. "I bet that little cottage soaked up a lot of magical power over the years."

Dawn nodded. "It did. Holton's mama made all of these little cottages for her kids over the years. They got one every Christmas."

"Wow," Justin said. "I'm not trying to get cocky, but if we have *this* kind of magic on our side, it's gonna be an early night."

As if in response, hope surged through all of us. The rules governing the powers we'd discovered were still baffling to most of us, but they seemed in some cases to be a product and function of love and meaning, in others a certain proximity to trauma, but in all cases they emanated from personal strength. Looking back, I feel anger at how terribly the magic failed so many of us, but I'm also reminded of my mom's words as she spoke for the ETSOSD: *There are powers and forces beyond our understanding, but . . . but they're not perfect. That's . . . why the Order exists.*

Lee seemed to read my mind: "A quote from *Star Trek* springs to mind for me to the effect that evil will win unless good is very, very careful."

Justin nodded. "Right, Lee. Good point. So what's next?"

Dawn: "Mama said we had to draw our 'finest maps' to construct our citadel, the *good* citadel."

"What does that mean?" Kaitlyn asked. "Do we need to draw brand-new maps?"

Justin shook his head. "No, but we do need to be careful. Skelton transformed Enchanted Caverns into his own evil funhouse. We need to create our own funhouse on top of the Mystery Mansion." We all gave him a confused look. He continued: "When you were a kid, did you ever draw your dream house?"

Auntie Hanna smiled. "I haven't thought of that in years. Yes, indeedy, we did. When I was a little girl, I adored Nancy Drew, so naturally it was very important for my dream house to have several secret passages."

I was already drawing: "That's perfect. Let's add some secret passages. Lessee . . . how about from the old gondola house up to the roof?"

Mac was shaking her head, an inscrutable look on her face.

I asked: "What is it?"

"I'm not sure if I dreamed about this, or if I'm having déjà vu."

Kaitlyn: "With our luck, sister, probably both."

Mac nodded. "I bet you're right. How about a zip line?"

"Down to Statuary Row," I said. "Wasn't that what the prophecy said? 'Between the icons of myth'? There's a train track that goes right through Statuary Row and *right between* the statues of Narcissus and Echo."

Justin nodded. "Might be useful in case we need to get down there in a hurry."

By this point, we'd slid our maps back out to work on them. Kaitlyn had taken up a colored pencil.

"This place is gonna need a bitchin' sound system. Okay if I add gigantic speakers on every floor?"

"Good call," Jason said.

"Mind if I add a chapel?"

Justin had spoken. All of us smiled and nodded.

"Of course," Mac said. "That's a great idea."

"Just a small one, y'know. I'm not even that religious, but . . . it'd be nice to have a place to go. I always liked that room with the barrel. I'll slip it in there."

Jason started to talk but hesitated. Lee nodded.

"What is it, Occultsmith?"

"Dunno if you all knew this, but the Matterhorn at Disneyland has a secret basketball court."

I whooped: "Seriously? Cool! We've gotta add that!"

"That's okay?" Jason said, barely audible. I thought of his words in Globe of

Gaming, about trying to "see the Grid a better."

I tried to match his energy: "Yeah, it's okay. It sounds like fun."

"Thanks."

"Observatory," Dawn said, muttering to herself. "I saw an observatory, one with the telescope pulled inside." Off our semi-confused looks, she added: "Our visions? Ain't we all had 'em? I think the Grid was tellin' us what to include in our dream house."

Lee nodded. "We should add your observatory to the mansion's roof. Greater elevation makes for a better view of the stars. I had a vision of a strange little house armed with a pair of spectral-plasma cannons. I'll add it to the roof, as well." He gave a mischievous smile. "As well as a video arcade inside."

Mac prodded him. "You better let girls in your arcade. Kaity and I play just as many games as you dorks."

"Of course, Grid-Runner."

"I'll add my library inside. I had a vision of it by the chain-link web, near the princess's castle, where we saw—"

She stopped and looked at Dawn, whose eyes glazed over.

"It's all right," she said before indicating Enchanted Caverns on her map. "Now I guess we put the other cottage here to represent the evil citadel?"

Justin winced. "That's the one we lost. There was a little coal mine that was a dead ringer for this place." He nodded at Enchanted Caverns. Dawn produced the replacement cottage, the haberdashery, and set it on the attraction's location.

"It'll be enough," she said. "What's next?"

Multiple lightning-bolts licked across the sky in a blinding blossom. The thunder that followed didn't rumble so much as *bellow* at us.

Lee: "It occurs to me that we need to agree on a path between here and the Mystery Mansion."

It hit me instantly. "The danavreece." I grabbed it and flipped it open to the page I'd seen earlier, the one with Mom's map. It was blank, but I used the magic ink to bring her map back into view. I held it open for all to see. "This is it. *This* is our path between the citadels."

Kaitlyn shook her head. "Way to go, squirt." She checked the map. "Yeah, this has gotta be right. Look, ladies, it goes right through the mall. Remember the vision we all had, when we were trying to find Skelton's address?"

Auntie Hanna tilted her head. "What vision?"

Dawn: "We all . . . Well, it's hard to describe. We *felt* a train go by in the mall."

Mac nodded. "It reminded us of the night of Soddy Farm. We could hear

Hiram and Lee over in Dizzy Pines."

"Fascinating," Lee said. "Very well. Our course must pass through Misbegotten Avenue. We should get to work."

All of us added the mall and a set of train tracks between the two citadels. Mac used plasticine to add some topographical details—hills and mountains—while Lee sculpted Dawn's observatory and his strange little house and added them to Holton's Christmas saloon. Once finished, we exchanged looks.

Justin's jaw flexed. "All that's left is a gate. It's bad in there, guys. The Plaid Man's face was everywhere, and the whole countryside was swarming with monsters. Plus, there's Skelton. He could be anywhere. That's what we're up against."

Hanna: "We saw one of the bastards over in the mansion. It tried to take the pouch from me. Watch yourselves. They try to get in your head."

Kaitlyn raised her hand. "Soooooo . . . who wants to open the gateway to a realm of unspeakable evil populated by bizarre cosmic leviathans—*not it!*" Silence. "Tough crowd!"

I smirked. "We *all* have to add the gate to our maps, Kaity."

"I know. I'm just trying to lighten the mood. Let's do it."

Justin leaned in. "Anybody mind if I draw it first?"

None of us minded. Justin drew a small archway, but instead of adding *one* detail that was his own, he added several—he drew all of us as cartoons.

"Oh, those are so cool," Kaitlyn said.

Jason: "Wow. Really good."

"Expertly done, Captain."

"Likenesses are so hard," Mac said. "You've really got 'em down."

I was already working on my gate. "Justin, would you mind if I drew you?"

"No," he said, his voice swelling. "That's really nice of you, man."

Mac: "I want to add Justin, too."

Dawn: "So do I."

Everyone did. Some of our drawings were good, others not so good, but they were all drawn with love. Suddenly: *Vum-vum-vummm!* Nearby, a rectangle of fire burst from the pavement. A gate rose from it, as if lifted on an elevator. We approached it, noting everyone's little portraits, but this gate had some details we *didn't* expect.

"Hey," Kaitlyn said. "I didn't draw this."

Sketched around the gate's arch were an assortment of good memories from the past year. Kaitlyn and Dawn laughing at the Soddy Farm party. Jason hugging everyone back at the hospital. Kaitlyn standing up for Mac against Kimber Huntmichael. All of us telling Lee he was cool. Me and Lee leaping over the fence in the lair of Not Justin Johnson.

The real Justin approved. "Wow, you guys look like action stars."

We all paused a moment and shared a few laughs and anecdotes. Jason stood by, waiting to finish this, our final Smoky Mountain, by sketching it onto a sheet of glassine.

"Are you guys ready?" he asked.

We nodded, steeling ourselves.

Jason sketched the boundaries of our Smoky Mountain, and the gate came alive.

Jason

Blinding white light filled this new gate. Jason stared at it, sweat breaking from the small of his back. Once they entered, he knew was going to have to craft their locomotive.

And he didn't know if he could do it, even with the raw materials provided by the Order.

Mac led the way. "Only one way to go: in."

Jason carried their newly-crafted three-dimensional super-map and followed them into the gate. Electricity wiped through everyone, transforming them into their cartoon selves. They emerged into the same dark inversion of the Smokies they'd glimpsed during Justin's "Fearless Freep" dive: the sky was a harsh white haze, the sun a swimming inkblot, the clouds splotches of watercolor smeared across an uneven canvas. Like their other Smoky Mountains, this one floated in an endless void, but the central pathway was much larger. Previously, the pathways were about five to six feet across; now it was a full mile wide, but nevertheless, in the distance, the world dropped off into pure, blinding whiteness. The landscape seethed with activity and was a-murmur with distant threats. The sky was a sickening soup of the Plaid Man's face. Creatures of non-Euclidean origin and composition lurked and gamboled through the unholy countryside, their fangs and claws and shanks slithering into view like so many razor-sharp dorsal fins. And to top it all off, the Plaid Man's voice chanted on, forevermore:

"Dead dead already dead dead already dead dead already dead dead already dead."

But the worst was what awaited them in the park.

A twenty-foot-tall Lenny Skelton floated above the Gold Rush, their citadel, chanting a terrible litany that stung their ears. The park's whimsical skyline had been supplanted with inky-black spires and ramparts. In the middle of it shone their citadel, the Mystery Mansion—which, even from that distance, they could see was adorned with their magical additions.

"Look, there's my observatory!" Dawn said.

Lee: "And my cottage!"

But as if he sensed their entrance into his domain, the giant Skelton raised a flat palm and chopped downward, pulling from the heavens a torrent of pure black energy that slammed into their citadel. Out in the real world, outside the Anti-Sneakaround, red lightning flashed through the stark white sky like a splash of blood thrown against a dome of thin pearl. Skelton brought his hand down again and hurled more dark energy into the mansion. In tandem, red lightning flashed out beyond the Anti-Sneakaround.

Kaitlyn shoulder-bumped Justin. "Well, this definitely lives up to the hype. I am positively incandescent with fear."

The entrance gate stood behind them, their Smoky Mountain's boundary extending far behind Enchanted Caverns, which now looked like a graphite sketch of itself. Every few seconds, one of Skelton's victims bloomed from the roofline in startlingly vivid color and sounded a direful note. Dawn's jawline trembled.

"Those sweet baby angels."

Mac crossed over and hooked an arm around her.

"C'mon, bestie-bestie. Got a long night ahead of us."

Lee noted Mac's Terpsichore-by-way-of-Wonder-Woman look and said: "I like your new attire, Grid-Runner."

But that wasn't all that had changed: their *maps* had transformed, too. Light burst from between their pages as they merged together and morphed into a kind of magic crystal, its edges ragged, like that of a tree. The details of their maps glimmered like fiber optics. Everyone looked on in awe.

Kaitlyn: "How're we supposed to carry that thing?"

"I think we'll find out in time," Jason said, turning to Hanna. "You've got the magic pouch, right?"

"Yessir, I do," she said, producing it. "Y'all better stand back."

Using both hands, she released the Flambonium Airscoop, which leaped from the pouch in miniature form before flash-expanding to its regular size with an audible *zhoomp!* Their faces fell slightly upon seeing it.

"It's black and white," Dawn said. "Like everything else here."

Mac shook her head. "It's not his land. Not for long."

Jason's heart thudded against his sternum. *I wish I had her confidence.*

Kaitlyn prodded Jason and said: "So how's this work, shit-for-brains?"

Something howled in the distance. Everyone looked, their complexions pale.

"It's been different for every treasure. I've usually . . . thought about something. Something powerful." His voice grew quiet. "Something sad."

Kaitlyn's brow furrowed. "Sad? Like what?"

"When I made your Havoc Staff, I started with plasticine." His eyes welled up. "Man, that was a bad fucking day."

Justin walked over and put a hand on his shoulder. "What happened?"

"Dad . . . hit Kaity. The first time."

Kaitlyn: "I remember that day. I think it's one of the first things I DO remember."

"Trent flew off the handle for some fucking reason, coulda been anything, and Kaity tells him to shut his fat face. And he hit her. Over by the utility closet. In the kitchen?"

"In the old house, yeah. I banged my head on the door so hard it fell open. The ironing board slipped out. It's how I got this." She indicated her scar.

"Right," Jason said. "I'd already drawn my first few maps. I snuck out to the woods sometimes. But that night, I took out my plasticine and . . . made a weapon. I had this image in my head, that I'd walk down the hallway to his room, and it would transform into a sword, or a lightsaber, something. And then I'd smash the shit out of him. I never did."

Justin: "Good. He's not worth it."

Mac nodded. "Damn right."

Jason's voice thickened: "I'm sorry I didn't stick up for you that night. I wanted to. I remember feeling so furious . . . but I was so terrified. It felt like I was bolted to my seat; I couldn't move. He was so much bigger than us."

"Uh I know the feeling," Hiram said quietly.

Jason nodded and continued: "That night, when I went into the Sneakaround Network, I brought the staff . . . and it transformed into the Scepter of Chaos. It didn't have any powers at first, but the more I brought it to the Sneakaround, the more powerful it got."

Dawn propped her arms akimbo. "This is bullshit."

"What do you mean?"

"That don't make no sense. Inside our Smoky Mountains, we're *superheroes.* Everything we've made together—Castle GrayCrystal, the magic gates, the maps—has been . . . I dunno. Filled with love."

Lee intoned: "And honor and courage."

"Yeah. If the idea is Kaity's gotta relive some bullshit trauma, then I don't want no part of this. I don't care how high the stakes are." Suddenly, a train whistle sounded. The flambonium device had sprouted one from its hull. Dawn hooked a thumb at it. "Did I do that?"

Jason nodded. "I think so. Hey—do you all know those quotes that go at the beginning of books?"

Lee raised a finger. "The epigraph."

"Right, thanks, Cleric. The epigraph. There's one I'll never forget: it's at the front of that big Stephen King book that came out a couple years ago, the one about the evil clown? He dedicated it to his kids. (King did, not the clown.) King said: *the magic exists.*" He rubbed his brow, deep in thought. "I think everything we've done, everything we've gone through, everything we've learned, has prepared us for tonight. It's all been a part of the magic. Even the bad stuff."

Kaitlyn whispered: "It's all a part of the art."

THOOOM! Skelton hurled another wave of dark energy into the mansion, his action underscored by a flash of red lightning in the real world. Jason's jaw flexed.

"We better hurry."

Hiram: "I used to think bad stuff happened to me because I was a bad person. Because I deserved it."

Mac hooked an arm around him. "I still cry sometimes that I didn't get to tell Mom I loved her before she died."

Hanna sighed. "Oh, Mackenzie. She knew. She was just a hard woman to know. As long as we're sharing, I'll say that the other girls used to make fun of me something fierce back in the day. Told me I was ugly, that I looked like a man."

Mac looked outraged: "Auntie, you're *gorgeous.*"

"Seriously," Kaitlyn said with a nod. "Fuck those bitches. And there's nothing wrong with looking like a man, or a woman, or however you want to look."

"I know," Hanna said. "But I used to think the man upstairs had it out for me."

Jason: "Me too. I used to think God gave the other kids dads who were nice because they were good and I wasn't."

Kaitlyn hugged him. "When girls called me names, I thought they were right. I figured I deserved it."

Lee stroked his chin. "Sometimes I say things, and people laugh . . . and I don't understand why. I surmised that I was simply deficient."

Dawn's reaction was instant and furious: "Who laughed at you?"

Lee shrugged. "It doesn't matter."

She shook a fist. "I'll sock 'em one."

"Please don't sock anyone anything."

"Okay, fella," Dawn said before taking a breath: "I used to weigh myself every morning, and if I weighed more than a hundred-twenty, I wouldn't let myself listen to music I liked. I wouldn't look in the mirror. I used to write all kinds of mean stuff in my notebook about myself."

Lee hugged her. "That makes my heart hurt so much to hear."

Justin stepped forward. "Do I need to share something?"

Hanna shook her head. "Not if you don't want to."

"Okay," he said, nodding. "I just want to say: I'm really glad I know you all. Thanks for having my back, and thanks for reaching out to me the way you did."

They all hugged, and: *TOOT, TOOOOOOT!* The flambonium device's whistle blew. It changed shape before their eyes, its hull bristling with brass pipes and servos and switches. The device's steel casing melted into a dark black iron. A headlight sprang out of its front, while a crimson cow-catcher sculpted itself into being across its prow. Various steam readouts and dials peppered the train, while orange neon wrote in cursive across the side: *THE ITZA LINDA EXPRESS.*

They all approached it in reverent silence, admiring its every feature. Under its wheels, train tracks sank into the earth amid bubbling black blood. Jason held back tears, thanking the powers that be for the help in summoning this magical conveyance into being.

I could never have done this on my own.

His thoughts were interrupted by a soul-rending roar. About a mile down the track, the earth heaved upward like a chest rising to take a deep breath. In tandem, tentacles and grotesque, spore-spewing orifices sprouted from the forest, all of them flesh-like, and all of them covered in a now-familiar criss-cross plaid pattern. Hanna, clad in her futuristic armor, ripped open the train's door.

"GET ON BOARD, EVERYONE!"

They all scrambled aboard, but Lee lingered in gog-eyed thrall. Hiram grabbed his shoulder.

"Come on, Cleric!"

"The Sororal Order was right. We have, in the guise of this Smoky Mountain, summoned the Plaid Man *in corpus.*"

"I don't know what 'in corpus' means!"

Hiram pushed Lee up into his sister's arms.

Dawn yelled: "It's Latin for 'in body'! He means this whole place *is* the Plaid Man!"

Once they had all clambered aboard, Jason pointed forward.

"Hit it!"

"Hit *what?*" Kaitlyn said. "We've never piloted a magic train before!"

In the distance, dozens of monstrous stalks capped with millions of gogging eyes leered above the tree line. Hanna pointed at a slot in the engine marked *MAP.* "Maybe this is it?" Jason slammed their magic crystal super-map into the slot, and the train launched forward. They all whooped and hollered in glory.

Hiram's Journal

Our magic locomotive thundered across the spectral countryside, its passage accompanied by the spontaneous generation of more tracks that sliced through the Plaid Man's *corpus.* We trailed a wake of his sludge-like, black blood, the cow-catcher shunting aside monsters left and right. The inkblot anti-sun seethed angrily overhead in protest of the pain; howls of unholy anguish sounded all around us, but still Skelton maintained his assault on the Mystery Mansion. Kaitlyn pounded the Scepter of Chaos to activate it, her mohawk shimmying in the blazing-hot wind, while Jason activated an array of luminescent orange weapons. Wearing my Necron 99 look, I watched the terrain stream by in silence. Thunder rumbled across the landscape. Mac sidled up next to me.

"Is everything okay?"

"Oh. Yeah. I mean, no, I'm terrified, but yeah, everything's okay. It's just . . . I love Mom, right?"

"Of course you do."

"And I miss her, but . . . I barely knew her."

Hanna, looking super badass in her Man-At-Arms getup, eavesdropped. "You talking about Corrie?"

I nodded. "Yeah. I . . . I guess—uh I can't say this, it's awful."

"Go ahead," Hanna said. "You're safe."

"I wish I missed her more. That's awful, isn't it?"

Jason shook his head. "Nah, I get it."

"It's like, Justin, I'm so jealous of you."

"Me? Why?"

"You and your mom were so close. You could tell just by listening to the magic disks. I could tell when we spoke through the radio the first time. You really miss her. I feel like my parents were both strangers to me."

Justin nodded. "I hear you. Hey, I want you to know: relationships with your folks are tough, even if you like 'em. Did you notice I never mention my dad?"

I searched my memory banks. "Oh! I guess I hadn't. I'm sorry. I bet he was really cool."

Justin shrugged. "He was . . . fine. He never did anything wrong. Came to all my games, and when I started doing plays, he came to all of those. Said all the right things. Worked his ass off. I could see why my mom loved him, but . . . I never could figure him out. He . . . he was from a different time and had a different way of expressing himself. I knew he loved me, but I didn't always feel it in my bones the way I did with Momma. Families are tough."

We all grabbed hold of the railings as the train rounded a corner and momentarily rose onto one set of wheels before slamming back into the earth with a *splortch*. Black blood misted all around us. We crested a rise and brought the Blue Ridge Supermall into view. It resembled a stack of gigantic black bricks, its outline shaky and surrounded by dancing black sketch marks.

Kaitlyn cocked an eyebrow. "Yeah, families *are* tough. Our first mom, y'know, Marie, felt like she came from a different family sometimes."

"Yeah," Jason said. "Like we had this guest star in our house who also apparently shared a bunch of DNA with us."

Dawn prodded Hiram and said: "And I want you to know you're not alone. We didn't know our daddy that well, and heck, our mama was a sorceress all this time, right under our nose."

"Yeah," I said, gloomier than I meant to. The sky seemed to sense my mood. A bank of slimy clouds broke across the inky sun, casting the landscape in a sudden pall. Our locomotive's engine misfired, the sound like a rifle blast. We all started. Justin checked the fire but stopped, shaking his head.

"Don't even know what I'm checking," he mumbled.

Auntie Hanna gave me a squeeze. "I said this before, but: Corrie had . . . problems. She was a sweet woman with a big heart, and she tried her best, but . . . I don't think her life turned out the way she hoped it would. Deacon really swept her off her feet back in the day, which was lovely for her, but she never quite found her footing again. She loved teaching, but she always wanted a second act in life. After Deacon died, I think she had to make some tough choices to keep y'all afloat." She looked at Jason and Kaitlyn. "Jason, Kaity, I don't want to be too hard on your pop."

"It's okay. You *should* be too hard on the stupid asshole. Are you saying Corrie might've married Trent just for his money?"

"She hinted at it."

Jason touched his temple. "God. That makes me feel awful. Hiram, Mac, I'm so sorry you got trapped in our shitty family."

Mac shrugged. "I feel awful that we're the reason she was never happy."

Justin said with assurance: "That's not true."

Auntie Hanna shook her head. "No, it's not. No one made her do it. She made her own choices, and she could've made different ones anytime. I even tried to stop her from marrying that prick. Sometimes grown-ups make choices, and they're for reasons you can't possibly comprehend, based on events buried deep in their past. Sometimes we don't even know why we do certain things."

BANG! The train misfired again, slowing enough for all of us to lean forward slightly.

Justin smiled wryly. "And sometimes it's because they've joined an ancient magical order whose mission is to destroy the oldest evil in the universe." Everyone smiled in response, but Justin's mood darkened slightly. "Hey, I'm sorry I checked out earlier this year."

Kaitlyn shook her head. "Ohmigod, I *so* don't blame you."

Mac: "Yeah, you needed to take care of you."

The train's engine grew quieter as we slowed down. The mall was barely half a mile ahead.

Justin: "Thanks. I really thought Skelton was gone."

"We all did," Dawn said, her tone distracted as she checked over the side. "Is there somethin' wrong with this thing?" The train slowed more and more until we were barely crawling. Everyone ran to the sides to check, looking back in varying states of alarm.

Jason hooked a thumb over the side and said: "The tracks are sinking back into the ground."

Kaitlyn nodded and jumped up into the window frame. "You're right, shit-for-brains. Something's wrong."

Justin checked our magic maps. "Did we mess up the maps somehow?"

I don't know what it looked like when Mount Vesuvius erupted, but I bet it looked something like what happened behind us. Miles to our rear, Enchanted Caverns exploded, but not like a bomb—it exploded in *size*. It doubled, tripled, quadrupled, *quintupled* in size, growing larger and larger, its roof smashing into the "top" of the Anti-Sneakaround, but still it grew bigger and bigger, filling the imaginary space and smashing itself to bits. In Enchanted Caverns' place stood a gigantic, thousand-foot-high new iteration of Skelton's factory of nightmares, its roof adorned with the heads of his victims, all of whom vomited forth fountains of fire that arced down onto our train tracks and set them aflame. Twin streaks of fire raced across the dark countryside toward us as we slowed more and more.

"Oh my God," Dawn said, her voice flat from horror. "We needed that other cottage. Without it—"

The fire reached us just as we passed into the Blue Ridge Supermall, heaving us up and off the tracks. Our beautiful locomotive's cow-catcher plowed into the earth as we crashed into the dark, spectral inversion of Misbegotten Avenue and ground to a halt, our train's orange neon sign going dark. Ahead, the walls exploded outward, revealing the truth, revealing Skelton's gigantic avatar, which continued its attack on our citadel, wave after dark wave.

And now, we had no way to stop him.

We had failed.

Justin

The mall had become a dank dungeon in the Anti-Sneakaround, its walls covered with black wood paneling and dotted with the occasional wooden torch that burned with spheres of ghostly white light. The mall's stores had made the transfer to the Anti-Sneakaround, but instead of English, their signs had been replaced with unusual glyphs of illegible gibberish. Shelves and shelves lined their interiors, all of them packed with various otherworldly *objets d'art* that made no sense; nonsensical geometric shapes that had no business in three-dimensional space. Looking at them struck you dizzy with migraines.

Justin Johnson leaped off the train. The rest of the gang followed, Mac bearing a dazed Hiram under the shoulder. They absorbed the horror and truth of the view and took stock of their situation. Kaitlyn, clad in her punk attire, summarized it best:

"We're fucked."

Hanna hadn't quite figured it out: "Can someone explain to me what the hell just happened?"

Jason sidled over, activating his weaponry and scanning the scene for threats.

"Holton's other cottage was supposed to stand in for Enchanted Caverns."

Justin nodded, activating his own array of armaments. "But Skelton tricked us."

Dawn: "He disguised himself as Holton's siblings and snagged it from us."

Realization dawned on Hanna's face. "Our map had a weakness."

Lee: "And Skelton was able to exploit it. His magicks still poison Enchanted Caverns, and here, in this realm, he has even more power."

Dawn, gleaming in battle-maiden glory, pulled her battle axe. "Do we gotta just *bum rush* the son of a gun?"

Jason touched her armored forearm. "Please don't."

They held each other's gaze long enough for everyone but Justin to notice; *everyone but Justin* because he was retreating under a dark haze of shame. When Holton's siblings had appeared at Enchanted Caverns earlier, his instincts had told him something was wrong. It was too convenient, too *perfect* for them both to show up right at that moment.

But he'd handed over one of the cottages anyway, because why *wouldn't* he? And now he'd doomed them all.

The rest of the gang had gathered before him, Dawn waving, Kaitlyn snapping her fingers.

"Justin? *Jussstiiiin?*"

Mac and a still-woozy Hiram staggered over so the latter could tug his sleeve.

"Justin? It's okay," the little guy said. "It's not your fault."

Their voices were drowned out by the cheers of a high school football crowd. It was Friday night, *the* Friday night all those years ago. In the distance, stadium lights shone through a sheen of falling mist. West Chim High was just wrapping up a win over Pigeon Forge Central. The evening's air was heavy with moisture and redolent of petrichor. Justin had pulled up in his squad car to find a spitting-furious crowd of parents gathering around Skelton, who had hidden under the bleachers. Justin knew he was facing a moment of truth, a test of his mettle and character.

He couldn't fail it. He *didn't* fail it.

But a mad stroke of fate gave the devil an escape. No force on earth could have predicted or stopped it. And Justin Johnson was left to shoulder blame and guilt he never deserved. Intellectually, he knew that to be so, but in a far-off heart, he still felt responsible, and every night when he prayed, he spoke each of their names in remembrance and reverence.

"It's not your fault," his friends all said.

His friends.

His *family.*

Justin returned to them, blinking away visions of the past. He activated his suit's every weapon: cannons and lasers and steel gauntlets that encased his fists. Everyone, Hiram included, gave a brave smile.

"Thank you," Justin said, and as if in response, an unearthly howl sounded from the shattered head of the hall. Everyone wheeled around. Stalking into the mall was an assemblage of geometric shapes that all floated in the vague silhouette of a ten-foot-tall wolf, its head a stack of shifting pentagons, its legs a quartet of jittering piles of hexagons and triangles and circles. A pair of floating red diamonds stood in for eyes, their centers smoldering like embers, their corners trailing plumes of rosy steam.

"It appears to be a relative of the Gmork," Lee said. "But constructed of polygons."

"A polygmork," Hiram said. They shared a look that said, *Cool name.*

They all arrayed themselves for battle, Jason sketching out a pair of orange cannons; Mac wielding her boomerang-bow, its bowstring a line of crackling fire; Kaitlyn pounding the earth to activate the Scepter of Chaos; Dawn wielding her battle axe; Hanna fumbling with her wrist cannon before switching it on with an audible *whump*; Lee standing forth with Compassion at the ready; and even Hiram, clad in his Necron 99 look, found a length of wrought-iron that he held like a quarter-staff.

Jason inched over next to Dawn.

"What do you think its weakness is, Mountain-Master?"

She shrugged. "Beats me. Better cut off its head to be sure."

"Nope!" Hiram called, looking through his sextant. "It's got a weak spot under its belly."

Jason smiled. "Just like a certain dragon." He addressed Mac: "Think you can hit it with an arrow?"

"Does Kira know how to roller-disco?"

"I'm gonna assume that means 'yes.'"

Everyone—and every*thing*—coiled to strike, when suddenly, a disk of flaming steel blades flashed out of nowhere and struck the polygmork right between the eyes. It reared onto its hind legs, howling, before it spun around and galloped away. Voices sounded from the left. The gang turned and was greeted by an astonishing sight:

Half a dozen women, all of them clad in various leather jackets, chain-mail breastplates, gauntlets, and work boots, came running out from doorways, some of them ripping off flips and back handsprings. Like the Sneakaround Gang, they were animated, but instead of cartoons, these ladies looked more like moving oil paintings. Their composition spanned generations and ethnicities. One white lady appeared to be a nonagenarian, while another was about Mac's age. Their apparent leader, a Black woman wearing a motorcycle jacket, baseball cap, goggles, and an armored kilt, stepped forward. She was armed with a bladeless sword-hilt. When she swung it, its blade illuminated like a smear of gold paint.

"*You better run!*" she screamed at the polygmork's retreating form before stowing her weapon and tipping her hat. "Begging your pardon, everyone. Name's Sheila, Sororal codename Swordmaiden. We've been expecting you."

Everyone gaped at her. Justin said, "You knew we were coming?"

Sheila nodded. "We're a part of the resistance effort. Revelation General stationed us in a Lodge a few light-years away but called us back when she got wind of Skelton's plan."

A few light-years away? Justin thought. He was about to ask a question when Hanna tipped her helmet to Sheila.

"If I'm not mistaken, Ms. Sheila, we've met before. You delivered the Order's first package to my house."

"Yes, I did, and apologies if I came off a little strange. I hadn't been earthside in a spell."

One of the resistance fighters, the ancient woman with waist-length white hair, pointed at their locomotive. Her voice sounded piped in from another century:

"Did you . . . *make* this?"

Justin propped his arms akimbo, smiling. "We sure did!" he said before feeling a stab of insecurity. "Why? Is there something wrong with it?"

The women, Sheila included, were pacing around it, slack-jawed.

"I've never seen an occultopsychic construct this size before."

"Or this *detailed*. Great gods, the love and energy that must've gone into this."

Sheila crossed to Justin, tucked her hat under her arm, and extended her hand.

"I can see why Revelation General named you Captain," she said.

Justin took her hand but also shook his head. "It was a team effort—"

Sheila's voice was a siren: *"All right, ladies! Assholes and elbows! Let's make ourselves useful before this monster turns the universe into hell!"*

The women sprang into action, some generating power constructs like Jason's, but instead of orange light, they were rendered in oil paints. They created giant levers and winches to hoist the train out of the ground.

Kaitlyn gave a small wince. "If Skelton pulls this off, is the universe really going to turn into hell?"

Sheila, who was cranking one of the levers, shrugged. "Beats the shit outta me! Any time Revelation General sends us on a mission, I just assume that's what the bad guys're after. Helps keep me focused!"

Jason stepped forward. "What can we do to help?"

As Jason and Sheila conferred, fell voices whispered to Justin on the wind. He frowned, searching his pockets until he produced his momma's photo. Meanwhile, the nonagenarian, who wore a floor-length chain-mail dress, floated over to Hiram and offered him a piece of candy.

"Everyone else has a weapon, sweetheart," she said. "Why don't you?"

The words of Justin's momma echoed in his mind: *There's going to be a fire, when all's said and done, little JJ, and I need to ask you to put it in there.* He walked around the train, stepping over one of the levers, which was being cranked by a pair of women wearing matching sets of post-apocalyptic football pads. He was semi-conscious, guided by forces beyond his reckoning, as he wandered up into the engineer's compartment.

Jason

"Everyone else has a weapon, sweetheart. Why don't you?"

Jason walked over. He could tell Hiram was stuttering, so he set a hand on his shoulder and silently asked if he could field the question. Hiram nodded, accepting the candy.

"He has a weapon," he said. "Well, he has a *treasure*. It's a sextant. Hiram, wanna show her?"

"Uh sure," the little guy said, relieved someone had helped him communicate. He handed it over, transferring the post-apocalyptic assassin look to the old woman, but rendered in oil paints. "It does all kinds of things."

The woman started to respond just as something shrieked. An amorphous black viper lashed out from one of the storefronts. With shocking speed, she snatched it out of the air and squeezed, her knuckles turning white, then red, as she briefly bared her teeth from the effort. In a splattery burst of black ooze, she crushed it in her fist and slung its remains to the floor. Everyone gawked in awe.

Jason: "Why didn't they send *you* on this mission?"

Hanna leaned over. "I had the same question. Also, nice to see some other old-timers on this detail."

The nonagenarian cocked her head at the train. "I couldn't do that. Wouldn't even know where to start."

Another woman, this one the teenager, paused her efforts to dislodge the train and stepped over. She wore cargo pants, a vintage football jersey (No. 54), and forearm gauntlets. Her blonde hair was in braided pigtail-buns like Princess Leia. Black streaks ran under her eyes, while a medieval ball-and-chain mace hung from her belt. Hiram blushed.

She said: "Revelation General sent the right people for the right jobs. Have faith in that."

"Got it," Jason said, smiling. Their interaction seemed to summon Dawn.

"Nice mace," she said. "Where'd you get it?"

"Elna helped me craft it back in the day," she said, indicating the old woman. "I'm Deena. You?"

"Dawn," she said, proffering her hand. They shook, smiling warmly.

Elna addressed Jason: "So, did you plan on doing some sightseeing?"

Jason frowned. "Huh?"

"You sent him into battle with a sextant? What, is he going to *look* at these creatures to death?" She returned the sextant to Hiram.

"Oh. I hadn't thought of it like that. I guess I wanted to make some treasures that weren't violent."

Elna and Deena shared a look that said, *That makes sense,* but still, Elna shook her head and undid her necklace. She presented it to Hiram.

"Oh, gosh," he said. "I don't want to take this, ma'am."

She pointed toward the Gold Rush, where the Skelton's ritual continued to destroy the mansion.

"You're going to need it, trust me, and I have plenty others." She returned the sextant and wrinkled her nose. "And I'd get that sextant checked out."

"Why? What's wrong with—" *SMASSSSSH!*

Every lever and winch failed, dissolving into magical mist. Sheila threw her hat to the ground.

"Dammit! We'll never get this thing out!"

Jason suddenly noticed an absence from their ranks:

Where's Justin?

Justin

It all made so much sense. Justin stood among the racket of repairs and shouts of frustration, staring at his momma's photo. In the engineer's compartment, stationed underneath their magic-crystal map, were the twin sliding panels of a coal oven. He opened them to reveal a roaring fire.

There's going to be a fire, his momma said.

His hand drifted forward, bearing the photo closer and closer to the fire. Flames licked at its corner.

Mac's voice: *"Loooooook!"*

Justin snapped out of it. Everyone spun toward either end of the passage. Two packs of polygmorks, each at least ten feet tall, crowded into either end of Misbegotten Avenue. Sheila was waving him out of the train.

"Get down, get down! We need you!"

Justin leaped out of the train, fully armed, and slid next to Sheila, who was wedged between Jason and Mac at the vanguard. Mac drew her bow and shot a flaming arrow right into a polygmork's growling maw. It yelped and fell back.

"There's no time," Mac said. "We've got to get Mom's ashes to the Mystery Mansion before it's too late."

Jason shook his head. "But what about the train?! We need to finish it, we need to finish the voyage!"

Justin took his shoulder. "You and me, we'll stay and get the train out." He addressed everyone else: "The rest of you, *get going! Run!*"

Hanna held up her hands and called: "Wait!" From her backpack, she produced a pair of walkie-talkies. *Real* ones. She handed one to Justin. "I figured we might need these."

"Good call," Justin said, pocketing the walkie.

Hiram pinned on the necklace and sparked a whirlwind of lightning that outfitted him in gleaming red armor. His usual bandolier, goggles, and epaulets appeared on top of the armor, courtesy of his sextant. The necklace transformed into a whip that appeared to be a chain length of rubies. When Hiram lashed the whip, a flaming disk of spinning blades—the same they'd seen earlier—flared from its end with a high-pitched wail.

"Cooo-oo-ol!" Hiram said. "Thanks, Elna! Oh, what's your codename? Mine's Dreamweaver."

"No codename for me, dearie. Just Elna will do."

Hiram smiled. "Okie-dokie. Nice to meetcha, Elna. You ladies sure are cool!"

Mac led the charge. "Enough of the *bon voyages*, let's *gooooooo!*"

The six of them sprinted forward, each of them attacking with their various weapons, all of them making short work of the polygmorks, which parted like a dark sea to allow their passage. Jason and Justin turned their attention to the top of the hall, where the other pack was vaulting forward. Sheila and the women of the ETSOSD ran into the fray, trailed by a screaming Justin and Jason.

Hiram's Journal

We fought our way out of the mall, running full tilt, magical weapons firing in every direction. Kaitlyn's scepter zapped beams of purple-and-orange energy, Mac fired arrow after flaming arrow, Dawn swung her axe through anything that moved, and Lee played defense, fending off blasts and slinging Compassion into the occasional unlucky spectral creature. Auntie Hanna was still struggling along, her helmet all catawampus, her wrist cannons misfiring. I ran over and helped orient her.

"Don't think about doing it, just *do it,* Auntie!"

"Don't wait up for me! Keep running!"

Skelton's ritual continued like a massive, dark thunderstorm over the Mystery Mansion, which peeked over the tree line to the west, the Wow-Zo roller coaster's tracks looping around it. I'd never run more than a quarter-mile in my life, and now we had a two-mile sprint across hostile, accursed land before us. Skelton, heretofore about twenty feet tall, had expanded to thirty or forty, his chants roaring across the landscape. Whatever he was saying wasn't meant to be heard by humans; your brain rejected it as some kind of malformed input. I swear I felt blood trickle from my ears.

A swarm of dark insects in the shape of a six-armed creature crested a rise before us, followed by five more of its kind, followed by six more, seven, eight—

Mac pointed: "They're cutting us off!"

As we neared the edge of the parking lot, a platoon of spectral midnight-creatures arrayed themselves to our left, forcing us to run up the hills to the north, heading toward Ober Gatlinburg. We ran and ran, my chest burning, my belly wobbling and bouncing as I slung my flaming razor-wheel downhill to hold off an advancing flank of unearthly horrors. Dark creatures, their faces peppered with trypophobic pockmarks, recited the Plaid Man's litany: "*Dead dead already dead dead already dead dead already dead dead already dead.*"

They were forming a *moat* around the Gold Rush.

"Up! Up! Keep going up!" Mac yelled, firing an arrow that dropped a three-headed bat from the sky. We all followed her, forming a perimeter, the ground like sand under us, our thighs churning uselessly through it as we passed into a dark forest, the air hot and dry as a sauna, all of us wheezing and sweating. Trees that resembled dripping black watercolors streamed past us as we ran and ran, taking out any monsters that crossed our path, until a dark—but welcome—shape emerged:

"A way-station!" Auntie Hanna yelled, leading the way.

A stone hut, about ten feet wide, with a wooden, chalet-style roof, stood on a platform about twenty feet in the air. A spiral staircase rose to a wraparound porch. A rusty old steel mechanism sat in the hut, empty and idle. Lee ran down to help me up the hill.

"Admiral, it's a gondola switch station. Come!"

We clambered up the spiral staircase, bringing the whole mind-blowing sight of the Anti-Sneakaround into view. We'd generated a roughly twenty-square-mile island of reverse-existence Smoky Mountains in our Smoky Mountain, all of it floating in an endless white void, its sky filled with the endless, iterating faces of the Plaid Man and a single inky blot that was the anti-sun.

With the high ground, we were able to blast away a decent perimeter around the way-station, which, like its real-world counterpart, had no cables or gondola cars. A pathway through the forest ran along the same parallel as the switch station, starting in Ober Gatlinburg and ending down at the Gold Rush park. We caught our breath. Kaitlyn deactivated her scepter and slid to the ground, holding her face. She produced flask and took a pull.

"Anyone else?"

We all declined, except Lee, who hadn't even heard the offer. His face was whipping back and forth, his animated glasses growing larger and larger. I took his shoulder.

"Admiral, what's wrong?"

"Where's my sister?"

Jason

He established a battlefront, his cyberpunk gear sketching out a plasma cannon that bolted itself into the cobblestone floor. Part of him was relieved to stay behind; he didn't think his knee could handle a two-mile sprint. Justin, meanwhile, stood back-to-back with Sheila and produced a full-sized, rotating mini-gun from his midsection that fired hundreds of rounds per second. Sheila, for her part, relied on arcane gestures that summoned all manner of glowing creatures—temporary, ferocious familiars—that tore their enemies to shreds. The rest of the ETSOSD irregulars had arranged themselves into a battle formation. Elna, the old woman, had re-armed herself with a locket that outfitted her with a pair of spinning, luminescent blades.

Justin yelled: "We can't do this forever! We've gotta get this train moving, and I think I know how!"

Jason threw up a hand. "Well, then *do* it!"

Justin

Justin clambered back up into the train, pulling out his momma's photo, slamming open the oven, his hands shaking as he lowered it into the fire, knowing she'd want him to make the sacrifice, knowing it was for the best, when suddenly, he was on his knees, a sudden upsurge in momentum knocking him to the floor as a chorus of cheers—marred by one outraged voice—sounded from outside.

"Goddammit, Elna, no way in hell am I gonna let you give that up! You'll be defenseless!"

Justin staggered down the compartment's steps to see Sheila screaming at a serene-looking Elna, both of whom stood next to a fully functioning Itza Linda Express, its neon sign blazing back to life. Elna's chain-mail attire had vanished along with her "oil painting" appearance, leaving behind a willowy ninety-year-old wearing a sundress and, of all things, a bonnet. She'd pressed her hand against the train's hull, where a pair of tiny twin faces smiled at each other.

She'd contributed her locket to the train's power.

Sheila was apoplectic: "That's the last gift he gave you! You can't give that up! I *order* you not to give it up!"

Elna shook her head. "It's a rational transaction. One token for billions of lives." She looked to Justin and said: "Get going. *Now.*"

Justin saluted. "Yes, ma'am. *Jason!*"

Jason nodded and fired off one more round. With a few taps on his forearm-mounted keyboard, his luminescent weaponry un-sketched itself and vanished. He turned, ready to bound onto the train, only for his shoulder to kick back from a blast of oozy-black energy. A creature of tar and pitch, a ten-foot juggernaut of steaming oilslick, stomped out of a storefront like a miniature Balrog, its mouth asmolder with gold-and-crimson energy. It disgorged another blast of black muck that struck Jason again, knocking him flat. Justin leaped off the steps, activating a pair of wrist-mounted cannons, only for his volley to get preempted by two things: The first was a spinning battle axe that whined past his ear, while the second was a familiar voice:

"Justin! Don't lose your mama's photo!"

Justin spun, beaming. "Dawn!"

Her battle axe buried itself into the juggernaut's forehead with a wet *scruntch!* Dawn Dockery strode back into the mall wreathed in a halo of blue-and-red light, her jaw set, her teeth bared. She raised her hand to summon her axe, which tore out of the felled juggernaut's head and returned. She pointed at Justin.

"Don't do nothing crazy with your mama's photo, y'hear me?"

"What?" Justin said, his eyes widening. "I didn't. How did you—"

Dawn hoisted Jason, his shoulder splattered with black slime, to his feet. "Y'all right?" she asked.

Instead of answering, he kissed her. The women of the ETSOSD laid down covering fire for the moment while Justin looked on, smiling his ass off.

Jason pulled back. "I'm all different kinds of great. Glad you came back."

"Me too," she said, blushing. "My lands, but you're tall. We need to *git!*"

Hiram's Journal

An orange streak blazed across the countryside. We all cheered from the way-station, jumping up and down and hugging each other. Auntie Hanna's walkie-talkie squelched.

Dawn spoke: "Did y'all make it to a way-station?!"

Tears flowed from Auntie Hanna's eyes: "Dawnie? Little Dawnie? Where'd you go?"

"I'm on the train with Jason and Justin. *Listen,* did y'all make it to some kind of way-station for the gondola?"

Kaitlyn grabbed the walkie: "Yeah, we're pinned down up here! What the hell's going on?! Why'd you ditch us?!"

"We're gonna get y'all into the Mystery Mansion, but first, we're gonna take out Skelton."

Skelton's gigantic avatar was looking more and more like the Plaid Man every moment. His clothes had vanished, leaving behind a featureless body. His mouth was frozen open in a forever-chant, an unearthly, unholy bellow sounding from his bowels and shaking the spectral countryside. His ritual's "thunderstorm"—the black column of energy that blasted down onto the Mystery Mansion—had grown heavier and darker until it was nearly opaque. It hammered at our shining citadel like a Niagara Falls of pure evil, the onslaught grinding away our dream house brick by brick and beam by beam.

Now I grabbed the walkie: "Uh *how* are you gonna take him out?! He's almost done! It's almost done! He's destroying everything—the mansion, Justin's chapel, your observatory—"

"That's the thing, Hiram," Dawn said. "It ain't an observatory. It's a *gondola station.*"

I almost dropped the damn walkie. We all stared at each other, slowly nodding, the truth of it all finally emerging from behind a dark cloud. Lee propped his hands on his hips and shook his head.

"My vision wasn't that of a cottage at all," he said. "It was a—"

"Lee," I said, my voice a strangled whisper. "Oh, my God, Lee. Everyone. Look at us."

Our animated appearances had become transparent. It was like we stood in clear plastic shells that depicted our magical, animated selves. Our citadel, the Mystery Mansion, was slowly coming un-seamed under Skelton's onslaught. Kaitlyn touched her head to find her mohawk gone.

"Oh shit, guys. He's winning. And he's killing our magic."

Dawn

Her little brother's vision was what finally tipped her off. Ever since the night they saw *Back to the Future Part III*, when they shared their visions with each other, Dawn had been puzzling over Lee's, worrying at it like a stubborn knot, turning it over in her mind.

Why would he have a vision of a house with cannons on it?

Tonight, when Lee sculpted his little house from plasticine, the answer came into slightly better focus. Lee was smart, but he was also a supernerd like Hiram, so when he saw a cottage with a pair of steel cylinders secured to its roof on a pivot, he naturally thought of the giant laser-cannons from the Death Star. Why wouldn't he?

But they weren't cannons. They were the cable-grips for a gondola car.

She had cracked the code as they ran up the mountainside toward Ober Gatlinburg. She didn't even get as far as the switch station. She never even *saw* the switch station. All she saw was a scar in the forest, the pathway that had been cut for the old gondola line. The instant she saw it, her mind delivered up the image of her observatory, which (now that she really thought about it) didn't look like an observatory at all. Her "observatory" stood about three stories tall, with an asymmetrical dome bisected by a fifteen- or twenty-foot opening. She had always called it an observatory, even though the dang thing didn't even have a telescope. She just assumed it had always been retracted into its dome.

The instant she figured it out, she turned on a heel and sprinted back to the mall, certain in her soul that she didn't have enough time to explain everything to everyone.

If my observatory ain't an observatory, then Mac's library ain't a library and Justin's chapel ain't a chapel.

Kaitlyn had complained about their mission being like advanced calculus, but to Dawn, it all suddenly seemed like arithmetic. She knew they'd need Justin's photo in the Mystery Mansion. She didn't know for *what*, but as she ran back to the mall, she had a terrible feeling that Justin was about to use his photo for . . . she didn't know what. *That* part eluded her for the time being, but she had a terrible feeling that if they entered their citadel without all of their icons and treasures, they'd be finished.

The Itza Linda Express rocketed down the tracks on a wake of the Plaid Man's blood, its orange neon signage an ambient haze that attended their passage. Dawn passed the walkie back to Jason, who hung out the compartment's window, while Justin tended whatever magical fire powered the vehicle.

Over his shoulder, he asked: "How'd you know about my momma's photo? That I needed to keep it?"

"The Grid," Dawn said with a shrug—and a gasp. Justin's sunglasses were disintegrating, floating into the sky in millions of glittering particles. She looked at herself and found that her gleaming armor was fading away. "Ohmigawd, y'all, *look!* Our costumes are disappearing!"

Jason, leaning out the window, pointed. *"This is it!"*

They rounded the final corner, bringing the Gold Rush park into view. Like everything else, it was a dark counterpart of its real-world self, its front gates a pair of gnarled steel batwings. Halloween decorations still adorned the park, all of them converted to their dark analogues: shimmering, irrational shapes had replaced the cornucopia, while the scarecrows had transformed into leering monstrosities hewn from polyhedra with *omega* number of sides. Its attractions had all been replaced with blurry-bizarre, headache-inducing, non-Euclidean hyper-shapes over which were scrawled illegible hieroglyphs that drilled into your mind. Jason swung back into the compartment, his costume completely gone.

"Whadda we do when this thing crashes?"

Justin, who'd also completely returned to normal, made a fist. "We jump."

They bulleted through Hootin' Hollow, zoomed through Christmasville—which looked like Clive Barker had taken over for Santa Claus—and made a hard right turn toward Statuary Row.

Where they saw him.

Standing right where he was supposed to.

Between the statues of Narcissus and Echo.

There were two Skeltons. One stood between the two statues, holding Sandra's book, still his normal size and appearance, while the second hovered in the sky above him, a massive, fifty-foot shadow version. A ring of black mist billowed out from the first Skelton's feet, while behind them both, the black waterfall of evil continued its inexorable, crushing cascade down onto the Mystery Mansion.

And still, the Itza Linda Express sped along.

They were a hundred yards away. Fifty. Thirty.

"Get ready!" Justin yelled.

Twenty. Ten.

"NOW!"

They flew amidst the slowing of time. Dawn had heard that your life flashes before your eyes. They were right. A highlight—and lowlight—reel flickered past: meeting Jenny, Lee being born, Jenny moving away, meeting Mac, hearing she was changing schools, learning she was at the top of her class, meeting Kaitlyn, learning about the Lodges . . .

All of it good and bad, happy and sad.

Justin

Justin Johnson had bad nights sometimes. He had nights where he'd wake up crying and wishing it could all go away. Wishing it could all end. He never thought about doing it, but there were times he thought about how nice it would be if something happened, something he didn't see coming, to end it all.

Those nights had grown further and further apart since he met Tony . . . and these kids.

He used to think he wanted a good life, not a long one. Now he damn well wanted both, and for the first time in a while, he felt like he deserved it.

When he leaped off the train, he felt one hundred-percent certain they'd all survive. He didn't know why he felt that way or what would ensure their survival, but he knew it in the deepest and truest corners of his heart and soul.

Jason

How'd he pull it off?

Jason gave no thought to living or dying when he jumped off the train. His eyes were locked on Skelton—the smaller one, the *real* one—searching for any sign of his maps. If he was going to die, he wanted to at least know how he had done it. How had Skelton made contact with the Plaid Man and made his way from certain death into the Sneakaround?

That's when he saw it.

Of course! That's how he did it! He

Hiram's Journal

A hundred-foot sphere of orange light blossomed at the foot of the giant, spectral Skelton and *swallowed* it, along with the dark, hammering waterfall. As the orange sphere dissipated, an explosion of ectoplasm—like the icing we'd seen so many times—splashed up and across the tree line. A shockwave rolled across the land, changing things.

As for us, our treasures and animated selves shimmered back onto our bodies to a chorus of cheers.

And as for the Mystery Mansion: once the Plaid Man's pitch-dark waterfall vanished, our citadel shone back into existence, a lone outpost of good amidst an evil land. Dawn's observatory/gondola station popped back out of the roof like a mushroom growing in time-lapse, while Lee's little gondola carriage reassembled itself next to it. More orange lights illuminated the mansion's windows, while the entire building's facade flooded with color once more. Kaitlyn shook her scepter over her head in triumph.

"Awww, yeah, big bro! You did it! We did it! We—"

As the gigantic splash of ectoplasm settled, plumes of smoke rose up from it, followed by the quiet thunder of the crash itself, which echoed across the countryside. All air left our lungs. Auntie Hanna took the walkie from me.

"This is Auntie Warrior," she whispered. "Come in, Captain. Come in, Mountain-Master. Come in, Occultsmith."

The walkie responded with nothing but static. Below, the moat of dark monsters was growing wider and wider, its front inching closer to the base of our way-station. Mad howls rolled up the mountainside. Auntie Hanna tried again:

"This is Auntie Warrior. Come in, Captain. Come in, come in, come in, *anyone.*"

Suddenly, salvation: "We're here! We're here! We made it! *We did it!*"

Jason had responded, setting off another round of jumping, hugging, and cheers. Hanna grabbed Mac in one arm while she spoke, tears streaming down her face:

"Well, if you ain't the sweetest voice I heard since Woodstock! You're all there?!"

Justin, speaking from some distance, responded: "We're stuck in some kind of weird goop, but we made it!"

Mac took the walkie, looking down the mountain. "You better hurry and get that gondola going, guys. We're trapped up here, and they're coming on strong."

"Copy that," Jason said.

Lee leaned in: "Is my sister uninjured and fully functional?"

Dawn, also speaking from a distance: "I'm here, Lee! We're goin' as fast as we can! Just sit tight up there!"

More howls sounded. We all exchanged looks that said, *Oh shit.*

Kaitlyn powered up her scepter. "Game faces, motherfuckers." She covered her mouth. "Oh! Sorry I called you a motherfucker, Auntie."

Justin

It was a candle.

Upon colliding with Skelton, the Itza Linda Express exploded into a mass of ectoplasmic icing that engulfed him, consumed his colossal dark avatar, and served as a means to break everyone's fall. A radiating wave of ectoplasm caught them all when they jumped. It felt like landing on a waterbed and affirmed Justin's confidence that they were going to survive. The wave of ectoplasm rapidly solidified, all while the locomotive accordioned together into an uneven cylinder marred with rivulets and drips and waxy bark.

The end result was what looked like a giant candle, thirty feet tall and twenty feet wide. It was a near duplicate of Devil's Mountain, with a flat mesa at the top, ribbed sides like corduroy, and a wide, fluffy base. It was in that fluffy base—the result of the hardening of the initial radiating splash of ectoplasm—where Justin, Jason, and Dawn had landed, all of them lodged halfway in and out of the ooze.

Jason's walkie-bearing hand stuck out of the wax, along with his head and a leg. Justin was buried up to his waist, while Dawn was buried radially, her entire right side stuck in the goo. Justin dug into the glop around his waist and scooped it away. It had hardened enough to hold them, but it was still hot enough to mold and move.

"Guys, guys! You can dig yourselves out! Quick, before it hardens!"

Their magic treasures helped with this task, of course. Jason whipped up a set of laser-cutters that sliced him free, while Justin activated his mini-gun and blasted his way out. They both hit the ground, slipping and sliding in the ooze as they ran around to help Dawn, who couldn't quite reach her trapped side. They freed her in moments, checked their inventory, and arrayed themselves at the head of the candle, facing in toward the Mystery Mansion.

Toward their citadel.

Just like they'd drawn on their maps, a zip line ran from their current position, Statuary Row, up into a new doorway that must've led into the old gondola house. Ten-foot rock 'n' roll speakers stood at every corner of every floor. Dawn's gondola station stood on the far side of the building, Lee's carriage next to it. The mansion looked like its old self, but somehow *more.* Its colors were super-saturated, like a photo with an ultra-long exposure. All of their new additions glowed the same fluorescent-luminescent orange of the Grid.

"She's beautiful," Justin said. "We did good."

"Yeah," Dawn said with a nod. "Now let's get in there and—"

A new voice: "It's a sight to behold."

He had melted into the wax, Skelton had. It was like someone had carved his face into the side of the magic candle and let it melt in the sun for a day. His lower lip dripped down his chin, revealing his teeth in a permanent grin. Wax had filled both his eye sockets, filling the empty one and pushing his remaining eye out onto his cheek, where it dangled by the ocular nerve. All of this was rendered in ghostly bluish-white wax.

Occultsmith, Mountain-Master, and Captain Tennessee stood before him and crossed their arms.

"I did the right thing," Justin said before Skelton could speak again. "That night. No matter what anyone else says. I couldn't let those folks sentence you outside the law. But that was out *there,* according to the laws of man. In here, we're playing by different rules and different laws. It's over. The ritual's over, *your* ritual's over, and we're gonna go in there, into our citadel, and finish ours. We can't make things right. We never could. But we can do what little we can to help those kids on their way. And we're going to seal away the Faceless One for all time."

Skelton hissed and wheezed. Laughter.

"But the priest done said 'speak now or forever.' Ain't no stoppin' 'em from coming together."

Fear filled Justin's lungs with cold sand. "What?"

But it was too late. The candle was consuming Skelton, millions of tiny wax-drops eating away his face like a swarm of insects, chewing away his forehead, eyes, chin, and nose, leaving behind only his mouth, which continued to wheeze and whistle with his final malevolent mirth.

He was gone.

Twin sensations beset Justin: an immense unburdening at Skelton's passage, and a sharp-sudden terror that he had left one final trap for them. Something spilled from the wax: Elna's locket. Jason took it and stood. "I'll hang onto this." He looked back at the candle and clicked his tongue in disappointment. "Damn, I wish we could've seen it."

"Seen what?"

"His tattoo. That's how he drew his map. Someone else must've gotten one, too. Another prisoner."

Dawn shook her head. "But what the hell was he talkin' about? *Who's* 'coming together'? He ain't never seen the ritual. Dr. Sorora encrypted it."

Justin shook his head and started running. "Can't worry about that now. Come on! The gang's waiting on us!"

Hiram's Journal

The darkness was encroaching, growing closer and closer every second. A wave of inky, oilslick creatures broke against our way-station's supports, all of them maintaining the Plaid Man's dark chant, even though our train had just cut a gash across evil itself. We spread out around the small balcony that encircled the station, firing off shot after shot.

But they were gaining.

"Didn't it work?!" Mac said. "Did they hit Skelton or not?"

Kaitlyn shrugged and fired off a bolt. "Did we even *need* to hit him? If those ETSOSD biddies had been more specific, we wouldn't be playing Twenty Questions up here!"

"It's Mom's ashes!" I yelled. "That's the key. We need to get her to the Space-within-Spaces, or it'll never end!"

"Over here!" Kaitlyn called. "They're forming a ladder!"

We all rushed over to see the creatures climbing one on top of the other, forming a linking pile of oily, pitch-dark bodies like a chain of ants crossing a pond. Kaitlyn unleashed an ear-splitting scepter blast, but they kept climbing and climbing—until they stopped.

All of them. Every monster surrounding us froze like statues. A trypophobic tableau surrounded the way-station. Auntie Hanna grabbed the walkie.

"Fellas, whatever it is needs to get done over there, *do it now!* We can't hold out much . . . much . . . oh, sweet blue Jesus."

The creatures started moving again, stacking on top of each other to form a tower of bodies that rose up to our level, where they formed a vertical ring of bodies, like a hoop for a Lovecraftian Evel Knievel.

No, not a hoop. An arch.

A gate.

Shimmering black light flooded this new gate and from it emerged a colossus, a veritable mountain range of a man, his legs like redwoods, his face a grim sculpture. He wore slacks but no shirt. His torso was an atlas of suffering, covered with thousands of intersecting black lines, all of them bleeding and swollen. He was unrecognizable at first because of his eyes. They were gone, and in their place a pair of horrors had implanted themselves and spawned thousands of wriggling, seething villi that blossom-slithered out from his sockets and crept around his skull, some of the villi snaking into his ears, while others created a demented lattice down his neck, lancing into his blood vessels and staining his flesh an otherworldly off-black.

He spoke with a voice that was an unholy, reverberating abomination: *"WHY IS IT SO TERRIBLY, TERRIBLY DA-AA-ARK?"*

He was covered from neck to waist and from wrist to wrist with tattoos. The tattoos depicted all of West Chimney Top, Gatlinburg, the Gold Rush park, Tennessee State Pen, everything.

It was Trent.

And he had turned himself into a map.

Jason

They burst into the lobby, magic weapons drawn. Unlike the rest of the Anti-Sneakaround, their citadel was the *real, actual* Mystery Mansion with all its normal sights and smells. Justin's and Jason's animated glasses fogged as they passed from the arid exterior to the standard humidity of a July evening in the Smokies.

Dawn paused. "I'm heading up to my station. Justin, you headed to your chapel?"

"Yeah," he said. "But I've got a feeling it's not exactly a chapel."

"It ain't," Dawn said. "Be ready for anything. Jason, do you remember where—"

The walkie squawked with Hiram's voice: "*—ent! It's uhhh-ennnt!*"

Jason: "What? What?"

Mac's voice came over: "It's Trent! Oh God, it's him it's him it's *him! He's the map! You've gotta—*" Feedback shrieked over the walkie, slowly fading as an extra-cosmic wail sounded across the countryside. Mac was still screaming, her voice close at hand now: *"Hanna! She's hurt! Oh, my God, her arm! He's coming for you! Hurry!"*

Blood-curdling screams blared from the walkie. Time somehow stopped and dilated at once for Jason, who stood stock-still, his breaths echoing in his head, his heart pounding, all of his senses shutting down as his vision narrowed to a pinprick focused on the walkie.

Was this the Plaid Man's plan all along? To merge with Trent? But he doesn't know the ritual. How could he—

Dawn pushed it away from his face.

"Move."

Hiram's Journal

The world slowed in his presence. I felt so stupid, so *naive* that we hadn't counted on them—Skelton and the Plaid Man—having one more trick up their sleeve. I screamed into the walkie, stuttering but bulldozing through it:

"*—ent! It's uhhh-ennnt!*"

Jason returned with: "What? What?"

Mac, who was firing off flaming arrow after arrow, screamed: "It's Trent! Oh God, it's him it's him it's *him! He's the map! You've gotta—*" Trent's jaw unhinged and stretched to a grotesque length to allow for an unearthly howl that flash-silenced our hearing. His throat spewed boiling black bile everywhere. Lee jumped in front of us and blocked it with Compassion, but the bile hissed and steamed, eating through the shield. Auntie Hanna shrieked and hit the ground, her right arm coated with the black ooze.

Mac grabbed the walkie: *"Hanna! She's hurt! Oh, my God, her arm! He's coming for you! Hurry!"*

Justin

Portraits of mad scientists flew by as they ran and ran, dipping underground. Halloween decorations still covered everything, the park having been trapped in amber since its closure after Jenny's death.

Murder. After her murder.

They emerged into the barrel room, which had changed. The hanging punching bags had transformed into luminescent orange columns, the silly circus signage had become stained glass, and the spinning barrel had been filled in with some kind of turbine or jet engine, all of it the same bright, glowing orange. Dawn turned to Justin.

"I guess this is your department, Justin. Jason, Mac said she put her library in—"

"In the chain-link web room, next to the castle. I'm on it. Who wants the walkie?"

A moment's indecision gripped them before Dawn made the call:

"I think Justin should keep it."

"Got it," Justin said, taking the walkie. "Do what you gotta do, and then let's meet up at Dawn's gondola station."

Jason and Dawn ran out, looping around the sides of the barrel-turbine device, which Justin approached, his mom's photo in hand. *She said there was going to be a fire. But there was a fire on the train, and apparently, I wasn't supposed to put this in it.* He read the inscription again:

JJ's big night! Love, Sue. AYF.

Justin surveyed the turbine, examining every inch, utterly baffled until he rounded the side and found a small picture frame set into the wall. It bore a small brass plaque with the letters *AYF.* He slid her photo into it. Nothing happened, and for five terrible seconds, he felt like giving up. He made his mind up to do it for those five seconds—and no longer.

He kneeled and bowed his head.

Momma, I was never religious like you, but I always respected it. You found so much of yourself in church, and I've got a feeling the Order recruited you there. He chuckled. *I bet they made a play for you the second they saw what a firecracker you were.* He shifted to speaking aloud: "Momma, thank you for raising me to be the kind of man I am. I'm not perfect, but time and again, I've made the right choices when it really mattered. I don't know if this counts as a prayer, but by God, I mean every word."

A new voice: "Amen."

Of course it was her, but it was *more.* Gone were those tired knees and her frayed blue dress, and in their place was a snapshot of her in a moment of purest joy, beaming and lambent, her mind fixed on the present, mindful and serene. The tears came fast and hard for him. Justin held up the plastic disk that contained what he thought were her last words. He was laughing and crying so hard he could barely speak. The moment coalesced into a perfect few beats when everyone said everything they were supposed to in what precious little time they had.

"You're a *sorceress*, and you don't even tell me about it?!"

She laughed. "My little man's got a big mouth. You can't hold water, much less a secret that big, and I didn't want you carrying that burden. You were already carrying so much."

He'd fallen into her arms without realizing it. He still felt joy, yes, still felt bottomless happiness at seeing her, but the last few years' grief came crashing down on him, and he needed his momma.

"It's been so hard. So hard. So hard without you. I didn't think I could do it. So many nights I thought I couldn't."

"But you did. You *did*, Justin Joseph Johnson, and even when there was no room at the inn, you found a way for you and your new family." She leaned back and looked him in the eyes, motionless and confident in the truth she was speaking. "Because that's what they are. And they're lucky to have you in their lives." She held his face and lowered her voice: "They're lucky to have you in their lives."

Sobbing, he nodded. "Yeah."

WHUMP. Whirr-whirr-whummmMMM! Radiating heat, the turbine spun to life, throwing orange light everywhere in a rotating celebration. Justin's chapel flooded the mansion with orange energy, lighting up the whole place like a Christmas tree. He beheld his handiwork.

"I think we've got a heartbeat."

She nodded. "Now what I want to know is: How are you gonna explain all this nonsense to Tony?"

Justin almost busted his gut, he laughed so hard.

Dawn

Lucky for her, Auntie Hanna's secret passage cut diagonally through the whole building. When they entered the Flambonium Airscoop room, now empty, they spotted the passage to the right, slashing up toward the roof like an empty stairwell. An orange cable stretched through the passage, Auntie Hanna's zip line down to Statuary Row. Dawn, her armor clanking and gleaming, ran over and leaned into the opening, testing her footing.

"I'm gonna run up this thing," she said. "You go on ahead to the library." Jason started to run, but she called: "Hold it!" She tapped her lips. With a goofy grin, Jason kissed her and ran from the room.

A dark climb up awaited Dawn, so she launched into it. The secret passage's floor was the same polished hardwood seen around much of the mansion, easy to walk on when it was flat, tough when it was angled sixty degrees. She scooted her way up and up, using her axe as a climbing staff, keeping her eyes locked on the orange light that glimmered above. She passed a doorway to one of the dark ride's control rooms. Wheels and mechanisms like a giant, steel grist mill lay dormant and gathering dust. She climbed and climbed, but paused.

Something dark blocked the passage above.

"Who is it?"

A cigarette lighter ignited and scooped a familiar, flickering face from the black.

It was Jenny Miles.

Dawn screamed.

Jason

As he ran through the enchanted forest, the smell of sweat, wood, and rubber hit him. It was coming from up ahead. He ran over the suspended bridge, darted around some trees, and emerged into the chain-link web chamber to find the web missing.

A basketball court had replaced it.

It was a full-size court, ninety-four feet from end to end. A set of bleachers sat on the far side of the room, and to their left, the passage into the dark ride's loading zone. A steel rack held a dozen basketballs. Jason had a tradition: any time he entered a new gym, he had to make his first shot. As silly as it was under the circumstances, he ran over, snagged a ball and executed an easy layup.

"Nice," he said to himself as he spotted it:

The library. Mac's library.

More bleachers sat at the end of the court and served as a makeshift staircase up to the library's double doors. Jason clambered up, only to pause at its threshold when a horribly familiar sound plucked his ears:

Sobbing.

From the top of the bleachers, he turned. Below, sitting where he sat last October after he fell, was Hiram. He wore shorts in the cold because they were all that fit, with his legs extended because he was too chubby to comfortably cross them. His Masters of the Universe T-shirt inched above his big belly. He hunched over, his cheeks round and red from crying. He looked half his age in that way kids do when they cry. Jason remembered this moment and how he'd felt.

He'd felt snide, sneering pity for Hiram. All he could think was, *Wow, he's really going to feel humiliated he cried like this in front of everybody, the fat fuck. What a pussy.*

That's actually what he'd thought, and he was reminded of Kaitlyn's words the night they all confronted him: *I told you one thing you did to me. I could sit here and tell you a thousand.* Jason had a history like that with so many people he'd bullied over the years.

Until his family stopped him.

They had to nearly break his nose to do it, but they'd fought like hell to help him change, help him see the Grid. Jason realized he was now crying in repentance and shame. If this had happened *now,* if Hiram had fallen and hurt himself after Jason had finally seen the Grid, he'd take him in his arms and carry him to safety, whispering comforting words to him all the way. And if anyone made fun of him? Hoo boy, they'd be in for it.

Tonight, without realizing it, Jason had already taken Hiram in his arms, carrying him up the bleachers and into his big sister's library, which existed in an impossible space. The double doors sat on an exterior wall, and yet this room somehow sat beyond it. Bookshelves, all of them hundreds of feet tall, swept around the room. Like the rest of their "dream house" constructions, this one glowed fluorescent orange. In his arms, his memory of Hiram faded into an orange mist that scattered away, leaving him with only his *real* memories, which he contemplated as he searched the library for clues as to what to do next.

He hadn't taken care of Hiram that day. He had bullied and humiliated him, pressing every button he could, adjusting his technique to inflict the maximum amount of damage. He had a stutter? Good, let's exploit that. He's fat? Great, he must be insecure about it. He's nervous around girls, like any kid his age? Even better, let's humiliate him in front of one so he has a complex about it for the rest of his life. Jason did it for no other reason than to amuse himself. It provided an afternoon's mild diversion.

But after he stormed away from Trent to go meet Jenny that afternoon, everything changed.

He'd met her behind the mansion, at the staff entrance. She'd changed out of her costume into a sweater and jeans. She beckoned him inside, showing him all the mansion's secret rooms, including the hallway to the old gondola house . . .

That's where his memory mostly went dark.

He remembered bits and pieces. Flashes of horror. A scream. Skelton's disguise; they'd thought he was a musical performer. He was even carrying a guitar.

Jason touched his head where Skelton had struck him. He'd hit him twice.

The first blow caught him across the jaw. It rang his bell but didn't knock him out. The second one was bad. It got him in the soft hollow on the side of the skull, between the temple and the ear. But it *ended* him. Jason remembered only the faintest, most fleeting of images after that second blow.

He counted himself lucky he didn't remember more. Skelton struck Jenny first, but his mind had lost that memory. His imagination had constructed a reasonable facsimile of it, and it was enough to wake him in a cold sweat almost every night.

"It's not your fault."

He spun, expecting to see Jenny, but instead he saw her mother, soaking wet and wearing a faded T-shirt for the band Heart. She stood in a puddle of water, her toes turning blue. He felt suddenly ridiculous in his cyberpunk get-up, so he doffed his 3D glasses and returned to his normal, animated self.

"I'm sorry I didn't go to the funeral. I . . . I just didn't think I'd be welcome."

She nodded, her appearance slowly changing. A dry outfit replaced her wet one, while a cane appeared in her hand. She walked closer.

"I understand," she said. "And you're so young. This quest has been so much to ask of you. But you need to know it wasn't your fault, and you need to know I would've been happy to see you there. I know it's hard to deal with these kinds of feelings and fear, but trust me, the older you get, the more you'll have to deal with them."

Jason nodded. "I understand."

She vanished. Another unholy howl shook the walls, accompanied by a banging at the front door.

It's Dad. Oh God, he's trying to get in. I've got to hurry.

He took out the *Occultopsychic Phenomena* book and jogged around the library, wishing he had the walkie so he could ask Mac what this room was supposed to do. Another terrible *bang* from outside rattled the bleachers, reminding Jason of a time when his dad kicked in his bedroom door. He was a kid again, small and scared, and he didn't recognize his dad anymore.

Trent's voice rolled through the mansion: *"THINK YOU CAN HIDE FROM ME?"*

Suddenly, the floor shook Jason off his feet. The library flashed an instant, blinding orange, the surge accompanied by a *thrum-thrum-thrumming* from somewhere in the mansion.

What the hell was that? Was that Justin? Or maybe Dawn, up in the gondola station?

Trent's voice came again: *"OPEN THIS DOOR!"*

A window stood at the far side of the library. Jason ran to it and tried to get a look at his father, only to notice something far more interesting:

He could read everything.

The outside world was still the Anti-Sneakaround, but all of the signage in the anti-Gold Rush was legible, each sign bearing one of Skelton's dark messages:

I WATCH FROM THE FOREST, I WATCH FROM THE TREES.

SHE'S CRYING BECAUSE SHE'S UGLY.

WE'RE WATCHING YOU RIGHT NOW AND ALL THE TIME.

And more of the same. On a wild hunch, Jason opened the *Occultopsychic Phenomena* book and flipped to the pages that detailed the dark rite to join the Plaid Man with an earthly host. At first the letters evaded his eye, seeming to dance away from his focus, but slowly, they faded into focus, one character at a time, until he found he could read every word.

When he did, his heart skipped three full beats in absolute terror.

Lee

"It's Trent! Oh God, it's him it's him it's *him! He's the map! You've gotta—*"

His prayer of three months ago sprang to mind as his shield dissolved. Trent, now in the guise of an acid-breathing demon, sprayed them all. Lee had jumped in the way to block it, but a black sheet of bile had deflected onto Auntie Hanna's arm, the one that bore her enchanted wrist cannon. Both of their magic treasures failed under the onslaught of Trent's evil, returning them to their normal but animated selves. Everyone screamed. Trent unleashed an earth-shaking wail and launched himself toward the mansion, soaring through the sky like a devilish Superman. Hanna crumpled to her knees, wailing in agony.

Mac grabbed the walkie: *"Hanna! She's hurt! Oh, my God, her arm! He's coming for you! Hurry!"*

But Lee's confidence in the mission remained intact.

I do not ask You to help us, O Lord. But I wouldn't object to You hindering our foes.

Hanna doffed her jacket, the sleeve of which was boiling away. Kaitlyn dumped some of her bourbon on Hanna's arm, which seemed to neutralize the bile's effect somehow.

"Figures," she said. "You all right, Auntie?"

Hanna cradled her arm. Burns covered it from wrist to shoulder. Lee examined her.

"Those could be second- or even third-degree burns. You need medical attention."

"How?" Hanna said through clenched teeth. "We're miles away from an exit, and this old lady's come too damn far to give up now." She struggled to her feet. "I'll finish this with one fist if I have to."

With Trent's attention aimed elsewhere, the onslaught started back up again as thousands of creatures scrambled and clawed their way up the way-station's legs. Hiram swung his spinning blades back and forth like a giant yo-yo, sweeping enemies aside, while Kaitlyn and Mac blasted enemy after enemy into splats of black ooze. Kaitlyn stalked around the balcony, eyes wide in growing panic.

"What the hell are they *doing* in there?! We need that gondola!"

That's when the mansion exploded—with *light*. Orange light flooded every nook, cranny, and crevice, every grouting, groove, and shingle, every windowpane and wainscoting. The mansion surged with power, followed by the triumphant voice of Justin Johnson crackling over the walkie:

"Guys, guys! It's Justin! I think I just . . . *activated* the mansion! Are you all right? Is Hanna hurt?!"

Hanna leaned over: "Hurt but hangin' in, Johnson! What's your twenty?"

"Heading over to the library to help Jason. I think I know what it is!"

Mac: "It's not a library?"

"No, it's a control center!"

Dawn

She lost her grip and started to slide down the passageway.

But Jenny saved her.

"Upsy-daisy!" she said, pulling her the rest of the way up into her gondola station, where she found herself standing on a tiny patch of ground amidst a small pond. Little stones and lily-pads dotted the water, which spanned the width of the station. Overhead, an opening in the ceiling gave view of the Anti-Sneakaround. A giant pair of mechanical wheels stood to either side of her, motionless. A small steel platform hung out over the pond, next to the opening, presumably where passengers would disembark from the gondola.

But the *pond*.

Dawn recognized it slowly, then all at once. At the same time she realized she was wearing her Rainbow Brite T-shirt, only it was brand-new, its colors fresh-from-the-store vibrant. Jenny, all of seven years old, bounded from one rock to another, squatting down to look for tadpoles, beckoning to Dawn. It was where they had met, down by the lakeside cottages; the same place where Dawn would meet Mac years later.

Jenny turned and smiled. "This way, bestie-bestie."

If Dawn had thought she was done crying, she was wrong. In swimming slow motion, she followed her old friend across the water and up a small staircase to the platform, where she could see the way-station that held the rest of the Sneakaround Gang. Jenny took her hand. Dawn saw that they were both grown again, but she was still wearing her Rainbow Brite shirt, now threadbare and faded. Jenny gave her a shy look.

"I recognized you that day."

Dawn was crying too hard to speak, but her expression said, *You did?*

"I'm sorry I didn't say hi," Jenny said. "I had had a rough few years leading up to that day, and I didn't have it in me to play catch-up with you. I'm not perfect, and I didn't know that was all the time I had. I thought I'd get another chance to say hi again. I wish I had. I think we could've been bestie-besties again."

Still sobbing, Dawn said: "*I'm* sorry I didn't say hi. I was intimidated. And I saw you flirting with . . . y'know."

"I know. All this crap seems so important in the moment, doesn't it? But you wanna know something? A few years from now, none of it'll matter. What matters is love. What matters is the family you've chosen. What matters is doing right by the people you love. I hope you'll always remember me. I hope you'll mourn me. But I hope you'll be happy. We always think we'll have more time for everything, but then the day will come when we won't. I hope you'll *live.*"

Dawn nodded. "I will."

Jenny hugged her and whispered: "And one more thing: *wait here.* You'll need to be here to catch it."

She vanished in a cloud of orange mist.

"Catch what?" Dawn said. "*Catch what?!*"

A shadow appeared overhead, cast by a dark angel. Dawn barely recognized him. Black ooze and villi encased most of his head, while tattoos carved his torso into a topographical map of hell. His maw was a doorway to hell, his vomit darkness. He clenched his fangs, slick with black blood, and reared back, unleashing another wail that echoed across the land. His empty eyes met Dawn's.

Oh, my God. The opening. There's nothing keeping him out! He can come right in!

He must've read her mind, because he bulled his shoulders and flew directly at her.

Hanna

Even as a cartoon character, her arm hurt like hell. Hanna tore the remains of her jacket in half to fashion a sling and steeled herself. Trent continued to pound away at the mansion's force-field. She and Lee huddled behind everyone else as they fended off the continuing attack of monsters.

They were *missing* something.

Some clue, some extra trick, some unknown spell they had to cast. Hanna had a lot of faith in the Order, but she had to admit Kaitlyn had a point about the sense in communicating the instructions for a world-saving mission in what was essentially code.

But they got us this far, she thought. *If only we could get that gondola going, we could smash right in—*

"We could smash right in there," she said, her excitement growing. She called: "Kids, kids! I think I've got it!"

A twelve-legged horror leaped onto the railing just in time for Kaitlyn to blast it to bits.

"Whadda you got, Auntie?!"

"We need a cable, a *gondola* cable."

Mac used her boomerang-bow as a melee weapon, beheading a trypophobically-pockmarked monstrosity that hurled itself at them.

"I had the same thought, but I figured the cable'd be in the mansion."

Hanna shook her head. "What if *we have the cable with us?*" While keeping their eyes on the fight, everyone exchanged glances. By this point, Lee had stood to survey the divide between them and the mansion.

"Auntie Warrior, I think I see what you're driving at. If I interpret your drift correctly, the answer lies with Admiral Dreamweaver—"

"—And Ms. Mackenzie." Hanna addressed Mac: "Don't ask me to remember all those codenames. I can barely keep your real names straight." To Lee: "And yes, I think if we put their treasures together, we can make this happen."

"But the Anti-Father's in the way."

Lee's spontaneous name caught everyone off guard, instilling them with an ineffable dread that coiled around their insides—but they rallied.

"We need a diversion!" Mac shouted over the otherworldly howls of a starfish-shaped blot of midnight, which she quickly shot out of the air. Grabbing the walkie from Hanna, she squelched it: "Guys, guys! Are you there? Who's there?!"

Jason

The book had fallen open to a page headed with the words:

DARK RITE TO MARRY A COSMIC CELESTIAL TO AN EARTHLY

HOST.

Jason buzzed through it in seconds. It only had a few steps, this ritual, but what made his heart seize was what *preceded* this ritual:

It had a prerequisite.

God, they even use the word "prerequisite" like it's a grammar textbook, he thought in a white-hot haze of panic. *How on earth did they miss this?* The prerequisite for the rite to marry a cosmic celestial to an earthly host was being carried out right now in the form of another ritual. Like Sandra said, this other ritual was dozens of pages long and called for scores of components.

The prerequisite ritual was the *DARK RITE TO DESTROY A CITADEL OF LIGHT.*

Another voice: "Jase!" Justin came running in, wide-eyed and hooking his thumb behind him. "Cool basketball court. We need to find the control panel."

"Control panel?" Jason asked, flipping the page. "Control panel for what?"

Justin's eyes fell on the book. They both fell into a moment's deep concentration.

Justin swallowed. "Is it just me, or do these steps to merge the Plaid Man with someone look really, really familiar?"

Jason reviewed the steps—there were only three—and shook his head.

"Yeah, but he doesn't have Mom's ashes." In the back of his mind, Jason realized he'd referred to Corrie as his mother. The Freudian slip warmed his heart in spite of their peril.

Justin: "Are you sure?"

The facing page included the rite for sealing away the "Faceless One, Original Evil." Both rituals' final steps had to be carried out in the "Lodge-within-Lodges." To seal away the Faceless One, they would need to scatter Corrie's ashes in the Lodge-within-Lodges. In order for someone to merge with the Plaid Man, they would have to breach the Citadel of Light's defenses and destroy it from the Lodge-within-Lodges.

Corrie's ashes would serve as a catalyst, or as the book cryptically put it: "The bodily sacrifice of a Sorceress-Adept must be willingly sacrificed to complete—and activate—the rite." Jason read aloud: "If successful, the Faceless One would transmute the length and breadth of hill and dale, from heat death to conception, from it all to it ever, from the now to the never, into its own damnable encompassment of sorrow and suffering."

Jason and Justin looked at each other with bugging eyes.

Justin: "He's gonna turn the universe into hell."

Jason grimaced and shook his head. "Now, are you *sure* that's what it means—"

SMASH, SMASSS-S-S-H! The rafters rattled and shook, raining dust and plaster.

"Pretty sure!"

"He's trying to get in," Jason said. "And we're all trying to get to the Space-within-Spaces. We've got to get them in here with Mom's ashes *right now*."

"Looks like it's another race."

They looked around and saw nothing but books, shelves, and a bookstand.

"There!" Justin said, pointing. They ran over and set the *Occultopsychic Phenomena* book on it, but nothing happened. Deflated, they looked around again. No clues jumped out at them. No giant lever. No magic words or magic spells came to mind. Their minds were blank, both from confusion and from a growing fear that they were going to fail their mission.

But Mac saved them all: "Guys, guys! Are you there? Who's there?!"

Jason squelched the walkie: "Mac?! Listen, I think Trent's trying to merge with the Plaid Man, and all he needs are Mom's ashes to do it!"

"What? How?"

"No time to explain! What do we do in here, in this library?! How do we turn it on?"

"No fucking clue, but I *do* know you need to get Trent away from the observatory—I mean, Dawn's gondola station!"

"Why?!"

"Because of magic stuff! Just make it happen!"

Justin took his shoulder. "I'm on it. Stay here and figure out this room."

He took off. Jason raised the walkie: "Mac, I need some help with this library. I don't know what to do."

Dawn

SMASH! A starburst of orange energy marked Trent's collision with the mansion. A force-field surrounded it, powered by their love and their magic, and it was holding.

For now.

He backed up and attacked again: *SMASSS-S-S-H!* Another fading starburst marked his strike-point. Dawn scanned the room for clues. There was the landing platform, the stairs, and the gondola's engine itself. She wasn't an expert on gondola stations, but she figured they needed some kind of cable.

Wait! What's that?

She leaped off the platform and splashed across her spectral pond to the other side of the room, where, concealed behind the shimmering orange illusion of her gondola station, was an emergency fire hose enclosed in a glass locker. She smashed it open and tied the hose's end around her axe. That done, she leaped back to the steel platform, wondering how she was going to get Trent out of the way of her throw.

But when she looked, she found the sky empty.

"Hot damn," she said to herself, preparing to throw. She was about to let loose when the high-pitched whistle of incoming munition stopped her.

She was under attack.

Justin

He almost slipped and fell in a patch of black ooze in the Flambonium Airscoop room on his way to Hanna's secret passage. After checking to make sure it was clear, he reached into his robotic midsection and pulled out a rope capped with a carabiner, which he hooked to the luminescent orange zip line.

"I sure hope this magic crap holds," he muttered as he jumped and zoomed through the mansion's innards and back out into the Anti-Sneakaround, where his lungs burned with every breath. Disengaging the carabiner, he landed nimbly and sprinted around the side of the mansion. Trent, looking every inch like an airborne demon, pounded at the observatory/gondola station. *Diversion, diversion,* he thought as he ran over to the giant candle, scaled it in a single bound, and stood atop it.

A bullhorn slid from his sleeve and amplified his voice: *"Hey, asshole!"* Trent's face whipped toward him with a saurian snort. Justin continued: *"Yeah, you! Have a taste of this!"* He fired his mini-gun, sending round after round of hot lead flying in zooming parabolas at Trent. One of them struck home, a black splatter-burst marking the entrance wound. Trent circled around in an attack pattern aimed directly at Justin, who stood his ground, his mechanical suit producing dozens and dozens of cannons, missiles, guns, and blasters.

I hope this'll give you enough time, guys.

Mackenzie

Auntie Hanna was a genius. The moment Trent—the Anti-Father—changed course to attack Justin, Hiram and Mac climbed onto the way-station's railing, Mac passing the walkie to Kaitlyn.

Jason spoke: "Mac, I need some help with this library. I don't know what to do."

While laying down covering fire, Kaitlyn called: "Hey, it's Kaity. Describe it to us, shit-for-brains—*holy shit, look out!*" She blasted a spidery-looking creepy-crawly that leaped at Mac. "There's gotta be more than just books in there if it's a control center. Here's an idea: *pretend you don't have shit for brains and look really hard.*"

Mac and Hiram held hands for balance. She readied her bow.

"You ready, goofball?"

"Ready spaghetti," Hiram said, so deadly serious that she had to stifle a laugh in spite of the dread in her stomach. *Jason said Trent was going to merge with the Plaid Man, but how?*

Jason's crackling voice distracted her from that worry for now: "Okay, okay. *I don't have shit for brains, I don't have shit for brains.* There's tons of bookshelves. A stepladder mounted on a rail."

Mac pulled her flaming bowstring. "Go for it, goofball!"

Hiram wound up and threw his shrieking armored disk as hard as he could, letting the chain draw farther and farther out until it had spanned half the distance between them and the mansion. Mac fired a flaming arrow, aiming for the dead-center of the disk.

Kaitlyn addressed Jason: "Climb it!" She blasted a creature that looked like the silhouette of a pterodactyl.

"More bookshelves," Jason said. "A podium for a big book, like a dictionary, and—*oh!* I see something!"

Mac's arrow was a bullseye, carrying Hiram's chain on a gentle, soaring arc across the divide, where it sailed through their force-field and landed in Dawn's station. Hiram's ruby-chain ignited, connecting them to the mansion on a cable of golden fire. Hiram, no longer armed, returned to his normal but animated self.

They all shouted: *"Yes!"*

Mac grabbed the walkie. "Oh *what,* Jase? What do you see?"

"The ladder's mounted on a railing. The railing runs around the length of the room, and there is—I'm not making this up—a *dance pattern* drawn on the floor. How the hell'd I miss that?!"

Kaitlyn laughed. "Amazing what happens when you don't have shit for brains, huh?"

A smile spread across Mac's face. "Jase, I hate to do this to you, but I think you have to dance."

"No problem! But dance to what?"

Kaitlyn bounded onto the railing with them, smiling. "I think I know."

She leveled the Scepter of Chaos at the mansion—but had to suddenly leap out of the way of a whirling blade: Dawn's battle axe, which lodged into the side of the way-station with a *thunk*. From the wraparound balcony floor, Kaitlyn pushed herself onto her elbows and squealed with joy, pumping her fist at the sight.

The axe trailed a remarkably long length of fire hose.

"Now all we need is shit-for-brains to get that gondola going!" Kaitlyn said.

Hiram pointed. "Look! Justin's in trouble!"

Standing atop the magic candle, Justin was struggling for his life. Trent was attacking him with dive after deadly dive, but even worse was the candle itself.

It was swallowing him.

Justin

"Cry havoc," whispered Justin Johnson, who had once played a mean Marc Antony at NC State. "And let slip the dogs of war." He unleashed hell, standing atop the magic candle, blasting away at whatever the hell Trent had become, his animated bullets striking home but not slowing him down. Justin ducked to dodge Trent's first pass, his passage accompanied by a wave of boiling air.

Poor bastard's body temp must be in the two hundreds, Justin thought, somehow summoning sympathy for a man like Trent. He'd spent the last three months working with Hanna to find a way to emancipate the four kids. No way in hell were they going to grow up in that house, not after everything he'd done.

But those were quotidian concerns for another day. If Trent survived whatever Skelton had done to him, he'd have to answer to him, to Justin Johnson, Sheriff of West Chimney Top. The man was a menace, and if he'd helped Skelton plan all this, he would face the consequences, no matter how outlandish the story. Justin wouldn't even need to emancipate the kids.

Trent would simply go to jail.

Unless he finds a way to merge with the Plaid Man. But there's no way he could've read the book. The ritual was encrypted.

A golden filament of flame rocketed from the way-station to the mansion, hooked onto something, and drew taut. Trent made another pass that Justin fended off with a volley of missiles, all of them trailing smoky jet streams and knocking him back fifty feet at a time with each hit. Something else flew out from the mansion—a rope?—but before Justin could figure out what it was, he fell.

No, he hadn't fallen. He'd been *pulled* down.

"What the—" A wail and a laugh cut him off as his legs sank into the wax, which boiled and bubbled as it consumed him. Between his legs, a face rose through the muck, still ghostly bluish-white, his eye still dangling by its nerve, his teeth bared in a permanent, lipless rictus-grin. Justin screamed and blasted him with a forearm cannon, only for the shot to splatter harmlessly into the candle.

The mouth spoke: "I ain't done with you yet, JJ Flash! I ain't done with you yet!" Twin bubbles produced a pair of protruding, skeletal arms with half a dozen joints, both of which coiled around Justin's legs and pulled him deeper and deeper, all while *his* mouth, the devil's mouth, continued to taunt him: "Drowning's the worst way to go. I done me a few that way, watched 'em suck it into their lungs, their eyes buggin', their arms flappin'. You're gonna die down here with me, JJ Flash. We're one, you and me, our destinies intertwined."

Hiram's Journal

Without Auntie Elna's necklace, I reverted to my standard post-apocalyptic assassin look. Hanna and Lee had lost their magic treasures entirely, which meant almost half of us were defenseless. All of us contemplated our next moves, frozen with fear and indecision, but thankfully, we had a surfeit of leaders on the team. Auntie Hanna, standing on the wraparound balcony below Mac, gripped her ankle.

"You've got Corrie. You have a treasure. You have to help Jason get that gondola up here."

Mac nodded, her Artemis armor catching the firelight. "Agreed. Kaitlyn, I need to help Jason in the library. We need music, and you need to help Justin."

Kaitlyn took a pull of bourbon and ran her fingers through her mohawk. "On it." She leveled her scepter at the mansion and fired, blasting one of the speakers, all of which suddenly blasted forth with a familiar song—the same song Mac had used to audition for the Sisters of Athens. We all knew every lyric. Mac jerked her chin at Justin.

"Kaity! Get going! He needs you!" Kaitlyn nodded and vaulted off the platform, landing below and swinging her scepter into the face of a bile-spewing specter whose head was below its shoulders. She sprinted into the woods toward the mansion. Mac continued: "Jase, you don't strike me as the kind of guy to go to *Rocky Horror* shadowcasts, but—"

"Are you kidding?" he laughed back. "I never told Dad, but I used to play Rocky at one! I've still got a video somewhere."

Mac shook her head. "I think I know what Dawn's getting for her next birthday."

Hanna prodded her and said: "Focus."

"I think you know all the steps, Jase. I trust you."

Jason

"I think you know all the steps, Jase. I trust you."

Jason found himself in a packed room. Bodies rendered in the glowing orange light of the Grid appeared all throughout the library: his friends, his family, his teachers, his coaches, everyone. But one face stood out:

Marie. His mom.

She stood in the back, wearing the last outfit he'd seen her in, a simple sundress, and waved. Sorrow nearly stopped him in his tracks, he missed her so powerfully and so suddenly. As the familiar song began, Jason hesitated. After all, he had a bad knee.

This is worth the pain, he thought as he threw himself from the ladder—and stuck the landing. Pain flared in his knee, but he harnessed it, channeled it, ripping off all the familiar jumps and steps. He found an ecstatic center he never knew he had, a truth that glowed within him and held a dialogue with his grief. He knew grief was a good thing; it kept the departed close at hand, their memories clear as crystal, and as he danced, he spoke to them in his heart, telling them he was sorry for straying from the path—and ignoring the Grid—for so long.

The song drew to a close. He fell still and bid farewell to his audience, who vanished one by one, until only his mother remained. She applauded, blew him a kiss, and fell back into the arms of a man who materialized behind her.

His dad.

But it was him years ago, before Mom died, before he strayed from his own path, before he became the creature he was that terrible day. He winked.

"Miss you, Jase."

And they were gone. Jason ran to the podium and placed the book on it, laying it open to the page depicting the twin rituals. Thousands of tiny slices opened across both pages as the book quavered to life. Invisible hands sliced and folded the pages, slowly crafting a control panel. A lever was clearly marked: *ENABLE GONDOLA MECHANISM.*

He threw it.

Above, ancient, magical mechanisms groaned to life, telling him he had accomplished his mission. Smiling a sad smile, Jason ran from the room, trying his best to ignore the dread deepening in his stomach. It was a dread that needled and prodded and poked him with an incessant question; a question whose answer was so terrible he dared not answer it.

Most of the people in that audience were dead.

Does that mean Dad is, too?

Hiram's Journal

We had only one chance to get it right. This damn thing was moving *fast*. In terms of magic craftsmanship, mine and Mac's cord of flaming rubies seemed to be holding up better than Dawn's John McClane ad-lib, the fire hose, which was already straining and tearing. All of us locked arms and waited as Lee's carriage swung around the station, and—

"Hold on!" Mac yelled.

—scooped us up. We soared, we flew, we hurled ourselves into a spectacular-shining unknown, the four of us crowding into a luminescent orange carriage that was bursting with delightful details: stained-glass windows that showed me and Lee in our animated Sneakaround costumes; wainscoting carved with quote after loving quote, including Lee's declaration of love for me from *Star Trek II*. A stained-glass light fixture swung and rattled overhead. Weirdly, it dangled a cord, but when I pulled it, all that happened was the bottom of the fixture swung open like a door and revealed a nest inside. A glowing orange bird chirped at us.

This moment was *happening*.

Heck, it still *is* happening for me. I cherish this perfect moment, when our looney-tunes plan came together, even though we weren't out of danger yet. I think of it all the time and shake my head, smiling, and maybe call up one of the gang and share old war stories.

But it was happening now, and in those ten or fifteen seconds when we rode from the station to our citadel, I opened my entire sensory apparatus as much as I could, soaking up every detail. It's funny, for a story that traffics in nostalgia as much as this one does, I never feel nostalgia for this moment, because it's still happening.

It will happen.

It did happen.

It's always happening.

I'm there right now, next to my big sister, my best friend, and my sweet auntie. I stored this moment in a shard of flawless crystal that I keep close to my heart. I never want to forget a single detail, and I hope and pray I'll remember it as vividly on my deathbed as I did then, and as I do now.

Kaitlyn

Sometimes she really hated being short.

Not all the time. Most of the time, it didn't move her needle. She carried herself with enough brashness and energy to deflect any demeaning jokes that came her way, but once in a blue moon, she wish she'd inherited their dad's height. That night in the Anti-Sneakaround, she cursed her short legs for slowing her sprint through the haunted forest to help Justin. Luckily, she was armed with a long-distance weapon, which she deployed right, left, forward, and backward as she slalomed around the jittering, non-Euclidean anti-trees that composed this weirdo forest, blasting away any and every enemy that crossed her path. Running over a small hill, she brought the remains of the Itza Linda Express into view, which looked like a giant candle. For the first time that night, Kaitlyn remembered what her step-mom had said months before:

We'll all have a part to play in the park. The candle.

Justin wrestled with some kind of wax-creature that grew out of the candle. Most of his animated weaponry was buried in the wax, out of reach, leaving him vulnerable to Trent's attacks from above.

Trent's attacks.

Trent. The Anti-Father.

He swooped around the magic candle like a hawk, darting in to attack Justin, who still had his wrist-mounted cannons accessible. He fired off shot after shot, but still her father dive-bombed one of her best friends, his voice a stomach-turning simulacrum of what it once was.

"YOU THINK YOU CAN HIDE FROM ME? I WATCH FROM THE FOREST, I WATCH FROM THE TREES."

Kaitlyn's bad arm ached in response to his subwoofing voice. Above, something crashed into the mansion. *Is that the carriage returning?* she thought as she hurled herself onto the candle next to Justin.

"Yo! Give me your hand!"

"Kaitlyn! Holy shit, is it good to see you, girl!" They locked hands, and she pulled him out, but there was a problem: his vest was stuck in the wax and slid off his frame, returning him to his normal, animated self. Slick with magic wax, he hugged Kaitlyn. "Thanks for the save!"

"IT'S A PLEASURE WATCHING YOU CRY."

Her father zoomed by again, knocking Justin off the candle. Kaitlyn swiped at him, missed, and suddenly found *herself* sinking into the wax. When she saw what was pulling her down, her mind nearly disintegrated into a sheer-shocking terror-state. The face of Lenny Skelton, rendered in bluish-white wax, grinned up at her, his visage flanked by a pair of grotesquely jointed arms that wrapped around her legs.

Skelton leered: "Hi there, little number nine. Hi there, little number nine. Hi there, little number nine."

She sacrificed her treasure without a nanosecond's thought, raising the Scepter of Chaos over her head like a broadsword and plunging it into Skelton's mouth, her lungs emptying in a desperate screech.

"No, no, no, no! We killed you, killed you, killed you! You're done done done done DONE!"

Her downward thrust pushed her up and out of the candle. Skelton's teeth chewed at the scepter—wetly, his lips smacking, his teeth clacking—his spirit still alive somehow, still fighting, still *there.* Kaitlyn stood in a moment's indecision that was broken by a friendly voice:

"Here," he said.

Justin took hold of the scepter with her, momentarily assuming her mohawked, punk-rock look. They both closed their eyes and willed the following to happen:

The scepter ignited.

Flame erupted from the ram skull's brow and shot skyward, flickering twenty feet high. They let go of the scepter, their punk-rock costumes fading to leave behind only their normal but animated selves. Both of them leaped from the candle, expecting another attack from above, but none came.

Trent had flown up to Dawn's gondola station, where there was a breach in the force-field.

Dawn

It was happening. The station's massive wheels squeaked and squealed and groaned as they began their massive spin. Of course, she hadn't been under attack moments before. It had only been Hiram's magic weapon, the spinning disk, carried across the divide by one of Mac's flaming arrows. Dawn had caught the arrow in her armored hands and looped around the gondola's massive, mechanical wheels.

As if drawn by magnets, Lee's gondola carriage tipped over and linked to their improvised cables, swinging slightly from the momentum before the apparatus sent the blazing-orange carriage flying toward the rest of the gang. Dawn waited, her gleaming armor fading away to leave only her normal but animated self.

Footsteps from behind made her spin around.

"Dawn!"

"Jase!"

She splashed across the pond to him, where they embraced and kissed. Overhead, the carriage crashed back through the opening, smashing part of the wall along the way, and slammed to the platform. The fire hose whiplashed around the room, having snapped from the weight. Like their locomotive, the gondola-carriage dissolved into a bed of ectoplasm that broke their landings. Everyone slipped and slid to their feet, beaming.

"Dawn! Jason!" Hanna said.

"Bestie-bestie!" Mac yelled, leaping off the platform and sweeping Dawn into her arms. Hiram and Lee jumped down and ran over to hug everyone.

Lee grabbed his sister's hand and pumped it. "That was an inspired improvisation with the fire hose!"

"Thanks, Lee, but—" She scanned the group. "Where's Justin?"

Jason's face fell. "Where's Kaity?"

Mac slipped her boomerang-bow into its scabbard. "Justin distracted Trent and got into trouble. Kaity went to help him."

Jason bolted for the door. "We've gotta help them!"

"Jason!" Hanna shouted. "We've got to get Mac to the—whaddaya call it?"

Lee: "The Space-within-Spaces."

"Right," Hanna said. "If we get Mac there, we can end this in a stroke."

"Wait!" Mac said. "Jason, what was that talk about Trent merging with the Plaid Man?"

"THERE'S NO POINT IN EVEN TRYING."

Trent, the Anti-Father, darkened the sky. A jagged hole like a smashed picture window glimmered overhead—a breach in their force-field. Their reaction came instantly, all of them diving for the exit, but it was too late: Trent morphed into an amorphous black splatter of ink that slashed into their citadel and reconstituted itself into his unearthly shape before them, blocking their way.

Hiram's Journal

We all stood in silence, slowly backing away from him.

"There's no point in even trying." His voice had risen to its normal register. His appearance was still stomach-turning, but he *sounded* normal: "It's done. Both rituals. He came to me in my study and told me a special truth, that I'd been right all along. Did you know that? All that guilt I'd been carrying, everything they said—'you're an abuser, you're a monster'—was bullshit. If anything, I took it *easy* on you—" (his face seized) "—*LITTLE SHITS*. But it's done." He produced a steel box that froze our souls.

"Oh, fuck," Mac whispered.

It was Mom's box. For her cremains.

The Anti-Father continued: "Destroying this citadel was the hard part. Merging me with him will be easy. Once this place has been destroyed, all you need are three things: an offering of blood from the Sentinel of the Hightower, which you provided on your trip over here; an offering of flesh from one of the Sentinel's lieutenants, which Skelton provided; and finally, an offering of love from one of the Order's initiates, which in this case is your stupid dumb fucking bitch of a step-mother."

"You switched them," I wheezed, my chest devoid of air. "You broke the ward and switched boxes."

He gave me a pitying look and shook his head. "Of course I didn't. The Order's a joke, but their ward on her crypt was too strong, even for the Sentinel." He sounded like he was chatting with us. I flashed on Skelton's offhand demeanor at Soddy Farm.

Hi, Jason. Good to see you again.

He continued: "And their enchantment on the book, *Occultopsychic Phenomena,* was too strong." The black villi infesting his skull suddenly writhed forth, expanding their grip and encasing his entire face in oozing black moss. His voice dropped into a dim depth of hell and wailed forth: "*But no one put a ward on your bedroom, little Hiram and Mackenzie, little Hiram and Mackenzie, no no! No ward for you!*" He opened the steel box to reveal it was empty. "*We didn't switch out her ashes, we switched out—*"

Searing torment clawed at me. Imagine a nightmare where something creepy-crawly sneaks into your bed; that's what had happened inside my coat. Razor-sharp talons lanced into my ribs. I tried to scream but only emitted silence. My aviator helmet was closing around my skull like a vise, while my duster coat had melted into burgundy-red ooze that coated my every inch, my goggles melting into my face like someone had poured hot wax over my head.

My cartoon costume had come to life and was trying to kill me.

Everyone jumped to my aid as I tipped backward. Jason swiped at me, and a pseudopod of red slime snaked out from my chest and into Mac's backpack, from which it yanked the steel box—the *real* box—filled with Mom's remains and delivered them into the waiting hands of the Anti-Father.

I managed to wheeze three words: "*Get it out!*" I tried to indicate my pocket, but my arms were glued to my sides like a layer of shrink-wrap was sucking shut around me. Jason plunged into my coat up to his elbow, took hold of the sextant-walkie, and wrenched it out—

—*ohmyholygod WHAT IS THAT*—

—a dozen arachnoid legs, their joints gnarled and hairy, sprouted from the sextant, from which suddenly blinked a pair of slitted feline eyes. A maw of dripping fangs slurped open across its middle and *snap, snap, snapped* at my face. Jason slung the snarling spider-sextant across the room. Once disconnected from me, the slimy-red coating vanished, and I returned to my normal animated appearance. Sound and sight snapped back, too, bringing with it a volley of screams from everyone:

"*The sextant! The sextant!*"

"*He switched the sextant!*"

"*He's gone, he's gone, oh my God, he's gone!*"

From my hands and knees, I saw it was true. The simulacrum of the sextant skittered toward us, but Kaitlyn blew it to bits. All of us spun toward the secret passage, where a wisp of inky black smoke was all that marked Trent's exit.

We slid down Hanna's secret passage to the Flambonium Airscoop chamber, where we landed in a heap, jumped to our feet, and sprinted through the enchanted forest, through Jason's gymnasium, the mirror maze, and into the load-in area for the dark ride.

Dawn was wailing: "We're too late! We're too late!"

Mac screamed: "Shut up and keep running!"

We flowed around the long-dormant ride vehicles, through the Chamber of Maximum Science, past the perpetually pratfalling Zygor, through endless space . . .

. . . and onto one, final floating pathway.

We crowded together, me, Mac, Dawn, Lee, Jason, and Hanna, all of us here, here, finally *here* in the Space-within-Spaces. Like the rest of the Smoky Mountains—the ones we'd constructed—this was a single stone pathway floating in endless space. I huddled next to my big sister, expecting the world to already be ending, but it wasn't.

The Anti-Father floated on a wave of black mist, holding the ashes . . . but doing nothing.

The mist rapidly dissipated along with the sickening villi and growths that infested his eyes and flesh. A button-down materialized on him. He de-aged twenty years, his skin tightening across his face, his eyes clearing up, his smile widening. He stepped forward, bearing the steel box, his eyes locked on Jason.

"You nailed that dance, kid. Man, I tell anyone who'll listen, Jason's the most talented kid around. He's smart, he can write, he's a great athlete. He can do whatever he wants, and damn! I had no idea you had a dancer inside you! Made me and your mom really proud, it did, and I bet your step-sister appreciated it, too."

My head swiveled toward Mac, whose face stretched in grief and horror at his invocation of her.

Trent propped his arms akimbo and continued: "This citadel is a work of art, guys. The library, the observatory, *little* Lee's *little* cottage—" (he chummily pointed at him) "—everything. You guys really nailed it." His voice jumped an octave. "Remember how it used to be, Jase? Before Mom died? We had that little place, and we watched that cat give birth late one night? We watched a million movies. You were making little short films at the time, and I held the camera. We went camping on that little island, got dinner from passing fishermen. Those were good times. Special times. Times we can have again. When I was outside talking with your friends, I thought, 'I bet Jase is worried about his old man,' and I'm here to tell you, I am A-okay, and what's more is—we can have those special times again. All you have to do is . . . well, I think you know what you have to do." He released the steel box, which floated over before us, right in between Jason and Mac. "The ritual calls for an offering of *love*. Someone who *loved* your step-mom has to give the offering." His eyebrows rose as he gave a small, contrite wince, a look that said, *Shucks, sorry I even have to bring this up!* "You have to destroy her ashes, kiddo. Take care of that for me, and let's get outta here and go get a burger at Darryl's, whaddaya say?"

Silence. The endless vacuum of virtual, magic space emitted a faint hum. Nobody moved, but we all had an eye on Jason. Turns out, we were watching the wrong person.

"Oh, FUCK you!"

With both hands, Mac yanked the box out of the air and slung it into the Space-within-Spaces.

Where it *clanked* to a landing on something.

Something invisible.

Jason

Mac broke the spell, bless her heart. For a single, awful, distending instant, Jason considered the Anti-Father's offer—because that's what he was, the Anti-Father—but as soon as Mac's voice rang out across the sparkling void, his mind rebooted and set him on his next mission:

Help scatter her ashes.

The steel box had landed on a small platform out in the abyss. Jason's cyberpunk glasses didn't reveal the platform, but they *did* reveal something else: the floating alien creatures they'd all seen in the ride before. Some resembled jellyfish, while others were vaguely humanoid in appearance. They floated thousands of "miles" away, their expressions unreadable but seemingly benevolent.

Oh, God. Why are they here? Do we need to deliver her remains to them?

The Anti-Father was still talking, still wheedling, still pleading, still plotting: "I'm not in any rush, Jase. Just jump out there and bring me that box, and y'know what? Mom's waiting for us! Marie! Ha, ha! Turns out she just got lost a while back. Never even got sick. She's got a table all ready for us. All you have to do is—"

What happened next brought a smile to Jason's face for the rest of his life, which was a happy one, incidentally. Jason had been one step ahead of everyone, including Hiram, until this moment. The kid *flew*. You'd never know he'd balked at jumping three months ago or that he had any doubts about his athletic ability whatsoever. He also wasn't wearing Jason's 3D glasses or any other magic treasure, which meant that without an instant's hesitation, he'd leaped into empty space.

He landed heavily, crashing to his knees, spinning around and taking up the steel box. He hopped to his feet, the motion suggesting a more athletic goofball than he let on. Jason doffed his glasses and held them up.

"Yo! Buddy! Catch!"

Jason flipped his glasses to him, his cyberpunk costume vanishing and leaving only his normal but animated self. In the corner of his eye, he caught Auntie Hanna giving him an approving smile. Hiram snatched the glasses out of the air and slipped them on, assuming Jason's cyberpunk superhero form in a tornado of lightning and electro-crackling daydreams. He stood on the invisible platform, clad from head to toe in neon-lined leather and denim. He looked great. He looked brave. He looked *complete*.

And when he saw the floating creatures, he sighed.

His sigh was so nakedly joyful, so sincere, that it relieved Jason of whatever stress he was feeling in that moment. He looked at the thing that had once been his father and shook his head, half in pity, half in triumph.

"You're finished."

Hiram's Journal

To say they looked like angels would be an understatement. They looked like every dream you wish you could remember. They looked like a feeling you couldn't describe but which you knew would change your friends' lives forever if they felt it.

They looked like a perfect memory.

I stood wearing Jason's cyberpunk costume, holding Mom's remains and wondering how I was going to deliver them to these creatures. The answer, of course, came from my fellow flag officer.

"Admiral Dreamweaver!" Lee called. "The boomerang!"

"Of course!"

"*NO.*"

It shook our existence. Gone was the artifice, the defense mechanism, the last-ditch effort to fool us, and in its place was pure malice, pure hatred. In the coming weeks, we'd learn that Trent had somehow opened a correspondence with Skelton, who had been sneaking art supplies and letters onto death row. Skelton had snuck ink and needles into his cell, carving tattoos into his own flesh. The details of their conspiracy would remain shrouded in mystery, amplified by myth-making, tall tales, and legend.

Only we knew the truth.

The Plaid Man had infected Trent directly. He'd chosen Trent because he embodied the banality of evil. His world revolved around himself and his pain and neuroses; he had no interest in changing, repenting, or growing, and as such, he was susceptible to the insidious evil of the oldest demon in all of existence.

He was also just a huge fucking asshole, so fuck him.

He'd spent the last few months sneaking away to get himself tattooed with the exact maps Skelton called for, and somehow, Skelton had communicated the rules and protocols for his dark ritual to him. (We never found out exactly how.) He had slipped into mine and Mac's bedroom to steal the sextant, making it easy to decode the ritual. Their only roadblock was the ward protecting Mom's ashes, but they'd created the phony sextant to retrieve them at the last possible moment. That our abusive step-father had knowingly conspired with a serial killer to turn the universe into hell remained our collective secret.

But in that moment, all we knew was that a creature of boundless dark malevolence stood before us as we teetered on the precipice of Armageddon.

I called to Mac: "Throw the boomerang that way, as far as you can! They're waiting!"

The Anti-Father's voice boomed louder: *"THERE'S NO POINT IN EVEN—"*

It lanced through his chest, impaling him and lifting him off his feet. They both held it, four hands between them, both of them dressed like punk-rockers, beautiful and bad in their dreams. Its flame was still flickering from the brow of the ram's skull, the ram wearing a collar of wax from which grinned the jagged smile of Lenny Skelton, his likeness captured forevermore in bluish-white wax.

Kaitlyn and Justin, who had snuck in the back door, dropped him to the floor, where he shrank, his bulk and mass withering away, leaving behind his *real* self: the wisp of a man he was, gog-eyed and frightened in a hotel hallway, shocked by his own evil, stunned at how horribly he'd mismanaged his life, how far afield he'd strayed from redemption and repentance. He looked up at us, his jawline quavering like an infant's. Kaitlyn and Justin stepped around him, their punk-rock costumes fading away.

Mac and I met eyes. It was time.

She slung the boomerang into the infinite. I hurled the box after it. They snapped together, flying, flying, and flying, faster and faster, gaining speed, shattering the room with a sonic boom, flying even faster and blasting us with a spinning flashstorm of pure white, the first time anything had broken the *light* barrier, the historic moment known only to us in the confines of this strange realm, the boomerang flying faster and faster, breaking *another* cosmic barrier, growing closer and closer to the strange creatures that floated in the endless beyond.

Mac's animated costume faded, and with it, *all* of our costumes faded.

We were no longer cartoons. The effect faded, leaving behind only us, us, the real us, all of us standing in the ruins of a kooky old amusement park ride, watching as the roof opened up, shaken asunder by a sudden earthquake. I was still wearing Jason's 3D glasses, but their work was done. I wasn't a cartoon anymore. I was just me, Hiram Deacon Gresham, standing side by side with my friends.

With my family.

Mackenzie

She had traversed their citadel without meeting one of its denizens.

Until now.

In the great-cosmic faraway stood one of the curious alien creatures, but as Mac squinted to get a better look at it, its form changed and morphed and transmuted into one she knew very well: that of her father, Deacon. Was it really him? Was he an angel, and were they getting a glimpse into heaven? Mac didn't think so. She surmised that whatever powers guiding them and the ETSOSD operated on a level of abstraction far beyond human understanding.

Regardless, she was so very happy to see him.

"Dad," she said, speaking amidst a fermata of endless *now-always*.

"Hey there, Big Mac," he said. "I don't have much time, so let me say: I miss you. I'm so sorry I had to leave you. I'm so sorry I had to leave your mom. I would've given anything to stay, but they told me a simple and brutal truth: just because we got to come here doesn't mean we get to stay here. I was furious. I screamed and begged and pleaded. But they told me I was done. It took a cycle and a half—from bang to crunch and back again—but I finally got my mind around it. I'm here. You're there. *But.*" He smiled and winked at her. "When word got around about this operation, you better fucking believe I was first in line behind home base."

Mac knew if she tried to answer, she would break down in tears and might ruin it all. Instead, she made ready to throw the boomerang, but her father held up a hand to stop her.

"Hey," he said. "I can ask one more thing: How's your little brother doing?"

Mac sobbed, smiling so big. "He's great. You'd like him."

"I bet I would." His gaze flickered, his eyes shifting this way and that. He clasped his hands before him. "You better get this over with. I love you so much, Big Mac."

"I love you, too, Dad."

"Throw true. Throw true. Throw true."

Lee

Lee and Hiram watched so many great movies and played so many great games on their sleepovers, including any number of fantasy action-adventures. One commonality they shared was how, when the good guys won, the bad guys' castle or ship or fortress would, for some reason, explode.

"It happens in *Krull*, it's suggested in *The Lord of the Rings*," Lee said. "I would even submit Khan's death in *Star Trek II* as an example."

Their defeat of the Plaid Man reminded Lee of Khan's death.

After Kaitlyn and Justin dropped the Anti-Father to the ground, he diminished but didn't die. Which made sense. They had impaled him with one of Jason's magic treasures that itself was covered with the ectoplasm of the Anti-Sneakaround, which *itself* was suffused with the evil soul of Lenny Skelton. The combination was lethal only to the Faceless One, and only in the moment when Corrie's ashes had been properly interred in the Space-within-Spaces, but Trent was spared.

His mission failed, he vanished from the Anti-Sneakaround to later be found by the police. The eight of them remained to watch the villain's castle explode. An earthquake—the third in three months—rattled the West Chimney Top/Gatlinburg area and sheared off the Mystery Mansion's roof. Overhead, fireworks filled the sky. We'd lost track of time in the Anti-

Sneakaround. An entire day had rolled past, bringing us to the evening of July Fourth.

I'd forgotten it's our nation's birthday.

An epicycle spun up in Lee's mind, one dedicated to preserving memories. In the years to come, he and his fellow members of the Sneakaround Gang would regale each other with tales of this moment, of its magic, its piercing beauty . . . and awe-inspiring terror. Around the world, people reported that you couldn't hear but *feel* it. Orbiting telescopes captured video of a great rift that opened in the Ocean of Storms and snaked like a dark bolt of lightning across the Sea of Tranquility.

To the Sneakaround Gang, they saw more than that. The latticed face of the Plaid Man rose out of the moon's surface in relief. His wail could be heard only by them, a distant keening from half a galaxy away, all of it accompanied by fireworks, both authorized and illegal, that showered the night sky. The ritual complete, his face faded away but left a visible crack that circled the moon's surface and emitted massive sheets of dust and rock. It was like the moon was exhaling after holding its breath for countless millennia.

This exhalation produced the biggest meteor shower since the Leonids and forever reminded Lee of Khan's death in *Star Trek II,* in which the superhuman prince perished in an explosion that generated a new planet. Lee would always think of this parallel, because while the Fourth of July 1990 marked the death of the Faceless One, it also signaled a new era for everyone.

Everyone.

Sandra

It was months ago, a few nights before they went to see *Back to the Future Part III.* They worked it out so all their kids were spending the night at Trent's, and they could have a night to themselves over at Sandra's. After that first kiss in the Mystery Mansion, they'd met in secret, sneaking down to Knoxville or, in one case, taking a quick road trip over the mountains to Asheville and Cherokee. Sandra had opened a bottle of wine, but Corrie never touched the stuff, always saying, "I saw enough drinking around my house growing up."

That night, Sandra got a taste of how Corrie could actively ignore a person. They were approaching an inflection point in their relationship, and they needed to talk about it, but Corrie had been resisting the subject for their last few dates. Sandra loved her, but they were almost out of time. She tried an indirect approach:

"How much do you think they saw?"

Corrie rubbed the inside of her arm. Her sessions had not only darkened her veins but hardened them as well, and they always pained her. She joked that they made her look "punk rock," though.

"Not much," she said. "I think Hiram saw our battle schematic, but he didn't know what it meant."

Sandra nodded. "They're powerful. You should be proud."

"I am. It's just . . . I want something for me."

Sandra Divine Dockery, Revelation General of the East Tennessee Sororal Order of Spiritual Defense, remained perfectly still. Corrie had just opened a door through her personal wall the *slightest* amount. One false move, and she'd slam it shut again. Sandra let the silence persist. She didn't even sip her wine.

Corrie looked over, her eyes welling up. "I thought we'd be homeless if I didn't marry him, but I was wrong."

"You did what you thought you had to do."

"Hanna always gave me these looks, but I've got two kids. The bills pile up."

Sandra knew Corrie blew money on things other than her kids, but now wasn't the time to fight that fight.

Corrie: "I knew I could make it work, but it felt so scary to be alone."

Sandra took a gamble and nodded. Corrie looked at her in astonished relief.

"Yeah?"

"Of course. After Hank died, I was terrified."

"But you made it work."

"I worked two or three jobs. Back-to-back shifts. Dead on my feet. But the main thing I did? I *asked* for help."

Corrie nodded, chuckling slightly in spite of her tears. "Hanna says I can be pretty bullheaded about that. I don't know *what* she's talking about." She smiled at her self-deprecation, and the door opened a little wider.

Sandra weighed her next words. Corrie had worked hard to keep her current house, and both she and Deacon asked for a lot of help, but after he died, she simply stopped. She never explained why. Sandra knew they would have to discuss that at some point, but not now. She knew it was time to let her save some face: "You're being hard on yourself. I mean, aren't you asking for help now?"

Corrie nodded. "I don't know if I can live around here when we do this."

Sandra knew that wasn't true. East Tennessee was her home, her power-point, and no way was she going to let any kind of bigotry force her out of the Smokies. But once again, she elected to let her lover—and very possibly the love of her life—save face:

"Where would you want to live?"

Her eyes took on the soft focus of someone looking at a distant horizon. She hooked an arm over the back of the couch, and they twined fingers. She spoke in a soft whisper:

"I want to go west. Alone, just the two of us. The kids could come out later. But west. I'd love to start late and drive into the sunset. Drive all night. Take interstate forty across the desert. New Mexico, Arizona. Sleep during the day and drive at night. Listen to a deep-desert radio station and then go find it. I always wanted to do that, y'know. Be a deejay at one of those desert radio stations. Broadcast from a little shack out in the middle of nowhere. I'd put on coffee. Have the place to myself. You'd be listening from home. Maybe we'd land somewhere in Arizona. A ranch. Lots of land. I'd go into the radio station every night and play whole albums. I'd put on *Graceland* or *Tumbleweed Connection*. I'd only stop when I flipped the record and say something silly like, 'Hey you, out there in radioland. Hope you're keeping cool on this hot summer night.'"

Sandra laughed through her tears.

Corrie continued: "I'd play 'Burn Down the Mission,' and I'd sing along, knowing you were singing along with me back home. I'd come home in the morning. We'd have lots of pets—cats and dogs. They'd run out to greet me. The kids would be away at school by this point. We'd sit and watch the sunrise, and I'd fall asleep in your arms."

Sandra smiled. "That sounds great."

Corrie didn't say anything for a long time. Eventually, though, she wrinkled her nose and glanced around the room. She stood, crossing to the kitchen.

"Are you looking for something?"

"Do you have any orange uh juice?" She opened the fridge.

"Yeah, it's behind the Vernor's. Thirsty?"

Corrie got a mischievous glint in her eyes. "I want a screwdriver. Can we make screwdrivers? Or what's the other one with orange uh juice?" She took out the carton.

Sandra stood and crossed to the kitchen. "Fuzzy navel."

"Right. Can we make cocktails?"

"I'd love to."

Hiram's Journal

It was over.

We stood in the Mystery Mansion, the ride having returned to normal, the Anti-Sneakaround having dissolved, our magic treasures having done their duty, and all of us having returned to our normal, *non*-animated selves. Trent, strangely, had vanished, but none of us was worried about him staging another assault. The earthquake had ended, the moon had cracked open, and the meteor shower had begun.

We'd completed the ritual, except for one part.

Justin walked over. "Now all we have to do is find Itza Linda."

CLANK. WHUMP, WHUM WHUM WHUMMM. Behind us, the Mystery Mansion's ride vehicles started up again. All of us frowned and exchanged looks. Jason hooked his arm around Dawn.

"Did one of you turn on the ride?"

Kaitlyn elbowed him. "Shit-for-brains, I think we *all* just did."

Dawn snuggled into Jason's embrace. "We need to get on, don't we?"

I nodded, my skin tingling. There was a moment's hesitation as we decided who to sit with. Our personal dynamics had shifted so much over the last six months. We surprised each other with our choices:

Jason and Justin sat together.

Mac and Auntie Hanna.

Kaitlyn and Dawn.

Lee and I sat together, admiral and admiral.

We rode through the ride's final moments, the ceiling gone, the sky alight with meteors and fireworks, all of us giggling at Professor Wizardo and Zygor's mishaps, the cars carrying us through the load-out area—and into the forest. The park was gone, and in its place, we found ourselves in the woods near our old house. Ride-tracks had appeared in the forest, rising from the earth as we coiled through the woods, accompanied by the cheerful chorus of fireworks.

We slowly crept to where I knew we were going:

Itza Linda.

We rounded a corner, bringing the wooded glen into view. Star-sprays of fireworks lit the summer sky, accompanied by meteor after meteor, the air heavy with the smells of honeysuckle, clover, and maple sap. It smelled like summer and simpler times, but we all knew those simple times were gone. We rode closer to the glen. A slight depression sank in the middle of it, and unlike the last time I'd been here, the depression was no longer empty.

The traincar was there, the same Old West-style caboose I'd seen months ago in my late-night walkabouts, the same one Justin had drawn on his maps, the same one we'd been trying in vain to find all this time. It was there, real and solid and true. Its windows were the same intricately crafted stained glass that depicted a bizarre array of otherworldly shapes coiling around a locomotive. The only detail that had changed was the writing across the side.

When I first saw the traincar, written across its side were the words, *Zo vaxap dis en zo flestulo.*

Now it said: *For everyone who couldn't be here.*

The ride vehicles faded away, leaving us standing around the traincar. All of us turned to the same person.

"Justin?" I whispered. "Do you want to go first?"

He nodded. Light flared around the doorframe when he opened it. He went inside, passing through a blinding white barrier. We all followed and emerged into a small, dusty, trapezoidal room. A school-desk sat in one corner, while a tiny pocket door sat in the wall.

It was the Office.

But it was empty.

Justin fell to his knees, burying his face in his hands. His sobs shocked us in their ferocity. He was screaming in grief, pulling his hands away to ball his fists in frustration and in fury. Auntie Hanna dropped to her knees to comfort him while everyone else staggered around in confusion. For whatever reason, I tapped a store of serenity inside me, searching my memory banks. Something was rustling around at the fringes of my thoughts. I picked at my lip as fireworks thundered outside.

"Dad, Dad."

Maybe I was thinking, maybe I was talking to myself. Like I said, I get those mixed up sometimes.

Mac walked over, her lower lip trembling. "What'd you say, goofball?"

"Dad. Dad. Little buckaroo. His Peace Corps stuff. Where'd he keep it?"

She shrugged, waving something away from her face. "I don't know. Mom never told me."

My eyes locked on what she'd waved away. I thought it was a spiderweb, but it wasn't. It was a pull-cord for a light. When I saw it, something random Mom said came back to me: *I don't want to clean your dad's stuff out of the attic.*

"The attic," I whispered. Mac was still with me.

She leaned in. "What?"

"Where's our attic?"

"We don't have one."

I frowned. Fireworks kept going *bang bang boom.* More of Mom's words echoed in my head: *The attic's hard to get to, so I think the architect added the Office for some extra storage. Your dad used to keep his Peace Corps stuff in there before I moved it.* When I asked her where Dad's Peace Corps stuff was, she said: "It's, uh, in the attic."

I'm pretty sure I said that part aloud. Mac and I made eye contact, her understanding growing. My memory called up the image of my first visit to the Office. I was on my knees, patting around the inside wall in search of a light switch. I'd flicked on a light. *Bang.*

Time and moments collided. *Boom.*

Suddenly, I was back on Lee's gondola-carriage, flying through the Anti-Sneakaround sky for those ten precious seconds. I was there then. I'm there now. I will always be there, reaching up to pull a cord dangling from the light fixture that hung from the ceiling. Instead of turning on a light, it opened a small door and allowed a bird to escape.

Time and moments collided. *Bang.*

We were all standing in the old gondola house back in March. It was almost the same shape and size as the Office. A cord dangled from the ceiling. Justin had pulled it . . .

Skelton moved their remains often. We all knew that. Itza Linda wasn't a single location, fixed in time and space. It was wherever they were. His victims. Those children. Those sweet baby angels, as Dawn called them. My map of West Chim had fallen out of my pocket at Soddy Farm, and he'd claimed it to use for his own dark ends. I'd drawn our house on my map.

Including the Office. *Boom.*

Gedda Brusha. Bang. Get the brochure.

High reason. Boom. Hi, Jason.

Feels Balmy. Bang. Feels slimy.

And when I'd first heard the name "Itza Linda," I'd heard more.

Itza Linda Adda. Bang bang boom.

Standing in the Office, I remembered six words I'd said over and over:

Spaces create shapes.

Shapes hold secrets.

Behind our old house was a rise in the earth on the same parallel as the Office, but that wasn't the only space unaccounted for. Mac's bedroom had a built-in desk that swelled out of the wall right over the Office. Its drawers were weirdly shallow, I always thought. In the Office that night, I looked at the light switch. Why would there be a light switch *and* a pull-cord?

"Itza Linda Adda," I said just as a massive firework shook the ceiling. Somewhere above, a bird chirped. "It's, uh, in the attic."

I reached up and pulled the cord.

And a door opened above us.

Lee

He had honestly felt insulted.

Earlier that night, when he and Hanna Blackledge ventured into the Flambonium Airscoop room to collect the device with Jason's magic pouch, whatever evil powers were arrayed at the Plaid Man's behest had presented Levi David Dockery with an image so simplistic and rudimentary that he contemplated filing a formal complaint with the powers that be.

They'd shown him his sister.

Presumably, the forces of darkness had thought it might rattle Lee to show him his sister delivering a confessional about how difficult he was to live with, how confusing his mannerisms, how strange and byzantine his thought processes.

He was insulted . . . then amused.

The idea of his redoubtable sister speaking of him like he was some kind of liability was so laughable to Lee that he almost didn't notice the upset on his Auntie Hanna's face. But as soon as he did, he let Compassion fly into the smirking face of whatever wight or wendigo the Plaid Man had conjured.

Hiram's Journal

". . . whatever wight or wendigo the Plaid Man had conjured."

Lee was regaling me with the tale of his and Auntie Hanna's mission to gather the Flambonium Airscoop for—what?—the twentieth time since they'd moved to the top of the hill where Auntie Hanna's sprawling house stood. Hammers banged and bandsaws whirred as construction workers milled to and fro, carrying two-by-fours, tools, and bags of cement. The skeleton of a new Victorian house stood a few yards down the hill from the guest house, where Auntie Hanna was sipping iced tea, her arm still in a sling.

Lee and I had been sitting in lawn chairs at the foot of the driveway, waiting for a delivery. We spent a lot of time in those lawn chairs that summer, watching the sky. Everyone did, because the sky had a new addition: a sweeping, striped plane that circled the Earth, tinged blue from the atmosphere. From where we were in Tennessee, they looked broad and flat, while folks down in Ecuador saw only a straight line that bisected the heavens.

The Earth now had a ring system.

No scientist could explain the sudden, catastrophic seismic event that had split the moon in twain. Only we knew the truth. Regardless, when it split, it shattered into trillions of pieces that slowly accumulated in Earth's orbit. For a month, we had meteor showers almost twenty-four hours a day, but as the system stabilized, the showers ebbed, leaving us with a new reality. Lee liked to joke that we should change Earth's name to Genesis, in honor of *Star Trek II.*

When we finally found Itza Linda, I realized that the world keeps getting bigger for everyone. New continents keep appearing, new rooms keep getting discovered, and sometimes, your home planet gains a ring system. Mac didn't know about the attic above the Office, but Mom assumed she knew about it, the same way Mac, in turn, assumed I knew about the Office.

Now the entire world had passed such a threshold together. There would always be a time before and after the rings. In time, there would be generations born who only knew of the Earth with a ring system. In the future, kids would ask me what it was like before the ring system. Sometimes a youngster would give me a funny look when I mentioned a time *before* the ring system, and I'd realize I'd assumed they knew about it, just like Mom assumed I knew about the Office and Mac knew about the attic.

Some mysteries remained unsolved. We never pieced together all of Skelton's plan. One detail that nagged at me was Trent's security codes. Was it a coincidence his numbers spelled "Pharaoh," or was he already in league with Skelton then? We also never figured out how that dang Tilt-A-Whirl wound up in Radagast's Oak.

The Mystery Mansion had collapsed on the Fourth of July. We mourned its passing, both as a place of childhood wonder and as the setting for one of our first adventures together. In our citadel, we had crafted a place where we could all store the pains and traumas of the past few years. We'd never be free of those experiences—no one ever is—but in storing them there, we could at least keep them in a place where they could be properly processed and reckoned with.

But back to that delivery.

It arrived in the hands of our Aunties Elna and Sheila, who stole out from the forest, their passage heralded by a flash of otherworldly light. Even outside the Sneakaround, Elna seemed to float, while Sheila maintained her usual martial posture, checking behind every shrub and tree, a combat helmet bobbling on her head. The delivery was a manila folder filled with papers, which Sheila dropped in my lap with a fist-bump while Elna dropped candies in our waiting hands.

"Be careful with this one," Sheila said. "I'm pretty sure this asshole's trying to turn the universe into hell."

They vanished back to parts unknown. We brought the folder back to the main house, where a slender Black man wearing horn-rimmed glasses emerged holding a pair of T-shirts.

"Fellas, fellas! I finished 'em! Housewarming gift!"

He presented the shirts to us. One said, *Nakatomi Plaza Christmas Party 1988*, the other *Dr. E Brown Enterprises, 24hr Scientific Services*. Lee and I whooped. He took the Doc Brown shirt, as it was clearly smaller and intended for him.

"This is a perfect recreation, sir!"

I was marveling at the Nakatomi Plaza shirt, giggling. "I love this *so* much. Thank you, Tony."

Lee raised a finger. "But I still don't understand how Marty was able to return to the future but not remember his own past."

Tony nodded. "He didn't. Marty leaped from one parallel reality to another and replaced the Marty from *that* timeline. In that timeline, his parents were successful."

I chuckled. "But he still hung out with a kooky mad scientist?"

"Yeah," Tony said. "I think Doc and Marty would be friends in any timeline." He noticed the folder. "Oooh, is that what I think it is?"

"Yessir," Lee said. "Is the captain within?"

"Yeah!" he turned. *"Justin! It's here!"*

Justin Johnson emerged from the back of the house, accompanied by Jason, Dawn, Kaitlyn . . .

. . . and Sandra.

She'd healed up well, with only a slight scar snaking across her forehead. She stopped before us and smiled.

"How are the aunties?" she asked.

"Quite well, Mother."

"They're great," I said, bouncing. "Can we read it, can we read it?"

Sandra raised a hand and took the folder, walking out toward the construction project. Sandy wanted to keep her best warriors close, because even though the Faceless One had been defeated, there were other evils out there.

Justin had explained everything to Tony his first night in town. He'd taken to it without question. Jason was already working on new magic treasures, while Justin had formalized our mapmaking. We could generate a Smoky Mountain connecting locations on *earth* in minutes, but now Sandra had us looking at maps of other places.

Other planets.

Other solar systems.

Other galaxies.

Hanna was in convalescence but preparing herself for more adventures. Kaitlyn was getting ready for a gap year, while Mac was getting ready to apply to colleges. Lee and I had forged an unshakable friendship. Jason and Dawn were the talk of the town, only topped by Justin and Tony, who were open about their relationship.

And their adoption.

After Trent went to jail, Justin, Tony, and Auntie Hanna teamed up to raise us. Hanna adopted me and Mac, while Justin and Tony adopted Jason and Kaitlyn. They got some flack because they were both men, but seeing as how Justin was a hero to all East Tennessee, they made it happen. Sandra was there, too. We all had four amazing parents, one of whom was also our Revelation General, Sandra Divine Dockery. Their new house was for her and her kids, yes, but it was also a standing *nexus profundus*, as well as the new headquarters for the East Tennesse Sororal Order of Spiritual Defense. Its doorways led to places remote and wonderful depending on the maps we drew, and standing in its center was the eight-pillared statuary we'd seen in our first Smoky Mountain. Its final three pillars, empty at first, now held superheroic renditions of Justin, Auntie Hanna . . . and Jason.

We sat spread across the main house. Kaitlyn and Mac stood to the side, whispering and giggling. Lee and I grabbed the couch next to Dawn and Jason, who was looking at Auntie Elna's locket. His parents smiled out at him. Dawn gave him a squeeze. Justin and Tony stood over by the kitchen, arm in arm. Sandy stood before us, briefing us on our next mission. I tried to concentrate, but I couldn't get something out of my head—two words:

Strong bones.

Skelton had coined the phrase. Coming from him, it was rancid and corrupt . . . but I couldn't shake the sentiment. There was something alluring about it, something I liked, something that resonated. I hold these competing feelings: the contempt and the fascination, the hatred and the pride.

We *do* have strong bones. All of us.

I'm taking those words back. They're mine. They're ours. They belong to us now. We found each other and came together, forming a family of choice, a Sneakaround Gang that's got strong enough bones to take on any menace— terrestrial or cosmic—that threatens East Tennessee.

So come and get us. We're ready.

September 2020
May 22, 2021

Acknowledgments

Gar Anthony Haywood, Teffanie White, Ed Greer, Stefano Terry, Shawn Marek, Ashley Glenn, Karl Mueller, Corey Finkle, Jordan Byrne, Beth Woodward, Meg Eden, Nathan Quinn, Adam J. Schwartz, Paul Kreuger, Dick Couch, Christia Crocker.

And of course, to my lovely and amazing wife, Lauren Rock, my family of choice.

About the Author

ROBERT J. PETERSON lives in Los Angeles with his wife and two cats. His other novels include *The Odds* and *The Remnants*.

www.ingramcontent.com/pod-product-compliance
Lightning Source LLC
Chambersburg PA
CBHW050944210726
48287CB00004B/1129